# Diary of a Nightmare in Williamson County

## A NOVEL OF THE NASHVILLE MONARCHY

# SHERRILYN KENYON

Strange Lit Publishing
Peachtree City, Georgia

This book is a threat to national
security and must be destroyed!

*~A U.S. Trustee in Nashville*

"A must read for any law student or lawyer. A captivating tale that realistically portrays how much harm one single out-of-control judge can do... And how little those who are supposed to protect our rights will do for those who need it most. A chilling tale of injustice in modern-day America."

~Nancy J. Rainer, Appellate Attorney


"I'd say it *(Diary of a Nightmare in Williamson County)* was unbelievable, but having been a Tennessee attorney for over a decade, I know all-too-well how often this sort of thing happens in our courtrooms. Thank you, Sherrilyn Kenyon, for being brave enough to take the bullet and shine a needed light on the American Injustice System."

~Keith Hatfield, Knoxville Attorney

*Let the bodies hit the floor...*

*~Drowning Pool*

ALL GOOD NIGHTMARES BEGIN *as a beautiful dream.* I had survived the nightmare of a horrible childhood to build what I'd deluded myself into believing was a great life, with a great career, three amazing sons and a man by my side I thought was dependable, and relatively good.

Granted, he had moments that in retrospect should have been giant waving red flags that warned me to grab my babies and run, such as screaming, lunatic fits over absolutely nothing at all; like when the kids had left their dirty socks on the floor, or *someone,* usually him, forgot to rinse out a dish in the sink.

Yeah, I was an idiot for not leaving him when I had a chance. I won't even try to deny it.

But we all delude ourselves into thinking that this was the best we could do.

That *this* was what we deserved.

After all, no life was perfect. That was what everyone said, right?

Mine had always been flawed. So, I'd done what I did best.

Made do with an asshole in tin foil, instead of a knight in shining armor that we'd all been promised would ride in one day on that fucking white horse.

*You know, the wolf in the proverbial sheep's clothing.* That animal that no one saw coming until it ripped out your throat.

Why not? Those around me seemed to envy my life, even though I kept assuring them all that there was nothing about it worth envying (this included talk show hosts and interviewers who'd told the world how "charmed" my life was—I was sure that they'd said and thought the same thing about Tina Turner while she was married to Ike). God knew that everyone had thought John Wayne Gayce and Ted Bundy were sweethearts, too. And let's not even discuss the BTK and how wonderful everyone thought he was.

Just like the police who'd returned the victim to Jeffrey Dahmer thought he was "normal" and "harmless."

Until they found the bodies.

They kept telling me how lucky I was even though loud, screaming sirens went off constantly that no one should have missed. But as with blaring car alarms on the street, no one paid attention to them.

As we've seen with couples like Ike and Tina, and on so many episodes of *Forensic Files*.

People were too busy being jealous. Too busy focusing on the bright and shiny coating, and not on the glaring rust underneath. All they saw was the sleek, pretty hood that distracted them from the rods that kept knocking, loud and clear.

Face it, I once lived in what some would term a mansion, with more cars than people to drive them, and to those who didn't know better, I appeared to have all the money in the world. Because of authors like Nora Roberts and J.R. Ward who had family money long before they began writing and who proudly flaunted their wealth in the faces of others, the general public thought that all authors were ungodly wealthy when the vast majority of us weren't.

How could *I* possibly have any problems?

But as I've always said, grief and tragedy were equal opportunity tormentors.

Injustice was far more blind than Justice. And unlike Justice, Injustice wasn't a whore who could be bought and sold if you knew the right people and had enough money.

No, Injustice and Tragedy preyed on us all, regardless of birth, religion, social order, or race. They were merciless beasts who took pity on none and who spared no one.

And on March 7, 2018, those bitches decided to move their asses into my home, take up permanent residence, and party like it was the end of the world.

Because it was the end of *my* world.

Now, I won't lie. I'd been sick for a long time. As in years and years of mysterious illnesses that no one could figure out.

The symptoms were awful and scary. Fatigue, choking on nothing, vomiting, swollen and bleeding gums, bloating, antaxia, hair loss. Constant stomach upset. Joints that ached for no reason, and horrifying headaches that wouldn't leave me no matter what I eliminated from my diet or added to it.

Brittle bones and teeth; as in I would bite into yogurt or yeast rolls and shatter a tooth. *That* kind of brittle.

My bones, themselves, ached all the time. I had trouble swallowing. My eyes would swell completely shut, and my lips would tingle and yet no one could tell me what I was allergic to even though I seemed to keep having a severe allergic reaction to everything and yet nothing at all.

My sinuses stayed infected and throbbing. All kinds of respiratory troubles that had never existed before. Backaches. Dizzy spells. I had strange vitamin deficiencies that the medical community blamed on everything from stress to menopause.

No one could figure out what was causing it or how to fix it.

All I knew was that every day when I woke up, I was in brutal agony that had me struggling for every breath. And there were days when I couldn't get up at all.

Yes, I was a crabby bitch. Who wouldn't be? I felt like complete and utter shit from morning, noon to night. There was never any let up from the unending misery.

I was so weak at times, I couldn't walk across the room without help and if no help was there, then I was trapped in my chair. Trapped in my brutal agony. I had to take breathing treatments and carry an inhaler everywhere I went. If I tried to eat, I would choke on my food and more times than not, I would vomit whatever I was eating right back up.

Not that it mattered. I couldn't taste what I was eating. Everything had a weird metallic ick to it that wouldn't go away. My mouth, lips and tongue stayed numb, or they tingled to the point of distraction. It was so weird.

"Hey, Dad! Mom's choking! I think she needs some help!" My oldest son, Maddox, had been panicked about my inability to eat a single meal without dire consequences a couple of weeks before he'd left to teach in Japan.

At only five-eight, and with pneumothorax that could strike him immobile at any moment,

Maddox couldn't lift much and had to be careful, or his lung could collapse. I'd always adored my brown-haired little cherub, with his kaleidoscope blue eyes.

That day, we'd been having lunch at home, and he was trying his best to help me as I struggled with a peculiar foam that seemed to close up my throat any time I attempted to eat something. No matter how small a bite I took, it was as if my food expanded like the "Foaming Bubbles" cleaner. It invaded my mouth and throat, and solidified until I choked on it, forcing me to my knees where I'd gasp for air.

It was insidious.

And painful.

I would invariably begin regurgitating. Wheezing. Unable to catch my breath at all.

It was terrifying to experience. Imagine the worst asthma attack of your life, compounded by a thick substance clinging to the walls of your throat and epiglottis. And I would vomit up ten times whatever I'd consumed.

No one could tell me why, or what caused it.

My husband, Lester Theodore Manly, III, or "Les" as his mother had so graciously nick-named him (because she hadn't emasculated him enough with her constant insults and poor clothing choices she'd forced on him as a boy and young man), had shrugged it off. "Oh, don't worry, son. She does that all the time."

"Yeah, but she's turning blue! Dad, I think she's in trouble!"

Still, Les hadn't cared.

Unlike the time, days before, when his assistant, Karen Hogg, had fallen out of the same chair, and he'd rushed her off to the emergency room in case she'd injured herself. Then, he'd been panicked with worry.

*God forbid, the mighty Hogg might fall.*

But when his cash cow was wheezing and turning blue at his feet?

*Fuck it! Let the bitch die.*

In retrospect, *that* should have been a major clue about what he and his assistant were doing, in more ways than one, behind my back. But while I was on the ground, fighting for my life, it was easy to miss such important warning signs.

Hindsight, as they say, is 20/20.

Just as I should have known by the weird relationship he had with a mother who'd thought so little of him that she'd given him the name of someone she hated, then a nickname that made his "name" sound ridiculous.

Of course, she was only one-half of the parental unit that Les swore he despised: Lester and Elaine "Snooty" Manly. The same pair that had refused to help us at all while Les went to law school in a futile attempt to gain their love and respect, and to find the self-esteem they'd torn down and ravaged while he was a boy living under his mother's scalding, embittered tongue.

His mother's most commonly uttered phrase? "You made your bed you can lie in it."

She used that phrase for all the most inappropriate things.

It was something she'd even said to my oldest son, Maddox, when he'd made the mistake of reaching out to the only grandmother he had while he was on the brink of suicide, living near her in college.

Wasn't she a paragon of virtue?

Grandma had actually told my pain-filled boy that his agony was his own fault because his generation was lazy. "You made your bed you can lie in it." Instead of getting in her car and going to him to make him feel better as any decent, loving grandmother would do.

Instead of lifting him up and helping him, she did what she'd always done. Kicked him down harder, and stepped on his precious, baby fingers as she tried her best to pry him off that ledge he was barely clinging to.

Just as she had blatantly and coldly refused to help my middle son, Caleb, after his car wreck, when he was also in town with her, not long after she'd buried her oldest grandchild, Taylor.

Caleb had an injured back and a totaled car, with no way to get help or to a doctor.

Neither she, her husband, nor Les's nurse sister (Taylor's mother) who also lived in town could be bothered to help my child. Or even call him to see if he was okay. Rather, it was my elderly aunt with gout, who was even older than Snooty, who had to drive in from over five hours away to take care of him.

And this after Snooty had already caused her eldest grandchild to commit suicide by turning her back on Taylor's pain and allowing the world and others to abuse her. Just as it had abused her children while she not only gleefully turned a blind eye...

She gloated to them about their mental and physical misery.

Or worse, after Snooty had aided in the abuse of her own children.

But then, that was what Snooty did best. Put down others so that she could float to the top like the piece of shit she truly was.

How cold was this portly, shallow wretch who fancied herself the Southern version of Princess Diana, but who lacked Diana's sophistication, taste, beauty and heart?

I've met maggots that I admired more. At least those parasites recognized what they were and didn't lie or try to disguise their real intentions behind a high-pitched cruel laugh.

Now before you think that I was completely heartless where she was concerned...

After she refused to ever pay a single cent of her son's law school bill or even purchased a single meal for him while he attended it (knowing we were starving the entire way through, which she thought was amusing), and while knowing her grandson, Maddox, was on life-support, fighting for his newborn life, what was Snooty's biggest concern the day Les graduated law school?

"I want a photo of me and my son in front of the school with its name on it!"

How I wish you could have heard her hick accent as she spoke those words. She fancied herself the elite sophisticate, in her always tacky designer-wear while driving around in an outdated BMW. But really, when one hears the expression, "lipstick on a pig," it conjured the near perfect image of who and what she truly was.

While she might pass on a good day as a bad Martha Stewart knock-off (low rent version) if you squinted hard enough, the minute she opened her mouth, that illusion she was trying so pathetically to create was shattered by the godawful thick North Georgia hillbilly accent. Seriously, it should come with the *Deliverance* dueling banjos in the background. There was a reason my mother had nicknamed her "Saucer-head." And it wasn't because of her bad haircut, or the fact that she'd been bleaching it blond for so many years that I wasn't too sure the bleach hadn't shriveled her Narcissistic brain.

But back to the point, her concern wasn't returning to the hospital where my baby, her second-born grandchild whose birth she'd missed, was alone, fighting for his frail life. Snooty wanted a photo to show her pretentious friends that she hadn't been lying about her son, the lawyer, from a campus where he'd never taken a single class, or even stepped foot on until graduation—which she would have known had she ever possessed a nano-ounce of maternal instinct.

All the law school classes were at a satellite campus in Jackson, Mississippi where we lived, and not at the main campus in Clinton where the graduation had taken place.

Naturally, this was after the two-hour grueling ceremony where Snooty had spent the entire time lecturing her son on what a loser he was because he hadn't graduated at the top of his class like all those other "intelligent" students or berating him because he didn't have a job waiting on him like they did, either.

'Course those students weren't all law students, and most of them came from families that had helped them through school and encouraged them with their studies. Not families who reveled in their children's penury and misery and gloated to them about how happy they were to see them suffer and fail.

"I need all my money for retirement, son. Sorry you're starving and having it hard, but you made your bed. You can lie in it."

"But Mom," Les would always whine. "Your parents helped you!" Her parents had been dirt farmers and trash collectors who'd scrimped and saved their whole lives, not white-collar, college-educated Narcissistic assholes.

"And I've spent all that money, Les. You just *had* to get married *(she'd originally thought I was pregnant when he told her we were getting married—sorry, Snoots, I was not your teenage daughter who finally got married while pregnant after she'd aborted two other children before that).* It's your job to take care of things, Les. You made your bed. You can lie in it."

As a friend of mine once said after spending a couple of minutes with old Snooty, "that woman doesn't have a kind word or thought for anyone." That included her daughters, her husband, her son, her grandchildren and her friends.

Snooty Manly was a nasty piece of work and didn't bother to hide it.

She'd always hated me because unlike Les who took her cruelty in petulant stride, I dished it right back, like my mother had taught me to do.

*I don't start shit. I finish it.*

As my mama used to tell me, "Terri, you ever start a fight, I'll beat you every step of the way home. But if someone else starts it and you don't hand their ass to them, I'll beat you twice as hard."

Not Les.

He drew up into a fetal ball until his attacker went away and then he'd go for their back with a knife, because that contaminated fruit grew straight off his mother's rotted-out limbs. And he'd suckled venom and poison straight from Snooty's shriveled, heartless tit.

Only someone that emotionally bankrupt and cold could do what Les Manly did in March 2018.

At three in the morning, we as a family had carried my eldest baby, Maddox, to the airport so that he could begin his great adventure, teaching in Japan. His dream job that broke my heart, but I knew how much it meant to him.

Scared for my baby, I choked back my tears, knowing this was what he wanted.

I had to let go, even though my innate tendency had always been to protect my kids above all, and from anyone who would do them harm. As the old saying goes, *when they're little they step on your toes, and when they're grown, they step on your heart.*

My heart broke as I watched that eager smile on his handsome face. Hopeful and brave, he waved back at me, then shifted his black backpack over his thin shoulders.

I rarely cry in public, but that morning, I was bawling as if my heart had shattered. My baby was leaving. It would be a year before we'd see him again.

Les had refused to book him a return flight.

"We don't know exactly when he'll return, so it would be wasteful."

Wasteful from a man who'd never saved a dime of what I'd earned? God, at the money he'd spent on absolute bullshit. Such as a million-dollar lawsuit I didn't want filed in the first place. He had two Rolexes he'd insisted be bought and then refused to wear because they bruised his tender little wrist. Expensive Shinola watches, and others he wouldn't wear for reasons unknown. And he once took a Porsche back less than twenty-four hours after buying it because he decided that he liked the one he'd traded in better and wanted it instead.

Yeah, that was a costly hissy fit.

But he didn't want to spend a couple extra hundred dollars on a return flight for his son after he'd made me set fire to five thousand dollars a week before on a paid-for vacation trip I'd bought him for Christmas because "I just don't feel like going."

Yeah...

He was such a pinchpenny.

Of course, everything was always about Les or Baby Huey as I now liked to call him. It was why he'd canceled having dinner that same week with the dean from my former college. He'd told them that I was too sick to go when the truth was, he was too eaten up with jealousy that they kept honoring me over him at a school that he'd graduated from and that he'd forced me to withdraw out of to tend to his little baby feelings, twenty-seven years before that day.

God, the stupid things we do when we're young. It pained me that at a time when we had so little world experience and knowledge, we made the decisions that we'd spend the rest of our lives paying for.

What a cruel twist of fate.

God had a sick sense of humor, and I was really tired of being the punchline.

"What if something happens? Maddox should have a way to get home." I was always paranoid about things going wrong and my kids being harmed. Life had a way of sucker-punching you when you least expected it. It was the one lesson I'd learned the hardest.

And I'd been to enough foreign countries to know that they didn't like it when you couldn't give them an exit date. They always wanted to know that you weren't there to stay, and that you planned to leave.

Les had scoffed at me. "Everything's fine."

So, I watched my baby vanish into the busy airport crowd, praying for God to keep him safe for me.

My youngest son, Nick, helped me back into the car. Even in height to me, Nick was almost an identical copy of my middle son, Caleb. Except he had a charming, mischievous glint in his brown eyes, and unlike Caleb, he'd never had a problem with me playing in his head full of dark curls.

Caleb had always tended to be moody and out of sorts for no reason, much like his father.

Nick was ever cheerful and sweet. There was no duplicity in his innocent smile, and his biggest worry had always been dealing fairly with others.

Out of all three of my children, Nick was the most like me, which had led us to quarrel more than I had with my other two. We were both stubborn to a fault and would hold our ground until doomsday. We had a very strict moral code, and a rigid sense of what was right and wrong.

Our integrity would not be compromised for any reason.

And we would argue any point we were trying to make into the ground.

That was what I adored most about my Nick. And it was what drove me craziest.

Maddox was like my little brother, Esteban Norman Woods. They couldn't have been more alike in looks and actions had Esteban been his father.

It was weird at times. First, I raised Esteban, and then I raised his doppelgänger.

Caleb was the most like his father. Moody. Secretive, and always holding something back. Not that it was his fault. Les had trained him to be that way.

They were even close in height. Same dark brown hair, and angry caustic putdowns for a world that they believed had done them wrong, even when it hadn't.

Because they were so similar, Les had been a lot harder on Caleb than he should have been. Right down to accusing him of lying and stealing even when Caleb hadn't even thought about it.

I couldn't count how many times I'd had to run interference between them because of Les's unfair abuse of his middle son.

"He's just like my sister, Annette! I can't stand her, and I won't tolerate him acting like her, either! You can't ever believe a word he says. He's nothing but a liar!"

I would roll my eyes at Les. "He's nothing like your sister!" For one thing, my son had a heart, which Annette must have had at one time until her mother devoured it.

But Les wouldn't listen. "You don't know what you're talking about, Terri! I can look into his eyes and see it! He'd climb a tree to lie before he'd stand on the ground to tell the truth."

Les said that to me a lot about Caleb.

Unfortunately, the sentiment was echoed by Caleb's friends and teachers who'd all talked about how much Caleb lied. But again, it wasn't Caleb's fault. It was what Les had taught him to do.

Les was so cruel to my child. He once publicly humiliated poor Caleb over a Ring Pop sucker that Caleb had won in school for doing well on a paper. Because Caleb hadn't told Les about it, and they had just come out of Kroger when Caleb pulled it out of his pocket, Les naturally assumed Caleb had stolen it, even though my children had never stolen anything in their lives.

Stealing was a Manly trait, not a Woods' one.

You have to remember that Les judged everyone based on what "he" would do.

And that told the world everything it needed to know about Les Manly. He was a barking dog who telegraphed his crimes.

This was extremely important to keep in mind. He constantly projected his sins onto others.

Because he was a lying thief, he naturally assumed everyone else was, too.

Especially his sons.

Poor Caleb.

Rather than believe his seven-year-old who was mortified by the accusation, Les dragged him roughly back into the store, and made him hand over the Ring Pop he'd won and apologize to the manager. Then he dragged him home, screaming at him the entire time.

In that moment, he'd stolen away his son's achievement and his innocence. Les was real good at doing that to all of us. We were never allowed to have one minute of success or one minute to bask in any kind of happiness before Les turned it into a moment of utter and complete embarrassment for us.

He was his mother's son.

After all, Snooty wrecked Maddox's graduation.

Twice.

When Les returned home with Caleb and told me of the event, I looked at him like he was the idiot he'd been. "Did you ask his teacher?"

"Why would I do that?"

Because his son might have been telling the truth. God forbid a father should ever believe his highly intelligent son had done well in school. But why should Les think that since he'd never done well in anything? He'd graduated at the very bottom of all his classes, with a Hail Mary.

For that matter, why should a father back his child when his own parents had never once backed him into anything other than a corner?

But then, Les had no reason to doubt his son's words either, other than his own neurotic idiocy.

You should have seen the "der" stare on his face. It was as priceless as the time he came into my office to announce, "Uh, Terri, the kitchen's on fire."

I had a moment while working where I thought it had to be a joke because no one in their right mind would come in and be that calm if the house was actually on fire. Then I remembered that I'd married a complete and utter moron. If anyone would be nonchalant while the house burned down, it would be Les Manly.

And of course, the Emperor Nero who'd fiddled while Rome burned.

So, I ran to check it out, and sure enough. My kitchen *was* on fire.

Les, in his infinite "wisdom," had dropped an entire handful of pasta onto my gas stove and instead of using salt to put the flames out or grab the fire extinguisher under the sink, or a pan to smother the flames, or nine hundred other intelligent things he could have done to put it out, had casually walked over to my office to get me, and had left the rapidly burning fire unattended with three small children and two cats to fend for themselves while the flames spread throughout my kitchen.

Yeah, he was *that* bright.

So that day after he'd traumatized my little boy in Kroger who was upstairs crying his eyes out, I calmly asked his teacher if he'd won a prize for doing well on his paper.

Come to find out, Caleb had won it, just as he'd said.

Les had been the biggest jerk of all time, and my son had been publicly humiliated for no reason other than the fact that his father had wanted to look like a big shot to the Kroger store manager.

Yeah...

And sadly, the lesson Caleb had learned that day was that even when he told the truth, he got beat for it in public, and that he shouldn't bother to do well in school since any reward he received would not only be taken from him, he'd be traumatized over it (again, this rang familiar).

Father of the year.

For the record, Les never apologized. That was the kind of human and father he was. He would never admit he was wrong on anything, and he jumped to the worst, most ludicrous conclusion of all time.

Like when he first filed the lawsuit, he forced on me in 2016, and we found out that the other author was out of the country on a trip. He said and I quote, "oh my God, she's jumped the country and won't ever come back! With her money, why would she? She'll just stay abroad forever and won't face justice! What are we going to do now?"

Like that made all the sense in the world. Rich people always gave up all their U.S. homes and holdings out of fear of a simple civil suit, instead of allowing their lawyers to battle it out in court.

Yeah.

Les had a severely damaged thought process that he somehow thought was "brilliant."

The rest of us, however, simply found the inner workings of his mind painfully hard to follow.

And on that morning when we left the airport after dropping off Maddox, Les was unusually quiet, but since it was before dawn, I didn't think much about it. Honestly, I was glad he wasn't rambling on and on with his usual nonsense.

Everything "seemed" normal.

I should have remembered that "normal" was a word that fell between neurotic and nosebleed in the dictionary.

As a girl, I'd never had it. Born Terri Ann Woods, I grew up in the poverty-stricken area of Riverdale, Georgia, in a place where things tended to explode into violence without warning.

Constantly.

So, chaos was my familiar stomping ground. *That* I could handle. As they said, a tiger lies low not from fear, but for aim. When things got quiet at my childhood home, they were indeed taking aim and about to go for your throat. That was the quiet before the storm and you needed to duck and cover.

*Or run for the door.*

I should have known that morning a storm was gathering. But Les had lulled me into complacency, like Alexander the Great with the Indian army.

*Walk your horses downstream as if nothing's going on. A few at a time, day by day, until your enemy's no longer paying attention.*

*Then strike hard and fast, and stab them in the back, right between the shoulders. Because from there, you can still reach their heart and they won't see it coming.*

Les was the soulless, sneaky coward Snooty had raised.

*Like begats like.*

His mother should be proud of him. Too bad she was incapable of praising anyone other than herself.

After we returned home and because I was so sick, I went to lie down for a few minutes. I knew Maddox wouldn't board for at least two hours, and he had an hour until he reached Minneapolis for his layover. I'd need to be up by six to check his gate connection and make sure he made it.

Nick headed upstairs to bed.

Les followed me to our room and crawled into bed beside me. Everything seemed fine.

Fine—Freaked out. Insecure. Neurotic. Emotional.

How could I ever forget that acronym? My older brother's diatribe about women whenever they said they were, "fine."

"The most frightening word in the world, Terri, is when you ask a woman if she's okay and she shoots back, with 'I'm fine.' 'Cause fine is the *last* thing she is. About to kick your ass is what she's about to do."

*Freaked out. Insecure. Neurotic. Emotional.*

Les had always joked with everyone that he was the woman in our relationship. He knew I was self-conscious over the fact that I'd been raised with boys and had been mocked abysmally in school for being a lesbian. Not because I was one, but because I had many friends who were, and for the fact that we were poor, I'd often had to wear the hand-me-downs of my male cousins we were helping to raise.

Not to mention, I'd taken a girl to the prom at a time when no one did so. Of course, I hadn't thought anything about it. My best friend had wanted to go and asked me to the junior prom, so I went. No big deal.

Except people were judgy asses.

People like Les. And his humor was forever cruel. But then mockery and shame were what I'd cut my teeth on, so I thought nothing about his caustic barbs that often bled my soul. That was mother's milk to me.

As I've so often said, my dad was a drill sergeant, and he was my sympathetic parent. Having someone criticize and belittle me was all I'd ever been exposed to.

Little did I know, Les was luring me in for the kill, because that was what Les did.

With a peculiar bipolar mix of entitlement and persecution complex, Les had been blessed early in life with one thing going for him; the ability to appear harmless and meek to disguise his ruthless, cold heart. Like a lumbering, lovable panda bear. So cute and adorable as it innocently chewed on its bamboo. How could that awkward, tubby teddy hurt anyone?

Yet it could shred you to pieces if you got too close.

That was Les. He even moved like some arthritic old man with a walker.

And that was when he was eighteen.

Right at six feet, he wasn't tall enough to appear off-putting or dangerous. He had a lean build and a pudgy beer belly that was in no way intimidating as it reminded you of some old, swayback mule. Big brown eyes that held so much stupidity in them that no one would ever think him capable of plotting any kind treachery (my mistake).

Or holding any kind of thought for that matter, other than, "Honey, where's my brain?"

That was his cryptic coloration. That screwed up bit of nature that allowed creatures who should be prey to camouflage their movements, identity, or real intentions and blend into their environment to give them an advantage around predators so that when they, the prey, attacked others, no one saw them coming.

Until it was too late.

That had been the downfall of many who were lulled into underestimating ole Les. His little lisp and that effeminate demeanor were edged with a brutal need to prove himself at the cost of anyone who got in his way.

Even his own sons.

Remember that he was born with a severe persecution and inferiority complex that only worsened after his parents abandoned us in Mississippi and turned their backs on his suffering while we were homeless. It, and our homeless poverty that he'd tried so hard to deny in spite of the fact we lived that way, left a festering wound in him that had never healed.

A wound that made him lash out at everyone like a rabid, wounded animal.

Including his own sons.

And me.

The ones who were by his side, suffering, through it all, and who'd loved and supported him, while the rest of his friends and family had abandoned him to it. His children who once worshiped the ground he'd walked on. The saddest part?

So had I.

Before he'd turned on me, too.

I slept for about an hour on that fateful morning of March 7, 2018.

In that one hour, my entire life changed.

I got up, wanting to protect my Autistic son. He was on his way to a foreign country to live on his own without the backing of his school or a friend. While he'd been to Japan before, he'd gone in a group to study, and had lived in a dorm.

This was entirely different.

He had no security blanket. No one to watch out for him when he arrived there. I was terrified. It was a big adventure, and he would need his parents' full support as he navigated the world that often left him baffled and confused. He'd been so nervous the days before he left.

Les had assured him that everything was "fine."

"Don't worry, son. Nothing's going to happen while you're away. We're here for you. I'll hold down the fort." Les had said those words to him. Those *exact* words, knowing he was lying to his own son with every syllable that came out of his venomous mouth.

That same week while I helped my son pack to leave, Les had stolen every single cent from Maddox's trust fund that I, not Les, had earned for him and put aside to ensure Maddox wouldn't have to worry about anything. That none of our sons would have to be homeless or stalked by creditors as we'd been.

That was the most pathetic part of all this. Les had stolen from his own children, for no reason other than selfish, pathetic greed.

No. Worse, he'd stolen from them because he was jealous of his own sons that he'd fathered. *Jealousy.*

How many times had he said, "I wish I were one of them. They don't appreciate anything."

Neither did he. I was the one who'd worked twenty hours a day, seven days a week, three hundred and sixty-five days a year with no break and no let up. Tending my sons and making sure they had everything they needed. While Les sat his ass on my couch and "delegated" everything from meals to having light bulbs changed.

Literally.

He did nothing for any of us, other than hire someone else to do it. It was why my sons had dubbed him "the Great Delegator."

"Oh no! Don't make me have to call someone to raise their voice to you! That would be too much work for me! You're hungry? Let me text your mother to get you food. You need help with homework? I'll text someone to do it for you, son!"

I have the records and employee statements to prove it. He didn't even put gas in his own cars.

He was *that* lazy.

Honestly, I was amazed he hadn't found a way to pay someone to wipe his own ass. Although, he had found a way to have someone come to the house to put toilet paper on the racks and in the bathrooms. To dye and cut his hair for him and the boys. To give him facials and massages. And pretty much everything else.

Just not the actual ass-wiping.

Only the ass-kissing.

Les even had his trainer from the gym, Pat Hanson, come over to work out with him, and he paid for people to go to the gym with him so that he'd have the illusion of having friends.

And to the movies.

He called them "friends" even though Les had to pay them to get them to do anything with him.

Weird, I know. My friends would go to things like that with me for free.

They even paid *my* way sometimes and bought my popcorn.

But then Les really was *that* hard to get along with. No one had ever been his friend for long, unless he paid them.

He couldn't even find enough friends to be groomsmen for my bridesmaids during our wedding. I had to cut my bridesmaids in half because he didn't have enough friends (and keep in mind that he'd been in a fraternity where his best friend was the president... until the day they debrothered him).

Never once in our marriage had he said, "thank you, Terri, for the wonderful life you've provided for me. A life I could never have given to myself or you or the kids."

Because he was a failed loser who'd quit at absolutely everything he'd ever done in his entire life.

*Everything.*

He kept trying to quit law school during every semester from Day One, but I wouldn't let him because I knew if he quit, he'd have blamed it on me.

"I had to give up law school to feed you, Terri! It's all your fault! I'd have been a lawyer if I wasn't married to you!" (Completely not true).

Instead, I dropped out of school and worked three and four jobs (even while pregnant) to keep him going in law school while he worked none.

And he dared to accuse my children of being ungrateful and lazy?

He was Lord King Asshole of Ingrates.

At the time he abandoned us without any warning whatsoever, I had two homes completely paid for. All cars were paid off. We had no debt (or so I thought—no one had bothered to tell me that he'd taken half a million dollars out against my house that had been paid off so that he could leave me with over a million dollars cash in his pocket). My sons all had college funds and trust funds.

We were set and should have had a nice future with no financial worries whatsoever.

Beyond the American dream.

Because of all *my* hard work while he sat on the sofa and didn't even help the kids with their homework or make a single meal.

And for no reason whatsoever, he'd ruined us in a matter of months and completely bankrupted everything I'd ever worked for.

*All* of us.

Even himself.

In particular, he'd ruined our sons. For no logical reason.

Lust? Greed?

Jealousy?

Each of those has a part, but in the end, none of it made any sense because his brain didn't work like a normal brain. That was why they said that truth was stranger than fiction. Because fiction, unlike real life, had to make sense.

Characters, unlike real people, have to have a logical motivation for their actions.

But you couldn't fix a broken mind. There wasn't enough duct tape in the world to hold that hot mess together.

I won't ever understand how, even as broken as he was, Les could prey on his own children. How anyone could steal from their babies.

How he'd found a court system so broken that it allowed him... no, encouraged him to rob us blind.

Knowing what he'd done to us, without any remorse and for no reason, and that he'd continued to abuse and torture us for almost three years without any let up or mercy whatsoever, how could anyone ever doubt that Les had tried to kill me and our son?

That Les had killed our beloved cat, and tried to kill another?

It happened every day in the news. That nice old man next door who went psycho and killed everyone.

"He was such a nice guy." No one ever saw it coming.

What I never dreamed was that the psycho was in my home.

Sleeping in my bed.

That he'd fathered my three special needs children. And while they were very high-functioning and intelligent, they were still special needs and had trouble navigating this complicated world where they couldn't always interpret or understand the people around them.

Especially their father's erratic insanity and emotional instability that never helped them gain any form of clarity on human behavior.

One minute he'd be fine and the next he'd be throwing things and screaming. Over something as simple as a box of something he'd ordered that had been delivered to our home that would cause him to go into a Rage-Virus level hissy fit.

There had been a huge, permanent scar in my foyer where he once tore the floor up during one of his more stellar tantrums.

My sons each have trouble understanding rather basic things, such as social cues and tone modulation. What was appropriate and when, even when I tried to explain it. Autism and Asperger's have their own unique ways of processing information and defining the world. There was a special beauty to it. But other people have trouble appreciating it the way I do (because I have it, too). And strangers have trouble recognizing what was going on with my sons as they, unlike my Cerebral Palsy sister, don't have any apparent physical signs that they weren't quite like everyone else.

Like I have with my hearing problems and dyslexia.

Even when I've tried to explain that I couldn't hear properly or that I was seeing, hearing or thinking out of order, people often thought I was kidding. Believe me, there was nothing funny when you really couldn't process information. Others quickly got frustrated and angry and lashed out.

Or worse, they mocked you.

I've been on the receiving end of it enough to know that I didn't want my children treated so cruelly by an impatient world because people didn't want to take the time for those of us who needed just a few more minutes to understand what was going on.

I've worried every single day of their lives about what this world would do to them, because I knew that the world had never taken mercy on me.

I'd had to fight tooth-and-nail for everything I've had since the moment I took my first breath and wasn't smart enough to exhale it and let go of this life. My boys were defenseless babes in this harsh landscape.

That scared me most of all.

While all three of them kept me up at night with fears of what might come for them, Maddox was the one I worried about most. He'd spent weeks in NICU when he was born, and I was told on two separate occasions to pick out funeral clothes for him.

Every mother's worst nightmare.

When his monitor kept going off in the hospital because he wasn't breathing, I grabbed a nurse who looked at me and said, "oh honey, he's just a little wimpy white boy. We don't expect them to live, anyway, so we don't worry about them until they start turning blue."

I've never wanted to hit anyone in my life more than I wanted to slug that nurse when she'd said those callous words to me. I couldn't believe any human being could be that cold and unfeeling.

And that any hospital was stupid enough to put such a person in charge of newborn babies while they were fighting for their lives.

That was one of many reasons I'd left Jackson, Mississippi to move my children to Franklin, Tennessee. A place that looked so "perfect" on the outside.

Just like *Mayberry*.

But then I'd forgotten that *Mayberry* was far from perfect or ideal. It was a freakish landscape that lacked all color and was only one channel click from *The Twilight Zone*.

So much for thinking I was giving them a better life.

Yet my Maddox had beaten those dire odds he was given. He'd always been my fighter.

Which didn't mean that I didn't worry about him. It was what a mother did.

So, when I got up to check on Maddox and to make sure his lungs were holding, I saw that my bed was empty.

Weird.

Les had almost never gotten up before me. Ever. After all, he fashioned himself the good old Southern plantation owner in charge of servants aplenty to cater to his every hedonistic need.

In fact, when he found out from my uncle, Carlos, that I had Native American blood in me, Les said, "Cool! I always wanted to have my own squaw!"

Yeah, I should have divorced him then, but there was a really good reason I didn't.

And we will get to that. But in the meantime, I was on the hunt for my missing husband.

"Where in the world are you, Les?" He typically slept ten to twelve hours on any given day. To call him lazy was an insult to those with a preference for sleeping as their favorite pastime.

Not to mention, he knew that Maddox was flying out of the country with a severe lung condition, and that the changes in pressure could cause his lung to collapse. We'd been told, repeatedly, to never put him on a plane without knowing where a hospital was when we landed.

Maddox had had his lung collapse spontaneously in the past.

So, I went to Les's office to see if he was there, looking for new cars to buy. His favorite pastime; wasting my hard-earned cash, instead of working to earn his own money.

Or watching the news so that he could complain about the world and how he was getting screwed over, even though he wasn't doing anything more than sitting on my couch, living off his hard-working wife.

His office was empty.

"Probably at the gym." That was the only other place he'd be as it had his only "friend," Pat Hanson, there. The trainer he'd hired for his workouts, though I didn't get it. You couldn't tell by Les's Scotch belly that he spent three to four days a week at the gym, and thousands of dollars working out to maintain his pudgy physique.

The only workout I ever saw was him lifting his coffee cup, that had more Scotch in it than coffee, to his lips.

And it wasn't Pat's fault. He tried. Les just wouldn't cooperate. Pat would push him, and Les would just sit down and refuse to do anything.

Literally.

Like the mule he was.

I'd been to the gym enough with him to know. Les was that useless.

Besides, Pat was more his therapist than anything else. Since Les didn't have any friends, he talked to Pat more than he worked out. But it got Les out of the house and out of my hair, so it was worth it.

I headed downstairs to my office to start working, and to check on Maddox's flight and text him the information.

Since I had a hair appointment that morning, I knew Les would be back soon. He never allowed me to go anywhere or drive myself any place.

"You're too sick, Terri. You don't need to be driving. You could get hurt, and then where would we be?" He'd even confiscated all my car keys, and if I ever raised the garage door for any reason, he'd come flying down the stairs like a madman to yell at me for even thinking of leaving the house by myself.

He was *that* terrified that I might leave him.

It was why he kept all our money in his accounts and doled it out to me like I was a kid. And because he had such abandonment issues from his heartless mother and psycho dad, I tolerated it.

I couldn't do anything without his watching me. Not even swim or shower. Over the years, I'd never understood why he was so concerned and obsessed about it. I was a grown woman.

But it wasn't worth a fight. I simply accepted his weirdness and thought it stemmed from his pathological fear of abandonment. One so bad, that he often stood on my toes to keep me planted by his side.

"Don't leave me!" His favorite whine whenever I had to travel for business (or go to the bathroom). One so bad that he'd often tried to sabotage my plans.

"Les, the plane won't wait for you to shampoo the rugs! I have to go, now!"

"But the boys spilled a Coke."

"Steam clean it after you drop me off."

I couldn't count how many times he'd done things like that. So, in my mind, there was no doubt he'd be back to drive me to my hair appointment.

Hell, he'd practically kicked Maddox out of the house. "You have to make him leave, Terri! He's grown! Get him out of here! He's a bad example for Nick! He doesn't need to see his brother sitting in his room, all day, doing nothing now that he's graduated from college."

Because seeing his dad sitting around doing nothing with a law degree on the wall had ever been a bad example?

Oookay…

Besides, Maddox wasn't doing nothing. He was writing, which told everyone what Les thought of my career choice and what he used to say to me before my writing had started paying all the bills—in other words, Les accused me constantly of sitting around, doing nothing.

"Of eating bon-bons" all day long.

"He's graduated, Terri. He needs to go! You have to kick him out of this house!"

"Uh, no, Les, I don't. This is his home as long as I'm here."

Then, the last couple of weeks when Maddox was packing, "Don't leave me, son! You can't go! You have to stay here! I don't know what I'll do if you're gone!"

Les really was *that* psycho, and unreasonable.

So, without much thought about his whereabouts, I answered emails and texted Maddox his flight information from the brown armchair I had strategically placed in front of my three wall monitors where I spent an average of twenty hours a day because Les was too good to hold down a job and help me pay our bills.

As he told our sons, "you're descended from royalty. You don't have to do menial tasks and labor. That's why we have servants."

Yeah. I wish I were making that up.

And yes, I know I should have divorced him. I admit freely that I was a fucking idiot.

Everything seemed normal, until it was time to go to my hair appointment.

No Les.

I texted him.

No response.

*What the hell?*

He never allowed me to go anywhere alone. Seriously. He even went to the bathroom with me about half the time.

Or stood outside the door while I went.

I hadn't been to a hair appointment on my own in years. He wouldn't even let me make the appointments or contact my hairstylist.

I ended up being late because I had to hunt down a set of car keys that Les had hidden in his office desk drawer, and then go tell Nick that I was leaving. Since he'd stayed up all night with his brother, he went back to sleep.

Off I ventured to my hair appointment, and about an hour into it, I pulled up the strangest email of all time.

*Gone to check on my parents.*

*~Lester Manly*

"What the fuck?" I said those words out loud.

Now to most people that note might seem "normal," but there was nothing *normal* about this.

First, he'd signed his whole name to it like I, his wife of twenty-seven years, was a stranger.

Or like he was setting up something he intended to present to a judge.

Second, his parents lived in Georgia, not Tennessee. Over five hundred miles away, and Les hated to drive. So much so, that in the past, he'd always paid to have a driver take him on long car trips.

More than that, he hated his parents.

No exaggeration.

He. *Hated.* His. Parents.

In ways you could not imagine.

Les and I had been together for thirty years and married for twenty-seven. In twenty-seven years, Les had never, ever left home to stay overnight somewhere else without giving us weeks of warning about it.

Who did?

For that matter, he'd never packed his own bags, and no bags had been packed before he left. At least none to my knowledge. Nor was Les a quiet person when he got up in the morning. Or if, on any rare occasion, I was trying to nap because I was sick or might have had surgery.

Or one of my notorious cluster migraines.

He was famous for yelling at everyone and slamming every single door in the house. So much so, that he'd pulled some of our doors off their hinges. *I swear to God, that is a true statement.* He was so abusive about it that I would often sleep in my chair in my downstairs office just so that I could get a nap without his shouting antics causing me to wake up in a panic.

Remember what I said about his cruel streak?

He knew that my grandparents used to wake me up with a belt-buckle across my back in the mornings. And that I have severe C-PTSD whenever I hear a door slamming while I slept, or someone shouted unexpectedly as my grandparents would often enter my room that way prior to beating me.

It was why I'd married what I thought was a Beta personality type. I didn't want shouting in my home.

But, as I said, that was how Les lured you into thinking he was this quiet, sweet man.

He was not.

His screaming was so psychotic that my eldest son once ripped the intercom straight out of his wall because Les was using it to scream obscenities at him, and then filter loud, obnoxious music into his room while he was getting ready for school.

While Maddox was a patient, sweet boy, everyone has a breaking point, and Les had pushed him too far that morning.

Les had a way of pushing everyone too far. It was why he couldn't maintain any long-term friendships unless he did it by rarely spending time or seldom talking to his "old" friends.

That was also why I refused to have an intercom in my office. I didn't want Les to use it to torment me.

Mornings in our home were like a war zone because of Les and his absolute need for control, and his problems managing his anger.

If he was up, everyone was up. He prided himself on that cruelty. No one slept on his watch.

Not even if you had cluster migraines and were lying on the floor of the bathroom, puking. Just ask my friend and fellow author, Nikki Kane. She had not only witnessed him doing that to me, she had chewed him out for his cruelty over it.

The third reason that this made no sense?

And please pay close attention as this was why I'd been trapped in a twenty-seven-year marriage with a madman.

His father was a known pedophile who was the son of an even better-known pedophile.

Not being mean. And this wasn't the case of a woman in a divorce making false allegations. I would never do that to anyone.

I wasn't Les.

Being an abused child, I was born knowing that no one wanted to believe you whenever you said someone had been molested. That was the trap.

It was what had kept me in this travesty of a marriage to a madman.

It was why no one wanted to report *that* crime. Why you had to think long and hard before ever reporting it.

Because the pedophile wasn't the one they'd be trying in court.

The victim was.

First you were raped by the predator and then you were raped by the system.

Everyone knew this.

We all knew that the authorities and society as a whole dismissed the most under reported crime with the lowest percentage of false claims simply because no one wanted to deal with the reality that every few minutes someone in this country was raped and a child was molested.

And society wondered why people put up with years and years of abuse and never came forward.

From personal experience as both an abused child and an abused wife, I can tell you why we don't.

Because as bad as the abuse was, it was absolutely N-O-T-H-I-N-G compared to the cold-hearted ruthless abuse put on you by society, the authorities, the court system, and others once you found the courage to come forward and tell someone what had been done to you.

Then, the real abuse and nightmare began from the accusations that you were lying, to the ones who said you deserved it or that you brought it on yourself. That was the last thing a survivor needed to hear. Our egos were already tattered, and our hearts broken into shards.

But the hardest assault of all to endure was the sick apathy of the system that was so broken it refused to do its job and protect not only you, but your own innocent children.

Or worse, those sick psychotic bastards who began victim-shaming.

That was why people stayed.

Why no one dared to speak up.

And that was what had happened to me and my boys.

Repeatedly.

It was had what trapped me as a little girl in my hell at home. And what had trapped me in a miserable marriage with a monster.

As society always did, it took the word of a known pedophile and abuser over ours. Because those disgusting sons-of-bitches knew how to blend in and appear so "proper" and "nice" which was how they lured their victims into their sick and twisted hands.

Go Ted Bundy. Jim Jones. Jeffrey Dahmer. Men so charming that no one believed they could harm anyone.

Not even the police.

For the record, there were other witnesses who could and would verify the Manly secret, and other long-established evidence that proved his family's guilt.

Let me reiterate that these were well-established facts about the Manly family to those who lived in their communities— Grandpa Manly had even been burned out of a town in North Georgia back in the day.

And he was the only machinist in their tiny town that they relied on.

The fire that the town had set to drive him out had been so hot that all the metal in his shop had been melted down to nothing. In spite of his needed and necessary skills, the entire town had stood there and let the Manly business burn to the ground to get rid of him.

He'd fled to the other end of the state.

Les's own house had burned down because of arson when he was in high school. He, his parents and sisters had lost everything they owned in that fire.

And they're not the only two pedophiles in the Manly family. I can't remember if it was

Grandpa Manly's father or brother who was a Sunday School teacher. But whichever Manly relative it was, one morning, in a small Tennessee town, while Mr. Manly was teaching his Sunday School class, a posse rode in, dragged him out in front of his students and killed him in front of the entire Sunday morning congregation.

Not a single member of the church, who had witnessed the entire event, had said a word against the men who killed their Sunday School teacher in front of his class and their congregation. No one was arrested or convicted for such a blatant, premeditated murder that happened in front of so many people.

We all know what that form of Southern justice meant.

"He needed killing." And the town had condoned it because his crime had been severe.

Normally, I don't condone violence of that nature, but when people prey on the innocence of others and threaten a child...

I wouldn't have said a word, either had I witnessed their vigilante justice.

But what galled me was that Les had failed to mention his family's proclivity for pedophilia prior to our marriage.

Prior to our having children.

Something like that should be a legally required disclosure, much like a blood test before marriage. And there needed to be severe repercussion in this world for those who failed to disclose such a horrific fact, because that one detail was what had trapped me into my marriage with a psycho.

Since the moment I had birthed a child and Les had dropped that unexpected bomb on me, I had lived with that Sword of Damocles suspended over my throat.

That demon of "My God, what if?"

Unlike me, Les's mother had known what she was getting into. According to both Les and his sister, she was a victim of his grandfather herself. What I'd never, ever understood and what both Les and his sister had always hated her for was the fact that their mother knew what she'd married into, and then exposed her own children to the pedophiles instead of protecting them.

"My God, Terri! After I told her we'd been molested, that selfish whore would take us to my grandfather's house that my father had bought for him after he'd molested him and his sister, and made us sit at a table with him and act like nothing had happened. What kind of fucked-up bitch does that?"

I couldn't have agreed more. And I'd been sickened by the sight of Snooty since the day I learned what she'd done to her own children.

What his father had done.

I have extreme sympathy for victims, but having been one myself, it didn't excuse victimizing another. In fact, that worsened it because you knew better. It was why I believed that the punishment for those who'd suffered it should be worse because we knew how brutal it was. How much damage the victim suffered.

We knew not to carry that forward, and it was our obligation to stop the cycle of pain.

My husband had duped me into believing he carried the same feelings and convictions about that, and about protecting our children from the monsters in his family.

Les's feigned outrage and hatred for both parents was such that I assumed he understood why it was imperative that we build up a substantial nest egg for our three Autistic sons who would need that money to protect them from not only the world that wouldn't understand them and their needs, but from his sick and twisted parents.

To that end, I made sure to warn any, and every person who had a child around me that my in-laws were a family of known pedophiles, and those who protected pedophiles. Just ask Nikki or Celestial Blackstone, or anyone else with kids who'd ever been around my in-laws over the years.

I told them all what the Manlys were.

My only regret was that I couldn't bring charges against his family.

Since I wasn't a Manly victim and none of their victims were willing to testify, there was nothing more I could do to protect those around us.

When Les's sister had finally wanted to come forward and expose them a couple of years ago, she'd reached out to her brother.

Les and I argued over his unwillingness to back her.

"It's the right thing to do!"

"I don't know, Terri. She's adopted and they're my parents."

"Who've done nothing for you or their grandchildren! My God, Les, you took a dump on your father's desk in high school because you hated him for what they did to you. Now, you won't back Katrina? I don't understand."

Another true event. When Les was in high school, which was a military school owned by the Army, he'd committed a felony by breaking into that school after hours, and then vandalizing his father's office. His pièce de résistance had been defecating on his father's desk and leaving it there, along with his broken sword that had been engraved with Les's name for his "loving" dad to find in the morning.

The ultimate act of humiliation for his father to make him a laughingstock to his peers. Something no normal human would do.

Another story I didn't learn about until it was too late.

Les was so proud of the event, that he also bragged about it to his own sons.

That act of ultimate defiance was on his permanent record. While he wasn't arrested for it, he was suspended from school. That event, too, had witnesses and records.

And after I learned just what a psycho I was living with, I went to three different attorneys during the course of my long marriage, and they all said the same thing to me. "Terri, unless it's your husband molesting your kids, there's no way they'll deny him custody. Your in-laws will have access to them, and you can't stop it. There's nothing you can do today that will keep him from gaining custody of his children."

*Let's hear it for the modern American courts that threw our children to the wolves to be ravaged and devoured.*

Having been one of those young lambs they left to be slaughtered, I wasn't about to sacrifice my children for my happiness. I'd made that vow long ago, and I'd kept it.

I wasn't Snooty Manly. My kids had always come first, and I would bust hell itself wide open before I allowed anyone to harm them on my watch.

Unlike Les, I was determined to raise my children free of the nightmares I'd known as a kid. They would not pull a bed across their doors at night and live with the stark terror that I'd known.

Not now.

Not ever.

So, when Les had said that he'd gone to check on his parents whom he had spent our entire marriage insulting and hating, it seemed a bit farfetched.

Remember that this was the same father who when Les had been told that the man had been diagnosed with cancer had said and I quote, "Good, it's about time Karma caught up to the old bastard. I hope it's painful and that he burns in hell. I can't wait to piss on his grave."

His sister said a very similar thing about both his parents when I'd told her they had cancer (she hadn't spoken to them in years).

Les was even crueler about how he felt toward his mother. "I hope Satan rapes her up the ass every day of eternity."

For thirty years, he'd referred to her as "the selfish whore who sold my virginity for her vanity. The bitch who had no use for her children and should have been sterilized at birth."

So, you can see why his note that he'd gone to "check on my parents" seemed a little bizarre to me, and greatly out of character for him. "I've gone to set fire to my parents..." *that* I would have believed.

Especially since we were in the middle of a hostile lawsuit Les had started under my protests, and that I was under the gun for. In fact, I was being publicly brutalized by the monster he'd awakened when I'd forewarned him what was coming (he'd laughed dismissively at my concerns), and then he'd allowed the attorneys he'd hired to put a gag order on me so that I couldn't even defend myself against the outrageous lies that bitch and her crew were spewing.

Lies that had put a serious hurt on my career.

As Les had said all throughout that lawsuit, "The one thing I've learned out of this is how to steal a bestselling series and get away with it with no repercussions."

Apparently, he'd learned a whole lot more from studying her and her tactics.

*How to ruin a life and further victimize the victim.*

That gag order had been done behind my back and without my consent—against my explicit orders to each of them that I hadn't wanted any kind of gag order in place, especially since my opponent wasn't complying with it.

Lucky me (please read with all intended sarcasm) that my lawyers had a conscience and refused to have her up on the contempt motions she deserved for violating the very gag order that her attorneys had insisted on having.

Wow!

For our team, Les had hired scrupulous lawyers who played by the rules and who refused to harm the other party's reputation, while the other party's attorneys went wild on my reputation and didn't care that I was the innocent victim of it all (boy, doesn't this sound familiar).

Meanwhile, Les was beside himself over the injustice of my being publicly brutalized, while the bullies got away with their crimes.

He constantly beat up the very attorneys he'd hired for their failure to defend me and go after the other side for their incessant lies, and for publicly attacking me and ruining my career.

This was truly ironic, and I ask you to remember that Les was my virulent defender against all their ridiculous claims that he would later use himself to smear me with in less than twenty-four hours after he forced me into a settlement with their side.

That was the real hypocrisy that Les committed against me and his sons.

He copied and pasted the same exact insults and phrases they used against me in his own divorce filings. He even hired the other author's attorney, to attack me and represent him, after spending three years calling the author and her attorneys liars for making the same bullshit accusations that he used against me, after he'd given my attorneys evidence to prove that those allegations were false.

Les used the same exact allegations against me after refuting them.

*What a guy.*

And there was no pulling Les back from the debacle he'd started and continued to inflame by insisting we carry on with his whole "we have to make them pay for ripping you off" scheme.

See, that author wasn't the only author or person he wanted me to sue. He had a whole jolly "sue" list of people he wanted my attorneys to go after before he got the idea to divorce me.

That had just been Case Number One.

Well, that wasn't exactly true. He'd actually hired the attorneys to go after someone else first. But right as he was directing them to file suit on that poor slob, Author Dumas had made the mistake of getting his attention drawn to her by doing something incredibly stupid.

Something that Les, my agent, and my attorneys had warned her, her agent, her lawyers and my publisher not once, not twice, but thrice not to do.

Trample all over my trademarked series.

Seriously. How many Cease and Desist warnings had to be sent before you and my publisher learned to steer clear of a property that you all knew full well existed, because you'd been told three times in the past to get your asses off it?

By the way, that was the law. Once you knew a property was in existence, you were required by law to steer clear of it.

Les's grand plan had been to take the money that we won from that case, and then pick up on the original case to continue to sue that first person he'd wanted to go after, then systematically go after a whole list of others he wanted to "bring down" for treading on my property.

That was his "get rich" scheme.

As Les had said so many times to me and our sons, "If something ever happens to you, Terri, I'm going to mop up on your trademarks and make sure those bastards pay for ripping you off!"

Given all that, and the fact that he had been talking just days before to the attorneys about making sure he could still go after the other "plagiarists" who were "stealing from Terri," I couldn't believe the rat-bastard had run out of town at the pinnacle of this case he'd been so hellbent for me to file.

It didn't make sense.

Until he hired her attorney to represent him against me.

But I'll get to that in a bit...

*As they say, corruption in Williamson County runs deep.*

All I understood at that point was that my phone had begun to explode from the lawyers who were desperate for information they needed for the Dumas case. Information that I didn't have because it wasn't my case.

It was Les's lawsuit, and he was the "Manly Command Center" that he'd dubbed himself, and keeper of all details where the Dumas lawsuit was concerned.

"You can't be trusted with files or emails, Terri. You'll lose them." That was his answer for keeping me out of everything to do with our lives.

My credit cards. My car keys. Information regarding my home and our sons' education files. Even invitations to parties that I was invited to for my organizations (organizations he wasn't even a part of and that didn't have his name on them). I was never allowed to have anything. Not a single piece of mail.

Nothing.

"I" couldn't be trusted.

*Feel free to laugh at my stupidity.* God knows I do on a daily basis, because I was the idiot asshole who'd married this jackass.

Now, I was being hammered by attorneys for all this information that they needed as of yesterday, and I had no idea where any of it was being kept in this massive home Les had also insisted we buy in a neighborhood I despised with everything I wasn't worth.

Why? Because everything was always about Les and what Les wanted, my wants and thoughts be damned. I had to placate Baby Huey at all times or suffer his giant, petulant fits. It was why I had to make posts on social media about how great he was and put him in the dedications of all my books.

If I didn't...

There was hell to pay, and I didn't have time to deal with it. I was too busy having to raise my children because he couldn't be bothered with them, and to build my career, while dealing with an awful lawsuit, and a debilitating illness no one could figure out.

All the while feeding his massive ego.

'Cause he was always watching and always pouting.

Lurking in the shadows.

Worse than Big Brother. *If you ever want to be really creeped out, watch any of my YouTube videos and pay close attention to where my eyes go during them.* He was always off camera, watching me, and I was watching him, watch me. I was looking at him before I answered a lot of questions.

*Keep an eye on my expressions and read between the lines. People who are victims of abuse will see the tell-tale clues.*

They are bone-chilling.

Just as the photos of him with his hands firmly planted on my shoulders, holding me in place. Or of his feet pressed on top of mine.

He was always in control. It was why when he left, my sons and I were like children in a candy store. We threw our arms out and leaned our heads back and spun around in giddy delight.

"We're free!"

Nick had said it best. "The reign of terror is over!"

Even Caleb's friend, Abraham, who was tutoring Nick noticed the difference as soon as Les was gone. "The house is so much lighter now. Brighter. I've never seen you guys so cheerful."

But we should have known it wouldn't last. Such sick, psycho bastards can never let go of their victims. Once they sink their fangs in, they never, ever let up. Not until they suck every last bit of life out of us.

Damn them for it.

And there I was, physically ill, on deadline, and I needed to go out of town for a major event with Nick. Not to mention, I had depositions coming up in two weeks and we had to have the information Les had hidden wherever.

Or had taken with him. No one knew because he refused to share information with anyone. It was all a sick game to him.

*What the hell, Les?*

*What the hell?*

Meanwhile my eldest was on a plane to a foreign country with a severe lung condition, while my other two were getting ready to graduate, and I was trying to help them all as best I could, while dealing with a sick and injured body.

My phone was still blowing up from lawyers who couldn't get the answers they desperately needed, as well as my pissed off Hollywood people and an agent who'd been betrayed and subpoenaed for no reason whatsoever.

I returned home after picking up lunch for Nick. "Hey, baby. Did you know your dad had gone to Georgia to see his parents?"

Nick scowled at me. "What? Dad wouldn't go there. He hates his parents."

"That's what he told me. Did he call or text you?"

"No."

So, Les hadn't said a single word to his favorite son (he made no bones about how much preferred Nick over his other two sons—he bragged about that to their faces and rubbed Maddox's and Caleb's noses in the fact that he preferred Nick over them) that he was leaving or planning to go away for an extended stay.

Nick had known nothing about his father's trip.

By now, I knew something big was up. For him not to tell Nick was major.

Had he even gone to Georgia or was he somewhere else?

Les was such a liar, he could be anywhere. After all, he wasn't answering the phone or texts. He wasn't emailing me back.

His assistant, Hogg, was at my house with a simpering smirk that said she knew he was doing something despicable.

My mind went wild with the possibilities. What were the two of them up to?

Or was Les just being childish as usual? Was this his way of paying me back because I'd dared take a research trip to finish a book last fall after *New York Comic Con*, rather than come home where I couldn't work because he'd moved Hogg into my home and that obnoxious, screaming banshee had made the house so unbearable that I couldn't work in it?

Yes, you read that correctly. My husband had moved an unmarried woman into my marital home, on top of me and my sons, where she'd walked around in her underwear, screamed at them in fits of rage, and claimed my home as her own.

She'd invited her friends and family over whenever she wanted and treated me like an invalid child. To her, this was her home and he was her husband. We, my sons and I, were the unwanted houseguests.

Les was okay with that.

If you doubt it, again, watch the YouTube videos where Les had forced her on me, and you can see exactly the abuse I was suffering at both their hands.

And how weak I was and unable to stop them.

Hogg even went so far as to tell others, "We're not going to really decorate for Christmas this year."

*What the hell?*

*We?*

*Bitch, this ain't your house...*

*It ain't your family.*

For that matter, she'd even offered to write *my* checks to my employees to pay them. Without *my* permission.

On my bank account.

An account she was *not* an authorized user on.

The balls on this cow were unimaginable. She even had her own personal mail delivered here as if she were the owner of my home.

*Who does that?*

But here, in the great state of Tennessee, they tell me that this wasn't proof of an extramarital affair.

*Are you kidding me?*

Even though I had two witnesses who heard and saw me tell Les on two separate occasions, "Get her out of my house. I'm sick of seeing you on top of her all the time. You have to make a choice. Me or the sister-wife. You can't have us both. Either she goes or I go. Choose!"

And less than six months later, he filed for divorce and to this day, more than two years later, they're still together.

Let me repeat: two other witnesses saw them in intimate encounters with each other.

While she lived in our home against my wishes.

My witnesses saw them embracing. Snuggled together. Even drinking together.

In the dark. On my couch.

Hogg also confessed to a third party that they were having an affair, and my aunt and another, separate, third party caught them intertwined.

How was *that* not proof?

Welcome to the great state of Tennessee. Proud land of the Dipshit. That should be our official state animal.

Instead of being the Volunteer State, we should be called the State of Corruption. Because according to two separate independent studies, we were the third most corrupt state in the Union.

The third of fifty.

And according to an independent Harvard study, Nashville was one of the most corrupt cities in this great nation.

Yee-haw! Never have I seen a state or city so proud of the fact that it runs on dirty deals and underhanded policies and politics. Everybody here talked about the corruption, especially in the judicial arena.

Yet no one would stop it.

Hell, we even ran Super Bowl commercials about how corrupt our courts were. Even named the judges that were scamming our citizens and violating their rights.

And no one would do anything to stop it.

Not our AG, DAs or any political incumbent.

But I wasn't most people. I came from a long, long line of those who weren't afraid to speak up when we saw something wrong. Who defended those who couldn't defend themselves.

Even so, I was about to get screwed big time by that corruption and their racketeering!

I should have seen it coming, but I'd been sick for so long. So sick that the May before Les had left, when I'd attended a writer's conference in Atlanta, every single person who saw me was convinced I was going to die.

Including me.

One friend, Catherine James, an author from Australia, went back to her room after seeing me and told her roommate that there wouldn't be any more of my Night-Seeker novels. "We're going to be writing Terri's eulogy before the end of this year."

She wasn't the only one who made that dire prediction. My lifelong friend, Kay Williams, who'd grown up just a couple of streets over, was a professional nurse and writer, too. When she saw me that same weekend, she was deeply worried. And not just because I was on a heart monitor for a weird tachycardia that had appeared out of nowhere.

I looked bad. Wane. Pale. Frail. I kept having tremors for no reason. Uncontrollable shakes. Confusion so bad that I couldn't even remember the name of my cousin who was more like my niece. The very baby girl I once held on my knee and had helped raise as if she were my own.

It was so bad that when one of my other childhood best friends showed up, I grabbed onto her in a restaurant and started crying in her arms, because I honestly thought that I would die soon and never see her again.

Kay was terrified over my condition, but she wasn't able to check in with me as Les had forced Karen Hogg to go with me on that trip.

Yes, you heard that correctly.

Karen Hogg.

That annoying, cloying creature who'd been hired initially to tutor my children and then ended up as Les's secretary/assistant/paralegal, and lap mate. Somehow, this repellent thing had wormed her way into our lives, and we couldn't expel her.

All of us complained about her constantly.

Les complained about her, too. But he'd run off all my reliable help and had secluded me from my friends and family.

One by one. Systematically.

Even worse, he refused to let me hire more. "We need the money for the lawsuit, Terri!"

Foolishly, I thought he was loyal to his sons, if not his wife.

Until the day that abhorrent beast waddled her way in.

I will never forget the first time I saw her sitting at my black kitchen farm table with that supremely fake smile and heinous laugh she thinks is oh-so-charming. For whatever reason, Hogg believed herself to be a pin-up showgirl with flawless looks. I'd seen her toss her frizzy, badly cut blond hair over her shoulders and flirt outrageously with men.

Married or not.

And I knew what those men said about her behind her back, including Les. Too bad she didn't. Even Les would tell me that he didn't want to be seen in public with her.

"It's awful, Terri. People think she's my wife. Last thing I want is for anyone to think I'd marry *that*."

I should have realized then that the "lady" doth protest too much. Had I not been so sick, I might have caught on and asked myself, "Yo, Terri? Why would anyone assume they're a married couple? How were they behaving in public that it would give other folks *that* idea?"

After all, I'd been out to eat with Les a number of times when they'd asked if we wanted one or two checks.

So, if they hadn't assumed he was my husband, why would they assume he was hers?

Why was he feeling the need to assure me that they weren't?

Just how public cuddly were they?

For that matter, why was he always taking her out for lunch, anyway when he was forever insisting that we not "feed the help" (or servants as Les liked to call them)?

And on family outings? Why was she making it a point to sit beside him on all those trips?

And why did he pay her outrageous hourly fees whenever she went with us to those family movies and such?

What kind of slag charged thirty to sixty dollars an hour to watch a movie or go to the opera with a family?

Yeah, that was the kind of slag or should I say "paid escort" Hogg was.

What else could you call her? Is that not the very definition of a prostitute? A woman of questionable virtue and morals who charged a man for her company to either spend the night with him while his wife was out of town, or to go with him to events where people believed she was his "girlfriend" or "wife?"

Les was the one who told me people thought she was his "date" or "spouse."

He was constantly taking her places and paying her for it and having her stay overnight at my house with him whenever I left town.

Never mind the whole she's "living with us" nightmare.

Hmmm...

Anyway, under normal circumstances, those rampant rumors from my neighbors and others would have clued me in that they were behaving inappropriately.

That, and Karen Hogg's constant bragging to my face about all the men she'd screwed, married and otherwise. How they were all dying to have her, regardless of her Ursula-the-Sea-Witch looks. Oh, to have her self-esteem. But sadly, my mirror was not only brutally honest with me.

It mocked me for fun.

I clearly saw my short, stubby stature. The lines on my face that got deeper every year. And my once black curly hair that had begun to fall out by the handfuls and go completely straight for no reason whatsoever. Like my mother's did when she had chemo to treat her cancer.

It was so bad that two different hairstylists had expressed their deep concerns to me. "Terri, you need to talk to your doctor. Hair doesn't fall out like this. And it never changes texture unless something's really wrong with someone." Dalton would know. She'd been my hairdresser for years. We hadn't changed products or done anything different than we'd been doing.

Yet there was no denying that my hair was a lot thinner than before.

My alternate hairstylist, Sharon, who filled in whenever Dalton wasn't there, said the same thing. They both urged me to have my doctor look into it.

And I did.

It was a mystery as to why my once incredibly thick hair fell out even when I laid my head on a pillow. I literally couldn't run my hand through my hair that I didn't pull out an entire fist full of hair.

"You should check with someone, Terri. I'm worried." Rio was another friend who'd been with me for years and who did facials for my sons and Les.

Rio watched as I grew weaker, and my symptoms worsened. She also saw how much hair was left behind on pillows or in my chair whenever I got up.

How much my eyes swelled closed.

I simply never gave much thought to the timing of it all. How those symptoms coincided with the arrival of Hogg into our lives...

Karen Alice Hogg.

My, how she was aptly named. As if fate had known what she'd grow into and had decided to stick her with a warning label for others. Or maybe "petty bitch" would have been a better moniker for her.

Though I try never to judge anyone, I couldn't help it where she was concerned. There was an innate smugness that permeated the air around her and it rubbed me the wrong way from that first meeting. An aura of cruelty that clung to her like a bad smell. Condescension dripped from her lips with snide comments that had often made me want to slap her plump jowls.

I didn't want her tutoring my sons. I didn't want her in my home.

For whatever reason, Les was unreasonable where this creature was concerned. "Why don't you like her? She's a preacher!"

So was Jim Jones, Andy Savage, Jimmy Swaggart, Peter Popoff, Aimee McPherson, and countless others who killed, maimed, lied and swindled others.

Preachers who preyed on weak minds.

Like Les's.

Not to mention the pervert my grandfather had brought home when I was a little girl, but I won't talk about that disgusting piece of shit I've relegated to my past. Needless to say, I was skeptical of so-called clergy, especially when they used their frocks to infiltrate people's lives and gain unwarranted trust.

As my father often said, trust was something you earned. It didn't come from the clothes you wore or the lies you told.

And you damn sure didn't demand it.

Besides, as a member of the faith, Hogg should know that gluttony, lust and envy were three of the seven deadlies, and yet she embraced them all with open arms.

Never mind the child abuse she meted out with greedy fists. You could hear it on her lips every day as she spoke about her "students" and their parents.

Not with kindness, but with bitter, mocking hatred.

She was a soulless slag unfit to be near children. It was why God had made her barren, and if our laws had any decency, she'd be banned from any occupation that allowed her near anyone under the age of thirty.

For that matter, she should be locked up for what she'd done to my Nick, alone. My kitchen table was scarred from where my son had dug his fingernails into the top of it while she mentally tormented him with insults that tore him down until he became a shell of his former self. While she cruelly belittled and berated my son, Les had not only encouraged her, he'd participated.

If I ever came into the room, they'd both turn on me and start shouting. "Go back downstairs! You're distracting Nick. He can't focus if you're in the room!"

To this day, I can't believe that I ever listened to them. I knew that Nick wasn't happy, but he'd never said a word to me about what they were doing.

Until after his father was gone.

"Because Dad said that shit rolled down hill. He told me that if I said a word to you that he'd make it worse for me."

I was so angry at God for letting that happen. For the fact that I was so hard-of-hearing that I couldn't tell what they were doing to my baby.

*Why is there no justice in this world?*

Had I only known, I would have stopped it. I was so angry at myself.

My heart broke for what they'd done to my baby while I was too sick to know about it. How many more children had Hogg torn down and destroyed? I knew my sons weren't the only ones.

And that stung most of all.

"She needs to go, Les."

Les refused to protect his children. "She's here to help."

How? My wonderful, chipper Nick had turned belligerent from the moment Hogg had come into our lives. With his previous tutor, Rebekah, he'd been a straight-A student. He'd been happy, popular in school, and outgoing.

Everyone loved my Nick.

In no time of having Tutor Hogg around, he'd become withdrawn and sullen. He'd begun secluding himself in his room and locking his door.

"It's just puberty. He's in a new school."

At first, I thought Les might be right. I'd had a very hard time when I started high school—because of my own Autism, I didn't do change well and the transition from middle to high school had been extremely difficult for me. Nick was having an even harder time, and he hated change as much as I did.

In less than one year, both of his brothers had gone off to college. Half of his friends had been sent to a different high school, and his favorite tutor had left to move on to a university in a different state.

Nick's favorite saying had always been, "it's different. I don't like it."

Maybe that was all that was wrong with him. My wonderful Boo would be back as soon as he acclimated. After all, he was incredibly bright. He was in the top one percent of Mathletes in the country.

Besides, I kept getting sicker with every day that passed. So sick that Les had refused to allow me to drive to Atlanta that past May.

"Someone needs to go with you and make sure you're okay."

I stupidly thought he had cared.

Sadly, I couldn't have been more wrong.

Instead of being there to help, Hogg had been sent to drive away everyone who was close to me, and I do mean *everyone*.

Even my editor ran from me as soon as she saw Hogg in the hotel lobby, and then, she canceled our dinner reservations. Probably because my editor was afraid of what the bill might be if Hogg came along (if you've ever seen Rebel Wilson's character on the train in *Hustlers* then you know what it was like to take Hogg out to eat).

For the record, that was not a comment on her weight. It was one on her selfish greed and Narcissism.

When Maddox had come up from the university he was attending in Georgia to stay with me for the weekend, would you believe Hogg had the nerve to tell him that he wasn't welcomed there?

In his mother's room that I was paying for.

She actually told him to go sleep in the hallway.

I told Hogg that she could sleep out in the hallway if she didn't like it. My sons were always welcomed wherever I was.

She, however, was not.

Next, she'd tried to expel my other two best friends that I grew up with. Joan Hart and Candice Jones.

Luckily, Candice (the one I had cried on) was a psychologist. Petite and frail in appearance, she had vibrant red hair and a dazzling smile as big as her heart. As usual, she'd shown up to spend the weekend with me and Joan had helped her to hide her suitcase in my room so that Hogg wouldn't run her off, too.

Tall and in-your-face, Joan doesn't listen to much of anyone. She's ballsy to the nth degree and doesn't intimidate easily.

Hogg had the nerve to say to both of them, "you can't stay long. Terri has a curfew and bedtime. She needs to rest."

*Like what? I'm five?*

These were the people who loved me and cared about what happened to me. Not the angry slut screwing my husband that Les had sicced on me that I couldn't stand to be around. The same micro-managing slag who had made the driver Les had hired so angry that he had to stop the car and get out to calm down. That was how condescending and demeaning this creature was to everyone around her.

Including Les who was too dumb to realize how much she insulted him to his face.

Candice looked Hogg dead in the eyes and pertly said, "uh-huh." Then sashayed right past her as if she wasn't there.

Later that day, she took me aside. "Terri, that is one toxic bitch. You have got to get her out of your life."

The funny thing? Candice doesn't cuss.

Nor does she ever treat people that way. The fact that Hogg had rubbed her the wrong way was impressive.

And an important indictment against Hogg.

Hogg had done the same thing with Kay Williams. She'd made sure that Kay, a veteran registered nurse who loved everyone, except Hogg, didn't have access to me.

She even tried to tell my own cousin and personal assistant, Lyra Wheel, that she couldn't stay with me and that she'd have to drive more than an hour to and from the event each day.

*Could you believe the nerve of this Hogg?*

Since the moment she was born a few months after me, Lyra had been like a sister. She was my blood.

More than that, she was my actual hired personal assistant who traveled with me to events to work them.

Not Hogg.

And Hogg had told her, what? That she wasn't welcome to stay with me?

Of course, Hogg felt entitled. After all, Les had allowed his slag to move into my home with us so that he could fondle her openly and flaunt it in all our faces.

I wish I were making that up.

And if that wasn't the gall to end all gall, Hogg actually wrote a hall pass for Joan to give her permission to bandy about the conference.

Yep, you heard that correctly.

Anyone who has ever attended a professional conference knew that you needed a badge to get in and out of them. Because Joan had picked up Maddox at the airport and had come in late, Joan hadn't picked her badge up yet, and I needed her to go check on something for me.

"Karen, give your badge to Joan so that she can go downstairs." I didn't give her mine because the people running the event would know Joan wasn't me since I was a guest of honor.

Joan didn't want to answer any awkward questions as to why she had my badge.

A few minutes later, Joan handed me the piece of paper that Hogg had given her.

> *Please allow Joan Hart into the book*
> *area. She needs access to do an errand.*
>
> *Thank you,*
> *Karen Hogg*

"Are you effing kidding me?" Like anyone at the convention would give two shits about Hogg and her paper pass?

My jaw had fallen to the floor.

Joan laughed. "I know, right?"

Rolling my eyes, I gave her my badge and decided they could ask questions about why she had it if they noticed the name on it. "She's a fucking idiot."

"Don't insult idiots."

"You're right, Joan. I'm sorry. They're good people. She's a shit-stirring whore."

Hogg's antics that entire weekend were so deplorable that by the end of it, I was done with her. During the course of it, she'd made two fans run away in tears. One, because she'd insulted her weight—she, honest to God, had called one fan fat to her face. Another one, she'd screamed at like a banshee in heat, for not seeing that the line began in a different spot. Which was an easy mistake to make, given the size of the crowd, and layout of the event.

Another fan, she insulted over a gift the fan had brought for me.

Poor Joan and Lyra had to run after them to comfort them. Not to mention, the way Hogg kept sending the poor volunteers after drinks and food for her to rudely slurp during the entire signing, while telling them it was for me. Anyone who had ever seen me at an event knew that I refused to eat while I'm signing as I don't want to get ick on someone's books. And while I might sip a little at a signing, I had never finished a whole bottle of anything.

Again, I refused to be rude. My parents had taught me manners and respect.

*I'm not a Hogg.*

Hogg went through I had no idea how many bottles or how much food.

I've never been more embarrassed, which given the fact that I've been seen in public with Les and his mother since I was eighteen said a lot.

The horror of *that* humiliating weekend will be forever seared into my memory.

Right down to the fact that Hogg ordered the VP of marketing for my publisher around like he was an errand boy, and then had the nerve to flirt with him.

Even after I told her he was married.

"I don't care!"

Please keep in mind that this slag was a Methodist preacher and was a pastor (or so she claimed). Shame on them for ordaining such a repellent, immoral creature!

And when I returned home, all Les could do was tell me why I needed to hire Hogg as my full-time assistant and to kick my cousin to the curb.

"I'm sorry, but Hogg doesn't ever need to go out into the public again. Keep her away from my fans and away from me. She is never to have anything to do with me or my business. She's repulsive and has no idea how to talk to anyone!"

Instead of listening, Les took it as a personal challenge to entrench her further into our lives. And to replace me with her.

I really had no idea how far he would take it.

Or how vicious he would become.

I had a viper in my home, and it was about to turn lethal.

**N**ICK NEEDS HELP WITH SCHOOL, so I told Karen she can stay here, and not have to drive back and forth to her parents' house."

Stunned like a deer in the middle of an interstate at rush hour, I gaped at Les as he stood in my office, behind my chair. "Did you suddenly find your missing sense of humor?"

Was he out of his effing mind?

He looked even dumber than normal. "What? She's only trying to help."

*Yeah, herself to our lives.*

"No, Les, she's not. Nick hates her. Caleb hates her, and Maddox will kill her if she's in this house, all the time." She was already spending way too much time here, and our kids couldn't stand the condescending bitch. No one could stomach her.

It was why she'd been run out of, not one, but three different churches.

As noted previously, people had begun to think she was his wife.

There were nights when she didn't leave until two in the morning, and it was killing Nick who had no break from school. He was going from eight in the morning until two a.m.

What they were doing to him was inhuman, and against any sort of decency.

Pretty sure the Geneva Convention had a mandate that said even POWs couldn't be subjected to torture this grueling.

I had no idea how she was supposedly teaching other students because she was billing us full-time.

Not to mention her lies about being a pastor, when she was here on Sundays.

Obviously, the lying slag wasn't in church on Sunday, and she damn sure couldn't be a pastor if she was spending all that quality time with my husband.

For those who don't know, anyone could be a preacher. It really wasn't hard. Nowadays, you could even be ordained online.

Different faiths had different qualifications for how you could become one. My grandfather and uncles were Baptist preachers. And depending on which sect of Baptist you were, they had different rules for how to become ordained. Some required seminary, and some required you to apprentice with another preacher after being "called" by God to preach, or in some sects of Baptist you could simply be "called."

In its purest form, *preacher* just meant that you spread the word of God by preaching the "good word."

You became a pastor when you had a church congregation that you were responsible for. That meant that you had a lot of responsibility. So, when I said my uncles and grandfather were preachers, they were pastors who were in charge of their churches, and who "preached" to those congregations on Sundays and on one weeknight, along with the other responsibilities that the head of a church took on, depending on the size of the congregation.

Hogg called herself a pastor, but she was lying her ass off as I knew for a fact that while she was staying and living in my home, she wasn't going to church on Sundays or Wednesday nights.

Or ever.

That meant that she had no congregation and therefore was not a pastor, while passing herself off as one.

That, for the record, was a crime in the state of Tennessee.

*Thou shalt not bear false witness.*

She was one heck of a preacher, eh?

Never mind the commandment about coveting and false prophets.

And Les defended the conniving, lying hypocrite he'd brought into my home against his entire family. "She's the best help we've ever had."

No, she wasn't.

"She treats everyone like shit, Les."

"You hate everybody!" Les and his famous gaslighting technique.

"Not true. I only hate assholes. She's Queen Sphinctera, and I don't want her here."

"She's moving in. Nick needs it."

Seldom had I been angrier.

*I got the cookie for you.* The old joke me and the boys used about Les. He always did that. Whenever he wanted something, he pretended he was doing it for you. That damn martyr complex he had.

*How dare you not be grateful after all I've done for you. "I" didn't want the "fill in the blank," I just tolerated it because* you *wanted it.*

Gah, for the times Les had pulled that crap on us.

You never knew what the truth was with him. He was such a manipulative liar. Case in point, for years he'd told me that Maddox had only wanted to attend Belmont University here in Rankville, oh, excuse me, Nashville. That it was the only university Maddox had applied to.

Then Les had told Maddox that Les had applied to Vanderbilt for Maddox and that Maddox didn't get in.

Let me repeat that.

Les had told Maddox that he, or rather, one of his paid henchmen (Hogg), had submitted a college application for Maddox to Vanderbilt. *I'm rather sure at this point that most everyone in the country knows just how illegal that is.*

It was what put Felicity Huffman, Lori Loughlin (and others) in jail.

It was also fraud to put in an application for someone else while pretending to be them, and without telling them that you'd submitted an application on their behalf.

Had Les or anyone else actually submitted an application to Vanderbilt or Brown where my child had really wanted to go, Maddox would have easily gotten in. My child scored so high on the ACT that he was accepted into the genius society, Mensa, based on his score alone. He also graduated from one of the best high schools in Williamson County, with honors. While I question its integrity, Williamson County, was on record as being one of the best school systems in the country, which was why I had stupidly moved to that hellhole.

And Maddox had slept through all of his honors classes while maintaining straight-A's in them.

He'd also founded a number of clubs in high school, started his own business, and was a multi published author before he graduated.

My multilingual son was an amazing overachiever who graduated from Belmont in three years, while exploring the world.

Unlike the total piece of utter shit I'd married who had dared to insult my son and called the boy lazy.

But Les had never been able to stand the thought of his sons doing better than him and so, unbeknownst to me while I was sick and fighting for my life, he'd deliberately sabotaged them.

Not only had he sabotaged my child, he'd made Maddox feel like crap and had insulted him for not getting into a school he'd never even applied to.

More than that, Les had allowed old Snooty to insult my baby at his high school graduation, just as she'd done to Les when he graduated law school.

"Look, Maddox. These other students got into all these colleges! This one girl even got into Emory!"

I sneered at the dried-up pedophile's whore. "Maddox got into every school he applied to. As for Emory, so what? They let me in, and my best friend graduated from there with a 4.0. Besides, that school's built on the land that used to be my family's dairy farm."

All true.

And it had shut that heinous slag up.

Les knew he'd deprived his son of going to the more prestigious schools Maddox could have gone to. That he'd short-changed his son's future, and then allowed his useless pedophile-protecting mother to mock my baby at his own graduation over it.

That was the kind of monster Les Manly actually was.

Let me repeat that Les was a liar. Nothing out of his mouth was ever the truth.

And he had no soul or heart. How could anyone do that to his own children?

While he was doing that to Maddox, he pulled Nick out of high school so that Hogg could become his full-time teacher, and Les could overpay the sow an overinflated salary to bolster her overinflated ego.

Under her brutality, Nick went from being in the top one percent of Mathletes in the country to being unable to finish a test because of her mental abuse of him.

While Maddox was brilliant and he knew how proud I was of him, Nick was even smarter. Even Maddox talked about that. But within a short period of time, Les and Hogg ruined Nick's brilliant academic future because Les couldn't stand the thought of his sons succeeding, and thus proving what a loser, he actually was.

Let's face it, Les had failed at everything he'd ever done in his entire life. He'd said it best years ago when my sons had found my Peanut Bowl Championship jersey from when I was a kid. Because it was a football jersey, they'd naturally assumed it belonged to their father.

"No, kids. It's your mother's. I was always a bench warmer."

And he was.

In everything.

Les couldn't cut it as a lawyer. The entire time he was in law school, he'd kept trying to drop out. He'd only finished law school because *I* had refused to allow him to quit, and he'd graduated at the very bottom of his class.

He'd failed in every job he had ever attempted with sorry excuses that the other workers were always picking on him.

Failed as a father.

Was a miserable husband.

He'd betrayed every friend he'd ever had, and turned on them, or walked away and ignored them.

He couldn't even finish the lawsuit he'd started.

It reminded me of an English class we both took when we attended the same college. Our professor had us write, as morbid as it was, our obituaries.

Here was what I wrote for mine:

> Today the world mourns the passing of #1 *New York Times* bestselling author, Terri Woods. Beloved by her fans and family, she leaves behind a legacy of work that she hopes will be cherished by her devoted readers. Known for her philanthropy, she spent her time divided between her children, fans and work, trying to make the world a better place. Please don't send flowers. Terri would have rather you spend the money on your favorite charity and to donate it in the name of your own loved ones. Likewise, Terri doesn't want a funeral or viewing (other than to please make sure a Catholic priest gives her Last Rites, and that she's buried with a copy of her latest book, photo of her family, and a rosary). Instead of mourning, she asks for her loved ones to hold a good old-fashioned wake with a lot of singing and dancing, and to have a party with the money she's set aside for it. Enjoy your life while you can, and please remember her fondly. Her only wish is that you smile when you think of her, and that your life was made better by having known her.

That is the actual assignment I wrote, and I could use it if I died tomorrow. If Les died tomorrow, his would read:

> Lester Manly passed away alone. Hated by his sons and estranged from the wife who once adored him, he will be missed by no one. Those who knew him, eventually hated him. He did nothing with the law degree his wife scrubbed toilets to give him. He stole the money his wife had set aside for their children and wasted it on utter selfishness. He did absolutely nothing with his life, except be a burden to everyone he ever met. He will not be missed. No one will even care that he lived. The world, and in particular, his family is better off now that he's gone. They are finally at peace.

How I wish that wasn't the truth. That I didn't regret having ever met him. And it wasn't the eulogy or obituary I'd hoped to write for the father of my children. But the sad truth was, if he died tomorrow, my sons would refuse to attend his funeral. They would celebrate and welcome his death.

As would I.

They prayed for it every night because they were tired of him interfering with their lives and seeking to do them harm. Seeking to lash out and destroy them because he was *that* jealous and hate-filled for his own children.

Their worst fear was that something would happen to me.

"Mom, please. You have to get better. Don't leave us alone to deal with him." At least once a day, my boys said that to me. They came to check on me constantly.

Because they were *that* afraid that Les would outlive me, and that they were going to be stuck in this mess that their own father had created for no other reason than he was bored.

How tragic was that?

Why?

Because their father didn't care, and he didn't love them, and they knew it. He was a heartless sociopath who was more than willing to destroy them and their futures to get what he wanted.

When Nick got into a Harvard program, Les mocked him for it.

So did Hogg.

Whenever Nick talked about wanting to study politics, they laughed at his aspirations.

"You can't do it. You don't know how to deal with people."

That was untrue. Before Hogg had infiltrated and took over our lives, Nick had been one of the most popular kids in his school.

Everyone had loved and adored him.

He'd proudly marched into the principal's office like he owned it, sat down and had conversations with her as if he were her peer.

When we took him to Chuck E. Cheese, he'd charmed every worker in the place and walked out with half the prizes. Anything he'd wanted, he'd gotten.

And he did it all without hurting anyone.

By his simple, unassuming charm and open warmth.

And those two worthless, jealous bastards criticized and gaslighted him until Nick withdrew into himself entirely.

Because they couldn't stand the fact that they knew he had the potential neither of them did. That Nick could have done anything he wanted.

The world had been his oyster and they were repellent ogres.

Damn them straight to hell for their cruelty and their sabotage.

How sick in the head was a man who would destroy his own son before he'd even had a chance to get started?

And so began the lock-down of me and my children at Les's behest. My boys were my last line of defense against Les and his ever-growing insanity and paranoia that was being hand-fed by the megalomaniac he'd found.

With Hogg firmly entrenched in my home, they were able to cluster my sons on the third floor and do their best to strip away their self-confidence and dignity.

"You can't go downstairs. Your mother is working and too busy to see you."

Something my boys should have known was a lie. I'd never failed at any point in their lives to stop whatever I was doing whenever they needed me. Even in the middle of the night, I'd pause in my writing and make Ramen Noodles or cookies for them.

Whenever they needed me, I'd hold them in my lap for hours and type while I rocked them to sleep or while they chatted to me. I owned dozens of photos of those precious moments.

Even while I was on deadline, if they wanted cookies, I'd put my work aside without a single word of complaint and make them for my boys.

Day or night. Because I knew how fragile life was and that at any moment anything could happen to take it away. I had never squandered a second when I could have been with my children.

Until I was too sick to move. That was what Les really stole from us.

Years I could have been with my kids.

But they couldn't get past both Les and Hogg.

I was too ill to climb the stairs, and so I was basically living in my office. An office that kept getting locked and with my arthritis, I couldn't turn the doorknob to get out.

Why couldn't I get out of my room?

Just a few dozen months before Hogg had come into our lives, Les had hired Cisco McCullough to be our "tech" guy, and Cisco had put electronic locks on my interior office door that would automatically lock me in whenever the door shut. It had such a tight seal that I'd have to call to others to help me open it.

Les would be furious. "Why are you locking your doors? Why are putting your hate on me?"

What kind of insane question was that to ask someone, anyway?

"You're the one who insisted the locks be put on my door and that they lock automatically,

Les. I closed the door because I can't stand that thing in my face whenever I get up to go to the bathroom."

The locked door had nothing to do with him. Everything to do with the massive Hogg who wouldn't leave me alone.

But in his mind, everything had to do with him—the beauty of a sick Narcissist.

If I ever moved from my open office, Hogg would appear right in my face. "Where you going?"

*To piss.* Not that it was any of her business.

I couldn't move without her being on top of me. She literally camped herself right outside my office and watched over me like a warden.

She even had the audacity to come into my room and search through it whenever she felt like it.

Even my pocketbook.

I couldn't stop her. "Les, get her out of here!"

"You're being unreasonable, Terri. She's only here to help."

I got so sick of hearing those words. Especially whenever I found the strength to climb up to the middle floor and I'd find them huddled together under blankets, giggling in the dark.

"It's disgusting, Les! Highly inappropriate!"

"We're not doing anything."

"No? You're sitting in the dark, on my couch, underneath a blanket on top of her, and drinking wine?"

*Seriously? Can someone please tell me what about* that *would be considered "appropriate?*

My own aunt caught them, cavorting.

And they jumed apart like two horny teens in the back of a movie theater, facing an usher's light.

Um-hmm...

Not to mention, Rio had been in the car with them the day before Maddox went to Japan and she'd seen Hogg place her arm around Les and caress him.

But none of these events counted as an affair?

Only in the state of Tennessee was it okay for a married man to move an unmarried woman into his marital home with his wife and children, and act as if she was his second wife, and it not be seen as an affair. Especially when the wife and children were protesting for the woman to get out because they were flaunting their caresses and flagrant behavior in front of her, her children, friends, and family.

Yeah...

And unbeknownst to me at the time, Hogg had run off my longtime personal assistant, Kiki MacDavis.

Ironic really. Kiki had always been so afraid and paranoid of any and everyone coming after her job.

"I love it here. Please, don't ever make me return to being a teacher!"

She'd been a special ed teacher and she loathed everything about it. Those were the only words I'll write about what she said because the rest of it was so repugnant and harsh that it doesn't bear repeating.

However, I have a lot of witnesses who have heard her say that and more, and she knew it. I'd gladly produce those witnesses, any time. Anywhere.

And twice on Sunday.

Kiki knew that I spoke the truth, while she did nothing but tell lies about me.

In fact, she lied so much that she went to great pains to make sure our friends never met.

Because the minute they compared notes on her stories, they'd know her for the two-faced liar she really was.

Was she a world class singer who was in a band in high school because she came from a family of singers, and she could pass for Joan Jett?

Or the pathetic "I can't carry a tune" mother who sang so badly off-key that her own son used to put his hand over her mouth and say, "Mama, don't sing?"

Which was it, Kiki? You never could make up your mind as you flitted back and forth between those tales.

Yeah, she really couldn't keep track of all her lies because she told so many different stories to so many people. And they changed more often than my socks.

She had more faces than a hundred-headed hydra.

Sadly, at first, Kiki had been great. But over time, she became lazier than a sloth stuck in molasses.

"She's not answering emails or doing anything!" My writing partner, Deanna Schell, had been the first to start complaining about her.

Once Les had hired Hogg to be his own personal assistant in 2015, the two of them, along with Cisco, had gone on an all-out campaign to get rid of Kiki.

"She's lazy and worthless." Les insulted Kiki every time we talked. "My God, Terri. Look at her! She's so useless, she won't even fill out her time sheets properly. All she does is copy and paste! You know you can never trust anyone whose ass is wider than her shoulders!"

Funny he should say that about Kiki when that applied to Hogg more so than her...

And he loved and adored Hogg for all her useless laziness.

"I need an assistant, Les." And loyalty at that time had meant more to me than competency. Stupid me that I thought Kiki was loyal.

*God, I'm so gullible and trusting.*

"You need to hire Karen!"

Hogg joined the conversation, because for some reason, she thought she mattered to me. "Kiki's way overpaid. I wouldn't tolerate her for a minute. What does she do, other than copy and paste her time sheets and lie about what she does?"

Cisco would constantly come into my office to complain about her. "I'm having to do Kiki's job again. Does she ever do anything? What are you paying her for, anyway? She's all the time pawning her work off on me. I'm sick of it!"

It was a constant barrage that wasn't helped when Kiki's own daughter, while having lunch with us and Les, outed her mother. "She doesn't do anything all day, except watch TV, and gossip on the phone."

I looked at Kiki who turned red in the face. "I work all the time!"

Yeah, just like at PensaCon where she charged me overtime, but instead of doing the job that I was paying her overtime for, she used volunteers to do it. Then, she had the nerve to work on a side job right in front of me and Joan who was sharing a room (that I was paying for) with her at the event.

That didn't endear her to Les, either, who complained about her even more. He also began harassing her, along with Hogg's help.

I was too sick to stop them.

By the fall of 2016, Kiki quit, citing that she was having family troubles. Which was true. According to her and what she'd been telling me and others, her husband had been beating her son and she was so afraid of him that she'd begun drugging him into a stupor at night with the Valium his doctor had prescribed for him. According to what Kiki told me and others (and who knew if it were true given her proclivity for lying), she gave him so much that "he just sits in his chair at night like a zombie, stroking his little dog. Hell, he can't even get an erection anymore. Which is good for me. I'd rather take care of myself, anyway. Who needs a man?"

Her mood went from being overjoyed over her husband's zombie state to outright terror when he wasn't being drugged by her. "He's going to kill me one day, Terri. I know it!"

She'd even run away from home a few times to escape his temper. "I don't know what to do. He needs to get help and he won't go! He's nuts. You know he buried a knife between the legs of his ex-wife and her lover before he divorced her! God only knows what he might do to me one day if he finds out what all I've done!"

I tried to help but didn't know where to start. One thing about the hick county where she lived, outsiders weren't welcomed and given the corruption in Williamson County, I could only imagine how much worse hers was. Besides, she lived next door to her parents and grandparents. Surely if she were in any real danger, they'd help.

Still, I missed her.

We'd been good friends, or so I stupidly thought.

Remember what I said about weak minds?

Kiki had always prided herself on being a *master* manipulator. On knowing how to "get back" at people. She proclaimed to the world that she was the Queen Bee of Passive Aggressiveness.

"I can stir shit and turn the world against anyone faster than you can blink." That was what Kiki had always bragged about.

She paled in the presence of Hogg. And she'd just been outplayed by the real slag who wanted her job.

As I've always said in my books. It was the one you didn't see coming who got you in the end.

Kiki had been outplayed by two of them: Hogg and Cisco.

Les was insistent that I hire Hogg to replace her once she was gone.

I was aghast. "When the devil shits an icicle."

"Terri! Be reasonable. Hogg is the most professional person we've ever had working for us!"

Really? Was that why my fans left in tears at my signing in Atlanta? When had professional ever meant someone mocking another fan's gift that she thoughtfully brought for me?

Or belittling me to my publishers, peers and readers?

As Maddox so often said, it wasn't just that Hogg was obnoxious and rude.

Hogg was intentionally malicious.

"I cannot take her into public ever again! She's horrifying and she treats people like shit!"

"She was only trying to help." I loathe that phrase to this day because of Les, and how much he overused it.

*And let's not discuss the hall pass issue again.*

Yet this was what Les was insisting I hire? A Narcissistic lunatic who thought the world was her grand stage.

Actually, I believed that Hogg suffered from Histrionic Personality Disorder. Narcissism was just a "fun" bonus of that lovely condition.

I knew for a fact that Les had it. Sadly, I didn't realize it until we were well into our marriage. Thank you, *Desert Storm*, for cutting my engagement short. Otherwise, I might have seen it in time to save myself.

Save my children. I might have had an opportunity to find a decent partner to be a father worthy of them.

Anyway, there was no chance of my hiring Hogg to do anything, in spite of the fact that Les kept putting her in charge of our lives.

Literally.

He even paid her to watch TV. Paid her to be his legal secretary even though her only exposure to the law was episodes of *The Good Wife*, and, with the help of Cisco, gave her unfettered access to my entire life. Including my emails, and databases that she wasn't supposed to touch.

"Gah, Terri! What's wrong with you? She needs them for the lawsuit."

The other answer from Les that I hated.

"She's running my store into the ground!" Not to mention, all my publishers and fans were complaining about her. And don't get me started on those who were in charge of events where I was supposed to be in attendance.

"Who is this Mildred person? She's horrible and obnoxious!" That was virtually unanimous from anyone who had to deal with Hogg and the pseudonym she'd given herself.

And what I didn't know then, but would discover after Hogg had left, was that she'd intentionally and willfully broken customs' laws with my store and had sabotaged me and my orders to make herself look good.

Never mind all the times she'd lied about her hours in order to steal more money from my company.

All this with Les's blessing.

After all, he'd told Cisco to lie about his hours and I had his handwritten memo to prove it:

*Cisco, you're leaving money on the table.*

*~Les*

That money on the table was *my* money. Money that belonged to my sons. Not Les. Money I had earned and he had no right to tell Cisco to pad his hours to steal money out of my children's mouths so that he could bribe his henchman.

By Christmas of 2016, I was terrified at the thought of this new creature from hell becoming any further entrenched in my life as Cisco had become.

Fate intervened.

My cousin, Lyra, came to visit with her mother and daughter. My aunt, Belinda, was there when I was born and had always been like another mother to me. That kind, sweet vision we all have of a doting mother figure.

She was my Hallmark mom.

I loved her so much!

Belinda was fluffy and sweet with dark hair and soft eyes. Married to my uncle, Darryl who was a Baptist preacher, I'd never heard a cross word pass her lips.

But even she'd noticed that Les's demeanor and attitude toward me and our sons had completely changed.

In the past, they'd been good friends and he'd always referred to her as "Aunt Belinda."

Suddenly, he was spending all his time with Hogg and had no use for Belinda whatsoever.

Or me and our boys.

"He doesn't look right, anymore. What's wrong with him, Terri? Is he sick?"

I had no answer. But as I was talking to Lyra, she told me how frustrated she'd become with her new job. For a moment, I thought God was speaking.

"Want to come work for me?"

Lyra was ecstatic.

At least for a short time.

"You don't want to do that." Les had pulled her aside later, away from my hearing after I'd made the offer. "Terri doesn't have a lot of family left on this side of the grave, and I'd hate for you two to get crossed up. You know how Terri is."

Lyra scowled. "Of course, I do. I've been with her my whole life. We're more like sisters than cousins."

"Just think about it, Lyra. I'd hate for something to happen. If you work for her, she'll run you off."

For the record, I'd never run off anyone.

Remember what I said about Les putting his sins on everyone one else?

He was the king of projection.

What Les had meant by that was that he, Hogg and Cisco were about to embark on an all-out campaign to get rid of Lyra the same way they'd gotten rid of Kiki, and others before her.

It would be psychological warfare at its finest.

In their minds it would be easy to get rid of her, because they'd done what everyone else had. Took one look at Lyra's tiny, angelic appearance, with her sweet, slow Southern drawl that could melt the heart of the Grinch faster than Cindy Lou Who, and thought, "Pushover. Simpleton."

But Lyra wasn't a Manly.

We were blood, and we were cut from much stronger stock than that.

As my uncle, Carlos used to say, "we don't run. Sometimes we might want to. Sometimes we probably ought to. But we don't ever run."

A Woods would stand their ground until doomsday and beyond. Like my grandmother used to say about my grandfather when a guy honked a horn at him in traffic and pissed him off.

"He just sat there, light after light, calm as you please, and didn't move an inch. He'd still be sitting there to this day if that man hadn't pulled around him."

Lyra was no different.

Yet they didn't make it easy on her. I couldn't count how many times she'd called me in tears, and making her cry was a hard thing to do. She had the mettle of steel inside that tiny body.

She sent me their emails where they'd picked on her and withheld information, not to mention, I knew how they talked about her, and to her. The textbook definition of workplace bullying. Hogg went out of her way to be rude and insulting.

To her face and behind her back.

"Lyra doesn't need to be dealing with people. She's too stupid."

As if Hogg had any room to talk.

I was appalled. "Everyone loves her." Unlike Hogg whom they all hated.

"She doesn't understand things."

Yes, she did. Such as the fact that Hogg was a bitch and didn't need to be living in my home or near me and my boys, and especially not underneath my husband at night, on my couch. Most anyone, other than Hogg and my husband, seemed to understand that. Why those two couldn't comprehend that their behavior was wrong and disgusting, I'd never understand.

My favorite example of them underestimating Lyra was when the magpies were trying to get my promotional hats through customs.

"Lyra can do this."

All three had rolled their eyes at me. "It's too complicated for her."

They were the idiots, not my cousin. Obviously, as months had gone by and none of them had been able to get the hats into our custody. "She did customs work at the airport for over twenty years. She can do this."

It took me weeks until I was finally able to wrestle it out of their hands and give it to her.

Lyra had the hats to us in a matter of days.

So, one little, tiny Southern lady was able to accomplish what a lawyer, a dark web expert, and a supposed pastor/tutor had been unable to do over a period of months.

Still, they refused to show her any respect.

Anyone else would have been long gone over their collective bullying and insults. But Lyra was too worried about me to flee. God had sent me an angel and she was on guardian duty.

Though Lyra couldn't keep Hogg from moving in with me as she lived in Atlanta while I was in Franklin, she made the trip back and forth quite often. Because she saw how rapidly I was declining under their "tender, loving" care.

Lyra was terrified they were killing me.

The weirdest?

May 2017. Remember that Lyra and Maddox had both come to stay with me at the Atlanta convention where Hogg was present?

Hogg made sure to document her care and "feeding" of me that entire time so that Les could see what she was doing.

How weird was that?

Only the buffoons who worked for the Williamson County police department and local DA wouldn't think so.

Because normal people knew that "normal" people didn't take the time to carefully document and record the fact that they'd "fed" another fully capable adult for their husband.

Nor did husband's pay them the grand total of one-thousand-four-hundred dollars to feed them for a weekend when they were not their assistant.

Yeah.

And remember that Lyra and my friends were there that weekend to help me at the event. So, I really didn't need any extra hands.

Les had told me that Hogg had gone along because she was a "fan" and had wanted to meet other writers. I had no idea that he'd sent her along to "chaperone" me or to be my "handler." Never mind "feed" me.

For that matter, I didn't know we were paying her until after he'd filed for divorce, and I saw her employee records.

I was appalled by the amount.

Should I also mention that my husband withdrew ninety thousand dollars in cash, out of our joint account, the week I returned, and it went missing?

To this day, I don't know where that ninety grand went or what it was spent on.

Or should I say whom?

Only those working for the Williamson County police department and DA's department wouldn't think that was suspicious, either.

Especially given the fact that during that weekend while all that money went missing, Lyra and I split our meals.

And Maddox did what he always had done. Finished off whatever I didn't eat.

Guess what happened...

*Pretty sure you know.*

That weekend, all three of us became deathly ill. Lyra went from a size eight to a size two because of the "illness" she "contracted" from eating my food.

It took her months to recover.

Maddox, after that one lone weekend, and for the first and only time in his life, became suicidal for no reason whatsoever, and after that solitary event, ended up quitting grad school and moving back home.

If you look back at him in old photos during those few months when he was at home, eating from my plate, he looked like a death camp survivor. No one believed he was the same person.

Yet within no time of his leaving home...

No more vacant stare. His thoughts cleared up.

His hair became thicker...

His skin color improved.

Hmmm. Three people made sick. All sharing the same symptoms.

All after one weekend where we shared food. To making a miraculous recovery in no time at all.

Ironically, we thought we'd contracted "food poisoning" from the hotel cuisine. We definitely got the *poisoning* part right, according to my toxicology reports.

*But I'm coming to that.*

This was May 2017.

Three people. Deathly ill.

At home, I had two cats who were also sick from eating off my plate on a daily basis. I just hadn't made the connection that, like my son and cousin, we were all sharing the same symptoms.

Kitty and Naveena had been ill for some time.

It was only after looking back, particularly at pictures and records, that I realized it'd happened to us at the same time, and that our symptoms were identical. Alopecia. Same thick, weird goo in our eyes that had a rubbery texture. It would cause my eyes and theirs to seal shut. I kept going to my regular doctor and optometrist thinking I had some kind of weird eye infection that wouldn't clear up.

No one knew what it was, either. It was so painful that I couldn't work at times. I couldn't see straight from it.

It literally felt like thick, smelly snot was leaking out of my eyes.

The cats would cry for hours in pain. They were disoriented and/or dazed.

Just like me.

Like Maddox. They vomited constantly and couldn't keep down food, either.

They went from being these beautiful Bengals that everyone complimented when they saw them, to looking like mangy zombie cats no one wanted to touch. It was heartbreaking.

Then one day, Kitty vanished.

"Where's my cat?"

"I had her put down."

I gaped at Les. "What the fuck? Where is she?"

"She was cremated."

I've never been so stunned in my life. The heartless bastard had murdered my cat without telling any of us. Without any warning.

Maddox was as furious as I was. His college was less than twenty minutes from our door. "Why, Dad? Why wouldn't you tell me you were putting down my cat?"

"I didn't want to interfere with your classes."

"That's bullshit!"

And it was. Maddox was the Straight-A student who'd slept through all his classes.

We knew Les was lying. We just didn't know at the time why.

To this day, my son refuses to forgive him. The saddest part? Christmas 2018 when my baby had surgery and was coming out from anesthesia, Maddox was crying as if his heart was broken for his Kitty. Calling his father a monster for murdering her and not letting him say goodbye. I've been never hurt so badly in my life as I was when I heard Maddox's unrestrained pain.

"How could you not let me say goodbye to Kitty! You monster! I hate you!"

I had to explain to the nurse who was present that I wasn't the one who'd put his cat down. Because she had looked at me like I was dirt.

Thankfully, Nick was there. "No, it wasn't my mom. My dad's a piece of shit."

*Again, who does that?*

The answer was obvious. A man covering up his crimes. Because in the past, we'd always buried our pets.

To this day, there were tombstones in our backyard of our lost fur babies. We'd never cremated one. Ever.

Why else would Les take my girl, without any warning and kill her, and then have her vaporized?

He wanted nothing left behind that could be tested.

More than that, he took her to a vet we'd never used before to do it so that the vet wouldn't have her case history, either.

Then afterward, do you know what he said to me?

"Naveena has the same rare disease that killed Kitty. There's no cure for it. She's going to die the same way. Our other kitten will ultimately get it, too, and die. Naveena will never get any better and will have to be put down soon."

For the record, he was lying.

Naveena started getting better the day he left.

Just like I had.

Just like Maddox.

All the years that Neveena had been sick and vomiting... hairless.

It all went away. None of it ever returned. Naveena completely recovered once there was no one here to tamper with my food.

Only an idiot working for the Williamson County police department or the DA's office would believe that to be a coincidence.

What was it that the FBI BAU criminal manual said?

*Once is an occurrence.*

*Twice is coincidence.*

*Three times establishes a pattern.*

Unless you lived in Williamson County, Tennessee. Land of the laziest law enforcement I had ever seen. It wasn't that we didn't have crime here. It was more a matter of the fact that we didn't have anyone willing to investigate a real crime.

I was told that by the head of their department, by the way, while I stood in the center of their police department and had two witnesses with me. They wouldn't even write it down or take a report. They expected the victims to keep all records of the crime for them.

"Get yourself a notepad and jot down whenever something happens. Keep a record!" Direct quote from Chief Shit-For-Brains.

Just as they expected the victims to pay for all the toxicology tests and to provide the police with expert witnesses.

And yes, that was the truth. The worker in the lab and the director of the TBI verified that.

In Williamson County, the victim was expected to pay for the tests.

Which meant if you were a victim of a crime in Williamson County and couldn't afford justice, you were screwed.

Seriously, we have no departments here that were set up to handle any kind of real investigation, according to their own detectives. Just look into the nightmare of the Holly Bobo case and what they put that poor family through.

It wasn't just me.

This was the most horrible place on earth to live.

Because, and I would be repeating this a lot so that everyone fully understood the horror, we were ranked in not one, but two separate studies done by well-respected sources as the third most corrupt state in the United State of America. And according to a Harvard study, Nashville was ranked as one of the most corrupt cities in the Union.

This was the real *Hotel California*. Once you checked in here, you could never leave.

I wanted out of this godforsaken hellhole more than anything, and they wouldn't let me go.

This wasn't just a horror show, it was the shit-show of all time, and I was cast against my will into the starring role.

By the fall of 2017, October to be precise, Hogg had taken up full-time residence in my home and had every intention of becoming the new Mrs. Manly and was flaunting it in my face, and that of my sons'.

It was nauseating.

She was brazen because there was nothing I could do.

*Karen and Les's Work.*

Those notes were left all over the place for me to see and find.

They were slowly erasing me.

When they spoke of me to others, or whenever Hogg emailed people about me, including my own publishers and fans, it was as if I were their child or a sick parent, they were taking care of. They made me sound like an incompetent invalid.

"Terri's not feeling well."

"If we can get her to wake up, I'll ask her about it."

"Terri's got another headache and is locked in her cave."

"It's been crazy here all day."

Nasty comments meant to undermine and belittle me to the world.

Meanwhile, the truth was that I would be lying in my chair, unable to move or even breathe at times, and I could hear them laughing together. They would bring me food that looked like it'd been left out for days.

Les was forever bringing me milkshakes and smoothies. No sooner would I drink one, than I'd throw it up. It happened so often that I'd begun to fear I'd become lactose intolerant.

When Lyra came and saw me in my chair, she honestly thought I was dead at first.

Until she touched me, and I moved slightly. "I'm getting you out of here."

While Hogg and Les were upstairs "cavorting," she gathered my things and took me to my office, which was a little cabin in the woods a few miles away from the house.

It took Les hours to realize that we'd left. But once he did, he was furious.

Lyra and I prepared what I needed for my trip to New York to see my publisher, and to get ready for *New York Comic Con*.

I couldn't understand why Les was so mad that I'd left my home. After all, Hogg had told Lyra on numerous occasions that she couldn't stay "in my room." Hogg's "room" was the guest-room in my home that Hogg had taken over and claimed as her own.

The list of her affronts went on and on.

Hogg even went so far as to write out checks to people on my accounts that she wasn't authorized to use. When Rio was over and gave a facial to Nick, Hogg smugly looked at her and asked, "How much do you get paid? I'll write you your check."

Rio laughed in her face. "Les writes my checks." Even though he wasn't authorized to use my account, either.

But then, Hogg had an obsession with finding out how much everyone made.

Later, I would learn that she'd used that to sow discord among the employees.

That was what shit-stirring slags do.

Along with making snide, lying comments to everyone. As soon as she'd see Rio, she'd always make some kind of statement to put me down. "Did Terri yell at you, too?"

"Terri never yells at me."

"Must be nice."

Rio scoffed. "Must be you. I've been coming here over a decade, and I've never seen or heard her yell at anyone."

While that was not one-hundred percent true, it was ninety-eight percent true. I never liked to yell. Ever. Remember that I grew up in a war zone. It pretty much took an act of God to get me to the point that I yelled at anyone for anything, especially when I was mad.

Normally, when I was angry, I walked away until I'd calmed down. Or my voice dropped an octave lower.

If I didn't have my hearing aids in, I couldn't tell how loud I was talking. Because of my Autism, I'd always had modulation problems. Something I overcompensated for by speaking in a tone so low that most people asked me to speak up. However, if I was excited and my hearing aids weren't on or if I'd left them out, I often spoke loudly because I couldn't hear how loud my tone was, and I was often too excited to pay attention.

Again, though, that wasn't yelling. That was because I was hard-of-hearing and Autistic. I've seldom yelled at people intentionally.

I don't like to be rude to anyone. Ever. My parents were exceptionally rude, on purpose. My mother had a razor-sharp tongue that let blood everywhere it went. It really should have been registered as a lethal weapon.

In fact, she prided herself on it. As a child, I would rush ahead in stores to warn clerks and others, "give her what she wants, or it won't go well for you."

Or in my mother's own words, "Listen to me, inbred. Either you'll do what I want or tonight when you go home, you'll still be so upset from this encounter that you're going to scream at your spouse and beat your kids. Either way, I'll get satisfaction from this. You tell me which way you want it to end for *you*."

That wasn't a made-up story.

There were people in this world, I was quite sure, who were still in therapy from a fifteen-minute encounter with my mother.

And as noted in some of my comments, my tongue could be pretty sharp as well. As was my brother's, Esteban's, and basically everyone else in my family.

We came out of the womb with biting sarcasm that could leave scars on a soul that would never heal.

Since I knew this about myself, I intentionally withheld my comments from others, all the time. The proof was in the pudding... or video. *Watch any interview with Hogg.* Whenever I curled my lips in and around my teeth, I was thinking of a vicious retort along the lines of something I'd written here.

But rather than be my mother or father, I withheld it.

*I've always done that.*

Unless someone condescended on me or attacked me first.

Then it became war.

Yet truth be told, I didn't always defend myself. If given the choice between walking away and being a bitch, I normally chose to walk away.

*But don't ever flip my bitch-switch.* That was when I could become my mother. Not only caustic, but funny.

That was the deadliest combination in the world, which was what I'd learned from my mother whenever she'd attack.

As my brother so often said, our mother was like a head injury. Funny as hell when it happened to someone else, but beyond painful when it was you in the line of fire.

Let me reiterate that my only goal in life had been to live in peace. *To live and let live.*

So as much as I hated Hogg, I'd seldom ever spoken to her in my home. I basically ignored the sow and interacted with her as little as possible.

Glared at her all the time.

For that matter, I was known to spray holy water in her direction whenever I passed by her, as it was scented with sage.

One) I kept hoping to drive the evil out of my home.

Two) she stank, and I was freshening the air that she contaminated.

Who wouldn't?

I had a slag living in my home, talking shit to my face and behind my back. She was pawing at my husband in front of me, stealing my property, being rude to my fans.

The creature from Trailer Park 9 abused my sons, and lied to my publishers, while trying to ruin my career. She was eating me out of house and home; refused to leave my house. Made a disgusting mess all over that she refused to pick up (she left used Kleenex's everywhere). Drove my car and tore it up. Knocked two doors off the hinges in my home, broke chairs and knocked holes in my walls. Tore up my favorite outside chair and ripped a hole in the rug that had been given to me as a birthday present. Then, had the nerve to damage my hot tub. All the while charging thirty to sixty dollars an hour to wreck my life and destroy everything I'd spent my lifetime building!

*I swear to God on the souls of my parents that was only some of what she did!*

And let's not forget that she not only carefully documented feeding me the weekend I was so sick and that my cousin and son became ill while eating from my plate, but that she also made sure to always remove the food I'd eaten from my home every night after I ate it.

Always.

Every day while she was here, she made sure that every single meal I consumed was taken away from my home under the pretense that she was taking it home to her dog.

But if you'd ever seen a photo of her dog, then you'd know that poor puppy didn't look well-fed.

That dog looked malnourished.

How suspicious was *that*, hmm?

Even better? According to the tests that were run on my hair, blood and nails, the compounds that were used to poison me were all found in a common supplement that was sold at the *Vitamin Shoppe*.

Do you know what came to my house that I still have?

A discount postcard from the *Vitamin Shoppe* with Karen Hogg's name on it.

In all the many months that she lived here, I never once saw her take any kind of vitamin or supplement.

None whatsoever.

Nor did she ever talk about taking any.

Even better? This photo was taken while Hogg was living in my home. It was obvious that she'd moved in by her extensive stack of clothes and CPAP machine that she had in "her" room.

But if you looked on the nightstand where she had placed them, there were two bottles purchased from the *Vitamin Shoppe*.

Could they have been some of what had been put in my food?

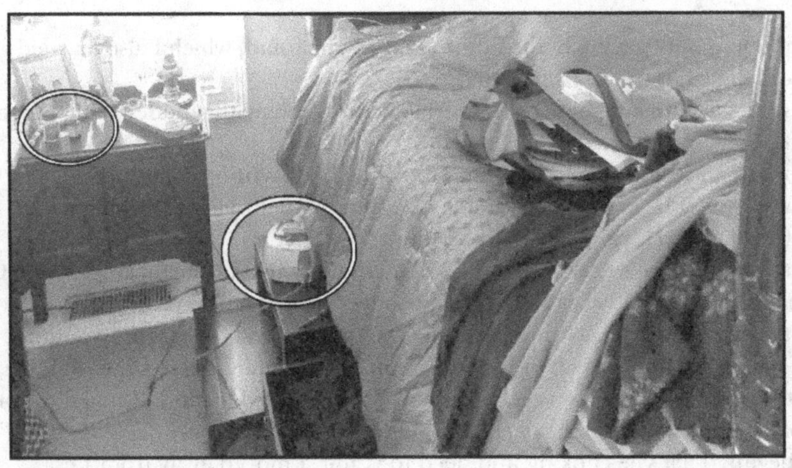

Only an idiot working for the Williamson County police department and their DA's office would believe all that to be a mere coincidence.

So, had I ever yelled at Hogg?

Yes, when she came out of *my* guestroom in *my* house in the mornings in her underwear to yell at the top of her lungs at my sons.

When I found her on *my* couch snuggled up against *my* husband beneath a blanket, drinking wine and drunk with him (look back at that photo and on the nightstand where she'd left an empty wine glass).

When she would yell at me and insult *my* children and *my* husband.

"Get out of *my* house, you fucking bitch!"

No one yelled at my kids or insulted my husband. *I* didn't yell at them, and no one else would either, especially not in their own home.

As Caleb once said to his principal when he was unfairly sent to the office, "you better call my dad. You don't want my mom up here, right now."

*I will voraciously protect my children. That is what I do.*

But it was rare for me to yell.

That I learned from my drill sergeant dad. You go an octave lower, and it was a lot scarier. People listened to *that* tone.

Les, on the other hand, yelled a lot.

And that he did the next morning when he showed up at my cabin with food for us. "We need to talk about *your* behavior."

I laughed in his face. "My behavior isn't the problem. You cavorting with Hogg in front my children and me, and everyone else, is."

"She's nothing to me."

"Then fire her."

"I will."

"Then do it." I made the mistake of biting into the food that he'd brought for us to eat. As usual, he made sure that mine was marked "special."

He stalked after me, like I was his prey. "I don't know what your problem is, Terri! Karen is wonderful. Nick has his best grades with her."

Not true. Nick had always been a Straight-A student. However, before Hogg, Nick had always done his own work. Since Hogg had come into our lives, Nick had stopped doing his work because he refused to work with her, and that bitch was writing all his papers and doing his homework *for him*.

Les was intentionally paying her to commit academic fraud, which I also learned after he left, and Nick told me what they'd been doing.

How was *that* Nick making better grades? He wasn't making the grades at all. Hogg was doing all the work.

For that matter, I would soon learn that Hogg had been writing college papers for Caleb, too.

"Nick hates her!" I began having trouble breathing. My throat was closing up.

"You're the one who invited her to live with us!"

I glared at him, unable to believe he'd dare say that to me. Was he fucking crazy? God, how I despised his gaslighting. "I hate that bitch! I've never invited her anywhere."

Les was the one who kept inviting her to meals, movies, and other family outings.

"Well, if you cared about Nick or his education, you wouldn't be so unreasonable."

"You're the one who doesn't give a fuck about Nick or his education. If you did, you'd get that bitch out of our home and off his back! You're destroying our family because of *her*!"

Then it began. That vile choking and need to vomit. I moved away from Les.

He continued to stalk after me. Lyra moved back, terrified. She'd never seen Les act like this. While I knew of his violent outbursts, he normally kept them carefully hidden from others.

Unable to breathe, I threw my burger into the sink and ran to the bathroom to vomit.

Still, Les pursued me, screaming at me. I honestly don't remember what he said, all I could hear was the loud ringing in my ears.

When I came out of the bathroom, I was sobbing and struggling to breathe. "I've had it, Les. Get her out of my life! You can't have us both. You need to make a decision. Her or me. Either divorce me or get that bitch out of my house!"

"Fine! She's gone. You want her gone? I'll get her out by this afternoon."

He didn't.

*Another Les lie.*

According to Maddox, she'd started crying when he told her she needed to leave, and Les had allowed her to stay.

After all, her feelings were so much more important than those of the wife he'd been married to for twenty-seven years, and the mother of his three sons.

The wife who'd worked twenty hours a day, seven days a week. Three hundred and sixty-five days a year to provide him with his cushy life.

The unemployed, worthless Hogg was so much more important than the wife Les was living off of and abusing.

*Made sense, right?*

I didn't think so, either.

Lyra and I went to New York as planned. Originally, they were supposed to depose Dumas and her people in New York that week, so I'd intended to be gone twelve to fourteen full days.

The depositions ended up being canceled, and then my Friday meeting was canceled, too.

Thank you, Les, for your interference with my business.

With nothing to do after I finished my meetings and my signing on Thursday, I called Les late that night to let him know that I'd be home earlier than planned. It was just before eleven that night when we'd made it back to our hotel room.

I was exhausted.

"Hey!" I was actually excited to hear his voice.

"I can't talk right now. Karen and I are watching a movie." I heard the slag giggling into the phone, meaning she was right there with him.

Les always watched movies in the dark, and I knew from seeing them together that they were snuggled up on my couch again.

It also meant that Hogg was still living in my home. In spite of his promises that he would fire her and get her the hell out of my house, she was still living there and making sixty dollars an hour of my hard-earned cash.

Abusing my sons.

I was sick to my stomach.

Unable to believe it, I hung up and shook my head.

First, I'd spent hours signing books in front of my former booth space where one of my publishers had taken up residence in my absence from the convention. Les had insisted I stop going to New York Comic Con because it was too hard on the family, even though it injured my career.

He refused to even let me send my crew up there to keep my space.

But what really sucked was that instead of hyping my books like they were contractually obligated to do, my own publisher had hired an author known for plagiarism to write a very similar series that I'd pitched to them before they'd hired her. Now, instead of promoting the *New York Times* bestselling books I'd written for them, they were hyping hers in the same spot where my books had once been sold.

*So much for loyalty and ethics.*

Wait...

What?

Yeah, it was true, and I had the witnesses and evidence to prove it. Years and years ago, I pitched my Young Adult series to the senior VP of my own publishing house. Instead of buying my Young Adult series that they'd been "so very interested" in, they had turned around and signed a writer whose only claim to fame was a well-known plagiarism scandal to write an eerily similar premise to the one I'd pitched to them almost a year before they bought hers.

Truth.

This while I was *a New York Times* bestselling author for their very own publishing house.

With a different series. Not the series they really wanted to get their hands on (I know this as the VP and publisher kept telling me that), then ironically stopped pursing me for that YA series after the other author had been signed. We had spent almost a year talking about my YA series and her plans for how she wanted her house to be my "new home" and how they were going to be my one and only publisher.

Hmmm...

Wish I was lying. It'd be easier to swallow than the betrayal I was handed.

Even after my lawyers sent my publisher a cease and desist, telling them that they couldn't use my trademarked series name in or on that author's books, they went to the Library of Congress and put my series name on her first book, too.

A full year after my lawyers had told them not to use my trademarked name. My publisher knowingly put my series name on her book at the Library of Congress.

I had to repeat that because it was just so unbelievable. Things like that weren't supposed to happen.

Especially in publishing. We'd all been told from Day One that the big publishers had more scruples than this.

It was a lie.

They did that, all the while knowing who I was (as I was under contract with them), and that what they were doing was both legally wrong and immoral.

It didn't stop them.

They did it with the entire world and publishing industry watching them.

Shame on every author out there who backed them against me, without stopping to think that this wasn't a matter of my being "jealous" of anyone. It was a matter of one little author trying to save her worlds and series from a giant publisher who was determined to squash us all.

Just like all the writers who'd attacked me, thinking to bring me down. None of you could be bothered to find out the truth before you jumped on me.

The reason?

That had become a standard in this day and age. *Believe the lies and do no research.*

What scared me most was knowing that they'd gotten away with it. The fear that I wouldn't be the last victim.

Because what they did was so brazen. So in our faces. They'd deliberately taken down a number one bestselling series.

Two of them, actually.

Good job to everyone who ignored me when I tried to get help. Way to stand by and allow an author's rights and hard work to be stripped from her.

Maybe we should "accidentally" put *Harry Potter* on this book and see what happens. After all, it would be an "accident." Just like when, two years after the Library of Congress event, they "accidentally" released, not once, not twice, but three times, her books into stores with my series name on them, too.

Because those mishaps happened all the time.

*Right...*

That particular time, my publisher had told me that they'd ruin my career if I didn't stop complaining about them treading all over my trademarked series.

That was why I had a gag order placed on me.

They feared the truth.

*I do not.*

So, all day long, I'd been in New York with bile in my throat over the injustice of it all.

How could this have happened?

Where was God? Why had He forsaken me? And why was my nose being rubbed in it?

Now a second lying slag had taken up residence with my husband in my own house.

It was more than any human should have to endure.

I looked at Lyra. "Do you need to get back home?"

"Not really." Luckily, her daughter was grown.

"Fine. I need to finish up my book." My other publisher had been riding me with spurs to get it done and I couldn't concentrate in that house with that thing stalking me and not allowing me to breathe. "We'll go to Virginia. I can finish the book and do the research I need for the next one."

In spite of the fact that I grew up in Georgia, Virginia had always been my ancestral home. There was something about it that succored me like a mother's touch. Since my mother's death, it was where I'd always headed for comfort.

And I needed comfort right then. Since my parents had died when I was young, I needed to feel the touch of my ancestors.

So, I rebooked our flights.

Suddenly, my phone blew up with Les needing attention from someone other than his live-in girlfriend. "What are you doing?"

"I'm going to do research." I hung up on him.

The next thing Lyra and I knew, our reservations were being changed. Les and crew were trying to force me back to Franklin, Tennessee.

"Stop it!" I directly told Hogg to get out of my emails and my Trip-it account.

I changed the passwords.

Cisco let her back in. I knew it had to be him as neither Hogg nor Les had the abilities to do it. And Cisco had access to all my passwords. He'd set it up so that he could infiltrate all of our devices for Les.

In the end, I finally won, and got to Virginia, but they didn't make it easy. And it cost me thousands of dollars to undo what they'd done during their hissy fit.

Then, by the beginning of the week and after only a few more days away from them, I'd started noticing something even stranger...

Lyra had ventured out to explore while I worked to finish my book.

When she came back that afternoon, we went to grab a bite at a local tavern.

When I sipped my stew, I gasped. "I can taste this!"

Lyra frowned. "What?"

Tears filled my eyes as I ate my food because for the last, I don't know how many years, I'd had what I called a "numb tongue." There was a weird metallic taste in my mouth that wouldn't go away. My doctors and dentist had blamed the symptom on everything from a toothpaste allergy to sinuses.

But suddenly, I had taste buds again. I was elated! The food was amazing!

What I didn't know at that time was that Les was frantic at home. Maddox had caught him crying outside, on the back porch. "You okay, Dad?"

"I've messed up everything. I really, really screwed up!" He continued sobbing.

In a panicked frenzy, Les called Lyra's mom. "You have to force them to come home, Belinda! Karen and I need to feed and take care of Terri."

"Feed her? Les, she's a grown woman and doesn't need anyone to feed her. She's been feeding herself since she was a kid."

Meanwhile, my sinuses were also clearing up. The weird, funky eye goo that had refused to go away was no longer there. I could see without straining. I didn't ache. All those weird ailments were slowly getting better.

I felt great!

Until I got home.

Les acted as if nothing had happened. No apology for his sick behavior or the tantrum he'd thrown.

No apology over the fact that he had yet to let his Hogg go.

Nothing.

Yet, for the first time ever, he had food waiting on me when I arrived at home.

"I'm not hungry. Lyra and I ate on our way in."

"Oh my God, Terri! I went to all this trouble. The least you could do is eat it! You're so thoughtless!"

Lyra and I exchanged confounded frowns. *What the hell? Save it for later.*

Instead, he threw it in the garbage.

Whatever. I chalked it up to another Les tantrum.

The next morning, Lyra went home and by nightfall, I was feeling terrible again.

"I think I'm allergic to Tennessee." I said that. My eyes were swelling shut. My lips were burning.

Once more, I couldn't taste food.

Within days, I was sick, wheezing and too weak to get out of my chair.

While Hogg wasn't officially living at my house, she was still coming over and staying until one or two in the morning. Only now, there was a darker smugness to her.

Les hired her and her friends to do "inventory" on my store items because by then she'd run off all my help.

"It's a toxic work environment." That was what Peyton had told everyone, including Rio. "I can't stand Karen. She's horrible!"

Rio couldn't stand Hogg either. She belittled her every time Rio came over. So, Rio, a svelte tall blond, did her best to ignore them.

Les had begun having me sign things, but I thought they were for the lawsuit.

Just like the inventory. That was what he told me, and my eyes were so bad that it was hard to read.

Besides, I trusted him.

We'd been married for so long, why wouldn't I trust the man who'd sworn every day that he loved me and his sons? That he was here for us and would always be here for us.

*Till death we do part.*

I didn't know how literally he was intending to take that.

Nor did I realize that he was about to take my trust and turn it into my biggest nightmare.

**M**ADDOX'S DEPARTURE WAS looming.

For Christmas, I'd bought Les a trip to Savannah, Georgia to tour with my Dames group, and visit our middle son, Caleb, who was in school there.

Les made me cancel it. Five thousand dollars down the drain.

For no reason.

Stranger still, Donna Handsoff, showed up on my doorstep, out of the blue.

Portly, round and with no remarkable features, Donna had been Les's friend in college who'd wanted to date him and made no bones about her crush, even though she knew I was his girl-friend. Which was weird as he'd always told our sons that she was *my* friend when I could barely tolerate the judgmental gossipy two-faced shrew.

Ironically, she hadn't aged, but mostly because she'd looked fifty when she was twenty. She still had that puritanical snootiness that reminded me of Les's mother. That holier than thou, nosy attitude that I found repellent.

*Judge not lest ye be judged.*

She was one of the bible-thumpers who somehow always missed that phrase when they were waving their bibles at others. The kind of Christian my granddad used to mock. "Honey, parking yourself on my pew come Sunday morning doesn't make you any more a Christian than standing in my garage makes you a car." I could still hear his voice in my head as he so often said those words.

She was the kind of person who made other people shudder whenever someone said, "I'm a *good* Christian."

Because you knew instinctively that they weren't.

Or in my grandfather's words, "Do good and it will shine. When you have to open your mouth to opine your good deeds, then you ain't living or doing right by nobody. Not even yourself."

That was Donna. And she brought along her equally odd daughter, Grace. Because every good bible-thumper had to give their kid a biblical name, just so no one would ever doubt how "god-fearing" they were.

Donna had been married until the day she'd learned her own husband was sleeping with fourteen-year-old prostitutes.

Interesting that she'd end up married to *that* given her crush on Les. Maybe the police should hire her. Obviously, she could sniff out a pedophile and those with ties to them like a pig on truffles.

Now, here she was at my house.

Again.

For no reason.

Absent for the vast majority of our marriage, she now kept turning up on my doorstep with peculiar excuses ever since her divorce from her pedophile had started.

Les had been spending a lot of time with her. But I hadn't thought anything about it because I wasn't a jealous person. I figured if Les had wanted her, he'd had the chance in college to claim her and had dated me instead.

Besides, he called her boring and ugly. He shuddered the one time I'd asked him in college if they'd ever dated.

Never mind the fact that there had been no Donna for all those years.

According to him, she'd looked him up on Facebook after the divorce and had started sniffing around. He was just being "nice" to her because he felt sorry for her and her circumstances.

"She doesn't have any other friends," he claimed.

And since Hogg had taken over my guestroom as hers, Les took Donna and her daughter to my office cabin to spend the night. "That is if it's okay with you?"

I had no idea what he meant with that snotty tone. "I don't care."

But no sooner had he vanished than the lawyers contacted me with more upsetting news.

Because of the lawsuit Les had insisted we file.

Whatever had been going on between them, Donna had left the next morning without saying goodbye to me or my sons.

Meanwhile, I was so sick, I was calling my friends and trying to get them to come visit me. Because I honestly didn't think I was going to live much longer. My breathing was labored, and I was getting weaker and weaker.

The doctors could tell me nothing about my condition. No one had a clue what was wrong with me.

Within two weeks of Donna returning to Georgia, Les went missing.

He refused to answer his phone.

I emailed him frantically. "You left us with no money and no debit card! Where are you?" I didn't even have cash to buy a pizza, and I was about to head out of town and needed money.

No answer.

He didn't care that Nick and I were broke, and he was off "having fun." That was always his sick, twisted delusion whenever my job had taken me out of town on business.

"It must be fun to vacation all the time. I wish I could go... " Fill in the blank of the name of whatever place I was in.

No matter how hard I, or my travel companions tried, we could never make him understand that I wasn't off "having fun" without him.

What an author does was hard, grueling work.

Not that meeting fans was grueling. That was the only light that made it all worthwhile.

But the rest...

Authors were lugging suitcases so heavy that no one wanted to carry them. Our publishers would pick crappy hotels that rarely had bell service or room service. So, we were in unfamiliar places where we were starving as they didn't feed us on the plane, and we couldn't find food in towns we were unfamiliar with (and this was years before all the cellphone apps). We would have maybe an hour, if we were lucky, by the time we arrived at the hotel to prepare for our event.

An event that would last for hours.

Hopefully, the event would go off without a hitch, but often we'd arrive and find out that the store was understaffed, or we'd have chairs that didn't work properly and I have a severe back condition.

I'd had signings where the store didn't even realize I was coming. The fans had nowhere to sit. They expected us to answer questions for three hundred people (or more), with no PA system, even in a mall situation where background sound competed with my already hoarse voice.

So, by day three, we'd have no voice left and were so hoarse that we could barely speak above a whisper.

We might catch some fast food on the way back to the hotel, if any restaurant was still open. And we might get six hours of sleep before we'd have to get up and go to the next city.

That could go on for as long as three to four weeks.

All we ever saw were airports, hotels and bookstores. There was no time to do anything else as we were always on deadline for the next book and couldn't afford to take any time off to just focus on the tour or event.

Or sleep.

At a conference, it was basically the same thing. We were there to work. We came in, loaded with promotional materials for the fans and event, met fans, and usually we did events outside the conference plans where we met up with other authors to network or with fans to grow our relationships with them, and to get to know them better. We had meetings with our editors, and other publishing professionals who were there and talked business, morning, noon and night.

This was completely contrary to the lies Hogg had written to my publisher, by the way. She, like Les, had to put me in the worst light imaginable.

"Terri needs a bigger car for all the costumes she's packed. You know how she is." Anyone who had seen my photos from the RT Atlanta convention in 2017 knew that I hadn't worn any costumes, at all, that entire weekend. I was on a heart monitor and could barely stand up without help. What I had packed, was a whole lot of giveaways for the fans and booksellers. My costumes were reserved for events such as DragonCon, which were separate and worn because they were expected at those events.

However, Hogg knew that I wasn't in the best standing with my publisher at the time and used that as a chance to twist the knife in my back.

For the record, it was Les who'd wanted the car that they insisted my publisher pay for (which also didn't help my strained relationship with my publisher that Hogg had damaged). I had planned to drive down, alone, but he had refused to allow it.

"You might get hurt. The least they can do is hire a car for an event where you're being honored. You're one of their best authors. Surely, they can get you a car for that event. It's the least they should be willing to do for an author of your caliber."

Yeah, bullshit. What he meant was that he wanted his hired gun there to isolate and "feed" me without any witnesses.

Because that event had worn the old Hogg out.

Why? Those events usually had us booked from seven or eight A.M. until eleven or midnight. And again, we were always on deadline, so we were trying to find time to work while we were working. I was used to those hours and being exhausted. I didn't expect my publisher to do anything as they normally didn't do anything for any author at any level.

I wasn't treated any better than anyone else and I didn't expect any special treatment.

Unlike Les and Hogg, I understood how the business worked and the last thing I wanted was to piss off my publisher.

Just like that fall when they'd wanted me to do a signing at New York Comic Con. By the time I'd been invited by my publisher to sign in their booth, there wasn't enough time to notify a local store that I'd be in town.

"Dang it!" I'd said to Lyra. "Wish they'd told me earlier. I could have done an outside signing for those who couldn't afford to attend Comic Con."

"I can arrange a signing for you."

I'd stared at Hogg like the idiot she was. "No, you can't."

She'd preened in front of Les and smirked. "Sure, I can."

I'd rolled my eyes so far back in my head that I'm still surprised I wasn't left blind from it. "No, Hogg, you can't. I used to be a bookstore manager. I worked for a book distributor. The largest one in this country. And I've been a writer for more than thirty fucking years. It takes a minimum of three months to arrange a booksigning for a store."

"No, it doesn't. I can do it."

"Let Karen do it. She's incredible. She can do anything." Les had smiled.

I'd looked at Lyra and again, rolled my eyes. "I don't care how 'special' she is, unless she's Harry Potter and can magically transport books from a warehouse in Tennessee to New York, she can't get this done."

They laughed at me.

Why not? I had oversimplified the long process of the store having to go through their higher ups to get permission to hold the event and then get permission to order books and schedule additional personnel for the event as that was a budget concern.

Then there was the additional store budget for advertising and event coordinating with the publisher.

They wanted and needed time to let their patrons know about the event, and of course, they did need a couple of weeks to order a few hundred copies of a book to get it from out-of-state to the store and no one wanted to overnight ship a few hundred copies of books as that was cost prohibitive.

As I'd said, it took months to plan one of these events.

In the end, after the idiot had nagged and bothered my publisher and everyone else, they had learned that I was right, and the mighty Hogg did not possess any kind of magical superpowers.

Yet Les continued to think that she was some kind of wonderful beast who could supplant me.

And I won't say that my job wasn't "fun." Because the truth was that anytime I was able meet my wonderful fans and grow closer to them, I loved the hell out of it. That part was always incredible. It was what I lived for, and it made all the other bullshit worthwhile. However, it was also a lot of hard, strenuous work. There were weeks of prep leading up to it, and days of unpacking once we returned home.

Les could never get the "work" part through his jealous, petty mind. Probably because Les had always refused to work and knew nothing about it. He went from job to job, being fired or highly criticized by his colleagues for his lazy work ethic and inability to think ahead. Or because of his neurotic obsession that he was being persecuted by the women in his office. Someone was always fixated on him and "picking" on him.

That had been his rant for years.

"They hate me because I was born." This included his own mother and father. "They always treated my sisters better than me! Even Katrina, and she's adopted!"

And there was always one "woman" in his office whom he claimed became fixated on him and who made it "so that I can't work in peace."

"They" were always tattling on him or spying and snooping.

"I can't take it anymore, Terri! I have to quit! I know Andrea is listening in on all my phone calls and reporting me to my boss!" He'd spent years being medicated for depression and whatever other matters kept him from holding down a job.

Of course, none of those medications had helped because he wasn't clinically depressed.

*Histrionic Personality Disorder.* That was his Alphabet Soup problem.

He was the very definition of it.

By 2004, I was making enough money that I bought him an office of his own in Columbia, Tennessee.

Even that didn't last. Year by year, he took on fewer and fewer clients until 2008 when he quit entirely because, "it's just too hard with the new bankruptcy laws. I'm afraid I'll mess up and get disbarred."

In 2009, he closed his law practice entirely, and then made my life at home utter hell as he couldn't understand that when I'm sitting in a chair, typing, that *was* work.

Maybe it was because of the back injury I sustained while having Caleb (they accidentally yanked the epidural out of my spine and almost paralyzed me), that required me to sit in a recliner. A regular armchair or office chair caused my back to spasm and my sciatica to act up in a most excruciating way. I even had to prop my knees up in bed and be very careful of how I slept, or I wouldn't be able to walk the next day.

Every time Les looked at me lying back in my armchair even while I typed, he'd sneer, "you're playing again, aren't you?"

He did the same thing to the boys.

They'd be busy doing their homework, but if they ever stopped for five seconds, he'd barge in and accuse them of being lazy and of doing nothing.

Remember what I'd said about him projecting his sins onto others?

Yeah.

I also had a tendency to work with my TV on because I have three very loud children who often had even louder friends over. Since I wasn't Les and I didn't want to constantly scream at them for being rambunctious boys, I found it easier to simply turn the volume up and ignore them while they played and ran around the house.

It was what I'd had to do at home when I was a child and my older sister, who was completely deaf, would start making loud noises. Since she couldn't tell that she was being loud and obnoxious, and there was no way to make her stop, we had to find ways to drown her out so that we could focus on our homework and other tasks.

I'd chosen to drown her out with loud heavy metal music, so I could work under the loudest of sounds.

"You're not working, Terri! You're watching TV!"

I got so sick of his endless accusations. Les could never understand that the TV was to keep me focused because "he" couldn't focus with a TV on. And of course, if he couldn't do something, no one else could either.

Which made no sense as he wasn't able to write a book and knew nothing about it, so one would think that a lightbulb would have come on in his head.

But we weren't dealing with a normal, sane person. That was why I'd had years and years of, "Terri! We don't need to call a plumber! I can do it!" And of course, he couldn't because he'd never done it before. Which meant that it'd cost us twice as much since we'd have to call a plumber to not only fix the original problem, but whatever else Les had screwed up while attempting to make repairs he had no idea about.

Even so, I was always supportive of him. "At least you tried." Because I was raised in such a negative household, I went out of my way to be kind to him and to not repeat the abuse his parents had heaped on him. The abuse that had been heaped on me.

My reward?

On March 7, 2018, Les abandoned me and his children, and ran back to the parents who'd abused him and allowed others to do so, too. Parents who had forced him to be nice and respectful to his molester until he was a grown man.

"Don't you ever embarrass me in public, Les." That was Snooty's primary concern.

Nothing else.

It was also what had caused us to cut short our engagement. When Desert Storm had broken out, they had activated Les who was an IRR (Independent Ready Reservist). He was terrified that he'd be sent to war, and when he wasn't home to make a payment on his truck that they'd repossess it from him.

So, he'd talked me into eloping early.

"Whatever you do, Terri, don't let my parents have anything of mine if I die over there. They don't deserve it. I hate them!"

That degree of hatred should have clued me in that something in him and them wasn't right, but I was young and at the time had my own issues with my parents who'd been extremely neglectful. But while I had those issues, I'd never *hated* my parents. I'd only felt disappointed by them.

Les's level of hatred was psychotic at times. He railed against them both for their selfishness and their inability to protect their children.

"They owe me! They treat strangers better than their own blood! I'm sick of my parents not having a dime or time for their own kids. They brought me into this world, and they owe me!"

Remember those words, because they have echoed in my head since the day he left.

So, so many lies.

Or it at least showed Les's total mental breakdown that he had in March 2018. His cold-blooded selfishness and lack of regard for his own children.

Just how much he had in common with his heartless mother and pedophile father.

After my panicked lawyers from the Dumas case in March 2018 had finally gotten ahold of him, he led them on for a bit longer. He was still telling them that he planned to return home, even though he knew full well that he was already meeting with a divorce attorney and had stolen his children's futures.

That he had no intention of returning.

But what was most disgusting was that only two weeks before this—at the end of February— he'd learned that my primary Intellectual Property attorney, Peggy Millhouse, no longer had a conflict of interest.

Three years before, he'd gone to Peggy to file the suit, but at that time, her law firm couldn't clear her working on the case.

Things had changed since then.

At the last minute, he'd called Peggy to help him because he was frustrated with the other lawyers he'd brought in. But of course, she had to get up to speed with what had happened during those three years. So, to the tune of over *one hundred thousand dollars*, Les had her join the case.

One hundred thousand dollars blown in less than a month, while knowing he was leaving and had no intention of allowing us to finish the suit he'd insisted I file.

And after committing that kind of money to her and promising her that she could take over as lead counsel to continue a case he had no intention of finishing, he vanished on her.

Vanished on us.

His parting words to me and his son?

"I need a break."

From what?

Sitting on my couch, watching movies? I was the one under fire because of his rank stupidity.

No one was attacking him in public and calling him names.

Insulting everything he'd ever done and making up lies about him.

He'd also promised to meet us in Biloxi at CoastCon that weekend.

Another lie. He'd never intended to join us there.

What I learned during the interim of his "vacation" in Georgia was that one week before he'd abandoned us, he'd cleaned out my sons' bank accounts. He'd stolen more than half a million dollars I had set aside for our sons' futures.

In their names.

What was wrong with this country and its laws that you couldn't close out a safe deposit box unless all parties signed off on it, but you could wipe out an entire family and remove *all* their funds without so much as a phone call to them to warn them that their father or your husband was stealing you blind?

Our banking laws seriously need to change.

My youngest son was barely eighteen. Like his brothers, he'd been told his entire life by his father, "You don't have to worry about your future, son. You have a trust fund and everything you need is there for you. You will always be taken care of. I've made sure of it."

What he meant was that *I* had worked my ass off to see to it that my sons had a future.

He'd done nothing but waste my money and lie to every one of us.

His comments rated right up there with why they never needed to learn how to do simple things, like change a lightbulb. "You're descended from royalty. You aren't meant for menial labor. It's beneath you, son!"

Another Les trait I didn't learn about until after he was gone, and my sons finally confessed to me the horrid things he'd filled their heads with.

Yet Les had stolen every cent of their money and futures in one heartbeat, without any warning, while lying to them and me, and fled to another state.

Not a single word.

Maddox had learned about his father's treachery the moment he landed in Japan with no return ticket.

I'll never forget that panicked call. "Mom! Help! I've got no money. I can't pay for anything! My card isn't working. What's going on?"

"Are you okay?"

"I am, but my credit cards and bank card aren't working. I called Dad and he said he didn't know what was wrong."

Another lie. He knew exactly what he'd done to his son. That he'd stolen all the money and locked up his accounts or closed them.

That was the kind of shit-turd Les was.

His son could have been arrested and deported in a foreign country and he didn't care.

I'd never thought anyone could be lower than his parents. But Les had found a way to replace them as the lowest form of scum on the earth.

"Don't worry, baby. I've got your back." I had Amex overnight him a credit card from my account, and I immediately contacted the bank to transfer money to him so that he could set up an account in Japan and not be arrested for vagrancy.

What kind of monster would do that to his own child?

The same rat-turd bastard who would have his lawyers haul me before a judge a year later for contempt for "transferring" money to my son while he was in desperate need.

The same rat-turd bastard who would then try to get me into trouble with a bankruptcy court for transferring money to my son to keep him from being arrested for vagrancy.

Les was just that sick in the head. And please keep in mind that he'd never earned one single cent of any of that money.

But what really stuck in the craw was that Maddox didn't spend one half penny of what I transferred into that bank account for him. All I did was set up a U.S. account for him so that he could go to a Japanese bank to show them that he wasn't indigent. The money I transferred to him remained in his U.S. Bank account that had both our names on it for the entire time he was in Japan.

And I provided him with a credit card that allowed him to set up his accounts and get started until his teacher's pay kicked in and he repaid me what I'd advanced to him.

When he returned to the United States, I transferred the money back into my account.

All of it.

And for that, Les's lawyers hauled me before a judge to make me look like the criminal Les was, and had my home illegally searched and my property illegally seized.

My civil rights violated.

While neither me, my son, my accountant, CPA, nor my lawyer, all of whom were there that day in court, were allowed to say a single word in my defense.

I was denied my basic civil rights. The rights that my veteran father had given his life to protect. Had spent his life protecting.

There was a special place in hell for every one of them who robbed my children, and I hoped to see them all burn for it.

All my rights, and those of my sons, were violated.

Because I did nothing wrong.

But I'm getting ahead of my story again.

What kind of person would do this?

The son and grandson of pedophiles who had extreme entitlement issues. The same person who'd spent decades ranting against his parents for what they never gave him.

For what they *owed* him.

At least the pedophile and his handmaid who aided him in getting victims had earned their money they denied Les. They hadn't stolen it from Les's own account after it had been placed there by the one who'd earned the money.

How sad that the pedophile family had more morals.

There were no words for what I felt about a miserly slug who could do such a sick thing. At least I have the comfort of knowing everything I owned, I earned.

Everything Les had, he'd stolen out of the mouths of his own children and from a wife who was stupid enough to think at one time that she'd loved him.

That she'd trusted him.

But that was not the worst betrayal.

Nope. Not even close.

That would be a few days later while I was getting ready for Biloxi.

The first bitter betrayal came when I learned that "someone" had given over the names of my would-be financial backers for the movie my producer had spent nearly a decade working on.

We were all set to have the "big" meeting that would finally get everything moving, when I was told by my attorneys that our potential backers had been subpoenaed by the opposing counsel.

To quote my agent, Bob, "Hollywood execs are like pigeons. They scatter if anyone throws a pebble at them, and it's virtually impossible to ever get them back. Buddy, you didn't just throw a pebble. You hit them with a boulder."

In the beginning, I had no idea who had done such a thing. I couldn't imagine how Dumas and her team could have found out about our would-be backers.

We weren't required to give over names unless we had a deal in place.

And no deal was currently in place. We were only in talks.

Until the paperwork was signed, we had no obligation to tell them about it.

Later, I would learn that Les had been the one who'd done this to all of us. He was the sole reason that there was no television or movies for any of my series.

He'd sold us out and told the other side all about the coming meeting.

And because of his cold, callous actions, members of the team had ended up being fired.

For no reason other than to ruin the deal before it was made.

Which made no sense, right?

Why would he destroy what he wanted to be a part of? The money he wanted to live off of?

It was like some twisted part of him was so afraid of success that Les had to destroy it to make sure that he could never have it. We've all heard about these things, but until you saw it for yourself, you simply couldn't believe that it was real.

It was.

I knew because it'd happened to me.

Sadly, real life, unlike fiction, doesn't have to make sense and there was no explaining an insane mind. Les was so fixated on ruining me and destroying my career that he was so jealous of, that he didn't care or think about what it was costing him or his sons.

That was why we have the expression, cutting your nose off to spite your face.

Les was the king of that. And it was always my biggest complaint where he was concerned.

Well, that, and his failure to think ahead. He was never able to do that, either. Play a game of chess with him and you'd want to scream. Les couldn't think ahead to save his own life.

He even lost at checkers.

To a five-year-old.

The one thing I'd learned from my childhood was that you couldn't fix crazy. There wasn't enough duct tape in the world to hold that mess together.

A warped mind was just that: Warped. And you'd go insane trying to apply reason to it.

So, there I was, my deal busted, being hammered by another lunatic who couldn't be reasoned with, Amy Dumas, whom I'd told both my husband and attorneys from the very beginning to leave alone unless they were prepared to have the fight of a lifetime.

The attorney Les had hired had smirked at me. "She won't fight. They'll have insurance in place. Trust me. No one wants a long, drawn out court battle. We do this all the time. We'll file the complaint, and they'll hush it up, real fast to keep from being embarrassed. It's what they do."

I was the one who'd rolled my eyes. "Trust me. She won't do that." She had the reputation for being one nasty piece of work. And vindictive as hell.

Everyone in the business knew that about her.

And what had Les done when things got bad?

Ran out on his own lawsuit, back to his mother whom he swore he hated. We had no idea why.

All we knew was that out of the blue and after all his assertions to the attorneys that week that he was in it for the long-haul and ready to go to trial, right as I was heading to Biloxi and right before the depositions he'd been begging for got started and he brought in a new attorney to the tune of one hundred thousand dollars, I received an email saying, "Terri and I have a difference of opinion on how the suit should progress. As a result, I will no longer be 'financially responsible' for the cost of this case."

*Beg pardon?*

*What?!*

Actually, my exact words had been, "what the fuck?"

That wasn't what he'd told his only friend and workout trainer, Pat Hanson. Just days before he'd skipped town, he'd told Pat that the lawsuit was going great, and we were going to win it. He had *no* doubt.

Then as soon as I was gone, he'd flown back to town to clean out my home and told Pat out of the blue, "I'm getting divorced and won't be back."

Pat knew about the divorce before I did.

Months later, Pat would tell my son, "I've known your dad for years. He never does anything without agonizing over the decision. Over the years, I've had a lot of clients get divorced, but it's never come out of the blue like this. All Les ever said to me was how much he loved your mother and his life. This was nuts."

That sentiment was reiterated by everyone.

Especially the attorneys.

Yet Les had told our sons that he'd been planning the divorce for months. While lying to everyone else.

Even our attorneys in the Dumas case.

Insane, yes?

"How could he leave? He loves you and the kids." So many people had said that to me.

But I knew what was going on.

The Hogg had gotten into his head and made it her playground. Little snide comments such as, "You better have fun now, Les, while you can. Terri will be home soon."

As if I'd ever put any kind of damper on his happiness. Or restricted him in anyway. After all, I was the one he'd chosen to be with.

At one time, I was the only happiness he'd ever known.

Unless that was another lie, he'd told me.

He had unfettered access to all my accounts, and what I would learn later, he had accounts of his own that I knew nothing about.

At multiple banks.

The accounts I'd opened for our sons, he kept closing and pulling the money into his own accounts, without telling me.

Remember, I wasn't allowed to touch "his" mail. Not for any reason whatsoever.

"You'll lose it, Terri. You're not responsible enough for it."

Even though I was the one who'd built a multi-million-dollar career. "I" was the one irresponsible?

Not the one who ran out on the family at dawn after stealing everything from our children.

Um, yeah. How did that work, again?

And please remember that in the months leading up to his abandonment, I'd not only been on a heart monitor, but had been forced to take infusions intravenously to keep my organs from shutting down.

All the while Les had stood there, watching my pain (and photographing it). Watching me struggle to breathe.

To live another day.

Knowing why it was happening and what was causing it...

*Him.*

He'd said nothing to anyone because it was all his fault.

Bastard.

All the while, I thought what a wonderful, dutiful husband I had to come with me to all those doctor's appointments. To sit with me while I received my infusions. He was so concerned.

Never knowing that the real reason he was there was to steer the doctors away from the real cause of what was going on.

*Him.*

He was there to blame it on:

*Terri doesn't sleep.*

*She's in menopause.*

*She's "always" been like that, even when I hadn't.*

*Do you think it could be "fill in the blank" with something ludicrous?*

Meanwhile, he'd buy supplements for me to try. "This will help you, Terri. I've done research about it online."

How scared he must have been all those hours, terrified that the doctors might uncover what he was doing to me. That one of us might catch on. No wonder he'd been so impatient in their offices.

Not mindful at all.

Plotting and insidious.

Now, he was gone.

And so was that computer where he'd done all his "research."

He even told on himself when he left. He'd asked for everything in his office to be returned to him. His desk. His printer. His chair.

But not the computer.

Because he took it with him.

Then he lied under oath to the judge and told the judge that he had to buy a brand new one because he had left all his things at my home and didn't have access to a computer.

Only a Williamson County detective and DA would be so stupid as to not be suspicious that a man would steal his computer, destroy it, and then lie about it under oath.

Haven't we all seen that episode of *Forensic Files?*

And what was his reason for abandoning us in the middle of the night?

Les claimed that I was threatening to harm myself.

Oh, okay. Because everyone had always been told that the smart thing to do whenever someone was suicidal was to leave them alone.

With their teenaged son and drive fourteen hours out of state.

In the middle of a ghastly lawsuit where the suicidal person was being attacked constantly.

Um, yeah. That made no sense whatsoever.

And only the Williamson County police, and DA could be so stupid as to not see through that lie and become suspicious from it.

Not to mention, everyone knew that suicides tended to run in families.

Sadly, it was a Manly quality.

Les's niece had killed herself over the abuse their family had heaped on her. His cousin had walked herself into Atlanta traffic and other members of his family had tragically ended their own lives.

My heart bled for them.

But not once had it been something found in the DNA of a Woods.

Homicide? That, unfortunately, had ended the life of a number of my family members, who'd been killed by other people. Because we stood up for ourselves and others. We never backed down.

We refused to run away.

When there was trouble, we helped others in need.

No Woods had ever committed suicide.

My family was directly descended from Charlemagne. Rollo. The Plantagenets of England. Verified by more than one highly respected outside historical and genealogical society.

A fact that had often angered Hogg. "There's no way you have *that* lineage."

But my hereditary was beyond contestation and had been thoroughly combed through and substantiated.

"Suck it, bitch." My words to Hogg.

And Snooty.

That, too, had been a major source of pride for Les. Since he was the descendent of dirt farmers, he was over the moon about my illustrious European DNA.

So much so that during the divorce he'd had the psychosis and nerve to demand my certified genealogy papers that proved I was related to royalty.

How sick was that?

*Les, you don't own me, and you aren't entitled to my genealogy or lineage.*

That was mine.

*You. Don't. Own. Me.*

For whatever reason, he never could get that through his head. Marriage had never entitled him to my family or my heritage.

Would you believe he'd also asked for my babydolls that represented my family members? He'd had the nerve to claim that "I" had bought them for him, as if I would have bought porcelain dolls as a gift for my husband?

Seriously?

In what world would *that* make sense?

As I said, his mind was broken, and his reasoning was beyond comprehension.

His attorney should have been embarrassed to even put that on a piece of paper.

She was the only one I'd ever met dumber and more shameless than he was. And I should have known something was up the moment he abandoned us.

Hogg was still in the house, with a simpering smile on her repugnant, hideous face. A face that I'm sure was the same one possessed by Medusa whenever she turned men into stone.

In the case of Hogg, she turned my stomach. Which was probably good as I'm quite certain that was the only reason I wasn't dead, because I was pretty damn sure that was why he'd left her there.

She was to finish the job he'd started.

As we all knew, no one in their right mind would abandon their home if they honestly thought for one minute that their wife was threatening suicide.

That made no sense at all. Especially if she were there alone with his eighteen-year-old son.

And not after he'd recently had his niece and other members of his family commit suicide after they'd been abandoned by his family.

"How could they leave Taylor all alone, knowing she was suicidal and in pain? What's wrong with my family, Terri? They're so fucked up! They don't care about anyone, but themselves. My parents are the most selfish bastards on the planet. Why can't they just die!" Les's incessant rant.

He'd said it so often that even my kids could quote it.

So, no. It made no sense for him to leave behind what he claimed he believed was a "suicidal" wife after all those months of lamenting what horrible people his parents and sister were for not being there for Taylor.

"I should have been there for Taylor when she needed me. How could I have let my niece die!"

The only rational thing that made sense was that he was leaving the state so that someone else could "poison" his rich wife who was worth millions, and make it appear to be a suicide...

What better alibi, since everyone knew that the spouse was always the first suspect the police had whenever someone died from anything other than "natural" causes.

I had no doubt that Les thought he'd created the perfect scenario. Because his actions that week, and those of his accomplices, would become more and more suspicious as time went on.

As odd as they were before, that was the tip of the iceberg that was heading straight for me.

And like the Titanic on that fateful winter's night, it was too late for me to steer clear of it and avoid the disaster he'd charted for no reason other than petty greed and jealousy over the fact that he was too lazy to get a job and earn his own way in life.

*Oh, what a tangled web we weave when we practice to deceive...*

HOGG WOULDN'T GO HOME. Nor would she leave us alone. Nick and I were still trapped in the house while I attempted to make ready for Biloxi.

The heifer continued to insert herself where she wasn't welcomed.

"You want me to pack for you?" God, she had the round face of a hamster. Right down to the buck teeth and nasty, whiskered jowls.

"No." After all, I'd seen how she dressed, and I didn't want to look like a bag lady, pushing a shopping cart.

Or worse, a painted-up clown.

Which was weird now that I thought about it. Les had always said that clowns scared him, and yet when she put on her makeup, that was exactly what she looked like.

A painted clown. With garish blue eyeshadow only on her eyelids, and overly large, dark red circles on her cheeks.

No one had ever taught her the fine art of blending.

Hmm...

Anyway, trying to escape her in my home was like trying to get a spider web off after you'd accidentally walked into it. And trying to avoid her was the same.

She lurked around every corner.

You'd be minding your own business and boom!

It was all over you!

Cloying and gross. Hanging on and clinging, no matter how hard you tried to brush it off. Then your skin would crawl for hours afterward because of the aftereffect of having been near her.

Kind of like the way the stench of shit lingered on your shoe after you'd *finally* scraped it off. Even though it was no longer there, you could still smell it and you deeply regretted not watching where you'd stepped.

That was what a Hogg-encounter was like.

"Why don't you call the police?" My buddy Candice was always rational, which was what made her a great psychologist. But as I'd said, trying to apply sanity to the insane would just make *you* go crazy.

"Because I can't. She's not my employee, she's Les's. If I call the cops, he'll tell them that I'm irrational, and that Hogg has his permission to be here. Since he's also an owner of this house, and she's working here under his authority, I can't legally ban her. She has all rights to be here." Which was what Les wanted; for me to look crazy to other people such as the police.

Both of them, for that matter. He and Hogg had been trying to set me up as some insane loon so that he could claim I was losing touch with reality and have me committed.

It was also what he'd been trying to do to Nick.

He wanted all of us gone and out of his way.

"You're being ridiculous."

"You don't know how he's been with her here, Candy. And how he's been treating us. He keeps trying to have Nick committed. I found the papers in his desk. I don't trust him, anymore."

"Then, tell her to leave."

"I have! Believe me. The bitch won't go!" That was my life. I couldn't get the elephant out of the room.

Literally.

"I don't get it." I'd called Joan after I heard about her aunt passing. She was every bit as insistent as Candy. "Just tell the bitch to go."

"Joan, I have, and she won't." No one could understand my plight, and I was the first one to admit that it was implausible. Until you were here to see it, firsthand, it didn't seem real or possible. Yet, it had happened and there really was nothing I could do to get that bitch out of our lives. "I'm trapped. Please come work for me! I'll give you a raise."

Joan was the only one I knew who could stand up to them and make them back down.

If someone else was here, Hogg might get out of my house and go away.

I was desperate for help, and no one would come to my aid.

"I'll have to talk to my mom." Joan was her mother's primary caregiver.

"Okay, but please think about it." I had to whisper to keep the Hogg from hearing us.

Meanwhile, I honestly thought Les had skipped town to run off with Donna Handsoff. That made more sense than he'd have gone to his parents. And it explained why Donna was here days before he'd abandoned us, and why he'd made so many phone calls to her right after he'd left.

And why Hogg was still in my house.

"Tell me where you are!" I demanded that he give me an address for where he was staying on his voice mail and in emails.

Les refused. He wouldn't even tell the boys his location.

And the real reason why I didn't think he was in Georgia came when Caleb called me in Savannah in the middle of the night because he was sick.

"Baby, what's wrong?"

"My ear is killing me." Like me, Caleb has had severe ear problems his entire life.

"Do you have a fever?"

"I do."

"You need to go to the ER immediately. If your eardrum bursts, you could have permanent hearing loss." That was what had taken the bulk of my hearing when I was ten years old, and why I have to wear hearing aids. "Did you call your dad?"

"Why would I do that?"

"He says he's in Savannah with you. Has he not told you?"

"No."

"Call him and tell him to take you to the hospital."

Needless to say, Les didn't do it and Caleb's eardrum ruptured that night.

Father of the Year.

Which made me wonder if the bastard was in Savannah at all or lying to everyone.

Where was he?

Just days before I was to leave for CoastCon, the strangest thing of all happened.

March 11, 2018. Les had been gone for four days.

Out of the blue, I received a text from a longtime friend, Frank Colson, who said he was in town and wanted to know if I could meet him for dinner.

It was odd. Frank hadn't spoken much to me since the Dumas crap had started, but Nick and I were sick of Hogg being on top of us, and I figured a little break would be good for my Boo.

We went out to eat at Chili's just down the street from my house, where we talked about much of nothing. Nick had a test that night, online, and he was stressed about it.

"Don't worry, babe. You'll do fine. Relax and have a good dinner and then tackle it like the champ you are."

It was after Frank had left a couple hours later that Nick came down to my office.

"Uh, Mom, I have a problem?"

"Can't log on?"

He shook his head. "Karen took my test for me while we were out eating."

I was stunned. "What?"

Looking as sick as I felt, he nodded. "She flunked it and then pretended to be me and emailed my favorite teacher about it." He held his phone out for me to see the email. "What do I do? She made me sound like an idiot and I love that teacher."

Flabbergasted, I kept the phone in my hand and read what she'd written while she's pretended to be my Nick. "That fucking bitch! How stupid is she that she can't even pass a high school English test?"

And this was the dumb cow that Les had wanted me to use to "edit" my books? Pah-lease!

She couldn't even write a coherent email. Oh my God!

"I'll take care of it."

Nick panicked. "Mom! Careful. It's academic dishonesty. They'll throw me out of school!"

"I know, baby. Don't worry."

But that was easier said than done. For one thing, Les had never allowed me to have access to their school accounts after he'd quit work. I had no login information, or anything else.

"This is my job. You go make money for us." His stock answer for everything.

It didn't matter that I'd been the parent in PTA or that I was their homeroom mom, and had helped with all their homework long before we could afford outside tutors (and many times even after we had tutors), and done all school activities for the majority of their lives.

He was the "man in charge" from then on, and he cut me out. Which meant that he just hired other people to do it all. Les couldn't be bothered.

Seriously. It was so bad that Joan often joked about when the boys were in San Diego with us for Comic Con and had spilled a Coke in our hotel room. They'd looked up at her and said, "We need to call Horace."

She frowned, confused by that since our handyman, Horace, was back home in Tennessee. "Why?"

"To clean up the Coke."

Because that was what their father had taught them. Call Horace for everything. Since Les refused to do anything for himself, the kids didn't have to do it, either.

Ridiculous.

And even though he paid Hogg to tutor my children (let me reiterate that she was terminally stupid), all of my children had continued to come to me for homework help because Hogg should never have been allowed to tutor anyone for anything.

By her actions, Hogg had left my baby in a bad way. Having taught in the past, especially at places like Mississippi University for Women, I knew this had to be handled with a lot of delicate care.

Since I didn't have any contact information for Nick's school, I went to Hogg's boss, Angelo Flora. He owned the tutoring company she worked for, and I decided that would be the best place to start.

As soon as he took my call, Angelo was confused. "Um, there's a problem. Karen hasn't been your tutor for over a year."

Now it was my turn to be befuddled. I felt my jaw go slack. "There is a problem. She's been working as my kids' tutor right up until she took that test."

"I'm looking at her records. She hasn't been tutoring for you."

Come to find out, Les and Hogg had violated her work contract that they both signed. A contract that said Les was never to hire one of Angelo's people outside of his tutoring service. Ever. Hogg had also signed a separate agreement saying that she wouldn't work for any of Angelo's clients.

Ever.

That said it all about the kind of people they were. Especially when you looked at the hours she was billing Angelo and us. She had double-dipped even worse than Kiki had, all the while she'd been whining to Les and tattling on Kiki for doing the very thing that she was doing to Les and Angelo.

*My, my. How do hypocrites stomach themselves?*

Hogg had used her own crimes to turn Les against Kiki and made him begin tormenting and bullying Kiki for the very lies she was telling.

Ironic, right?

And this from a woman who went around bragging to everyone about how she was a Methodist pastor.

Shame on the church that had ordained her, and that allowed her to continue to use its name and endorsement to swindle and abuse people.

So, what did Les have to say when his son confronted him over what the Great Hogg had done?

"You took the test, Nick."

"No, Dad, I didn't. I was out eating when it was taken."

"We were sitting at the pool when you took it."

Nick scoffed. "No, Dad. Here's the email that I didn't write. I couldn't have written it because I was sitting in a restaurant at the time it was sent, and the restaurant didn't have wifi and it blocks all cell phone signals so that you have to pay to use theirs."

What my research into the matter quickly uncovered was that Les had been paying Hogg to falsify information for schools.

*Let me repeat that.*

Les and Hogg had been *falsifying* information for not only Williamson County schools, but other school systems as well. And Williamson County Commissioner, John Alaimo, not only knew this for a fact, he had the nerve, during my divorce, to sue me on behalf of his client for almost *seventy thousand dollars* for Les's criminal behavior in defrauding the Williamson County schools and for violating their academic *dishonesty* policies.

Judge Bubba Joe Dinky screamed at me in court, on record (I have the transcript and recording), for being unreasonable and not cooperating with Alaimo and Dinky's former law firm, Ogles & Steal (before Dinky became a judge, the law firm had been called Steal-Dinky-Williams and remember that latter name because the *Williams* part was going to come into play real soon, too).

Wasn't this just a jolly fun crew of corruption?

How would you like for Alaimo to be your Republican county commissioner who ran on a platform promoting "family values," and to protect and improve the schools where you lived? So much for all his bullshit about nanny states, and all that other rigamarole he and Les supposedly stood for.

How I so loved a liar, said no one ever.

I supposed that Alaimo's principals didn't apply when his client was a fully able-bodied lawyer who had never worked a real job and wanted to live off the welfare of his disabled wife and three special needs sons.

*Hypocrites unite.*

God, for all the rants I'd been forced to endure for three decades from Les over how much he hated those "able-bodied" people on welfare who refused to work because they felt entitled. "Those people" who felt like the world owed them something when they were simply "too good" to work a real job.

His tirades against "wealth redistribution."

Seriously? And here he was, the worst of the bunch.

He not only refused to work, he'd stolen from the very family that had trusted him.

The only family that hadn't abused him.

Stolen the future from his special needs children.

And in so doing, they put us all on welfare by the end of it (*I'm getting there*).

The worst irony? Les's main attorney had the audacity to show a photo in court of his office in my cabin where he'd stolen the sign he used to keep in our house.

That sign?

"He who will not work, shall not eat."

Yeah...

There was so much irony there, I could write a country song.

I guess the others were right when they vilified you, Les.

*You are the devil. You did steal from us, you old bastard.*

*All of you.*

And you did it with the full cooperation of the Tennessee State government, and none of the agencies I went to would help me.

None of them.

Not the ACLU. Not the governor. My state reps. The FBI. The police. ADA. IRS.

Nobody. And I tried them all.

Every one of them stood aside with their lame-ass excuses as to why their agency couldn't or shouldn't get involved while all my rights were taken from me. I went from being a hard-working, upper middle-class woman capable of supporting her family, and others, to being put into bankruptcy by a system that stole my voice from me.

While I was denied due process.

My home was illegally invaded and then stolen from me.

All my assets illegally seized. I was robbed by my government and held hostage for more than two years.

And I was arrested without due process and jailed in America for no other reason than I had to go to the bathroom because of the kidney and liver damage Les had given to me from the poison he'd fed me.

Third most corrupt state in the Union. Nashville was one of the most corrupt cities in America.

Too bad Felicity Huffman and Lori Loughlin hadn't lived here. No one would have ever prosecuted them in this state. Most likely, they'd have baked them cookies, and taken them to the opera.

Because no one here gave a single shit that Les had paid Hogg to take tests, write papers, and falsify college applications for *my* children.

Or committed tax fraud and blackmail in open court.

Apparently, fraud and extortion in Franklin, Tennessee, was okay. Impersonating a student and illegally taking a test for that student, was okay, too, with our law enforcement and judicial systems. I knew that because I'd filed the report and the detective just shrugged it off.

And it was especially okay with our Williamson County Commissioner who was defending the perpetrators and insulting me for daring to question the villain.

While robbing me in the process.

Hell, they were even willing to assist in suing the parent who was attempting to get justice for their child. And all the while they bullied and harassed me and my sons, his law firm had the audacity to advertise against bullying on their own web site.

How sickening.

Even locking Maddox out of his own personal email account and pretending to be him with his employers was fine by Tennessee standards. Apparently, no one would ever prosecute criminals for cybercrimes even when they were caught red-handed, and you could show the police the emails you had going back and forth, bragging over the fact that they were in other people's emails without their knowledge or permission, while those people were away from home and even out of the country at the time they were in their emails.

And I could do you one even better. Old Judge Bubba Dinky was on record telling me that he'd put me in jail if I didn't hand over the private, personal information of hundreds of thousands of my fans and put them at risk (I'll get to that, too) with a dark web expert who had a history of violating other people's privacy and of hacking accounts.

Wasn't *that* scary?

But you calmly go to the bathroom before you wet yourself because you have kidney disease, and you were sentenced to ten days in jail for it.

That was why this book was called *Nightmare in Williamson County.*

No one here cared at all what the law was. Not the Attorney General. Not the governor. Not the local DA, and definitely not the police. They couldn't be bothered to enforce our laws.

Never mind our Civil Rights.

The judge said it best, "I don't care what the law is." I have that on a transcript, by the way.

And when I told that to the Tennessee Judiciary Board of Review, do you know what they responded with?

"It sounds to us as if you didn't like the judge's opinion." And I have that in writing, too.

Not that it mattered. After all, that same Board was the one that went up to the Tennessee Senate and testified to the fact that they refused to take action over any complaint brought against any judge for anything.

*And yes, I'm going to repeat that.*

The judge said in a courtroom and on a transcript, *"I don't care what the law is."*

For the record, that wasn't an opinion, Mr. Judiciary Board of Review. That was a terrifying declaration of war against our citizens, and a flagrant disavowal of a judge's job.

So maybe you sons of bitches might ought to rethink your policy against dismissing all complaints filed against judges and start actually reviewing them and doing the job you were given.

*Maybe you should take your jobs seriously or give them over to people who will.*

But then what were a few felonies and criminal impersonations between citizens and friends?

*Y'all come on down! We'd love to have you here in Franklin, Tennessee. Every criminal's welcome! Just move on in. It's a lovely place to live.*

*Want to poison your wife and kids?*

*Ah hell yeah! That's fine. We understand. We want to kill ours, too. It's all good. Don't worry! We got people on the bench who frequent prostitutes and belittle women all day long! They'll take good care of you and your needs. We have lawyers who pay no attention to any form of conduct or ethics! So, don't you worry, now. Ain't no such thing as a Board of Review.*

*No one here will ever prosecute you!*

*It's all good!*

*For that matter, what's a little credit card or bank fraud? We got your back, brother!*

In the end, I would have to say that the news was right, after all. If you were one of the "privileged" class in the great state of Tennessee, you could get away with murder, or in Les's case, three cases of attempted murder and the death of a cat.

Personally, I had never really believed that until all this started. I thought it was just venom spewed by people who were angry and looking for an easy excuse to blame others for their own failures.

But it was real.

It happened to me and my sons.

Here in Williamson County, Tennessee.

Little did I know then that my nightmare had just begun.

Three days after Hogg had committed her latest felonious act against my son with his schoolwork, Nick and I went to Biloxi for CoastCon.

Les didn't show up in Mississippi as he'd promised Nick. A liar was always a liar. In fact, while I was there, I received another email from him that he was turning payroll over to me.

Something he'd never allowed me to touch before or even see. I knew nothing about it. And he dumped it in my lap while I was at a major event.

While I was greeting fans and embroiled in the lawsuit he'd dragged me into against my common sense.

Suddenly, I was getting calls from my bookkeeper, Nancy Harrison, asking me even more questions I couldn't answer.

"Well, it's nice to finally speak to you, Terri." Les had always kept us apart in the past. "He always said you were too busy for it."

I sighed at Nancy's words.

Les had said that to a lot of people about me. My banker. My friends. My family. Even my children.

It was called isolation. A trick that abusers commonly used on their victims.

Les was afraid I'd leave him, so he kept me locked away from the world as much as he could. I should have changed my name to Rapunzel.

While I liked to have people over and throw parties, Les had run everyone off. Year by year, until I'd become a prisoner in my own home. Too sick to fight him. And as a writer, who needed a lot of quiet time to work, it was extra easy to accomplish that isolation.

The only people he allowed to stay were his chosen few who aided him with keeping me in seclusion.

He'd even run my brother off for a time. Why? Because my brother had seen through him. "He's a fucking weasel, Terri. Spineless piece of shit, unfit to be called a man. You need to dump him and find someone who can be an actual role-model for your boys."

Believe it or not, Les actually agreed with Esteban. He knew he wasn't a role-model for his sons. It was why he kept trying to get me to send my boys to stay with Esteban every summer.

"Think of everything your brother could teach them!"

Such as what I learned when Maddox was twenty-four; his father had never once taught any of my sons how to use a hammer or screwdriver.

How pathetic was it that I, their mother, had to teach them such basic skills after the weasel I married sat on our couch for the entirety of their lives, watching old movies and lamenting over the fact that there were no real men any more?

Oh, that irony.

Les had been right all along.

Things my brother could have taught my sons—Working on cars. How to play sports. Basic home maintenance. A good, moral character. Strong work ethic.

Shouldn't their father have been the one to teach that to his kids?

Instead, he'd taught them how to run out on your family when the going got tough. How to steal from your children. How to lie to their faces.

How to fail at everything.

Maybe he showed them something, after all. They now knew what not to do.

Most importantly, they now knew who they didn't want to be.

"Les, my brother lives in the most dangerous part of Atlanta and has a ten-foot electric fence around his house! With barbed wire. I'd really rather you choose a safer environment for my sons to have summer camp."

I should have realized then that Les was trying to get rid of us all.

*Some things no one wants to accept...*

That every night when you closed your eyes, you were lying next to a cold-blooded monster who was one step away from killing you. I stupidly thought the only monsters in his family were either dead or living hundreds of miles away.

I should have known that evil like that was too infectious to simply die out. It only got more cowardly with each subsequent generation. But I knew that I hadn't allowed the horrors of my past to impede me. I had risen above.

I'd never struck my children. Never caused them harm. I'd gone out of my way to make sure they were safe. Happy.

Case in point, when Maddox was around four, we were at my mother's house and he did something she disproved of, my mother glared at him. "You want a spanking, boy?"

Maddox beamed up at her. "Yes!"

Aghast, she turned toward me.

"He doesn't know what a spanking is, Mom. I've never hit my kids."

I was emphatic that they would never fear me. Never know the horrors of my childhood. Just as I didn't want that kind of drama or trauma in my home. That they would never have to pull their bed across their door every single night the way I'd done as a child because they were afraid to close their eyes and feared to sleep because they couldn't afford to relax their guard for even a single heartbeat.

I'd made a vow to myself and to my babies.

I failed us both.

While I knew at this point that Les was a far cry from my Prince Charming, I wasn't quite aware of how close to Prince Evil he was.

Honestly, I thought him too lazy to do much of anything. After all, he couldn't get off the couch to do something as simple as change a lightbulb. At this point, he was a permanent growth sprouting out of the sofa cushions.

With his new henchman in place, Cisco, he seemed content enough with everything. Right down to ordering Cisco to put gas in the cars whenever they ran low.

I knew there was something a little creepy about Cisco, but he seemed to be a typical computer Geek. Antisocial. Rotund with this air of unwarranted superiority.

Cisco hated everyone and wore it like a badge of honor. He'd finished high school with a Hail Mary, never gone to college and yet, according to him, he was the most brilliant person on the planet, ever. He should be in charge of the whole world, except for the fact that he had no ambition, and a recreational drug habit that I kept telling Les concerned me.

"We can't replace Cisco. We need him."

"But he's got some really weird ideas that I'd rather not have the kids exposed to." For one thing, he hated women and was a pathological liar. His mother had abandoned him when he was two, and, according to Cisco, his father had illegally smuggled him into the U.S. and forged documents to get him into the country.

But no one listened.

No one cared.

No matter who I tried to tell these things to, my words fell on deaf ears.

Like Hogg, Cisco stayed even though I had a sick feeling in my stomach anytime he came near me, and it wasn't only when he made groping passes at me when Les wasn't looking.

In fact, it was so bad that I couldn't even work at my cabin whenever Cisco was there. I refused to be alone with the creep. He was way too handsy.

Kiki was as bad as Les. "I think Cisco's kind of pathetic. He needs a mother-figure. Poor thing. No one should be abandoned like he was. That's what's wrong with him."

She felt sorry for him, and he talked about her like she was a dog behind her back.

"Kiki's an idiot. I'd fire her if I were you. She lies about her hours. What does she do all day? You're paying her for nothing." He went from me to Les with those complaints until he had Les hating Kiki, too.

Of course, Cisco also talked about Les the same way. "I don't know why you married him. What does he do all day, other than sit on your couch and spend all your money? I wouldn't put up with it. Does he do anything other than scream at the kids? What is his damage? I couldn't stand to be married to such an idiot."

And that was the biggest reason I wanted Cisco gone. Having been raised around such negative people, I kept hearing my grandmother's voice in my head. "A dog that totes a bone will carry it."

If he talked about other people like that, I figured he was saying shit about me behind my back, too.

I wasn't wrong.

What I didn't know was that a perfect storm was brewing, and my boys and I were right in the middle of the hurricane's eye. Les had assembled the ideal team of unscrupulous users, liars and thieves who would do anything for the all-mighty buck.

While Les thought he was sealing my fate, it was his own goose he was cooking.

He was just too stupid to realize it.

W HILE I KEPT WAITING FOR Les to show up in Biloxi as he'd promised so that he could explain his bizarre behavior, my phone wouldn't stop ringing with lawyers and my accountant.

For one thing, I was heading into depositions for the Dumas case in less than ten days, but because my ever-treacherous husband had fired off an email saying he would no longer be financially responsible for that lawsuit, I had no attorneys.

*What?*

That was what I kept saying.

Here was the problem.

Les had started that ungodly lawsuit against my protests and all commonsense. From day one, I had known it was not going to go the way he and the lawyers had told me it would.

Unlike Les, I wasn't stupid or delusional.

I was well aware that all lawyers lied. They were in it, not to win, but to get paid.

Much like the doctors when my cousin Michael had been diagnosed with cancer at age eight. They had looked at his mother and told her that he had a thirty percent chance of survival.

"We have to do everything we can to pull him through. He has a chance to survive!"

Once they'd run her out of all her insurance and had bankrupted her and she'd sold her home and everything else she could to pay for his treatments, then it was, "well, he *only* has a thirty percent chance of survival. There's really nothing more we can do. You should take him home and make him as comfortable as possible until he dies."

How I really wish I were making up that story.

Lawyers were the same way. They'd fight only as long as you had money to throw at them. As soon as it was gone, so were all your chances of winning.

Remember that I had been married to one for multiple decades, so I wasn't being harsh. I'd been around enough of them to know they had well-earned their reputation.

At least the majority of them. I have a tiny handful of lawyer friends who are unique among the jackal horde.

As in I knew three out of hundreds who weren't like that.

Anyway, because Les was a chicken-shit bastard, he had refused to be deposed by the other side's attorneys and had been panicking (just like Kiki) since the moment they'd said they were going to depose him. He'd emailed every one of our attorneys saying that since he "served as my attorney every day" that he couldn't be deposed.

That he had "immunity."

Dumas's lawyers were such money-grubbing douchebags that they deposed my other attorneys, which made Les shit his bed. I would say literally, but that would be gross.

So, he fled his bed to Georgia.

Why he and Kiki were so terrified of depositions, I had no idea. Les had been pushing for depositions for the other side since the moment the suit was filed. And I agreed because I knew how ridiculous the lies were that Dumas and her team were telling. They were so bad, that I knew her lies would fall apart instantly if we could get to them before they could unite and get their lies coordinated.

However, my side didn't keep their word to me. I'd been promised those depositions immediately.

Over a million dollars spent and years later, still no depositions.

I wasn't happy as I wanted the truth out to the public. *When you live a life of integrity and honesty, you're not afraid of the truth.*

Why was Les so scared?

Why was Kiki so terrified that she quit a job she claimed she loved in the middle of the night, with no warning?

Kiki had told Joan that she didn't want to be deposed, because she was afraid she'd go to jail over it.

It made no sense.

I knew exactly what Dumas and my publisher were afraid of.

And earlier in the suit, Les had offered to sign the Non-Disclosure he'd forced all our employees and contractors to sign. My lawyers had told him that they'd simply add him on as a client and so that, too, would cover him for attorney-client privilege.

This was a very important fact to this tale as Les drafted the Non-Disclosures for my company that said any lie or dissemination of private information about me or my family to the public was harmful to my future, and detrimental to my career and earning potential. There was a lot more to it, but that was the gist of the Non-Disclosure Les drafted and was fanatical about making everyone sign and enforcing whenever someone broke it.

He'd even fired people such as my longtime cleaning lady, Shelly Carson, for talking about my sons in public.

Les made everyone who came into my home sign off on that document. Cisco, Kiki, Hogg, etc.

I was surprised he hadn't made our sons sign it, too. He was that paranoid. And yes, he'd gone after people for breaching it.

Because of that paranoia, and his insistence, my attorneys could no longer represent me (according to them) without acquiring his permission to do so.

Yes, you heard that correctly. In this modern-day era, I, the one who had earned all the money and paid for those expensive attorneys, wasn't allowed to have those attorneys represent me without my husband's permission.

I felt like I had in Columbus, Mississippi when the doctor had come into the examination room and told me that even though I had insurance coverage, they were denying it because they didn't want to pay any more money on my policy—my back-to-back high-risk pregnancies had cost them a lot more than the insurance company had anticipated.

So, because they were denying coverage, my doctor was going to cut me open for a major abdominal surgery without anesthesia.

Oh yeah, I wish I were making that up, too. *The horror of being told that they plan to do major surgery with a local...*

There were so many reasons I had wanted out of Mississippi.

And it was a sad statement and a full indictment against the state of Tennessee that I would sell my soul to Satan to be back in Mississippi over Tennessee any day of the week and twice on Sunday.

Because Mississippi was unfairly picked on, especially when compared to the psychopaths who ran the state of Tennessee, who were so proud of the fact that they were so far behind the times that they flaunted it.

Seriously. What can you say about a state that proudly has a monument for Nathan Bedford Forrest right there along the main interstate for everyone to see?

The entire state should be required by the federal government to post warning labels at the state line to put the innocent on notice that they were entering an unholy land where the laws of the U.S. Constitution and commonsense do not apply.

Remember that this was the home of Bufford Pusser of the *Walking Tall* nightmare, and that we'd had governors in the past who'd sold pardons to hardened felons. You wouldn't believe all the stories I'd heard about the utter bullshit that went on in this state and especially my county.

Again, everyone here knew how corrupt Williamson County was and no one would stand up and stop it.

*But I'm getting ahead of myself.*

Because I was still at the beginning of my nightmare where one man with one email could deprive a woman of the lawyers she was paying her hard-earned money for.

Lawyers who would later claim that he wasn't their client even though I had been told that they'd added him on as a client to the Dumas case to cover his ass.

And I had the emails from them to prove it.

So why then did I not have lawyers suddenly if he wasn't their client?

Yeah, it was that messed up, and it hurt my head, too, as I tried to figure it out.

Anyway, I was dealing with *that* stress while having to put on a smiling face and greet fans all weekend long. Not to mention, trying to figure out payroll for the first time ever and send money to Japan for my son who had landed over there without a working credit card because his father had stolen every dime out of his account.

My son had no money to eat on and had no place to sleep or stay.

He was in jeopardy and could have been arrested at any moment for vagrancy.

My baby who had been assured by his own blood father as he was putting him on that plane that everything would be fine, was sleeping on the ground at night with only his leather jacket for warmth. The same father who'd abandoned him to homelessness before that plane had left the tarmac in Nashville.

*Let's redefine the word "bastard" to the name "Les Manly." Make it synonymous the way everyone associates "Benedict Arnold" with "traitor."*

*No one wants to be a "Les Manly" do they?*

Anyway, my cousin Lyra and her mother and daughter had come in to help as I was too weak to do it on my own. But the peculiar thing was that G2 (name replaced to protect the guilty) was supposed to come to Biloxi and help that weekend, and at the last minute couldn't make it.

It was odd that Les's little friend he loved so much had banged out on me, but I was so distracted with everything that had blown up that I paid it no attention.

Until she showed up on the last day.

At the last minute.

Acting weird.

As a rule, I wasn't paranoid. Like most children brought up in an abusive home, I was good at reading people. You had to be. Your life and health depended on it.

The minute G2 came in, I knew something wasn't right with her.

I just didn't know what, other than the fact that she didn't hang on the way the "dingleberry" normally did. It felt as if she were fishing for something.

But once the event was over, we parted, and Lyra and her family headed back to Georgia while Nick and I returned home to Franklin.

Still, I had a bad feeling on that long car ride back. Les was supposed to be waiting at home for us.

He wasn't.

We arrived just before midnight.

When the garage door opened and I saw my '64 Mustang in the place where Les kept his Porsche, I knew what the bastard had done.

My Mustang normally stayed at my office cabin.

Which meant he had driven away in our family SUV and then came back to steal his sports car.

I admit I was furious. For one thing, he barely knew how to drive my vintage car and he'd touched it. The one and only time the idiot had driven it, he'd opened the hood and for some reason used a flashlight to disconnect the battery tender from it so that he could move the car.

Not knowing what Mr. Moron had done and assuming no one could be the idiot Les was, I drove my car and then when I opened the hood to reattach the battery tender, I found the flashlight still sitting on top of the battery.

Yeah, he was *that* level of stupid.

After that, I forbade him to ever touch the car again as I didn't want it permanently damaged by his incompetency.

That thought was foremost on my mind as I opened the door to our house and stopped dead in my tracks.

It looked as if my home had been robbed. Les and his Hogg girlfriend had raided my house while Nick and I were away, working all weekend. He'd stolen furniture, silver, photographs, jewelry, everything.

Whatever he'd wanted.

He'd even stolen Nick's theater tickets. And sold my precious fish out of my Koi pond.

Even Nick's cat, Mochi, that he used to comfort himself with whenever he was upset. A cat that had been given to me as a Christmas present that Nick had taken up with after Les had murdered his Kitty.

Other items that belonged to the boys were missing as well.

But the sickest part?

On the island in my kitchen was a dozen roses with a note. Well, not exactly. He'd taken an old anniversary card that he'd given me and wrote inside it.

*I still want to be married.*

*Please call me.*

*~Les*

The real kicker was the handwritten note from his slag that she'd placed on top of it.

*I hope you work out your marital problems.*

*Call me if I can help.*

*~Karen*

There was no way to describe the nauseated sensation in my stomach. The cruelty of those actions of the two of them robbing me and my sons and then to have the sick gall to leave that for us to find on our return, knowing that Les had already been talking to his divorce attorney and had no intention of returning, at all.

That he'd already paid the attorney retainer (something I'd learn later). That was what a sick, lying fuck he was.

Sick lying fucks they both were.

I'd never done anything other than take care of this psycho bastard while he berated me.

Poisoned me and made me so sick that I could barely walk. Had left me so sick that I had required multiple infusions to keep my organs from shutting down.

I knew I should have left him years ago.

Damn the disgusting family courts of this country for the fact that they would have given him custody of my children so that his pedophile father would have had unfettered access to them.

The dumbest statement made to me to date, bar none, had to go to a federal attorney here in Tennessee who actually said, and I quote, "I still don't see why you stayed with him. It's not like he would have custody of them *all* the time."

Thank you for that ultimate level of stupidity that made me feel sorry for your wife and children. That total lack of regard that you had for anyone.

According to the Tennessee Bankruptcy Trustee and what he'd said, it was okay to molest a child, so long as you didn't do it *all* the time.

In one nutshell, that was what was wrong with the entire judicial system of this country and let me reiterate that it came out of the mouth of an actual federal attorney, assigned to my case.

And it was that rampant, callous stupidity that had kept me bound to Les and his sick family for all those years.

Because I always thought that anyone with a minuscule amount of brain activity would know that it only took minutes for a child molester to ruin a child's life.

For eternity.

Seconds to molest a baby.

And there was no way to repair that damage.

What kind of sentient human could make such an asinine, inhumane comment?

Who said that?

Well, I knew who, and so did he.

Fortunately, I loved my children. They have always come first in my heart, and they always will.

That rated right up there with the absolute idiot who'd said when the Dumas case broke that the whole reason I brought it was that I "must be jealous of her."

Jealous of what? An author so pathetic and uncreative that she had to steal a series in order to have one?

Seriously?

Like Les, everything she had she'd stolen, and she knew it.

So, what in the world would I have to be jealous of? I wasn't the one trying so desperately to be someone else. Nor was I the one who had to lie about everything for fear of others finding out the truth.

I was a Woods. We didn't do that. We stood tall to our principals.

And our integrity wasn't for sale.

So, I threw the flowers out and kept the card to remind me what a lying piece of shit I'd made the mistake of putting my faith in.

The worst mistake of my life was falling in love and trusting the wrong person. Putting him through law school while his own family and friends had turned their backs on him.

I should have realized how rotten he was when not even the pedophile and the slag protecting the pedophile wanted anything to do with him.

*Said it all, didn't it?*

After the flowers and those notes that said Les wasn't returning, I went to my computer and summarily told Hogg not to bother coming back to my home ever again.

I was done with her illegally writing papers and taking tests for my children. With her impersonating them and me, and illegally submitting college and job applications for them, breaking into my email and doing all the other questionable and illegal activities Les had paid her to do on his behalf.

Since Les wasn't here and had put in writing that he'd abandoned his family and was no longer living here, I could finally ban her from our lives and my presence.

Would you believe the bitch had the audacity to then try and bill me *fourteen hundred dollars* for stealing my husband, money and property out of my house while I was off working with my son?

She also had the gall to bill me an additional two days of work *after* I told her not to access my servers or anything else.

Really, she was a disgusting piece of work.

I had to continually remind her that she was not and had never been *my* employee. That was why she wasn't on my payroll with my other employees. It was why at the bottom of each and every one of her invoices she had clearly stated that she worked for Les Manly, *Attorney at Law*. That all her work was done under *his* supervision and at *his* behest.

Not mine.

Unlike Les, I had standards. It was even in my employee handbook that my people were required to keep their work area clean.

After I got Hogg out of my home, it took three of us, Lyra, Joan and I a full two weeks to clean out her sty where she had left half-eaten food, bags of chips, cookies, empty bottles, and dirty tissues all over my den.

How had she gotten anything done, eating, drinking and dripping all over the place?

She really was a Hogg. But what thoroughly pissed me off was the moment I realized just how incredibly manipulative she'd been, and how stupid Les was.

That skank knew what I did about my husband. Les was severely OCD and couldn't stand a mess.

As sick as I'd been for so long, I would clean out her nasty work area whenever I could manage it, and she would pile it up again to irritate Les and cause strife between us, because she knew that it was an irritant to him that she could blame on me.

Before she'd come into my life, that area had been spotless, and it'd been spotless since the day she left.

While she'd been there, Les had constantly berated me about the mess that she had caused and that she kept filthy.

Not me.

The moron known as Les could never figure out that the main problem in his life had been the Hogg he'd let into it.

They deserved each other.

How I wished you could have smelled the odor of her in my home. We had to fumigate the room for a month to get it back to normal.

At least I had the comfort of knowing I couldn't compete with *that*. Nor would I want to.

So glad that was what he'd left me over. Because when everyone saw them together, they laughed at him for his stupidity. Just as they laughed at him for throwing away the life everyone had envied him over.

Only Les could be *that* stupid. But I was so grateful that he was gone, because had he not left, I'd be dead now.

By his hand.

Anyway, after he was gone, I also realized that the idiot had left me with no running car to drive.

Seriously. Les had taken the family SUV and then flown back into town to steal his Porsche.

Those were the only two cars that had been running at the time of his departure because he'd been that afraid of my leaving him.

While I have an Audi, it'd been sitting up for all the months/years Les had refused to allow me to drive anywhere and so the battery on it was long dead. The same was true for Caleb's Corvette he'd left behind the four years he'd been in college.

Maddox had wrecked his Jeep months before he left, and since then, he hadn't been driving it. Which meant it wasn't working, either.

In fact, that first month Les was gone, it cost me over fourteen thousand dollars in repairs to get our cars running again.

If you were thinking about my vintage Mustang... The car was older than I was, and the problem with driving a car older than you when you weren't a young whippersnapper?

It required a battery tender on it at all times as the battery had a bad habit of going dead real fast.

Les hadn't returned the tender with the car.

Not to mention, it was a convertible that leaked every time it rained, and it rained all the effing time in Nashville.

That meant there were only two cars I had that worked. And Les had called Cisco in from out of state where Cisco had moved off to once Les had forewarned him of the pending divorce (this I learned about later) to drive the company car so that I wouldn't have it.

That car would also stop working the minute Cisco left town, how ironic was that?

Nick's car was the only one that worked, and since I had deposition preparation all week downtown, I couldn't leave him stranded without any transportation, and even his car had an engine warning light on it that needed to be taken into a shop that week.

Which meant I was screwed.

There were literally no cars I could drive.

None.

I had to call my cousin in from Georgia to come and take me back and forth to Nashville for my deposition preparation.

Which was good, because having Lyra here was what saved my life that week.

Seriously.

I was on the phone, calling her to ask her to come up for the morning while surveying the damage Les and Hogg had done when I walked into my bathroom and saw the strangest thing of all.

"Lyra... you're not going to believe this."

"What?"

"All my hairbrushes are out on my countertop."

"Huh?"

I stared at a dozen hairbrushes that someone had carefully lined up on a towel beside my sink. Not in one bathroom, but two of them. "Someone cleaned out all my hairbrushes." I took a photo of it and sent it to her.

"Are you serious?"

"Yeah."

While it pissed me off, I understood why Les had robbed my house. But why would anyone in the middle of robbing my home of cash and other valuables take the time to clean out all my hairbrushes?

And leave them so carefully placed?

"Terri, you don't think he poisoned you, do you?"

I scowled at Lyra's question. "What?"

"You know, all the crime shows I watch? That's how they catch people. They always find poison in people's hair."

"That's weird."

But the whole thing was weird, there was no getting around it.

"Are your guns still there?"

My blood ran cold at her question. "Hang on."

I ran through the house to check the two gun safes where we kept them. Les's was empty. And mine...

He'd reset my code so that I couldn't open it.

*What a piece of shit.* So, I picked it up and when I did, I realized that there was no sound inside. It, too, was empty.

"No. They're all gone."

"You need to call the police. He's nuts."

She wasn't wrong.

In that moment, I was terrified. One reason being that I had told so many people over the years that my fear was he'd kill me if I ever tried to leave him.

It hadn't been a joke. After all, he had a history of mental health issues. Remember what I'd said? He was so afraid of my leaving that he used to stand on my toes to keep me planted by his side.

Everyone knew that control freaks were dangerous when they left. Because they always had to be in control.

Les was insane about controlling us.

It didn't make sense that he would leave.

The roses didn't make sense.

Then again, Les had never made any sense with anything he did.

He had fits of depression and rage. There were scars all through my house where he'd thrown things during those fits. Deep gouges in my hardwood floors. Plates he'd shattered.

Not to mention the fact that he'd been a raging alcoholic through most of my marriage.

And he had all my guns and was most likely entrenched at my cabin that rests on seven-and-a-half acres of heavily wooded land.

*Easy to hide a body there where no one would know.*

I'd seen this movie.

Lyra was right. Anyone who knew anything about violent people and bad marriages knew that the most dangerous time for a spouse was when their abuser left. That panic that set in with them. It was usually when they killed their spouse. I had a dear friend and fellow writer who'd been murdered by her husband during a divorce.

How many times had I told my friends that if I ever tried to leave Les, I was afraid he'd kill my children?

Or kill me. Because he was so afraid of being alone.

This was the man who had always said that he wanted me to die first so that he could be buried on top of me.

He was *that* sick.

That controlling.

All through law school he'd made me sit in the room with him while he studied. I wasn't allowed to make any kind of sound whatsoever. I couldn't type or even turn the page of a book because it'd distract him. But I had to be there because he couldn't stand being alone.

Even after trying to drive Maddox out of the house for all those months, on the eve of his leaving, Les had cried and begged Maddox to stay.

That's how unstable Les was. How his mood swings were so unpredictable and erratic.

"I hate you! Go away!"

"No! Don't leave me! I don't want to be alone. I love you so much!"

Being around him was the most unsettling, horrible feeling in the world. I'd always said that it was like walking on eggshells. He was a violent toddler who couldn't make up his mind.

I just never knew how far he'd take it.

*Still didn't.*

Not to mention, my brother was a former police officer, and my guns were registered to me. I knew from him that I'd be required by law to report a missing gun that was no longer in my possession.

So, I called the police to make the report.

And forgot that I lived in one of the most corrupt places in the country.

The Williamson County officer who came out was bored and unconcerned. "You're married."

I showed him the fact that my home had been robbed and the notes left behind. "He took all the guns and has a history of mental problems."

"So?"

Was he kidding? "In my age group, the third leading cause of death for women is homicide. Usually at the hands of their domestic partner." *One would think a fucking cop would know this.*

"Look, there's nothing I can do. You're still married."

"Could you at least make a note about the fact that he took my legally registered handgun from me and that it's no longer in my possession?"

"No."

And he didn't. He didn't even file a police report about it. *Let's hear it for Williamson County, shall we?*

*To this day, I still don't know where any of my guns are, and the courts won't make him return them.*

Which made me completely vulnerable to a dangerous spouse. We'd all seen that this cake don't bake. No matter how many times you'd read those instructions.

What could possibly be the most likely scenario for a spouse's missing registered gun?

And why wouldn't Les return them?

Guns were Les's weapons of choice.

Not mine.

Anyone who had ever read one of my books knew this. My characters seldom used guns.

I think that was why Les wanted to get me alone before anyone knew he was planning his divorce.

Because I had a bad, bad feeling in my stomach about it. That kind of warning that Gavin de Becker talked about in his book, *The Gift of Fear*. I knew in my heart and soul that something didn't feel right.

Les and his crew were being entirely too sneaky.

Sneaky people were never up to any good.

And remember what Les had been going around, telling people.

He was afraid that I was suicidal.

That I would "kill" myself.

Luckily, I had lawyer meetings and couldn't meet with him that week.

Besides, Les wasn't the only one acting weird.

Lyra came in at first light with her mother and daughter, along with my best friend from childhood, Joan Hart. They are my family.

Since all this started, Joan had been in touch with Kiki MacDavis who had been telling her all kinds of screwed up lies.

As if Kiki knew Les was leaving me, even though I hadn't been in touch with Kiki. She had been lighting up Joan's phone, trying to out a wedge between me and Joan.

"Is Terri talking about me?"

"No, Kiki. Since you quit, she hasn't mentioned you."

"Good. I don't want to be on her radar." Then Kiki was pissed off that I wasn't talking about her. "She's obsessed with me, you know?"

Joan rolled her eyes because she knew I wasn't. That I really couldn't care less what the trailer tramp of Rural Tennessee was up to. I had much more important things to focus on.

Like my incredibly gifted sons, wonderful fans, and a successful career.

All the things that Kiki lacked, which was why she had time to Facebook-stalk me and call Joan to see if I was as obsessed with her as she was with me.

*Get over yourself, Kiki.* As my mother used to say, "you're not a twenty-dollar bill. The rest of the world doesn't love you."

And she wasn't the only one acting squirrely.

Cisco had come in from Michigan right after Lyra and crew and had wanted to know if he could stay at the house instead of the cabin where he was supposed to be staying while here.

Had I not had so much going on, I would have stopped and asked myself why Les had Cisco come down from Michigan if he knew he'd intended to leave.

Yeah, I admit I was being stupid. But let's face it, I had a lot of balls I was juggling that week. And creepy Cisco was the least of what was vying for my attention.

When he asked, I was a little put out, but Cisco complained about not wanting to stay with Les at the cabin.

"He's an idiot, Terri. I don't want to be there with him."

I understood that. I wouldn't want to stay with a crybaby either. And at the time, Cisco claimed that he despised ole Les and found him, and this is a direct quote from Cisco, "a whiny bitch who needed to go find a job and stop ordering me around like I'm his slave. If I stay over there, I might kill him." I had witnesses to him making those comments, by the way.

Since Maddox was in Japan and I had so many other people staying in the house—Joan, Lyra, Belinda, Nicole, Nick, and Nick's best friend Ed, I finally agreed as I still thought Les might come back from his tantrum at any time.

Not to mention, my house was filled with so many guests. What was one more person?

I paid no attention to Cisco as I went about my business, but I should have.

While I was off with Lyra at the law office, preparing for my deposition on Friday, Cisco was busy texting with Les and rewiring the security in my home and at the cabin.

He was allowing Les to be able to spy on us.

Additionally, he was printing tons of evidence for Les, deleting files from my computer and my sons'. Maddox lost months of important documents and emails. As did Nick, and Cisco made sure that Caleb's entire computer was removed from my home. Cisco was in constant contact with Les, and the two of them were cooking my goose while I was dealing with the case Les had started and abandoned.

*What a guy, eh?*

Meanwhile, I was downtown in Nashville, trying to get Les on the phone to bring necessary files to us for deposition preparation.

He refused. "You've moved your employees into your house. Get them to bring you the files."

It was such a weird comment, and he was so angry and explosive over the fact that I had people in the house with me.

*Too* angry and explosive over the fact that I had additional people with me.

Why?

With the exception of the one employee he'd called in from out of state to do his dirty work, they weren't my employees who'd come to stay with me.

They were my family.

My cousin, her daughter, my aunt and a friend I'd grown up with who was more like my sister than a friend.

The only one of them I was paying at the time was my cousin.

Besides...

"They don't know where the files are. *You* do and it's *your* case."

Still, he'd refused to return home and get the files we needed, even though it was costing us tens of thousands of dollars for him to be an asshole.

This went on for days.

By Wednesday, I realized that I didn't have the files I needed, and that Les wasn't going to cooperate in any way. He had dug his heels in, and he was forcing my hand.

The lawyers were as frustrated with him as I was.

Worse, he kept sending me emails that nauseated me. "End the suit, Terri. We should be holding hands in Williamsburg. You're destroying our family."

That was when I learned that Les had stolen more than half a million dollars out of my children's accounts without my knowledge or consent, or that of my sons' and taken it, along with all the money for my store and had placed it all into his own private account out of state.

He'd robbed all of us.

More than a million dollars was missing.

And he was proud of it.

He was holding my children's money as blackmail.

My career was being held by him as blackmail.

I couldn't pay my attorneys. He had every dime of my money in his hands.

I was broke.

No, I was fucked and fisted.

As always, he was in complete control of my life. If I didn't end the suit that he had started against my wishes and that I had told him was a bad idea, I would lose everything I had. So yet again, I had no choice about anything in my life. I had to do what Baby Huey said.

I settled the case on Thursday, and I was disgusted.

I'll never forget sitting there with Peggy Millhouse, the attorney Les had brought in less than two weeks before he knew he was leaving us to the tune of over one hundred thousand dollars under the pretense of having her take over the case so that she could litigate it.

The bastard had royally fucked both her and me with his lies.

"You are being remarkably calm given what's happening with your douchebag husband."

I sighed at Peggy's words. "Unlike him, I've stood over the graves of my brother, my nieces and nephew. I know what's important in life. My kids are alive and well. This is only money. It's not important. He's an idiot. I'm not."

The one thing my life has taught me. Perspective.

Too bad Les had never learned that.

Over and over, he'd told Lyra and our attorneys that he couldn't afford to go broke on the Dumas lawsuit that he'd insisted I file. I have dozens and dozens of emails from him stating that.

"We have to stop the bleeding. We cannot afford to go to trial (after he'd promised me that we would and told the attorneys that we would 'go all the way,' and had brought in Peggy to refile the suit and begin again and take it to trial). I can't afford another hundred thousand dollars on this suit!"

What he meant was he wouldn't spend it to sue someone else, but that he'd spend a whole lot more than that to ruin me after it ended.

So please remember what he'd said that about the Dumas case, as the grand stupidity of all time was about to take place.

I settled the case around six in the evening on March 22, 2018. Lyra drove me home. She, Joan, her mother and daughter were supposed to go home that evening.

Since I still didn't have a car that was drivable, I asked Lyra to run me to the grocery store before they left.

The interesting thing about where I lived was that there were two ways out of my neighborhood. We went down the back road.

If you left the front way, there used to be a little market restaurant that had since closed. We came home that way. As Lyra and I passed it, we happened to see something very peculiar.

In the vacant lot, two cars were parked.

Hogg's total POS Buick that no one could mistake with Les's pin head and her round, badly cut frizzy 'do sitting across from my company car that held Cisco's rotund trollish form.

Lyra slowed down so that we could get a better look at them.

We weren't wrong.

It was definitely the three of them, and they were having a meeting.

No, they were plotting something.

*At the end of my street.*

*What the ever-loving fuckage?*

I gaped at her, and she gaped at me. This was not acceptable.

Stunned, we went home and told the others what we'd seen.

Joan and my Aunt Belinda immediately made the decision that no one was leaving that night. Not while Cisco was there in my house. The last thing Nick and I needed was to be alone while those three were plotting whatever foulness they had in store for us.

A little while later, Cisco returned.

It was then that I noticed he was carrying food.

Joan scowled at him. "Don't you want some of Terri's leftovers? They're amazing!"

"No. I don't ever eat the food here." He held up the bags in his hands. "I always bring my own."

*Since when?* Les used to always bitch about Cisco being the human garbage disposal. That was one of his massive complaints about the man. How he'd inhale whatever we had on hand. How he'd come in the door and hit the fridge, then our pantry.

It also made me realize that Les had cleaned out my fridge and pantry when he'd left, too. I'd thought him an asshole for that, much like when my dad had unplugged my mother's freezer when they'd divorced so that her meat would ruin.

But...

Given that and the fact that ole Hogg had always removed the food I ate from the house... it didn't get thrown out like my sons' or Les's food.

*My* food, alone, was taken away so that no one else could eat it or that it would be in our garbage cans.

Just like the email Les had sent to Peyton. "Bring your own food to the house and put it in the downstairs fridge. We're no longer sharing food."

*What?*

Les had instructed Peyton to keep his food separate from mine. That was the strangest email I'd ever read.

For that matter, about the time I'd begun to get ill, Les had switched over to using only paper plates and plastic cutlery for the entire family.

Plastic cups which he'd always bitched about in the past if I ever bought some for a party (he'd said it was wasteful).

And all of our metal spoons had gone missing.

Why?

"Hey, Les? Where are the spoons?"

"Kids must be throwing them away."

But my sons had never used spoons. They ate with forks...

Why had someone tossed out all our spoons? Why had Les begun using disposable products? Was it to ensure that he and his girlfriend weren't getting any poison residue by mistake?

This was looking more and more sinister given what Lyra had proposed about the hairbrushes.

Given the fact that I could taste food again now that Les was gone. That I was feeling better than I'd felt while Les lived here.

Chills washed over me.

And as the night went on, I tried not to think about it. But when I got the call from my attorney that Dumas and crew were trying to change the terms of our agreement, it was hard to think of anything else.

"Tell them to turn the plane around and come back to Nashville. I'm not playing this shit. I didn't want to settle to begin with."

If they wanted to continue the fight, so did I.

In the end, Sal Tiller, Dumas's attorney caved. "Well, the one thing we know about Terri, she will fight."

That I would. To the bitter end.

But I was human and by midnight the stress of it all was enough that I was having chest pains. I went to look for my insurance card only to learn that Les had taken it as well.

I texted him and he yelled at me.

Deciding I didn't want to wake anyone, nor did I want Nick to be with me if I died of a heart attack like my mother, and other family members had done (my father survived one himself), I drove myself to the emergency room. The last thing my baby needed was to have *that* kind of memory.

My kid brother was still traumatized over having discovered our mother's body on the couch when he woke up in the morning.

"She was right where I left her, Terri! Why did I go to sleep? I should have stayed with her!"

I've never been able to convince Esteban that it wasn't his fault. That he did nothing wrong.

I never wanted to do that to my children.

So, I figured if God wanted to call me home, it would be best if I were alone for the journey.

At the hospital, I texted Les to tell him where I was. Stupidly, a part of me thought he'd show up at the ER to check on me.

Why not? The case was settled. He'd promised me that the minute I finished the suit we'd be "walking hand-in-hand in Williamsburg" and that he'd come back.

Instead, he continued to yell at me through texts.

So, I texted Maddox in Japan. "Love you, Bug." I didn't tell him where I was. Just in case I died. I wanted him to have that. Likewise, I texted the same to Caleb and Nick.

At dawn, they released me with orders to have my heart monitored again, and to reduce my stress and follow up with my doctor.

All I kept thinking was that it was March 23.

On March 23, 2004, we buried my mother. Everyone knew that date. Les was well aware of it because I'd told him and all the lawyers that I didn't want to be deposed on the anniversary of my mother's burial. Not to mention my grandfather died March 23, 1984.

March 23, 2007 was the day my goddaughter and her psycho mother had tried to have me arrested for car theft after I'd given her a safe home to escape to because she'd sworn her mother was physically abusing her. And this after I had loaned her over three thousand dollars to buy her car back from her mother who had repossessed her car from her, because she was dating a boy her lunatic mother didn't like.

She was supposed to pay me back for the car.

Needless to say, she didn't. She trashed my cabin and left it in the middle of the night, on my mother's birthday; after having committed credit card theft, and embezzling tens of thousands of dollars from me and blackmailing me.

In the end, she was arrested and did get a felony conviction. But that was after she and her mother had filed a false police report and tried to have me, and Esteban arrested. (As a side note, you should have seen my face when I learned that ole Les had been in touch with them during the divorce. For what? Character witnesses from people we had to sue, and that Les had thrown into jail? They're such known liars that even in the small town where they lived, the police had refused to deal with them. They wouldn't even let us leave the car with them for her to reclaim it.)

The police had been adamant. "We don't want nothing to do with that bitch! Don't you dare leave her car with us!"

And that was what Les had gone to speak to and sought out as witnesses against me?

Okay, then. My witnesses were lawyers, nurses, psychologists and decent, law-abiding people. His were known scumbags who'd robbed me and perjured themselves under oath...

*Like attracts like.*

Guess it was true. *Birds of a feather flocked together.*

Anyway, I really hated March 23.

Knowing that it was a historically bad day for me, Les chose it so that it would have the deepest emotional impact.

He was that big of a rat-bastard.

Even after knowing I'd spent the night in the emergency room with my heart and knowing that I'd been on a heart monitor for a heart condition.

After sitting with me while I had infusions because my body was trying to shut down.

Anyone still believe the man wasn't trying to kill me?

The entire day had been strange.

First, Cisco was supposed to leave that morning.

"I need to head back to Michigan."

"Okay, go."

He didn't. The troll kept trying to get to my phone, which was weird. "I need to check something."

Then I caught him in my office, lurking about. Joan and Lyra were with me. "What are you doing?"

He had this creepy smile. "Don't you know that Cisco knows and sees all? There's nothing I can't get into!"

It sent a chill down my spine. The three of us exchanged a nervous glance.

What *was* he up to?

Then he vanished upstairs.

Just before five, the end of the workday, the doorbell rang. Les had hired the scummiest bitch of an attorney in the business.

While I was working to feed my family, Lyra answered it and brought me the papers. Cisco followed her, but she and Joan wouldn't let him into my office. That overpaid bastard stayed on top of me that Friday for Les so that I couldn't call an attorney. He and Les wanted to make sure that I wasted three of my ten days and that I'd spend all weekend worried sick about Les's twisted cruelty.

Even sicker, Cisco was trying to record my reaction for Les. That was how twisted the whole lot of them were. After all the hundreds of thousands of dollars I had paid that handsy, twisted Cisco for lying on his time sheets and stealing from my family.

To my credit, I refused to show him anything but a smile. I knew what he was up to.

And why.

At the end of the day, I am a direct descendant of Charlemagne and Eleanor of Aquitaine. William Marshall.

The blood of Vikings, warriors, kings and presidents flowed in my veins.

I was my father's and mother's daughter and I refused to shame them. We were strength incarnate, and while we might stumble, it took a whole lot more than trash like Les Manly, Karen Hogg, and Cisco McCullough to take us down.

*This too shall pass.*

And that little bald-headed bastard prick would never shake my confidence for his master overlord. Cisco could French kiss my ass first.

And then I saw him heading toward my son. I motioned to Lyra to intercept him.

She headed him off and ran interference while I called my little brother, who I'd nicknamed the Hellhound. For reasons unknown Les had always been terrified of Esteban. Which I found hysterical as my little brother would never harm a soul.

Whatever.

When I got on the phone with my brother, that was when Cisco got nervous. He knew we were onto him and suddenly he couldn't get out of the house fast enough.

Not to mention, the moment I was on the phone he started shaking so badly, he couldn't even hold on to his keys.

Was he afraid I was talking to the police?

Or was there something else?

What we found later was a large stack of printed out papers from my email accounts that he'd made illegally for Les that he'd also forgotten in my office.

Stupid troll.

But then, Cisco had left so fast, you could see a vapor trail behind him.

For all his big talk over the years of how bad ass and fearless he was, he ended up being the same scared little bitch as Les.

Cowed by four tiny women. Hell, Lyra's twenty-year-old daughter, Nicole is only four-feet-nine and weighs less than eighty pounds.

How pathetic was he that Nicole had caused him to practically piss his pants?

And to think, he was only surpassed by the maggot he served with his simpering Igoresque obsequiousness. You could even hear him say, "Yes, master" whenever he talked to Les. He practically dragged one leg behind him.

Honestly, I don't know who was more pathetic or cowardly. Cisco who ran from the teensy Lyra and Nicole, or Les who was so weak that he didn't even have the balls to tell his own sons what he'd done that day.

Or tell the wife he'd abused for years, that he towered over, that he wanted a divorce.

Rather, he just wanted to keep abusing us.

I called Maddox in Japan who was floored.

"He did *what*?"

"Your father served me with divorce papers."

"No, he didn't."

"I'll scan them in for you." And I did. After all, I was being accused of witchcraft and other items so ludicrous and outrageous that to this day, I couldn't understand how his attorney hadn't lost her bar license for writing such unfounded stupidity on paper.

A normal human being would have laughed him out of her office. She damn sure wouldn't have put her bar license on the line for such idiocy.

Especially idiocy that violated my First Amendment Rights.

I guess that was why he had to scrape the bottom of the barrel to find a shyster who went to the *Nashville YMCA Night Law School*. And yes, that was a real thing here in Nashville. *Google it. I dare you.*

It even had a dean there named... brace yourself.

Judge Joe C. Loser, Jr.

Only in Nashville, Tennessee could you find something that embarrassing. *Seriously. Google it. While I'm highly creative, not even I could make this shit up.*

And only in Tennessee could a bitch that stupid ever pass a bar exam with a degree from a school with those "astounding" qualifications, (by the way, that school wasn't accredited by the American Bar Association, so her degree wasn't worth wiping your ass on outside of this state).

And neither was the two-bit attorney Les had hired.

Because one of my favorite allegations that the stupid hag made was that I believed myself to be "morphing into my characters."

While they'd kept beating me up over the fact that I couldn't be trusted to give testimony because I wrote for a living, I had to say that his attorney, Bonnie Jo Cockburn, should really consider trying her own hand at fiction writing. That slag could give me a run for my money any day of the week. She was quite the delusional author. Not a word of truth in anything she put forth to the court and everyone in Williamson and all surrounding counties knew this about her, and no one cared enough to try and stop her.

That would floor me, except as I'd said repeatedly Tennessee was the third most corrupt state in the Union.

And only in a city so corrupt would they tolerate an attorney that every single lawyer and judge in town knew for a fact was an absolute liar. That everything out of her mouth was utter fiction. Yet no one would discipline her for the bald-faced lies that she told in court and never backed with facts.

Things that should have her disbarred according to the Code of Conduct put forth by the Tennessee Board of Professional Responsibility.

*Want to know why they refused to discipline her?*

"You're not the one who is paying her. We only take complaints from people about their own attorneys."

Oh, okay. So, all attorneys in Tennessee were allowed to lie and break every single code in their charter.

*Just don't do it on your own client.*

Tennessee was *that* fucked up.

This was the most disgusting indictment against the state of Tennessee I could imagine (at least at that time).

Cockburn had been so flagrant in her lies during her cases that she had run off a combat vet from the very country he had spent his life serving and had bled for. She had made him give up his own children because she lied and set him up—this story from the lips of his own tear-filled mother who'd begged and begged for justice to no avail.

His mother contacted my attorney after she saw what Cockburn had done to me in the local paper. She wanted a class-action suit against the bitch, but no one would help us.

Why?

First, I hadn't been able to find an attorney willing to sue another attorney, no matter how egregious their actions.

Second, because Bitsy Dullard of the Tennessee Board of Professional Responsibility kept refusing to take any action against a woman who should not only be disbarred...

She should have been tarred and feathered.

According to Ms. Dullard, "no action will be taken against any lawyer in this state unless you are the one paying for them."

Which really made no sense when you thought about it. I *was* the one paying Cockburn, because Les had no income. The money he had was the money he'd stolen from me and his children, and he'd admitted that under oath.

Repeatedly.

For the record, stealing money from your spouse and hiding it out of state was supposed to be against Tennessee law.

Unless you happened to live in Williamson County where the judges apparently didn't care what the law was.

I had two of the judges say in open court that they didn't care what the law said. They really were that disdainful and open about the fact that U.S. laws don't apply to this state or to their courtrooms or citizens.

Not to mention, the shameful Williamson County judges kept making me pay for the frivolous SLAPP motions that Cockburn and crew hit me with and forced me to pay for their fees, instead of disciplining them for harassing me as they should have done.

As any normal or decent judge would have done.

I knew this as I had judges in my family who had presided over courtrooms that followed state and federal laws.

Yet even so, Ms. Dullard refused to discipline Cockburn.

Yeah, Tennessee was that fucked up a state. *Never move here. Don't even visit.*

*If you do live here, leave. ASAP.* Because the corruption here made the machine-gun gangsters of Old Chicago look like posers.

*And baby, you ain't seen nothing yet.* I was just getting started.

Cockburn, a former realtor who, according to her own words got out of the field because she couldn't make a living as one, also owned a construction and mortgage company (how was this not a conflict of interest?).

*Oh yeah, I live in Williamson County, Tennessee. Never mind.*

She had only been an attorney for about five minutes. Slight exaggeration. But she was so green, she reeked of afterbirth. No one knew much about her other than she was such a stupid, belligerent bitch that the handful of attorneys who'd had the misfortune of dealing with her wanted nothing else to do with her, and that she had to leave the only law firm she'd worked for because her kids were out of control.

At least that was the rumor among the other attorneys in town.

Well, there were other rumors, too. Such as she'd had so many husbands at this point that she no longer bothered to count them or change her last name, and that the last one came and went so fast that the ink hadn't even dried on their marriage certificate before she'd kicked him to the curb. *Which made you wonder why, didn't it?*

Theories abounded around town, and some concerned a certain judge who currently presided over my case who used to be the partner for the firm that Cockburn had worked in.

Why Les had picked this fatuous loon, one can only imagine that it had to do with *that* rumor, especially given his diatribe against licensed idiots practicing law. "God, Terri, why did Dumas hire a moron! If she'd hired a decent attorney this would have been over, and we wouldn't be broke!"

So, what did he do? Hire an even dumber, more belligerent version than Sal Tiller, whom he'd insulted and ranted against for years.

But wait...

What was it I'd just said?

Les had ranted against Sal Tiller.

For years.

So, who did Les and Cockburn hire to help her with this case?

Dumas's attorney, Sal Tiller. *Spoiler, I know, but I had to drop that bomb here.*

No one would believe that shit. *But we'll get to that in a few.*

Right now...

April 2018, I should have known from the idiocy of her brief what to expect, but even I was floored when Cockburn walked into the courtroom.

Dressed like a two-dollar hooker in spite of the notice on the courtroom door against wearing revealing clothing, she came barreling through the double doors like the barroom bruiser she was. Total low-class skank. I had friends who'd done better in heels their first time in drag than her klutzy Bessie-the-cow stumble. Too bad no one loved her enough to tell her how unattractive that gait was.

*Honey, whoever said you were sexy must have been your mother. Trust me, you're not. Button up that shirt and learn how to properly walk in your heels or buy lower ones. Bouncy boobs aren't pretty. Strap up and get a bra that fits.*

*Your baby sister who came with you into court should have loved you enough to tell you this. Obviously, she doesn't. That means that she's laughing with her girlfriends behind your back. As my mama always said, "every woman needs two friends. One she can be friends with and one they can talk about behind her back."*

*You are obviously the one they're talking about.*

*And do something with that godawful nest you think is an attractive hairdo. For the love of God, please go get a new stylist and stop going to whatever cheap, strip mall, dime store hairdresser you've found. You look like you've just come out of the broom closet from a walk of shame. While that may be the look you're going for, I assure you that it's not becoming. As a professional woman, I am highly offended every time I see you in public.*

*Stop it.*

*You're embarrassing the rest of us, and we're being judged by your sloppy, slutty appearance. We've had to fight too hard to have you single-handedly set us back fifty years.*

*If you want to walk a street corner, that's fine. It's a perfectly good career choice and with your questionable intelligence, it's probably a viable option for you, too. Please, do so.*

*But if you wish to continue working in the legal profession, then for the love of God, get an image consultant, remove your heinous photo off your emails that are obvious holdovers from your former career choice so that you don't look like a hyena chewing cud. Buy some clothes that fit and read a book that doesn't have pictures in it.*

*Also, sign your entire name on your letters when you're filing court documents and sending letters to colleagues.*

*You look like a grade school moron when you just sign your first name. You're not Madonna, honey. No one's impressed and you're not that important.*

*It's highly unprofessional, and it makes you look like an idiot.*

*Okay, diatribe aside.*

This... it was so hard not to insult her, seriously. I had such an impossible time calling her an attorney because she was such an embarrassment to everything, including humanity. The fact that she wasn't born sterile caused me to doubt the very existence of God. Because really, why would a benevolent being be so cruel as to curse an innocent child with a mother like this sub-life, inhumane, self-absorbed bitch?

How could any divine being do that to anyone?

Anyway, Cockburn came in and the first words out of her mouth in court were absolute blackmail.

No, seriously.

It was on record. I sat there, and all that went through my mind was that old *Saturday Night Live* skit from the seventies, "Jane, you ignorant slut."

This lunatic with a degree from a part-time community college law school stood before the judge and said in her hick, bitchy voice, "Your Honor, when she sees what I handed to her attorney, she's going to want to settle immediately before any of this is made public."

*Beg pardon?*

*What?*

*You want me to pay you off so that you don't embarrass me publicly? Is this not the very textbook definition of extortion?*

*Let's check it, shall we?*

*Why, yes!* According to *Black's Law Dictionary*, the preeminent authority of all attorneys everywhere, the definition of extortion is:

*Any oppression by color or pretense of right, and particularly the exaction by an officer of money, by color of his office, either when none at all is due, or not so much is due. Or when it is not yet due. Preston v. Bacon, 4 Conn. 4S0. Extortion consists in any public officer unlawfully taking, by color of his office, from any person any money or thing of value that is not due to him. Or more than his due. Code Ga. 1882.*

Wow! There you go. Law School 101, and she failed it right out the gate and Williamson County judge, James Woodly, didn't even blink as she violated my most basic right not to be blackmailed in his kangaroo courtroom.

Strike one for Williamson County, Tennessee. One of the most corrupt places to live, according to numerous independent studies. No wonder Harvard thought so little of Nashville, eh?

I would say I'd expected better from an attorney, but she did graduate from the *YMCA Night School of Law.*

Was it any wonder that only sixty-one percent of their graduates passed the bar?

That I believed, if she was what they extolled as one of their top graduates (and they did, by the way).

What I had a hard time believing was how this thing in a way-too-tight suit and low-cut blouse was one of the few that passed.

And Judge Woodly sat there on his bench and let her blackmail me. Not a word about how inappropriate it was.

Why was I even surprised, given that Woodly, who was supposedly ex-military, also sat there and let her commit an act of Stolen Valor in that same three ring circus he called a courtroom. As the daughter of a decorated Army veteran who served his country with true honor and distinction in two wars, I am sickened to the core of my soul by that wretched slag as she lied and dishonored my father, and all the men and women who have served this country and bled for our rights in an effort to smear me while lying about that sorry sack of shit she was taking stolen money to represent.

That said it all about what a lowlife, sleaze-ball she really was.

"Your Honor, my client is a distinguished veteran who served his country with honor."

*Yeah, right.*

Let me set the record straight about her "client." Les Manly stole his Army Vet Recs when he left my house because he should be jailed for his dereliction of duty, and he knew it. The last thing he wanted was for anyone to see them and hold him accountable for what he'd actually done— because running from responsibility and his crimes were the only thing in life he'd ever been good at.

Yes, you heard that correctly.

Not only had Les come home during *Desert Storm* while the unit he'd been assigned to at Fort Eustice was deployed into war, after he'd dodged that bullet and pissed his BDUs at the mere thought that he might have to be shot at, he never put on his uniform again. Believe me, I knew exactly what an Army uniform and duffel looked like, and I never again saw them after his near miss with war.

Even though he went to college on the G.I. Bill and owed his country service every year from 1990 until 2001 when he retired his captain's commission (because of 9-11 and the fact that he was scared to go to war), he never once met any of his military service obligations to the United States of America.

*Never.*

That also meant that he owed Uncle Sam a rebate on all that money that had been paid to him to get a degree. A degree he blatantly refused to use. That wasn't an honorable veteran who served his country, it was a scabby piece of shit who lied.

One who reneged on his deal.

To Uncle Sam.

And to his family. Just like he'd run out on our marriage and all the vows he'd made to me and his sons.

Meanwhile, Bonnie Jo Cockburn had stood up in front of a former Army Ranger and lied to him about it. Tried to curry favor from the judge by extolling service that her client had never completed and assigned military honor to him that he most definitely didn't deserve.

*As the daughter of a man who trained soldiers at Ft. Benning, bitch, I am offended by every breath you draw. How dare you spit on my father's memory and on the service he, and the rest of my family members gave. On the service of all the true servicemen and women, and their families, in this country. You need to be held accountable for what you've done.*

*So, does he.*

The fact that Woodly insulted and criticized me while he took up for and defended a coward and the lying slag who helped him steal the futures I'd worked my ass off to save up for my special needs children was disgraceful. Children that Les had proudly announced in that court-room he wanted absolutely no responsibility for, and that Cockburn wanted me to sign a paper saying I would assume all financial responsibility over them as if she had never ruthlessly stuck it to the fathers of the babies she'd unfortunately spawned.

My decorated father rolled in his grave, while all of them dishonored the very code he'd taught me to live by.

God. Country. Family.

Truth. Honor. Dignity.

*You, Woodly, are a disgrace to both the uniform you once wore and the robe you currently don.*

Not only was Woodly okay with her committing Stolen Valor in his courtroom, he knowingly allowed her to breach my Dumas settlement, even while, on record we told him that both Cockburn and her client were breaching it in open court.

And yes, you read that correctly, too.

After all the hell Les had put me through to settle the Dumas case; after all his broken promises of how we'd be "walking hand-in-hand in Williamsburg" and would have our "happy" nuclear family back together again if I "just settled that case that was tearing our family apart" (instead of it being that disgusting hag Hogg that he'd brought in on us), he breached that effing settlement that he'd forced me into because he'd robbed me of all my children's money, and left town without any warning.

Then Les filed a divorce on the anniversary of the day I buried my mother after I'd spent the night in the emergency room.

That's that kind of scum-sucking animal we were dealing with.

And it got even better.

Cockburn then allowed him to commit tax fraud on the stand, under oath, in open court, thereby putting both of us and our freedom, and all our finances at risk.

Really.

And that, too, was okay with Bitsy Dullard and the Tennessee Board of Professional Responsibility, because apparently that was protecting your client and their best interests...

*Um... okay, how?*

This was the one that floored and baffled me most.

I bought my writing cabin in 2006 after Baby Huey began stalking me in my home all the time. "You're not working, Terri. You're goofing off."

That was all I heard, constantly. I couldn't get anything done for Les bothering me.

And after the death of my mother, I was falling farther and farther behind on deadlines because, for whatever reason, Les could never get it through that thick thing he called a brain the concept that a writer needed time to *write* a novel.

Little fairies never magically appeared in the middle of the night to do this for me like the cobbler and his magic shoes. I had to sit down and think, then I typed.

Then I would sit and think.

And I typed more.

That was how this whole process worked. It was not a novel concept.

Or I guess, maybe it was.

But for whatever reason, Les had never fully understood that. Much like Nick when he was six and wanted a really expensive toy and I told him that we couldn't afford it.

He looked up at me with that adorable cherub face and in the most serious tone said, "Just go write a book, Mama."

*Yeah, I'll get right on that, kid.*

*See you in about nine months when it's done.*

*And then a year from now when they finally pay me for that work.*

Les had always had the same mind set. With a six-year-old, I expected it. From a grown imbecile who took a week on average to write a single email, I would think he'd know better.

But I forgot that Les was a first-rate idiot who made idiots look like they should be the cast for *The Big Bang Theory*.

Or running the courts and police department of Williamson County, Tennessee.

Anyway, so there Les was, looking creepier than even his pedophile father as he sat on the stand and out popped, "the cabin is a family retreat, Your Honor. Terri hasn't used it for writing in years."

*In years?*

What delusion was this?

Did my hard-of-hearing ears fail me yet again?

That was not what our tax records had said for the last twelve years. It was not what our tax audit had said from a couple of years before. And it was not what Mr. Dumbass had told the IRS agent who'd audited us.

Was he high? Had he forgotten the multitudinous conversations with our CPA and book-keeper?

The whole IRS audit nightmare?

Every single year of our owning the cabin, we had written records of it being used *one hundred percent* for business. And business only. That yes, while people stayed overnight there, they were *businesspeople* who did so.

People who were there for *business* reasons.

With the one exception being Donna Handsoff, right before Les abandoned his family.

We had sworn to the IRS every single year of our ownership that we never used that cabin for personal reasons and until Donna, we hadn't.

Furthermore, there was nothing in that cabin of a personal nature.

Nothing. It was all my business stuff. Fan gifts. Costumes. Writing essentials. Books, etc.

Everything in the cabin was also written off our taxes as a business expense.

*Everything.*

Because it was.

The only exception being some of the clothes I'd taken there a few days before he'd left for a photoshoot.

That photoshoot? They were my new publicity photos that my publisher had paid for.

Again, all business.

Everything in the cabin, from the water cooler and high-end photocopier to my numerous computers and desks were all business items that were written off my taxes as *business*.

*Does any of that sound like personal items in a family retreat to you?*

*Me, either.*

In fact, the PC was still on with my latest novel displayed from where I'd left for CoastCon with the full intention of returning so that I could pick up where I'd left off.

I even had a half empty, capped Coke waiting for my return on my desk because I thought I'd be able to finish it.

Stupid me for not anticipating a court order that had banned me from my own office.

Where I worked and supported several families.

More than that, I routinely had another local author who came over for regular writing sessions with me at the cabin, and who'd finished a couple of her books there, too.

The kicker?

She was the wife of a Williamson County sheriff's deputy. How was that for a witness?

Some of you probably knew her. You might even have seen her and the books that she wrote at my cabin on some of my YouTube videos.

Yeah, Woodly. *Suck on that and be embarrassed why don't you?* You allowed a fucking jackass to take possession of my business office and ban me from it because you didn't believe a twenty-first century businesswoman could own an office in this day and time.

Yet you bought the lie that a family would own a "retreat" less than two miles from their home.

Because what? Every family owned a retreat next to their kids' school?

*You are an effing moron, aren't you?*

Could someone please explain to me why any of these people allowed this kind of perjury to go unanswered and still have bar licenses?

Or judgeships?

Oh, and Woodly wasn't the only judge to give him a pass on this perjury.

We'll get to Judge Bubba Dinky in a bit.

In the meantime, Woodly allowed this stupid slag to get up there and for all time, put on record a felony that could land us both in jail for tax fraud.

They really should move the courthouse into a circus tent. After all, false advertising was also illegal. The citizens of Williamson County should know what they were getting for justice and instead of robes, our judges needed to be painted clowns because that was what they really were.

Truth.

They didn't give two shits about justice or their oaths of office.

That for the record, was on the record.

And that wasn't all that was going on with Cockburn. She had even more surprises for me.

There to testify against me for my witchcraft was none other than Hogg, herself, the woman who had physically and mentally abused my sons and who had abused her own special needs sister in front of others, but...

Brace yourself.

Kiki MacDavis, out of the blue, and for no reason whatsoever made an astonishing appearance that day.

Because she, unlike the decent other people Les had contacted who'd laughed in his face when he tried to coerce them to testify against me over something so ludicrous, jumped at a chance to commit perjury and lie about something she knew I'd never done.

Yes.

Kiki.

The woman who had professed to my best friend and who had told Joan, repeatedly, that she didn't want to be on my radar. That she was afraid to testify in the Dumas case because she didn't want to go to jail. The same one who had said that she'd drugged her own husband because she swore to me and others that she was afraid of him.

Why would she be there?

Especially given the fact that she knew I, and plenty of others, knew how much she'd always professed to hate Les? "I prefer manly men. But I guess you love him, Terri." That was a direct quote out of Kiki's mouth.

*Judge not lest ye be judged.*

Just like the time I saw her and her friend, Sister Teresa, the scam artist and "spiritual warrior" perform an actual blood ritual in front of me while I was working.

No wonder she loved the Salem Witch Trials so much. I guess Kiki saw herself as Ann Putnam.

But I wasn't Martha Corey. And I would not go quietly to the gallows without letting the world know exactly what Kiki had done.

You lied, but I spoke the truth and I had witnesses aplenty.

Unlike you and Les, I had always told the same story.

You were the ones whose story changed, and the world knew that, too.

And one day, Kiki, you would face that Maker you feared who knew the truth, too.

*Thou shall not bear false witness.*

And that you did. For no reason.

Because there Kiki sat, right beside them in court, refusing to look at me or Joan whom Kiki had been chatting with on the phone just a few weeks before about how much she hated Les and had resented him for making her do work that we were overpaying her for.

That was the thing about Kiki.

Liar to the end.

She lied about the hours she worked. The job that she did. How much I paid her (and it was a lot, contrary to what she'd told others). She billed me for the time she spent working for other people. The time she spent at the ballfield with her kids, and while she was making and selling her own products.

Never doing the job I was paying her for, even though Les kept giving her raises. Even while he complained about her.

Even stranger... What I learned by going through her employee records was that Les, unbeknownst to me, had been sending her money orders in addition to her salary. She also had benefits and retirement that I knew nothing about.

*What the hell, Les?*

Why pay her so much, without telling me, all the while you complained incessantly about her? Just what was going on between them?

Meanwhile, Kiki, behind my back was telling everyone how underpaid she was while being way overpaid, especially since she wasn't working.

In fact, she only worked about three hours a week while billing me forty (often claiming overtime) and was making way more than she'd ever made in her life, plus benefits. Not to mention, I spent thousands of dollars a year buying her clothing, luggage and designer pocketbooks.

Even Thanksgiving meals for her family.

Thousands more a year on her travel and meals.

Yeah, she was a treacherous, lying bitch.

But what was really interesting, and peculiar was after Les left, and I threw Hogg out of my home. Joan, Lyra and I were cleaning out Hogg's space.

In the cabinet that was in the area Hogg had claimed as her own, where she had set up her "basecamp" from where she ruled me and my sons with her tyrannical cloven hoof, I found one of Kiki's prescriptions.

Now this wasn't a happenstance thing like Kiki was over one day and "accidentally" left prescription bottle. This was a full box of Albuterol vials.

Hidden in a medicine cabinet.

The kind of vials that went into a prescription nebulizer.

Had I failed to mention that while robbing my home on the weekend of March 16th, one of the items Hogg and Les had made sure to steal was my personal nebulizer that I used on an almost daily basis for breathing treatments?

*Oh yeah, I did.*

How could I be so careless as to forget about something that important?

Because that was *not* the kind of medicine or box someone just casually tossed into their purse and traveled with.

Ever.

This was something critical that you needed when your life depended on it.

Like an EpiPen.

Ironically, it was also the same, exact prescription that my doctor had put me on once Les had poisoned me to the point that my respiratory system had begun to shut down. What my life depended once those ailments had progressed to horrible wheezing spells and horrific bouts of bronchitis that wouldn't clear up.

Wasn't that interesting?

Yet here was the same exact kind of vials that I would have innocently poured into that missing nebulizer that Les had stolen out of my home without any thought as to what might be in them and inhaled directly into my lungs. From a woman who'd bragged about her medical family and her father, the lab tech.

I could still hear Kiki's hick accent, "I was raised in my dad's lab. I used to help him run experiments. Why, I know so much about medicine, I could be a nurse, like my mama and sister."

A woman who had diabetics in her family.

*Access to needles.*

See where I was going?

And I still have that box of medication with her name on it. I would love to know if it was simple insurance fraud Les was committing with Kiki, or something a lot more sinister.

Because the one thing I realized as I saw her sitting there, all buddy-buddy with them in that courtroom was that while I'd traveled with her, none of my mysterious symptoms had ever once improved or dissipated.

*Not once.*

My numb tongue, dizziness et al remained in place. It wasn't until I had begun to travel with Lyra that my symptoms began improving and vanishing.

That Les had begun panicking.

Kiki was the one who had started lying to people and accusing me of drug use, while telling me that she was my best friend. "I love you like a sister. We're family."

Yet she had lied behind my back about me to everyone.

Even Joan. And tore me down with those lies.

Why would she do that? And why lie about drug use when everyone who knew me knew I had never taken anything? I don't even drink.

In fact, my doctor fusses at me because I often forget to take my blood pressure medication.

I won't even take Tylenol or Advil.

And why was Kiki so afraid in the Dumas case of being deposed?

"I can't be put on a stand! They can't depose me. I don't want to go to jail!" She not only said that to me, but to Joan and Les, and countless others. I never could understand her irrational fear.

No one went to jail for a deposition in a civil trademark case.

But if Les had been paying her for something else that she was terrified might come out in discovery or depositions...

*That* made sense.

*That* would explain why she was on the verge of a nervous breakdown at the mere prospect of having to be deposed when all I was asking her to do was tell the truth.

It might also explain why her laptop that I'd bought for her had gone missing (along with the desktop that Les had removed from our house). Neither of those computers have ever again seen the light of day.

"I don't want to go to jail, Terri!"

For what? Saying, "yes, I read her manuscripts, and was her assistant before the other author sold her first book?"

How hard was that?

There was nothing in that case that Kiki would have been asked that would have put her freedom at risk, and yet, she who refused to "lie under oath" when no one had asked her to do that in the Dumas case, sat in court to swear under oath that I was a witch and that I practiced witchcraft.

Facts that were, first, irrelevant, and stupid. Even if I were a witch, who would give a shit?

Freedom of religion is a constitutional right in this country, and Wicca is a recognized religion.

However, I was not pagan, nor was I Wiccan. While I have many friends and even family who were those, I happened to be a Catholic and she knew this. She'd seen the rosary and holy water I traveled with. Along with my rosary bracelet. For Kiki to testify otherwise, was perjury, and she was willing to break the law for Les, and that *could* get her arrested.

So, if she was willing to get arrested then, what else had she done for Les in the past?

Not to mention, she was breaching her Non-Disclosure Agreement to testify for him.

Subpoena or not, breaching that meant that I could sue her for breaking our contract. Her fear had always been losing her trailer, and she was putting it all on the line.

For a man she had spent our entire relationship telling me she loathed.

What on earth could make her risk her home, her family, and her freedom when she didn't have to?

All she had to do was say no.

Les had contacted a lot of other people to testify, or should I say, lie about me in court, and they'd all refused.

Because they had consciences and weren't about to lie under oath.

Why would Kiki? Unless he was holding something else over her head.

The plot was thickening, but Williamson County Detective Lynn Lazy wasn't listening.

No one was.

I kept waiting for old Rod Serling to tell me that I'd just fallen into *The Twilight Zone*.

After all, Les came into that courtroom on the first day looking twenty-five years older than he'd looked when he left my house.

It was scary.

And he appeared stoned out of his mind. I barely recognized him when he walked in. He looked like an extra off *The Walking Dead*.

Instead of the dark-haired man we knew, his hair had gone stark white. Les was hunched over and shuffling his feet, unable to meet anyone's gaze. Looking at him was like staring at the portrait of Dorian Grey.

Spooky as shit.

The last time I'd seen anyone age like that overnight had been my mother after my brother had died.

Or after weeks of chemo.

This wasn't someone who had "left an unhappy home for greener pastures" as he'd claimed.

Keep in mind that after he left, everyone who saw me had commented on how much healthier and better I looked.

Everyone.

No one could believe the difference in my appearance. Everything from my hair, to my skin, to my health.

Meanwhile, he appeared a hollowed-out shell of his former self.

And he was following his mother around like Forrest Gump or some little puppy begging for scraps. Whereas he'd been calling her "Grandma" in the past, he was now calling her "Mummy" as if he'd had a brain tumor.

Worse? He wore ugly, mismatched expensive clothes that she'd obviously picked out and forced on him. His mother never had any taste. Once hillbilly trailer trash, always hillbilly trailer trash. He used to mock her for that.

Nick and I looked at each other with a wide-eyed stare.

As bad as all that was, Les continued to lie his ass off while he was on the stand, under oath. "I assured Nick that I would pay for his college."

*With what? His arrogance?*

Or the money he'd already stolen directly from Nick's account?

*How generous of him to offer to pay for Nick's classes with Nick's own money.* That pretty much summed up Les's entitlement in a nutshell.

What was even more galling was that Les and Cockburn had a court order to lock up all of Nick's college funds the moment he'd left.

After Les had stolen every single dollar out of Nick's account without any warning whatsoever and left him broke, and then stranded his brother in a foreign country, penniless, Nick was a little "tense."

*For those without Autistic children, let me explain.*

Children and adults with Autism don't like any kind of change in their routine. They don't cope well with abrupt and unexpected changes in their lives or environment. No one really likes it, but those with Autism *really* had a problem with it.

It caused them to withdraw into themselves.

Nick was having severe panic attacks. Overnight, he'd lost his brother. He'd lost his father. He'd lost his cat that he needed to help calm himself.

His home environment had been significantly altered with no warning, because his father had stolen items out of the house, including items that belonged to Nick, and left it in a mess. For all he knew, I would be gone without warning, just like they'd done.

That was where he was living in his head, and I couldn't get through to him that I wasn't going anywhere.

That nothing else would change.

Nick's ability to trust had been shattered.

It would be hard on anyone. But to someone on the Spectrum, it was a lot harder to cope with.

His own father, who had told him his entire life that he was his favorite child, and that Nick would never have to worry about his future because it was all taken care of, had robbed him of everything.

He was expecting me to do the same.

That would have been debilitating for a "normal" child. For one with Autism or Asperger's, it was a special form of hell and Nick was in a mental meltdown over it all.

His anchor, Maddox, was across the world, in another time zone. Caleb would only scream at him whenever he tried to talk to him.

The only other anchor he had, his cat, had been stolen by his father who refused to return Mochi to him. And instead of trying to help Nick, Les had turned Nick's words against him in court, after Les had sworn to Nick that he wouldn't do it. That was why Nick's best friend was spending the night at our house so much.

Nick needed someone he trusted implicitly, who wouldn't lie and backstab him.

To him, I was another parent and his parent had already crushed him. One parent was no different than the other.

He could trust a friend.

I was trying everything I could calm my baby down. To do so, I called our broker and had him explain to Nick that his college fund was safe, and that Les couldn't steal that money from him, especially after Les had already told Nick that he couldn't go to the college of his choice like his brothers had done after Nick had kept his grades up and was on the verge of graduating with a 4.0.

"Sorry, Nick. All your money's gone. You'll have to go to the local community college. That's all we can afford for you because of what your mother spent on the lawsuit."

The lawsuit that Les had started that I had settled the moment he was gone. Not because Les had walked out the door with his sons' trust funds that their mother had set aside for them.

Les the liar.

For the record, every single check written to the lawyers in that case, was written by Les, prior to his departure.

*Every single one.*

And he'd done it on my account that he hadn't been authorized to use. Thank you, Tennessee for refusing to prosecute him for fraud and for theft, which he should have been put under the jail over.

Just because we were married, it didn't give him the authority to misuse my business account that he wasn't a signatory on. To write checks for whatever he wanted to, without ever consulting me, while I was too sick to stop him.

While I was fighting for my life.

Which I didn't understand. In other cases, they'd put spouses in jail for misusing a spouse's credit card, even when the spouse that was misusing the credit card was paying it off.

They still were prosecuted and jailed for the crime.

But if you wrote a check on your spouse and closed out their safe deposit box without letting them know and robbed them and your children of over a million dollars.

That was all right.

I, personally, hadn't spent a single cent on lawyers. As I said, it was his lawsuit from the beginning to the end. And he hadn't been man enough to see it through after having his wife publicly barbecued over his stupidity after I'd told him time and again not to do it.

Yeah.

Anyway, the broker had spent a long time on the phone with Nick, explaining to him how his college fund worked. He'd assured Nick that his money was still there, and that it was safe from Les's greedy hands.

That helped. What helped even more was when the Dumas money came in. I took Nick to a local bank and opened a CD account. We put one third of the settlement into that new account with our names on it and locked it up so that no one could touch the money for five years.

Security.

With Autism, it was all about security and routine.

I allowed Nick to pick out the stocks we invested in for the CDs at the bank so that he was in control of what happened to the money, every step of the way.

And would you believe that Les would spend more money hauling me into court for trumped up contempt charges, and on lawyer fees to get at that money than what I put in there just so that he could make me look like I was doing something underhanded to the judge when I wasn't?

You heard that correctly.

Les burned up every single dollar of Nick's money, and more in attorney fees than what I put aside to make Nick feel safe for no other reason than to smear my good name before the judge.

In less than three years, every cent of it would be gone.

That was the kind of dipshit asshole he was.

To what avail?

He allowed Cockburn to get rich from stealing money from his Autistic child.

What did he get out of it?

I was publicly insulted and made to look bad before a judge who had a prior conviction for prostitution that everyone in town knew about and laughed at behind the judge's back.

Ooooo!

In the end, it left Les broke, and his son hated him for it. More than that, it left his son with no sense of security.

And would you believe that Les blamed me for the fact that Nick refused to talk to him?

All true. All of it.

I had married the dumbest idiot ever born.

Les couldn't accept the fact that the real reason Nick hated him was because Nick had been in that courtroom that day, and heard his father lying.

He'd heard his father tell everyone present that, after having stolen all their money, he wanted absolutely no responsibility for his sons whatsoever.

And he'd heard Les's biggest lie of all, "Your Honor, I called up my broker and had him explain to Nick that his college money was safe."

Les stated that under oath. He committed perjury, again, and took credit for my phone call. Like Nick didn't know which parent had made the phone call with him that day.

Cockburn might be that stupid.

The judge might be that stupid.

But Nick, the broker and I, as well as the broker's assistant, all knew the truth.

Les had committed perjury. He had never once, called the broker to discuss Nick's money with Nick.

"I told Nick that I would scrub toilets to get him the money he needed for college." Uh, yeah. I'd love to see that since Les had never once scrubbed out a toilet.

Period.

Just ask my old friend who'd found my wedding rings in the guest bathroom soap dish after they'd gone missing for almost a year. I'd taken them off and placed them there in our old house so that I could scrub out the bathroom toilet and sink by hand, even though I'm allergic to most cleaners.

Obviously, Mr. "I do everything" had never cleaned out the only other bathroom in our tiny house or he would have found my wedding rings. They were obvious in a place where he went to take his daily dump.

What skeeved me most was the fact that he must never have washed his hands afterward or he would have seen them.

But the point was that Les had never lifted a single finger to help me. Yet he took credit for everything.

Was that why Les had thrice stolen all of Nick's college money from him?

Again, Nick wasn't the idiot, thank God, that his father was.

And it crushed him to hear those lies. Just as it crushed him for his father to demand we hand over Nick's beloved electric keyboard to him when Les didn't even play.

That had always been Nick's other solace whenever he was upset. He would play his electric piano for hours on end and would write songs and record them.

First, Les took Nick's cat. Then he demanded the baby's keyboard.

He was systematically trying to break us all.

The kicker? Les had always claimed that he hated the piano and keyboard because it reminded him of his pedophile grandfather and father, and the molestation he'd suffered as a boy.

"It makes my skin crawl to hear someone play the piano." That was why he'd made Nick play it with his headphones on.

Yet he'd demanded his son's most treasured item.

*What a guy.*

Nick also heard Les proudly admit on the stand that he'd stolen all their money from them, deposit it in an out of state bank account, and then spend it for his own benefit. "Yes, I took their money. It was put there for their futures. If they needed a house or got married."

"Did you spend any of it?" Woodly asked.

"Just two thousand dollars, Your Honor. I bought a new computer because I didn't have one at the cabin."

Pardon?

*Just* two thousand dollars?

Why would Les need a computer *that* expensive? Unlike me, Les never did video or audio editing. He didn't do graphics work. His software was all paid for.

The most he should have ever paid for any computer was a few hundred bucks.

But let me back up a second and reiterate that the cabin was *my office.* There were over twenty computers and laptops kept there, including a brand new one that I had bought at Christmas that year.

It was only three months old at the time he commandeered my office.

There were no shortages of computers or computer equipment in my "office" cabin.

Oh, and let's not forget the brand new one that ole Les had stolen out of my house when he'd abandoned the marital home. The same computer that would have held all of his internet searches for things such as...

*What he could have used to poison his wife and sons.*

Items he could have bought to poison his wife and sons. You know, things we like to call...

*Evidence.*

*See for yourself.* There was no computer left in our marital home. He'd taken it and his laptop.

I tried to point that out to my attorney and the detective when Lynn Lazy came to my home to see the damage Les had wrought.

My first attorney refused listen.

To this day, no one, including Detective Lynn Lazy, had made Les produce that missing computer, nor had they made him provide any explanation of what happened to it or why Les had to buy a brand new one right after he'd taken his brand new computer from our home that March day.

Had we all not seen this episode of *Forensic Files* or *Dateline*?

Why would anyone take a computer out of a house and destroy it so that it was never seen again?

Where were those intelligent detectives who wanted to solve a case and see justice done for a family who'd been preyed upon?

Oh, I forgot!

None of them live in Williamson County, Tennessee.

In the end, Woodly allowed the bastard to keep all the company cash that he'd stolen from my company safe.

Every single dime, even though he'd admitted that he had stolen it and that he'd wrongfully closed out my sons' trust funds and taken that money out of state.

The money that ran my business.

Just as Woodly allowed him to keep my office where I worked and kept all my work files and company equipment and inventory and business licenses, because here in what I like to call the Twenty-First century, women apparently weren't allowed to own an office outside of their home. At least not in Williamson County, Tennessee.

Not if their husband committed perjury and tax fraud on the stand and proclaimed their office a "family" retreat. Even though the wife had photographs and the wife of a Williamson Country Sheriff's Deputy to testify otherwise.

Not even if the wife had YouTube interviews and books launches in that office.

None of it mattered. The office was whatever the husband proclaimed it to be, and the wife who'd busted her ass for thirty years was just out of luck.

Woodly also allowed Les to keep all the cash he'd stolen from my grown sons.

Let me reiterate that.

The judge gave him the money he'd illegally stolen from his grown sons, without their knowledge or approval. Why was this not a crime? If anyone else stole money out of someone else's account without their permission, they went to jail for it.

But it was okay in Williamson County for a spouse to deliberately hide more than a million dollars in assets and transfer them out of state, away from their adult children, who weren't part of the divorce.

Then commit perjury on the stand about it.

Sure.

The judge also let him keep both cars, including the family SUV, even though I didn't have a car at that time in running condition, and everything else Les wanted.

Even Nick's cat that my Autistic son needed to keep calm, and even though I had evidence to prove Les's abuse of our other pets had caused their deaths.

Apparently, it was also fine to murder pets (and that was a plural s on the end of that) in Williamson County, and not get into trouble for it.

Because Woodly didn't even want to hear the facts or review the evidence about pet abuse. "I don't have time for it."

Never mind see the evidence of child and spousal abuse.

Because then, he might actually have to do his job and protect us.

We were left out in the cold. The lying, thieving, psycho bastard got everything.

This was Williamson County, Tennessee where a modern Twenty-First century woman was being accused of witchcraft and denied her right to speak up and defend herself, her sons and her pets.

As my attorney had proudly announced to a room full of other attorneys, and Les during the Dumas case, "Honey, this is Williamson County, and you're a woman. Don't be expecting to get any kind of justice here."

And my hell had just begun.

RIGHT AFTER THAT COURT DATE, I realized that Les had stolen the theater tickets I'd bought for Nick. My sons and I were huge theater buffs.

Les wasn't.

Theater was my major in college, at one time. I'd been in countless productions, both on stage and behind it. I'd always loved theater and being a part of that world.

Nick took after me. He had a number of plays that he adored and one of them was *Wicked*.

I'd taken him and Maddox to see it in town a few years back and had promised him that if it ever came back to Nashville, we'd see it again.

So, the minute I heard it was returning, I'd purchased four tickets to see it, thinking that Les would still be part of the family.

Instead, Les stole every single one of them. Even though he hated the theater and had made me walk out of countless productions over the years because he refused to sit to the end of the shows.

They bored him and he didn't want to get stuck in the crowd, waiting for the car to be pulled up from valet.

He was that big of a brat.

In fact, I couldn't even begin to catalogue how many shows I'd had to leave before and during intermission because Les was too bored to stay.

Opera, ballet, *and* theater.

He hated them all, and I adored them. My wants and needs had never been important.

Only Les's.

I'd bought season tickets to each of them and had supported Nashville's TPAC for years.

Since Hogg had shown up and I'd been too sick to go, Les had started giving my tickets to Hogg so that she could pretend she was someone special in my great seats.

And it broke my heart, because it'd always been one of my favorite things in life. Something I shared with my boys.

It was bad enough that Les had taken my joy from me, but to steal it from Nick...

Unconscionable.

But what Les had forgotten was the fact that I'd worked in theater for years. That I'd been a proud patron of it for even longer.

Because of that, I knew how ticket sales worked. As soon as I realized the baby's tickets were missing, I called up my lady in concierge and reported the tickets as stolen and had them reissued.

No one stole my child's pleasure on my watch. Not when I'd worked so incredibly hard to make sure my boys were taken care of.

The theater held them at the box office and on the show night, I took my son to see his favorite play, along with Lyra and Joan. We'd just gotten our drinks and were moving toward our seats when lo and behold Nick and I came face-to-face with none other than old Snooty herself.

*God has a sick sense of humor.*

And far too often, I was His punchline.

That night, God was looking for a belly roll.

There Snooty stood, nose-to-nose with her own grandson.

*Do you know what she did?*

Nothing.

She turned her back on him and moved forward toward Les who had his back to us and couldn't see us in the crowd.

Not a single word was said to her grandson. And she only had four grandchildren left after she'd driven one to suicide.

The two of those asses were dressed like they were important. Like they were the ones who'd slaved, night and day, three-hundred-and-sixty-five days a year, twenty hours a day to pay for those tickets.

It was sickening.

But that was fine. Let them pretend to be honest, good people.

I slid over with Nick and entered through another door.

Then I paused to watch as they were turned away with their stolen tickets.

Did I feel pleasure?

No. I was sick, to be honest. Sick to my stomach to think that any "man" would so selfishly rob his son of what that boy loved most for the pedophile whore who had left us homeless in Mississippi. The bitch who had taken such sick pleasure in our misery.

Who had rubbed her own abused son's nose in it, every day.

She had laughed in Les's face when he'd asked her for help. "You made your bed, son. You can lie in it."

How could he ever forget that? Her callous cruelty for all those years?

Instead, Les had carried that soulless bitch who'd turned her back on her own grandchildren up here in a car I had paid for, while knowing he was depriving his own son of what gave his son pleasure to pamper the same bitch who had knowingly allowed his own sons to starve, and wallow in poverty.

How could anyone be that sick in the head?

My mother had always talked about someone being so sorry she wouldn't throw piss on them if they were on fire. I wouldn't spit in their mouths if they were dying of thirst.

I only prayed that there was a God in heaven and that they both got exactly what they deserved.

Not for me, but for what they'd done to my children.

And because of their cruelty, I bought my son the backstage experience that night. He got to meet the cast and the crew. It was one of the most magical nights of his life. And I will forever treasure the smile on his handsome face and the curious questions he asked, as well as that delighted twinkle in his eyes as he saw everything behind the scenes.

*So, thank you, Les.*

Nick and I had a wonderful bonding moment that we wouldn't have had if you'd been with us. You would never have allowed us to stay.

We loved every minute of our night.

Just as we've loved every minute of every single one, we've had without you.

**Y**OU LOOK LIKE A MILLION BUCKS!"

I smiled at Lynn Gates, the receptionist at my dentists' office. "Thanks! Everyone's been saying that." And they had. While Les might be looking older than his mother (those showing up in court had believed she was his girlfriend he'd left me for), everyone I ran into, constantly commented on the fact that I appeared younger than I'd looked in years.

It was beginning to scare me.

But not as much as the check-up at the dentist's office. Since my boys were in high school and for reasons no one could explain, my teeth had begun to literally rot out of my head. I went from having little to no cavities to massive decay. Everything imaginable. Root canals. Veneers that came off for no reason. Two implants; one that failed so badly, I spent a year with no tooth at all, while they had to regrow my jawbone so that they could try the implant again.

To this day, I have a nasty place in my jaw where it still hadn't grown completely back.

It was rough.

I'd been told before Les left that all the veneers needed to be taken off and redone because of the inexplicable decay. Decay I had since learned was caused by the heavy metals that had been fed to me over those years.

As a side note, since Les left, I'd not had a single cavity. Once whatever he was feeding me got out of my system, all my dental troubles, including the swollen and bleeding gums had vanished and never reappeared.

Not a single one.

How was that not evidence that something weird had been going on?

Thank you, Detective Lynn Lazy for not wanting to do your job. He should be ashamed of himself.

They all should.

"You're looking so much better." Jamie beamed.

"Thank you."

Jamie was the hygienist. "How's your headache?"

"Pardon?"

She motioned to the window. "It's raining. Don't you have a headache?"

I paused as I realized that I didn't. For the first time in years there was no vicious migraine, and it was raining. I always, always got migraines when it rained.

Now, I knew something was definitely wrong.

It was time to go to the doctor, and have this shit checked out for real. I couldn't deny it anymore. Les had done something to me.

Too many "coincidences." Too many things had ceased happening since he left. No one was as sick as I'd been for as long as I'd been ill and got better for no reason.

That only happened in Hallmark movies and miracle plays.

So, I called the doctor and made an appointment.

I fully expected Angela Hera to laugh me out of her office. I'd been going to Angie for years. Really, having a patient haul in a bag of hairbrushes was a little strange. I admitted it.

Nervous and feeling ridiculous, I second guessed myself a million times over while Lyra and I waited for her to come into the room where we sat.

When she joined us, it was with her ever beautiful smile. "What's going on?"

"Promise you won't laugh or think I'm crazy?"

Angie arched a brow as she sat down across from me.

I took a deep breath and forced myself to continue. "You know all the weird ailments I've been having? The headaches, backaches, vitamin deficiencies, infusions, and everything else that we haven't been able to figure out?"

"Yeah?"

"Well... " I opened the bag to show her what I'd brought with me. "Les has filed for divorce, but before he left, he cleaned out my hairbrushes and I know this sounds weird, but do you think he could have poisoned me?"

I really, truly expected her to laugh.

She didn't.

Instead, she sat there stone-faced.

Then she flipped through my file. And flipped some more. As the minutes ticked by and she didn't laugh or comment, I became more nervous.

Finally, she looked up. "We need to get you tested."

*Ah crap.* She all but confirmed it with those hollow words. "You think he did it?"

"I don't know."

But she wasn't laughing at me and that said a lot.

"Any idea what he could have used?" I asked.

She shook her head. "I don't even know what kind of tests are out there for something like this. Give me a few minutes. I have to go look this up."

It wasn't a few minutes. Lyra and I sat in her office for over an hour while she tracked down someone in town who could run a broad-spectrum test for any and all mysterious compounds. Because we didn't know what we were looking for, a lot of different things had to be screened for and screened out.

There was only one lab in town that could do it.

Angie gave me the address and we headed over.

Luckily, I was the only one there. The tech was an adorable young woman.

"So, what are we doing today?"

Again, I felt like a fool. This was unfamiliar ground and not something I'd ever thought I'd be standing on. "Please don't laugh. I think I might have been poisoned."

She scoffed at me. "Honey, that happens all the time. It's one of the things we get most often in here. You'd be amazed at how many people try to kill their spouses in this town."

*Wait. What?*

My jaw dropped.

She wasn't kidding. Come to find out from all the attorneys and lab people I'd spoken to since, it was, indeed, a very common occurrence that no one talked about, and that neither the police nor the judges took seriously, given the fact that it was a popular means of spouse disposal.

In fact, in spite of it being a regular and I mean *regular* as in brushing your teeth and putting on socks, occurrence here (no exaggeration) in this hellhole of a place, our police department refused to even have a toxicologist on staff, or any means to test for it.

At all.

Williamson County expected the victim, at an exorbitant cost to themselves, to go out and do all the testing, collect all the experts and then, maybe, just maybe, they *might* consider doing something to the culprit.

But only after you'd been killed and if your family continued to press them over your dead body.

Of course, because you were the one who'd paid for the test yourself, you'd already lost the case. Defense could now argue that the chain of custody was tainted, even though the lab took special care to preserve that chain of custody.

After all, *you* paid for it.

Then again, it wouldn't be nearly as biased as a Williamson County judge who refused to listen to any allegations of poisoning, whatsoever.

Even if a spouse admitted they'd done it.

*True example from another case, by the way.*

But since we didn't have any lab people at the police department and no tox experts, the police were the ones who told us to go out and do it at the same lab that my doctor had found to run the test.

I had the emails from Detective Lynn Lazy where he'd told me that was what I had to do and if I could get a doctor to validate the test, then and only then, they would pursue it.

Not only did I get the test and the doctor, I got a specialist.

They still refused to pursue any charges, in spite of all the detective's promises and those of the director of the Tennessee Bureau of Investigation.

Why?

Because I wasn't dead. Had I died I would have been a priority. But because I had the audacity to survive the attempts made, my life and Les's crime didn't matter to them.

I had that in writing. Our local, world-renowned medical facility wrote that to my doctor. "She's not dead. It wasn't fatal."

How dare I survive Les's attempts on my life. Or that the police hold him responsible for putting lethal compounds in my food that are all carcinogens.

The fact that I had exceptionally high levels of arsenic and twenty-one other extremely suspicious compounds in my blood, hair and nails that no one could account for by any normal means was okay by them.

It didn't kill me.

No need to worry.

*You're still alive, Terri. You should take the win and go on with your life as if everything's okay.*

*Even though he was still trying to ruin and destroy your life, and those of your children.*

Even though those metals would most likely cause the same kinds of cancer that killed my parents.

*Fuck it! Get over it.*

How dare I be upset that someone had caused me to spend years of my life in misery. In-and-out of the hospital. That I had been robbed of my health and mobility. Been forced to spend hundreds of thousands of dollars on infusions and other painful medical treatments because he was an asshole.

One of the police even tried to excuse it by saying that the levels could be explained by eating fish. My best friend from high school who was, ironically, a toxicologist and pharmacist laughed when I told her what they were arguing and showed her the reports.

"Honey, you'd have to be a dolphin to eat enough fish for these levels. And unless you've changed all the years I've known you, you don't eat fish. As for the other stuff, I don't know how you'd come into contact with it. That's stuff you find in a nuclear plant."

And she would know. Her father was a nuclear physicist.

It was also the same kind of substance found in hobbies and other places both my hubby and his girlfriend were known to frequent and do.

Not hobbies of mine.

Not to mention, my friend was right about my diet. My idea of seafood was hush puppies or the cheddar biscuits at *Red Lobster*.

Even Dr. Oz had agreed with her when I appeared on his show. When he saw my test results, he said that his own levels were nowhere near as high as mine and that he'd been contacted, personally, by the health department because they were concerned about how dangerous the levels were for *him*.

Keep in mind that he eats fish all the time.

I don't.

And my levels blew his "elevated" ones out of the water.

My other best friends who were in the medical field were every bit as aghast.

One was stunned by the levels. "How are you still alive?"

The other was appalled. "How can they look at this and not arrest him? My God, Terri! This is not something you see from a 'normal' patient."

Oh, how I wish I were making all that up.

Sadly, it was true. Here in Williamson County, one of the richest counties in the country, they simply didn't care.

*Attempt to kill your spouse? We don't give a shit.* That should be the county's motto.

One husband even admitted on the stand that he was drugging his spouse, and the judge shrugged it off.

*True case.* He let the man go because the wife didn't drink the whole thing, and therefore didn't get all the effects of the drug in her system. So apparently, ruffying your spouse was okay.

*Yee-haw, Nashville!*

Please don't let your daughter, sister or mother near this place. My treatment at the hands of their courts and law enforcement explained so much about the Vanderbilt rape case. I was amazed anyone was ever arrested, never mind convicted for it. Had it not made national news, I doubt anyone would have paid for that crime.

Yet even so, there was a part of me that didn't believe it was real.

A part that didn't want to think that the man I'd been sleeping next to for twenty-seven years was *that* cold-blooded and twisted.

That he could sit there, day after day, and watch me physically deteriorate before his eyes, knowing he was the cause of it all. To go with me to every doctor and specialist's appointment and stand by, stone-faced, while the tests were run, fearing that they'd find out he was causing it.

No wonder he wouldn't let me go to the doctor alone.

The fact that he looked me in the eye, day after day, while plotting with others to steal from my children and divorce me. All the while telling us that he "loved" us and was a dedicated family man who reviled those who filed for divorce because they were scum dogs.

"An affront to God." That was what he called divorcees.

Hating on his own sister for how many times she'd divorced. "Can you believe that slut kept her husband's mother's china cabinet? She claimed that she wanted it for Taylor to protect her inheritance. What a fucking bitch! My sister is insane!" He'd railed against Annette for years over the way she'd done the father of her child.

Yet what Les did to his own family made Annette look like a saint.

But I didn't want to accept the fact that, as crazy as he'd always acted, he had actually poisoned me.

Surely, those symptoms were menopause like Les had kept trying to convince me.

It wasn't.

The tests came back. One by one.

By the time the last one came in, I knew the truth and there was no more denying it.

Because I wasn't the only victim.

Everyone seemed to forget that major detail. The other victims kept getting lost in obscurity.

Simply because Les didn't care who else ate my tainted food in his quest to control and/or kill me, so long as I got the bulk of it.

I was one of five actual victims.

My greatest regret was that I was too sick at the time to realize it before it was too late. Two of his other victims were Lyra and Maddox.

As far as we knew, Lyra was only dosed the one time as I'd mentioned during the Atlanta trip.

Meanwhile Maddox ingested who knew how much over how long a period. My poor baby. Because his father had ranted so much about "wasted food," Maddox had wanted to be a good son and so he'd finished off my meals whenever I didn't feel up to it.

That was what terrified me. I had no idea how much my baby ingested or what the long-term effects of it would be for my son.

He could have died, and no one seemed to care. Especially not the man who'd fathered him. But when I looked back at his photos during that time, it was so obvious. He was so pale and drawn.

Not to mention, sick, too. He'd also had documented medical problems then that have since gone away.

Same vitamin deficiencies. Bleeding gums. Numb tongue. His hair fell out. Same pain in his bones. Weakness.

Mood swings.

The same, exact symptoms that I'd had.

All his symptoms vanished when he went to Japan and was no longer eating after me. And none of those symptoms had returned.

The other two victims were my cats, Naveena and Kitty. Nav was the one who made me realize that they were victims, too. When Les had left, she was virtually hairless. My boys affectionately called her "baboon butt" because all her hair had fallen out across her rear first. Her once beautiful Bengal coat was so splotchy and dull. She appeared spacey and out of it.

Like me.

Nav had respiratory problems and threw up constantly.

"She has the same rare disease as Kitty and will die from it. There's nothing we can do." That was what Les had said.

But Nav was recovering, and her new vet said that he'd never heard of such an illness.

The longer Les was gone, the better Nav got. And we weren't doing anything different than we'd been doing before.

Her diet hadn't changed.

Nick had even bought himself a new cat to replace Mochi.

Nav was again playful, like a kitten. Her hair, like mine and Maddox's had started growing back and it returned to its original "glitter coat."

In no time, she looked like her old self.

For the first time in years.

And Nav began eating from my plate again. Something I hadn't realized that she'd stopped doing until she began begging for food while I was eating. Putting her little paw on my hand to get a bite from me.

I had just sat down with Nick when suddenly Nav was there. She practically took a piece of chicken out of my hand.

"What the heck?" I laughed and put her back on the floor.

She jumped up on the table, meowed and pawed at my hand.

"Wow," Nick said. "She hasn't done that in a long time."

I froze at his words.

He was so right.

Kitty and she used to always circle me while I ate, begging for food. It would make Les crazy because I'd tear them off small bites and drop them at my feet.

"Stop doing that, Terri! It's not sanitary!"

I didn't care. They were my babies, and a lot more sanitary than the Hogg he'd let in who'd left her nasty, used tissues all over the place.

But at some point, over the past year or so, as she'd gotten sicker, Nav had stopped wanting to eat after me.

Kitty hadn't.

And Kitty had gotten sicker and sicker.

Until Les had taken her without warning and had her killed and cremated.

*Holy shit.*

Nav must have known intuitively that something was wrong with my food.

Why hadn't I paid attention and realized that in time to save her sister?

Because I was too sick, and out of it.

What were the odds that all of us would be ill at the same exact time, eating the same exact things, and then would recover during the same exact time frame?

The FBI BAU handbook.

*Once is an occurrence.*

*Twice is a coincidence.*

*Three times establishes a pattern.*

And we had five victims.

Les had killed poor Kitty. The cat that Les had put down without any warning and had *cremated* so that I had no remains to test and compare.

You couldn't say it was environmental because nothing in our environment had changed. Not to mention, I had my water tested and everything else that I could.

Nothing was tainted.

The only thing different about our environment was that Les and Hogg had left.

If only Detective Lynn Lazy would act upon what he knew had happened. But in spite of seeing the reports, and of assuring me that if I could find an expert who would testify about the results that they would prosecute for it, Lynn Lazy had yet to arrest Les for what he'd done to us.

That was what truly sickened me. The authorities knew he had done this. That he'd had a long history of "dosing" my children—I had called poison control on him for years, and even had a witness to him overdosing me in Jackson, Mississippi when I'd flatlined and had to be resuscitated because of his bad act against me.

They refused to act on it.

Not even after Les threatened harm to the witnesses who could verify what he'd done.

We all knew for a fact that he'd done this to us. Why else would Les call my aunt up in panicked voice? "You need to make Lyra bring Terri home so that *we can feed* her."

Who said that?

Why would he make sure he cleaned out my fridge and pantry when he left?

Threw out our spoons and made us eat off disposable dishes.

How much evidence did they need?

Anywhere else, the police would have done the tests and provided the experts for us. I'd spent tens of thousands of my own dollars and provided my own experts and still they wouldn't lock up an attempted murderer. They'd rather have him on their streets and in their stores, running lose among innocent people. The son and grandson of known pedophiles who had so little regard for others that he would kill off his own son and wife for money.

That he took photos of me writhing in my hospital bed, in utter agony in the emergency room, so that he could keep it, like a serial killer with a trophy.

Yeah, that was who I wanted living in my neighborhood.

Sure.

But it got even better!

According to the judge's own order, Les wasn't supposed to alter my business office at all. I was supposed to be able to film my live book signing there as I'd always done in the past.

As he knew I was scheduled to do one when he illegally seized my office from me by committing tax fraud and perjury on the stand.

Could someone please explain to me where, outside of Williamson County, it would be acceptable for a non-working spouse to move into a working spouse's office while that spouse was away on a business trip and take it over with all their records and work, and then bar them from it and never allow them to gain access to their office and work again?

To their necessary work files?

Then turn around and hold the working spouse in contempt of court for not handing over the work documents and files that were in that office where the non-working spouse lived because the working spouse had been banned by a court order from their office and couldn't get them without violating that court order.

How was that for a Catch-22?

That was the unreasonable nightmare these bastards had put me into and forced me to live under for over two solid years while they robbed me blind.

This was why I was now in bankruptcy. Caused by the man who'd made me settle the other lawsuit he'd started against my will because, "We couldn't afford to go bankrupt on attorney fees!"

So, his answer?

Sue himself and burn down the money even faster? The same, finite amount of money that he needed to see himself through the rest of his life because he was too lazy to work.

At least with the other suit, there was a chance of being paid with money that didn't belong to us.

The true idiocy of not one but *three* judges in this hellhole where I lived who had allowed his madness to continue and grow out of control.

Instead of protecting the marital estate, as they were charged with doing, they allowed him and his jackals to set fire to it and watch it burn.

And there was nothing I could do to stop them.

Nothing.

That was the law. I was at their mercy, and they had no mercy to give.

Scariest part? I wasn't the only professional woman in this county. There were a lot of us. And that list included Taylor Swift, Reba McEntire, The Judds, Nicole Kidman, and a whole lot more.

My worst fear was that this wasn't only Tennessee.

That this might be the rest of the country, too. And everyone needed to wake up before you found yourself an innocent victim in a similar reign of terror.

Because the only crime I'd committed was marrying a sociopath and spending twenty-seven years working hard and taking care of my family.

My biggest mistake was thinking that there were laws in this country that would protect my children and I, and if they failed that there were organizations and people in place who would help us.

I couldn't have been more wrong.

No one had ever told me that when I signed my marriage certificate that I was surrendering all my Constitutional Rights. This was America.

Until you were married.

All your rights went out the window.

And in violation of the judge's orders, Cockburn allowed Les to not only destroy my office where all my records and files were kept, but to tear up all my fan gifts and to pile them like garbage into one room.

Why not? That was what he'd always thought of my writing career that he was now claiming he wanted to live off for the rest of his life.

It was what he'd always thought of me.

And much like Solomon's Baby with the fake mother, it proved beyond a shadow of a doubt that he had absolutely no hand in building my career.

If he had, he wouldn't have been able to destroy it any more than the mother could stand by and see her child butchered. But he hadn't helped to build it and he was insanely jealous of it.

Which was why he'd torn my fan gifts apart, right down to shredding my most beloved and personal ones. That amount of rage against me was bone-chilling and showed a level of hatred and obsession that was terrifying.

Everyone around us knew he'd always been in complete control of us. It was why they all, including the bankers and accountants, rallied to my side when the divorce began. They knew how badly he'd treated me over the years.

How badly he'd treated all of them in my name.

That unwarranted and hate-driven destruction that the court had allowed to go unanswered showed what all the law enforcement agencies and all government officials thought of me and my children.

*We were nothing.*

My work was nothing.

It was easy to be a bestselling author. Anyone could do it, or so Les had always proclaimed. Although, if it was so simple, why couldn't he do it?

Why couldn't he get a job and support himself? After all, he'd spent decades railing against welfare mothers and other "welfare" recipients who refused to go get jobs at McDonald's. Why was he suddenly too good to go put in his application after screaming about them?

Then again, he couldn't even make it as a lawyer and let's face it, Cockburn and her "friends" had the I.Q.s of a chickpea. If they could make a living, being brain dead, surely Les could make a living at it, too.

Cockburn was so proud of his wanton destruction, that she brought photos into the courtroom and bragged about it to the judge. "Your Honor, he's piled up her belongings in one room. Here's a picture."

I couldn't believe that the judge didn't say a word about them violating *his* orders. Violating the laws against wanton destruction of marital or personal property during a divorce.

About them violating me and my fans.

But what I found truly repugnant was that any judge in Williamson County, home of Country Music, had so little regard for someone's fans. That the judge would tolerate such willful and wanton destruction of property by an attorney and her lawyer client, and to let it go unpunished.

But not a word was said.

And there was no doubt that Les had done this. He had stomped pieces of my personal costumes to the point that they no longer worked, and had shredded my clothes and other gifts, which showed a clear mental breakdown and a disturbing amount of hatred toward me and his children.

And my career and fandom.

That, alone, should have concerned everyone in law enforcement, especially given the fact that this man, with a history of mental illness, made sure to take all the guns out of our home with him when he'd left.

And lied about having them.

Really? That didn't set off any alarm bells with Williamson County officials?

And they wondered why spouses ended up dead.

Why abuse victims were so afraid to leave. Because law enforcement would never, ever help us, even when it was so obvious that our spouses were deranged and dangerous.

When we were afraid for our lives and terrified to be left defenseless in the grips of an apathetic court system that would only intervene once we were dead.

I firmly believed that God would grant me justice one day, and that all of them would all pay for the injustices they'd allowed to befall us. But it didn't make it any easier to swallow.

*Woe to those who enact evil statutes. And to those who constantly record unjust decisions.*

*What will you do on the day of Judgment, in the calamity that will come from far away? To whom will you run for help, and where will you leave your wealth, so you won't have to crouch among those in chains or fall among the slain?*

*Isaiah 10.*

Whatever Les did to me, the judges acted as if it was okay. As if I deserved it. One by one, the Williamson County judges had signed off on, and continued, encouraged and propelled his abuse of us.

Nothing like state sanctioned child and spouse abuse to warm the cockles of a heart.

Just like no one would punish Les for violating the court order and invading my home or my storage unit. He came and went as he pleased. No one would enforce that, either.

No matter the evidence given to them or the police.

After all, Les had a magic wand between his legs that gave him special powers in Williamson County so that the laws of the U.S. didn't apply to him.

Instead, Cockburn hauled me into court in August to split our bills where the Whore of Babylon boldly lied again about what I was already paying.

Woodly wouldn't listen to either my attorney or me because apparently if you were a woman in Williamson County, standing before him, you had no rights to speak—as my attorney had forewarned me in that crowded room during the Dumas case. "Honey, this is Williamson County and you're a woman. Don't expect any justice here."

It was also reiterated by the new IP attorney I'd hired that summer who was a former business partner of my Williamson County judge. "We don't try cases down there if we can help it. No one in their right mind wants to go before a Williamson County judge."

Wow. That was how rampant and brazen the injustice was.

But after April where the judge had openly and proudly declared on record, "I don't care what the law is." I'd decided that I needed a more aggressive counsel.

One who would file a motion of contempt on Les when he violated court orders by coming into my home and storage units and removing property out of them.

Or destroying property inside them. Really, was that too much to ask?

Not to mention, my original attorney was costing me too much. I'd already paid close to one hundred thousand dollars to her, and she was telling me it would be three years to settle this divorce.

What that translated into in attorney speak was, "I've got a client who can buy my Christian Louboutin shoes, and I'm going to milk this bitch for every dollar she's worth."

I had just come off Les's three-year lawsuit that had cost well over a million dollars and didn't have any more money to spend like that. Contrary to what everyone thinks, I wasn't J.K. Rowling, and Les had stolen the majority of our money when he left.

All my attorney fees were being put on credit cards and I was spiraling toward bankruptcy. The only one who seemed to understand that was me.

Because of the lies of Dumas and her unconscionable team that they'd hammered me with for years while I wasn't allowed to say a single word about any of their bullshit, my career was in trouble and my publishers were pissed off. I needed to be writing and rebuilding my career, not fighting the Idiot Cockburn who kept filing insane allegations such as witchcraft with every brief and trying to rewrite my past with Les's new lies where he double downed on the what he'd called bullshit in his own emails days before he left.

My favorite was the summer of 2018 when an article came out, like thousands of them before, that talked about our being homeless in Mississippi.

Les, himself, had written to our lawyers during the prior lawsuit that we were homeless. He'd told that very same tale to our children and friends for decades.

The words had come out of his own mouth, countless times. "We were homeless in Mississippi."

Because we *were* homeless. That was a fact.

Snooty's own words about the matter, "you made your bed, you can lie in it."

Didn't matter to her that we had her grandson and that I was pregnant with another. Snooty was too busy taking in a young girl from Hawaii to live with her and her pedophile husband (*are you as creeped out by this as I was then and still am?*). All their funds were going to the little girl and her parents to pay for all kinds of extravagant things such as jet skis, private school tuition and airfare back and forth to Hawaii.

There was no money left for such trivial items as a single pair of shoes for my son, or baby food to feed him.

Or for their natural granddaughter's, Taylor's, Christmas.

In fact, I remember Snooty and Les Senior having to hide more than half of the girl's Christmas gifts because their granddaughter, Taylor (the one who committed suicide as an adult because of their neglect and abuse) was coming over and they didn't want her to know how much more they'd given the girl they'd taken in than they'd bought for their own flesh and blood.

Baby Huey had whined, bitched and moaned about that for years and years.

I had to listen to it until my ears bled.

"How could they do that to Taylor? She's their blood! How could they steal from their own granddaughter for a stranger? I hate my parents! I wish they were dead!"

*Given all those rants, how could you steal from your own sons, Les?*

And after all those decades of abuse, and of listening to Les rant about his "pedophile parents" as he, himself, called them, and their sickening ways, I now had Cockburn threatening to sue me for defamation over a well-established truth that her own client had established himself.

From his own mouth and emails.

That we were homeless in Mississippi.

In fact, Cockburn bullied, harassed, threatened, and constantly insulted me over the very facts that Les, himself, had been putting into emails to our lawyers in the Dumas case less than two weeks before he'd abandoned us.

She was that incredibly stupid and vicious. Like a complete idiot, she refused to vet anything.

Too bad the Tennessee Board of Professional Responsibility refused to uphold their own code that said no attorney could knowingly present false testimony or knowingly misrepresent facts to the Court.

One of my favorite lies that Cockburn had begun telling to the Court was about Les's own family:

They were "rich" and therefore would not have left us to suffer.

*Pardon me while I laugh.*

We've all seen that movie about selfish parents who lavished themselves in luxury while their children wallowed in poverty. How many times had Children's Services come into a home where the children had no food, but Mom and Dad had a brand-new car?

Yeah.

"Gussied up pigs" was what we called them in Georgia. Mama Snooty was from the same itty-bitty hick town where my family originated, except my family had old money there.

For all the airs that Snooty put on, her parents didn't finish grade school and were dirt farmers who were barely literate. Her father was a janitor. She was raised on their dinky farm that she despised and ran from as soon as she could find her own cock to suck and get free. Even if that cock was attached to a pedophile, she didn't care. Snooty had always been the one who would do *anything* to deny her past of penury.

My grandfather's family had founded the county she'd come from, and they were judges, lawyers and senators. Pillars of that community. Postmaster, doctors, pharmacists, and the owners of the local quarry.

My grandmother and her sisters went to boarding schools. My great-grandmother was the daughter of the family that had the first house with electricity in all of Atlanta. Even my father's grandmother was college educated.

My grandfather and uncle were Lockheed engineers, in addition to being real pastors (not the fake one that Hogg tried to pass herself off as). My sister, brother and other relatives owned their own businesses, as had my father once he'd retired from more than triple decades in the army.

Esteban not only had his own business that he'd run since he was a teen, but he'd been a major trophy-winning motocross and race car driver. And he'd had his own rock band for years.

Les's pedophile father was the son of a pedophile who was run out of town for molesting children. We've established this. Old Daddy Manly was a Lieutenant Colonel in the Army so hated by his own men that one of them had taken a shot at his head and ended up serving time for it.

Another interesting fact, Old Daddy Manly had come out of the Army with the same salary as my father who'd retired with the rank of Sergeant Major. My father went on to found his own company that spanned four states, while Daddy Manly went on after his Army retirement to work at a youth detention center (don't get me started on that as it creeped me out to even think about it).

Mama Snooty was a schoolteacher.

Hmmm…

Weren't they lovely people that they kept ending up around kids all the time?

*Wouldn't you like to have this family living next door to you?*

And Les wanted to complain in the divorce that I kept the circle of pedophiles and their pimps banned from my home.

*Ya think?*

Let me reiterate that my niece, Taylor, was dead and buried because of these sick psycho animals who should have been jailed decades ago. That Les, himself, so hated Papa Manly for what they'd done to him and others, that Les risked jail time to commit a federal crime by breaking into an Army military facility and taking a dump on Old Papa Manly's desk.

And now Les was defending them?

Yet no one wanted to believe this man had had a psychotic break of some kind?

Right…

Anyway, all I'd say was that my father could buy and sell Les's worthless parental units twice over, and my grandparents made my dad look poor. The problem was my father didn't share his wealth and neither did my grandparents.

I'd come from a long line of people who disinherited their kids because they believed that you should earn your own way in life. Not steal or take from others.

Too bad the Manlys didn't teach that to their children.

But I would take my Narcissists over the Manlys any day. The Manly bastards wouldn't even buy their own grandchildren shoes when they were shoeless. During our twenty-seven-year marriage, they had spent less than five hundred dollars total on presents to their grandchildren.

When we were needy, my parents both bought us a car, and my father bought us our first home. Even my little brother bought us a car when we didn't have one.

His parents insisted, against doctor's orders that had endangered the life of their second grandson I was carrying, that we return the car Les had paid for in college that he'd borrowed from them while I was pregnant and was supposed to be on bedrest. Even though they owned and had parked in their driveway three other cars, that included two Corvettes.

They put their own grandchild's life at risk for a car they didn't need that Les had bought in college and left us with only the one car my father had paid for, while we were being hounded by creditors and in the process of having the home my father had bought, repossessed if we couldn't come up with the money, on our own, to save it.

How much were those house payments?

Two-hundred-and-eighty dollars a month.

That was the kind of sick psychos they were. They allowed their grandsons to go homeless for less than what old Snooty spent a month on a single pair of pants.

And they only had a grand total of five grandchildren, before Taylor's suicide.

Which meant they now had four grandchildren.

Les and I were the parents of three of them.

But honestly, I was okay with their selfishness. If having them spend money on my kids meant that I had to let those sick bastards molest or abuse them to the point that my children killed themselves or became what Les was, then I would gladly buy the toys and shoes myself.

I wasn't his sister. My kids weren't for sale.

However, I somehow jumped across that channel and now lived in *The Twilight Zone.*

Once the douchebag abandoned us of his own freewill, every time I gave an interview or wrote a social media post that had nothing to do with him, and that stated facts that had long been established by Les, either before my grown sons were born or in diapers, out trotted the poorly coifed Cockburn with her threats that I could no longer say those things that I had been saying for thirty years.

Because the truth hurt Baby Huey's tender little feelings (or insulted his pedophile family) and didn't mesh with the new lies he was now telling people.

And they dared to accuse me of not living in reality?

Seriously?

*Don't whitewash your past, Les. You've got too many witnesses to what really went on.*

Not to mention, that was called interference with business relations. *Really, Cockburn, take a refresher class on your law. I know you're new to your profession, but shut-the-fuck-up.*

Every time she spoke, I heard my mother. "Better they should think you're stupid than for you to open your mouth and remove all doubt. Speak with purpose. Not stupidity."

People like Cockburn needed to learn that not everyone would bow down to the Queen Bitch, no matter how much she bullied them.

I was one of those people. I would stand up and say, "enough! Be humane!"

What I wanted to know, though, was where the hell was her mother or father? I would be ashamed if that was what I'd raised.

But then I could never defend someone I knew for a fact had stolen money from his special needs children, either. Never mind stand up as she had in court and proudly proclaim that my client ripped off his special needs kids and should be entitled to keep it because my "attorney" client was too lazy to hold down a job like everyone else.

She told my attorney that he had no intention of ever working a job.

Especially being a single mother, herself. That said it all about what a soulless piece of shit Cockburn really, truly was.

Can you imagine having the embarrassment of introducing *that* to your friends and teachers as your mother? Her kids must have been traumatized from birth. No wonder the rumor around town said that her kids were so out of control that she had to quit working in Dinky's firm to stay home and ride herd on them.

Given that she was their example for morality...

As they say, the apple doesn't fall far from its tree.

*Whoever sows injustice reaps disaster, and the anger he uses for a weapon will be destroyed.*
*Proverbs 22.*

But what was more sickening than her was that creepy, twisted goofy grin on Les's face while he watched me being insulted in the courtroom. It was reminiscent of the children in my sister's special needs school who were laughing when they didn't understand what was really going on.

I just sat there, along with Nick, thinking, "you idiot. They're burning up every dime of our money to insult me. You're not going to have anything left and you're laughing? I knew you were stupid, but damn, you've taken this to a whole new dysfunctional level."

But I guess that was okay. When he was working as a door greeter while Cockburn was vacationing on the money he'd burned through, who'd be laughing, then?

And how could the judge not tell that there was something seriously wrong with him? Les would wave at his sons in court like a mental patient.

Now, I'll be honest, when the poisoning first came to light, Maddox didn't believe it.

This was his father. The man who...

Well, he'd never done much for him.

"Hey Dad, can we play ball?"

"I'm watching a movie. Don't you want to play Nintendo instead?"

That was a real example and conversation between them.

"Hey, Dad, I have a project due for class. I have to build a crossbow. Can you help?"

"I'll call Horace."

Horace Underway was the caretaker for our house and my cabin. He ended up being more of a father to my boys than Les ever was.

But the problem with Horace was that whenever Les asked him to do something, like help the kids with a project, Horace built it himself and showed up with it completed.

What happened to Horace?

No one really knew. Les had told me and the boys that Horace had "gone crazy." Les's default excuse for anyone who contradicted him. That Horace was "strong-arming" him for more money.

Once the divorce started, I contacted Horace. "That's utter bullshit! I never asked for more money. That stupid bastard sent me an email, out of the blue, and told me that my services were no longer required. He never would take my calls and he refused to tell me what I'd done wrong."

Seemed I wasn't the only one that Les couldn't face after he fucked them over. My own, personal belief, given that Horace's departure coincided with when I started getting ill, was that Les had wanted him out of our house as Horace would have been the first to notice something wasn't right with me.

More than that, we often employed the extra help of Horace's wife from time to time.

*Know what his wife's other job was?*

Nurse.

How coincidental that Les had removed the one person who saw me every single day and who came with a nurse who'd known me for years at the same exact time my "poisoning" symptoms began manifesting?

*Once is an occurrence.*

*Twice is a coincidence.*

*Three times establishes a pattern.*

One by one, Les had ridded our family of everyone who would have become suspicious so that they wouldn't see what he was doing to me. Horace, Polly, Deanna Schell, Aaron and numerous others.

As a result of Les's refusal to move off the couch and Horace's eagerness to please the man who'd ultimately stabbed him in the back for no reason, my boys never learned the most basic life skills. Such as how to work a hammer or screwdriver.

Again, I wish I were making that up.

As Maddox said in his own words, "Dad just sat on the couch, yelling for us to do homework with someone he paid to do it because he couldn't be bothered to stop changing channels, and come eat. He really wasn't good for much else."

Even so, no one wanted to think that their lazy-ass father was capable of poisoning their mother.

Or them.

Until Maddox confronted him.

Les didn't react like a normal person. He didn't ask or respond in the way normal people do.

Being intelligent, Maddox picked up on that right away.

"She poisoned herself."

What kind of answer was *that*? Maddox was as baffled as I was. Why would I poison myself for a divorce I didn't know was coming? In what alternate bizarro universe would that *ever* sound logical?

Then, Les couldn't keep his stories straight. Within a single paragraph, he'd change what he was telling Maddox. "I just needed a mental break. I'd only planned to be gone for a few days."

Yet he had stolen all of the kids' money more than a week before his departure and put it in an out of state bank account?

What? Was he planning to transfer it back?

Not to mention, we had a vacation for a week planned a couple of weeks prior to his leaving that he'd made me cancel. If he needed a mental break, wouldn't that have been one?

Oh, and don't forget that had he simply told me at any time that he needed a break or vacation alone, he could have taken one.

Hell, I'd have gladly allowed him to move into my office and live in a legal separation. All he'd had to do was ask.

No one would have objected. Because we couldn't stand him and any time he left, we did what we had dubbed the "Barney Dance of Happiness."

As Les used to tell my sons, "When the cat's away, the mice will play." And without him here to scream at us, we had a modicum of peace.

There was that.

Then, in the next breath, he told Maddox, "I couldn't take it anymore. I had started planning to divorce her last year."

Couldn't take what? Any more *Turner Classic Movie* marathons? That was all he did.

His daily routine was:

- Sleep ten hours.
- Get up.
- Yell at the kids.
- Have Terri order his breakfast.
- Make coffee and pour Scotch into it.
- Go to the gym.
- Work out with trainer.
- Come home and shower.
- Make coffee and pour Scotch into it.
- Leave to spend money.
- Have lunch out with Hogg.
- Come home.
- Make coffee and pour Scotch into it.
- Yell at Terri and children, then order Cisco around.
- Make coffee and pour Scotch into it.
- Spend some more money online while watching TV.
- Make coffee and pour Scotch into it.
- Yell at Terri to order dinner.
- Yell at Terri because he had to open the door to get the dinner she ordered.
- Make coffee and pour Scotch into it.
- Take dinner downstairs to Terri and yell at her again because she was too weak to walk upstairs to get it.
- From his indented place on the couch, watch Hogg abuse Nick while Nick attempts to do homework, and continue watching movies.
- Make coffee and pour Scotch into it.
- Snuggle with Hogg on family sofa in front of the entire family while the two of them

drink wine.
- Pour straight up Scotch to help him sleep.
- Go to sleep.

That really, truly was his average daily schedule. His life was *so* incredibly hard, wasn't it? No wonder he had to run away from all the stress and anguish of it.

With more than a million dollars in his pocket.

Remember that my job required hours of isolation in order to do it. Unless I was traveling for work, I was in the house, twenty-four hours, seven days a week.

Locked in my basement.

That meant that the boys came to me when they had problems. They didn't go to him because he was worthless at listening and even more worthless with advice.

"Why are you complaining, son? You don't have any *real* problems. I wish I had your life. You have no idea how lucky you are." That was always Les's answer to everything because his cushy life was so incredibly strenuous.

He could have strained a thumb muscle flipping channels, don't you know?

Funny how everyone who knew us and saw how pampered Les was had said the same exact thing to him. How lucky he was to have a wife who never bothered him and never asked him to do anything for her. Who left him alone to spend all the money she worked her ass off to make, while he sat on his couch ordering what he called his "servants" and "man-bitch" around to serve *him*.

"Dad, I broke up with my girlfriend."

"You'll get over it. Have you seen my coffee cup?"

His lack of regard for his sons had left them cold and seeking me every time.

My boys came to me for everything they needed. Night and day.

Les knew it, and it infuriated him. He'd proudly scold them. "Don't bother your mother! She needs to be working! She doesn't have time for you kids and your made-up problems!"

Remember what I'd said about Les being the King of Projection?

Whenever Hogg would get Nick so wound up that no one could calm him down, they'd have to help me upstairs to "deal" with him because Les and Hogg had him so traumatized that he'd mentally shut down into a giant ball of anxiety. It would take me hours sometimes to get Nick back into a normal state after no more than thirty minutes of that bitch's abuse.

That was why I kept telling Les to drive that demonic slag out of my house. She was so evil, I would spray holy water at her as I passed by her.

I wasn't ashamed to admit it. I kept hoping she'd burst into flames.

Or melt.

In my defense, it did work in *The Wizard of Oz*. Surely, it would work on the Hogg.

But no matter how awful she was, Les refused to make her leave, and he allowed her to mentally destroy his son.

I really did begin referring to Hogg solely as a "demon." In fact, I told everyone around me that I had a demon living and infecting our home, because she was one. And I tried everything to exorcize her from our lives that she was hellbent on ruining.

It became a running joke so much that even my boys took it up and called her "the demon lurking in the darkness of our lives."

Les didn't find it funny at all.

And their bullying of us worsened. So, did Les's gaslighting. It became so bad that he even began doing it to Maddox.

"It's your mom who drove you to Japan."

"No, Dad. It was Karen."

"Karen was trying to help."

"Karen's a fucking a bitch and I hate her."

"No, you don't."

"Yeah, Dad. I do."

"No, Maddox, you don't."

Yes, Maddox really did. And the more he spoke to his father who kept gaslighting him, the more unhinged he realized his father had become.

"That fucker is crazy!" A direct quote from my son.

"I don't know what's wrong with him."

"I do. He's fucking crazy!" Another direct quote.

And as Maddox started feeling better, too, he realized that he'd had the same symptoms I'd had and that since he'd left home, his health had improved substantially.

His brother sent him photos of Nav, and he saw that all her fur had grown back and that she was playing like a kitten.

*As they say, seeing is believing.*

All doubt left Maddox when he came home in August, and he saw for himself that I was no longer sick. Not only that, but he also saw how much I had physically improved.

I went from being a housebound invalid who couldn't cross the room without becoming winded back to a vibrant woman with energy to burn.

Damn Les to hell for all the years of good health he'd stolen from me and my sons. All the time I could have spent with my kids, doing things and having fun. That was what truly angered me.

More than the money. More than the lies.

The fact that I could have spent time with my boys and have been active with them instead of curled up in a pain-filled ball of utter agony. All the hours and days I'd spent in and out of doctors' offices, hospitals and outpatient visits.

All the surgeries and tests. The infusions and monitors.

Because of one fucking monster who knew exactly what was wrong with me. One who had sat there, feeding me more of it, either to control me for whatever sick-in-the-head reason he had.

Or to watch me suffer and die.

And if anyone doubted that, then his behavior since the day he'd walked out of here, where he'd harmed himself and his sons more in his insane quest to cripple me proved beyond any reasonable doubt that he was not only capable of what I was saying...

He was guilty. Plain and simple.

Because no sane, rational person would ever do what this man had done do us all. Those around me have all said that if they weren't here to witness it then none of them would believe it. Every single friend.

Every single lawyer.

"In all the years I've been doing this, I have never seen a divorce get this dirty this fast. Not even when the wife was caught in bed with a man. And honey, you haven't done anything to him. What the hell is his problem?"

"If he was like this during your marriage, I doubt nothing you're telling me. He is insane."

"You know as a lawyer, we meet a lot of irrational people during divorce, but that thing you married takes the cake."

"Yours is the divorce from hell. I'm amazed you haven't blown your brains out." That was a direct quote from more than one attorney.

Even Cockburn and his other attorneys called him crazy to my attorneys.

How sickening was what?

Not to mention, how weird was it that after twenty-seven years of marriage (thirty years of knowing each other) and with three children, including one who graduated from college only a couple of weeks after Les filed for divorce, Les had never once attempted to call me to discuss anything.

Not once.

He wouldn't even look at me.

To this day, he has attempted absolutely no communication with me whatsoever.

None.

In other words, he'd lit out of here like his tail was on fire, or like he was running from a crime he'd committed and never looked back.

And I had done nothing to him.

Nothing.

How was it that my sons and I were the only ones who thought that his behavior was abnormal?

The man had stolen over a million dollars in cash and property (over two million if you included the cabin), left while we slept, without a single word to anyone and had never once tried to talk to me.

Even more peculiar?

When he took his passport with him, he left the receipt for it on his desk where his stolen PC used to be so that I'd find it.

Why?

He also made sure that he took the birth certificates, social security cards and passports for my sons.

My adult, grown sons.

Only Maddox had his passport with him, and he'd had to fight Les to get it right up until the day before he'd boarded the plane to Japan.

"Dad, they require that I have documentation in hand when I get there. I can't work in Japan without a passport. Would you *please* hand it over?"

Seriously, how off was it that Les made sure to take everything he'd need to jump the country?

He also took my social security card with him, along with my birth certificate.

Oh, and I forgot to mention the lovely phone call from the branch manager of a bank I had no idea that we'd banked with.

"Ms. Manly? Did you close out your safe deposit box with us?"

I was stunned when I got the call. "You mean the safe deposit box I didn't know I had at your bank? No, ma'am, I didn't. Why?"

She became nervous, then. "You weren't in our branch on Wednesday?"

"Since I didn't know I banked with you, no. I wasn't."

She couldn't get off the phone fast enough.

What I learned was that Les had opened three more accounts for my sons with that bank, and closed them, too. Along with over a hundred thousand dollars more that was missing. And who knew what was in the safe deposit box that someone, *not me*, had helped him to close out.

No doubt, that was why he'd needed to take my documents with him.

And how was it that Detective Lynn Lazy didn't think that was worth investigating, either?

Who was the bimbo impersonating me?

Hogg? While she looked nothing like me, the bimbo was close to my age.

Or was it Donna Handsoff? The "Godfearing," Jesus-freak, hypocrite divorcee who'd had a crush on him since college that Les had brought to my cabin days before he'd abandoned his family?

I wondered if Hogg knew that he'd been staying with her during the months since he'd abandoned our home.

The beauty of paying his bills, I had his records. So much for the whole "He who divorces his wife becomes an adulterer" verses in the bible. Guess Les and Donna had somehow missed those.

And they weren't the only two women he was "seeing."

On the peripheral had always been Nick's godmother, Buffy Brewster.

Buffy and I grew up together. I'd known her since middle school where I'd felt sorry for her. An unattractive, socially awkward, often rude misfit who used to scream out such charming things as "Hey, Tight Ass!" to men from the bus window as we passed by them. She had no friends. No one liked her and all my friends harassed me for the fact that I let her trail after us like a lost puppy.

"Gah, Terri! Do you always have to bring that tramp with you?"

I couldn't help it. Yes, I'd always known that she was a pathological liar and that you couldn't trust anything she said. That she was abrasive and obnoxious, but I was a sucker for the disenfranchised.

The more people picked on her, the sorrier I felt for her.

It took her forever to find a guy willing to date her and then she ended up marrying the man who bailed her out of the drunk tank on their first date. She still had the bail bond from it.

"I know he's not good-looking and that I don't love him, but he takes care of me." Buffy's words to me the day before her wedding.

Over the years, I'd grown to call her my dingleberry. *You know, that annoying little turd you can't get rid of that hangs onto your ass no matter how hard you try to scrape it off?*

That was Buffy.

And she had the nerve to call me right after Les had left, and act like it was out of the blue and she was "just checking on me" for no reason.

As if.

See, that was the thing about Buffy. There was always an agenda. She never "just" called. All the way back to middle school. She was a user to the nth degree.

Let me go back to what she'd said about her husband.

"I know he's not good-looking and that I don't love him, but he takes care of me." She was so cold-blooded and calculated that she went to work for Delta Airlines to be a pilot scheduler for the sole reason that she fully intended to snag herself a pilot to marry so that she'd never have to work again.

And that was exactly what she'd done. She nabbed herself a pilot she didn't love so that she wouldn't have to work.

In high school, she'd only called me whenever she wanted something. "Hey, what are you doing?"

"Nothing."

"Are you going to the mall today?"

That translated to, "I want to go to the mall, but I don't have a car and need a ride. And before we get there, I will ask you to run a number of other errands for me, including stop at the bank, but none of those errands will include putting gas in your car that I'm wasting, or buying you food to thank you for driving me. I won't even say thank you. What I will do is spend the entire day telling you how much better I am than you are and how much greater my parents are than yours, etc."

*That was Buffy.*

Likewise, she showed up at your house with photos of hers and her family, showing them off to everyone and bragging.

*You know the Buffys of the world. I'm sure you have a few in your life and they annoy the shit out of you, too.*

The reason I'd put up with her over the years was because I knew the truth. While on tour, Deanna Schell and I had once taken her up on the offer to go stay with her in her massive Victorian mansion in New Jersey where she lived with her pilot husband who was also once very publicly shamed for being drunk on a flight he was supposed to be piloting, and their two kids.

We arrived and watched in horror while her husband brazenly and proudly abused her in front of us. I'd never seen anyone be so open about their abuse in my life. He berated and belittled her with every word out of his mouth.

He wouldn't even allow her and their kids to have air-conditioning on their floors of the house. I knew Buffy dressed in rags and that he doled out his money to her with a cruel fist, but this was truly pathetic.

So, out of pity, I cut her a lot of slack.

Until the day at DragonCon (a convention in Atlanta) when I came back from a panel and caught that little slut sitting in the lap of my husband, eating french fries off his plate.

Then I promptly threw her out of my room.

Because of that single event, to this day, Nick referred to her as "the french fry 'ho." In fact, that was the only way my sons knew her as she was never around them because I knew what a two-timing slut she was. I'd always tried to keep her away from my husband as best I could. But over the years, she'd made it a point to Velcro her muffin to his crotch as often as she could.

For that matter, she flirted with every man she ever got near, and made it clear that she was after mine.

I gave her props there that at least she had the balls to tell me she wanted him, unlike Donna.

So how could Buffy think for one minute I would be so stupid as to forget all the photos she'd sent me of her having dinner out with my husband while I was away working?

"Hey, Terri! How are you? How's Les and the boys?"

Like I didn't have the phone bill to know that since Les had left, he'd been talking daily to Hogg, Donna and Cisco? That he hadn't spent hours talking to Buffy and Kiki?

They really underestimated me.

"They're great, Buffy. How's your hubby and kids?"

"Wonderful! Doing great! Getting ready to graduate." She bragged on and on while I pretended nothing had happened. I wasn't about to give her anything as I could tell she was only calling to pump me for information.

I even had her on speakerphone so that Joan and Lyra could listen in.

Joan and I have never forgiven her since the night in high school when we found a backstage pass for Adam Ant at a concert. I had driven us to it. Joan had gotten us the tickets, but Buffy who had contributed nothing more than her annoying company, snatched the pass out of our hands and ran off with it before we could blink. We were the bigger fans, by the way.

After a few seconds, she came running back. "Damn. He left already."

*No shit, Sherlock.* All fans of Adam knew that he always left the venue immediately once he finished, hence why it was on the ground.

But by the time we made it home, somehow, she'd "caught a glimpse of him leaving."

By schooltime on Monday, her lie had grown to where she was telling everyone she'd actually gotten backstage to meet him.

Yeah...

Today, that lie was all about how she'd spent time with him, and she'd look at both Joan and I to corroborate it. Like we didn't remember the whole truth.

As I said, she was a pathological liar of titanic proportions. It was why when she'd first called to tell me that her husband had been arrested for drunk piloting, I thought that was a lie, too.

Until I saw it on CNN.

She was such an attention-seeking whore that you never knew what the truth was. Much like Cockburn, Buffy only moved her lips for two reasons, to give a blowjob or a lie.

And she proved that a couple of weeks later when she tried again to get information from me for Les.

This time, I didn't answer her call as it just *happened* to be the very day I'd been in court. "Oh Terri, I'm so sorry about my earlier phone call. I had no idea you were going through something so awful. How thoughtless and insensitive of me! Call when you have a chance."

*Bitch, please! You're not my confidante.* I learned that in middle school when you stuck a dagger in my back for no reason. I don't ever forget treachery.

*Les, you idiot, you've heard that story from me enough that you ought to know better than to send Buffy in for information. I never forget a turncoat.*

Buffy was my dingleberry, not my friend.

Something proven even more so a few weeks later when my "other" phone rang. The number that was our work phone and that Les had given her as his.

"Hey, Les! It's Buffy. I'm here in town. What's your address?"

*What the actual fuck?*

She had come to Franklin to meet up with my husband? And yes, he was still legally my husband. The divorce wasn't final yet. Even though he'd been spending time with Donna (I had the records to prove it) and kept showing up in court with not only Hogg, but according to his attorneys, her parents, too, and now Buffy sans her husband and children.

Wow!

Tell me again how this wasn't considered inappropriate spousal conduct?

And unlike Les, I had real, dyed-in-the-wool friends. Had had them for decades.

He had users that he had to pay.

All my real friends were appalled by the whole herd of this treacherous nest of vipers.

Especially Cisco who, when told to get out of my life, locked up my emails and refused to let me back in. Much like Les who, through his attorney, had promised me that Les would continue to help run my business any way he could.

Yet the minute I asked his attorney for the electronic files he'd stolen on that computer that he'd taken out of my house that had mysteriously vanished, he refused to hand them over.

"She has copies of her employee handbook in the filing cabinet." Cockburn had the nerve to write that to my attorney.

Yes, but they weren't the *electronic* files that needed to be updated that Les had drafted and that I had paid thousands of dollars to a lawyer to approve. You know, *my company property.*

How that wasn't interference with business, I had no idea.

But then Cockburn was an even bigger idiot than the client she represented.

This was the same ignorant slag, who when I demanded that they hand over my office computer that was at my, you know "office" that Les had taken over without warning where my PC had been left on for my return, and that held my latest novel and all the chapters I'd been working on, told me to go and I quote, "sweet-talk Cisco and have him hack into it to get a copy."

"I beg your pardon?"

Okay, in reality I actually said, "What the fuck?"

The guy I had fired for illegally hacking into my files, emails, and accounts, and those of my kids without my permission and deleting them for Les? This bitch had told me to give him access so that he could do it again?

In writing.

And the police, the court and *my* counsel were all good with this?

Here in the Twenty-First century.

What backwards, inbred hellhole did I live in that they had never heard of how wrong and illegal that was? I had the actual emails between Hogg and Cisco where they were bragging about hacking into my computers and files and email accounts while I wasn't home. Talking about rifling through my personal data. Yet no one in this town would prosecute it.

Thank you, Tennessee District Attorneys and Attorney General. May you all rot for your dereliction of duty.

I wish I were making this up.

How many human and civil rights, or laws could one county violate and tolerate?

Oh, I couldn't even begin to count them all.

Again, this place needed to be knocked off the map and remember this was the home of Taylor Swift and Nicole Kidman. *Girlfriends, y'all need to move. Because sooner or later, you're going to be in court here, and God have mercy on your soul.*

But back to Cockburn's email to my attorney for a minute. What modern day woman told another woman that she needed to "sweet-talk" a man to get back her legitimate work files? Especially a slag who had such nasty little memes on her "professional" site as "What do I have to bring to the table? Boy, I bought this table."

That was how ole Cockburn saw herself, and yet she was tearing down another woman for a POS who'd stolen money from his children?

Under the word "hypocrite" should be the very photograph that this ugly, hyena-faced bitch who walked like she had an eight-foot dildo perpetually wedged straight up her ass appended to all her emails.

And you'd love her hashtags: #bossbabe #bitchybarrister Because she thought her shit didn't stink.

That was how unprofessional this skank was. No wonder with all the great schools in town, the only law school she could get into wasn't ABA approved.

Nashville YMCA Night Law School.

Just made me so proud that this was what the idiot had burned through my children's savings to make rich because he was too lazy to go get a job.

Or a real attorney.

Wow. I could really pick them, couldn't I?

*Father of the year.*

*Go sweet-talk a criminal to hack into your necessary work files to get them back so that you can pay me to publicly insult and humiliate you.*

*Yeah. Cockburn is one stupid skank.*

In fact, she was such an idiot that within weeks of having been told by Woodly that there was no alimony because her client had stolen over a million dollars from me and his children in cash, this slag had the nerve to hit me up with *an eighty thousand dollars* a month alimony demand for him.

I hope you choked on that amount because I did.

*Eighty thousand dollars* a month

For the record, I didn't make that kind of money. I'm not J.K. Rowling. If I made eighty thousand a month, I wouldn't be writing. I'd be off on an island, retired.

Now I realized in her pathetic little mind that she probably couldn't comprehend anything more than mani-pedis, blowjobs, and how to get cum stains out of her skirts and blouses, and that she probably believed that everyone on the *New York Times* made that kind of money. Hell, maybe she thought that she could bully it into existence by her sheer stupidity. But it didn't work that way.

I wasn't Rumpelstiltskin. I couldn't spin straw into gold. Especially when my latest book was sitting in the very cabin I'd been banned from by the court order she had stupidly filed after her client committed tax fraud and perjury; while she, herself, was refusing to allow me to get the PC, or hand over the PC that had my latest book on it.

How could she not follow that pure, basic logic?

No one could simply duplicate work already done. Writing wasn't like making a widget. Once you'd written it, you couldn't redo it. If you lost a file, it was catastrophic.

Why was Cockburn too stupid to comprehend that? I guess the Nashville YMCA Night Law School never made her write a single paper to get that degree that obviously wasn't fit to wipe my ass on. Otherwise, she'd understand that you couldn't simply sit down and remember everything you'd written the first time.

Hell, she couldn't even remember her lies from one moment to the next.

By her own rampant stupidity and Les's, they had set me back for a year on my deadline.

She also had the nerve to ask for a copy of every book I'd ever written to be autographed to him. After all, in his delusional, drunken mind he was an "integral" part of my "family" business.

*What the... ?*

Since when had writing *ever* been a family business?

How could any person write that demand in a court document, and not burst into flames for that lie alone?

Or at least have laughed when Les had asked for it.

Cockburn's nose should be so long by now that she could masturbate with it.

I thought every human on the planet knew that writing was a solitary venture unless you were in a co-authorship with someone, but those were rare as most writers didn't play well with others.

We were, by our natures, horrible introverts. This was a long-established fact that everyone over the age of two knew about us.

*For the record, let me explain Les's "contribution" to my solitary business.*

We were at Comic Con, San Diego. Me, my sons and my crew. We were busting our asses from seven in the morning until after nine at night to get the booth up and running because we were on a very tight and strict deadline, and if the booth wasn't upright and functioning when the doors opened, it would be a catastrophe.

We'd been there since seven A.M. with no food and no water. I called Les at noon because we were hot (there was no air-conditioning as they don't turn it on until they've shut down the back-loading dock) and tired, and starving. Les, for the record, was asleep in the hotel room because he was too good to help us do any of this.

"Hey, can you call and get us some pizza and some water?" I hung up.

Kiki's phone began to ring. She answered it.

It was Les. "Can you order pizza for everyone?"

Now let's play, "How fucking stupid was Les Manly?"

If I could have spared Kiki to make the call or fetch the pizza, wouldn't I have told her to do it since she was standing a whopping three feet from me?

Obviously, Kiki was needed. The piece of shit asleep in the hotel room had the time to go get food and bring it to the civic center for us, because he had nothing better to do with his useless life.

And for that phone call to order my assistant around, the rat-bastard thought he was entitled to half of everything I'd ever earned by busting my ass for three decades?

Please remember what I'd just said. My children were at the center *with* me, helping to set up the booth. Les was alone, sleeping in the hotel room.

He was not the Happy Homemaker who gave up her career and life to drive the kids around and do everything for them while Hubby made the money, and never came home at night.

Let me repeat. My children *were at the center with me* while he was alone in the hotel. Sleeping.

I was at home more than he was as he would often abandon the kids and vanish with no word to anyone. When he was home, he was a drunken slob who parked in front of the TV where he ranted about politics and how everyone picked on him.

This piece of shit literally did *nothing*. I couldn't ram that home enough as I had his uselessness well-documented.

By him, ironically, as he'd required all his "servants" to keep meticulous records of everything they did.

Such as putting toilet paper on our racks.

Picking up our children from school.

And going to the gym with Les.

While he paid them gross amounts of my money to do so because he had no friends.

But stupid me, since Lord Dumbfuck left in March claiming he didn't want to go broke from the Dumas lawsuit he'd started, and he had hired Cheap Floozy Thundercunt of the dubious law degree to represent him instead of a real attorney with a brain, I figured he'd want to get the divorce over with before we spent another million dollars, plus, on attorney fees.

I forgot how seriously stupid he actually was.

And I seriously underestimated the greed of Attorney Lack Wit who had made her living off dog bite cases. Anyone who loved to go after beloved family pets to have them put down...

Well, that said it all about her morals and compassion, didn't it?

Heartless whore, through and through, who had no problem representing a man who'd tried to murder his wife and child, and who proudly admitted under oath that he'd stolen all of his sons' futures.

*Because they were being mean to me!*

What that translated to in Les speak was, "Terri refused to come home when I demanded it and she'd hired an assistant I couldn't control with her money! Oh, the horror! Someone stop her before she leaves me on her own and I might have to go get a job!" *I have to start hiding everything and hit her with divorce papers before she comes off anymore of the drugs I've been shoving down her throat and can walk on her own again!*

Hiding everything included more than a million dollars he bought in gold coins that he stole out of my house.

How do we know for sure?

Caleb confessed it to both of his brothers and me, in independent conversations. "Dad is such a *great* guy! He gave me almost two hundred thousand dollars in gold bullion!"

The kicker? None of our sons knew that we had *any* gold sitting in the safe that Les had raided with the help of Hogg.

I mean, I knew that Caleb could be the liar Les had always accused him of, but he normally didn't make up stuff like that.

Not to mention that I got a postcard a couple of weeks after he said that to let me know Caleb had set up a "Wealth Management Account" at a bank where we didn't do business.

Hmmm...

And still no one would investigate my missing gold or make Les answer for it.

To quote my little brother, "Bitch, if having an Amex Black Card, spending my wife's money while driving around in a Porsche and having my wife lavish me with gifts is mean, chain my ass to the wall, motherfucker!"

After all, Cockburn didn't care about her own kids. She admitted in April 2018, that she knew Les's father was a pedophile and she'd shown up in court with his mother.

So, keeping company with pedophiles didn't bother her at all. Any more than being so thoughtless about her children that she had her home address listed as her office on her public website.

*How did I find this out?*

It wasn't intentional. Because I never dreamed any mother even as low-rent as Cockburn would be that reckless and stupid when it came to their own children. I foolishly thought other mothers were like me.

*Protect your young at all costs.*

I forgot how many selfish Snootys were out there.

Well, during the April hearing where Cockburn demanded basically everything in my home that Les hadn't already stolen with Hogg, including my deceased mother's soup bowls she'd left me that were mine when I was a girl—along with my grandmother's dishes—Cockburn had the nerve to claim that I'd cut off the cable at my cabin.

*Say what, bitch?*

Here were the facts. There had never been any cable at the cabin because Les refused to let me have any. "If you want cable, you need to come home for it. You're over there to work. *Not* play."

Remember, the cabin was an office. Not the home or a retreat as those two had lied about in court and Les under oath so that Les could steal it away from me with the judge's blessing.

Could the idiots of Williamson County not look up the legal definition of "perjury"?

"Someone who knowingly provides false testimony or statements while under oath to the court or a judge."

Yet Cockburn had no problem lying to the judge, and on record. And apparently, in spite of his lies throughout the Dumas case to the contrary, Les had no compunctions against perjury, either.

So, after that April hearing, I packed up what few items Les had left behind and waited for them to tell me when we'd exchange them for what I needed from my office, such as my work computer that held my latest novel-in-progress on it.

And my deceased brother's property that I kept at the cabin, along with items of my mom's, my sons' and my fan gifts that meant more to me than anything.

Les never responded.

I was left holding the bag, and worried sick that he had destroyed my mother's and brother's belongings, along with everything my fans had given me.

—|—

In August, Maddox returned from Japan with his fiancé, Maiko. They came with us to the next hearing because that was how every girl wanted to meet her future in-laws.

In divorce court.

Really, Les, you were a rare piece of work, and I wished to God that I had never laid eyes on you.

After the ordeal was over where Woodly made a total ass of himself yet again by berating me and calling me a "train wreck" when I dared to ask that they return my work computer and my son's cat he needed to stay calm, Snooty had the nerve to approach us like we'd just gone out to a church picnic together.

She was smiling like it was Prime Rib Day at the country club. Snooty, who was in her eighties and supposedly broke either her leg or foot depending on the lie Cockburn was telling in court, showed up with a cane and high heels?

Seriously? An eighty-year-old?

Cane and high heels.

I broke my foot at the same time, ironically, that she did. To this day, I was still in a walking boot and the injury hadn't healed. Supposedly, ole Snooty had cancer, and let me repeat, *was in her eighties*.

My mother had cancer and broke a bone so I knew broken bones for cancer patients didn't heal within a matter of a few weeks to where the bitch could strut around like a young debutante in high heels.

Either that or how much poison had Les fed me that I had yet, two years later, to heal? That was how brittle my bones had become because of him and what he'd done to me. An eighty-year-old woman with cancer healed faster than an athletic woman half her age, without cancer.

Hmmm...

Anyway, this repulsive, pedophile-protecting bitch had the nerve to approach us like Les hadn't robbed his sons of their futures and lied to them.

"How you doing?" Snooty asked me.

"Shut-up." I walked off as I no longer had to be polite to the dried-up whore who'd sold her children's virginity for her comfort, and who aided her piece of shit son in the theft of my children's money.

Maddox tried to get away but ended up cornered. He introduced his girlfriend.

Tiny and beautiful, Maiko was shy and timid. She was always dressed impeccably and had a smile that would rival the sun for warmth. She bowed to the grizzle-whore who also asked her how she was doing (Snooty was such a riveting conversationalist—she really kept you engaged with her spork-dull wit).

"I'm a little nervous."

"We don't speak Japanese here. Speak American, now!"

For the record, Maiko spoke flawless English. She didn't even have much of an accent. Snooty was simply fluent in Stupidity. It was, after all, her native tongue.

The look on my son's face was priceless. Contrary to what Les thought, I didn't teach my sons to hate him and his parents. They did that all on their own with ignorant, hateful and racist comments such as that one.

Even after that fiasco, Les insisted that they go to a movie with him and his mother.

That was the biggest mistake ever.

For him.

Bonus round for me because the more time he spent with his sons, the more they realized what a scabbing bastard he was, and how little they wanted to do with him.

That he had no redeeming factors, whatsoever. And the more he tried to convince them that he didn't try to kill their mother, the more they knew he was lying, as none of his excuses, lies, or buckled reasoning made any sense.

If only Detective Lynn Lazy would interview him, he'd see for himself how guilty Les was. Which meant that Cockburn knew it, too.

Shame on you. But then a slag had no shame. That was why she could sleep at night, knowing that she'd spent every dime of money I'd scrimped and saved for my children while she'd lied about me on public record, and harassed me.

*Forgive me for being redundant, but the horror of it all had so thoroughly scarred us.*

Our courts might have refused to hold her accountable, but I pray to God that He doesn't disappoint me, too.

Anyway, my sons had always hated Les's parents. Because his parents were always wretched.

While they'd loved their father at one time, Les having stolen all their money and his continued lies had turned their stomachs more than I ever could.

And mostly because Maddox had a new realization while speaking to his father.

Remember that Maddox had already spent a whole year in Japan before he'd left in March 2018?

Back in 2015, he'd gone there to study and didn't come back until 2016. So, he'd spent a full year, 2015-2016 in Japan. Before that, he'd been to Istanbul.

Even after he came home in 2016, he didn't live here as he was off at college.

For part of 2017, he was in school down in Georgia. He'd also spent time in Seattle and Vancouver. My boy liked to travel.

So, when Les told him that he'd had to leave us without warning, because he couldn't be left "alone" with me without Maddox being here in the house to run interference, Maddox called him out on his bullshit.

Les had been alone with me, a lot.

"She's so violent."

"Dad, Mom has never been violent. She can't even get out of her chair. She can barely lift her head."

"You don't understand, Maddox! I can't be alone with her."

"She can't leave her office without help. And you're never alone. You have a million people in and out of the house, all the time."

For that matter, I could barely breathe and had an oxygen machine and nebulizer both plugged in next to my office chair where I was having to sleep because I was so weak that I couldn't climb the stairs to get to my bedroom.

But a grown, six-foot-tall man who'd been in actual knife fights was afraid to be alone with someone almost half his size. A woman who became winded from going to the bathroom.

Yeah, something sounded rotten in the State of Tennessee to Maddox, especially when ole Les began insisting Maddox should always feed me.

"You have to be home! She won't eat from me!"

The truth was whenever I did, I got sick. *Real* sick. Remember those violent choking episodes when Les had given me food? That weird foam that would collect in my throat? Within minutes of eating, I was projectile vomiting. My body would cramp and seize.

Not knowing any of this, Maddox would bring my food to me. If he was at work or off with friends at mealtimes, his father would insult and scream at him for not being home.

Then Les began to ask him if he could delay his trip to Japan. "Can't you wait a week or two?"

"No. I need to go, Dad."

There was no rhyme or reason for any of this. Any more than there was a reason as to why Les refused to buy a return ticket for Maddox.

The more Maddox refused to postpone his departure, the more Les turned on him and the angrier he became.

"You know, Mom. The more I think about it, the more I believe that bastard was setting me up to take a fall for him. If you'd died and they'd done an autopsy and found the poison, who better to blame than the son who'd fled the country? The son who was taking food to you."

Something Les's own attorney, Cockburn, affirmed in her own response to our first motion on

April 27, 2018. In fact, she hanged her own client with just a few words.

First, she claimed that Les had been wanting to leave me and would have left me sooner if he'd had the chance.

Really? Then why had Les begged for Lyra and me to return from our New York trip? Why was he so hysterical when he called my aunt, Belinda (and her sister heard the entire call with his hysteria and was a witness to this), demanding that Lyra and I return home immediately?

If he was so miserable that he couldn't stand my presence, would he not have been rejoicing at my absence and not demanding my return?

Could he not have left then? Or during any of my other monthly business trips I was taking in those days?

Why had he canceled a five-thousand-dollar trip when he could have taken that trip to get the "few days of rest" away from me that Cockburn claimed he was doing when he left and never returned?

Why had Les thrown the tantrum of all time when Lyra came and took me to the cabin to spend the night away from home? He literally stalked us to my office and screamed at me for daring to leave my home that was less than three miles away to go to my office without his permission.

I had a witness to his fit.

In fact, I had three. Aside from Lyra, he'd screamed at both my sons over my leaving home without his permission.

Lastly, if he'd wanted "a break" from me, we had another home that he had sworn in a court statement was "a retreat" that he could have gone to for a few days and not run off to the pedophile family (his own words) that he'd spent our entire marriage hating, criticizing, and saying that he wanted nothing to do with.

That was corroborated by his own sister when I called her and told her that he'd left us.

"He's not at his parents'." She had been adamant that her brother would never visit *his* parents.

"Yes, he is."

"My brother wouldn't do that. Why would he do that? We hate them. I didn't even know he was having contact with them. He *hates* them. Last time we spoke, he said he wanted nothing to do with them ever again."

Yet in their response, his attorney wrote:

> His son was leaving for Japan on a single entry visa application. Husband is unsure if and when, if ever, their son will return to the United States. Husband held on until the morning of March 7, 2018 so he could see his son off to Japan.

What? Les knew that the visa was temporary and only good for a year. He'd had long discussions with me and our son over this fact. So, he knew to the day when Maddox would be forced to come home or risk arrest and deportation.

Unless, as Maddox realized, he was setting up his son whom he'd ensured knew all about his inheritance and how much money Maddox would get should something happen to his mother while he was away in Japan.

The same mother Les was making sure Maddox fed for every single meal and screamed at the boy if he wasn't home to do it.

And Les had a witness to those facts.

Hogg.

Not only was Hogg a witness, but she'd also been telling my fans that my son took food to me. In spite of the Non-Disclosure Agreement that she'd signed, and the fact that she was supposedly a pastor (*sorry I have to roll my eyes which makes me blind for a minute*), Hogg had been telling my fans all about my family and how I would refuse to come out of my office, except to eat and yell at her.

And by the way, for a "pastor" to tell items that had been told to them in private and she was telling my fans that she was our "minister" was a crime in the state of Tennessee.

What the ever-unimpressive Hogg failed to mention was that I was too sick to leave my office.

That I was "angry" because my husband had moved another unmarried woman into my home who kept leaving notes out for me to see that confirmed their inappropriate relationship, who was abusing me and my sons, and screaming and belittling us, and my staff to the point that my sons were locking themselves in their rooms, and that I was being locked into mine by the self-locking doors Cisco had installed. And that my employees kept quitting by saying that they couldn't tolerate her.

I had to scream to get someone to let me out of my room because they kept taking my phone from me.

So yes, I was a little perturbed.

I don't think it unreasonable that any woman would be upset to work all day with eyes so swollen from the poison they were feeding her that she could barely open them, eyes that kept getting sealed shut with some mysterious icky goo. That whenever I would stumble upstairs, I found my husband under a blanket, giggling with Hogg after I'd been working all day to feed their voracious appetites. Really, I wouldn't think that was unusual. Pretty much anyone would lose their shit in that situation.

And really, I was too sick to lose mine. It took all my breath to breathe.

In fact, I couldn't get through a meal without laying my head down on the table to rest. That was how sick I stayed.

So why would Hogg lie about my condition to my publishers, colleagues and fans?

For the same reason that both Hogg and Les had started telling everyone that Maddox had "rage" issues of his own. That he was "out of control" and was always attacking other people (which was also untrue).

Setting up alibis.

I had actual YouTube videos where my eyes were so swollen back then that I had to wear glasses over them, and even then you could plainly see how ill I was. I was dying in front of the entire world.

No one noticed.

That was what was terrifying, in retrospect.

I had a million witnesses, and these bastards were getting away with what they did.

Because Williamson County was *that* corrupt (and everyone here knew it).

Both my sons who were living in my home and who saw what Les and Hogg had done to me and my cats—my son who was also poisoned and who saw my cousin get sick, had absolutely no doubt that they had gotten away with attempted murder.

Therefore, I had nothing to do with my sons' current attitude about their father. They were grown men with very stubborn minds.

Truth was, I didn't hate Les. I thought he was pathetic. I pitied him for his stupidity, and for the fact that he had ruined his life for no reason other than his unwillingness to get a job.

He'd had the dream and thrown it all away.

I was only sorry that I had the misfortune of being tied to him, and I was extremely sorry that my poor sons shared his genes.

Thankfully, I was bred from much, much better stock that I was pretty sure would override his inferior DNA.

At any rate, after my sons returned from the movie, I had to listen to Maddox go on and on about how much he hated his father and grandmother.

For hours.

"Gah! He's such a controlling, lying asshole! I forgot how much I hate him!"

What could a mother say to that? "Sorry."

"No, Mom. You have no idea! Remember when I was at SCAD?"

Of course. Both he and Caleb attended Savannah College of Art and Design in Georgia. "Yeah."

"Well, I owe you an apology."

"For what?"

"I spent a lot of money."

"I know." Tuition there wasn't cheap.

"No, Ma. It wasn't tuition. See, when I came home, I knew that Dad was going to be his asshole self and so I wanted to teach him a lesson about going through my things all the time. So, you know I had a gay roommate, right?"

"Yeah." To Les's extreme hissy fits, all my sons and I have a number of gay friends.

"Well, I had my bud take me to his stores and buy all this transvestite stuff."

Eyes wide, I glanced to Joan and burst out laughing. Not for the reason that Maddox thought. "Holy shit! *That* suitcase!"

"Wait! What?"

It took a few minutes for me to stop laughing. "I found *your* suitcase." Only I hadn't known it was Maddox's.

It was Les's suitcase with his name on it. "I thought it was your dad's. He'd stashed it in Caleb's closet. I found it while I was cleaning up—" Actually, I'd found it while searching out files and jewelry Les had left scattered all throughout my home to make everything as difficult for me as he could—"and opened it. I thought holy God, what kind of kink was he into?"

It had every kind of transvestite makeup and clothing item, which I knew because I had once lived with one when I was in college. And as Maddox had noted, it wasn't the cheap stuff. It was the good stuff that they really used.

"Well, I wanted to make it convincing."

I laughed harder. "That you did."

"What I didn't know was that Grandma would open it first."

That put me on the floor as I imagined Snooty's face. This was the bitch who had threatened to boycott my wedding if I had my transvestite best friend for a maid of honor.

*Oh, to go back in time...*

"I love you so much, Maddox. Best practical joke, ever!" And it must have been good for Les not to have even mentioned it.

Then again, that might have been what got me divorced.

All because Les didn't have the balls to talk to his son.

Whatever.

Of course, tearing down his sons was what Les, like his mother, did best. Nick was still trying to get his life back together from all the damage Les and Hogg had done to it.

Over the summer, I'd helped Nick get into a Harvard program. I wanted him to see that he could do anything he set his mind to. That he was still competitive in this world no matter what Les or Hogg had said.

How did they respond?

"It's not really Harvard. They'd let in anyone."

Not true.

But that was Les in a nutshell, like his mother. Always tearing everyone down. His sons. His wife.

How sick were the modern laws that allowed an abuser to continue to abuse his family even after he was gone?

He was a beast, and I was glad to have him out of my life, and that of my kids.

Sad to say that the only time I cried after he left was the day that I found out he'd stolen the money from my sons.

How awful that I was married to him for twenty-seven years and I hadn't shed a single tear when he left. I honestly felt relieved. Like a tremendous burden had been lifted from my shoulders.

If only I could get him to go away. To leave us alone and never come back.

That was the problem that we kept having.

The monster and his hyena refused to go. They were worse than Jason Voorhees.

Remember what I'd said earlier? That I fired my first attorney because she told me it would be three years and I wanted him out of my life?

Well, he had been in no hurry to go, and the shyster hyena he hired was only interested in milking my sons' money for every penny. All Cockburn wanted was to haul me in for trumped up contempt motions to discredit me and try to find some semblance of credibility for herself, even though everyone in town laughed at her behind her back.

To try and get them gone and to gain justice for me and my sons since the police didn't seem interested in any themselves, my new attorney came up with the strategy to file a civil suit against Les.

No matter how much evidence and witnesses I turned into the police, and it grew exponentially every day, Detective Lazy refused to do anything.

Even when I had third party witnesses who told him that Les had been inside my home in violation of a court order and had committed criminal perjury.

And remember that I had not one, not two, not three, but four different security companies willing to testify that Les and Cisco were using my "smart" home against me.

That was what Les had Cisco come back into town to do.

It all came back to that threat Cisco had made to me in front of witnesses. "I see all and know all. There's nothing I can't get into."

Even Cockburn knew this, hence her whole, "Sweet-talk Cisco and have him hack into your computer to get your files to you" after I'd hired someone to lock him out.

I had it all in writing.

They had infiltrated my entire home and hacked the system where they'd sabotaged my pool, causing thousands of dollars in damage (to go along with other sabotage Les had done such as removing the trap in my outdoor sink and costing me thousands in waste before it was discovered).

Cisco had left my cameras online so that Les could spy on us. He also took the cabin security offline so that I couldn't see that Les was taking marital property from my storage unit and storing it at my cabin. Or see what they had been up to the week before Les had filed for divorce.

My burglar alarms kept going off and sending the police to my home, night and day.

But the worst?

They piped a recorded heartbeat through my entire home for three days straight, until I was forced to have the entire smart system gutted out of my house.

Now I knew some people were going to try and claim that it was a "wiring" problem.

It wasn't. Let me go back to what I'd said. I had four very competent and well-respected companies send their technicians out to my home to review my system.

It wasn't wiring.

They all said the same thing, including the company who had originally installed the system in my home.

The heartbeat was a recorded loop that someone was piping into my audio system to harass me.

"Cisco is a dark web expert. And I'm telling you, right now, that when I was putting this in, they did some questionable things. In fact, Mr. Manly had me fly a software engineer in from Utah to customize this system for him. The two of them wouldn't even let me know what all they were doing to it. And he was such a bastard about it, that he nearly gave me a nervous breakdown over this job. I've never met anyone I hated more."

I knew the man wasn't joking or kidding as I saw a note in Les's writing from another company where he'd written in an angry scrawl. "Refuses to do business with me."

That wasn't Mr. Bishop's company. It was another Audio-Video company in town who knew Les. Obviously, they'd talked.

Les's reputation was well-known in this community.

In fact, Les's temper and assholishness had become legendary.

Just ask the poor manager where we've bought the majority of our cars.

And that wasn't all John Bishop had told me about Les's relationship with Cisco. "I overheard a lot of things between the two of them. Things that had me wondering about how close they were, if you know what I mean."

He wagged his brows.

Which got me to thinking.

Not long after Les had hired Cisco, for an entire year he became inexplicably impotent. He blamed it on his prostrate.

Then he blamed it on an "accident" at the gym.

Trusting my husband, I didn't think anything more than what he'd told me.

Until John started telling things he'd overheard passing between Cisco and Les, all those weeks and months he'd been here at my home. Along with other rumors I'd heard from people about Les.

And the fact that since Les had left me, he'd spent an inordinate amount of time with young men...

*You know...*

Things that during our marriage he claimed always made him nervous because of his family history.

Hmmm...

*What's the old saying? Where there's smoke, there's fire? It does begin to make one wonder, doesn't it?*

Maybe he wasn't just with Hogg, Donna and Buffy.

My sons kept telling me that he was shacked up in the cabin with a young friend of theirs...

And the one thing that all the companies were emphatic about, "Turn your home into an island. If it has a hard drive in it, take a diamond drill bit to the drive and destroy it. If Cisco touched it, don't ever use it again. If it's ever been on your Wi-Fi, you need to just scrap it all and start over somewhere else."

In the end, they pulled enough electronics out of my home that it cut my electric bill in half.

Three wheelbarrows full.

We also learned that Les had contacted every contractor who worked on my home and set it up so that my three-acre lawn would be destroyed. He turned off the maintenance equipment. Sold my Koi fish out of my pond. Removed the trap from my outside drain so that it would leak.

Then popped a hole in the drain by the drive.

Thousands upon thousands of dollars of damage to my home.

All the while refusing to hand over the names of the people I needed to contact for service to repair his damages, and after removing all information about my house from the filing cabinets so that I would have no idea who to call for help, while having Cockburn haul me into court to demand the very records ThunderCunt (sorry for the C-bomb, but she's earned it) had charged tens of thousands of dollars to copy.

He even took all of my sons' files and hid them in their closets—which was what I'd been searching for the day I found Maddox's suitcase.

It was like watching someone pile every dime of money I'd ever earned onto my front lawn and set fire to it.

That was bad.

Worse? Being hauled before an arrogant ass of a judge who cursed me out and insulted me as if *I* were the problem, not the idiot and his lawyer who had started this stupidity without any warning.

*I* was the problem?

I who wanted out of this nightmare and couldn't make them stop.

*Let's hear it for modern day sexism.* 'Cause everyone knew that no man could ever act like a psychotic bitch. That no man had ever, in the entire history of humanity, ever been known to stalk and kill his family, or harass them because *he* was fucking nuts.

Men *never* killed their wives with things like Visine...

Look it up.

North Carolina. And before that, a woman had done that to her husband in South Carolina.

*Want to hear another "weird" coincidence?* When the woman killed her husband in South Carolina by poisoning him with Visine, guess who'd lived there and would have seen it on the news?

Karen Hogg.

Yeah, and those monsters had no intention of going away or leaving us alone.

I was sick of it all. I wanted Les gone. He'd tortured us for years and now, with the help of the court and his greedy hyena, he continued.

State sanctioned spouse abuse.

How was this possible?

He'd left us of his own volition, after robbing us, and was refusing to move on. My sons and I wanted all traces of him out of our lives.

And no one would help us.

Why wouldn't the judge make them go away? That was what had been so impossible to believe. There should be a limit on how long any divorce could take. Instead of a minimum time, there should be a maximum term. No divorce should ever last more than six months. This shouldn't become a shyster's full-time job to make them rich.

That was bullshit.

Nor should it be a means for an abuser to continue their abuse of their spouse with the full backing of the state courts.

It was beyond ridiculous.

In an effort to try and break their psychotic grip after they'd complained to the judge that I was the one holding things up when clearly I wasn't, I immediately called a moving company as soon as I walked out of the courtroom in August. I arranged for the company to pick up all the boxes of Les's that I'd packed in March when Les filed for divorce and deliver them to what I thought was Cockburn's office on the first available day the moving company had for the move.

Two days after the hearing.

I used the address that Cockburn, herself, had posted on her own legal website as her office.

Any normal human would assume that it was a place of business, right?

Guess again.

Half an hour after the movers left, I got a call. "Ms. Manly... we're um, standing in a yard."

"Of an office."

"No, ma'am. This is a neighborhood."

I was stunned.

Turned out, in violation of zoning ordinances for Williamson County, Cockburn was illegally running her law office out of her home in a regular subdivision.

According to our county laws, you could not have more than one business in your home (and she was running three of them) if it was in a regular neighborhood on a postage stamp lot.

Nor was she supposed to have a business where she'd regularly meet clients in her "office" like a lawyer does, nor have a "staff" that came and went unless you had more than two acres.

I knew she had a staff in violation of that law, because I'd had to pay her tens of thousands of dollars for that "staff" to duplicate papers that she later claimed in court she didn't have so that she could up her bills to get even more money from me.

I reported her violations to the county. Why wouldn't they do anything?

*Hold on...*

Let's hear it for the sick Peyton Place known as Williamson County.

This place was so backwards that you should be afraid of it. Remember, it proudly flaunted a statue of Nathan Bedford Forrest right on the side of the main interstate and in the town circle of Franklin stood another similar shrine that they were all so proud of. One that they routinely hold ceremonies and festivities around.

Nashville loved the fact that it was entrenched in backward thinking and corruption. And it had no intention of changing.

This wasn't Mayberry.

It was Amityville and the demons were swooping in for the kill. My horrors were just starting.

**W**OULD YOU BELIEVE *that Cockburn had the nerve to file a motion complaining over the fact that I had "dropped" Les's stuff in his driveway? Of course, you would. If you've been reading this far, then nothing would surprise you.*

Then again, it was *my* driveway. After all, I was the one who'd bought and paid for every bit of it. Every single inch, not the ogre who sat on my couch.

Not to mention, it used to be my office before ole Les had committed tax fraud and perjury to steal it from me.

But all that aside, I wanted to stay focused on her "perjury." Because everyone knew that it was against all law codes for an attorney to go into court and file misrepresentations of fact before a judge, right?

Apparently, Cockburn missed the night they'd taught ethics in her part-time law school. And Bitsy Dullard expected the judge who'd said, and I quote, "I don't care what the law is" to ride herd on this out-of-control, lying attorney who worked in his old law firm.

Because everyone knew that lawyers were the most ethical people around. Right up there with used car salesmen and grifters.

For the record, I had tried to take her perjury to the judge. His response?

"I refuse to hear it. I don't want to ruin a 'good' lawyer's reputation."

Seriously? He'd said that while in a separate case he was ruining a good lawyer's reputation because Dinky, with no evidence whatsoever, suspected that the lawyer had outted him for his arrest record for solicitation.

*No, I'm not making that up.*

So why then, in my case, was Bubba Dinky so worried about ruining Cockburn's reputation while he was raining down holy hell on an innocent man?

Wonder if that was special judge code for "I'm getting some on the side from this ugly slag?" *Seriously, you do have to wonder.* Because, as creative as I was (and let's face it, they pay me to be creative), I couldn't come up with any other definition for "good" that old Bubba Dinky could possibly mean. In my experience, good lawyers didn't lie, and they didn't have their clients commit perjury in open court.

Only a judge who'd once been arrested for prostitution would consider her a "good" lawyer.

Anyway, I didn't have anything dropped in the driveway.

Because Cockburn and Les had refused for months to exchange the items that I needed, such as my work PC where my latest novel was languishing, I was trying to facilitate the exchange of our belongings after she had Woodly insult me over it in open court.

I won't even begin to chronicle the insults that stupid ass leveled at me while he ran a three-ring circus in his kangaroo court. *Before you pronounce your judgement, dumbass, you might want to learn some facts*. Last I checked that was what a judge was *supposed* to do.

Just not in Williamson County, Tennessee.

*I'm not the problem here.*

Cheap 'ho and Baby Huey were the ones who wouldn't budge.

Come to find out, Dipshit wasn't even living at my stolen office (after both of them lied in court and said that he was). Only in Williamson County would they take away someone's necessary business office and give it to their spouse because it wasn't like I had, oh say, my work product and other essential work items in my office, right?

You know, the very work documents Cockburn kept hauling me into court over that most normal people kept in their office...

Such as files about their business.

I had no idea where Cockburn kept her work files (maybe in the cheap hotel she used between johns er, I mean clients), but I kept mine in my office. Since she didn't have a real office, I guess that explained why she couldn't understand where those documents were kept.

To her, office meant home. *Same thing!*

But for those of us who worked and had an office, we kept items such as our business licenses (that I didn't have access to for all those months because it was hanging on the wall of my office that they'd banned me from) at those places.

Which begged the question to Judge Stupid; what kind of family retreat had a business license hanging on the wall?

Nor would the insulting shrew who worked for the State of Tennessee send me another business license when I asked for a copy of it at the State Office.

"We already sent you one."

When I read those words in the Secretary of State's letter, I suddenly channeled my mother, "See, Terri, this is why it's illegal for brothers and sisters to marry. This is what they end up producing as offspring." Then my mother would look back at the clerk and sigh. "Tell me, because I simply must know... Is your level of stupid painful? And was it congenital or did you grow into it?"

Very few people have ever brought out my mother in me.

The vast majority of them have lived in the State of Tennessee and most of them, I met during the course of this divorce.

Or in the Manly family.

Apparently, I was the only person who'd ever needed a duplicate copy of their business license for any reason.

Who knew?

Anyway, after legally stealing my office away with a lie and perjury before the court, Les was living in Georgia. He was even paying utilities there.

This while I was stuck paying over two-thousand-two hundred dollars a month rent for Caleb's apartment in Savannah, Georgia, thanks to Les who'd bought him one of the most expensive apartments in town, while knowing he was going to divorce me and leave me holding the bag.

How stupid of me to assume that after stealing my office out from under from me and after his attorney swore in court that he was living in my office that Les would still be staying at my office forty-eight hours after the court date where he demanded the stuff I'd been trying to give him for months, and that Cockburn would not be in her "office" at one o'clock in the afternoon. How ridiculous of me to ever entertain such farfetched notions about people!

No wonder they'd called me delusional, eh?

That was what I deserved for having the moving company take the couple of dozen boxes and a few pieces of furniture to Cockburn's "office" at one in the afternoon, when any normal human would be in their law office with a secretary. After all, Cockburn had been charging for her "assistant's" time.

And I knew that I always had someone in my "office" during office hours.

*Even more stunning?*

Cockburn's neighborhood was directly across the street from our old neighborhood in Spring Hill. The same neighborhood where one of my dearest friends currently lived.

Here was proof that God truly hated Les, and of just how small the world was.

All those years he'd spent going after Dumas...

The very weekend he turned chickenshit and left because he was terrified of a deposition, guess who I'd met?

My enemy's enemy's best friend. I was at a Con where the good Lord dumped into my lap a programmer from the old fan fiction server where Dumas got her start. The same server that she'd been banned from for plagiarism all those years ago.

Just wait, it got better.

That server was pivotal in our case. See Dumas had always claimed that she'd never, ever heard of me (even though I had emails from her friends and publisher that she knew exactly who I was, and the fact that her best friend had proclaimed her an expert in my series years before her first book was published).

This person could prove what a liar Dumas was. Because she was a programmer on *that* site at the same time that Dumas had been banned. My new friend remembered all the old scandals and had all kinds of fun-filled facts, information, and most importantly, records and phone numbers. She was still in contact with people and witnesses about Dumas's bad behavior.

People who hated Dumas and who would come forward to see her burn.

More than that, she knew and remembered the fact that my fiction was the second most popular subject on *that* server at the time, and that there was no way for Dumas to be there and not know all about me. Because they all knew about me back then as I was all over that server.

Even *she* knew of me, and she doesn't read my type of fiction.

And the weekend after we met, she was going to a conference to meet up with an old enemy of Dumas's because they were still good friends.

If Les had only waited one more week to leave...

What a fucking moron.

And my new friend lived in the same neighborhood as his attorney.

Oh, the irony of *that*.

It was a small world, after all.

I mean, really, what were the odds?

Only my luck would be that screwed up.

So, I closed my jaw and listened to the movers. "What do you mean, no one's home?"

"There's nobody here. What do you want us to do?"

Given how much they were charging by the hour, I didn't want them to wait.

"Fine, take it to my ex's." I gave them his address, which was less than a mile away from Cockburn's "office," and his phone number.

Five minutes later, they called back. "He's not here. No one's answering the number."

"Are you kidding me?"

"No."

I groaned. "Open the gate and take it up to the porch."

Those were my instructions to them. I didn't tell them to "dump *it* in the driveway," as Cockburn had lied.

Whether they did that or not, I don't know as I was banned from the cabin and couldn't legally oversee what they did with the stuff Cockburn and Les claimed he had to have and that I was "holding up" from being delivered to him. I have multiple witnesses who will verify that I'd told them how to manually open the gate and get up to the porch of the cabin to put the boxes and furniture in a safe place.

According to Cockburn, the major liar who had yet to tell a single truth in the case, they dumped it all in the driveway. Although, I find that hard to believe as I have never known a moving company to do something like that when they could get sued for it.

And why would she start telling the truth now when everything else out of her mouth had been a lie?

Face it, my favorite lie to date, outside of the witchcraft was that I threw all of Les's belongings onto the lawn and he had to get a metal detector to find it all.

Seriously?

How stupid was Marshmallow Brain? I lived in an HOA neighborhood. That HOA would have fined me had I done something *that* stupid.

Better yet, when I told my sons about it, they asked the intelligent, logical question that none of the idiot judges thought to ask.

"Where did Dad get a metal detector?"

We don't own one and Les was too lazy to rent one, not that there was any place in town that rented such an item. Hell, I don't even know where you'd go to buy one. It would take a few days to get one here, and by then, I'd have been back from Biloxi.

Not to mention, where was his receipt and photos of everything on my lawn? He so loved to photograph everything, such as weird chemical bottles in his hands that I hadn't known we had.

Or him and Cisco rifling through my storage unit to get boxes and files that Cockburn kept saying he didn't have when I'd told them that I couldn't locate those items because he'd already stolen them.

As the photo above clearly showed, Les had possession of all my "contract" files and all the other items that they kept hauling me into court over with contempt motions by claiming that I was withholding them (as a side note, he returned that tag to me months later as he took it with him during his pillaging). Meanwhile none of the fucking judges would look at the photographic evidence that proved Les had the files or consider the fact that they had banned me from my office where the files were kept.

The facts couldn't be argued. That was ole Les's body parts in the photos.

Somehow, the moron judges believed that I could shit my files out my ass and make them appear out of thin air. I guess they'd bought into old Cockburn's lies that I was a witch who had the magical powers to make things manifest at will.

Hmmm...

Yeah, we had some seriously dim bulbs on our trees around here. And rather than clip them back so that something good could grow, we gave them robes and put them on our benches to preside as judges.

Anyway, Les had sworn he was living at the cabin. He wasn't supposed to be paying for a caretaker in my office. Shame on the judges for depriving me of my workspace and costing me thousands of dollars because they refused to believe that a woman in the Twenty-First Century could have a business and an office outside of her home.

But old Cockburn and Dipshit weren't through messing with my business and interfering with my life.

Cockburn had a paying, idiot client, and she was milking him for everything she could. Ethics, common decency, and rules of conduct be damned.

**D**RAGONCON FELL EVERY YEAR during Labor Day weekend. I'd never realized how much stress and misery Les had put on me until the first year we did it without him being there. Damn.

Twenty-seven years of complete and utter hell because of one selfish bastard.

It was amazing how much agony and stress we put ourselves through without realizing it.

Of course, I'd had no choice.

With pedophile in-laws, I'd been trapped.

But for the first time since before I was married, I was able to take a deep, miraculous breath and enjoy it. There was no psycho Kiki acting like an out-of-control, pouty bitch who was afraid my fans were giving her "cursed" amulets to hex her so that they could take her job from her (wish I were making that up).

No booth drama from Cisco throwing his tantrums and bitching about my readers because he didn't want to do his job and sell items to them or answer any of what he called "petty and annoying" questions about the books he refused to read.

Why wouldn't he read them? "In case I don't like them. I'd hate to have to give you my completely honest opinion of your work."

Too bad I'd never given him my completely honest opinion of his.

No Peyton complaining about my son Caleb or making snide comments about Nick or Maddox, while shit-talking Cisco, Caleb and Les behind their backs, either.

None of them handing out all my inventory "for free" because they didn't want to pack it up.

"That's the point of the booth," Cisco had said on more than one occasion. "To do promo, not sell."

No, Dipshit, the point was to try and break even so that we could afford the event.

And this was what Les had wanted to replace me with? Idiots who understood nothing about how my business worked or what we were there to accomplish.

Said it all about his business acumen and how he'd contributed to my success.

*Not at all.*

I couldn't believe how calm and smooth everything went with a mature, adult team that actually worked together to provide service to my readers.

What a novel concept!

As usual, my publisher used the party at DragonCon to launch my latest release. Everything seemed to be going well.

Until those peculiar attacks against my books and me personally began on social media.

How ironic that they accused me of "cutting and pasting" when they were all "cutting and pasting" the same exact complaints everywhere.

Don't get me wrong, it wasn't the first time my books or I had been attacked. Or even attacked with something outlandish.

In fact, since ole Hogg had come sniffing around my husband's truffles, a lot of "weird" things had happened.

*Let me explain.*

Back in 2013, not long before the Whore-Hound had shown up, I'd published the book in my Night-Seekers series that was the twin brother to one of my most popular books that had come out a couple of years before then.

It took off like a rocket and the fans were giddy. However, since the books were about twin brothers, that meant that I basically rewrote Book One with a few added scenes and more dialogue from the twin's perspective. After all, being identical twins, the two characters had shared a common life, and a lot of the scenes had to be redundant, with the only changes being that the scenes were now told from the twin brother's point of view.

The thing about having a rabid fan base was that they knew every nuance of every character. If you so much as changed a single comma, then they began to have conspiracy theories as to why.

"Why do you think the comma was there in this book and then moved in the later one? It has to be important! Otherwise, she wouldn't have done it!"

"Why did character X have a conversation with character B in this book, and then when they have the same conversation in another book, she changed it? Did she forget what they said to each other?"

Fans would eat you alive if you changed one single thing (or if a copy editor changed it because s/he didn't realize that there had been a previous book you'd pulled that conversation out of, and you didn't realize they'd tampered with it on the edits). So, I meticulously made sure that when I wrote that second book nothing was "tampered" with.

Except for one thing...

Because the book was well over one thousand pages in length (the size of four full length novels, and then some), and my publisher was already squeamish over the production costs, I removed a scene to make room for more "fresh" and original content.

I didn't think that scene was necessary. It was the brother's wedding where the twin wasn't there for long. He basically walked a bridesmaid down the aisle and didn't really hang around once the reception began. He went in, did his job and left as soon as he could. We'd already read that scene in the previous book, so who would care if we skipped it in such a large tome so that I could put in new material?

Boy, did I ever miscalculate my readers' reactions.

I and my team had spent countless hours answering those emails over the years to say why I didn't add one more scene to that already incredibly long book.

*Live and learn, right?*

That was what I thought.

So, when I was writing my next novel that had a character who was traveling through multiple books in the same manner, I made sure to grab every single scene, and all dialogue so that no fan would be upset that I'd left something out about that particular character from a previous book.

*Leave no scene behind* had become my mantra. Because my staff had threatened my life if they had to answer any more emails about why a scene hadn't been included or if they had to say that, "yes, Terri knew about that particular scene when she wrote the current novel, X, but due to the length of the book and the fact that it'd been covered previously in the prior novel, Terri chose not to include it in the character's main book. We're so sorry that it distressed you."

That was August 2016.

The Hogg was in the house.

And a lot of interesting things had happened around this time, so please bear with me as I set this little nugget up.

To fully understand it all, we had to go back to the beginning of 2016 when Les, against my will, talked me into filing suit against Dumas. I had warned Dipshit and crew that they didn't want any part of this nasty bitch they were about to piss off.

For one thing, I'd had years of showing up to interviews where, swear to God on a bible, reporters had said to me, "oh thank God, you're not that bitch. That's right, you write the *other* Seeker series."

Literally, I have witnesses to this being said to me, on more than one occasion.

Likewise, Dumas had been handed awards with the name of my series on them and had to have people correct it. To this day, I have YouTube videos of other authors who knew better, on panels with me, calling my series by the name of hers. Hell, for that matter, a few weeks ago, I was in a sales meeting with my own Night-Seeker publisher who accidentally said the name of her series during our sales meeting for my Night-Seeker books.

And it wasn't the only time.

They'd done it before and after, and half the times they hadn't even realized it.

For that matter, everyone, except me, had made that mistake at some point, even my own lawyers in the middle of my lawsuit against her. It wasn't helped by the fact that she inserted the name of my series in front of hers as an indicator for the bad guys in her series just to be a cute little contrary bitch after my lawyers (and my publisher she currently wrote for) told her that she couldn't use my series name.

Or for that matter that her series name was taken from the name of one of my major characters that had been long established before she ever published her first novel (or got out of grade school).

So how they could make any kind of real argument that there was no confusion whatsoever between our series was absolute legal bullshit and nonsense that would never hold water with anyone who had an IQ above five.

Which meant that all judges were too fucking stupid to get it.

In fact, one of my attorneys, who was now a federal judge, was having dinner with a colleague and the colleague made the offhand comment, "Well it's not like Dumas called them the Night Ghoul-Seekers."

"Actually, she did do that, too."

Swear to God, she inserted my series name in front of her series to turn them into villains.

"Oh shit! How stupid is she?" said the lawyer.

*I'll leave that for you to figure out.*

Anyway, you could get away with a lot when your own publisher knowingly hired a fan fiction writer to steal your Young Adult series out from under you. And rubbed your nose in it, especially when their higher ups had threatened you and your career if you didn't sit down and take the fact that they intended to screw you if you breathed a word of what they'd done to you.

*Thank you, Sid & Shyster.*

And every bestselling author, or any writer who had ever created their own unique premise, needed to live in absolute terror of what they'd done to me.

The worst? They had taught New York publishers how to legally tear a #1 bestselling series out of the hands of the #1 *New York Times* bestselling author who'd created it and get away with it.

As Les had so often repeated in our house, "I have learned how to legally steal a series out from under the author. Now I know how to make millions."

*God help us all.*

Unlike Les and the team he'd hired, I'd read Sun Tzu, and I knew that something was weird about Dumas from the get-go.

She was too in the shadows and had too long and dark a history of screwing people over.

Royally, and was too good at it.

Not to mention her past had been meticulously whitewashed once she had her dubious contract in hand. And I don't mean a little. Professionally done. Clinically done. In a way that the average person couldn't do.

Scrubbed in a way that a politician would do, and that took a lot of money. Something the average author, especially a young, brand new one, wouldn't have a clue about. Something a new author would *never* know how to do.

Never mind the fact that publishers, as a rule, refused to take on authors who had a well-known plagiarism scandal in their background. That normally sent them skittering into the hills as most publishers never wanted to be sued.

In all the decades I'd been in publishing, I'd never known of a publisher who would willingly go near an author like that.

Never mind indemnify an author with such a background. They typically threw us under a bus, because we were a dime a dozen to them.

For every author out there, there were ten thousand more waiting in the wings, willing to cut the throat of whatever author was on the list to take their place and write the next book at one-hundredth of the price that author was being paid just to have a shot at the title.

And every publisher and editor were more than aware of that fact and used it to their advantage.

So, their uncharacteristic relationship set off every red flag in my head.

Which was what I'd warned all of them about. "Find out who she is and who she's related to. No one has a movie flop as badly as hers did and then comes back with a TV series, unless they're related to someone extremely important and is loaded for bear." Unlike the Confederacy of Dullards that Les had surrounded himself with, I knew better than to go up against someone like that. It was why I'd left another extremely well-known plagiarist of mine alone.

You couldn't win against that kind of money, and everyone knew it.

Except for unscrupulous lawyers who were too willing to screw their clients for profit.

If you had no money, you had no case.

If you had a lot of money, you had a case until they'd sucked every dime out, and then it was time to settle.

*Everyone* knew this.

Except Les who was an attorney.

They assured me that I had to "stand up" for my rights, or else I wouldn't have been able to use my trademarked series name for the TV and movies that we were getting ready to go into production on.

"I've seen it happen a hundred times," the lawyers had said. "Because Dumas has changed the name of her series, you're screwed. She can come back on you later and block you from using your series name, even though you wrote it years before she did and were a number one bestseller before her first book came out."

Well, that was my luck. And that was the consensus from everyone I talked to, and from every law book I read.

If we didn't go to court now, we'd be in court once my series came out, and then I'd be the one having to defend my pre-existing rights to use my series name from the thief who had knowingly violated all my rights to my trademarked series because they had bullishly gone ahead and used it, even after I'd taken all legal actions to block them that I could.

How was *that* for our legal system?

"People think better of you when you're the plaintiff."

Another lie they'd fed me, especially given that no one knew how rich Dumas actually was. Or the fact that she'd spent years lying to her own fans. She was a spoiled bully whose entire background was littered with all the people she'd ruined, and she was very proud of that.

You had to love this business.

Anyway, they had bullied me into their lawsuit, and I was sicker than I'd ever been in my life.

No sooner was it filed, than I'd learned that my attorneys, naturally, had lied to me every step of the way.

"We're going to come out swinging and hit them hard! Don't worry, Terri. We have a PR firm who will help with any negative media that comes up!"

They didn't.

"Oh, I'm sorry, Terri. I didn't realize that my firm doesn't do that. We don't have *any* PR people."

*Are you kidding me?* What kind of high-profile law firm in Nashville didn't have anyone to deal with the media for their cases and clients?

Not only that, but none of them had listened to me. Les had hired Hogg to be his "legal" assistant for our all-important case.

Why? I was the one who had tutored Lord Dumbfuck through all his legal classes in law school. I was the one who had prepped him for suits and had helped him write briefs for years.

Hogg was qualified to pick out cheeseburgers and low rent clothing.

She was a bad tutor who couldn't properly punctuate a sentence. The ever-fatuous Hogg was barely literate. Remember that this was the moron who'd failed my child's high school English paper online after Les left, and who could never submit the correct paperwork for my children in their classes.

Nor did she get their papers in on time.

At fifty, she lived with her parents, had been thrown out of multiple congregations, and her only other means of gainful employment?

Working part-time at a retail store.

The same job I'd had in high school.

Only then, I'd been an assistant manager. So, as a teen, I'd been more accomplished than Hogg had managed in her entire lifetime.

What was Hogg's biggest accomplishment in life?

Other than sabotaging the futures of innocent children?

Talking another underachieving, low-functioning troglodyte into believing that she had a brain in her head. That *she*, who had barely eked by and graduated summa cum nothing at a state university with no more credentials than the state school Les had garnered his bachelors from was somehow more accomplished than a man with a law degree.

But then when you graduated at the bottom of your law class and refused to work at all, I guess you believed an out-of-work retail clerk who was employed as a part-time tutor belittling children who had been run out of multiple churches on a rail, was much more accomplished than you.

And that she was worth throwing away your entire family and life for.

Why not?

We all needed change. I guess Les had figured that it was time he earned the name his mother had given him, and a major step down in lifestyle was what was in order.

Who didn't dream of plunging themselves into an abyss?

*Oh wait, everyone.*

In the end, I supposed it was true what they said; like attracted like, and these two losers had bonded together over their mutual disdain of me and my children. Because we were what they could never be.

Intelligent.

With goals and futures, they could only dream of having.

After all, I had single-handedly built my career long before Hogg had slithered near my home. So why not hire this incompetent imbecile with a massive superiority complex, and who was incapable of following directions to anything, to write the complicated legal briefs for his major lawsuit regarding my worlds that Les had never bothered to read?

I mean really? Who would know my worlds and characters better than I would?

Obviously, the magic Hogg who had somehow consumed them by osmosis simply by being in my home!

So, all my examples for the case and suggestions about it were thrown out and Hogg's were used instead.

Les had hired her to the tune of sixty dollars an hour to "know" my series better than I.

I tried to warn them all. I told them what to use. They didn't listen.

When the suit was filed, I was publicly barbecued as I'd predicted. Really, my name should be Cassandra. Just like the Geek princess, no one listened to me.

There's nothing like a public roast. But then I'm used to it. I grew up in a family where that was their favorite sport.

Even better, the attorney Les had actually hired didn't put his own name on the case, for whatever reason.

So instead of it being a full partner and a major trademark attorney name that was well known in the business, it looked like Les had gone out and hired a newbie, which I have the bill and emails to prove he didn't do.

Thank you, Les, for that, too.

Les, however, was horrified, especially over the fact that I kept getting called crazy in the media. "How can they say that about you?" He sent tons of emails out to our counsel. "Terri's not crazy. These are her worlds. It's all *her* hard work! She did it all on her own! Why is it that any time a woman tries to stick up for herself or her work, her opponents call her crazy?"

*Remember that line from ole Les.* I had it in writing from him, over and over again, and it was important as he, too, began that litany for me the moment he left my home.

*Can we say hypocrite?*

Or a man who was trying to convince the world his wife was crazy so that when she told the world that he'd tried to kill her and their son, no one would believe her.

Exactly.

Anyway, Les was livid at the way I'd been hung out to dry by the attorneys he'd hand-selected.

And I was heading into a major event at Pensacola on the heels of being publicly shamed.

*Go me!*

On the way to PensaCon, I broke one of my teeth on a yeast roll in the airport.

Yeah, I really did.

Now many people might have used that as an easy excuse to cancel the whole event and stay home. But I wasn't about to let my fans down for one minute. Some had bought tickets just to meet me, and for no other reason. Not to mention, I wasn't about to let the rumor grist mill think that I was afraid to be seen in public after the lawsuit had been filed. I wasn't the one in the wrong, and I had nothing to hide.

However, my tooth didn't care. It was killing me.

Kiki went with me for the trip, along with Les and two of my sons.

I'd also invited Joan who was driving over from Georgia, because I wanted every piece of support I could get. Given the online hostile attacks, I had no idea what I was about to walk into there, and I wanted to be prepared for the worst.

Kiki was acting weird, even for Kiki. You had to remember that she was a nut job on her best day. She lived in a trailer in Hickville, Tennessee County where she mocked every person there, especially the polka dot trailer of her crazy neighbor. Apparently, she had no lawn of any kind because the first time her daughter had seen mine, she'd wanted to know what the "green stuff" was in front of my house.

"Honey, it's called grass," Kiki had told her teenager.

True story.

Anyway, Kiki was always a little touched in the head. Convinced that everyone was out to get her and so jealous of her and her life that they even hexed her for it. She was so paranoid about that, that she often called in Teresa Richards who went by the name Sister Teresa, Spiritual Warrior, to "cleanse" items that Kiki swore were cursed.

Teresa had also been to Kiki's trailer a couple of times because Kiki's youngest daughter had a demon in the trailer that was out to get her, too.

Her older daughter and niece had also brought a demon home from some old house they'd once visited.

And my favorite story was the time at San Diego Comic Con when I took Teresa with us to help keep Kiki calm. The entire time we were there, Kiki swore that an alien demon from outer space was stalking her in the booth and kept coming by to glare at her. Even better, she came back from lunch, terrified because she'd seen a group promoting the upcoming show, *Damien*. They'd been in the street, chanting and singing.

"They opened up a portal to hell, Terri! Demons have come out now! You can *feel* it! The whole atmosphere of the convention has changed! Now everyone's so mean! Even the nice women at the Snoopy booth have changed!"

Needless to say, Kiki was all kinds of drama, all times of day.

But much of it was entertaining. Especially when she started seeing her demons everywhere.

Although one of those times caused her to come flying into my bed at DragonCon, because she was too afraid to sleep by herself in her room.

"Teresa let loose demons! I saw her! I have the gift from the Lord!"

I put her on the pull-out couch in my room with a Disney movie playing in the background, to calm her down.

Which was why I didn't pay attention to her acting like a nervous Chihuahua on caffeine while we were in Pensacola. I figured she'd gone back onto her fen-phen or whatever other weight loss drug du jour she'd had her doctor prescribe for her that always turned her into a jittery, screaming bitch.

She kept complaining about Joan coming in for the trip. Kiki could never stand the thought of anyone else around because of her paranoia.

G2 (name replaced to protect the guilty) was one in particular who'd always driven her crazy whenever she'd shown up because they not only looked alike, but their names were also similar enough that people confused them. "I don't need anyone thinking she's your assistant when I'm your assistant and getting us confused. I'm your assistant and that's all they need to know. G2 doesn't need to be thinking she's ever going to be your assistant. You need to make sure she knows that *I'm* your only assistant, and make sure that she doesn't come around the booth and hang out. No one needs to be confused!"

I really didn't care. I basically ignored Kiki's tantrums because they were as regular as Les's PMS. You could practically time them.

But once Joan got there, Kiki became even loopier than normal. "Terri's on drugs. Watch her!"

Joan knew it was utter bullshit.

I seldom took Tylenol even when I had a cluster migraine. I grew up in a house with a grandmother who'd treated everything with ice or heat.

And a mother who was infamous for her prescription med addiction. Having been there when she overdosed and almost died, I wasn't real keen on meds of any kind. The only thing I took regularly was my blood pressure medication, and I was bad to forget about it, too.

My poor doctor was forever reading me the riot act for the fact that I wouldn't stay on anything she prescribed for me.

If I took it at all. I seldom even filled the prescriptions I was given.

Still, Kiki tried to convince Joan that I was an addict. She took her into the bedroom where I was staying with Les and opened the drawer to my dresser. "Look at all those pills she's on."

Joan rolled her eyes. "They're vitamins."

Most of what was in the drawer were Les's prescriptions.

Still, all weekend, Kiki kept telling Joan to watch me. "Look how loopy she is. She can barely stand."

Yes, I was, but not from anything *I* was taking.

At least, not knowingly taking. In fact, Alec Vangelo, the guy who'd brought me in to sign at his booth, had to send his people out to get me Tylenol and Ambesol for my broken tooth because I didn't have anything for the pain.

That was how much of a "druggie" I was.

Throughout the entire weekend, I took less than six of those Tylenol.

But the real question was: why was Kiki so interested in promoting Les's agenda where I was concerned? Why was she trying so hard to convince Joan that I was on drugs when I clearly wasn't?

More than that...

Kiki started talking to Joan about fan complaints that I was "copying and pasting" books.

*Beg pardon?*

At that point in my career, I'd published over a hundred stories in multiple number one bestselling series.

For decades.

Some of my fans had been reading me for over twenty years. I was extremely active with my fans and in all that time, no one had *ever* once leveled that accusation at me.

Never.

As I'd said, the worst mistake I had made at that point in my career was not including a previously published scene from a book three years earlier. Hundreds of fans had complained that I had left it out.

However, while going through internet blogs, Hogg and Les had discovered a complaint from the fans of Dumas's that she had "cut and pasted" passages from her works into other stories.

"Damn! How bad a plagiarist is she that she has to copy and paste her own material?" Les had made that comment at least once a day.

Now Kiki was echoing it, only she was applying it to me when no one else had ever made it before.

Ever.

Hmmm...

Kiki made it for the first time ever at PensaCon.

Then it suddenly manifested through my fans in August 2018.

While Kiki liked to pretend that she was psychic and could see "demons" because she was "right with the Lord," as she'd often alleged. She was not. And while I'd seen her and Sister Teresa do a blood spell together in my cabin while I was trying to work (the stench of it all was repulsive), I had no faith in her psychic abilities.

Mostly because she was full of shit.

On all accounts.

But how very strange that suddenly I was being attacked out of the blue for something that I'd never been attacked over in my entire career.

Something that Kiki had "somehow" predicted that I would be attacked over six months prior to it happening...

*Yeah, right.*

Which meant that either Kiki or Hogg was behind it.

Only I didn't know that at the time.

Because of the lawsuit and Les's daily rants, I'd naturally assumed the attacks were spawned by our opposition. Who wouldn't?

My editor, Phyllis Waterford, who had been with me since before my youngest son was born was as baffled as I was. "In all the years I've been doing this, I've never seen an author get attacked like this and have an allegation made of this nature."

Remember that she'd been editing my books where I'd been implementing the same technique of using scenes from previous books to show different character perspectives for decades. I wasn't the only author to do this.

Most TV shows and serial movies had done it, too.

"Cutting and pasting" was a term that Hogg liked to use. It was what Hogg liked to do.

And after that, each of my books was attacked more and more viciously with the same exact "cut and pasted" complaints, until my publisher canceled one of my bestselling series, right in the middle of it.

Because of those well-orchestrated attacks.

That cancellation also came after my editor was sent to my house to spend time with me, to "see" what was going on there. After she had spent time with Les and Hogg...

My editor, who had been hugging me like a sister only a few months before she came to my home for that landmark visit, hadn't spoken to me since.

The one and only time she was going to, she took one look at Hogg and ran the other way in the hotel lobby, then canceled our dinner via text.

One can only speculate as to why.

But in August 2018, the lawsuit was over. While Dumas had lost in the end, she had no reason to come after me to attack my books, and every reason, including a court order, to stay away from them.

So, the new attacks on my latest release made no sense.

And it wasn't more of what had, ironically, become "cut and pasted" allegations that I was "cutting and pasting" scenes from previous books that they were making against me that August. There was something new.

Something unprecedented.

For this release, my publisher had decided to have me autograph over fourteen *thousand* copies of the book.

Let me repeat that.

My publisher had decided to have me autograph over fourteen *thousand* copies of the book.

This was important because I want you, as a reader, to imagine how many books that would be in your mind. And remember that the book that I published at that time was the size of four and a half regular novels. It wasn't the standard three hundred pages.

So, fourteen thousand copies would weigh as much as fifty-six *thousand* copies.

That book was so thick that only twelve copies fit per shipping carton, as opposed to the standard thirty copies of a book per carton. So, imagine that if they had attempted to ship *one-thousand-one-hundred-and-sixty-six cartons* of books to my home.

Where would I have put them?

Could you imagine the cost of all that shipping of books from New York to my house and back again?

This was crucial.

Because I was barbecued and fileted for the fact that I hadn't personally gone through *one-thousand-one-hundred-and-sixty-six cartons* and written inside the individual pages of each and every book.

*Thanks to Hogg.*

And I had the emails from her to the fans to prove that *she* orchestrated those attacks against me.

Not to mention, live witnesses who had since come forward, wanting to testify against her.

At no time had I ever told my fans that my publisher was shipping all those books to my home as it would have been logistically impossible to do such a thing.

I'd still, to this day, be opening all those boxes and signing all those books.

When Hogg lied to my fans about it, she knew it was logistically and financially impossible to ship that many copies to my home. Even with a regular-sized release, it still would have been over *seven hundred boxes* of books.

That would have been a lot of boxes to store in someone's home. Anyone who had ever moved would know how hard it was to walk around a large number of boxes that were in the middle of a room.

Never mind thousands upon thousands of them.

Whenever a publisher chose to do a promotion of this nature, they mailed to the author what were called "tip-ins." It was the title page of the book only, and then after it was signed, that page was inserted into the book and bound with the other pages.

Anyone who had ever watched a YouTube video of Brandon Sanderson had seen Brandon signing these sheets while he was interviewed. He and other authors did them all the time.

That was the typical promotion that I, and hundreds of other authors had done, all throughout our careers. It wasn't the first time I'd done one. Hogg had been here in my home when I'd done them in the past.

Even when I'd done tip-in signings, I would still get a few dozen boxes that my family would have to trip over for the couple of months that it would take me to sign them all. And Les would bitch and moan the entire time they were in the house.

This time, while I was signing them and since I wasn't doing it to the cadence of Les's whining complaints, I was happy and thought, "hey! You know what would be fun? I'll add something neat for the fans!"

Because I was thinking about the book and the characters and not listening to Les bitch about all the boxes and why it was taking me so long to sign that many tip-ins, I was hearing the characters talk to me while I signed. So, I thought that I'd add fun tidbits about the upcoming books to some of the pages as I signed them. Just random one-liners. That way, when a fan got one of the pages where I'd added a "clue," they could share it on my Facebook page for the other fans and use it as a way to come together as a community.

It was meant to be a delightful egg hunt. So, every few dozen pages, I'd add a random clue about a favorite character or a scene from an upcoming book.

I posted what I'd done on Facebook and in my newsletter to the fans to let them know to look for them in my August/September release. My intent was to make the fans happy and to help them befriend each other.

I forgot what a menacing, shit-stirring whore Hogg was. Since I don't maliciously twist people's good intentions or words around to harm others, I forgot about those malcontents who were only happy when they made others miserable.

The people in the world who live to turn others love for someone into cold-blooded hatred. For no other reason than they were miserable people, living miserable lives.

Suddenly, I was being lambasted by some of my biggest fans who were claiming that I'd said I'd be making "notes in the margins of the books," and that "I always lied to my fans."

*After all, Dumas had written in the margins of her books, why couldn't I?*

*What the effing hell?*

First, that was a total lie. Dumas had made notes that were in the entire manuscript and printed with every single copy as part of the print run. It was nothing like what I'd done when I hand signed the individual pages.

But for some reason, we couldn't get that across to the fans. They refused to listen to any explanation.

Someone was maliciously turning my fanbase into an attack mob.

Stunned to the core of my soul, I couldn't believe how vicious my devoted "fans" had become over something meant to make them happy. The rancor was unlike anything I'd ever encountered in my life.

My biggest fans now hated me.

For nothing.

No matter what we said or did as an apology, the attacks only worsened.

Since there was nothing we could say or do to placate them and our apologies and explanations only worsened the attacks, I finally told my crew to ignore them.

*If you don't feed a fire, it will burn out.* And the last thing I wanted my staff to do was hurt the feelings of any fan or reader.

Besides, we had New York Comic Con to focus on.

Which ended up being very interesting, indeed, as my old publisher, Sid & Shyster turned their entire booth around that year so that they gave a big blank white wall to us.

It had no ads on it, whatsoever. It was just one giant white wall.

Like a big white flag of surrender.

Funny, eh?

I thought so.

Especially since the year before they had been facing us with Dumas's books in my face while they smirked.

In 2018 after she'd surrendered the suit, they weren't flaunting anything. I think that said it all about what they'd done.

Anyway, while in New York, I learned a few more interesting things. One was from an old booth worker and fan, Julie. Aside from remembering Kiki's and Teresa's lunatic battle with alien demons that one particular year at Comic Con in San Diego, she also let me know how backbiting Kiki had been long before she quit, and how much she'd been violating her Non-Disclosure ever since.

Not that I was surprised. I knew exactly what a little troublemaker Kiki was. After all, causing drama in her hick town was what she lived for. And I'd seen her turn on everyone, even her own sister. Oh, the snotty stories I could tell Bethany about what Kiki really thought of her when she wasn't around. She'd always been so jealous of her little sister who was doted on by their parents. Not to mention the fact that her sister was so much prettier, smarter, and far more popular.

More accomplished.

And Kiki was well aware of that fact.

Kiki even preferred Bethany's daughter over her own daughters and made no bones about it to anyone. "Casey should have been *my* daughter. She's so much smarter than my girls! She's just like me and has nothing in common with Bethany. Bethany doesn't deserve her!"

There was a reason when Kiki had wanted Bethany to come work the booth in San Diego with us that I was aghast.

"It's for a full week, Kiki."

"I know."

"You're going to be with your sister, in a room, alone, for a full week."

"I'll be okay."

Really? Because the way she talked shit about her sister and how much she hated her, I really found that hard to believe. I expected an all-out bloodbath to ensue. But then Kiki backbit everyone when they weren't around. And even though she'd never wanted to work the booth and would only play on her phone while she was in it, she'd kicked out all my other workers whenever she felt they were threatening her position.

So, I figured since she hadn't kicked her sister out of the family, maybe we should give her a shot.

That hadn't lasted either. She could only suffer her sister a couple of trips before Kiki kicked her out of the booth, too.

As I said, Kiki never could stand anyone for long.

And Julie wasn't the only one tattling on Kiki, either.

Another longtime fan of mine whom we'll call Joslyn Marko, who used to attend my fan events and other conferences with me, told me all about how Kiki had been acting right before she left.

"If anyone complimented you or your books, she'd roll her eyes behind your back." Then Joslyn leaned in closer. "She's also been telling everyone you're a witch, and she's not the only one spreading that shit, either."

Come to find out, G1 and G2, both of whom were assistants for another urban fantasy author, were lying their asses off as my brother had forewarned. This after they'd given me a "charged" crystal from the author they worked for to "protect" me.

It made me wonder what lies they told about the author they worked for while they were on one of their legendary drunken binges at author events. *Honey, watch your back. Those two are never sober after hours. Have you seen how much alcohol they consume?*

It was frightening.

All they'd ever done was pretend to know information they didn't and talk about how so-and-so's career was tanking.

Not just about me. Ask them about Lolly M. Holly. Another popular author who was on panels with us. They lied about her, too. I can't count how many times I'd heard those lies myself fall from their treacherous lips.

Just as they were always talking about how my brother's baby mama abused her daughter and slept with every guy she came near.

They were the ones who'd told me that Baby Mama Drama had sex with my brother two hours after she'd met him. And that the reason it'd taken two hours?

He was hungry and had to eat first.

They were also the ones who'd told me about Baby Mama's sex tapes that she'd made while driving down the highway.

Indeed, according to them, she was not the saintly Christian virgin she portrayed herself to be to the world. If even one tenth of what they'd told me was true, then I was amazed BMD didn't burst into flames whenever she touched a bible. Never mind entered a church.

The one thing they said that I knew to be truth was that BMD had weaponized her daughter to use her against my brother and to control him.

There was something profoundly wrong with our court system that allowed our children to be preyed upon. Honestly, we didn't need lawyers for judges. We needed psychologists.

And we needed a panel of them.

Get those imbeciles off the benches. Was it any wonder why crime was out of control?

Thomas More had it right.

"For if you suffer your people to be ill-educated, and their manners to be corrupted from their infancy, and then punish them for those crimes to which their first education disposed them, what else is to be concluded from this, but that you first make thieves and then punish them."

We needed a court of common sense.

Not the idiots on parade that we currently had populating the kangaroo courts of America.

Absolute power corrupted absolutely. We all know this adage. And in American courts, the judge reigned as a king and executioner.

Topple the kingdom. The day had come. There should never again be a single judge presiding over another human being's life with no one overseeing them. Most of them are incapable of handling the responsibility of it.

They were too busy worrying about their tee times (and yes, I had that on a transcript, too, which had caused me to get screwed in the first hearing). My judge was so worried about getting to the golf course that he hadn't taken time to review evidence or listen to any argument.

He just wanted to get out of there, so he made a snap judgement based on his own stupidity and misconceptions that ruined the lives and futures of three innocent young men.

Woodly should be forced to pay back every single dollar he allowed to be stolen from them because of his own selfishness and the fact that he refused to believe a man could and would steal from his children.

Like that had never happened before.

*You fucking idiot.*

Over and over, judges have shown themselves to be incapable of handling the responsibility of their jobs.

It was time for us to take back our authority and say, "No more!"

As American citizens, we needed to stop their gross injustice and incompetence. I doubted if there was a single family left in this country who hadn't been touched by their corruption. I have yet to speak to anyone who hasn't had at least one horror story, or many more, of a judge who had done them or one of their family member's wrong.

No matter their social standing. No matter their race, religion or sexual orientation.

Everyone had been bitten by the injustice of America. By the brutality of our fucked-up court system that preyed on every last one of us.

Yet no one had attempted to do anything.

How was this possible?

What country did we live in that we were all so afraid? So beaten down by these monsters who had taken over our lives and who stole billions of dollars a year from American citizens?

Why have we taken it all this time?

*Speak up, America!*

Nothing had changed since Salem or McCarthy.

Except to worsen!

Whenever I'd been forced to sit in that courtroom, which had been roughly every five to ten months, weeks, days? for the last two years, I wasn't able to believe what I'd seen and heard. Not just in my case, but the other families who were being torn apart by these greedy animals.

For no other reason than to line their pockets with *our* money.

It saddened me that we were sending our beautiful sons and daughters into war to defend an ideal that no longer existed.

We didn't have a single king or queen.

We had hundreds of thousands of them, presiding in these kangaroo courts all throughout America that they'd turned into their private hell kingdoms, who could haul us in at a moment's notice and tear down our lives.

Destroy the lives of our children.

Strip us of our freedom and rights and throw us into jail for no other reason than breathing too loudly in front of them.

Seriously.

*Please, pay heed, and take notice.*

I never thought this would have been my life. Not after I'd spent the entirety of it never breaking rules, never getting into any kind of trouble.

Yet everything I had worked for, that I had saved for and set aside for my sons, was destroyed by these unconscionable thieves we'd elected.

Not in the White House or congress.

In our own backyards!

*Wake up, America!*

Today it was me they were brutalizing and terrorizing. But don't think for one moment that tomorrow, it couldn't be you. Your children. Your parents.

Your loved ones.

Don't think for one instant that *you* are immune. Whether you are male or female. No matter what religion, race or station you come from.

*Injustice stalks us all. Without mercy.*

Indiscriminately.

If you thought that I was kidding, then please, take one day of your life and sit in your local family court to listen and observe the nightmare for yourself. You would be appalled at the routine injustice taking place there.

Every time I stepped foot into court, it wasn't only my case that horrified me.

It was everyone's.

My brother's. My cousin's.

Those of the strangers who came and went, pleading for help, who were mocked by those crows on the bench who preyed on them and tore apart their lives, without any care or regard.

The more I heard, the more nightmares I had.

Because I didn't understand how these people hadn't been struck by lightning when they spoke.

Since the moment this had started and I'd been faced with the horrific hypocrisy of them, I'd struggled hard with my faith. It had taken everything I had to hold on to it.

Over and over, I heard my grandfather's voice in my head. "Without doubt, there can be no faith."

But it was so hard. Especially when I saw a lying hypocrite like Kiki MacDavid conduct an actual blood spell with another woman in front of me, along with other "spells" and curses that she'd done to other people, and then have her turn around and accuse me of witchcraft. To have a modern-day attorney such as Cockburn, put that in writing without any real evidence and spread it to others as if this were the Salem Witch Trials and to try and harm me with such insanity.

And for me to be condemned in Williamson County for it because I happened to have friends who were Wiccan and Pagan. Friends who would happily tell the world that I was not a Witch. And that list included Tasha Ewan and Selena Fox.

For those who knew nothing about those religions, Selena and Tasha were very well-known leaders, speakers and activists in the Wiccan and Pagan communities.

Believe me, if I followed their traditions, I would proudly own it and proclaim it. Just as I would if I were Muslim or Jewish or Buddhist or any other religion.

While I respect everyone's religion and held it sacred as well as their right to be whatever they wished, I'd chosen to be Catholic even though other members of my family were Baptist, Shinto, Methodist, Atheist, Presbyterian, Wiccan, Dutch Reform and Unitarian.

So why was I being unfairly persecuted by these lunatics here in Williamson County?

Just like Hogg putting on her "pastor hat" while she'd sat in my home and wrecked my marriage, abused my children and lied to my fans about me.

It boggled the mind, didn't it?

So, as I was reeling from all these liars, Joan came into the back of the booth after Joslyn had just left it. "You got a minute?"

"I'm supposed to be working." But what the hell? Couldn't really focus.

"You'll want to see this."

I frowned at her as she sat down beside me. The backroom of the booth was always very, very cramped. It wasn't a big room to start with and we kept it stocked with loads of giveaways for fans, all weekend long.

Because of the noise level at such events, you couldn't hear anything other than a loud, ubiquitous roar that droned in your ears. Not that I could hear much on my best day. I was very hard-of-hearing and had severe Tinnitus. As such, I normally had music playing in my hearing aids so that the only way I knew if anyone was speaking to me was when they waved at me.

Which was another lie that Hogg had kept perpetuating through my fanbase. I'd never "spied" on people in the backroom of my booth. I had the medical reports going back to my childhood to prove that I couldn't hear people who were sitting directly in front of me, unless I was paying close attention to them. It was why I was always hyper focused at signings on the people I was talking to while I was signing their books. I had to be. If I wasn't looking directly at their lips, I had no way of hearing what they were saying.

In this case, Joan put her phone in my hand that was logged into the fan emails.

It was a message from Cynthia Britain.

My stomach tightened. "Uh! I don't have time for this."

Even though Cyn had always been one of my biggest fans and greatest supporters, she'd been freaking out over the last couple of weeks. And had been one of the ringleaders in the tirades against me and my latest release.

Joan refused to take the phone back. "Look at the subject line."

I really didn't want to. No offense, but I was tired of her shit. And I was on the verge of telling Joan and the others to ban her from the groups.

I'd never liked negativity. No one needed that in their life. The world was bad enough.

*My rules. My house.* If you wanted to be ugly, you had the rest of the internet for it. When someone came onto my social media, I expected a modicum of politeness and decorum. I didn't want to see anyone attacked.

Not just me. Any author, and especially not another fan. I'd even banned people for attacking Dumas.

Joan gave me a peeved glare and tilted the phone in front of my face.

I looked down and read, "Hogg did it."

My eyes widened. "What the hell?"

"Yeah." Joan smirked. "Keep reading."

I did. It was an apology from Cyn. More than that, she went into great detail about how Hogg had been infiltrating my fan base for months and motivating them to boycott my books and email my publisher with absolute hatred toward me. "Is this for real?"

"I don't know. But I think we should find out."

So did I.

When we first called, Cyn was extremely nervous. She was terrified that I'd be mad. But I didn't blame her. It wasn't her fault. She'd been tricked. And in all honesty, I admired her for having the strength and decency to come forward and to apologize. Very few people would have had the courage to do what she did.

"I was talking to Karen, and she told me that she was having an affair with your husband. That was when I knew something was wrong. That there was a lot more to this than what I'd been led to believe. I'm so sorry."

"It's okay. You had no way of knowing."

"Yeah, but she painted you up to be such an awful person. She told me that you'd fired her in an email."

I laughed at that. "I didn't fire her. She never worked for me. My husband forced her into my life and business. What I told her was that she wasn't welcomed to come back to my house." Because she'd been abusing me and my children.

"She said she was your assistant."

I laughed even harder. "Never. She worked for my husband who kept trying to get me to hire her for that. I kept trying to get her out of my life."

"That's not what she's telling people."

Hogg had lied about a lot of things. Such as telling everyone that she told me to break my latest book in half and to publish it as two separate books.

As if I'd had any control over that. All publishing decisions of that nature were, by contract, in the hands of my publisher. I couldn't have done anything about it if I'd wanted. Another example of her trying to look important instead of being the piece of shit she was.

The funny part? She wasn't even in my home when I'd written that book. I hadn't even started the book until after Les had filed for divorce.

Lying bitch. It was why there had been so many misprints of the first cover. My publisher had had no idea of the size of the book due to the fact that I'd handed it in so late.

Cyn couldn't apologize enough. "I can't believe the person she turned me into. I knew something was wrong the night I heard her screaming at her mentally challenged sister. She's a monster! I couldn't believe the way she talked to her sister and insulted her. I've never heard anyone speak like that to someone so helpless. And the degrading way she talked about her students. She's an awful person."

"Believe me, I know."

More than that, she threatened Cyn.

"It was creepy," Cyn said. "She told me that she knew where I lived and that she'd come visit me. Her tone was totally sinister. It gave me chills the way she said it."

But Detective Lynn Lazy didn't see the threat in that, either.

Any more than he saw the threat of Hogg revealing more of their insidious plans for me to Cyn. Both verbally and in writing. "When Terri loses her shit after this divorce is over, we're going to take her worlds and do what we want with them. I'll answer *all* your questions then and make up what I want."

"How so, Karen?"

"I've got all her notes and databases."

That made my blood run cold. Not only to hear it, but to see the actual emails and texts Hogg had written stating their evil plans for me and my work.

Especially since Kiki had always bragged to others that she could "duplicate" my voice so well that no one could tell the difference between us (not true, by the way), and that Les had gone around bragging throughout the lawsuit that the one thing he'd learned during the Dumas case was how to "steal a number one bestselling series and not get caught."

In fact, that was what he kept saying to my sons who were writers. "Don't waste time creating your own worlds or series, boys. Just steal one and get rich overnight."

"Be a Dumas!"

Was that what they had planned for me? Had Hogg convinced him that they didn't need me, anymore?

But he should have known better.

He saw for himself that even though Dumas had taken so much, she didn't have the fan loyalty that I had. They had to keep propping her up, and coming back to my material, over and over, and hiring other authors to help her.

Duh!

And what had it gotten them all?

Sued.

And I'd won. Did he not think that I wouldn't do the same to him?

Oh wait, their plan had been to kill me. How could I forget that?

I guess had I been dead, I couldn't have done much to stop him, could I?

Yeah, that made sense. Kill me and they could take all my worlds and have their hack to write them.

Or commit me and I couldn't do anything.

Sheez, not even I could make this up. Truth *was* stranger than fiction. And sick minds made sick truth.

What was more was that Hogg didn't stop talking. She kept calling Cyn even while Cyn was pulling away from her.

Only now, Cyn knew the truth.

She heard it from the lips of my sons who'd told her exactly what Hogg and their father had done to them.

And to me.

Such as in November when Nick had surgery and I texted Les to let him know that his son was in the hospital.

He didn't care. Not a single text to ask his own son how he was doing. If he was all right. Nothing.

Same for December when Maddox had come home from Japan to visit and landed with a hernia. He was in the emergency room within hours of landing.

How did Les handle it?

He screamed at him in a voicemail. "How dare you have surgery and run up *my* insurance!"

Pardon?

When had he last earned a single dollar of his own money?

Contrary to the perjury of him and his lawyer in the documents they'd filed with the court it was 2008 or maybe 2009 (they claimed he'd stopped working in 2004). I was the one who'd paid their insurance and since Judge Woodly's orders in August where he'd told us to divide out our bills, I'd had a separate insurance policy for me and my sons.

What was Maddox supposed to do? Go back on a plane for eighteen hours with a hernia about to rupture to a foreign country and get surgery with no one there to take care of him?

That said it all about the kind of rat bastard dog Les Manly was and how much care he had for his own sons. No wonder he'd been able to steal from them and not blink an eye.

So much for his claim that he was the parent who'd always taken care of his sons, huh?

And why had Les needed his money at Christmas?

He was buying himself a seven-thousand-dollar show pony.

And Les didn't even ride them.

*Go ahead and ask me where that horse was kept...*

Not in Tennessee where Les was supposed to be living.

Les had the horse stabled in Georgia.

*Oh, and remember my work cabin?* He was renovating that to the tune of over *one hundred thousand dollars.* In fact, he'd spent seventy thousand dollars to pay for his mother's friend, a decorator, alone. And had spent over sixteen hundred dollars on curtains.

So much for the court order to not "misspend" or waste marital funds, eh?

And I was the one they kept hauling into court for contempt. *Please explain to me why none of the attorneys I'd hired would file one single contempt motion against him, yet his combined forces of attorneys continually manufactured contempt charges against me for things I hadn't done and lied on me to the judge's face.*

Yet no one would see them punished.

Meanwhile Dinky in his bathrobe on a bench never once asked them for one single bit of proof of their charges against me. Instead, he merely assumed because they were his former business partners that they were telling the truth and that because I owned a set of breasts, I must be the liar.

Of course.

How did this work in the American court system? I thought that form of justice ended with the Salem Witch Trials?

McCarthyism.

Oh, yeah, I forgot. I lived in Williamson County.

"You're a woman and this is Williamson County, honey. Don't expect justice here." How could I have ever forgotten that sage advice out of the mouth of my own attorney?

But let my son need a hernia operation and the world was coming to an end.

It was also during the Christmas season of 2018 that I got two very interesting phone calls for Les. One from another divorcee.

"Les, honey, is that you?"

Hmm... Mickey Watkins. The mother of my son Caleb's old school chum. She, too, was a decorator and had sold our former home. How weird that she would be calling Les. Les had always said he hated her for her "liberal" views.

More than that, he'd mocked and hated her son and didn't want him hanging out with Caleb because he was, according to Les, a drug addict and "bad influence."

If only she knew what Les had really thought of her and how he called her a slut and everything else under the sun.

Oh well.

The next call came from a man wanting to talk to Les about renovating my cabin to add a "false beam" in it. The kind used to "hide things" such as money or jewelry.

You know, the kind of jewelry and gold I'd been telling my lawyer and the police had been missing since Les had walked out the door of my home.

All that tied to the comments my movers had made a few weeks after New York Comic Con when they'd finally delivered my items from the cabin sans a few important things such as my deceased mother's dolls that Les had refused to hand over.

Despite the court order that said he was to return them.

Les had pissed off the movers he'd contracted with so badly that the poor guys had to take a two-hour break before they could travel the whole two miles from the cabin to my house in order to drop off my things.

No lie.

Or exaggeration.

Apparently, Les had risked their lives. Their words, not mine. "Is he fucking crazy?" Their words, not mine. Redundant on purpose.

Les had made them back all the way down a mile and half driveway in a truck where there was no margin for error, which could have killed them had they made a mistake as it was a sharp drop off on a horrifically bad incline.

The entire time they were moving boxes, he was following after them with a vacuum cleaner, telling them not to mess up "his" cabin. Bragging to them about all his plans for "renovating it" because he was going to sell it.

"This stuff's cool!" Dalton had said.

"It's my ex's," Les sneered, not knowing how bad it made him look to them.

Or the fact that they would later mock him over it.

"Would you believe after chasing us around with the vacuum cleaner all day, that creepy old bastard had the nerve to ask us to assemble his piano?" Dalton laughed. "Now, a nice lady like you, we'd have done it in a heartbeat. But an asshole... no! He's on his own."

Jake concurred. "If that wasn't bad enough, when we were leaving, he refused to sign off on the paperwork. That after screaming at us all day about how *he* was paying for it."

"He *refused* to pay for it." Dalton looked as disgusted as I felt.

Which meant that even though we had a court order saying the bastard was supposed to pay for it out of the money he'd stolen from me and my children, I had to pay for it out of what little he'd left us.

Oh, and let's not forget about the entire box of clothes he'd "returned" to me that weren't mine.

In fact, by their size and style differences, it was obvious they belonged to one or more of his girlfriends.

*Piece of advice: when you return your "spouse's" clothes, make sure they belong to your spouse and not whatever person you're screwing that week.*

Such a prince.

*Merry Christmas to us.*

Meanwhile, he was spending lavishly on the pedophile crew. What a champ!

And don't forget the horse that he happened to name "Penny." The same name as my stepmother who'd swindled me and my siblings out of our inheritance when my father died.

But the joke was on Les.

He should have remembered that Karma's a bitch. While Penny might have walked away with my father's millions, she didn't keep them. Her lawsuit with my brother wiped out a lot of it. Within a year of my father's death, she was left destitute, working a minimum wage job.

In the end, she killed herself, because she had no friends and no family who cared about her. Ended up cremated and forgotten.

That was what happened when you lied and stole from people.

Had she simply been decent with us, she would have spent her last years surrounded by a family that loved her.

Les had damned himself to the same fate. Even his own sister was horrified when I told her about his equestrian acquisition.

"Les doesn't ride. He hates horses!" Katrina was as stunned as I was.

"I know."

"Why would he buy one? All he ever did was complain about Annette and her riding them when we were kids."

Again, I was well aware of that. "All I can figure is he bought it as an FU to me since I lost my horses when my parents divorced when I was a kid." And every time I'd wanted to buy one in our marriage, he'd denied me.

But then trying to unravel a sick mind was like trying to solve a Rubik's Cube. Damn near impossible, and just as frustrating.

Especially when it came to his gift-giving for the kids. He only sent a card to Maddox after screaming at him over his operation.

For Nick, he sent a "furry" head. For those unaware, it was a fetish thing that was exceptionally creepy given Les's background and family history.

Nick was so creeped out by it that he shoved it in a closet and never wanted it mentioned again.

The next present was even worse.

A Dr. Seuss book.

But not just any Seuss book. *Fox in Sox.*

Now that might seem innocuous until you thought about it. One, Nick was never that big of a Seuss fan, and two, he was nineteen years old. A little old for Dr. Seuss.

The other reason, it was creepy as shit. It opened with the words, "this book is dangerous." And it went on to warn kids to keep their mouths shut.

Hmm...

And you'll never guess how it ended.

"Is your tongue numb?"

Remember what I'd said about my poisoning? Numb tongue was one of the major symptoms I'd suffered from. Of all the books in all the world for him to choose, what were the odds that he'd pick this one by chance?

Seriously? A book that had no meaning to my son or our family?

*One time is an occurrence.*

*Twice is a coincidence.*

*Thrice establishes a pattern.*

And this made him sick in the head.

That wasn't random. He was playing with me, like when he'd left the roses on my counter saying he wanted to stay married while knowing he'd already stolen all the money from my sons and deposited in an out of state bank account in his name only, and had made a deposit on a divorce attorney. After he'd gone through our entire house making a documentary for the divorce of everything he wanted that he hadn't already stolen from us. When he'd gone into our sons' rooms to "document their items and rather than use their names had said, "middle son's room." So effing creepy.

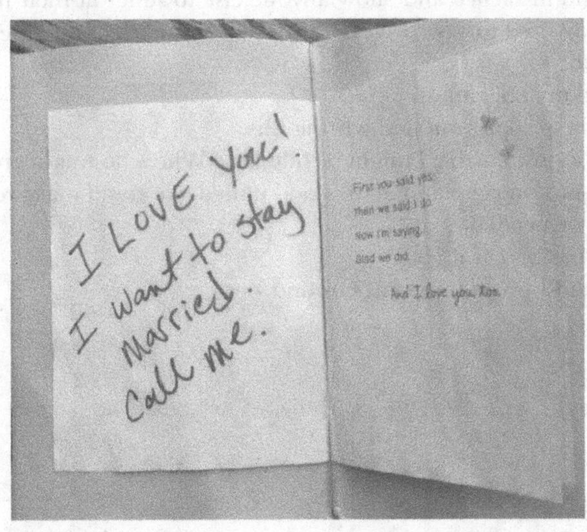

To quote his trainer, Pat Hanson, "The one thing I know about Les Manly, he never acts on impulse. Everything he does is methodically and meticulously planned out. It's why I couldn't believe it when he came in and announced out of the blue that he was getting divorced. In all my years as a trainer, no one's ever done that. He gave me no warning. Just poof. I'm done."

Cold-blooded.

The kind of man who could put his son on a plane to Japan and frame him for murder. The same person who could sit there and watch his wife struggle to breathe while they were having to pump iron intravenously into her to keep her alive, knowing he was the cause of it all.

Telling that wife how much he loved and adored her and their family, right up until the moment he walked out the door on all of them without an ounce of remorse.

That alone told everyone how sick in the head Cockburn was that she defended such a ruthless monster.

And she was a mother?

That alone should be grounds for her to lose custody. Because anyone that soulless and heartless had no business with children of her own. She was as much a sociopath as he was.

No wonder she was so terrified of my sons giving testimony. Every time we'd tried to schedule a deposition for them, she'd backed down, terrified of them speaking the truth. Because she knew what would happen if my sons spoke.

They would condemn their father and her for the monsters they really were.

None of them wanted the real story out.

That was why they'd gone to such lengths to discredit me. Just like Dumas. It was the only defense they had.

Funny how none of them had ever once presented any real facts. All they'd done from the beginning was call me names and use their lies and twisted innuendo to frame me.

Because the facts and evidence resided with me, and they had done everything they could to bury every bit of it.

How was this justice?

But I wouldn't go silently to my grave. My parents had taught me better. I couldn't do that. They had victimized too many others. I couldn't stop the ones who'd come before me that I didn't know about.

Yet if I failed to speak now, then I would be responsible for all the victims who came after. And I would not stand in silence and allow anyone else to suffer at their hands. Not if I could stop it. Like my daddy used to say, "I wear this uniform and fight and bleed in hopes that my children won't have to."

It was my duty and my obligation.

That was why I was speaking out and writing this.

In hopes that maybe, just maybe, I might be that little Who who was heard. Because one voice might be the one to start an echo and if we stood united, we could make real change.

Change was what we needed.

Because this wasn't as bad as it got...

Hell was coming and I was standing at Ground Zero.

JUST WHEN I THOUGHT IT COULDN'T get any worse, Cockburn decided to drag me into court on my mother's birthday. Not like Les hadn't known that date. Not after thirty years.

Just as I knew his mother had been born on 9-11.

As if it wasn't bad enough to be dragged into court, again, for nonsense, but no one had bothered to tell us that our judge had been changed.

Not even my attorney.

So, we walked in late to a new courtroom, and I was floored. While I was no fan of Woodly as we all knew, I honestly didn't think there could be anything worse than that arrogant idiot and his tirades against women.

I forgot that Williamson County was on a hell-mouth.

*Enter Judge Bubba Dinky.* My first impression of this love-child of Joker and Skeletor was that he reminded me of Steve Martin's character in *Little Shop of Horrors*. You know, Orin Scrivello D.D.S.? The dentist who lived to give pain to others and who kept sucking on the nitrous oxide machine between patients? That creepy smile where the audience could instantly tell something wasn't quite right in his head?

*C'mon, ladies, we all know* that *look.* The one that goes down our spines like a shredder.

And I was right. Come to find out, this "winner" had been arrested for solicitation of a prostitute.

*No surprise there.* He certainly looked the creepy type.

Dinky was let off those charges by his "buddy" who had since been arrested and jailed for the part he played as a judge in a major scandal where Judge Casey Moreland had attempted to frame a poor woman for turning him in because he was forcing her (and others) into prostitution with him and his "friends" who also happened to be in the legal profession.

Yeah, that was the kind of high-class people Dinky associated with and that Nashville put on their benches and in their courtrooms.

Rather than disbar Dinky as any normal state would have done for his arrest, Williamson County, Tennessee rewarded him by making him a judge!

And why not?

His father had been a judge and his brother was a judge. Brother Dinky had even sworn him in while knowing he'd been arrested.

Even Dinky's former business partner, Judge Robert E. Lee Williams was a judge. A name so stereotypically bad, I couldn't have made that up if I tried, and why would I do that to the South? I would like to pretend that we're not as bad as everyone thought we were.

But after living in Williamson County...

Yeah, we were.

This place was worse than those stereotypes.

I was surprised ole Dinky didn't wear a big white seersucker suit with a little black tie a la Colonel Sanders to trial.

Besides, why was I even surprised given that this was the state where one of our former governors used to sell pardons to hardened criminals?

*Everything for a price.*

*Third most corrupt state in the Union.*

Anyway, Dinky sat up there, all smiles and giggles, again reminiscent of Steve Martin's character, talking about how this wasn't personal. "It's all business."

*Yes, Judge Dipshit, it was personal as well as being business. Would you please stop wasting my time and money talking about how it was all wasting my time and money and shut the fuck up and let the lawyers speak?*

Really, someone needed to get a hook with this crazy bastard.

*Both sides and not just the side that used to practice with you in your law firm should be allowed to speak.*

In case you missed it while you were in law school, Dinky, that was how the court system in this country was "supposed" to work. Both sides were supposed to get to speak and present their cases.

*Both* sides.

E-q-u-a-l-l-y.

While I realized that it probably wasn't as entertaining for you to listen to both sides give you facts about the case you were supposed to be presiding over as it was for you to waste our time opining about your boring case history and dispensing your war stories, I can promise you that the only one being entertained by your stupidity was you. The rest of us were bored out of our gourds.

But apparently, he never got the memo. Or any base instruction on what a judge was supposed to do.

No one had ever been able to get a word in edgewise because he wouldn't shut up and listen.

But that wasn't all. Cockburn wasn't alone this time. She'd gone out and dredged up some new friends to steal even more money out of my children's pockets.

Other former business partners of ole Dinky's.

Because everyone knew that a lawyer getting a divorce needed three lawyers on his team against his wife when all the discovery had been done in a lawsuit her client and his wife had settled the day before he filed for divorce without warning her he was going to divorce her.

And he ran off with all that discovery and paperwork, and still had it all in his possession.

*Yeah. How does that work again?*

*Repeat after me, Judge Dipshit:* "it was a waste of marital assets to spend over *one hundred thousand dollars* to duplicate the discovery and records that had already been done in the Dumas case. Discovery that was only a few weeks old at the time the stupid son-of-a-bitch filed for a divorce and had all the records on his computer that he'd stolen from his wife's house."

Yet there I was, being hauled in again for the very records that Les had taken and that I'd already been billed by Cockburn for her to duplicate.

*What the ever-loving-fuck?*

Anyway, enter the dubious and extremely hideous Mika House who everyone in town knew was Dinky's personal protégé, and none other than Williamson County Commissioner and dough-boy stunt double, John Alaimo.

Well that certainly explained why old Cockburn could run illegal businesses out of her home and not get into trouble with the county, didn't it?

Why the rules and laws of Williamson County didn't apply to her?

*Nice to have friends on the inside...*

Oh, and I forgot to mention the best part of all this. Our local paper, *The Tennessean*, had just run an entire article about how Alaimo and House's firm that used to be the same firm ole Dinky had been a partner in (and had founded), might be doing something hinky with Dinky, literally, just prior to them making this appearance in my divorce case.

*Is it Okay for Lawyers to Spend Extracurricular Time with Judges Outside of Court? How Much Is Too Much?*

How much, indeed? Especially when they were from the same firm and had been in business together for years?

And then Dinky kept going on and on about, "these fine attorneys" to them while ignoring my lawyer.

That level of biasness was embarrassing. Last I heard, judges were supposed to be *impartial*.

Dinky most obviously wasn't, and everyone in town knew that about him. He was famous for it, point of fact.

*Welcome to my boot party.*

Dinky spent the entire time lecturing me on the fact that I hadn't turned over the discovery that Les had in my office that I was banned from going to by a court order. The same discovery Les had been overseeing the collection of in the Dumas case that was on his computer that Les had stolen out of my house.

*Remember Tennessee law:*

> **Rule 26.02: Discovery Scope and Limits**
>
> *The frequency or extent of use of the discovery methods set forth in subdivision 26.01 and this subdivision shall be limited by the court if it determines that: (i) the discovery sought is unreasonably cumulative or duplicative or is obtainable from some other source that is more convenient, less burdensome or less expensive;*

Yeah. What that meant was that since Les already had the information, and we could prove it as in my attorney attempted to give Dinky an email written by Les as evidence in court, that Les was harassing me and after a fraudulent contempt charge.

What did Dinky do? He not only ignored the evidence, he screamed at me and my attorney for an hour about how I better re-answer the questions I'd already answered (meanwhile Les had yet to answer a single one of the ones we'd given him).

*Favoritism much, Dinky?*

The bastard then went on to make me pay Les's exorbitant attorney fees to Dinky's former legal partners that I was already paying as Les had no job.

Yeah, Dinky was *that* underhanded and corrupt.

Or was he that stupid?

It was hard to tell.

The only satisfaction I had was that later that same day, I got to see an actual, real judge at work in Davidson County when we went up there to go after Hogg.

There, my IP attorney, Bob Harvest, was given permission to take her phone, computer, laptop, cloud account and iPad to seize all the files, emails, databases and all the other information she'd stolen from me and my sons. That included my sons' passport information, driver's license info and other things that were so illegal I still cannot believe Detective Lynn Lazy refused to arrest her over it.

I had irrefutable proof that she impersonated my sons. That she had stolen their identities, and no one would arrest her for it.

Welcome to Williamson County, Tennessee where identity fraud was apparently okay, too.

*Lori and Felicity, you should really be pissed off.* Why were you so severely punished, and this bitch got a free pass?

Where was the justice in this country? Why was it that our laws weren't enforced on everyone, equally?

Why did some get hammered while others went free?

I was sickened by it. Hogg and Les had done everything that had landed all those others in jail, and more, and no one would touch them.

Meanwhile, Cockburn and crew were trying to make me pay for Les being sued because they were impersonating my children and submitting false records to their school systems. Taking illegal tests for them and committing wire and mail fraud.

Wow. Just wow.

And remember that one of the attorneys after me happened to be a county commissioner for Williamson County.

Les admitted to Maddox that he applied to Vanderbilt for him, without Maddox's knowledge or participation. Had bragged to my sons that he'd gotten them into schools with false documentation. My sons didn't write essays for the schools he claimed they got into. I knew Les was too fucking lazy to write them. That meant Hogg had done it.

And Les said she'd done it, and I have her documentation from her that she wrote those papers. She proudly declared her actions on the invoices she'd handed in to Les so that he could pay her.

I've been to every law enforcement agency and academic institution to tell them about it.

No one would do anything.

Not even Williamson County Commissioner Alaimo who knew firsthand that they had defrauded the Williamson County school system where he was an elected representative, and this after he ran on the platform of improving our schools.

In fact, Alaimo was trying to force me reimburse Les for his illegal activities against our school system.

What a guy! And he was also a member of the Sons of the American Revolution. His ancestor must be rolling in his or her grave.

And just two weeks later, when Dinky was given my civil case, he laughed and laughed about the matter, as if a man attempting to murder his wife was hysterical.

I supposed to someone who bought and sold women for entertainment, and then was let off those charges by his friend and fellow judge who went to jail for framing an innocent woman, it was.

Then, Dinky said, "Let me explain this to you. I'm the judge for the divorce. I'm going to be the judge for this civil case and should there ever be any kind of criminal charges filed, *I* will be the judge for those, too. I do it all."

Well, now we knew why Les had never been charged with anything and why he wouldn't be so long as ole Dinky sat on that bench.

Why Les and his team of idiots were so cocky and smirky whenever they sashayed into the courtroom.

It helped when you hired the friends and former business partners of the judge. Friends who were defending the judge's questionable reputation in the paper.

*Now I know what you're thinking. That's a conflict of interest! You should get another venue or judge.*

Yeah. I thought the same thing myself.

But this was Williamson County, Tennessee. And I lived in the third most corrupt state in America; according to Harvard one of the most corrupt capitals in America.

Believe me, I tried.

*Three* lawyers.

I was stuck with this buffoon of a judge. Believe me, if I could have gotten rid of him and moved this to another county or judge, I would have.

Sadly, there were only a handful of judges here and I'm told that they were all like this. And everyone knew it.

They bragged about it.

Not to mention, the ones in Davidson County were also old business partners or relatives of Dinky's.

And don't forget that I had Woodly before him, and he wasn't any better. He was the first idiot who let Les take my children's money and spend it into the ground and who kicked me out of my office without hearing the evidence that it wasn't a "family" retreat.

That Les had committed perjury in front of him.

But now that we had Dinky on board and Cockburn had her friends around her, she was emboldened even more. Now, there was no stopping this out-of-control lunatic bitch.

Her first lie that day was that I'd hired a PR firm to assassinate my husband's character. As if anyone could assassinate the character of a family of known pedophiles.

They'd done that on their own.

Or if I could ruin the reputation of a fully able-bodied lawyer who'd stolen the futures of his special needs children.

I mean really, I had an international fan base with hundreds of thousands of people on my social media networks. I didn't need an expensive PR firm to tell anyone what a piece of shit I'd married.

I could do that for free.

More than that, I had emails that I'd sent to Les months before he'd left where I'd asked him to vet my contract with my PR firm because he was the one who'd told me to go out and hire them to deal with the Dumas bullshit.

Since we were coming up on the trial, he wanted me to have a good firm in place when Dumas continued her hostile lies against me. Ironically, it was all his idea. So, I went to a friend and asked her whom she'd used during her separate trial for infringement.

God forbid, Dinky should have ever actually looked at any evidence before he began his screaming tirade against me.

*Boy, did Dinky need his binky* that *day.*

Instead, he took Cockburn's ridiculous unsubstantiated accusation as gospel. "I have it on good faith, Your Honor, that she hired her company to bribe the *USA Today* newspaper months after he left."

What the hell? I'd never even had an article in the *USA Today* from my PR firm.

"Happens all the time," Dinky repeated.

"All the time, Your Honor."

"And it's not about the money."

"No, Your Honor."

*Oh, I'm sorry, Dinky, if you were having flashbacks over the fact that the media barbecued you for being arrested for hiring a prostitute. Or were you sore about the* USA Today *article that alleged you were being bribed?*

Because the way you acted, Dinky, with your buddies, I was beginning to suspect there might be some fire with that smoke they alleged. What other "good authority" could Cockburn have?

'Cause there damn sure wasn't any evidence since I didn't do it.

And old Dinky granted her motions without her having presented any evidence to him whatsoever.

Or allowing us to refute her preposterous lies.

For that matter, he wouldn't even allow me or my attorney to speak. He was a rare piece of shit that should be flushed down the toilet along with Les and their whole zoo crew.

I really didn't know which one to hate more. Mika House who looked like he'd been hit in the face with a shovel because someone got so sick of looking at that arrogant smirk that they'd tried to remove it by hitting him, or Alaimo who was a cross between a scared bear trying to take a dump and a brainless imp. You could tell Alaimo wasn't the leader.

As the old Southern saying goes, "ain't no light under *that* bushel." Which was funny as hell given that he'd told my attorney that Les's law degree wasn't worth the paper it was written on. Having been married to Les, I could honestly say as stupid as he was, he was a lot smarter than Alaimo. At least Les had the God-given brains to not violate his code of ethics for his bar license.

Williamson County Commissioner Alaimo, himself, was the one who came at me and tried to make me pay sixty-eight thousand dollars for Hogg's and Les's illegal actions against Nick's tutoring company.

*I kid you not.*

He put his own name on that travesty.

House was an arrogant dumbfuck of titanic proportions. Honestly, he reminded me of someone whose family had interbred so much that he was a genetically mangled byproduct who couldn't understand basic reasoning. That was half the problem with the divorce.

His IQ was so low and his viciousness so high that there was no place for the two to meet. These were not the people to hire for a divorce. To quote the intelligent lawyers I'd known, you could get a ton of flesh or a ton of cash. But you couldn't have both in a divorce.

Decide which one you want.

These stupendously ignorant morons were in it for bloodletting and to get as much money for themselves as they could.

Client be fucked.

Les was too stupid to figure that out. He was too drunk on the fact that he had someone willing to put their bar licenses on the line to publicly insult an innocent victim for him.

It was why we were now broke.

The questions they were hitting me with in January read like a third grader had prepared them. They couldn't even get Hogg's name spelled right, and it wasn't a hard name to spell.

They were either redundant, or irrelevant, and about half of the questions they asked hung Les.

Even so, they dragged me before Dinky and rather than read the questions, they pulled them out of context to make it look as if I wasn't cooperating (this was the third time I'd answered their idiocy and sent it back to them). Never mind the fact that Les had yet to answer any of the questions we'd given him.

At all.

In fact, to this day, I was still waiting on my answers.

Why wouldn't my attorney file a contempt order on Les? This had angered me all along. But then, my attorney had been hammered by the three of them, constantly.

Dinky wouldn't listen to my side because we had breasts. He made no bones about that. Truly the most embarrassing display of chauvinism and favoritism you'd ever seen, and it explained why Alaimo and House's firm was the great sausage fest of all time. I was amazed that the EEOC hadn't had words with them.

It was probably the reason Cockburn had left that firm. Or maybe it was the reason she'd worked there...

There were several theories I'd heard, and a lot of interesting rumors about her on the street. *I'll leave that for your imagination.*

Anyway, in February, after Cockburn very adamantly insisted that someone could bribe a major newspaper, I was contacted by my PR firm.

"We have a reporter from the *New York Magazine* who wants to interview you. Lily Ships."

I was a bit surprised. "Really?"

"Yeah. She wants to do an in-depth piece that has nothing to do with the lawsuit or divorce. It's all about how you rose from the beginning to become a number one bestselling author."

Finally, someone who wanted to talk about my books. I was thrilled.

It'd been a while since someone did an in-depth piece like that. About a year. *The Tennessean* had done it right as the divorce had started and Cockburn had threatened me over it. Ironically, that piece had been lined up before Les left, and had taken place just after I'd been served.

I was grateful to be on track again. These were the kind of articles we'd been after, contrary to Cockburn's lies to Dinky.

Ships arrived on Valentine's Day. *Ever get that creepy weird feeling?*

Yeah.

Moment I laid eyes on her. I opened the door expecting to see a real journalist representing such a prestigious magazine.

Nope.

I was confronted with what appeared to be the missing hobo orphan of Corporal Klinger from *M*A*S*H** and *Seinfeld's* Kramer. Dressed in a homely, cheap polyester Dollar Store top that was stretched out of shape and clingy black pants that emphasized the fact that she had spent way too much time at *Starbucks* with her Frap and cake pretending to be a pseudo-intellectual.

She reeked of entitlement, and one too many *Women's Studies* class, even though it was obvious that she'd never suffered a day of anything in her life, which was why she had to feel bad about herself and her pretentious, overprivileged upbringing. She reminded me of a former roommate I had in college who walked around all day on a hunger strike protest, sporting the shirt and button that touted her cause. Late afternoon, she came into our dorm room, removed her walking billboard items to go eat, and then returned to put the paraphernalia back on and continue her "hunger strike protest" afterward.

It was obvious Lily Ships was one of *those* kids that her parents had been forced to bribe the neighborhood children to come over on her birthdays because no one wanted to play with her.

You know the type: "It's okay, honey. They're jealous of you because you're so much smarter than they are. Here, baby, have another slice of cake. Daddy'll buy you a pony when he gets off work. Have some ice cream. One day, you'll show them how special you are, and they'll be sorry they were mean to you!"

How stupid was she?

Here was one of her usual stellar comments. "I have a friend who testified in court as an expert against your lab company, and he said that lab company was a joke."

"Really? You have a friend who took a lot of money to tear that lab down from someone who was trying to get away with something, or who had an axe to grind with the lab company, and your friend was paid a small fortune to help them do it. Now his reputation was on the line because he took money to say something bad about that lab, by someone who wanted to hurt that lab. That meant that forevermore, he had to tear the company down because he had been paid good money to hurt their reputation for the benefit of the person who paid for his testimony."

Yeah, we all knew about those "expert" witnesses and the fortunes they earned tearing someone or a company apart.

"Nuh-huh. That's not how it works! He gave a testimony in court about it!" Was she five? That was honestly my thought as she literally argued like that. Not because of her puerile responses, but because of her infinite stupidity.

"Yes, it is. How do you, as a journalist, not know that those so-called expert witnesses in court cases give paid testimonials?"

"No, they don't."

"Yes, they do. I just came out of a case, and I can assure you that they are very highly paid for what they say, or they're not used as witnesses. Which means, they are exceptionally biased when they give their testimony for or against anything, or they are weeded out and not used."

Yes, she was *that* stupid.

I've never met a "journalist" that fatuous who didn't know that "expert" witnesses were paid attack dogs.

Guess we know why print was dying, and why no one wanted to pay for fake news when they could get that junk free on Facebook.

What horrified me most was that people this lazy, and inexcusably corrupt, stupid and mean were getting paid good money to ruin other people's lives, and that there was no culpability for them.

At all.

But then, Lily Ships knew she was lying to the public, and that what she did was wrong, otherwise she'd have been proud enough to give out the name of the magazine she actually wrote for, instead of trying to ride the coattails of the legitimate parent company.

Not that I was giving a pass to the parent company, mind you.

Shame on *New York Magazine* for allowing itself to be used this way and for endorsing and sponsoring such a rag to exist on your coattails. It was still your reputation, and you should be sullied by it, because it was filth that you knowingly allowed. And by having a sister company that specialized in defamation and lies, it impugned your integrity and legitimacy, too.

And made your rag as much a laughingstock as *Vulture*.

As they said, one rotten apple spoils the whole barrel. And that scandal rag of lies was more than one rotten apple.

It was a cesspit of made-up bullshit you should be ashamed of, and because you allowed it to continue as part of your company, it made one wonder if you did any kind of real fact-checking for anything under your masthead.

I know I will no longer trust the *New York Magazine* for anything, and I wouldn't use any of their publications to wipe my ass with, even if it was a choice between one of their rags or a thorn bush.

I'd rather use a thorn bush.

And given the COVID-19 crisis, that was a potent statement as any paper to wipe with was important.

But I'd still rather have the thorns.

Lily Ships also had no measurable sense of humor as I made my standard joke when I opened the door about *the big yellow ball in the sky that burns us*. Most people laugh. I used that to judge whether or not I wanted to spend time getting to know someone.

Ships didn't laugh.

It confused her feeble mind.

Crap.

This was going to be a *long* interview. I had to explain to her about the joke as I would a toddler.

Joan came rushing over. "I finally found the alarm! Thank God!"

That damn thing had been ringing for hours. *Thank you, Les.* The idiot had put a carbon monoxide monitor off in the floor where no one could see it.

I was partially deaf so I couldn't locate sound. We'd been hunting the noise for hours.

Anyway, Ships came in and started looking around. My house was open and airy. I didn't have any blinds or curtains in the front. My kids refer to it as living in a fishbowl. From the street, you could see straight through my entire home.

Strike one for the made-up lies Ships printed.

I only had blinds in the rooms we used a lot.

Or, like a normal person, my bedrooms.

The one directly above was taken in my office.

That was what it always looked like in my office, except after dark when I'd pull my curtains closed. But I always opened it during the day and, weather permitting, opened the windows too so that my cats could sit in the window and get fresh air. Just like the one above it that was my "outer" writing area. There were curtains there that could be drawn and the door to outside was normally left open during nice days so that my dog could come and go as he pleased.

And I should think it was rather obvious from all the outdoor sections of my home that I must spend a great deal of time outside, otherwise I wouldn't have not one, but two outdoor monitors for my computer so that I could write outside.

Which would also explain why my office was a cabin in the woods and why I had archery gear hanging in my office and an archery range in my backyard.

Obviously, I wasn't a "shut-in" who never left the house. Because how the idiot missed my worn-out backpack of climbing gear, my extremely obvious and worn-out pink Butora Acro climbing shoes that were set next to my writing chair and my overly "well-loved" chalk bags as well as my numerous pairs of well-loved hiking boots (some with holes in them), was beyond me. And let's not even get started on all the other outdoor, worn-out sporting equipment throughout my home such as my pink golf clubs, roller skates, skateboard, baseball equipment, safety gear, et al. And given how feminine they were and their bright pink color in a house of all men, one would think it was obvious who owned which sporting gear.

She and Cockburn were cut from the same cloth. If their lips were moving, they were lying.

What I didn't know when I let her in was that she'd come here with an agenda.

Over and over, she kept asking me about witchcraft, which should have clued me in. I kept telling her that while I have friends who were Wiccan and Pagan, I was not. I even showed her my prie-dieu that I kept in my office. For those not Catholic, it is a small kneeling bench we use for prayer. One that had a small little ledge that held my holy water, rosary and bible. Everywhere you went in my home, there were a number of crucifixes and rosaries hanging on the walls or resting on shelves. Along with saint statues.

Really, you would have to be blind to miss them, along with the three holy water fonts I had mounted on my walls. Never mind the palms from Palm Sunday.

"But you have tarot cards."

"So?" I was once a professional tarot card reader. Had been one for decades. I had never hidden that fact.

How ignorant and intolerant could one woman be? Lots of people read and own Tarot cards.

Oh, wait, were we putting Cockburn in the running?

Then that became a loaded question.

The only person who had a whinier more grating voice the Lily's was ole Snooty.

And the more Ships talked, the more I got a bad feeling about her.

Especially when she was talking to my physical therapist, Mary Schultz.

"So, you're saying Terri isn't a witch?"

"Of course not. She's Catholic. I've known her for years. After Les left, he called me up and asked me if I'd ever seen her practice witchcraft and I laughed in his face."

Still, Ships kept trying to steer her in that direction instead of asking questions and "reporting" on them, which was what they'd taught me to do when I worked as a journalist.

I was so good at it, that I was a legend at my old alma mater. They still talked about a story I'd written at age eighteen, that was picked up by the AP wire and went viral before the concept of viral was a thing.

And this bitch was digging for dirt, not writing a story.

"You're being paranoid, Terri." My publicist kept trying to reassure me (you know, the same PR company Dinky had testified I'd bribed).

But that feeling wouldn't go away.

Again, I had *real* journalistic instincts.

And a conscience.

Joan agreed with me.

"So, like why do people read your books? Aren't they, like, dark?"

I just stared at Ships whose IQ shrank every time she opened her mouth. It was entertaining to watch her get dumber as time passed by. "You'd have to ask them. What they tell me is that the books speak to them. They relate to the characters. And they're not dark. They have a lot of humor in them, too. Occasionally they're serious, just like real life, because you have to have *conflict* for a book to work."

She tilted her head and stared at me with an opened mouth, befuddled frown. The same expression a dog had whenever it couldn't decide if it needed to eat or take a massive dump in your shoes. I believed that expression was commonly termed, mouth-breather. "But, like, aren't they dark?"

*Oh. My. God!*

I'd had more stimulating conversations with a disgruntled toddler.

Had Ships ever read something with actual words in it, she might have known that. That was the whole precept behind *fiction*. Goals. Motivation. C-o-n-f-l-i-c-t. Heavy emphasis on the *conflict* part. To quote Mark Twain, *there's no literature in heaven because there's no conflict in heaven.*

Guess we all knew how she'd gotten her job and it wasn't based on merit or intellect.

"Well, like, I don't get it. I, um, tried to read your book and I just don't get, like, why someone would read it."

Probably because I used multisyllable words.

Often.

Those could be confusing to dullards and fools like her.

Not to mention, I didn't have pictures in them.

"I guess you've had a very privileged life, then. For those of us who haven't been raised with a silver spoon, or with a mummy and daddy who think we shit gold, it makes sense."

And by the third time Ships had appeared at my home in the same ragged clothing that she got off the plane in, I was really being skeeved out by this bitch. My God, had no one ever taught her to bathe?

That the concept of *changing clothes* was a good thing? Her poor husband. He must have to hold his nose to tap that unwashed skank.

How highly unprofessional were you? You looked like nine miles of badly laid road that only worsened every day. I'd seen better looking roadkill.

In Southern Louisiana during August.

*Think about it for a second...*

And I wasn't the only one who felt that way. Everyone who talked to her reported the same thing.

"Was she a special needs hire? I kept getting the feeling that she went to the same school that your sister does." My favorite comment of all about Mrs. Ships that came from my aunt who never insults people.

"Now don't insult my sister. The people in her school are *much* brighter."

Trying to get Ships to understand anything was like explaining String Theory to a two-year-old in need of a nap...

And a diaper change.

She really was *that* stupid.

"Yeah, but why?" Ships asked that as much as a petulant child wanting to know why it couldn't have one more cookie before dinner.

That was probably the only thing she had learned in journalism school.

*Sweetie, bit of advice. Just because you ask, "but why," over and over, it doesn't make you an investigative journalist.* It made you sound like the fucking idiot you were. What made for a good journalist was knowing where the real story lay and having instincts about it.

Being ready to do actual research and go down rabbit holes you didn't know were there when you started. To pivot the story into the direction where actual news was.

*Most of all, keep an open mind.*

Not the open, slack jaw of a mouth-breather.

That was what had made so many good journalists famous, and why her "big" stories were nonexistent. Misquoting people, lying about what they'd said, and yellow journalism was just plain lazy.

Muckrakers were always forgotten and mocked.

I would sue you, but you weren't worth the time.

She started her story on Valentine's Day, when Cockburn and Dipshit had me in court because the jackass just couldn't stand going a week without seeing me.

I should have known something was weird because Les was alone that day and fled out of the courtroom like someone had lit his ass on fire.

That was suspicious.

And what I had no idea was how dirty these bastards were about to get, or how low they were about to sink.

**H**AVING LIED TO GET A SUBPEONA for my PR firm, agent and publishers, Cockburn still had no proof that I'd ever bribed the *USA Today* or any other news agency (because I hadn't). Something that made both her and Dinky look like the fools they were. What disgusted me to this day was that no news agency had ever come forward to defend themselves about that allegation.

*Maybe they do take bribes and I'm the idiot who thought they didn't.*

All I knew was that I had never bribed one because I didn't have the money to do it. Nor had something that scummy ever entered my mind.

Again, I had a massive online presence. When I posted about the poisoning, it went viral instantly.

No PR firm required. All the news agencies came to us to get more information about it. Another fact Cockburn misrepresented to the idiot known as Dinky.

My God, man, weren't you tired of being lied to and made a fool by someone you constantly complimented?

And on that morning in April, I was back in court for another round of stupidity because apparently Cockburn had no other clients and needed more financing for her side construction business. Bleeding Lord Dumbfuck dry was so much easier than getting a builder's loan.

How could I tell?

She was there, along with Shovel-Face, Alaimo, Chad Donut who had signed on to represent Hogg, and none other than Robert E. Lee Williams, Jr. who'd come on board to represent Cisco. And yes, you heard that correctly, the son of Judge Robert E. Lee Williams, Sr. Former business partner of ole Dinky himself.

What were the odds that the old band would reassemble to railroad me, and no one would stop them?

But here was the weird kicker about this one. Robert E. Lee, Junior was a ghost.

Seriously. I had tried to look this little bastard up online and couldn't find any actual law firm that he worked for. No contact info at all. On the motions he filed with the court, he only provided a P.O. Box. This little shit was shadier than the driveway for the Twelve Oaks Plantation.

The question was, why?

We all knew that old Daddy Bobby Lee didn't go to a real law school. Much like Cockburn, he was the proud graduate of the Nashville YMCA Night Law School.

But they let him be a judge here in Nashville, anyway.

*Third most corrupt state.*

So, here was the whole jolly reunion of Dinky, Williams and Cheatum. All the lawyers that were former business partners of the judge.

Interesting, right?

Same judge who, only a couple of weeks before this had refused to hear my legitimate case for perjury against Cockburn and Les. Why?

"I don't want to ruin a good attorney's reputation."

Didn't matter that they had committed tax fraud or had broken the law. Didn't matter that Dinky had spent nearly an hour glaring at me and lecturing me on what would happen if "anyone commits perjury in my court."

Apparently, he'd meant to add, "that only applies to you, little lady. Everyone else here can lie their ass off and I'm good with that."

Stupid me had thought it was a rotten trick when Cockburn lied and said she'd be late to court on Valentine's. My attorney had told me that we didn't need to be in court until around eleven.

Just after nine, I received the call telling me that I needed to be in court immediately.

Ever tried to rush a child with Autism after you'd told them a plan?

That day had been bad.

On this April morning, my little brother had driven up in a separate car. I took my sons with me, and we were in court, the day after Easter.

What I couldn't believe when we walked in was the sight of Les helping his father come down the aisle.

*Are you fucking kidding me?* He'd brought the old pedophile in with him? And sat him down near my children?

I couldn't have been more disgusted! Even worse, was Hogg and her ancient friend who sat across from them. My youngest son was drawn up into a ball, he was so traumatized by the sight of them.

Things that tested your faith in God.

Because we were the only case being heard that day as apparently Dinky didn't want any witnesses (not to mention the lawyers had to make sure that they were raking in every dime they could from me), we were put in this teensy, tiny courtroom.

I was placed behind the speaker's podium in a chair with my teleprompter in my lap. My attorney was seated at a table far off to my left and there was an entire row of Les's attorneys on my right. By the way, no one had ever explained to me why an attorney needed so many attorneys and why that wasn't considered wasting marital assets.

Anyway, I was wedged in there well and I was so close to whomever was speaking that all I could think was, "Motherfucker, you break wind and I'm going to kick you through that podium."

It was disgusting. I literally had a face full of male ass all morning. So close at times that it should be considered sexual harassment. I literally could tell whether or not these bastards had wiped.

I spent over three hours with all of them running their mouths, and most of it being Dinky with his side stories and rants about wasting *my* money, which he was culprit number one as he rambled on like some Alzheimer's patient who seemed to keep forgetting what we were there for. Not to mention, his belittling comments to me about how I needed protection, even against myself...

*What the fuck?*

No, Dinky Dick. What all citizens of this county and nation needed were protection from this kind of corruption and from Lord Skeletors, i.e. things like *you*, being on that bench when they had no business there.

Really, the condescending looks he gave me whenever I had a case in his courtroom, to the side winks he passed to his protégé Shovel-Face were gross and highly inappropriate. While I couldn't see them that day, I was more than acquainted with them from all my other times in court.

He might as well have said, "Don't worry, Mika. We got this bitch fucked! I'll see you on the golf course later. My next prostitute's on you, right, old friend?"

But as we were heading into hour three of waiting on Skeletor, my bladder was about to explode. One of the beautiful gifts that old Les had left me with was Kidney and Liver Disease. You had to love being poisoned.

I had no other reason to have those kinds of health issues and believe me, my doctors and specialists had run all the tests. No family history. No lifestyle choices that would cause them. No other known health concerns that would have led to them.

But everyone knew that the liver's primary job was to filter out *"poison"* and toxins from the body.

Anyway, because of my condition, I wasn't supposed to hold my water and I'd been holding it for a long time, and there was no sign of Skeletor shutting up anytime soon.

I was about to piss my pants.

As a result, I started looking around uncomfortably. But I knew I couldn't wait, so I passed a note to my attorney to tell her I needed to go.

She didn't respond. I sent over another note to her.

No response.

I was now in a critical state. So, I gently closed the teleprompter that had a delicate dongle on the side and set it on the floor at my feet.

Had I "stormed out" as Dinky knowingly lied about in his court report, I would have broken not only the laptop and dongle, but the foot of every bastard I had to climb over to get past so that I could make my way to the aisle.

Really, try climbing over people with a walking cast on. It wasn't easy.

Not to mention old Dinky couldn't see my face at all as I had my back to him. I was facing that row of attorneys where I was wedged, and one foot was broken where I'd sheared off part of my heel and the one without a cast had a broken toe and two fractured metatarsals on it. So, I was *very* carefully stepping so as not to harm the row of idiots who wouldn't make room for me or cause myself even more pain.

How could anyone storm out like that? Hell, I couldn't "storm" at all given the fact that I had two busted metatarsals, a broken toe, and had sheared off part of my heel.

And I had the medical records and X-rays to prove it.

For that lie alone Dinky should be thrown off the bench. The moment I stood up, my brother, a former police officer, was watching me as he was concerned that something was medically wrong. I walked right past the bailiff who was laughing at whatever was being said. Because I didn't have my teleprompter nor was I facing whomever was speaking, I had no idea was being said, and honestly didn't care.

I glanced over at my brother and kept walking out of the room to go to the bathroom.

After I did my business, I came out to see my brother standing there with my sons in tow.

"You're in trouble."

"For what? Taking a piss?"

Esteban shook his head and led me to a bench in the hallway. "Dinky's furious."

"For what?" *Taking a piss?*

"Look, I've seen these sister-fuckers a million times. Their dicks are the size of their pinkies. He thinks you disrespected him because you walked out."

"Oh my God, are you serious?" What kind of shriveled up ego did this idiot have?

Wait, stupid question on my part. I forgot that he was the pathetic kind of scab who bought and sold women as commodities.

"Yes. His brain capacity's smaller than his dick."

Which meant you needed a microscope to view it. "Christ Almighty."

By this time, my attorney, Constance Yabetz, had joined us. "Terri, what did you do?"

"Went to the bathroom."

"Did you really call Cockburn a fucking liar?"

Ever seen the movie *My Cousin Vinnie?* Know the scene where Ralph Macchio was going "I shot the clerk?"

That was what that moment felt like.

"No! *Cunt-hole Whore or Thundercunt.* That's what I call her."

"Well, she's telling Dinky you called her a fucking liar."

*Guilty conscience much, Thundercunt?* And even if I had mumbled that, which I hadn't as I was in pain from my foot and had my teeth clenched with the agony of two broken feet and a bladder about to burst, how would she know I was talking to her or about her since she wasn't the one speaking?

Wow.

*Ego much?* I supposed she did believe the entire earth revolved around that planet-sized ass of hers.

Why not? Her ass was large enough to form its own gravity.

Stunned, I stared at them.

"You have to go in there and apologize."

I gaped at my attorney. "For what?"

My brother went dead serious on me. "Terri, you have to do this. Listen to me. I've seen this a thousand times. That bastard will lock you up. Cater to his ego and do whatever he says."

"I didn't do anything."

"It doesn't matter."

By this time, my sons were crying and begging me not to go to jail.

I was in a daze.

How could this be happening? How could it even be real? Were we in grade school that I needed a hall pass to go take a pee because of a kidney disease that sorry sack of shit had given me that he should be in jail over?

Constance kept repeating everything my brother was telling me. "Whatever Dinky says, don't argue. Just agree. After it's over, you can go home. Just go in there and say yes."

*Are you fucking kidding me?*

After all the lies Cockburn had told and gotten away with, including this latest one, I was being dragged before Lord Skeletor and I couldn't even defend myself?

When had the USA become Nazi-fucking-Germany?

When did we put Tomás de Torquemada on a bench?

No wonder they'd accused me of witchcraft.

This wasn't Williamson County 2019. It was Salem, Massachusetts circa 1692.

This was not the country my father had bled and died for. And he'd died a horrible, agonizing death because of the shit they'd dropped on him in Vietnam and Korea. He had scars from the gas that had ruthlessly been dumped while he fought for us. Defending our rights, and those rights were now being denied to his daughter for a piece of shit who had committed dereliction of duty, and an out-of-control judge who thought himself God?

For that matter, I had a paralyzed hand from birth because of Agent Orange. My whole life, I'd suffered because my father had fought for rights that I was being denied by these animals.

Constance led me in there with two deputies flanking me as if I were the one who had tried to kill my spouse and who had poisoned my children and stolen their money.

Dinky refused to return my teleprompter to me. And this wasn't the first time he'd denied me my ADA rights.

In previous hearings, I'd also been mocked for my well-known dyslexia and belittled by not only him, but the whole zoo crew as well, over my hearing loss and learning disabilities.

More rights denied.

"You left my courtroom."

"Yes, sir."

"You called Cockburn a fucking liar loud enough for the entire first row to hear you."

My jaw hit the floor as the lie had grown bigger with each retelling.

On the first go-round, Cockburn had claimed that she didn't hear it. Someone had told her. Then I'd said it directly to her... how, I have no idea as I don't even know where she was in the courtroom when I left. And lastly, I was being accused of speaking so loudly in that tiny courtroom that everyone on the front row had heard...

As an interesting side note, the room was so small that had I done so, not only would the bailiff and judge have heard me, so would the court reporter.

They'd have had a record of it.

Cockburn was lying again, and it was as obvious as the judge's prejudice against me.

Not to mention, my brother had been there. With my sons and their Autistic friend. Had I spoken that loudly, not only would Esteban have heard me, along with the three of them.

And the wonderful and frightening thing about children with Autism.

They don't lie. They are frightfully honest.

Cockburn was right with her confession she was a fucking liar. But I hadn't called her on it.

Constance grabbed my hand. "Say yes," she whispered.

Even though it galled me to my bitterest core, I did what my attorney had advised me to do because I knew I wasn't facing a sane, rational person on that bench. He was drunk with his own power and filled with an undeserved hatred of me. "Yes, sir."

"Now you know I can lock you up for both of those."

No, I hadn't known that and the last time I'd checked, according to my American rights, you were supposed to tell me the consequences *before* getting a confession, judge.

*That was the law.*

Not that he cared. Remember what he'd said? "I don't care what the law says."

Come to find out later, Dinky, and brace yourself because you'll be stunned, was lying and misstating what the law said.

He couldn't legally lock me up as he hadn't heard me say those words that I didn't say. As a judge, he could only punish me for direct contempt, which was something he'd have to witness or hear himself or I would have had to do something to disrupt the court. Walking out of his courtroom didn't disrupt anything, especially since I'd done it quietly.

As countless others had done all morning during the hearing.

No one else had been hauled before the judge to be ridiculed and lectured to.

For that matter, he'd kept the hearing going after I'd left for quite a few minutes. The only reason it had become disruptive was because Skeletor got his itty-bitty, baby diaper in a wad, then had his tantrum over it.

Because Dinky needed a binky.

That had nothing to do with me.

Let me repeat: People had been coming and going all morning.

I wasn't seated at the Plaintiff's table. My going to piss had no bearing on anything.

Skeletor had lied on record.

Not to mention, he had all those "front row" witnesses and a bailiff and he hadn't bothered to ask for any verification about whether or not I had called her a name.

Nor had he asked my sons and brother, also on that front row.

Instead, he'd taken the word of the attorney who I'd had up on perjury charges a mere two weeks prior to this. The attorney he'd refused to punish for her crime (and perjury was an actual crime), because he hadn't wanted to "injure a good attorney's reputation."

But it was okay to put an innocent woman in jail who had never even had a parking ticket in front of her sons and leave them exposed to a pedophile.

Whatever happened to innocent until proven guilty?

That was a direct violation of *my* civil rights.

And don't forget that on that day when I'd brought my case to Judge Skeletor for perjury that ole Cockburn had been so scared, because I had her Dead-to-Rights on it, that she hadn't even bothered to show up for court.

She had completely chickened out.

Now my understanding of the law was that when a defendant doesn't bother to show you were supposed to get a judgement in your favor by default. Especially when you had all the evidence, and that defendant was a lawyer who knew better than to lie and present false testimony to the court to deprive someone of their money and/or property or rights.

Nope. Not in Williamson County, Tennessee.

In fact, my case didn't even get heard. Dinky refused to do his job, which was also grounds for having someone yanked off the bench, according to Tennessee's Ouster Law.

So why I was as stunned that day as I was standing there when he lied about the law again, I had no idea.

Never mind that little pesky constitutional right to be heard before a sentence was passed on someone so that the person being sentenced could tell the judge about any mitigating circumstances. Such as, I had a bladder about to burst and was threatening my health, had no idea I couldn't leave the room and oh, there was a pedophile a few feet from my child causing him to draw up in a fetal position on the bench.

Never mind the fact that every statement made about me that morning had been a lie, and I could prove it, yet the judge had refused to ask them for any evidence.

If they spoke, it was truth.

If I spoke, it was a lie.

So what did he care about taking away someone's freedom in violation of their constitutional rights? Or following due process?

Dinky denied me all of it.

And do you know what the Tennessee Board of Judiciary Review had to say when I reported this to them?

"Sounds like you didn't like his opinion."

*Excuse me, Shawn.* I had no idea how you got your cushy job, but failure to follow the law and due process, and misstating the law on record wasn't a case of my not "liking his opinion." That was a clear and direct violation of my rights and due process.

Refusal to hear a legitimate case brought into the courtroom because you didn't want to "harm" a crooked attorney's reputation wasn't a matter of my not liking his opinion.

That was failure to do his job. Judges didn't get to pick and choose the cases they heard. They were required to hear the facts of the case and then judge them.

Not toss them out on their whims because the attorney the case was being brought against used to work in his firm and was working with his little protégé.

That was what you were given your job for. To make sure these little bastards didn't turn their courtrooms into their own private kingdoms.

The mandate of the U.S. Court system dictated that the role of judges was to prevent abuse, oppression, and injustice. Not become the cause of it.

God forbid someone in the state of Tennessee should perform the job they'd been given.

I assumed it never occurred to old Dumbass Dinky that Cockburn had set me up in his courtroom as retaliation for going after her for her perjury.

Or maybe he was in on it.

Because let me tell you something even more interesting. That day when Cockburn didn't appear in court for perjury, she was supposedly up in Dinky's brother's courtroom in Davidson County.

Know what was going on there?

According to a friend of mine who was in that courtroom that day, a man went off and called the counsel a "fucking liar" and threw a fit in big brother Dinky's courtroom and was cited for contempt.

Only he didn't get jail time.

But really, what were the odds of that happening twice in a Dinky courtroom, especially when I hadn't said it?

Even more interesting? When you read the court transcript, it showed me calmly leaving and Skeletor having a fit about it once I was out of the room. Then, he went on a break. Ten minutes passed before Cockburn said a word about having been insulted.

Anyone with half a brain, and I realized that Judge Skeletor was working at one tenth of that capacity, could figure out that she had gotten together with her little crew of hyenas and set me up.

So much for the American justice system. Weren't we all proud this bitch got to go to the YMCA Night Law School so that she could come at me with her lies and unwarranted viciousness, and use it to also drive an American veteran who had defended our rights out of the country and deprive him of his children?

God bless America. I was so glad that I'd been forced to grow up without a father because he was off fighting for this slag's rights to do this to me.

Made me sick to my stomach to even look at them.

"Now I want you to know that I could have you thrown in jail for what you've done here today, but I'm not going to do that. I'm not. But you need to know that your behavior isn't going to be tolerated."

My behavior? Really. I was the only one acting like an adult in this entire travesty.

It was definitely not Skeletor who was throwing a toddler tantrum because I had to go to the bathroom and who was "demanding" respect that he didn't deserve because his fragile ego couldn't handle a woman leaving the room without asking *his* permission.

And don't get me started on Ms. Grade School bully bitch who was probably that skank who used to steal other girl's boyfriends and then beat the hell out of anyone who went after hers. You know that old-style Georgia junkyard beat down. Like my friend Milly had done in college when she'd caught her boyfriend cheating on her. She broke her nails off, one-by-one on the dash of my car.

"Milly! What are you doing?"

"Girl! I'm going to snatch that weave off that bitch's head and beat her with it."

And she had. It was quite impressive, and I could pretty much guarantee that woman never went after anyone else's boyfriend again.

That was the kind of old-school ass-kicking I was sure Trailer Trash Barbie Cockburn used to give other girls. It was probably why she walked like she still had someone's baseball bat wedged up her ass.

Someone had probably left one there during a brawl.

That was Cockburn to a T.

She was that repulsive bully bitch who knew that she was so worthless and stupid that the only way she could feel good about herself was to have someone else defend her and do her dirty work for her.

"Now, I want you to apologize to Ms. Cockburn."

Again, I gaped. I couldn't believe that as a grown adult, I was being told to apologize to a lying bitch for something I hadn't done when clearly this was retaliation from her.

Any human with half a functioning brain cell could take one look at her ugly face and tell she was lying.

We all know *that* smirk.

There I stood with that slag bitch simpering with her hyena face, knowing she'd lied and was getting away with it. She was proud of it. Behind me sat the pedophile who had gotten away with years and years of ruining the lives of children. That he dared enter a courtroom as if he were a "decent" human being. Les smirking and simpering, knowing he'd poisoned me, killed my cat, stolen all my sons' money and fucked me over and gotten away with it, and he was gloating.

Sitting next to the bastard who had put my boys in bed with him...

After Les had sworn to me that the creepy, sick bastard would *never* be near them.

I'd turned my back for five fucking minutes.

What had happened with their grandfather was something my boys had only just told me, right before this court date. I had no idea that it had ever happened until after Les had left, and Maddox had returned from Japan.

All those years, I'd known that something had caused Nick's personality to change.

Jason, the tech guy I'd hired to replace Cisco, who was also a youth minister had been trying to warn me since Nick had started going to his ministry group that there was something Nick needed to say.

I wasn't prepared to hear it. Any more than I'd been prepared to see that bastard in court that day.

It was more than I could bear. In one moment, everything came to a head.

So, without thinking, I asked a simple question. "Do you also want me to apologize to the pedophile family, too?"

Dinky scowled. "What'd you say?"

I repeated it, since it only made sense to my Autistic mind. He wanted me to apologize to Cockburn for something I hadn't done, and according to her lie, I'd said it loud enough for the entire first row to hear. So, shouldn't I be apologizing to all the people who'd victimized my sons and me?

God forbid we insert actual evidence and logic into a modern courtroom.

But again, because I was calm and I tended to speak in a low tone as I was partially deaf and any loud, sudden sound could cause feedback in my hearing aids, I repeated my question.

Again, Dinky got angry. "I can't hear you. You need to speak up."

"I'm sorry, Your Honor. I'm partially deaf."

"I know you're deaf!" At this point, he was screaming at me, and red in the face and at least he admitted that he knew I couldn't hear properly and yet he'd denied me the use of my tele-prompter. "You need to speak up so that I can hear you."

I repeated it again, very calmly.

And again, he yelled at me, "What did you say!"

"I asked if you wanted me to apologize to the family of pedophiles, too."

"My God," Les said behind me because he knew the cat was out of the bag.

"That's a disgusting allegation! How dare you say that! That's it! Ten days in jail!"

No, Skeletor. Disgusting was the fact that Taylor was dead from suicide because of this family of repulsive human beings who had been allowed to rape and destroy human lives.

Disgusting was the fact that Les was fucked in the head because of this family that had been allowed to rape and destroy human lives. The fact that the one decent in-law I had moved as far away from that family as she could get and that my sons and I had been isolated from her because of their disgusting acts.

And Cockburn not only knew that she'd put it in her filing that was dated April 20, 2018 when she also committed Stolen Valor, and claimed that I had "personal knowledge," which for those who hadn't gone to law school meant the psycho Cockburn was saying that I'd either seen or participated in Les's molestation that happened more than a decade before I ever met him.

Not a mistake. She had claimed, in writing, that I had "personal knowledge" of his molesta-tion *twice*.

Disgusting was that the Cockburn whore knew that she'd just framed me with a lie and then allowed me to be arrested for something she knew for a fact was the truth. That Les Senior was a pedophile and that his wife had helped him procure victims and had protected him over the welfare of her own children for decades.

Then the slag had stood by and said nothing as *you* sentenced me, an innocent person, in front of her.

What kind of mother could protect a pedophile and attack another mother who was protect-ing her children?

In that moment, I knew Satan was engraving a place in hell with their names on it.

Disgusting was Les's poor cousin who was so traumatized by the Manly's abuse that she'd walked herself out into busy traffic on a North Georgia interstate and killed herself to escape them (true story. Look it up).

His sister no longer had extended family as she'd chosen to live in Hawaii and to remove herself from them completely because of what they'd done to her.

The fact that his father was given a job at a Youth Detention Center after he'd already molested his own daughter was disgusting.

Even more disgusting was the fact that his parents had refused for years to leave Milledgeville, Georgia because they "couldn't" leave their doctors or whatever excuse du jour they'd made up. But the moment Les's other sister opened up a riding school for little girls, Papa Manly left a vapor trail selling his home and moving in next door to her in Savannah, Georgia so that he'd have a whole new supply children around him.

*That* was disgusting! That his sister knew for a fact Daddy was a pedophile and had allowed him that close to other little girls on a daily basis, along with her mother who'd stayed by the pedophile's side all those years after knowing what he'd done.

To his own daughter.

The fact that Les had taken the money he'd stolen from his own sons and bought a seven-thousand-dollar horse for his sister to use to lure more girls to that riding school that was next door to a pedophile...

*That* was disgusting!

The fact that *you*, Dinky, were allowed to sit on a bench, day after day, and not be disbarred after you were caught buying and selling women when it was obvious that you had no respect for us and no care for any child in your jurisdiction, was disgusting.

The fact that a Williamson County Commissioner stood there that day, defending the child molesting family and allowed an innocent voter, a mother protecting her sons, to be jailed on his watch and her basic constitutional rights denied to her and say nothing about how criminal and wrong their actions were, was beyond the pale of what should be acceptable or tolerated in our modern society.

For that alone, Commissioner Alaimo should be forced from his office.

The fact that Cockburn knowingly allowed an innocent to be jailed for telling the truth while she knew she was lying should be an automatic disbarment.

Most of all, the fact that you, Dinky, didn't even bother to read the motion where Cockburn admitted to the molestation and the acts of the Manly family should have required you to leave your bench. Especially after you'd lied in court by saying, "I've read it all. I know this case."

Either you were lying then, or you were more than happy to back the pedophile family against their victims.

Which was it, Dinky?

*Oh, wait...*

I forgot that this wasn't the first time Dinky had backed a pedophile and defended them. He, in fact, had a very public record of defending pedophiles.

Just as it wasn't the first time he'd lied on a court report. Believe it or not, one of the judges on the Tennessee Court of Appeals had taken Dinky to task for his lies and called him out by name when Dinky had "falsified" a court repot.

*Look it up. He did it.*

But that day, lying on the court report was just one abuse of his powers. He'd failed to ask a room full of witnesses who could have easily verified that I was telling the truth and that with one phone call to my sister-in-law who would gladly let the facts out of what had happened to her. That you denied hearing what my sons had to say about Les Manly the elder and his Snooty wife along with their father was truly the most repugnant miscarriage of justice.

God forbid a judge should ever protect a child, sitting in a room with a pedophile.

*That was what was disgusting.*

Instead, you left my children there, *unprotected*, and made them watch as the only one who had ever tried to protect them from the pedophile family that should have been put underneath a jail years ago was hauled out in front of them in handcuffs.

You left my children *unprotected* with those lying, unbalanced monsters who had done nothing but prey on them.

But then, why not? You, Dinky, were every bit the predatory monster they were.

In one fell swoop, you showed my sons that there was *no* justice in this country and destroyed their belief in our court system.

All the times that my brother, the ex-cop, and I had warned them that they could be shot dead at a traffic stop for no reason. To be wary of calling the cops for any reason because they, like you, could be so corrupt and far more dangerous than any actual criminals. You proved to them that day that we weren't being paranoid. That my brother wasn't kidding when he said that he'd left the force because he was sickened by the corruption he'd seen and that he refused to be a part of it.

They saw it with their own eyes.

Firsthand.

By the way, Cockburn, you should learn something, *that* was legal definition of *personal knowledge* that you failed to pick up in your night law school classes.

Firsthand experience. *To witness*. I couldn't have personal knowledge of Les's molestation unless I was a time traveler.

I supposed that explained the following article about YMCA Law School and why so few passed the bar after graduating from their part-time classes:

https://www.tennessean.com/story/news/education/2018/05/31/nashville-school-law-bar-exam-pass-rates/639257002/

Because here in Williamson County, one of the richest counties in America, an old, upper income woman should never have been arrested for complying with a judge's orders and telling the truth about a pedophile.

Yet I was.

Dinky, you were and are an embarrassment to everything that the legal system was supposed to stand for and were the epitome of what had dragged down the reputation of everyone who had ever practiced law. Judge Bubba Dinky. The fact that you had a brother and father who were judges was even more disgraceful.

And reader, if this didn't scare you to the core of your soul, I don't know what would. Because I was railroaded into jail.

How do I know?

Three days before I'd walked into that courtroom, my aunt had received an email from a fan who had been talking to Hogg who had warned my aunt that I was going to jail that day.

They had this all planned out before I ever stepped foot in there. It was why Hogg had come to this hearing when she'd never been to any of the others.

She wanted to see my humiliation.

Even my son had warned me. That was why I'd asked for Esteban to be there that day.

My aunt had refused to believe it. In her religious, innocent mind things like that didn't happen to good, law-abiding people in America.

Why would a team of divorce attorneys have the wife arrested when she was the sole bread-winner for the entire family (and others) and as Les knew and had written in his Non-Disclosures he'd forced everyone to sign:

> The privacy of Terri Manly is highly valued and you shall make each and every possible effort to maintain confidentiality with respect to all information and other material of every kind whatsoever concerning Terri Manly, including but not limited to documents, recordings, and pictures, however coming into your possession or otherwise discovered by you (individually and collectively, "Manly material"), expressly excluding information intentionally publicly disclosed directly by Terri Manly. You acknowledge that due to the particular nature of the entertainment industry, any disclosure or dissemination, whether or not inadvertently, or the Terri Manly material without Terri Manly's express written approval will cause severe and irreparable financial and other harm to Terri Manly. Accordingly, you hereby agree that you shall not at any time use or disclose, directly or indirectly, to anyone other than to Terri Manly or her legal representatives, any of the Terri Manly material and you further agree to keep all such information strictly confidential, private, secret and sensitive. All Terri Manly material, and all other documents, pictures, recordings, records, documents, business contacts (business associates), client contacts, readership lists or other materials in any way relating to Terri Manly, however coming into your possession, is and shall forever be Terri Manly's sole and exclusive property, and you shall not retain, copy and/or disclose any of them without Terri Manly's prior written consent, but shall at Terri Manly's written request, immediately deliver

to her any and all Manly Material which may come into your possession.

In addition, I expressly grant and assign to Terri Manly any and all monies or other benefits whatsoever received by or payable to me (or any designee or representative of mine) in connection with any use, dissemination, or exploitation of the Manly Material or any other information or material described in this agreement. Any such monies received by me, or on my behalf shall be held in trust for immediate payment over to Terri Manly.

Which meant that Les knew how devastating Hogg's attacks against me had been to my career. Especially given the fact that she'd used my fans to attack me.

The same vicious lies said about me by Dumas that Les, himself, had denied in his emails for years where he'd defended me to our attorneys during that suit. But after I came forward with the proof that he had indeed poisoned me, he began to "validate" the lies because the last thing he wanted was to go to jail for the crimes he had committed.

*Welcome to American Injustice.*

*And my persecution.*

*Discredit the victim and no one will hear them. They will be denied all justice.*

*Get a judge to help do it, and you were set for life.* You'd never do jail time for your crimes.

They were so swift to discredit me, regardless of the fact that it was about to bankrupt Les, that they had a copy of my arrest and mugshot out to my fans before I made it to the jail. And they made sure to post my mugshot with a picture of my latest book.

So much for his expensive Non-Disclosure, eh?

And how was any of this to supposed help their client in a divorce?

It didn't. Financially, it'd ruined Les since he was refusing to work and now my publisher was extremely upset to see their release next to a mugshot.

*But if he was a criminal, facing attempted murder...*

That was the only way this could help him, and it should tell everyone that his attorneys knew full well how guilty he and Hogg were in their acts against me. Just as they'd known that the Manly family were guilty of pedophilia and had done nothing to stop a gross injustice.

A repugnant crime.

All acts that should have them disbarred.

My bailiff friend, Bruce Meyer, was extremely sympathetic. When I arrived at the jail and came out of the car, there was twenty officers waiting for me in a circle. Billy clubs out. No lie.

I stared at them.

They stared at me.

*Do they want an autograph?*

That was what it looked like. Normally, when I saw a crowd like that, it was what they were after.

Finally, one of the women guards came forward. "Do you need any medication?"

"I'll need my Benicar for my blood pressure and my stomach meds."

She was even more confused. "The nurse will take care of that."

Then why was she asking?

Another guard came forward. "We were told you were out of control and angry."

I scoffed derisively. "I'm not exactly happy. Would you be happy if the pedophile who molested your nephew, sister-in-law, and kids was left in a courtroom with your boys, and you were hauled to jail because a sick-in-the-head judge wants to protect him? Not my best day, by far."

"Oh, Dinky," they said in unison. Again, no lie.

And then they dispersed.

Apparently, from their reaction, I gathered that Dinky did this sort of thing to women a lot.

As I'd said repeatedly, everyone in town knew what a corrupt scum-sucking piece of garbage he was, yet no one would do anything about it.

Tennessee, the third most corrupt state in the union.

*Number three.*

Ringleader: Dinky.

Later, Brian would tell me that Dinky had called ahead to have them "ready" for me. Apparently, he'd intended for them to rough me up.

Brian's exact words were, "We had been expecting a lion to come raging out of the car and instead this tiny little thing in a cast came out. So demure, frail and quiet. We didn't know what was going on. Instead of a lion, we got a kitten."

They were very to kind to me in jail. I spoke to a number of women who had been wrongfully seized. One poor woman had been shifted from jail to jail and held for a year because of an expired driver's license. All she wanted was to get back to her son as her husband had died in a car wreck. Her bond?

Ten thousand dollars.

*Are you serious?*

I was never more ashamed of Williamson County than I was sitting there that afternoon watching women come and go and knowing that those cops were well aware of the corruption going on around them. The injustice they were a part of.

Unlike my brother who had walked away when he saw how dirty the system was, they were a willing cog in this rotted out machine.

It was only worsened when the booking officer made a joke about my mugshot. "Hey, it turned out nice. Maybe you could use it for your next book cover."

*Shame on you.*

Not a one of you willing to stand up for what was right. Instead, you mocked someone you knew had no business there and who had been wrongfully sentenced.

Some of them were even ex-military and that truly saddened me. Obviously, none of them had been taught the code my father instilled in his soldiers and his children.

God. Country. Honor.

*Integrity.*

*To stand up for those who couldn't fight for themselves. To call out injustice when you saw it.*

*I wear this uniform and bleed in it so that my children won't have to.*

Was that kind of injustice what you went to war for?

*What you bled for?*

It definitely wasn't what my father had given up his life to protect.

I sat there all day, not knowing what to expect. I'd never been in trouble for anything in my life.

"You can make a call, you know."

I'd been trying, but no one would answer. They wouldn't allow me to have my phone, so I had no way of controlling my hearing aids to use a phone. Nor did I have any numbers besides Nick's.

Since I couldn't really hear, I couldn't use a regular telephone.

What I didn't know then was that because of what Dinky had done to me, no one knew how to get me out.

I'd been sentenced to ten days. Ten days for doing what I had been told to do. For nothing more than saying the word *pedophile* in America. Dinky knew what he'd done was wrong. I wasn't the one who'd lost my temper and acted out in court.

He was.

So, after much begging from my attorney, he'd decided to let me out on bond.

Which apparently wasn't done or proper, either. And since there were no protocols for letting someone out after they'd been sentenced by the judge, they didn't know how to release me. Whenever they tried to ask Dinky about getting me out, he threw another fit at them. "Just do what I said! When I tell you something, do it!"

Regardless of what the law was.

He really was that unreasonable.

Remember, "I don't care what the law is." That was the unofficial motto of the Williamson County judges. At least for all the ones I'd dealt with.

After hours and hours of being unable to get Dinky to calm down and answer their questions, the secretary in the jail finally said, "Fuck it." Literally. "Just take this," she'd handed me a piece of paper, "and show up for court tomorrow at nine. Don't be late."

Okay.

My brother and sons were waiting for me outside.

Esteban shook his head. "I've never seen anything like this shit in my life and I worked for one of the roughest jails in Georgia. What kind of fucked up hellhole do *you* live in?"

"Told you."

"Yeah." Also, keep in mind that our cousin was a parole officer and we had judges, lawyers and other officers in our family.

By the time I got home, Les and his crew had posted to all my fan pages and social media about my arrest.

I shook my head at their stupidity.

So, Einstein and crew, how on earth was that going to help your agenda of getting eighty thousand dollars a month in alimony from me?

*Remember what the idiot had put in my NDA?* They had just crushed my reputation.

For no other reason than speaking the truth about his family.

Not to mention, my publisher was already pissed off at me over the whole Dumas suit. So much so that they'd canceled a number of contracts and one of my number one bestselling series.

They'd canned it right in the middle of it, even though it was still a *New York Times* bestselling series and sold more than other series out there.

My agent had been able to move me to a new imprint there, but even they were getting a little tired of Hogg attacking every book that came out.

"It's not fair to the fans and it's not fair to us."

No kidding. Nor was it fair to *me* to work *that* hard on something and to have it unfairly bashed by a bitch with an agenda. Especially when I had the evidence in hand to prove this bitch was in my fan groups and was indeed the one behind the negative attacks.

That she was leading fans around in angry mobs to "bring me down." Not only did I have her emails and texts where she was saying this, I had the fans willing to testify against her.

Now they were smearing me even more.

But then I guess it was more important to keep Les out of jail for poisoning his wife, sons and cats than it was to make sure he had alimony. Anything to discredit me meant he was less likely to get arrested for the crimes he'd committed.

Great game plan.

Whatever. I'd learned from my family a long time ago to deal with humiliation. Cut my teeth on it, point of fact. My grandparents lived to publicly embarrass people.

Especially me.

And it wasn't like I hadn't just come off a three-year lawsuit where Dumas and her best friend, another bestselling author, had run the smear campaign of all time for the same reason. *Discredit the victim and distract everyone from the crimes the repeat offender keeps getting away with.*

But the one thing they hadn't counted on. There was no gag order now.

And I was a fighter. As my uncle Carlos so often said, "Woods don't run. Sometimes we might want to. Sometimes we probably ought to. But a Woods don't ever run."

And Cockburn and crew were bullies who weren't used to people fighting back.

So, with my next newsletter, I got to see just what a little bully bitch she was. And learned that the "bitchy barrister" as she liked to call herself really couldn't stand it when someone punched back. 'Cause old Cockburn cried like a scalded banshee when she came under fire.

That had always been what I hated most in life. Those who dished but couldn't take it in return.

*Don't start no shit. Won't be no shit.*

And the shit was on.

Les should have warned Cockburn that was the thing about us Woods. I'd become best friends with Candice in middle school when a bully threatened to beat her up. I didn't even know Candice then, but I knew how to fight.  She was new to the school and this cheerleader Neanderthal was shoving her around and calling her names because she could.

*Not on my watch.*

So, I got off at her bus stop (not mine) and told that bully, "you want to fight, bitch? I'm here to answer your call."

We'd been friends ever since. I've never been able stand anyone who picked on someone else.

My spine was made of steel.

Even Dumas's attorney, Sal Tiller, said that at the end. "The one thing we learned about her is that she will fight."

*Yes, I will.* To the bitter end and beyond. Even if that meant taking you to the throne of Satan and chaining you there so that I could spend the rest of eternity beating your ass.

I was a direct descendent of Charlemagne. I had the same blood in my veins as Richard the Lionheart.

*Don't tread on me, motherfucker.* That had always been our family motto.

I guess Hogg had convinced Les that after the Dumas shit, I'd be tired of fighting and would have settled quietly. Had he come to me like a grownup and said he wanted a divorce; it would have been simple.

Tennessee was a No-Fault state. Because we'd had all that discovery already paid for in the Dumas case, we knew exactly what we had in terms of assets.

Everything had already been paid for and done.

Had he hired an intelligent, experienced lawyer, he'd have been out of here before I caught on to his poisoning, and none of this would have happened.

Instead, Cockburn got bloody and nasty with the first filing. As my attorney said the moment she read that first motion, "My God, I've been doing divorces in this town for a long, long time with some of the biggest names in the business, and I have never seen anyone get this nasty, this fast. What is wrong with her?"

That was a long, lengthy list that would take days to delve into, and explained why Cockburn couldn't hold on to any man for long.

At the end of the day, my family had been taught to be fair.

Just like my brother and his wife when they divorced. They didn't even use lawyers. Esteban gave Gigi half of everything and set her up nicely. When the judge asked why they were splitting, he answered honestly. "I'm an asshole, Your Honor. She knew that when she married me. I'm hard to live with. She deserves better."

He had the judge laughing. "Well, that's about the most honest answer I've ever heard."

The real reason was because Gigi had decided she wanted kids and she knew Esteban didn't. So, they made a clean break, and wished each other well.

*If only I'd married someone with a soul.*

Instead, Les sucker-punched me after he'd put me down on the ground and lied about me. I didn't know if those lies were spawned by Cockburn telling him that he could get more money if he went for my throat, or if Hogg or one of his other henchmen convinced him to do it.

It was his biggest mistake. Woods are Weebils. We might wobble. But we will get back up.

Les was what my father used to call "terminally stupid."

Cockburn, even more so, because that "barrister bitch" couldn't be taught. *Einstein's definition. Repeating the same action and expecting a different result.*

But what killed me the most about it all was the fact that *The Tennessean*, which knew exactly how corrupt Dinky was, and had reported on it, refused to talk to me about my unjust arrest.

Yes, you heard that correctly. I contacted the paper directly. The same reporter who'd written that article questioning Dinky's possible corruption, and who'd written one on me.

So, when they claimed that I "couldn't be reached" to give a statement to them, the reporter had lied to the public.

Imagine that.

A lying reporter for a major newspaper.

None of us had ever seen that one before, right? Maybe Cockburn was right. Maybe the media could be bought, after all. They just wouldn't take *my* money.

I had a statement to make, and no paper wanted it. They were all too busy running lies on me that Cockburn, Alaimo and Les had fed them.

So, I went with what I'd done with the poisoning statement and proved Cockburn a liar again. I made my statement quite publicly on my social media sites and it, again, took off like wildfire.

Only, unlike the poisoning, no newspaper or blogger picked it up. They didn't want a story about actual corruption where someone had real evidence.

Or was Cockburn right, and they'd all been bought off by someone refusing to show me their spending statements as they'd been court ordered to do?

Someone who had yet to account for the more than a million dollars he'd stolen from me and his children? She sure had been adamant that she knew for a fact that the news media could be bribed. The only way to know that for certain was if she'd done it.

Because Cockburn had provided no evidence in the court, then or since, to prove that I'd ever bribed the media.

By the way, where was my male attorney while my brother was trying to bail me out?

Talking to Les's counsel. Couldn't be bothered to answer my brother's questions on how to help me.

Just like all those reporters who'd been so eager to help hang me over a lie Alaimo and Cockburn had told, who wouldn't come out and defend themselves against Cockburn and crew afterward. They allowed themselves to be accused of being bribed when they all knew that I was innocent.

Not a single blogger. Not a single paper.

No one.

But they let a judge and a lawyer get away with accusing them, and let my life be torn apart over those false accusations.

They allowed numerous illegal subpoenas to go out based on false testimony.

As a result, I'd lost all respect for any form of "news." They were nothing more than gossip rags.

*Truth be damned.*

*People be damned.*

Not that I was really surprised by the latter, I just thought that they gave a little shit about some form of the truth and that corruption would at least cause them to lift their eyebrows. Especially when they were the ones being accused.

Stupid me for thinking they'd defend themselves.

Not even the *USA Today* that was so clearly named and defamed in my suit could be bothered.

Anyway, after I got out, I tried my best to find a new lawyer as I knew that Dinky had it in for me and for Constance. Everyone had warned me that I'd be back in jail if I didn't do something.

Fast.

What I learned was that I had been blackballed in this town. No lawyer would touch me.

Not speculation. Confirmed by half a dozen lawyers. Straight from their mouths. And from the fact that no one would return my calls.

"No one's going to touch you."

"Everybody knows about your case, and they don't want to get involved."

*How's that for justice?*

No other lawyer would speak to me, except the ones I already had who all admitted that what was being done to me was fundamentally wrong, on every level.

"You can't fight Dinky."

"You're screwed."

"There's nothing you can do. Dinky hates you. You better stay out of his courtroom."

That was what I was told.

By everyone.

Les was panicking because he knew I had an expert willing to testify against him, and Detective Lynn Lazy had promised me that he would arrest him, never mind the fact he knew he was guilty.

He didn't care that his son had more surgery or that his son's fiancée was coming in from out of the country, and that we were trying to get her paperwork in order for immigration, and that I was needed at home to help our son with that.

Why should he, their father, care about anything other than himself?

They were ratcheting up their game as I was trying to find representation so that I didn't get arrested again over a single word, calmly stated, the next time my diseased kidneys and liver Les had destroyed forced me to go to the bathroom during one of Dinky's ridiculous, long-winded tirades. My attorney was now under persecution, too, and they did eventually arrest her for equally trumped-up charges.

Why? Because she had the nerve to run against the corrupt judges. I don't know how someone can be arrested for "interfering" with custody by the state that dropped their case and admitted on record that they had no business seizing the custody of a child from its mother. My attorney had been doing her job. She'd planned to surrender the mother to the state when they'd arrested them both.

All bullshit.

As I'd been told by other attorneys in town, the judges had it out for her and so long as she was my attorney, I was screwed.

Luckily, fate intervened.

*Or so I thought.*

Back in March, Maddox had found me a new employee for our store. Kate Raye. She was amazing. Tiny and blond, she was incredibly smart and well connected. Her husband was big in the music industry, and she lived nearby.

She was a godsend.

Outraged over what had happened, she'd immediately begun making calls on my behalf.

One of her friends knew an attorney in town, Melissa Magillicutty. Now, I tried my best to warn Melissa what she was getting herself into.

"Trust me, I know. I used to intern for one of the judges here in Williamson. I know *all* about them. I've had many cases in front of Dinky. He likes me."

I knew she wasn't getting it. "He *really* hates me."

"Yeah, but I'm willing to fight for you."

Melissa kept saying that, over and over, for the next two weeks until I had court again. "I'm going to fight for you."

"He's going to put me in jail."

"Terri," Melissa chided on her way up the court steps. "No one goes to jail in a civil trial."

"I did. A couple of weeks ago."

"You shouldn't have."

"I know. And I did. I'm telling you, that corrupt bastard is insane. And I don't mean Les this time. I'm talking about the judge."

She tsked at me.

Until our case was called.

The moment Dinky looked at me, he turned red in the face. Not a little flushed like an alcoholic might get after one drink. I mean the kind of red like a cartoon character one second before they launched into outer space.

Then, he began a three-hour screaming hissy fit against me. I recorded it, it was so bad. The other side really didn't have to speak a single word against me. Dinky did it for them.

He called me a monster. A buzz-saw. On and on, the insults flew as he threatened to put me in jail for no reason. In fact, he said, "Give me a reason. I want you in jail."

My friend who was a Davidson County police officer for more than fourteen years and who witnessed this said and I quote, "a person expects a certain level of decorum in a courtroom and from a judge. In all my years of law enforcement, I've never seen or heard of anything like that. He's out of control."

It was so bad, that Melissa who had sworn so diligently to fight for me, simply sat down and closed her mouth while Dinky continued to rage and shame her for daring to represent me. She didn't say a word during his repeated threats to put me in jail.

Again.

For what?

Paperwork that Les had in my office that I was banned from going to by a court order. Files that were on the computer Les had removed from my home that he refused to return to me (I have those emails from Cockburn, along with the statements she filed in court saying he did not remove a computer from my house, even though she knew he did). Photos of Les removing the files prior to the divorce and of him "planting" records in each of my sons' rooms in the house.

Meanwhile, Les had never once answered a single question we had sent him. He had violated his own court orders.

Instead of Les being punished for all the crimes he'd committed against me, the least of which was poisoning...

Dinky apologized to him for having to put up with me while he continued to insult, mock and threaten me on behalf of my poor put upon husband.

"The only reason I'm not sending you to jail today is because I'm going to give your new counsel a chance to catch up. She has no idea what kind of monster her client is and what she's in for. Since she doesn't know what she's done, I want her to have a chance at this. But I don't care if you have to work night and day, get it done. I don't care how much you might hate or dislike your client. Get it done!"

How I loved his cavalier attitude about my money.

And I didn't say a word. I just kept writing on my pad, "Vengeance is mine sayeth the Lord. I shall repay. He who justifies the wicked and he who condemns the righteous are both alike. An abomination unto the Lord. Keep far from a false charge, and do not kill the innocent and righteous, for I will not acquit the wicked. Ye shall not spread a false report. Ye shall not join hands with a wicked man to be a malicious witness. Ye shall not fall in with the many to do evil, nor shall ye bear witness in a lawsuit, siding with the many, so as to pervert justice. Woe to those who decree iniquitous decrees, and the writers who keep writing oppression, to turn aside the needy from justice and to rob the poor of my people of their right, that widows may be their spoil, and that they may make the fatherless their prey! What will ye do on the day of punishment, in the ruin that will come from afar? To whom will ye flee for help, and where will ye leave your wealth?"

Never pick on the granddaughter of a preacher who was punished by having to write bible verses and quote them all through her young life. I had read the bible that Cockburn, Kiki and Les thumped. And I knew a lot more than their two pithy quotes they used as memes on their Facebook pages to deceive people into thinking they were "good" Christians.

More than that, I understood it and lived by it.

*Do no harm.*

But even Jesus had his limits.

When you are persecuted in one place, flee to another.

The student is not above the teacher, nor a servant above his master. It is enough for students to be like their teachers, and servants like their masters. If the head of the house has been called Beelzebub, how much more the members of his household!

So do not be afraid of them, for there is nothing concealed that will not be disclosed, or hidden that will not be made known. What I tell you in the dark, speak in the daylight; what is whispered in your ear, proclaim from the roofs. Do not be afraid of those who kill the body but cannot kill the soul.

... Do not suppose that I have come to bring peace to the earth. I did not come to bring peace, but a sword. For I have come to turn a man against his father, a daughter against her mother, a daughter-in-law against her mother-in-law—a man's enemies will be the members of his own household.'

Matthew 10.

As my grandfather so often pointed out in his sermons, even Jesus had called for war.

*To everything there was a season.*

This was the time for war.

*For the Lord helps those who help themselves.* And the jackals had been circling my doors and doing iniquitous acts for far too long.

Not just to me. But to many more. I had a voice. It was my job to use it for all those who could not be heard. I would be failing in my duty if I didn't speak out. And unlike the journalists and bloggers who had failed us, I would not fail others.

I would do my best to be the voice that shouted when it saw injustice.

I didn't start this fight, but I was not going down in silence. They'd taken my voice when I was a child, but I was done cowering in the dark, trying to placate the monster that would not go away and leave me in peace.

Unlike the coward, Les, had turned out to be, I was showing my sons what it meant to be a human being. To stand strong on my principals and the honor code that my parents had instilled in me.

They would not make me a liar when I was not the one telling the lies.

They would not break me.

*One finger and one fist. I declare my independence. I declare my defiance.*

Fuck. You. Dinky, and all the Dinkys out there.

And so, I let him vent while I recorded his diatribe that was an embarrassment to the entire state of Tennessee. Over and over, Dinky threatened to lock me up again when I'd done nothing wrong.

"I ought to do it, too," Skeletor raged from his bench like a pathetic caricature of a shriveled-up old man who'd lived a corrupt life. "Poor Mr. Manly's been waiting and you won't cooperate."

Been waiting on the paperwork he stole out of my house and had refused to hand back to me? Oh, okay...

Where in the lawbook was that a crime to put a woman in jail for? But Dinky had already lied about the law and what he could do with it. Why should he start telling the truth about it now?

*Ah hell, let's just start making shit up and finding new ways to arrest citizens and torture them for no reason whatsoever!*

And wait for the best idiocy out of Dinky's mouth. "I don't understand why you can't get a copy of all your copyrights. Just pick up a phone and call the people who publish your books. How hard is that?"

*Well, let's see, Judge Dim Wit.* My books were published in over one hundred countries.

All over the world.

While I do speak quite a few different languages with some degree of fluency, I don't speak fluent Stupidity as you and Snooty do. Never mind Nigerian, sad to say. Nor Mandarin. Bulgarian. Russian. Hungarian. Thai. And on and on. How could I possibly call those publishers when I couldn't even read the name of the publisher on the contract? When I went to their websites, and they were written in a different alphabet than ours so that I couldn't even find a phone number to call?

For that matter, I couldn't even read the contracts. Yes, I signed them, but I was assuming that my agents had done their jobs and read them for me. Hell, for all I knew, I could have signed away my soul on those things. I had no way of knowing.

More than that, Dipshit and company were asking for all copyrights to be listed for everything I'd ever published.

*Ever* (repeated for effect).

Articles, interviews, art, photos, short stories, novellas, books, etc. That included, all cover art on the books, too, which no author had ever been given access to and had no knowledge of (which Les, and I was sure even the idiot Cockburn had to know as the legal copyright remained with the photographer or artist who created it and not with the author of the book).

I guess Cockburn had failed that course in her night law school, too.

Let me repeat that I could not read the languages that many of my contracts were written in. Some of them, I couldn't even discern the alphabet they used.

And here was the real kicker about copyright. Authors didn't have one per book or story or art.

There was the original copyright that was created when we began a story. That was called the "creation" copyright (since most of my stories were started before marriage, Les was *not* entitled to those, so what they were asking for was a giant waste of time and money—if only Skeletor would shut up long enough for someone to explain that to him instead of him going on and on with stories about when he was a lawyer... like anyone gave a single shit for his side chatter that was costing me thousands of dollars). Then, every single time we changed a comma, that created a whole new copyright. Those copyrights were listed in a book every time a new edition came out.

That was why there was often a number of copyrights listed in the front of any given book. If you have ever picked up a copy of a hardcover and looked on the copyright page, you would see a different year of copyright than the paperback version of that same, exact novel.

Same story. No difference. However, the paperback might have a copyright of 2002 and the hardcover might be 2009. Or the hardcover could be 2008 and the paperback 2009. Those were real examples from my books. Audiobooks of the same novel could have an entirely different copyright, too.

Likewise, every time my publisher excerpted one of my books in someone else's novel as an ad, that created a new copyright. Every edition of an eBook was a different copyright from the others. Every format had a unique and separate copyright.

Now, the problem of listing absolutely every single copyright when you had more than one hundred books, countless short stories, articles and interviews, in hundreds of countries the world over was more than apparent, yes?

No author in the world had ever kept up with all their copyrights.

No publisher either.

It was an impossible, Herculean task that Dinky was threatening me with. "If you miss even one of them, I will put you in jail for it!"

Okay, Einstein. There was no way to hand over a list and *not* miss something.

And that being said, according to Les (and I have it in emails he wrote) he was my *IP attorney* right up until the day he left my home. What he'd claimed in the divorce was that he was my "business manager" whose sole job it was to do my IP paperwork. So, all of this would have been the one, and only, thing he was supposed to keep up with as my IP attorney. Which begged the question, why would my IP attorney be requesting the very list from me that he was supposed to be compiling during the twenty-seven years he claimed under oath to have been working for my company?

And let me repeat Tennessee law in this matter:

> The frequency or extent of use of the discovery methods set forth in subdivision 26.01 and this subdivision shall be limited by the court if it determines that: (i) the discovery sought is unreasonably cumulative or duplicative or is obtainable from some other source that is more convenient, less burdensome or less expensive; (ii) the party seeking discovery has had ample opportunity by discovery in the action to obtain the information sought; or, (iii) the discovery is unduly burdensome or expensive, taking into account the needs of the case, the amount in controversy, limitations on the parties' resources, and the importance of the issues at stake in the litigation. The court may act upon its own initiative after reasonable notice or pursuant to a motion under subdivision 26.03.

In other words, Dinky was breaking the Rules of Procedure and he knew it.

Said it all, didn't it?

Never mind the fact that neither Les nor any of the illiterate troglodytes he'd hired could figure out that my publishers were all based in *New York*.

New York City... home of publishing. I thought every human over the age of five had seen the movies and read the books to know that all of the major publishers were based in the Big Apple.

Not like I hadn't talked about it extensively every day of the Dumas case with my kids and friends.

Wow.

Just wow.

And that, right there, said it all about how Les knew absolutely nothing about the "family business" as he'd claimed. Or that he'd even had a simple conversation with me about what it was that I actually did for a living, for twenty-seven years.

Anyway, I'd given them a list of all my published books, as that was what a normal, intelligent spouse would be interested in having as that was the only thing that generated income.

After all, it wasn't like I didn't have a printed-up booklet that we handed out to fans for them to use to go purchase every single title that I currently had in print.

That wasn't good enough.

Instead of becoming educated on the subject and asking a couple of questions so as not to look like the complete and utter moron he was, Lord King Judge Dumbass tiraded against me for not providing the impossible list, and told me how easy such a list would be to compile when he couldn't even comprehend what it was, he was asking.

"Why, I know when I was a lawyer, my clients didn't want to do paperwork. No one wants to do paperwork, but sometimes you have to do paperwork."

*No shit, Sherlock. Why don't you pick up a publishing contract? Or one of our marketing packets. Now, do our yearly IRS forms for foreign publishers so that we don't have to pay foreign taxes. You know, the stuff I do for fun!*

*Your paperwork was pussy league compared to what I do on a daily basis. Stop assuming your little microcosm of experience was everyone else's. The world doesn't revolve around your tiny brain, Dinky.*

*Get over yourself and shut the fuck up while you're wasting my time and money.*

Because really, sometimes, you had to shut up and listen. Especially when you were a judge, and you didn't know the first thing about the business you were presiding over. Guess you failed to attend that day in law school, too, hmm? No wonder you got along so well with Les's jackals.

*My God, with all those losers in the house, did your firm ever win a case?*

But then, that appeared to be systemic here. Woodly had done the same thing.

Two judges.

Two idiots.

And I'm told they were all this way, which was why no lawyer wanted to bring a trial here.

This entire county was seriously *that* corrupt.

Never mind Dinky's redundant rants about wasting my time and money that smacked of Autism he should be tested for. I swear to God, my sons and I have less OCD on a subject.

This was the horror of my constant shit show.

I should have filmed it for Pay-Per-View.

"Now, little girl, instead of arresting you again like I should." Dinky kept rubbing that in my face. He was real proud of the fact that he'd denied me due process and violated my constitutional rights. "I'm going to give you one more shot that you don't deserve. I expect you to answer these questions. I don't care if you have to work nights and weekends with Ms. Magillicutty, here, but I expect it to be done and be done in two weeks. Whatever it takes. Do you hear me?"

*People in Canada heard you, you ridiculous bitch!*

Hours later when he'd finally gotten as sick of hearing the sound of his own voice as the rest of us, and let us go, Melissa was visibly shaken.

Gone was all that self-assured arrogance about how she was going to fight for me.

"I'm sorry, Terri. I didn't know what to say. I was afraid to say anything for fear of making it worse on you."

"I tried to warn you."

"You weren't kidding."

*Do you want to know the real kicker?* After Melissa spent the next two weeks and fifty thousand dollars of my money answering those "important" questions that I'd already answered and given to them four times before that they "had to have," and had kept dragging me into court to be screamed at by Judge Skeletor, Cockburn, Shovel-Face and Alaimo decided that the copyrights and other information they'd been harassing me over weren't necessary, after all.

They didn't need any of it. They just wanted to drive up their paychecks and make me look bad to the judge.

To try to get me arrested again.

Tens of thousands of my dollars set fire to for no reason. An arrest conviction for no reason.

They were out to destroy my life and Baby Huey was only too happy to help them.

And please keep in mind that at this point, they had yet to answer a single piece of the discovery from us that had been due August 2018.

We were now in June 2019.

Where was *my* apology?

Neither the Judiciary Board nor the Tennessee Board of Professional Responsibility said any of that was a violation, either.

Apparently, this was how the State of Tennessee conducted its business. This was normal and routine for how they viewed and treated their citizens.

Unfair judges who made no bones about the fact that they didn't care what the law was. Lawyers who willfully lied and misconstrued facts and who had their clients commit perjury because they were friends with the judge, their former business partner. And they knew that their old buddy would never allow a case for perjury against them.

Even if that perjury put their client and the innocent party at risk for tax fraud.

The third most corrupt state in the Union.

One of the most corrupt cities in the country.

And in two weeks, they were about to break the laws of the U.S. Constitution.

Again.

This time, Williamson County Commissioner Alaimo, Shovel-Face and Cockburn all had the nerve to put their names on the complaint, itself, where they were asking their good ole buddy Dinky to arrest me over the paperwork and information they already had in their possession.

But that was only part of their corrupt little plan.

*Just wait for* this *humdinger.*

I KNOW I'M BACKTRACKING A BIT, but Joan, Nick and I went down to the courthouse, first thing in the morning after my dubious arrest like I'd been told to do.

It was supposed to be for a bond hearing over my release. The reason?

No one had known how to let me out because Dinky had done something he wasn't supposed to do.

All the way around.

There wasn't any paperwork for how to release me and every time they'd tried to ask Dinky about it, he'd screamed at them.

"Just do what I say!"

Sadly, the law was the law, and it wasn't whatever Dinky said when he said it. In spite of what he thought, he wasn't Lord King Emperor.

There was this thing called "Due Process" that Dinky had broken. So, all the members of law enforcement were baffled about what do to as they, unlike Dinky, were trying to follow the law.

Finally, the poor guys in the jail had thrown up their hands. "We don't know what to tell you. You've been here for hours for no reason, and this is ridiculous and wrong. We're sorry. Just take this paper and make sure you come back in the morning."

"Yeah, this is not what normally happens. We've never seen anything like this before."

I knew it was bad when everyone in the jail kept apologizing to me.

So, the next day, we went to the second floor, criminal clerk's office. As I'd been told to do.

They stared at me. "Uh, we have no records for you. Go to the downstairs office."

Okay...

Not what I'd been told, but who was I to argue?

We headed downstairs.

As soon as I told them my name, the entire office got quiet and the clerk I was talking to went white.

"Oh, we know who you are. You need to go home and call your attorney. Right now!"

That was ominous. And it freaked me out a bit. "I was told to show up here for court this morning."

The clerk touched my hand and in a quiet voice told me in no uncertain terms, "Honey, you need to go home. Now. Trust me. You don't want to step foot in any of the courtrooms here."

Direct quote.

"But the bail bondsman told me I had to do this, or I'd be in trouble."

"And I'm telling you right now that Dinky was in here yesterday showing his ass to us about you. He took all our heads off. You need to go home and call your attorney." Her tone was deadly serious.

So were the looks on all their faces.

The expression on my son's face was so grim that I feared he might cry.

Joan pulled me out of the room.

We went back to the car, and I tried to call my attorney. But she didn't answer.

So, I sat in the car, terrified to leave. "I don't know, Joan. I'm scared. What if this is another setup?"

She sighed. "You're right. Hang on." Joan left the car and went back into the courthouse while Nick and I waited.

"What's going on, Mom?"

"I don't know."

And I didn't. I called my brother who used to work in a jail, as a police officer.

He was as baffled as we were. "I've never heard of anything like this."

"No one has, bro." That was the problem.

"Let me call my friend." One of his best friends was a criminal attorney in Georgia. "I'll hit you back in a few."

I'd just hung up when Joan returned. "What'd you find out?"

"That Dinky wasn't supposed to let you go. Apparently, from what they were saying, he knew he screwed up. Instead of owning it, he screamed at them yesterday and acted like it was their fault. He threw one of his epic tantrums with them and told them to let you out, but none of them knew how as there's no precedent for releasing someone after an idiot unfairly convicts them."

"So, what do I do?"

"No one knows. You weren't supposed to be convicted or released."

As a result, I was in a fucked-up state of limbo where normal laws and rules didn't really apply to me.

And when my new attorney filed a motion to appeal the unfair and dubious conviction, would you believe Cockburn filed an objection to it?

Then charged me thousands of dollars for her objection.

While I was in bankruptcy.

Melissa was stunned. "I've never seen anything like this. People don't file things like this. What is wrong with her?"

I shook my head at her. "The bitch is beyond crazy."

"No one files a response." Melissa was horrified. "She refutes her own testimony in this. Is she stupid?"

I didn't comment as it was a no-brainer, much like Cockburn who constantly refuted her own statements in everything she filed. Even in the beginning. Such as claiming that Les didn't remove the guns from our home because he was afraid for his life. Rather, he hid them in our home.

*As we all know, that was what every responsible parent does. Take a loaded gun and all its bullets out of its locked and secured gun safe and hide it in a house with a teenaged boy and all his friends to find.*

Okay.

Sure.

As I'd said before, Cockburn had no business raising children if she believed that leaving children alone and exposed to pedophiles, along with loaded guns at their disposal was good parenting.

*The fact that this bitch was licensed to drive scared me. The fact she was licensed to practice law...*

*Was an embarrassment to the United States.*

Not to mention, Cockburn, as par for the course, couldn't even keep her lies straight. What happened that day I was arrested depended on her PMS and the day of the week. I supposed that this was why so many men had mocked women in the workplace.

*I get it. I wouldn't want to have to work with such an irrational bitch, either. Please don't judge us all by this crazy slag, and I promise I won't judge all of you by Les Manly standards.*

*Deal?*

Unlike Cockburn, my story hadn't deviated. Why no one could figure out who the liar was and who was telling the truth was beyond me.

My God, at this point, I couldn't figure out how any crime had ever been solved in this county. What? Do the police just randomly pick someone and argue them into a conviction?

Really, it was the only thing that made sense given what I'd experienced. Where the hell was the Internal Affairs and the FBI?

Where was the Department of Justice or Attorney General?

Could you stop ignoring our calls and letters and do something about these pathetic jokes you had in your state because I was certain that I wasn't the only one they were abusing. Pretty sure the governor of Tennessee hadn't created an official "Let's Screw Terri Day."

That was what I truly found terrifying.

How many more citizens were getting seriously harmed by these out-of-control lunatics?

These people were fucking nuts and needed to be investigated and stopped before they ruined even more innocent lives.

Meanwhile, they kept going and with every hearing, stripped away more of my rights without due process.

But wait for that promised humdinger...

AGAIN, JOAN AND I WERE HEADING into the courthouse. This time alone. For once, it wasn't for a hearing. I was putting in the paperwork for my legal name change.

I'd been asking my attorneys to get this done for over a year. From the moment Les had walked out, I had wanted my name back, and in most states a woman could get that as soon as a divorce started.

Many states, you didn't even have to waste court time and dollars by making an appearance. Unless you were a felon or your new name was something outrageous, the judge simply signed off on it in his office, sans court, and you got an official letter saying, "hey, you have a new name. Have fun with it!"

Not Tennessee, 'cause we were the land of backwards assholes!

And contrary to what ole Les thought, his name didn't make me famous. I was a *New York Times* bestselling author under another name long before I was one under his.

As Shakespeare said, "a rose by any name would smell as sweet."

And the last thing I wanted was the name of a known family of pedophiles associated with me.

I wanted the stink off my rose.

Even my sons wanted to change theirs. *Let's hear it for my progressive eldest.* He planned to take his fiancée's name when they married.

My youngest planned to take my maiden name.

I was so proud of my kids.

Anyway, we walked in and talked to the bailiffs (I was on pretty good terms with all of them now as they knew how badly I'd been mistreated by the system and judges) and headed to the clerk's office. The bailiffs would even tell my attorney to say hi to me whenever they saw her, and they stopped by my booth at a local festival all weekend long to check on me.

They were so sweet.

Just as I was finishing up the paperwork and fee, I heard a grating hick voice that made my blood run cold.

Yeah, God hated me *that* much.

Bubba Joe Dinky.

Complete with his faded jeans, plaid shirt and mullet.

And you could watch his presence wash over the women in that room like an arctic blast. When I'd walked in, they'd been happy and cheerful. Talking back and forth, greeting everyone who came in like old friends.

The moment the door opened, and Lord Skeletor came in, they shrank down in their chairs. Their eyes fell to their tasks or the floor. You could literally here them whispering, "I waited on the douche last time. It's *your* turn!"

Dinky was that creepy old man all women dreaded whenever he entered a room. The one who made your skin crawl because you innately knew he wasn't right, and you didn't want him near you because it was so gross. The kind of man who stared too long and his hands lingered. That kind of creep who always wanted you to sit in his lap when you were a girl...

Cringy all the way. That was the vibe you got from him.

C-r-e-e-p!

"How's my girls?" Skeletor beamed with that fake Pepsodent smile.

A mumbled response.

He was so stupid that he continued to try and flirt when it was obvious, they couldn't stand him. I'd never understood men who were *that* obtuse.

Or maybe he knew, and he was so in love with his power that he enjoyed making those women squirm.

Joan stepped forward to block me from his view. Luckily, I'm small enough that she towered over me, and he was too busy being creepy that he didn't notice.

I quickly finished my transaction with the clerk who was much more somber now and left.

Joan and I shivered on our way out. "Gah!"

"Yeah," I said. "He's repulsive."

But I was looking forward to putting him and Les behind me. And starting over without the pedophile name hanging over me like a sinister pall.

**B**Y THIS POINT, I WAS SICK of being hauled into court every two weeks. My money was being drained out faster than I could replenish it, and Les didn't seem to care that we were going broke.

The craziest part? None of their bullshit had ever been necessary.

We had documents for everything we owned and IRS statements for my income. For years. And Les was in possession of it all because of the Dumas case.

All Dipshit had to do was say, "I want a divorce," and we could have split amicably.

No attorneys necessary.

The fact that he came out the door swinging at me and insulting me with such ludicrous allegations from the beginning showed that he was afraid of something coming to light.

Why else go to all these stupid stunts that depleted our funds when he'd spent three years screaming at me that he didn't want to go broke on a lawsuit?

*Who was the crazy one, I ask you?*

More than that, my publisher was getting tired of having my name dragged through the mud with Les's antics. Hogg and crew were in rare form.

By this time, I'd learned that Cisco's girlfriend was in on the action, too.

On one of my Facebook groups someone had posted a message as "Doug Ramstein" claiming to be a friend of my sons' from school. They opined at what a great, wonderful father Les had been and how *I* must be crazy. That clued me in immediately that it wasn't a friend of my kids.

First, their friends had never stalked my fan pages.

I was just Ms. Manly to them. They'd never given two-shits that I was a writer. Never had.

Never would.

Second, contrary to Les's delusions and Cockburn's bullshit, Les hadn't raised my children, and all their friends were well aware of this. *I* was the one who made their snacks for them whenever they came over. The parent who conversed with them and made them dinner. The homeroom mother who was in charge of their parties when they were little.

I was the one who was always in charge of all their parties (birthdays, holidays and sleepovers), and the one who'd bought all the presents for their friends.

Kids never forgot who bought their presents.

Or cupcakes.

Les knew nothing about them or their friends. Other than being the spoilsport who would piss them off and irritate them whenever they were at our house so that he could drive them out. You know... *that* parent who always broke in on the kids in the middle of their fun and said, "Do you have to use so much ketchup? Why's that creepy kid here all the time? What's his name, again? Why are their parents dumping them here? Don't they have homes? Can't their parents ever have our kids over?"

I, personally, preferred for the kids to come to my house.

Les couldn't stand it and he was extremely obnoxious about it whenever they were here.

Not to mention, none of my children had a friend named Doug. And I would know as I was the one who filled out all the invitations for their classmates to invite them to parties. The one who wrote those names on Valentine's Day cards every year. The room mom for all their classes. You know, the one who volunteered for the PTA and school fairs, library sales, etc. I was the one who went on career day and who talked to their classes.

Not the I-refuse-to-work Les.

And let's not forget the important fact that they'd never even had a kid in any of their schools with the last name of *Ramstein*. But since Hogg's a tutor, she knew that Doug was a common name for their generation.

My kids didn't happen to have any friends with *that* name.

Idiot bitch.

So, I naturally assumed it was Hogg posting the attack. It sounded like Hogg, as it was written in her style and "voice." She'd said in her own email to Cyn that I knew her syntax:

> So, after reading those, especially Helen's, fans might think about making inquiries to TOR via TOR's site, comment section, or whatever address they have for questions about publications. They ARE the published.
>
> Comments should include a copy of the hint post and/or any post about the bonus scenes and alternate endings, especially where they contradict each other: posts from their author/ author rep.
>
> Fan comments should ask how many books had alternate endings, bonus scenes (I'm not sure when or if they were announced), how many had hints, where in the margins, how did hints get in the margins (can be an excited question about publishing), which vendors received the different versions of the book, etc.
>
> Folks could include what they've experienced and what they've learned from other fans: factual and clear.
>
> (reminder: post may say Carter, but it's the authors site, she's their author and TOR wanted her more connected to her fans).
>
> If you guys talk about this, try not to use my direct words or phrases from here. If there is a subpoena for emails with specific phrases, I'd rather keep it mixed up.
>
> TM might know my syntax, then again, she might be too self-involved to know, but I can't afford the risk of identification

I found the comment about cancel due to no stock interesting, (Helen's first comment below). It sounds like the normal cancel when pub date is pushed back and distributor doesn't have new date:  NOT something any fan wanted to hear when it's the 3rd or 4th book with dates pushed around that messed up preorders.

I'm finally getting sleepy and Dolly just came upstairs for some middle of the night love. I'll pet her a minute, if she doesn't run down the stairs; then make sure she wants to stay outside, and then try for sleep...

Hope you don't get this til morning!! You need sleep. It's ONLY Tuesday.

Sweet dreams or happy day!!!

That was the actual email that Hogg had written to Cyn where she'd outed herself and the emails that she'd been sending to other fans and groups.

It was only one of a number of them that have since been sent to me at the time of the "new" unwarranted attack that occurred in the fan room where I knew Hogg went to stir dissent among my fans.

> are people commenting on your pages since we know they can't comment on the main page.
>
> 10:10 PM

That was one of Hogg's texts to Cyn, asking if attacks were happening on my fan pages as my crew could block and delete them from my primary fan page that was owned by my publisher.

As for the other attack, I'd never once met Cisco's fiancée. None of us had, for that matter. Honestly, I thought he was lying about her as I couldn't imagine a woman who would willingly put up with his repulsive ways. So why in the world would I have ever assumed that Cisco's fiancée would have a dog in this fight that would cause her to put up a fake Facebook account so that she could come over to my fan pages and insult me for no reason?

Until my new IT guy, Jason, received an email Hogg accidentally sent to Cisco's old email account that was now Jason's.

Oops.

Here's a snippet from that actual email:

Karen Hogg did not post as Doug Ramstein.  Karen found out from Cisco McCullough on May 2, 2019, that the post was actually done by Cisco's fiancé, then girlfriend. He recently discovered Shirley had a profile for Doug Ramstein and made the post.

Cisco McCullough will attempt to obtain the facebook historical evidence of the post May 3, 2019. Cisco will provide his findings to Attorney Lee Williams.

Joan Hart, a lifelong friend of Terri, is Carter.

Karen Hogg does not have any alien profiles/accounts on facebook or other social media.

Now do you see why I'd continually said that the bitch was barely literate, and couldn't punctuate a sentence? This was what Les had hired at sixty dollars an hour to tutor my children. To write their admissions papers to college and to take finals for them.

No wonder my son's grades had slipped with this idiot "tutoring" him. Does this not explain why my son dropped from being in the top one percent?

Yeah...

The fact that any tutoring company would employ her was deeply concerning.

And she was lying to her own attorney in this. She did have fake profiles on Facebook. Although, they probably weren't "alien." The word is alias, you nimrod (look it up, Hogg, it is a real word). Provided you could figure out how a dictionary worked.

She'd posted as "Mildred" all the time in my email accounts, and I have the emails to prove it. She'd also posted as me and I have evidence of that, too, as she'd admitted it to other people, and put it in writing.

Again, why couldn't liars ever keep their lies straight? It made my head hurt trying to wrestle them all together.

And why was she even talking about Joan? Joan had nothing to do with anything, and she wasn't Carter. That would be Jason.

Didn't you just love how Hogg was always speaking like she was an authority on things she knew absolutely nothing about? She was long gone before either Joan or Jason were hired and had never worked in this house since they'd been here.

What a rare piece of shit Les threw his family away for.

But that was neither here nor there. With this email, Hogg had shoved Cisco under a bus, and they were all too stupid to realize it only proved that they were indeed in a conspiracy together to attack me and publicly destroy my reputation, which was what I'd been saying.

And what I'd filed a suit over.

In fact, in this text to Cyn, I think old Hogg said it best:



So, the question remained, why would Cisco's fiancée have bothered to create a fake Facebook profile so that she could pretend to be a young boy in order to attack the reputation and books of an author she didn't know and had never met?

To compliment and back a man that she had never once met?

Yeah, that made all the sense of the world, said no one ever.

I mean really, why would I think of Cisco's woman when I had tons of evidence that in the past Hogg was the one who'd led those attacks on my social media accounts?

And they dared call *me* delusional?

The arrogance of that one text said it all about Hogg and her delusions. This after she'd admitted to spending the night with my husband while my son and I were out of town. To her admitting that she would drink with my husband while I was lying sick in the basement, too ill to help myself.

Yeah, there was nothing immoral, illegal or inappropriate about that.

And the word was immoral, not amoral. Sheez!

I'm not the one doing illogical acts for no reason and, as a grown adult, jumping into fights where I didn't belong. Just how many people had they roped into this madness?

And who would willfully participate in such a thing? My God, do none of these people have lives? Where did they find each other?

1-800-Dial-An-Ass?

My friends would have laughed at me if I'd ever asked them to do such a thing, not that I ever would. We had far better things to do with our lives and time than make fake accounts and stalk people we didn't know for the benefit of someone else we hadn't met.

Even Cockburn was friends with Les on Instagram, Facebook, et al.

Again, who does that? I'd been friends with my attorneys for decades and we're not friends on Facebook or Instagram. And keep in mind that I was kind of famous, in the right circles.

Really pathetic for all of them that they had no real friends in this world. Only people they were currently using.

Maybe Facebook should consider creating new "groups" of names. Friends. Sycophants. Henchmen.

Dumbasses.

Not to mention that Cisco was a dark web expert who had always been insanely paranoid. Were we really to believe that his girlfriend was in his home, and on his computer doing anything that he didn't know about?

Yeah, right. And my kids have a meth lab in the hall bathroom where they keep six naked women and a rock 'n roll band.

With that amount of bullshit, I could start a fertilizer factory.

And I love that Hogg blatantly admitted that Cisco "will attempt" to hack his own girlfriend's account so that he could try and get evidence (I believe everyone over the age of five, except the idiot Hogg, realized how illegal that was).

Or wait. Could it be that ole Cisco was setting up his girlfriend to take a fall for him?

That could make a lot more sense.

Because I did have evidence of Cisco's cyber-attacks on me.

Right down to the fake, recorded heartbeat that he'd pumped through my house in January, that forced me to rip out every piece of electronics in my home.

And what did I do to him to make him hate me like that?

Not a damn thing, other than way overpay the piece of shit for nearly a decade while he stole from me by charging me for hours he'd never worked. Where he'd taken inventory that was supposed to be sold and handed it out because he was too lazy to pack it up.

Then, insulted my fans whenever he could.

He'd even accused one fan who had legally changed her name to one of my characters of being a thief. As if such a loyal fan would ever do that.

That was how insidious they were at isolating me from everyone and trying to destroy my fanbase and cause dissension in my home.

Dissension with my fans.

This was what Les had brought into our lives.

But then who could blame Cisco for illegally reporting time he hadn't worked and expecting to get paid for it? After all, Les was the one who'd written to him and said, "Hey, this is a forty hour a week job. You're leaving 'money' on the table."

Way to help your wife save money and watch our bottom line, ole Les. Love how you cavalierly threw my money away and documented the fact that you'd told an employee to falsify his time sheet to get paid for hours he didn't work.

And for helping Cisco to rip me and our children off, Les believed himself to be entitled to half of all my worldly belongings and all future income?

*Are you fucking kidding me?*

Les had stolen from me and my children for decades. Why should the law enable a thief to steal even more from us for the rest of our lives?

I thought we were supposed to have laws in this land to protect the innocent and punish the lawbreakers and abusers.

Never mind all the computer equipment that went missing from my home and storage unit with Les.

Equipment last seen in Cisco's possession.

This was the same psycho who when I was at Comic Con and discovered Cisco had shipped an entire giant road case of bubble wrap out to the west coast had the gall to attack me for it. All I did was close the case and look at his "friend" Peyton and ask, "why did you ship a case of bubble wrap out here?"

"In case we need to pack up something. Cisco said to."

Sighing, I shook my head and pushed it aside.

It had cost me three thousand dollars to ship that one container of bubble wrap. That was how stupid Cisco was and how wasteful with my hard-earned money. And he and Peyton had spent that entire Comic Con of 2017 telling my sons how they were going to "replace me" because they knew my business so much better than I did.

That they could run my business so much better than I could. Les kept repeating that, too.

How Hogg and they were a hundred times better at managing my business, because I was the one who mishandled and misspent all the money. Not them, and all the useless things they'd bought. Such as shipping a large container of bubble wrap cross country.

Les was even wanting me to hire the barely literate Hogg to copyedit my books.

You read her letter. Seriously?

Les had also said that to my sons who'd laughed in his face.

After all, I had built my company and career long before any of them were hired.

Had begun my career long before I ever married Les.

And made a lot more money before they came along. Funny how my income declined substantially once Les forced them on me and they started ripping me off.

Anyway, we were busting our asses to set up the booth while Cisco was back in the hotel room with ole Les. Hmm... Mr. Bishop's allegations about the two of them were beginning to make more sense.

Suddenly, Cisco came in, red in the face, and slammed down the toolbox. My sons and I, along with my four other crew members who were there to witness his hissy fit turned to stare at him.

"Are you okay?"

"No," Cisco roared at me. "I heard you've been talking shit about me behind my back!"

I glared at Peyton who'd gone over to get Cisco a few minutes prior to this tantrum. "I haven't said shit about you. And you need to curb your attitude or go home."

That was the kind of shit-stirring trash Les liked to keep around himself. Liars and thieves who schemed against people for no reason.

He was welcomed to them all.

*Can't wait until they turn on him, because they always turn.* Remember that these were the same bastards who used to pretend to love and adore me to my face, too, while talking crap about me behind my back to Les and Hogg.

And Kiki.

Meanwhile, they were telling me how much they hated Hogg, Kiki and Les.

And no, I was not making that up. It was all true and I had witnesses who could verify it.

I'd been dealing with this crap, nonstop.

Joan and I were talking about it when Skeletor came in and called court into session.

Since I was sure that I was going to jail, I'd made certain to wear my outfit from *A Handmaid's Tale.* I figured if I got another mugshot, I'd make a real statement with it, especially since Atwood's Gilead and Williamson County bore a frightening resemblance to each other.

They were so stupid they didn't even catch on.

However, it was more fitting for that day than even I had guessed it would be.

Skeletor cleared his throat. "Something interesting happened as I was coming in here. I was handed a piece of paperwork. It seems Mrs. Manly wants to change her name."

Gaping, I glanced back at Joan. My paperwork shouldn't have gone to Skeletor. It was the responsibility of another judge to oversee name changes for Williamson County.

But then as Skeletor had said, "I do it all." Even when he wasn't supposed to.

"Well now, I'm not going to sign this. I want Mr. Manly to think about whether or not he wants to agree to that."

*Are you kidding me?* When did the legislature meet and change Tennessee law? Nowhere was it written that my ex had to give his permission for me to change my name.

Nowhere.

Skeletor gave that creepy smile to Les and his hyenas. "Now, sir, you don't have to make up your mind right now. You take all the time you need to think it over."

*Were we in the Middle Ages?*

Well apparently, we were because he left my paperwork there, ignored it, and stuck me with a name that now gives me PTSD.

To this day, I'd been denied my name change.

But they were only getting started.

The first four hours were taken up with Shovel-Face calling in his buddy accountant. Dinky immediately began opining what great friends they were and how much he trusted him. How long they'd worked together, yada yada yada.

"Do you have a problem with him testifying?" Skeletor finally asked me after wasting a few thousand dollars in attorney fees.

My attorney looked at me.

"Yeah, I do."

"You can't," Melissa whispered back.

"Bullshit! He has no impartiality!"

But in the end, I had no choice as Skeletor threatened me with jail when I spoke up.

"You have an attorney! You don't speak in my courtroom. You speak through her."

Even when she refused to do what I told her to do. When I had every legal right to object to Dinky's "buddy" he was in league with giving false testimony against me.

Even so, Dinky put this lying, doddering imbecile on the stand.

My accountant and bookkeeper who were in court?

Not allowed to say a single word on my behalf for the entire day. Nor were they allowed to refute the perjury being spewed by Dinky's biddy buddy. Dinky refused to hear them because he didn't want his "good old friend" to be liable for his perjury and lies.

I couldn't believe it. I'd seldom seen anything more blatant other than Dinky's statement that I needed protection from myself.

*Oh, wait...*

I forgot the infamous judge statement that was on a transcript. "I don't care what the law is."

Yeah, that one trumped them all.

Next came Cockburn who wanted to *voir dire* me. Only one problem. They forgot my teleprompter, and we were in the big courtroom.

So began their usual mockery over my hearing problems.

See, Cockburn had this stupid belief that because her father was deaf, I couldn't possibly be hard-of-hearing.

Remember that she was dumber than the shoes I wore.

Apparently, no one other than Cockburn could have a deaf person in their family.

And if one person was deaf, then another couldn't possibly be hard-of-hearing.

Contrary to your terminal fatuousness, bitch, my sister was born deaf. My grandfather went deaf. My mother and father both lost most of their hearing by the end of their lives. And I've lost all hearing in my right ear and a lot of hearing in my left—well documented medical fact. There was a huge difference between someone who was born deaf like my sister, and one who cannot hear at all, and someone who was partially deaf, and hard-of-hearing.

If Cockburn's encephalopathy wasn't so pervasive, she'd know that. When you were partially deaf, you couldn't understand all the words and that made it extremely hard to follow conversations, especially in certain conditions. The worst part was that your brain often substituted words for what you thought you'd heard. So, the infamous "dinner for two" could become "dinner for crew."

That was funny when you were in casual conversation and you answered what you thought you'd heard, and people stared at you like you'd just grown two heads.

In a courtroom, that mistake was what caused Rebecca Nurse to be hanged for a crime she hadn't committed.

It could also cause you to be up for perjury charges, especially with a judge who'd already threatened to put me in jail if I missed even a single copyright by accident because he'd told me that he would assume I'd done it on purpose.

Whatever happened to innocent until proven guilty?

Oh, wait, that wasn't in Williamson County, land of the corrupt.

And given that Cockburn and crew were lying pieces of shit and that Dinky kept threatening to and had put me in jail over a lie this bitch had told with a smirking grin, I wasn't about to say a fucking word as an answer unless I knew exactly what these lying sacks of shit were asking me.

No mistakes. I couldn't afford them.

*Do you blame me?*

My refusal to be cross-examined without a teleprompter threw them for a tizzy. They ended up having to take me into a mediation room so that I could read from the court reporter's stand while Cockburn interrogated me.

Oh, what joy. I was close enough to smell her rotted out twat. *Woman, please learn to apply deodorant and for God's sake, brush your teeth and get some mints.*

I've smelled better polecats that were dead on the side of the road. In Georgia.

In July.

Every time I tried to answer, Dinky threatened me with more jail time.

Even when I asked if I could ask a question for clarification.

Seriously.

Meanwhile, Cockburn lied. Then lied again. She took entire emails out of context and out of the more than ten thousand emails she had received from my PR firm from her illegally gained subpoena when she and the judge had both accused me of using my PR company to bribe the *USA Today* newspaper, she read the only two that had to do with Dinky and her. "See, Your Honor. This is what they released to the public."

*No, bitch, it wasn't.*

"There are over ten thousand emails just like these."

*No, bitch, there weren't.* While I realized that Cockburn was too stupid to do basic arithmetic, the other emails directly attached to the two she had the judge read out loud after mocking me for the fact that I couldn't because I'm dyslexic were my PR folks telling me *not* to release that email. Again, my PR company said not to release them. Had Dinky read one more paragraph, he'd have known she was lying to him. And it really made me want to know where the ADA people were to help me with these bastards who blatantly broke the law (they ignored all my emails and letters as I pleaded for help).

Cockburn, in violation of Tennessee rules of procedure and code of ethics that said she was obligated to mention that the other ten thousand emails were all about release dates and interviews, and had absolutely nothing to do with her, him or the divorce at all.

Hell, a number of them didn't even have to do with *me*. They were emails about other clients my firm had accidentally sent over.

Instead, Cockburn knowingly, maliciously and willfully lied to the court. All done to prejudice the already unfairly prejudiced judge against me, and he was too stupid to catch on. I don't understand why my attorney couldn't object to it being entered into evidence based on that. But apparently Tennessee law was unlike any law code of any state I'd ever heard of.

At least that was what every attorney I talked to, told me.

More than that, he never allowed my attorney or me to speak up or have our turn to refute Cockburn's preposterous lies.

Not once.

Funny, Bitsy Dullard from the Tennessee Board of Professional Responsibility didn't think that was a violation either. Really? Last time I checked, that was misrepresentation and a violation of ADA law.

Not to mention, due process.

If I lied like that to a judge under oath, I would go to jail for perjury. After all, I was sent to jail for something I didn't do.

This miscarriage of justice was sickening.

It was as bad as the motion where Cockburn had claimed that I had threatened to kill two people, then only named one. "Her former best friend that she got in her car to drive to Georgia to assassinate."

Oh my God! Did I ever laugh, as did everyone who knew me. Thank you, Les and Cockburn, for that entertainment. It normally took me half an hour to get into a car.

Sometimes longer.

Les should know that as he'd spent thirty years screaming at me over the fact that I had to keep going back into the house because I forgot:

My glasses.

My shoes.

My purse.

My coat.

My phone.

My wallet.

My credit card (and I only had one).

My license.

And I could never remember where I'd left any of them.

Really, it was ridiculous. I admit that freely as it aggravated me as much as it did others. It really should be a comedy skit.

Oh, the person I supposedly went after?

Ironically, that bitch had threatened to kill *me* and Joan. I have that well documented because of what Les did to her daughter, we had to hire security guards for almost a year. Even my sons had to go trick-or-treating that year with armed security guards due to her *written* threats against us.

What was even more galling? Since the divorce had started, Les, whom I had email after email from him calling them liars and everything else, had since gone to their small Georgia town to get them to testify against me. The same women he'd called liars, whores, and every horrible name in the book.

Remember that he'd had her daughter put in jail for a felony and was single-handedly responsible for her daughter turning twenty-one in jail.

Hence the death threats against me and Joan.

Cockburn had the audacity to say that *I* threatened *them* when I had the receipt to prove I'd been forced to hire bodyguards. Never mind all the witnesses that year who'd seen those bodyguards at signings and such.

Yeah...

Anyway, hours went by with other such Cockburn falsities. "So, when Mr. Manly left, you had access to ten cars? Yes or no?"

"No."

"But you did."

No, I didn't. Dipshit took two of the cars with him and my son had a third car in Georgia with him.

That removed three of those ten. I might be dyslexic, but unlike Cockburn, I could count without using my fingers and toes.

Not to mention, the other ones didn't run, and I had the fourteen-thousand-dollar car bills in less than a month to prove that, too.

If only they'd allowed me, my attorney or accountant to speak we could have refuted her lies. With facts. God forbid someone put that on record in a Williamson County court. The court reporter's stand might have burst into flames if actual truth hit the screen she was typing on.

So much for American justice.

But at no time was my attorney allowed to respond.

Or object.

Cockburn kept going and going like the Pinocchio Energizer bunny.

Her next attack was on my son's company that he'd built by himself.

I plainly told her that "Black Hat Society is owned by my son, Nick Manly. I have nothing to do with it. At all."

They had no proof that I'd ever had anything to do with it. None whatsoever. And I had all the proof that it was all his.

Because poor Nick was so proud of himself for setting it up with his own funds, he'd made the mistake of showing his credit card to his father with the name of his company on it.

As usual, and in true Manly fashion, Les couldn't believe his son could do anything. After all, Les was a complete and utter fuck up incapable of dialing his own phone. How could his Mensa-level son ever be capable of starting his own business?

That couldn't be. Only Terri was *that* smart.

So, the lies and interrogation began.

I stared at Cockburn the Idiot. "The money in that account came from his job at AMC."

"AMC? What's that?" She screwed up her over-painted, hyena face.

I looked at Cockburn like the utter moron she was. "You know? The local movie theater. The only one we have in town?" My God, bitch, had you never lifted your head out of your date's crotch long enough to see the giant marquis or signs? Or were you not even literate enough to make out the giant A-M-C letters all over the one and only movie theater we had?

Wow. *She was special.* Les could definitely find the bottom of the barrel when it came to attorneys.

In the end, they proved nothing. But she kept insisting that I'd transferred "hundreds of thousands of dollars to my son's company" and that I was using that to hide funds from them.

Guess how much money was in his account.

*Go head, I dare you.*

*Less than one grand.*

*Idiot had spent thirty-five thousand dollars that day, alone, to strip his son of his entire savings that amounted to roughly eight hundred dollars. Aren't they awesome people?*

I never used my son's account for shit. And Cockburn put on no evidence of my doing that as I'd never done it. So, we wasted a full day of utter bullshit to the tune of tens of thousands of dollars.

The most she could show was that I'd transferred fifty thousand dollars into a single account and then wrote a check for that amount.

What she and her lying accountant forgot to mention was that the money went to the IRS to pay my taxes. I had to suppose that they never paid theirs so the concept of someone paying off their IRS debt was an alien concept for them.

Even after all her bullshit, Dinky was about to let us leave when all of a sudden, Cockburn went running up to Shovel-Face.

Next thing I knew, because I couldn't hear and didn't have a teleprompter in the big room, Dinky was telling us that we were to be held as prisoners in the courtroom. Me, my sons, Joan, and two other friends.

If we made a phone call or tried to leave, we'd be arrested immediately.

*What the hell?*

Bewildered, I stared at my attorney.

"They're going to seize everything in your safes at your house."

"Pardon?"

With absolutely no cause having been given or shown, and without allowing me, my accountants or my attorney to respond to their lies or to give any refuting evidence, Dinky had ordered that a trustee be appointed over me and all my accounts.

Me, *personally*, and all my accounts.

My freedom had been denied to me without any due process whatsoever.

Even my personal accounts, which was illegal for him to do, under the law.

And Nick's accounts. Nick who had nothing to do with the divorce and who was a grown adult.

*Also illegal under the law.*

By law, the useless Judge Dinky *only* had authority over marital property. *Nothing* else.

With no due process, they turned me into an indentured servant and took away my right to have any say in my life whatsoever.

In one heartbeat, every asset and dime I owned was seized and taken from me.

*With no due process (I needed to keep saying that as it was so unbelievable).*

*For no reason, other than I'd written an email insulting a corrupt judge who'd been arrested for prostitution and had no business in a courtroom.*

Didn't matter that Les, in violation of a court order, had been recklessly spending all our money on things like a seven-thousand-dollar show pony he had boarded in a state where he didn't live so that his sister could induce another little girl over while living next door to their pedophile dad.

Or that he'd run through every single dime of my children's trust funds that the judge had told him was his "alimony" and that he was under a court order not to mishandle or misspend.

He even spent money on women's clothing and at women's boutiques. Thousands of dollars.

*I* was the one who was now under what was basically house arrest and was stripped of all my rights.

*What the fuck?*

Joan stepped forward. "What about the jewelry Les took?"

"Where is it?" Dinky asked.

"In Georgia."

"He can return it when he has a chance."

*Are you fucking kidding me?* My home was to be raided like I was a drug dealer and this lowlife bastard who'd stolen everything while I was away working was to be allowed to leisurely bring part of his stolen items back whenever he got around to it?

From a state where he'd been committing perjury by saying he wasn't living?

Third most corrupt state in the Union.

One of the most corrupt cities in the country.

Not only did they seize all my accounts, but they seized my son's.

My grown, adult son's.

Literally every single dollar that baby had earned as a busboy cleaning up after people, which was a nasty job that he got in order to be the man his father never was.

To help his mother pay bills and to start his own company.

While his father spent three hundred dollars for a single meal at a time with the money I'd earned for Nick and went on shopping sprees at women's boutiques and biweekly hair salon and manicure/pedicure salons for hundreds of dollars a session.

Les dared do this while his son worked as a busboy just so his father could steal every dime he'd saved for no reason.

While his brother was sleeping on the floor in Japan, barely getting by.

Their father lived lavishly on the money he'd stolen from them.

Never mind the hundreds of thousands of dollars wasted on useless, brainless attorneys Les had spent to haul me into court every two weeks because he had no other form of entertainment.

They seized Nick's meager money out of his account and left him stranded at the gas station, unable to pay for his gas and no way to get to work.

Meanwhile, no one would force that bastard to go get a job like everyone else, including his sons. Or enter mediation so that we could put a stop to his stupidity.

And my abuse.

Rather, there stood Les with a law degree that I scrubbed floors to pay for, daring to claim that I had emasculated him.

*Brother, newsflash, it was your own actions that did that. It had nothing to do with me.*

I felt just like the old prisoners in Salem, Massachusetts who had to pay for their own torture while they were being persecuted and held in jail before they were hanged.

*Are you ready for this?*

They charged me thirty-five thousand dollars to illegally search and seize my home and take away my basic constitutional rights.

*Are you as sick to your stomach as I was?*

To this day, they'd continued to harass and badger me if I spent so much as three dollars of my own money for my business.

If I spent two dollars to buy myself a bottle of water while I was at an event.

Meanwhile, Les still had no restrictions on anything he'd spent at all.

How fucked up was this nation?

*Do you still believe that this is America the free?*

And if you thought for one moment that this couldn't happen to you, man or women, regardless of race and social standing, you'd better think again.

*Republican or Democrat, they are all lying to you, and you are one step away from being thrown into the gutter and forced to work with no rights whatsoever.* My agent had said it best, they intended to hold a gun to my head and force me to write.

For free.

Last time I checked, that was called slavery and was against the law and Constitution, but that was exactly what they planned to do to me.

Remember that my only crime was being dumb enough to get married when I was twenty-four. To believe for one minute that my abusive husband wasn't *this* psychotic.

And it got better. Remember those friends I had in court with me to witness the travesty?

After holding all of us hostage in his courtroom without reason, old Dinky then followed my friends to their car. He almost ran over Rose in the parking lot. Bastard had the nerve to roll down his window and smile that creepy smile at her and Rio.

"Sorry, ladies. I thought you looked familiar." Then he rolled up the window and summarily circled the parking lot to make sure he saw which car they got into.

Only he wasn't smiling as he watched them get in and drive off.

*Know what made that even creepier than what it already was?* Remember that Dinky was arrested for prostitution. Well, the judge who let him off was taking women who'd had minor violations in his court and using that to force them into prostitution for him and his legal buddies. When one of those women threatened to go public, she ended up dead from what was ruled a "suicide." Although, I had never heard of any thirty-year-old women shooting themselves in the face...

But after it'd happened, another woman who was being coerced by the judge who'd let ole Dinky off panicked and went to the authorities to tell them what was going on. While they were investigating that judge, he decided to try and hire someone to plant drugs in the woman's car so as to discredit her and have her arrested.

That was what had ultimately sent Moreland to jail.

So, Dinky following my friends to their car to see what they were driving wasn't creepy or sinister at all...

Yeah...

Anyway, when I told my friend who was a Marshall that they'd held us in my driveway without a warrant in hand, she was appalled. "They can't do that."

"We were told we'd be arrested if we interfered."

"But they can't legally do that!"

"Shelby, they did! What was I supposed to do? There was a deputy, threatening to arrest me and my children. When he took my brother's property and I told him that my brother would have a fit over it, he put his hand on his gun and drew it on me."

The deputy glared at me inside my home where he should never have been and said, "Is that a threat?"

What? That I was protesting the illegal seizure of property inside my home that the judge had no jurisdiction over?

That none of you had the right to steal what belonged to my children or family in a divorce? Property that belonged to my brother?

"No threat. Just a promise that my brother will be calling his attorney over this."

They took my mother's, grandmother's and great-grandmother's wedding rings.

My deceased father's wedding band. My deceased brother's wedding band. Jewelry that not only belonged to all of the above, but my deceased niece as well.

Family heirlooms of little monetary value, but that were priceless to me and my brother.

Their reasoning?

*I* might sell them.

They even took my baby bracelet with my name on it from when I was born. And a spare button to my coat.

My Daughters of the American Revolution pins, and my National Society of The Colonial Dames of America pendant. My National League of American Pen Women pins and pendant. My Jamestowne Society pin and pendant that proved I was not only a direct descendent from the royal Plantagenet dynasty in England, but also a direct descendant of Charlemagne and the royal Capet line in France.

These were all marked with my name and membership numbers. Why would I ever sell them?

They took the bubble gum machine ring my sons bought and gave to me for Mother's Day when they were boys. The little rock ring that Nick had made for me in third grade.

The Mother's Day ring I bought for my mother while I was in high school.

My mother's watch that my deceased brother had given for her for Mother's Day one year before he was killed.

The plastic handcrafted necklace my grandmother had made for me when I was six years old.

The list goes on and on, but you get the gist of it.

To this day, none of it had been returned to me. Not even my coat button. And they kept threatening to sell it all.

May they all rot in hell. Every human who had a part in forcing my babies to sit in my kitchen and who threatened them if they so much as went into their own rooms for the six interminable hours while our home was plundered.

And where was their father who was supposed to protect his sons?

Sitting in the fucking driveway with Cockburn. Laughing at the fact that he had orchestrated traumatizing his Autistic sons in their own home.

Oh, but, according to him, he had done nothing to make them hate him. I was the sole reason his sons refused to speak to him.

*Me. I did it.*

*Les, you really are a Narcissist, through and through.*

Nothing to do with the fact that the bastard plundered their trust funds to come pillage their home while they were held hostage in their own kitchen and threatened by an armed police officer if they so much as called their best friends.

While their father laughed about it in the driveway.

They also seized the operating cash for my store out of my safe and didn't bother to count it or leave a single receipt for anything they took.

Not one damn piece.

To this day, I had to take their sleazy, corrupt word for what was hauled out of here in front of my neighbors like I was a drug dealer.

My favorite part?

Shovel-Face on the phone with Cockburn and Dipshit. "He says there's a gun safe, too. I need the contents of *that*."

I glared at him. "Dumbfuck stole all of the contents when he left. I've told you that. Repeatedly. Remember, you mocked me for it in court." And he stared at me with his hideous, ugly inbred face. "I put it in writing and reported it to the police. Then he reset the alarm on my safe so that I can't access it. If you recall, you've been illegally threatening me by saying that I filed a false police report over the fact that he illegally stole my registered handgun from me."

I still had to produce the safe and though we couldn't get into it because the code had been reset as I'd said, he could plainly shake it to tell there were no contents.

Remember, according to Les, he'd taken all the guns from their safes and had hidden them "somewhere in the home," which we hadn't found. This after his original lie that he'd taken them all with him when he left because he was afraid of me.

Though I did find a single box of bullets in my tiara case.

*What the fuck, Les?*

We had yet to figure out his insanity on that one. Was he thinking I'd pack it in my luggage and get arrested at the airport? I never pack anything without going through it.

He was so screwed in the head that none of us could figure out his twisted logic.

I shoved the safe at his attorney. "Take it, Shovel-Face, I have no use for an empty safe." Gah, the bastard really did look like someone had slapped him for his arrogance. You know the old joke about a kid, so ugly Mom had to put a porkchop around his neck to make the dog play with him?

Mika House.

I prayed to God this thing hadn't spawned any children. Not only because it would be cruel to pass down genes so hideously ugly and stupid, but for his cruel, inhumane arrogance. No child should ever be raised in a home with something this inherently cruel.

God forbid he should date, never mind marry. I pity whatever human was saddled with this mutant life form.

I'd seen slasher movies and serial killer documentaries that were far less disturbing to me than that thought.

So, after robbing my home with no legal warrant, seizing all my money and that of my sons', with no legal warrant, and leaving no receipt, I was finally, after more than twelve hours of this grueling hell allowed to have my phone.

That was when I learned that while they knew we were being held hostage in my home and in court, old dip Ships had picked *that* day to unleash her "hit piece" on me.

What were the odds?

Really.

*Let's think about this.*

Cockburn accused me with no evidence whatsoever of bribing a reputable newspaper, the *USA Today*. "I have it on 'good authority,' Your Honor, that reporters can be bribed and paid for."

Yet she'd never produced any evidence whatsoever to prove those words.

None. Zilch.

Then all of a sudden, on a day Cockburn had handpicked, this reporter showed up and instead of doing the piece she'd pitched to me and my PR firm, she did a total hit piece *on me*.

The reporter had entered my home under false pretenses, claiming she wrote for one paper, while knowing for a fact that she wrote under their slash paper and not the legitimate one that she claimed.

That she wasn't a staff writer at that time, according to her, but a freelance writer...

The one and only kind of writer who could be bribed to do a hit piece because they were writers for hire.

I supposed that explained where Cockburn's "good authority" came from.

Even a three-year-old or Bubba Dinky could put that one together.

Not only had she unleashed the article while I was unable to say or do anything to defend myself as my home was being illegally searched and my property illegally seized, Les and Cockburn had their whole funhouse crew pile on to "validate" her outrageous lies against me.

Even Buffy had stepped forward. Remember the "french fry 'ho?" She claimed to have watched my kids grow up and to have been "part of the family."

My kids wouldn't know this bitch if they set her on fire. They had no idea who she was or where she lived. They didn't even know the names of her kids or if she had any.

The minute I said her name while talking to Joan, Nick frowned. "Who?"

"French fry 'ho."

"Oh! *That* skank. Why she's saying anything about you?"

"Ask your father."

The only thing Ships had gotten right in the whole article was my name. One of my favorite lies had to be where "someone" said that Les had told her during one of their multi-hour-long conversations after he filed for divorce that he came home to find me "casting a demonic spell" with a local psychic.

I'd never laughed so hard in all my life.

That local psychic was named Tasha Ewan, and she also reads for Taylor Swift and a ton of other local celebrities. She was not "satanic" or "demonic." Many of you have probably seen her on a lot of Travel Channel shows as she's quite famous herself. While she was Wiccan and ran the yearly Pagan Pride Festival in Nashville, Tasha had never even stepped foot into my current home until after Les left it.

He'd forbidden it. He didn't like for me to have any of my friends over.

So, unless he'd been channeling ghosts and summoning demonic spirits himself, he'd never seen shit. 'Cause we didn't do anything.

Why? Well, since Les had been poisoning me for so long, and I'd been so sick, Tasha hadn't come over. I'd been too ill to entertain guests. Remember that Les and Hogg had isolated me from everyone.

Told them I was "too sick" for company.

None of my friends or family had been welcomed here in a very long time. They had done everything they could to drive them away.

Even Lyra had been told that she couldn't stay here and wasn't welcomed in my home. Luckily, she was a feisty little Chihuahua who got in Hogg's face. "That's my sister, coz. Until she tells me I'm not welcome, I'm not leaving."

Tasha was also one of many who told Ships over and over that I wasn't a witch. If anyone would know that Tasha would. She was a world-renowned, leading authority and published author on the subject that all kinds of media had consulted with.

Which, again, got back to how stupid and lazy was Lily Ships.

Even worse, how sorry was their factchecker?

*New York Magazine* should be embarrassed that they pay her. More than that, they should be sued. Their rag wasn't fit to wipe ass with. I wouldn't even line Nick's birdcage with it. His parakeet might get cooties from shitting on it.

Obviously, *New York Magazine* knew this which was why they called their sister publication *Vulture*.

Because journalism wasn't disreputable enough. They had to take it one step further and turn it into something truly laughable.

My mother was right. The only real paper worth reading was the *National Inquirer*. At least they made no pretense about having real news.

They were honest in their dishonesty.

You had to respect that. And after all the lies printed about me in *The Guardian*, I wouldn't use it to wipe my ass with, either. Again, that old trick, "she refused to give us a comment."

Try asking me before you print that lie, *Guardian*. I would gladly speak. Any time. Anywhere. Truth doesn't scare me.

I remembered back when I used to think that journalists were worthy of respect.

Now I rank them even lower than lawyers and judges, and I think it was obvious what I thought of those.

So, what did I do once they left my home, and I was no longer being held illegally against my will?

What Cockburn had accused me of doing in front of Dinky.

*Fuck it.*

My bitch-switch had been flipped.

The slag had thrown me in jail for a lie, raided my home illegally, taken property of my children and brother out of my home and lied to the judge, accusing me of insulting her little feelings online.

I'd never once insulted her online or the judge. I'd shown complete ladylike restraint.

But now she'd gone too far because it was obvious that one of those online attackers had to be her. Not only that, but Cockburn sent her ex-husband over to my Facebook page to attack my fans. *How do I know?*

She admitted to it.

There were a lot more than these attacks, including one that threatened me, personally, should I go to the media again. Some of them more insulting toward me and even more threatening, but not appearing here because of the names that were used in the posts.

But here was my question; this was the ex who was only married to Cockburn for a few months. Why would he rush off to her defense after divorcing the skank?

That didn't even make sense.

Most men couldn't care less about such social media drama. And given what a vindictive whore Cockburn had been in *my* divorce, I could only imagine what a true cock burn she must have been in her multitudinous ones. And that she was such a nightmare that the poor guy couldn't even make it a year in the same house with her before he took off.

Yet we were to believe that her ex had come onto my site and not only insulted me, but he also *threatened* me.

*If she (Terri) goes to CNN, it won't go well for her.*

That, legally, was a terroristic threat. Especially given what he did for a living, and that he was an MMA type A bruiser who knew where I lived.

This sick, psycho bastard had come onto my site and publicly defamed me and my fans. Remember, Cockburn had admitted that this was him. Her ex. He had viciously and without any provocation verbally assaulted us, defamed me and my career, and issued multiple threats against me, and *that was* okay?

More than that, he released to the public information that was in a private email from the Dumas case between her and her friend. How was that for an ethics breach?

But I still had to wonder if it was even him?

Cockburn had also sent a few of her friends over to participate. They admitted they were friends of hers.

What kind of lawyer does that?

Funny, old Dullard from the Tennessee Board Professional Conduct didn't think Cockburn did anything wrong.

Wow.

Tennessee.

*You do us proud. Thanks for looking after your citizens.*

And after all my son's money was seized from his company, and he was left destitute—I got a call that weekend that even his personal account had been seized.

They took everything from us.

The Receiver they'd appointed had gone off on vacation and locked up all our accounts. We didn't even have money to eat on.

Again.

So, Nick quit his job. Why should he work when the money was deposited into an account he no longer had control of?

How could I argue for him to work to keep his father up in the "lifestyle" his father had become accustomed to while we were starving, and my son was wearing jeans and shirts with holes in them?

His father had even refused to return Nick's dress shoes to him that he'd stolen that Nick needed for work. For that matter, he'd refused to return our winter clothes to us that I had Cisco documenting he took to the cabin before ole Les stole it out from under me.

So, Nick and Maddox put their heads together and tried to think of something they could do to keep their father out of their pockets.

They decided to open their own online store.

"We have to do something to eat. What's wrong with the bastard?" Maddox was livid and I didn't blame him.

"Every time I make a dime, he steals it!" Nick wasn't wrong. His father had stolen and seized all of his money three times now.

Given that, they took Maddox's credit card and bought copies of the book the two of them had spent about a year writing together. They also bought a few copies of my latest book and opened their own online store.

That generated another court action from their "loving" dad.

My sons were told by Cockburn and crew that they couldn't open their own bookstore.

Really.

Not even to sell the book *they* wrote.

Les refused to believe it. "It's obviously their mother's work."

Really? 'Cause Maddox had his own online comic that he'd written and procured artists for, independent of me, for years. Les should remember it because he'd tried to take credit for it.

Even during the divorce.

In fact, here was a photo of my baby at his own booksigning more than a year before Les had abandoned us.

Maddox was so frustrated. "The bastard did nothing but tell me I was worthless the whole time I worked on it. He complained I was sitting in my room, setting a bad example for Nick."

"I know, baby."

"Now he wants credit for my work?"

Of course, he did. Les was doing the same thing to me.

All because he "fostered the environment" where we worked. By fostering, what Les had meant was that he'd created a hostile, toxic living space where we were yelled at constantly. That he kept us in a state of extreme agitation and was forever having people come in and force us up from our workstations.

Because he was bored.

Never mind that I was published before I met the bastard and was a legend at my alma mater for a story I'd written before I even knew he existed, I could never have been published without *him*, according to the voices in his head that had driven him mad. He was the sole reason I was a bestselling author.

And to think of the times he'd mock Kiki and all the others before her for making that claim. Wow.

Just wow.

Forget the fact that in third grade, Nick had set up his own store and had made three thousand dollars selling trading cards.

*In third grade.*

According to Les, my kids were incompetent without their lazy, useless father who refused to change light bulbs in our home.

Wherever would they be without him?

However would I have survived had I not married the albatross?

So ironically, after Les had sent an angry email to my aunt, Belinda, where he'd threatened her should she testify against him for the poisoning (and again Detective Lynn Lazy refused to do his job and arrest the psychopath for threatening a material witness), and then in the same email after threatening her and insulting her, Les had begged her to help him reconcile with his children that he had continued to insult, rob, and harm.

*Does baby need a tissue for his issues?*

Could something with a brain, so we knew that wouldn't be Cockburn, Alaimo, Dinky or Shovel-Face, please explain to the dipshit I married that whenever you threatened and insulted someone, they were not going to help you?

That when you lied, robbed, threatened and insulted your grown sons that they were not going to take it anymore?

Duh!

My aunt who I had never seen upset before was beside herself when his email hit her inbox. She couldn't believe he'd threatened her, then asked for her help.

"He's insane. That is not the same man I knew before that old Karen came along. What happened to him?"

"I don't know, Belinda. He's lost his mind."

More so because my kids had called him. In the creepiest voice imaginable, he asked Nick, "Are you safe?"

On a good day, I barely stood five feet tall. My sons were grown men and could easily overpower me. They had their own cars, unless the hyena crew got their way and stole them from them as Les was claiming that the cars I'd bought for my sons were marital property, and therefore "his."

Meanwhile, I no longer had a car. I also had two broken feet. Liver disease. Kidney disease. A bad back. Arthritis. And a paralyzed hand.

Yeah, I was one scary bitch.

*Was Nick safe?*

Not like I had pedophiles in my family tree, or that fathered me, or the snotty bitch who'd spent her life not only protecting her pedophile but helping him gain new victims.

*That would be you, Dumpling.*

And let's not forget the old Hogg that Les had hired who used to abuse and humiliate Nick in front of his father. So much so, that when we were driving past where Les used to slip off to meet her without telling me and leave Nick to wait for him in the car, Nick had a full-on PTSD meltdown. We had to pull over to calm him down from it.

That was how bad Les's and Hogg's abuse was of my son.

Nick didn't dignify Les's question with an answer. "Dad get your attack dogs off us. It's *our* store."

"No, it's your mother's." He so loved to gaslight.

"It's mine. Just like Black Hat was."

"That was your mother's."

"No, Dad. It wasn't. I told you that it was mine. I showed you my credit card with my name on it."

"You can't have companies that are tied to your mother's."

"It wasn't tied to hers. It's *my* trading card company. Sheez!"

"No, that name is hers."

Actually, the Black Hat Society was a name that belonged to a society of witches. I wrote a bunch of short stories back in the 1980s for a friend of mine who was in it as a lark for her and published a number of them.

I bought the domain I don't know how many years ago because no one had claimed it. Since I had the short stories and thought that one day I might return to them, I figured the domain would be a good investment. Just like I'd bought the domain for another series in 2005 and didn't publish the first book for that until 2016.

That was the nature of writing.

You never knew.

When Nick had wanted to start a company, I told him not to waste money buying a new domain as I had a lot of them. "Scroll through my list of unused domains and find something you like."

It was what I'd done with Maddox and his web comic. That was my sole contribution. I was in no way trying to pull a Les and claim any ownership of anything on my son's web comic. I just donated a domain to save him a few dollars so that he could spend it on inventory.

What I'd done for one son, I do for all. Unlike Les and his pedophile family, I refused to show favoritism.

Nick picked Black Hat Society not because of the witch element, but because of the gamer/PC reference.

If Les knew anything about my writing that he claimed he was a "vital part" of, or his own sons that he kept saying he "raised on his own," then he would have known a few things about gaming and trading cards.

As he'd said to my aunt, the truth would reveal itself, and it did every time he opened his fatuous mouth. It was obvious which parent was with the kids, and not on their phone, ignoring them. I had a lot of photos of Les on that phone, during holidays and birthdays, paying no attention whatsoever to any of us.

Anyway, Les continued on, trying to gaslight my boys. "You need to find revenue that isn't tied directly to your mother."

Maddox was aghast. "Old man, I'm her son. I came out of her body. You chose to leave this family. You're not a part of her. You need to find a source of revenue that isn't tied to *my* mother."

"I have a doctorate. It's hard for me to find work."

"You're a lawyer. Go get a job. Hang out a shingle!"

For the record, in spite of all the lies that Les and his imbeciles had told to the court, I had collected a number of voicemails from people trying to hire him as an attorney. He *could* work.

He refused to work.

Given that we had now paid two million dollars in lawyer fees to a bunch of nimrods, I would think that Les could hold his own. Especially since he had an actual accredited law degree and not one from the night school that was once headed by Judge Loser.

"Listen to me, Maddox," Les said, his voice turning hysterical. "There are real world consequences for what you've done! I'm coming after you! Do you hear me! I'm not going to jail! You're going to pay for what you've done!"

I wish I'd recorded how unhinged Les had sounded when he'd screamed that out. The hysteria of his tone. If there was any doubt to his insanity, it showed right then and there. The psychiatrist and psychologist that he'd been seeing twice a week hadn't been helping.

But then they were only as good as the lies they were being told, and he'd shown what a liar he was.

"I had every right to leave an abusive situation!"

"Christ, Dad! You were the abuser. No one ever did anything to you here." Maddox was the one who was beaten. Something I didn't know about until after he'd come home from Japan and told me. How I wish to God he'd confided that to me when he was a boy.

"You don't know what it was like living with your mother!"

"We live with her every day. She's not the one who breaks our stuff when we leave underwear on the floor. Or who has screaming fits because we don't come to dinner every two hours."

For the record, that was Les. When he'd first left this house, I hadn't realized how badly he'd abused my sons until Nick had accidently put this tiny, little black mark on my wall.

He'd practically had a nervous breakdown in fear that I would beat him for it.

"Honey, it's okay. Walls get nicked all the time."

He was hyperventilating. "But Dad always screams and has a fit."

"I don't. Let me show you how to fix it."

Nick had the same reaction a few days later while I was cooking, and he dropped his Yoo-Hoo all over the floor.

"Sweetie, we all drop stuff." I had a paralyzed hand and arthritis. I dropped crap more than I held on to it. "Grab a towel and we'll fix it."

It took a few months, but Nick learned the world wouldn't come to an end over simple human mistakes we all made. Over things his father had beaten him into a quivering pulp about.

That was why before Les had left and when he'd had Hogg here to reinforce his abuse, my vibrant sweet boy had turned himself into a stone-faced shut-in who kept himself locked in his room, night and day.

Nick was living in terror of his father and the Hogg he'd hired.

Now he no longer locked his doors. His doors stood wide open, even when he slept. He laughed and he joked.

He was back to being his sweet, jovial Boo self.

And Les had the nerve to ask if he felt safe.

His safety had begun the moment that Ass and his Hogg had left our home.

Finally, Nick grew sick of the mewling lies and hung up on him. "He's insane. That's it, Mom. I'm changing my name, too. I don't want anything to do with that man ever again."

I patted him on the back. "I'm sorry. I tried to find you a good dad. I failed you so miserably."

Maddox hugged me. "It's not your fault, Mom. He lied to all of us. Hid everything. He's such a piece of shit."

I couldn't agree more.

How could he live with himself? And what kind of attorneys thought that it was okay to do that?

Well, we knew that answer.

The kind of soulless bastards who took money from Autistic children and gleefully locked up their mother over a lie, in front of them.

What was more... when they seized all those items from my home, I kept demanding that they return my sons' class rings that had also been taken. When each of them graduated I bought them an 18 kt gold ring, which were exceptionally pricey.

My reason? My boys weren't dating so I knew they wouldn't give it to a girl.

It would be the only nice ring I'd ever be able to buy for them. None of them liked or wore jewelry.

I figured if they were to ever get into any kind of financial trouble and I wasn't there for whatever reason, they could melt the gold down and have some quick cash.

Or pawn it.

My only thoughts since the day they'd entered this world have always been how to take care of my boys.

They came first. In all things.

And those bastards had taken their rings illegally from my home. Rings that had each of their names emblazoned on the side of them.

Well, come to find out, those rings had quite the journey.

I knew other pieces of my jewelry had been stolen by Les when he'd left. I'd given reports of that to the police, my attorneys and the U.S. Trustee, none of whom would do a damn thing about his theft or the fact that he'd been hiding marital assets since before he left.

We were married, so apparently stealing from your spouse in Tennessee was fine. The police refused to even write up a report about it.

But out of the blue, Cockburn showed up with the Grand Larceny rings in her possession. Along with the registered copies of my sons' birth certificates. Nick's passport (Maddox had his only because he was living in Japan), and their social security cards.

Everything Les would have needed while living in the college town where he'd been staying to have someone pretend to be his sons.

Hmmm...

Why had he stolen all that? He wasn't entitled to it. He'd also taken my birth certificate and social security card with him.

It pained me that I hadn't known he'd had my sons' rings. Down in Georgia, my sons could have sworn out a warrant for his arrest. Maybe *there*, we might have gotten some form of justice.

Probably not, but I could dream. At least he would have been arrested for *one* of the crimes he'd committed.

Unlike me who was arrested for something I didn't do.

And the question was what else had he stolen?

Had he taken those rings when he'd left in March 2018 or when they'd been removed out of my house, illegally, in June 2019?

No one was talking.

They had all stolen so much from us.

Besides our gold and my jewelry, my son's graduation watch, their innocence and futures, as well as any dream of a secure future I'd ever had.

What was even sicker was that Les had left the stand for Maddox's pocket watch on Maddox's chest of drawers. But took the watch with him.

Just so his son would know that he'd left him with nothing.

And he'd robbed their piggy banks.

There was no justice in this world. I'd always known that.

But I couldn't take it anymore. It was time to let the world know what was going on.

Why my books were being delayed. I'd lived in silence for too long and had taken the brunt of everyone's anger.

Les's. Hogg's. My fans.

No more.

I posted to my fans about the illegal search and seizure to my home, and I named the whole jolly crew of hyenas and what they'd done and stolen.

How they'd traumatized my sons. Sons who couldn't sleep for days after the invasion.

What I failed to mention was that after Les had originally left, my first attorney had warned us that Les might be allowed to come into our home.

Nick had been so terrified of being robbed by his father that he'd gone into a panic. "What if he takes my cards?"

"He's not going to take your cards, baby."

"But some of them are worth a lot of money!"

Nick had been unreasonable. Because of what had been done and the fact that Les had a habit of stealing property from both Maddox and Nick for Caleb, he wouldn't be reasoned with. He was convinced that his father would return to take his *Magic* cards from him.

To placate him, I took him to the bank and procured a couple of safe deposit boxes. "These are yours." I handed him the keys. "You can go to the bank and put whatever you want inside them. You don't even have to tell me what's in them if you don't want to."

That succeeded in calming him down.

Until that June.

Ironically, Nick had never used the boxes. They'd stayed empty until Maddox returned from Japan, and then we'd closed them out.

They were part of the court order. Had Nick placed his cards in them, they would have been seized, too.

Without warning or common sense.

Without due process.

As a result, my Autistic sons were thrown out of balance, because this was not the way the law was supposed to work.

A father was not supposed to treat their families like this. Everything in the world was wrong. And anyone who had ever had to deal with an Autistic child or adult knew that it wasn't easy to get them back on track when something this unnerving happened, and they had no control over it.

How could I ever make it right for them?

Even I was traumatized. Because this should never have happened.

Castle domain.

They were not supposed to be in my home without a warrant. Without providing evidence. That was what we'd all been taught.

*They had none of that.*

Nothing.

And they had charged me for the seizure.

Better yet, that illegal search and seizure drove me into bankruptcy because I couldn't afford it. Nor could I afford the cost of the Trustee the judge had put over me and my sons with reckless disregard and no common sense or decency. I'd barely been hanging on financially because of the jackals hauling me into court every two weeks as it was.

Judge Dinky knew this. He was the one who'd said, "I don't care what it costs. You will do it."

After all, that was their great game plan. If they couldn't destroy my credibility with the public so that I couldn't get justice out of the system, then they would break me financially so that I couldn't pursue Les and get a civil conviction from him for poisoning me and my son.

That was what they did.

They, with the full backing and knowledge of the judge, drove me into bankruptcy so that I would be forced to drop my civil suit. It was called a SLAPP, *strategic lawsuit against public participation*. According to the Anti-SLAPP site:

> SLAPPs are used to silence and harass critics by forcing them to spend money to defend these baseless suits. SLAPP filers don't go to court to seek justice. Rather, SLAPPS are intended to intimidate those who disagree with them or their activities by draining the target's financial resources.

That was what they'd done to me from the beginning. It was state sanctioned spouse abuse. Endorsed by everyone, from the local to the federal level.

*And it could happen to anyone.*

Since I'd been falsely accused during that hearing of posting about Judge Dinky and Cockburn to my fans when I hadn't done it (the very nature of the Anti-SLAPP laws), I made a post about their illegal activities. They wouldn't allow me to speak in court, but they couldn't stop me from speaking outside it.

Which proved my point to Cockburn.

Cockburn had to immediately take down her Facebook page, and her law web site (a site that also violated the Tennessee Board of Professional Conduct's rules and regulations for what attorneys could have on their sites).

As I'd said on record, Cockburn, when you rolled your drooping, over-painted eyes at Dinky and scoffed to imply that I was lying like you did every time you moved your bulbous lips, I had never released anything about you to the public prior to June 2019.

While I didn't invite my fans to attack and had a long history of asking them not to do such a thing on my behalf, I couldn't control what they did when someone violated another person's civil rights.

They should be angry. Every citizen in this country should be up in arms over what had been done to me and my sons.

Because of that attack, I was now broke.

Flat busted.

What did the jackals care? They'd found a way to save their client from jail, while lining their pockets.

I had to drop my civil suit, not because it lacked merit, or as Alaimo went on the news and lied when he'd told everyone it was because I feared facing a jury of my peers.

It was because he and his dubious firm and accomplices had driven me into bankruptcy with their SLAPPs.

By the way, Williamson County Commissioner Alaimo knew at the time he made that injurious, false statement about me to the press, which was against the codes set up by the Tennessee Board of Professional Responsibility and was a disbarrable offense if ole Dullard would only do her job, that I was filing bankruptcy.

He knew that for a fact as they were busy hiring an extremely expensive bankruptcy attorney for Les.

Commissioner Alaimo was well aware that the only reason the case had been dropped was because they'd put a receiver over me and that I couldn't afford his outrageous three-hundred-and-ninety-five dollars an hour rate on top of all the other attorney fees.

(k)    The Receiver is hereby authorized to receive compensation at a rate of $395.00 per hour plus reimbursement of expenses from the Receivership Assets; provided, however, that all sums paid to the Receiver, his counsel or his employees shall be subject to final approval of the Court at the conclusion of the Receivership.

(l)    The Receiver shall provide to the Court an accounting of all assets and liabilities of the Receivership, as well as funds received by the Receivership and expenses paid by the Receivership, on a monthly basis.

As you can see, they handed the Receiver a blank check to write out of my funds, with no accountability to me.

> (f)     The Receiver is hereby appointed and authorized to manage and operate the
>
> Receivership Assets and other Collateral and to hire a professional management company, on terms
>
> approved by the Plaintiff, to assist with same.

The idiot judge gave full control of my company and business, that I had spent my lifetime building, over to the fucking moron who didn't even know that my publishers were based in New York.

How was this protecting my assets when they'd already allowed him to steal over a million dollars of my children's money and mine and spend it on such vital necessities as a seven thousand dollar show pony that he was keeping in a stable in a state where he didn't live?

*Are you fucking kidding me?*

More than that, the judge had even given him the authority to raid the homes of any and all my family members, and any and all employees.

At the Receiver's discretion.

What they gave him was shocking and abhorrent. A complete abolishment of my rights as a free American citizen.

> (c)     The Receiver is hereby appointed and authorized to employ and fix the
>
> compensation, salaries and wages for all persons, including but not limited to managers, agents,
>
> employees, servants, accountants and attorneys, as may be advisable or necessary in his judgment to
>
> discharge his duties hereunder for the management, conduct, control or custody of the Receivership

Servants. Did you happen to notice that word? That was what Cockburn and crew thought of people. And they dared to call me delusional? At least I knew what century I lived in and what country. We don't have servants in America, the last time I checked.

*What the ever-loving fuck?*

And that was taken out of the actual order that Lord Skeletor signed off on. I don't know what was more frightening. The thought that he hadn't bothered to read it and signed off on it, or the fact that he had read it and allowed them to abolish my civil and constitutional rights.

Either one should require him to be yanked off that bench.

Keep in mind that I had not been ruled incompetent and they'd put forth absolutely *no* evidence of my mismanaging my money.

This was done based on my insulting the judge in a private email and nothing else. An email Cockburn had obtained by an illegal subpoena when she'd lied in court:

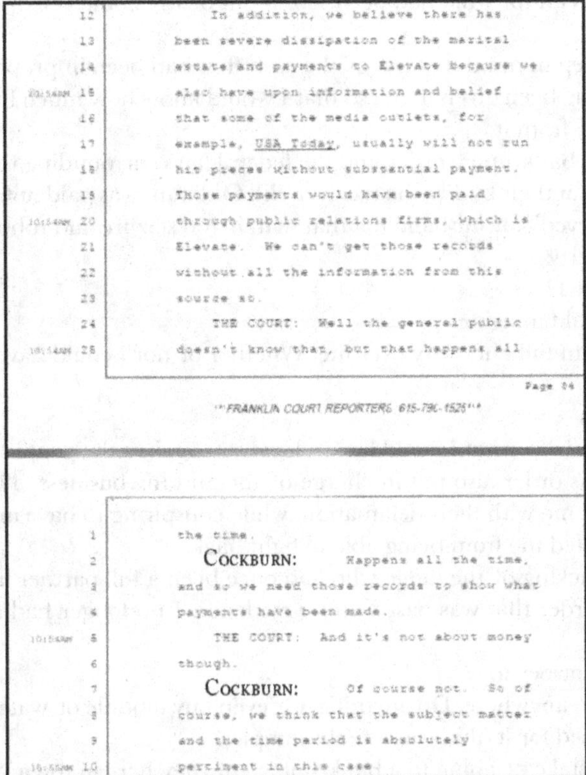

```
   12              In addition, we believe there has
   13         been severe dissipation of the marital
   14         estate and payments to Elevate because we
10:54AM 15    also have upon information and belief
   16         that some of the media outlets, for
   17         example, USA Today, usually will not run
   18         hit pieces without substantial payment.
   19         Those payments would have been paid
10:54AM 20    through public relations firms, which is
   21         Elevate.  We can't get those records
   22         without all the information from this
   23         source so.
   24              THE COURT:  Well the general public
10:54AM 25    doesn't know that, but that happens all

                                              Page 04

            '"FRANKLIN COURT REPORTERS 615-790-1525'"'

    1         the time.
    2         COCKBURN:      Happens all the time,
    3         and so we need those records to show what
    4         payments have been made.
10:54AM 5          THE COURT:  And it's not about money
    6         though.
    7         COCKBURN:      Of course not.  So of
    8         course, we think that the subject matter
    9         and the time period is absolutely
10:55AM 10    pertinent in this case.
```

*Yeah. Behold the perjury and lies for yourself.* The judge blatantly showed his bias and convicted me with no evidence because he wanted to think that his opponents had paid for the papers to write the truth about him.

*Third most corrupt state in the union.*

*And I lived at ground zero for this state.*

Another thing to note was that having a receiver put over me wasn't the same as being ruled incompetent which was the other lie Cockburn and crew had put out to the public about me to damage my reputation so that they could keep their client out of jail.

This was all their dog-and-pony show. But the cutest trick was this one:

As was plainly evident by the photo above, the order to come in and seize my property and invade my house was signed six days after they'd taken my items and those of other family members who weren't part of my divorce to an undisclosed location and after failing to leave me with any form of receipt for what had been seized out of my home.

*Six days after the fact.*

Oh, and please keep in mind that out of the cash that had been improperly seized and taken with no receipt having been given to me so that I would know how much had left my home, the receiver paid himself from it.

In violation of my bankruptcy order and the federal laws surrounding that.

They made sure that their buddy, the receiver, Bill Oldham, was paid upfront and every dollar he claimed he "deserved" for mishandling that search and seizure and robbing my children and family of their property.

How disgusted was I?

More than you could imagine.

They had given him full authority over me. Whether or not I could have attorneys. Employees.

Even my contracts.

He controlled whether or not I could have a legal suit against the people who'd poisoned me. The same people this order also put in charge of me and my business. The same jackals who had publicly shamed me with their defamation, while conspiring to have me arrested over a lie, and who had prevented me from being able to fight back.

All with the full backing of the judge who had once been a full partner in their law firm.

With that illegal order that was based on no evidence, I no longer had any control over my life, at all.

I had no rights whatsoever.

None. I couldn't go anywhere. Do anything. Or even buy a bottle of water while out in public without being harassed for it (that was a real example).

So, I made the mistake of going to a bankruptcy attorney here in town, Stefano Leadwits.

I had found him by calling a law firm that was recommended to me. Little did I know at the time, Les had beat me to that firm. They sent me to Leadwits, who obviously was either in on their side, or because they knew how incompetent and self-serving he was.

He promised me that in federal court, everything would be different. That the federal court would take precedence over the state.

"You won't have to deal with Dinky anymore. Don't worry. I've got your back."

I should have known better. One of the first things he did was call up Bill Oldham, who to his credit was polite. He had no idea that he was on speakerphone and that I could hear him. "She's a really nice lady. It's terrible what they've done to her."

Yeah. It was.

I made sure that Leadwits knew my position. "I want my life back. A writing career isn't something that can be managed by just anyone. They will screw it up royally. I have to be in charge or I'm finished."

"Don't worry. I've got this."

Yeah, he had it all right. He lied worse than Cockburn.

The first thing he did was apply to have a trustee put over me. Which I protested.

"If we don't have it, the other side will insist on it."

I was aghast. "I thought you told me that wouldn't happen in federal court."

But it was too late. He had my money and he'd already filed. I begged for him to get a dismissal.

He refused.

And against my wishes, he conspired with Martha Seaver, the federal U.S. Trustee to have a trustee put over him.

Tom Newhouse.

*What a fucking nightmare.*

Even the judge was aghast. "Why do you want a trustee?"

Leadwits rattled off bullshit. I was afraid to say anything because the last time I spoke up in a courtroom to protest the unfairness of something, I'd been sentenced to jail.

Instead of putting a trustee in who had experience, they picked a newbie who was immediately accosted by Cockburn and her lies.

I was doomed from the beginning.

Because another matter Leadwits had forgotten to mention was that the trustee wouldn't come alone. He'd have to hire his own attorney and guess who he picked...

My old friend Bill Oldham. The very asshole that I couldn't afford before I'd been forced into bankruptcy.

The same lying sack of shit who had driven me into bankruptcy by doing an illegal search and seizure on my home. And then filing a lie to the court when he did his report.

I was disgusted by the whole lot of them.

And I'd been told by other people who'd filed bankruptcy that what had been done to me *never* happens in bankruptcy.

But *it was* happening to me.

All of it.

Even though I was in a Chapter 11 that was supposed to give me full autonomy over my life and full say over what I got to keep or sell, I wasn't even allowed to buy Christmas presents for my own children, with the money I earned.

Oh, don't get me wrong, the ex and his team were paid almost *two hundred thousand dollars* ($200,000.00) by Newhouse out of my money that I earned.

But I was denied three hundred dollars ($300.00) to buy presents for my family and friends for Christmas.

And what was my Christmas/birthday present?

Another lawsuit from a hardworking man I had employed for years to do my lawn because old Newhouse refused to pay his fees.

"It's outrageous!" This from the trustee/attorney who was charging thousands of dollars to write a single letter.

I often found it ironic for any attorney, anywhere, to complain about someone else's fees.

Especially the man who'd hired his "friend" at one hundred and seventy-five dollars an hour to do redundant bookkeeping for me (and harass me), and his other friend at three-hundred-and-ninety-five dollars an hour to be "his" attorney. I was never told going into bankruptcy that I'd have to spend that kind of money, or I wouldn't have filed.

Yet Newhouse expected me to maintain a three-acre yard without *any* help and *no* equipment (I didn't even own a lawnmower), and dared to complain about a very legitimate bill from someone who sweated for a living?

Seriously?

It was humiliating.

And it rated right up there with the trustee and crew coming into my home and ripping my precious mementoes out of my hands to sell them off. My pocketbooks. My clothing. My furniture.

Everything.

I asked to keep one coat to wear to court, and it was denied. Even though it later ended up being sold for the same amount of money they had to "approve" me to spend on a replacement coat so that I wouldn't freeze.

Where on earth did that make any kind of logical sense?

Les got to keep his Porsche and Rolexes, and the family SUV that he stole.

My cars were being sold off which left me with nothing that I could drive.

Nothing.

I had gone into the bankruptcy with a plan. Since I kept getting slapped with ridiculous contempt motions every time I had to move money from my savings accounts to pay bills for things such as my IRS bill, I needed someone who could combine my accounts.

Then of all things, Newhouse waited until the COVID-19 virus struck to list my home for sale.

What was worse, he planned to sell the home where my business was located and where my son who was still in high school lived, but Les would get to keep my office and what he stole from me and his sons.

We were to be left homeless.

Why? Because Newhouse was so fundamentally stupid that he couldn't comprehend that I had bought and paid for both homes.

"Yeah, but he got a house, and she got a house. That's even."

No, you inbred moron, it wasn't. The marital home that I was in was to be sold to pay for Les's debt. Not even my debt. Every last cent would go to pay for the bills that Les had run up in legal fees.

All of it.

And Newhouse had testified to that very fact in front of Dinky.

I wasn't going to get a single penny from the sale of my home. Every cent was going to pay off Les's attorneys.

Every cent.

Meanwhile, Les was being allowed to keep my office that I had also paid for without any help whatsoever from him.

If Newhouse thought that was fair, then I hoped and prayed that his wife divorced him and took him to the cleaners, because really, this idiot made Les look like a rocket-scientist.

And this was what they'd put over me as my trustee. Someone who couldn't even figure out something *that* simple.

Yeah, I was in trouble.

That explained how it was that old stupid Newhouse arranged the next deal.

When I'd entered bankruptcy, I was only having to pay Les's lawyers after they petitioned their old friend for the money. Stupid Newhouse decided, against my existing court order, that I needed to pay Les not to work.

To the tune of over seven thousand dollars a month.

While I was in bankruptcy.

More than that, he also agreed to pay his jackals whatever amount they wanted.

All up to them. Whatever they wanted to bill me, he would approve.

Yeah, my attorney and I thought it was a bad idea, too.

"But I'm the trustee. You will do what I say! The last thing you want to do is go in front of Dinky!"

I was so sick of that threat.

In the end, I had no choice as Newhouse had all the say in my life. A fact that he took sick pleasure in reminding me as often as he could.

So Les, who had already blown through millions of dollars with nothing to show for it, was allowed to have more of my money than I was.

Meanwhile, every cent I spent for something as simple as a stick of gum was scrutinized.

In a few weeks after writing this, I would be sleeping on the floor in order to pay for Les's attorneys, not the bills I owed but for his attorneys.

Why?

Because Newhouse intended to take my bed and furniture to pay Les's bills, too.

When I asked about keeping the loveseat in my office to sleep on, Newhouse had scoffed. "Isn't that part of the other furniture?"

I was aghast. "But you're selling my bed."

He looked at the auctioneer. "It can be added to the auction, right?"

"Absolutely."

What killed me was that the items they were selling weren't worth much. I didn't have expensive furniture and most of it was worn down from years of use.

My newest sofa was nine years old. The oldest was seventeen.

Better still? The auctioneer charged twenty-five percent off the top. One quarter of whatever the gross of the item would go into the auction house's pocket, plus the fees of the trustee and all his friends.

So how much would I make off those items?

Nothing.

After all, how much was a well-used Coach bag from a decade ago worth?

Not a lot.

Used clothes that were also out of season and out of date, sold for even less. My coats were more than a decade old. I wasn't Princess Diana. My clothing would go for pennies on the dollar.

The reason they were being sold? Les and Cockburn had told them to sell them.

"She has expensive designer bags you can put up for auction!"

Newhouse agreed because he didn't like the thought of my keeping anything "flashy." A direct quote from that soulless bastard.

"It doesn't look right!"

Oh, okay, but the seven-thousand-dollar pony in another state was hunky-dory and the hundreds of thousands of dollars Les was wasting on his attorneys was fine.

Uh-huh...

And because of Les, I wasn't even allowed to keep my eighty dollar an hour bookkeeper that he chose before he filed for divorce. Nope. Ole Newhouse saddled me with one who charged one-hundred-and-seventy-five dollars an hour.

"Be grateful. She reduced her rate for you!"

Yeah, right. You saddled me with an unreasonable, stupid bitch who charged more than twice as much when my old accounting firm was perfectly able to do that math. And do it without insulting me.

He'd used a similar argument to get me to agree to Oldham. "If you don't agree to Bill, then my next choice charges over five hundred dollars an hour!"

Wow.

Just wow.

What kind of sick blackmail was practiced in Tennessee? Both in the federal and state courts?

*This* spendthrift was what the U.S. Bankruptcy court had put over my estate and me? Because he could make better choices?

I don't know what kind of fucked up Voodoo economics Newhouse was attempting, but where I lived, an eighty dollar an hour accountant was a shit ton better than one who charged over a hundred dollars more an hour.

I wasn't just paying the trustee, but every friend he could dredge up who needed a Christmas bonus.

And the real kicker that stuck in my craw? I was forced to cancel my appearances in London and New York where my fans had purchased tickets. Where the event itself had already paid for my plane ticket (he refused to reimburse them seventeen hundred dollars while paying out hundreds of thousands of dollars to the bastards who were mentally torturing me and violating my rights).

Yet every one of these attorneys, including the trustee, all ran out of the country for weeks on end to take a vacation at critical times during this nightmare while I was forbidden to pay back the poor event people who'd advanced the plane ticket money to me.

Even though I'd begged and begged for them to be reimbursed.

"Nope. Can't do it." That was all I was told.

Meanwhile, Newhouse paid Les over seven thousand dollars a month to sit on his ass and abuse me and his children.

To plot further evil against us.

Paying Les's attorneys, including Dumas's former attorney, hundreds of thousands of dollars.

While I worked, night and day, with a paralyzed hand to pay these ungodly fees they'd put on me. While I had kidney and liver disease that Les had given me by his wrongful acts. With two broken feet caused by the brittle bones left over from the poisoning.

I couldn't even get the surgery I needed for my feet because I couldn't afford the downtime, or the cost.

My checks that I wrote to pay for basic utilities were constantly bouncing because Newhouse doled my money out to me like a stingy parent who waited to the very last minute so that if I had an emergency, such as when I needed to go to the doctor for my bronchitis, I was told that I would have to get a bill from the doctor and submit it to Newhouse before he'd give me the money to pay for the visit.

I was aghast at this Catch-22. "Have you never been to the doctor before? No doctor's office bills the client. They all have signs up that say, 'payment due at the time services are rendered.'"

"I need a bill before I can authorize it."

*Are you fucking kidding me?* How was I ever supposed to go to a doctor again?

"We authorized a payment to the Georgia Internal Revenue Service. Why has that payment not been made?"

"I wrote the check out. I have no control over when they process the check."

Oh my God! I went through that every two weeks. That IRS check? I wrote it in September and for whatever reason, they didn't process it until December. I had no idea why. I didn't work there.

Newhouse acted like he'd never paid a single bill in his life. Like everything out of my mouth was a lie.

"No bill is ever due when you get it. It's always a month later!"

That really was how stupid this moron was. A few bills have a thirty-day leeway, but many, many more are "Due upon receipt." Or have a ten-to-fourteen-day window from when they arrive to when they were due.

Meanwhile, the trustee kept threatening to "break" all my publishing contracts. "You know I have the authority to cancel them all. I *will* do it."

I was so tired of being threatened and bullied by everyone around me.

Everything Newhouse had done to date had only cost me more money. Ten times what it would have had I not gone into bankruptcy.

Or in the case of Les and his jackals, hundreds of thousands of dollars more.

And while I couldn't have an attorney to go after Les for poisoning me, my son and cousin, and killing one cat while maiming another, Les was able to hire a five hundred dollar an hour attorney with my money that the trustee was paying him with to represent him in the bankruptcy and to further enslave me so that I don't know if I'll ever be able to get out of bankruptcy.

Yes, you read that correctly.

My idiot husband who was a bankruptcy attorney and who had hundreds of cases in Tennessee and Mississippi that he'd filed in a bankruptcy court, and had overseen, needed to spend tens and tens of thousands of dollars of my money on another bankruptcy attorney.

When I had consulted with Leadwits, my bankruptcy attorney, I was told that the federal judge would take precedence over the matter, and it would stop Dinky's madness.

"You'll be in a whole new arena, and you won't have that level of stupidity."

He lied.

Third most corrupt state in the Union.

The federal judge kicked it right back to Dinky. So here I was in bankruptcy, and I was being told that I had to pay the worthless piece of shit who refused to work, more than seven thousand dollars a month, while I was in bankruptcy.

For the record, that was more than I made.

Then I was given the almost two-hundred-thousand-dollar bill for Les's attorneys.

While in bankruptcy.

And I was now being told that I would have to continue paying them whatever fees they wanted as long as they submitted their bills to their buddy Dinky who was going to approve them because they were all his former business partners. So, Cockburn was about to get that eighty thousand a month she'd wanted, while I was in bankruptcy and couldn't pay my bills.

We all knew what that meant.

When everything I owned, including my contracts were sold off and I no longer had the money to pay their fees, they would lock me up and not let me out.

Because I had displeased my husband.

Right down to the fact that they'd allowed him to show up to my bankruptcy hearing and pull his chair right up behind me so that Les's knees were in my back the entire time.

Absolute control and domination.

Talk about intimidation. Meanwhile, his five hundred dollar an hour attorney that I was paying for was asking the most ridiculous questions in order to drive up his fee.

I had never been more appalled in my life.

Not until they tried to entrap me.

Again, over the money that I had temporarily transferred to my son's account while he was in Japan so that he could show them he had assets in America to keep himself from being deported.

At no time did Maddox ever touch those funds. And once he had his Japanese account set up so that he could live over there, I put the money right back into my account.

For that, they were trying to hang me.

Even worse? Les and his team of overpaid liars kept trying to say that I had transferred money to Nick when all I'd done was set up a CD account for his education to replace the money Les had stolen.

My name was on the account, too. Legally, it was *my* account.

I hadn't transferred money anywhere except to a different bank than we'd normally used after Les had thrown a tantrum with our old bank after the court order from Woodly where we were supposed to "divide" all our joint accounts.

We had one joint account.

Every time I put money into it, Les had stolen it out.

I called the bank and they refused to take my name off the account to stop that from happening.

"Are you kidding me? He was allowed to steal over half a million dollars out of my accounts without so much as a phone call from any of you, and closed them, and that was okay? But I can't take my name off the account and let him have it with all the money in there?"

Not without *his* permission.

That was the kind of fucked up country we lived in.

"We'll have to call him and make sure it's okay."

*Are you fucking kidding me?* I seemed to be saying that all the time these days.

My banker called him and even though Les and Cockburn had lied to Woodly and told him that I was the one refusing to have my name removed off Les's accounts and they'd just hauled me into court over that where I'd been subjected to Woodly insulting me for it, Les yelled at my banker and refused to allow me to remove my name from the account.

How screwed up was *that*?

As a result, I refused to put any more money into that account. He'd stolen enough money from us.

The account became overdrawn, and they'd finally closed it. But not before another man from the bank called me up to scream at me over Les's immature behavior.

"I tried to close out this account and you wouldn't allow it." Because I had to have my husband's permission to remove myself from it. Even though they allowed Les to close out all my accounts and steal all my money and close out my safe deposit boxes without *my* permission.

Where was the law?

"Well, be that as it may... " Yada, yada, yada.

I'd grown weary of the laws only applying to me and of them finding loopholes for Les to get away with his crimes and lies.

Such as why I was in trouble for transferring money between my accounts here in Tennessee to pay unfair bills, while Les was transferring hundreds of thousands of dollars between states to spend money against a court order.

Yet I was in trouble for a simple CD bond that no one could withdraw funds out of. No one had taken money and put it anywhere that wasn't clearly on record. Nothing of mine was being "funneled." Nothing crooked had been done with it, such as taking it out of state without anyone's knowledge and then spending it, against court orders on home renovations and women's clothing for a mistress while in the middle of a divorce.

Or on a horse that was being boarded in another state.

Everything I had done was "status quo" while everything Les had been doing was not.

But wait, it got even better. By the fall of 2019, Cockburn attempted to haul me into court for the insurance fraud that Les had committed.

Wait...

What?

Yes, you heard that.

Remember in August 2018 when Judge Woodly had told us to separate our bills? We were getting divorced, after all, and the last time I checked that was the purpose of a divorce—to separate from each other.

So, I went out and got separate insurance for me and my sons.

That fall when open enrollment began, Cockburn emailed to tell me that Les was getting insurance for us.

"Uh, no. Not after he tried to kill me." The last thing he needed was to keep spying on me and our sons, and our medical history. "We have our own insurance. He can go get his."

He didn't. Being the control freak of nature that he was, he went to the Marketplace and committed another act of perjury. The Marketplace where they tell you, point blank, that you were being recorded and that you cannot submit false information on your federal application.

It was against the law.

They were quite clear about this. It was even on their website.

Yet Les did. He not only proclaimed himself the head of a household that no longer existed, he also told them that my sons and I lived in Thompson's Station, Tennessee.

At the location where I had a standing court order that banned me from stepping a single foot on its soil.

Neither my sons nor I had ever lived there. That was where my business cabin was located.

My sons and I lived in Franklin, where I was the head of this household.

More than that, no one could legally sign adults up for insurance without their permission. My son, Maddox, worked for a private health coverage company. One of the largest in the country as one of their coverage counselors. So, I knew that for a fact.

You couldn't have double coverage if you signed up through the Marketplace, as that was the point of using them.

Most of all, you couldn't sign up in the Marketplace for a state where you didn't live. This was a big one. See, my son Caleb hadn't been a legal resident of Tennessee since he graduated college in April 2018.

That meant that he couldn't legally be on the same Marketplace policy as the rest of us because our insurance company wasn't licensed to cover him in Georgia, and they offered no network or services there. He must have a separate policy for Georgia where he lived.

Yet Les got coverage for him by lying, even though Caleb wasn't a legal resident of Tennessee.

How many laws did Les break?

*Let me count the ways.*

And Les knew he broke the law. Remember that my sons and I all had surgery at the end of 2018. The way our insurance worked, Les would have been notified of the procedures when they happened through his insurance, and he wasn't.

They notified me because I owned our policy that was separate from Les's.

Yet Les knew the boys had surgery. Remember that he'd yelled at them for it. So, Cockburn lied again to the court when she said Les didn't know we had separate coverage. I had proof he knew it in 2018 when he purchased his illegal coverage for all of us.

What was more, I had the emails to my attorney, telling him to drop it, pretty much every single month after that.

My new attorney, Melissa had told them repeatedly from April forward to drop the additional coverage.

Yet in August 2019, after all the other illegal acts the bitch had pulled, and after I'd filed for bankruptcy, Cockburn slapped me with a contempt order over the insurance her client had illegally obtained for all of us.

Not only that but she demanded that I drop my legal coverage to return to Les's illegal coverage so that he could spy on me and see the damage he'd done when he'd poisoned me.

The cherry?

Cockburn wanted an additional twenty thousand dollars to pay for his illegal coverage, plus attorney fees.

In the event I refused to pay this, they threatened to haul me back in front of Dinky, the judge who'd spent hours and hours threatening to arrest me if I so much as asked a question to clarify a question I didn't understand. The judge who turned red in the face as soon as he looked at me.

Every attorney, from the U.S. Trustee to my bankruptcy attorney to my IP and divorce attorneys told me the same thing. "It won't be in your best interest to take this to Dinky. He hates you. He will put you in jail. Don't do it."

In other words, every time I appeared before Dinky, there was an unnatural risk of my being sent to jail for no reason.

He had refused to allow me to speak or for my team to have any say whatsoever on my behalf.

Didn't matter if I had witnesses. Les's accountant, Dinky's old friend, was allowed to lie for hours on the stand. My CPA and accountant had been to court on three separate occasions and hadn't been allowed to speak one single time.

Last time I looked at the law, it was extortion to threaten to pull me in front of a known biased judge or pay an exorbitant amount for something that was clearly illegal.

Not to mention, it was illegal to profit from insurance that you weren't authorized to take out on four adults. That you lied to obtain when they clearly told you that it was perjury at the time you did it and taped you when you did it.

Yet no one, not even the Insurance Commissioner of Tennessee would do anything about this. Even though I had reported it and my insurance company had reported it. The insurance company could get into serious trouble for this.

I really did live in *The Twilight Zone*.

Believe it or not, when this was being hammered out, along with that almost two hundred thousand dollar attorney fee along with spousal support (even though Woodly had said that the money Les had stolen from our children was supposed to be his support and was supposed to last him until the divorce was final), I had in writing from my attorney that what Cockburn and crew did was indeed extortion against me.

And there was nothing I could do except pay it.

Why? Because if I didn't, Dinky would have put me in jail for nothing. That was the consensus from everyone. Dinky was so open about his bias that when my trustee first showed up, Dinky said and I quote, "My condolences."

As if I were the problem in this and not Les or Cockburn.

"I'm amazed you haven't blown your brains out." That was what no less than three of the attorneys I'd spoken to had said to me recently.

"It's obvious that Les is still trying to kill you."

That, too, was a true statement. And the state of Tennessee was a willing accomplice to his crimes against me. That was why I started writing this book. The world needed to understand what was truly going on in the modern court system and how horrific it was.

We have yet to progress past the days of Salem.

When I went to a civil rights attorney about my son's money being illegally seized, do you know what I was told?

"Yes, you have a case. But my firm will never let me go up against Dinky. You're going to have to go out of state to find help."

When my bankruptcy attorney tried to find help for my attorney, he came back with what I already knew. "Everyone in town knows about your case. They won't touch it."

I'd been blackballed and railroaded.

Every single attorney knew this, and they wouldn't return my calls.

This was a story that should send shivers down the spine of any and every American citizen.

When, after over a year of waiting, I'd finally received the records of what Les had spent do you know what else I learned?

Les had hired the very same attorney who had represented Dumas against us here in Nashville.

And no, you didn't misread that one. I had yet to get an explanation as to how that was even possible. Remember that Les breached the settlement his first day in the courtroom.

Dumas then threatened to sue me for six million dollars, as if the rich heiress needed any more money. If her husband was smart, he'd take her to the cleaners, as she had publicly admitted in numerous interviews that he helped her write her books and was her primary researcher. Not to mention, his name was on some of them.

Stupid bitch. Unlike Les who had never done shit for my books or career, Mr. Dumas could mop the floor with her, and there was nothing she could do.

And that settlement we made?

It covered not only me, but anyone who had anything to do with my company i.e., Les Manly self-asserted business manager, who was in on the drafting of that settlement (another perjury he'd committed under oath by saying he had no idea what was in the settlement that I had drafts and emails with his name on). So, explain how Sal Tiller could possibly represent the very person he should be suing according to the terms of the settlement he'd negotiated just a few months ago for Dumas.

I was so confused.

Welcome to Williamson County, Tennessee where U.S. laws don't apply. Since the Judiciary Board refused to hold their judges accountable for dereliction of duty, they didn't have to try a legitimate case. They could toss it out for no other reason than, "I don't want to destroy a 'good' attorney's reputation."

*Fuck the law. Screw what's right or decent.*

Even though the same judge had ranted and railed against perjury in his court. "I won't tolerate lies in here."

Really? 'Cause you did it every time Cockburn, Shovel-Face and Alaimo opened their mouths.

Seemed to me, Dinky, you had a problem with the truth. You couldn't stand it.

So here I was. Broke. My career in shambles. No rights. No freedom. I couldn't even buy Christmas presents for my sons because Newhouse had refused my request.

Just as he refused to allow me to buy them replacement sweaters for the ones their father had stolen.

Or for me to keep a single coat to wear to my ever-revolving court dates.

I had to beg like a starving peasant to attend any event with my fans, even when my fans were paying for it.

Newhouse was just as bad as Cockburn. Knowing I was in bankruptcy, what did he do?

Made it all worse, of course!

"We can't use your accountant. They're complaining about her because she likes you."

They, of course, being Cockburn, Les, Alaimo and Shovel-Face.

I shuddered at the bills from the new accountant, especially when they were constantly inflated by such brilliant questions as: "Explain to me these thirty dollars we haven't authorized you to spend for X Insurance. Why are you spending it, and can you stop spending it?"

Well, June-You-Overpaid-Loon. Obviously, it was for insurance, hence the "insurance" part of your question. Not to mention, you knew from Newhouse that I was in a divorce, which meant that I was under a court order to pay Les's insurance, so I had no choice, except to pay it.

Newhouse knew that, too, yet was too lazy to explain anything to her.

*Way to twist the knife in and inflate your salary at the same time.*

All day long, I was harassed with questions that were so insipid and stupid it was embarrassing.

"You spent three dollars. What's this for?"

"Same thing I spent it on last month. It's a backup feature on my website." She had asked me that question every single month.

"Where's the invoice?"

"There's not one. It's an online site that backs up. It's set to autodraft because sites like that will not do monthly invoicing."

My favorite question from her to date. "What's this payroll tax that's being taken out?"

*Are you kidding* me? Wherever did Newhouse dig this one up? Pretty sure the government wasn't picking on me and that I wasn't the only human in the country being forced to pay payroll tax. Whoever said there was no such thing as a stupid question had never met this woman.

Or Cockburn and Shovel-Face.

Definitely not Newhouse. He had humdingers that beat the shit out of the stupidity of the idiots he'd hired with my money.

Every day, there was something new that they threw at me, and it was never anything that I saw coming. Just when I thought I'd stomped out the fire, they found something new to ignite.

The latest act of Cockburn's insanity:

> Mrs. Manly is required to file a statute of use or a request for extension for the attached application by today. If she does not, the application will go abandoned. We had spoken before regarding our concern of recent abandonment of trademarks. Waleski is the firm Mrs. Manly hired to take care of these business affairs. What is going on? This trademark in particular is valuable. Today is deadline to file so can one of you please call Waleski and find out if this to be taken care of today?

Well, you could clearly see from her email what an imbecile she was. The only good thing I could say was that at least this time, she followed the correct protocol. Unlike all the times before when she'd called my agent up, without permission and demanded from him my records, instead of going through my attorneys for them.

However, I resented her and Les driving up my bills when they were all well aware of the fact that they were asking me to commit a felony, again.

Yes, they were.

Contrary to Les's lies to the court, he had been working as my IP attorney since he stopped doing bankruptcies. He had years of experience. More than even Sal Tiller.

The trademark referenced above was one Les had filed for just days before he abandoned his family.

But again, it got better.

As he was having Peggy Millhouse file the paperwork for the Night-Seeker trademark in movies and television, he was simultaneously informing ole Sal Tiller and Dumas about the talks I was entering into for a "possible" financial backing to get my project off the ground, after a decade of trying. Remember that Les knew he was under no obligation to tell them about the talks. We only had to tell them of any "deals."

We didn't have a deal.

There was no obligation to tell them we were talking to someone.

He knew Dumas's reputation and my attorneys had warned him that they would pull this shit and blow my deal.

Les did it anyway, knowing that he was about to file for divorce.

Since that day, they hadn't come back to talk anymore about any movie or TV deals.

*Thank you, Les.*

Now of all the people in Nashville who knew that I was no longer heading into production for the movie or television due to their actions, it would definitely have been Les and Sal Tiller who was Dumas's counsel here in Nashville when they'd issued those subpoenas.

Yet now, Tiller with Cockburn, had come knocking on my door, demanding that I renew a trademark that I could not legally renew as we weren't in production, nor were we likely to be heading into production because of what Les and Tiller had done.

Given that no one was returning my phone calls, I couldn't in good faith make that assertion to the U.S. government. And unlike Cockburn and Les, I refused to commit perjury.

Again, how was it legal for Tiller to be in the middle of this?

Or for Cockburn to continue to demand that I take illegal actions or commit perjury against the government?

Why wouldn't anyone help me?

Oh, that was right. I was broke and being blackballed.

This was my life, and this was why there weren't any new books until late 2021. Because I was constantly having to redo the same paperwork I'd turned in ten times. I'd have to go find receipts that were irrelevant.

Such as all day yesterday where I'd been harassed over that same jewelry that was illegally seized from my home. Remember that fun day?

So did I.

Yesterday blew up when Newhouse and Oldham couldn't find the jewelry that was removed from my home and walked out of here in violation of my insurance policy. They had a video of me telling them this.

Well, now some of that jewelry that I had at the time they'd done that had gone missing. More than that, Newhouse was threatening to report it to the insurance company.

*Fine. Do it.* I had the videotape of it being illegally walked out of my home and I would gladly give the insurance investigator one hell of a statement about that false insurance claim.

I was so tired of being accused and threatened.

Of explaining things I'd explained nine hundred times, while Les didn't have to explain anything. I couldn't buy a new pair of jeans to replace my son's pair that had holes in them (that was what I asked my brother to give me as a Christmas present—for him to buy my sons some pants that fit and didn't have holes in them). My attorney refused to write the contempt order to make Les return my sons' winter clothing or their shoes.

But Les was allowed to spend thousands of dollars on curtains at Williams-Sonoma and to buy clothing in women's boutiques that were clearly not for me, while claiming he wasn't having an affair.

All while I was in bankruptcy.

Meanwhile, my sons and I couldn't have Christmas lights and I was denied my request to keep one coat.

And my appeal for a conviction that never should have happened was being blocked by Cockburn who kept demanding more and more of my money, even while she continued to threaten me with bogus lawsuits, she knew she couldn't win.

Even my attorney was appalled.

"No one does this. What is her mental damage? She looks like an idiot."

But apparently, Cockburn didn't mind looking like a fool. I'd seen her wardrobe. Her mirror lied to her, and I wanted that one in my home, at least until they put me out on the street, which was their plan.

And how did I spend Christmas 2019?

I supposed the upside was that unlike Christmas 2017, I wasn't on the floor, puking my guts out from the poison I'd been fed by the man who'd stood in front of a preacher and sworn before God to love, honor and cherish me for the rest of his life, afraid that I wouldn't make it through the year.

That was the upside.

Because in 2017, not only I, but everyone who cared about me and who was around me then, including my fellow authors who knew me, were all convinced that I wouldn't live to see the end of 2018. Half of my friends and family were preparing themselves to write my eulogy.

On December 20, 2019, I was pulled in for a meeting so that I could be told that due to the direct actions of Les and his team of hyenas, my bankruptcy was going to be converted into a Chapter 7 after the first of the year, and that I would have absolutely no say in it whatsoever.

That they were going to come and take my car, my clothes and my pocketbooks, furniture and everything I owned to sell it off to pay for Les's attorneys who'd done nothing but make my life a living hell since the day the fucking bastard had run off like the coward he was.

Newhouse had said, "It's not your spending that did this, Terri. You don't spend that much. Your business expenditures aren't excessive. It's all the expense for his professional fees that are killing your budget and driving you over the edge. His attorneys. We have no choice. This is what's happening."

Because of Les and the idiot brigade he'd hired, not to settle this and get divorced, but to harass and torment me and his children.

It made no sense.

Yet they were taking everything I owned, including my publishing contracts.

My trademarks and copyrights.

I would no longer be able write in a single world I had created. Not even those I created before I ever knew that rank bastard existed. Nor would I own any rights to any of the tattoos any of my fans had on their bodies.

None of them.

My only prayer was that whoever bought the rights wouldn't go after my fans for royalties on those marks. That they wouldn't go after my publishers for the books they'd published that had my name and trademarks on the covers.

What I knew for a fact was that my publishers would pull every single book off the market because they wouldn't risk the possibility of the new owner suing them. It was what publishers did when they were under threat.

I wouldn't be able to sell any of my merchandise in the future or anything that I'd spent my entire lifetime creating. And all my future income would be gone as my publishers would cancel the remaining contracts because I wouldn't be able to use the names of my characters or worlds that Les intentionally trademarked.

Under the lying guise that he wanted to "protect" me.

What he really had wanted to do was make sure that he robbed his children of their inheritance and to snatch every single crumb from their mouths that he could.

Once we filed Chapter 7, I'd never write again.

Les was too stupid to even realize that I wouldn't be able to pay whatever licensing fees the new owner demanded so that I would be able use the very characters and worlds I'd created.

Contrary to what people thought, authors didn't make much per book. We made ten percent or less of the cover price. And our agents took twenty percent of our ten percent, and the government took half of what was left because we had to pay our own taxes for self-employment.

There was nothing left for me to pay a third party to use my characters and names.

So, my ex would get what he'd wanted from the beginning.

To destroy me.

He was as psychotic as I'd always feared he'd become.

What I never dreamed was that his abuse would be sanctioned and endorsed by the American government.

But I should have known that. This was the same government and court system that when I was a little girl, handed me back to the monsters who'd tortured me.

To this day, I hated that caseworker who I'm sure went home and patted herself on the back that she was doing a good job.

She almost got me killed that day.

Instead of helping, she'd set me up to walk blindly into a maelstrom when I came home from school.

"You think you know child abuse? I'm going to show you child abuse."

It was a promise my grandmother had made good on.

Thank you, Child Services. May you all rot in hell. Personally, I believed they should be held accountable for all the children they'd put in harm's way with their stupidity.

But hypocrisy was what America was known for. It was apparently what the country exceled at.

Just as no one had ever warned me that losing everything I'd ever worked for would be a possibility in bankruptcy. At no time was I told that the U.S. Government could come in and take over my contracts and nullify them. I thought the point was to help me get back on my feet.

Not cut my feet off and force me into poverty and welfare for the rest of my life. To steal away from me, absolutely every last thing I'd ever worked for.

Including my basic human rights.

My dignity.

Because a healthy, college educated lawyer flat-out refused to work and feed his family.

You sickened me.

But that was what they'd done. They had destroyed my family and taken away my ability to earn a single penny with which to feed myself or my special needs children.

I was left with nothing but tattered dreams, and a decaying house that I couldn't afford to repair.

Because of one madman who wouldn't stop tormenting me. Even the day after Christmas, first thing I received was an email from his crazy attorney, screaming about the fact that I'd allowed one of his illegally gotten trademarks to lapse.

*Brace yourself.* I couldn't afford to spend two thousand dollars to renew what was called an "Intent To Use" application with the United States Patent and Trademark Office for my Night-Seeker series that covered "motion picture films in the field of the paranormal and science fiction" (Class 9) and "entertainment in the nature of a series of television shows in the field of the paranormal and science fiction" (Class 41).

I couldn't legally file that as I knew my works were not going to be made into a movie or television.

Never mind the fact that I was in bankruptcy and didn't have a spare two grand laying around to pay lawyers again, something Cockburn couldn't seem to get through her exceptionally thick head, I already owed over seventy-seven-thousand-five-hundred dollars to my old Intellectual Property attorneys.

*Did your jaw hit the floor?*

So, did mine when I saw the bill that stupid, worthless bastard had run up.

See, one of the beautiful things Les had done when he decided to divorce me without telling me was that he'd gone out and started trademarking absolutely every last character and series of mine that he could think of. Every series and character that I might "someday" in the future work on. His thought being that if they were trademarked, by law, he'd be entitled to one-half of it in the divorce.

The lie he'd told me then was that he was "protecting it" for me and "our" sons.

"I got the cookie for you." Now you know why my sons and I make that joke about what a self-serving piece of shit Les was.

So, the day after Christmas, I was blind-sided with this incredulous letter from Cockburn where she again lied her incredibly large ass off.

> Gentlemen:
>
> You will recall on December 5th of this year our team brought to your attention the above trademark's impending expiration. The response I received from Bob Harvest, Mrs. Manly's counsel at Dewey, was the following:
>
> Please advise Ms. Cockburn and anyone else who might be interested that the intent to use application covers "motion picture films in the field of the paranormal and science fiction" (Class 9) and "entertainment in the nature of a series of television shows in the field of the paranormal and science fiction (Class 41).
>
> Since there are no projects on the horizon for that proposed mark in those fields, the applicant cannot file another extension.
>
> Despite (*I really wish someone had taught Cockburn proper grammar in school. She embarrasses herself every time she sent a letter or email.*) our repeated pleas for everyone to keep the business trademarks in a renewed status until the divorce court can make proper allocations and distributions, Mrs. Manly has been permitted to make false assertions to her counsel to bring harm to the marital estate and, in fact, the bankruptcy estate.
>
> Our team has had to spend countless hours as private investigators in order to provide those who need the evidence and information to make informed, educated decisions. Despite the evidence withing the past twelve months there had been interest from producers for television shows in the Night Seeker series, the above trademark, in particular, was allowed to lapse. Our team brought to your attention an unusual number of abandoned trademarks within the past 12 months. To our knowledge nothing has been done to rectify this concern. I am enclosing a more recent email dated September 3, 2019 between Unknown Producer and Mrs. Manly's literary agent. Mr. Producer produced an Old Cartoon and An Even Older Cartoon franchise. Mr. Producer is a fan and is seriously inquiring after the film/tv rights.
>
> Mr. Manly is renewing is request to have the above trademark application re-filed immediately and to reapply for any and all related trademarks which were previously abandoned.
>
> Very truly yours,
> Bonnie, Esq

In an exceptionally high school fashion, she only signed her first name on her professional letters and did so in a giant scrawl. One that a handwriting analyst would quickly tell anyone showed her low functioning IQ and immaturity (which was adequately demonstrated by all the typos and bad formatting that I intentionally left in). It also meant that she was full of herself and didn't value her family or others. She only thought of herself and was obsessed with money and ambition. She was all about appearance and showing off.

Funny, Les always claimed to hate the very thing he'd hired to represent him in court. He always called women like her "Femanazis" at home and ridiculed them whenever he had to face them in business and at the office. It was women like Cockburn who'd driven him out of the workplace, because they were always "picking on him" and "out to get him."

But that was neither here nor there.

*Let's begin to count her lies, shall we?*

The first one: Gentlemen? Really? Last time I looked, I was not a man, and neither was my attorney. Given the fact that this bitch had the extremely unprofessional and highly sexist meme on her "professional" law site that says: "What do I bring to the table? Boy, I bought the table." I found this disgusting. It ranked right up there with her demand for my tools and her extremely sexist assumption that all the tools in my home belonged to Les who wouldn't know what to do with a tack hammer if one hit him in his missing balls.

In fact, my response to them when she'd demanded my "table saw" was that he could have it on the day that 1) he correctly identified what kind of saw I owned (I don't have a table saw). 2) He could name the actual brand it was. 3) He could open the blade and show us that he knew how to use it (I knew that he would never be able to figure it out).

I was tempted to give it to him just so that he'd lose a limb. But then, he'd never use it. He'd only sell it for money.

Not to mention, all my tools were pink or purple, including my drill. Obviously, none of them belonged to Les.

Moving on...

My IP attorney very eloquently explained to her the law. I would think that even someone as low functioning as Cockburn could understand it. But then, she was constantly amazing me with the new level of stupidity that she sank to.

Yet again, she didn't fail to set a new record.

Let me reiterate that I was in bankruptcy. To keep those trademarks in a "renewed status" was costing me over *seventy-seven thousand-five-hundred dollars* for just three months.

And yes, you read that correctly.

That was how many bogus trademarks ole greedy Les had filed for.

Over *seventy-seven-thousand-five-hundred dollars'* worth. I didn't make that kind of money. Wish I did. Had I kept paying that, I'd have been in bankruptcy even sooner.

Not to mention, he had filed for trademarks in categories that I wasn't eligible for.

A *lot* of them.

Part of the reason that bill was so high was from me trying to understand and figure out what Les had done. I would submit what were called "specimens" to the attorneys, only to learn what an absolute moron I'd married. My counsel kept telling me that what I was submitting didn't qualify as trademark items and that the government wouldn't approve my application.

That meant that Les had filed false information and that I had no choice other than to abandon them as I didn't qualify for the trademarks.

Simple law.

You couldn't file for a trademark you weren't entitled to. You couldn't hold on to a trademark you were not entitled to. That was fraud and it was illegal.

At no time had I been lying to my counsel.

Les had. And Cockburn lied every time she parted her lips. And how could I bring harm to the bankruptcy estate when my trustee was the one who had to approve each, and every dollar spent on my attorneys? I couldn't even have an attorney unless Newhouse said I could.

Cockburn was *that* stupid.

So right here, she was lying to the trustee who knew she was lying, and Newhouse said and did nothing to cow this lunatic bitch.

He allowed her to continue, knowing every second she spent on this insane, illegal quest, she was gouging my estate and stealing money from my children.

Now let's consider those "countless hours." Obviously, the bitch was counting them as I'd been billed for every single second Cockburn had been on the clock.

After all, Newhouse had refused to allow me a few hundred dollars to buy Christmas presents for my family and business associates but had cavalierly handed over a check to that whore for almost two hundred thousand dollars of our money right before Christmas.

In other words, after Newhouse had illegally seized my son's money out of his account that had his name on it, by using threats against me and intimidating me with tales of how he'd drag me in front of Dinky if I didn't cooperate, or throw me into a Chapter 7, spent every dime of my son's money on this sow.

He'd done the same thing with Maddox's money. This wasn't money that I had "just" transferred into joint accounts right before I'd filed because I was trying to pull something over on the court.

Maddox's money had been in his account, and I could prove it, for more than two years.

Nick's had been there for over a decade.

In their own private accounts that Newhouse had illegally stolen.

Newhouse had absolutely *no* right to take a single dime of the money out of my grown sons' accounts.

Sadly, I hadn't known the law at the time and my worthless bankruptcy attorney, Leadwits hadn't said a word to protect me or my children.

He'd sat there and let them do it. Worse, he'd used the same threats of Dinky to "corral" me for them.

Even though he was in on and had backed Oldham into "dipping" illegally into my cash to be paid the thirty-five thousand dollars for his illegal search and seizure of my home, instead of having Oldham added to my "creditors" as he should have been.

Anything to scratch their own backs and steal from the innocent.

Welcome to Nashville.

Now this bitch was back at Christmas because *she* wanted a bigger bonus for her family off the backs of mine.

And Newhouse was all too happy to accommodate her.

Cockburn wanted another hundred thousand plus out of us.

Too bad they'd all robbed us dry.

And for all those "countless hours" how much research had the bitch actually done?

Hmmm...

I could tell you what she hadn't done. She hadn't bothered to look up the Hollywood producer's website which was, of course, part of his email before she went and "cited" that reliable Hollywood offer she was waving under everyone's noses.

When you went to the domain, it was an empty GoDaddy holding site.

Well, how serious an inquiry could it have been for my movie rights if the company didn't even have a company website up in this day and age?

Yeah. That was some serious detective work she'd billed me for, wasn't it? As for this "legitimate" company's work, well, their most recent project was over twenty years old.

Really, that was all you needed to say.

This "producer" she was flouting hadn't done a project since the 1990s. And those had all been cartoons.

Which, by the way, was what he'd wanted to do with my franchise. He hadn't wanted to make a movie or television show out of it. He'd wanted to make a short cartoon.

No real offer had ever been made and when I called my agent to ask about it because he'd never mentioned the project or producer to me, he said and I quote, "Who?"

Bob had to go look up his notes to remember that he'd even spoken to the guy.

See, that was the real kicker and Les knew this as he was married to me for almost thirty years. We got Hollywood "inquiries" all the time about rights. But they never panned out. People would constantly say that they had a project, but more times than not, it was with little to no budget and wasn't something they could actually do.

The one real offer we'd had, Les had blown apart out of spite.

That I knew for a fact.

It was why I could verify that we had no movie or show currently in the works and why I couldn't legally tell the government/Trademark Office that I did have a deal because that would have been perjury. And not even a bully as stupid as Cockburn was going to make me commit that crime.

And didn't you love how she'd said that she had "evidence within the past twelve months" and only showed one piece of it? She was famous for that kind of lying. Just like when she'd looked Dinky in the eye and read one single email and said, "there are tens of thousands of emails like this one."

There wasn't.

She was a lying bitch, and no one would bust her on it, even though what she was doing was illegal as fuck. Even though it was against the Tennessee Board of Professional Responsibility's mandates.

No one would stop her or discipline her while she ruined lives and used her bar license to threaten and intimidate.

It was sickening. How could anyone make an "informed, educated decision" when all they were being fed by her were lies and blatant misrepresentations of facts?

Even if that producer had made a serious offer, I still couldn't have pursued the trademark Les had filed. The trademark that expired was for live action. Animation was a separate filing.

Gah, the ignorant slut!

And with her brilliant intellect at work, she left off with the promise that they were going to continue to illegally renew those trademarks that I wasn't entitled to, that had cost me over seventy-seven-thousand-five-hundred dollars while claiming that I was the one who was wasting my marital assets and estate.

How does that work again?

And they were going to bill me for their work that they knew was illegal and for trademarks that I wasn't entitled to.

Uh, yeah.

Now you knew why Newhouse was so sure when he'd said unequivocally that Les and Cockburn were the sole reason that I was in bankruptcy and why I was going to lose absolutely everything I had spent my entire life working for.

Including all my trademarks and contracts and royalties.

It was their legal fees, not mine, that had caused this nightmare.

Because...

*Keep reading.*

I REMEMBERED BEING YOUNG and looking forward to the new year. A new chance to begin fresh. A year filled with possibilities and exciting opportunities.

They'd stolen even that from me.

From the first day of the year, I had a sick lump in my gut, because I knew they would be pulling some shit on me, and that this year would blow in epic chunks.

I hated being psychic.

Okay, that wasn't really my being psychic. *C'mon, you've been reading this. With odds like that...*

Well, we all knew the bastards were up to no good the minute they called off mediation in December and made no more good faith efforts for it. They had to be plotting something, right?

I supposed that made us all about as psychic as Sean Spencer on the old TV show *Psych*.

Sadly, as usual, we didn't know from which direction they'd strike. Because lunatics tended to be unpredictable.

Remember when the jackals got their big bonus payout of almost two hundred thousand dollars in November?

Well, it was like feeding a stray. And rather than help me drive off the pack of wild dogs to protect my estate (as a trustee was supposed to do), mine allowed it to be open season on what tiny little money I had left.

*Mazel Tov!*

This year was off with a bang!

Now, I should put a disclaimer in here, as I've been told to do. Newhouse couldn't *do* anything after he and Oldham, against the advice of my attorney, had consigned me to penury by giving Cockburn and crew a blank check from my estate and saying, "Have at it. I'm sure given all your past lies and bad acts that you'll conduct yourself responsibly."

Yeah, Newhouse was that fucking stupid.

After all, they were only out to fuck me. Surely, they wouldn't make *him* look like the idiot buffoon he was.

Needless to say, they did.

Newhouse's lie was that, "he had no choice," according to his boss, Martha Seaver. "There's a court order. He has to pay it!" Martha, whined to me.

"He *had* to pay it."

Didn't matter that he was there in the court the day the order came down and that he was the one who'd negotiated it with Cockburn and crew while railroading me into it with threats of jail if I didn't.

"You don't want to face Dinky. He hates you. He'll give them even more than this if you go before him."

Well, first, Dinky shouldn't have. Second, as my trustee, Newhouse, you could have spoken up that my estate couldn't pay that and taken it to the bankruptcy/federal court like you were supposed to.

But instead, what had he done?

Approved another two hundred, plus, payout to attorneys, and then tacked on his own one-hundred-and-eleven-thousand-dollar bill at the end of it.

How I wish I was lying.

He even paid Les's attorneys who had nothing to do with the divorce and Dinky knew he was signing away money to Les that Les wasn't entitled to.

Yeah. Newhouse railroaded me into an all-new feeding-frenzy by the state and the jackals. He'd refused stand up to the corrupt state judge or the opposing counsel he was so friendly with, or to his friend he'd handpicked against my wishes who was his own private counsel for the bankruptcy. The same man who'd been hired by Cockburn and who had done the illegal search and seizure for my home.

Didn't matter that the federal bankruptcy judge was the idiot who'd put the corrupt state judge who had it in for me back over me after I'd been assured that it wouldn't happen.

So much for the federal judge watching out for the government's money and my estate. What did she care?

After all, my bankruptcy lawyer, Stefano had told me over and over and over again that there was no way the federal judge would allow it to stay in the state court. "You don't have to deal with Dinky anymore. It'll now be in the hands of the feds and not those yahoos down in Williamson. It's a whole different matter now. Don't worry. They're not idiots here."

Yeah, right.

The federal judge was just as bored and uninterested in doing her job as those in Williamson County. Anything she could do to get out of her robe and go play as quickly as possible, she was willing to do. If it meant flushing someone's life down the toilet, so what?

It wasn't *her* fault.

How could I, as an American citizen, hold her or the trustee or the trustee's attorney-boss, Martha, responsible for *their* actions? This was the land of "blame someone else." Pass the mighty buck we stole from someone else.

After all this, I'd begun to believe that there must be a first-year law class that was taught to all students. Blame The Other Guy 101.

At least it would explain so much about Les's personality.

Anyway, it wasn't like there was a Tennessee Bar Association statute that required lawyers to report on each other for corrupt behavior or misdeeds that all of them ignored.

Oh, wait! Yes, there was such a statute! That statute also claimed that they could be disciplined if they failed to report on the attorney who ignored their oath of office or abused their bar license.

And power.

Want to see it?

> (c) A lawyer shall be responsible for another lawyer's violation of the Rules of Professional Conduct if:

(1) the lawyer orders or, with knowledge of the specific conduct, ratifies the conduct in- volved; or

(2) the lawyer is a partner or has comparable managerial authority in the law firm in which the other lawyer practices, or has direct supervisory authority over the other lawyer, and knows of the conduct at a time when its consequences can be avoided or mitigated but fails to take reasonable remedial action.

[4] For example, a lawyer who commits fraud in the conduct of a business is subject to discipline for engaging in conduct involving dishonesty, fraud, deceit, or misrepresentation. See RPC 8.4.

[6] A lawyer's conduct should conform to the requirements of the law, both in professional service to clients and in the lawyer's business and personal affairs. A lawyer should use the law's procedures only for legitimate purposes and not to harass or intimidate others. A lawyer should demonstrate respect for the legal system and for those who serve it, including judges, other lawyers, and public officials. While it is a lawyer's duty, when necessary, to challenge the rectitude of official action, it is also a lawyer's duty to uphold legal process.

[10] In any case, however, the lawyer is required to avoid assisting the client, for example, by drafting or delivering documents that the lawyer knows are fraudulent or by suggesting how the wrongdoing might be concealed. A lawyer may not continue assisting a client in conduct that the lawyer originally supposed was legally proper but then discovers is criminal or fraudulent. The lawyer must, therefore, withdraw from the representation of the client in the matter. See RPC 1.16(a).

And of course, there's my favorite part they had continually violated from the beginning:

RULE 3.1: MERITORIOUS CLAIMS AND CONTENTIONS

A lawyer shall not bring or defend a proceeding, or assert or controvert an issue therein, unless after reasonable inquiry the lawyer has a basis in law and fact for doing so that is not frivolous, which includes a good faith argument for an extension, modification, or reversal of existing law.

[1] The advocate has a duty to use legal procedure for the fullest benefit of the client's cause, but also a duty not to abuse legal procedure.

RULE 3.3: CANDOR TOWARD THE TRIBUNAL

(a) A lawyer shall not knowingly:

(1) make a false statement of fact or law to a tribunal; or fail to inform the tribunal of all material facts known to the lawyer that will enable the tribunal to make an informed decision, whether or not the facts are adverse.

(b) A lawyer shall not offer evidence the lawyer knows to be false.

(c) A lawyer shall not affirm the validity of, or otherwise use, any evidence the lawyer knows to be false.

(d) A lawyer may refuse to offer or use evidence, that the lawyer reasonably believes is false, misleading, fraudulent or illegally obtained.

(e) If a lawyer knows that the lawyer's client intends to perpetrate a fraud upon the tribunal or otherwise commit an offense against the administration of justice in connection with the proceeding, or comes to know, prior to the conclusion of the proceeding, that the client has, during the course of the lawyer's representation, perpetrated such a crime or fraud, the lawyer shall advise the client to refrain from, or to disclose or otherwise rectify, the crime or fraud and shall discuss with the client the consequences of the client's failure to do so.

(f) If a lawyer, after discussion with the client as required by paragraph (e), knows that the client still intends to perpetrate the crime or fraud, or refuses or is unable to disclose or otherwise rectify the crime or fraud, the lawyer shall seek permission of the tribunal to withdraw from the representation of the client and shall inform the tribunal, without further disclosure of information protected by RPC 1.6, that the lawyer's request to withdraw is required by the Rules of Professional Conduct.

(g) A lawyer who, prior to conclusion of the proceeding, comes to know that the lawyer has offered false tangible or documentary evidence shall withdraw or disaffirm such evidence without further disclosure of information protected by RPC 1.6.

(h) A lawyer who, prior to the conclusion of the proceeding, comes to know that a person other than the client has perpetrated a fraud upon the tribunal or otherwise committed an offense against the administration of justice in connection with the proceeding, and in which the lawyer's client was not implicated, shall promptly report the improper conduct to the tribunal, even if so doing requires the disclosure of information otherwise protected by RPC 1.6.

Comment

[1] This Rule governs the conduct of a lawyer who is representing a client in connection with the proceedings of a tribunal, such as a court or an administrative agency acting in an adjudicative capacity. It applies not only when the lawyer appears before the tribunal, but also when the lawyer participates in activities conducted pursuant to the tribunal's authority, such as pre-trial discovery in a civil matter.

[2] The advocate's task is to present the client's case with persuasive force. Performance of that duty while maintaining confidences of the client is qualified by the advocate's duty to refrain from assisting a client to perpetrate a fraud upon the tribunal. However, an advocate does not vouch for the evidence submitted in a cause; the tribunal is responsible for assessing its probative value.

Representations by a Lawyer

[3] An advocate is responsible for pleadings and other documents prepared for litigation, but is usually not required to have personal knowledge of matters asserted therein, for litigation documents ordinarily present assertions by the client, or by someone on the client's behalf, and not assertions by the lawyer. Compare RPC 3.1.

Misleading Legal Argument

[4] Legal argument based on a knowingly false representation of law constitutes dishonesty toward the tribunal.

Hmmm...

That meant that ole Cockburn was honor bound to tell the judge that Les's father was in fact a known pedophile when Dinky sentenced me for making a "disgusting allegation" that she knew for a fact was the truth and wasn't an allegation. After all, she'd put it in her April 20, 2018 motion against me (it was on public record, thanks to her). She'd spelled it out completely and used it to shame me in one of her very first court filings that Les had been molested, which was also against her Code as an attorney. Yet she said not a word after she'd lied to get me, an innocent victim, sentenced and shamed, publicly.

And the courts of Tennessee allowed that to stand.

*Shame on all of you.*

So many violations that they'd refused to sanction her over. It really was disgusting.

Just like the Tennessee Ouster law that would have allowed them to get a corrupt judge off the bench. Yet none of them would help me enact that either. Nor would they allow the obviously prejudiced judge to recuse himself, never mind demand that he go away, which was my legal right and supposed guarantee.

Even though I went to them with the petition and with more than ten times the required number of Williamson County voters to get Dinky off that bench that he shamed every time he sat himself upon it. Even though I had a petition with tens of thousands of names demanding someone do something in this county to give me a fair hearing.

We won't talk about the fact that they ignored all that. Or the fact that none of them would take my case of abuse to the federal judge to ask for help. Because the federal judge would have had the discretion to do something to intervene, had she chosen to do so.

But she refused to even hear it.

They refused to allow me to have a voice.

Never mind the fact that every single one of those attorneys had told me to my face that I could, under no circumstances, go before Judge Dinky because there was, and I quote, "no chance in hell" of getting a fair shake from him.

"He will put you in jail again."

Oh, for the times that had been said to me.

Nor was there, and I quote, "a chance in hell" of getting him to recuse himself from the case or of getting the case moved out of his jurisdiction.

"I just had a case where the judge wouldn't recuse himself. They don't do it here. It takes an act of God."

On January 2 (because the jackals were that greedy after having just been paid a fucking fortune), they filed a motion for (brace yourself) *over* seventy-seven thousand dollars to be paid to themselves for the honor of coming after me while I was in bankruptcy, right after they'd been paid almost two hundred grand.

Gotta love ole Dinky who was supposed to be "guarding" my estate and making sure it wasn't being raided by one party or the other, but as long as the party raiding it was your old business partners...

*It's all good. Load 'er up, boys! Come on back for seconds!*

So much for putting the wolf in charge of my marital henhouse. Let the raping and pillaging commence!

"Here, buddies, write your own check! Everybody take a turn!"

I felt like the town bike.

And my trustee, Newhouse, was in on it.

My attorney, Melissa, took a very modest pay, less than four thousand dollars a month. Her fees weren't included with the above outrageous amount. That seventy-seven-thousand plus bill was *all* Les's jackals.

When you combined the money they stole from me in three months, at Christmas and New

Year's where I was not allowed to even buy my boys a pair of jeans that didn't have holes in them, those bastards stole over three hundred thousand dollars from me (not counting the over one-hundred-thousand dollars tacked on to me by Newhouse).

*To sue me.*

For what?

Well, according to their notes, they were coming after me for defamation. Which, according to Tennessee law they couldn't legally do as I was Les's only form of income—that was why I hadn't filed a defamation suit against old Hogg the year before. My attorney had refused to let me file a suit because he claimed it would be too difficult to prove that she was the one who'd harmed my declining income as you *must* prove financial harm as a result of the person who was bad-mouthing you when you sued them for defamation in Tennessee.

"It's too hard to establish that they're the reason your income has fallen while you're in a divorce. Besides, Terri, she's a turnip. What would be the point? It's not like you could get any money from her even if you won it."

And forget ole Les. I couldn't touch him because he had no job at all. While my "status quo" had tremendously declined, his had risen off the backs of his own sons.

While the judges and trustees all signed off on it.

So, needless to say, Hogg and Les couldn't make a legal claim against me for defamation as neither of them had any income.

And let's not forget the most important fact of all. Everything I'd said about the two of them was one-hundred-and-fifty percent true. The whole "truth" argument also precluded a defamation case.

*Because you can't libel or defame shit by saying it stinks.*

And while I definitely had a case against each, and every one of them for their malicious defamation and libel, including Judge Dinky, I couldn't find an attorney in town who would represent me because I was blackballed.

*By them.* They'd gone to basically every firm in town to slander me and keep me from justice.

Meanwhile, I was in bankruptcy because of the lies they had all, including those sickening lawyers, told against me. While they had breached their oaths of office that the Tennessee Board of Professional Responsibility had refused to uphold.

No one would do anything about it.

At this point, I was as sick of writing bar complaints against the magpies as I was sure Ms. Dullard was of receiving them.

Here was the most recent one I'd written on this matter that week:

> The latest actions of Bonnie Cockburn, Mika House and John Alaimo are that they are currently refusing to allow me to depose their client by claiming that my bankruptcy has halted all divorce proceedings. Yet, as you can plainly see by the attached invoices, they are billing me tens of thousands of dollars for them to continue their actions against me in my divorce. Cockburn actually told my attorney, Melissa Magillacutty that my bankruptcy halted all further discovery, and yet as you can plainly see by the attached invoices, I was billed for their activities while I'm in bankruptcy. They've halted nothing. They are blocking me from conducting discovery on their client and from getting the justice I deserve while charging me for their continued harassment and frivolous actions against me.
>
> Melissa Magillicutty's contact information is attached in the enclosed affidavit. Please contact her for more information about how they are refusing to comply with the very codes you have been charged with upholding, and how they continue to misbehave and embarrass attorneys in this state.

If you want to see just how reckless they have been, and the lies that they have no problem putting to the court, just look at the attached document 2018.04.20 where Cockburn blatantly misstates facts and contradicts herself throughout it. At one point she indicts her own client by saying that he didn't remove my loaded guns from our home (which he did) but rather "hid them" in our house when we had a teen-aged son in residence. Not only is that a stupid argument, but it opens her client up for liability should my son or one of his friends find one of those registered weapons and use it to harm someone. Not to mention she claims that her client didn't take my shotgun and that it's at the cabin that I'm court order banned from visiting, which means that he has taken my weapon from me and I want it back.

Likewise, I have documentation that Les was in my Spring Hill storage unit at 6 AM that is located 30 minutes from my home, so obviously he left my home before her stated 7:30 AM time frame. That is not a "reasonable" time. And I have time stamped emails I was sending out at 6-9 AM that morning (and every morning as I'm always up at those hours, and as you know from when I've sent emails to you) to prove that she is lying about the times when I sleep and that I was definitely awake that morning, contrary to her lies to the court.

Further, she says that I "threatened to kill 2 people" and only names one, which is a blatant lie that I can prove as I'm attaching the bodyguard bill to show that I had to hire protection against the person she names who had stalked me for a year. I had to even have security guards for my sons against that lunatic.

Furthermore, she commits an act of Stolen Valor that is easy to prove. My husband committed Dereliction of Duty and never fulfilled his military obligation to the Army, and I can easily prove that, too, yet she touts him as an honorable serviceman while she accuses me of carrying a "bladed cross" through airport security. I've enclosed a photo of that "bladed weapon" along with the other items that are in my travel case. It is my father's service cross that is awarded to those who fight in foreign wars. My father died from wounds he received in Vietnam. I carry his cross and dog tags because they are all I have of him. He died while I was in my twenties and it is disgusting that she is allowed to lie and attack me in this manner. My other "weapon" is my pink pen that is made by "Smith & Wesson." As you can plainly see, it is an ink pen and not a weapon of any kind. The pen was a gift from a fan.

Furthermore, in this document, she admits that my husband was sexually molested and yet she allowed Dinky to convict me for contempt of court because I said my father-in-law was a pedophile in his courtroom. Dinky, with no investigation, assumed I was lying based on Cockburn's incessant lies and slander against me. Yet Cockburn knew for a fact that I was speaking the truth and said nothing while I was unfairly sentenced. This is an abomination and gross miscarriage of justice that no one will address.

This is fundamentally wrong. You have to know that. And I have complained repeatedly to you and the Judiciary Board. It doesn't do any good to complain to Judge Dinky because he refuses to hear any complaint against lawyers who used to work in his firm. This is a sick miscarriage of justice and I cannot believe that the Tennessee court system is this corrupt. Will you please help me?

That was the last of seven emails that I sent to Ms. Dullard within a one-week period, all with attachments to show how egregious and sickening their behavior had been.

These were some of the photos sent to her:

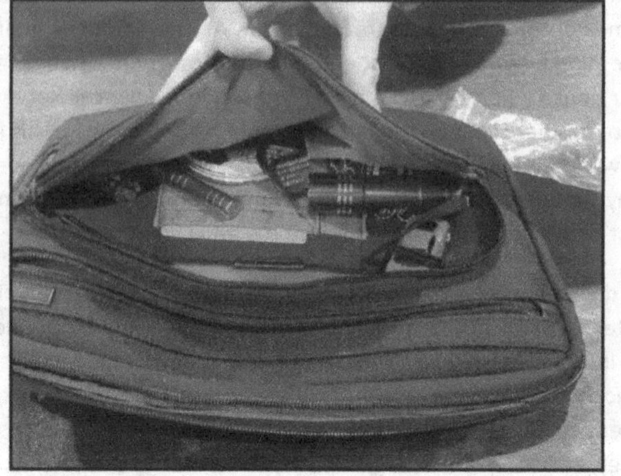

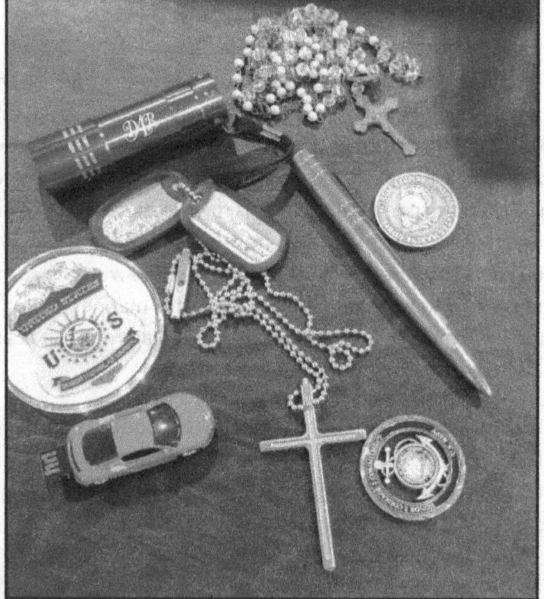

I should also make note that Dinky putting me in jail for ten days was also a violation of my Eighth and Fourteenth Amendment Rights.

But as the judge had said, "I don't care what the law is."

And they had proven it. Repeatedly. From the lawyers to the judges, to those who were charged with overseeing them. No one would stop this sick abuse.

God help us all.

*If that wasn't bad enough, ask me about the second week of January when they came to take my cars from me. The car I'd had for fourteen years.*

*I dare you.*

As always, the auctioneer and tow truck driver were on my side and were kind. Because they knew how badly screwed over the system was doing me. How wrong the others were.

Just as the insurance lady I'd spoken to who'd promised to keep me in her prayers.

They all knew how rotten Newhouse et al were for stealing from me to pay Les's bills that he was too lazy and sorry to pay for himself. And you could see it on their faces how sick they were to do what their jobs were making them do.

Mr. Extra Nice Tow Truck even said he'd be glad to come back any time I needed him. The reason?

While they were depriving me and my sons of our cars, my "neighbor" i.e. Les's old friend came barreling over.

"What's going on?"

As if we didn't know he'd been spying for Les. By the way, this wasn't the first time I'd been accosted in my yard by Mr. David Lickenfelt.

David had come over a few months back, out of the blue while I was taking groceries in and was trying to deal with my wonderful Orkin guy.

He was in my face, then, about my son's dog, Rex Luther.

As soon as Maddox had returned from Japan, he'd gone to a shelter to rescue his pet.

Maddox, being his hard-headed self, hadn't listened to me when I'd told him that cute little puppy was going to grow into one huge, monster of a Treeing Walker hound dog that chewed up everything.

And I do mean e-v-e-r-y-t-h-i-n-g.

At a cool hundred pounds, Rex doubled as a small horse and had become an aggressive chewer who would even nosh on rocks. We had to watch him carefully lest he turn my deck into matchsticks.

Well, ole Dave came over to me, screaming. "Your dog has been in my yard!"

"No, he hasn't."

"Yes, he has!"

"No. He hasn't. He never leaves my yard. I would know." Whenever we let him outside, Rex would sit right at my window and stare at me as if to say, "Hey, woman, I want in." And whenever he stayed too long outside, he would stand up on his hind legs and knock twice on the door to be let back in. Damned thing sounded like a person out there.

It was kind of spooky. He'd learned that from my Orkin guy, too.

With a smug smirk, my "neighbor" handed me one of Rex's brand-new toys. "Does this belong to him?"

Stunned, I gaped. "Yes, it does. How did you get it?"

"It was in *my* yard! As I said, your dog has been in my yard, digging it up."

Now I was scared. "No, he hasn't. My dog doesn't dig, and he didn't put it there. Trust me. You'd know if he'd been in your yard as he'd have chewed it up like a piranha. Why were *you* in *my* yard?"

He stuttered a bit. "You have a Beagle, right?"

"No, I don't. I have a giant hound. Bigger than me. Would you like to meet him?"

He sputtered more. "Well, I-I-I've reported your dog to the HOA. And they're going to come and take him. He's been barking all the time. We were walking along your fence, and we heard him the other day. We know it's him!"

"If you were walking along my fence, you were trespassing on my property, and he was barking because you were on my property illegally and he was doing his job. My dog stays in the house and you're not supposed to be in my backyard, walking across it." My fence splits my backyard in half. And Dipshit would have been trespassing and had absolutely no business there as there's no street or walkway behind my house, or that divides my property.

"Well, I've reported your dog and I have a camera to prove it's your dog!"

"Good. You'll have proof that it isn't, and I want the footage."

"Well, I hear your dog all the time. I'm retired now. I retired awhile back. I used to talk to your assistant and... "

Then he began rambling on and on about his old job and Hogg.

Not *my* assistant, I realized as he kept babbling. Les's.

Lyra had never spoken to this jack-off. And the more he rambled the more suspicious I became.

For a number of reasons.

Why was he so pissed off at me? As I'd said to him repeatedly, my dog stayed in the house the majority of the time. We rarely let him out. But one interesting thing.

Prior to Maddox getting that dog, someone had kept going into our yard.

A lot. We constantly found our gates opened. Yet once we had Rex, that had stopped. Whoever had been coming and going freely in my yard had no longer made free back there.

Also, why would old Dave have had *any* contact with Hogg while she'd been at my house?

In all the years I'd lived here, I had never, ever had any contact with my neighbor until *that* particular day. Not once.

Not even to say hi.

Or fuck off.

Not until that day and then when they came to remove the cars.

While I'd known he was friends with Les, who constantly complained about him, I'd never once met him.

Never.

I'd only heard Les talk shit about him and point out his house to me.

Had no idea this neighbor was "good" friends with Hogg or that he'd ever met her. So, I was stunned that he'd known her name and had met her so much that he kept referring to her and talking about how many times they'd conversed. More than that, he confirmed how many people she'd lied to when she gave out her occupation as "Manly Command Center."

Why was she so insistent on telling everyone that she was my assistant when I had hired Lyra for that job?

It was so weird.

And do you know what old Dave's job had been that he retired from?

Brace yourself.

Pharmaceutical Rep.

You know those guys who went around to doctor's offices handing out free samples of things like Lithium. The very things that had been found in my system that I had never, ever taken or been prescribed, and had no explanation for how in the hell it could have found its way into my blood, nails or hair.

Wasn't that one heck of a coincidence?

And guess where that camera in his yard was turned?

Straight onto my driveway so that it monitored who came and went. Not really *his* yard.

*My* driveway.

Hmm... How peculiar was that? Why would he have it only in one place and only aimed at my house. And my driveway?

Not to mention, on the day they came for our cars, there he was. In our faces so badly that both the guy from the auction house and Tow Truck Driver were acting as security guards to protect against him.

"I've reported your dog!"

"It's not my dog barking." It was actually the neighbor on my other side who has two huskies and a pit bull. Those were the dogs that came out and barked all the time. Even at two in the morning while Rex was curled up at my feet.

*I'm listening to them, right now as I type this, while my dog is resting in the house, asleep.*

Yet there Dave was, arguing with us while we were attempting to do something highly stressful.

Why?

"Can't you see we're busy?"

"You're not being very neighborly!"

Joan stared at him. "I don't live here."

"Are you the new neighbor who bought this place?"

She screwed her face up at him. Why would he think that or even know that the house was being listed? No sign had been posted.

Unless he'd been talking to Les.

It went to show that the rotten bastard was in contact with Les as there was no other way for him to know that the house was going up for sale.

"No. Now go away!"

He had to be expelled from the yard, and his behavior was so extreme and over the top that the auction house guy came back that evening to check on us.

He'd also heard by then that I'd written a book about the egregiousness of my unjust treatment at the hands of the court and others in Williamson County.

Another thing that floored me. *What the actual fuck?*

I'd only told my attorneys about my little diary I was keeping. Which meant that one of my attorneys had breached their attorney-client privilege with me.

Okay, only one of them, and I knew which one. You had to love this town.

I couldn't believe it. My diary that I'd been told by the Head Detective of Williamson County to keep so that I could document every underhanded piece of bullshit because and I quote, "We don't do that here. It's up to you to keep up with it." Because they couldn't be bothered to do their jobs and write reports.

And it meant that Frick and Frack and old Cockburn would be at my throat, along with Dinky soon over the fact that I'd written it, too.

*The hits keep on coming.*

By that point, I was so tired of being threatened and bullied, and of the games that they continued to play.

Not the least of which was their latest bunch of horse shit.

When I spoke to my friend who was a Davidson County police officer for over fourteen years, he said, "Yeah, it happens. Criminals are known to attack a victim's credibility and seek to put them in jail to keep themselves from serving time for their crimes. I've seen it a lot."

Which begged the question as to why the Williamson County DA and police acted as if they'd never seen or heard of this? Why they believed in helping the criminals victimize their victims?

There was something rotten in the county of Williamson and I wanted out of here so badly.

But they wouldn't let me leave. They had all my money in their hands, and they wouldn't allow me to buy moving boxes (my request was denied) so that I could start over where the shit didn't stink to high heaven. I was trapped in this never-ending nightmare for the crime of thinking I'd once loved a wretched piece of shit.

For thinking, for one minute, that there was something called an American judicial system, when there wasn't one.

Not at a state level and damn sure not a federal one.

# JANUARY 16, 2020

*I*AM NOW A THREAT TO NATIONAL *security.*
*Wait? What?*

*That got your attention, didn't it? Got mine, too. Let me tell you about this fucked up day…*

*Take a second and buckle your seatbelt. You're going to need it for this next fun-filled chapter I liked to call, Twenty Hours of Hell.*

I was supposed to have a meeting that morning with my bankruptcy attorney (Leadwits), my divorce attorney (Melissa), and the head U.S. Trustee lady, Martha Seaver, along with Joan who was coming in for moral support.

That was it.

I thought.

We were going to strategize on how to get me out of the bankruptcy while Les and crew had carte blanche to keep writing their own checks to sue me at will courtesy of ole Dinky.

Keep in mind that at this point, I'd been in a bankruptcy for over six months and Newhouse had yet to file a plan to get me out of it. All my money had been seized and none of it had gone to a single creditor. Rather all my money had gone to pay for my trustee and his furry little crew of friends AKA Les's attorneys and Newhouse's attorney and accountant who made my life utter hell.

Personally, I didn't see a way out given that all my money was going to lawyers and Newhouse kept writing checks for ten to twenty times what I was making.

I was praying for a lifeline, because after the day before where the auction house guy had come in and ripped out my heart by taking the car I'd bought my son for graduation, my car and the '64 Mustang I'd had for a decade and a half, that I had loved with all my being and protected as carefully as I had my children, I was gutted and bleeding. (For the record, almost every cent of the sale of that Mustang went to pay the auction house and nothing else).

Never mind the fact that they'd taken my purses and my coats.

Well, of course it was fucking freezing that morning and all I had was a thin sweater to wear.

Joan and I sat alone in the trustee's office, talking about how weird the night before had been. The fact that I'd been betrayed by my own attorney who had been talking about my diary that wasn't supposed to be mentioned.

Who'd betrayed me, again.

I was expecting this meeting to be my attorneys with one trustee. In walked my bankruptcy attorney with the other two. Newhouse and Oldham. And this wasn't a meeting on how to get me out of bankruptcy and how to help me.

It was an ambush.

No wonder the bastard had hung up on me when I'd called to talk to him the day before. See, I was always told that an attorney's job and oath was to *help* their client. That their first oath was always to their client.

God knew that Les's attorneys, *all* of them, had no compunctions against breaking any and every law they could for him.

Perjury. Check.

Lying to the media. Check.

Lying to the judge. Check.

Tax fraud. Check.

Benedict Arnold had been joking the entire time about, "When this is over, you're going to have one heck of a book about all this!"

"Yeah, I am."

So, as a lark, I'd sent him a copy of this as I'd been keeping tabs on all the dirty deeds as the detective had ordered. Stefano called me up at first, laughing about it and said I was a brilliant writer.

Then, instead of telling me I was doing something wrong by documenting the injustice being done to me (as I had been told to do), he not only handed it over to the head trustee but began giving copies out to everyone.

Without my permission.

Thus, breaking the law, himself. As anyone who has ever seen the FBI warning label on copyrighted products knew. It was criminal to disseminate any intellectual property without the express permission of the copyright holder.

I hadn't given him permission to start spreading my diary all over this fucked up town.

He also breached his attorney-client privilege and violated all kinds of codes according to the rules put forth by the Tennessee Board of Professional Responsibility.

*That* was what the auction house guy had been talking about when he'd come to my house.

And of course, they were all furious.

At me.

*The victim.* Not the attorney who'd breached attorney-client privilege.

Not the judge who refused to act impartially or legally.

Not the other attorneys they were all honor bound to report, or anyone else who was being unethical or breaching their fiduciary responsibilities.

*Nope, let's all jump on top of the victim and pummel her into the ground.*

Martha's nostrils flared. "I've sent this," she stroked my manuscript like an evil villain, "to my bosses in Washington! If you ever let this out, you'll be in trouble."

My jaw went slack. So much for helping me to get out of my bankruptcy. "Pardon?"

Martha sat there with her beady little eyes, glaring at me. Threatening me with who knew what. "You better *never* let this out... or *else!*"

*Or else what?*

Martha left it hanging there like a gleaming guillotine suspended over my head. A definite threat. Not a little veiled threat.

A *definite* threat.

Stunned, I couldn't believe that, yet again, my rights as an American citizen were being trampled. And for what? I'd done what they all had demanded I do.

Write.

The bitch sat there and said, "Obviously, you can write a book." She continued to stroke a copy of this very diary that she'd printed out (without my permission, thus breaking copyright law). "I don't see why you can't write more!"

Well, Lady Dipshit, there was a big difference between taking dictation of all of you persecuting me while threatening and intimidating me at every turn, as you violated my basic American rights, than creating a novel from scratch. Writers had to create villains, not have them be their living, breathing selves. I couldn't create the betraying assholes all of you were, because my mind didn't naturally go to the level of malevolent asshole where all of you dwelled. Without any effort on your own parts.

That was hard for me to do.

I wasn't a bitch or a betrayer.

I had to work to make my mind sink to the low levels where all of you lived. Because I found the behaviors y'all exhibited so morally corrupt and repugnant that my brain rebelled against it. So, for me to create the villains you were, was so far beyond my wheelhouse that it took a while for me to get there. I couldn't do it easily. I would say that I was sorry, but I was really glad I had to work hard to come up with ways to fuck someone over.

So, contrary to *your* stupidity, Martha, I couldn't sit down and write a novel as easily as I documented your abuse of me and my children.

But her threats to tear my life apart and do who knew what to me, weren't all.

"You are being punished for having written this book. In retaliation, I've told Tom to sell off *all* your jewelry. Every piece."

That included the bubble gum machine ring and the little rock ring with googly eyes my baby had made for me in grade school for Mother's Day.

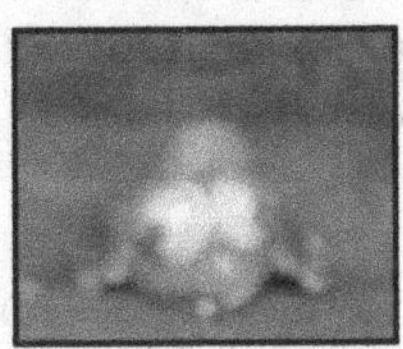

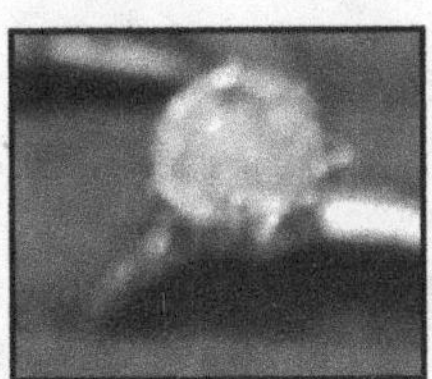

But, according to the Queen Bitch, they were being "kind." I could pick twenty pieces that they may or may not allow me to keep in the end, depending on whether or not I "pleased" them.

That was it.

Twenty.

Out of everything I had kept from my childhood and that had been left to me when my mother, father, brother, niece and grandparents had died, that were all cheap, junk jewelry they had illegally seized from my home.

Out of all the cheap junk jewelry they'd raided that belonged to my deceased mother and grandmother, including her fake brooches I'd played dress up with as a girl. My great-grandmother and her grandmother. My deceased niece's baby earrings and deceased brother's wedding band, and the Timex watch that he'd given my mother for Mother's Day before he died.

These heartless monsters who had come into my home without due process and without any reason, were forcing me to pick out only twenty pieces that included things such as my son's graduation watch, and his cufflinks.

Things they had no right to sell and no right to remove from my home.

I hoped and prayed that they all burned in hell.

And I prayed to God that He gave me a ringside seat for it.

*Want to know what else they told me?*

"Your husband calls all the shots."

I could only keep what he, the fucking bastard who had abused me for triple decades, allowed me to keep.

They were throwing me out of my house and everything else. And they were going to put me and my children on the street. "Without enough money for food or gasoline. We are cutting you off." Because they were *that* insulted. I had hurt *their* tender little baby feelings by writing down what they'd done to me.

Never mind the trauma they'd caused to my boys who'd been held hostage in their home without due process while *their* belongings were seized and removed from their home while dear old daddy had sat laughing in the driveway.

Forget their bank accounts that had been illegally seized by first the state and then the federal government.

Never mind the fact that these assholes had insulted me first. Remember, Newhouse had talked to Cockburn before me and went on attack from the very first phone call and called me names from the get-go and done far worse than that.

Newhouse had taken away my rights.

Not because *I'd* done anything.

Because Les and his crew had gotten into their ears, and they'd assumed the worst about me. Without allowing me to defend myself or my children.

And then acted against me and seized my property that they had no right to take.

Welcome to the country my father and numerous members of my family had fought and bled for.

Never had I felt more betrayed.

But wait...

It got better.

They were ordering me, yet again, to commit a felony.

Yes, they were. These four officers of the court, one of them with a Department of Justice stamped email and appointment, were ordering me to commit a crime. After sitting there and telling me that they could "not" defy Dinky's orders and that Les was in charge because under no circumstances could they defy any order that Dinky had written, Martha was ordering me to destroy all copies of this manuscript.

This manuscript that I was under both a state and federal court order not to destroy. Not just by Dinky *and* Woodly who'd deemed all my writing products to be marital property to be later determined who owned what, but even Martha's own boss, the United States government that had declared all my assets as U.S. property. I had been put under extreme threat should I dispense of, conceal or destroy *any* asset in my possession, I could go to prison for it.

Yet this stupid whore, in front of four other witnesses, was telling me to conceal and destroy a most valuable piece of property that could easily have gotten me out of bankruptcy had I been allowed to shop it out to publishers because she didn't want to be embarrassed or lose her cushy little government job.

Really?

Not to mention the fact that I'd been told to document every piece of dirty dog thing they'd all done to me by the head of the detectives in Williamson County.

*Don't you just love the irony of it all?*

Even better? Magillicutty didn't show. My divorce attorney was sick (or so she claimed). So, there I sat. My world being torn asunder.

Alone, with Joan.

No decent attorney there to protect me.

And when I started crying from all the threats they were leveling against me, Martha made me leave the room. Because *I* got personal.

*You think?*

"If you can't write, then you need to go get a job at Target."

Again, I gaped. Seriously? Martha dared to say that to me? "What about Les?"

"He says he can't work."

Oh, okay. They accepted that bullshit from a fully capable man with a law degree. Obviously, given the level of stupidity that they functioned on, brain activity for an attorney was optional. So, I had yet to understand why no one had forced Les to hang out a shingle. It wasn't like he didn't steal a million dollars as a startup fee for his company like Cockburn had done. That was plenty of money to fund a new office for him. Plus, he was living in my former office, less than a mile from where Cockburn resided and worked.

If she could work illegally out of her home, which was in a subdivision in Williamson County, then he could put up a shingle in my former office.

More than that, they were demanding that I write more to get myself out of bankruptcy, while at the same time refusing to allow me to publish the very book that was guaranteed to be a bestseller.

The book you were currently reading.

*What the fuck?*

How was that even possible? How was that not some kind of violation and conflict of interest?

Martha sat there, threatening me if I published this manuscript, while telling me that they were going to maliciously sell off everything I owned right down to my socks because I wrote this manuscript and if I didn't write more manuscripts to sell to get myself out of bankruptcy. She told me that her orders came to her from her bosses in Washington.

Seriously? They wanted me to burn a manuscript because they were embarrassed by it. Yet the government owned all my property and if I destroyed it, it would be a federal crime. So, if I did what they said, wouldn't that be destruction of government property?

I'd been told repeatedly by *all* of them that I could *not* destroy or hide anything of value, including any and all of my IP or else they'd arrest me for it.

*I swear to God, I'm a Heller novel.*

*Or an Ibsen play.*

*No, I am Kafka!*

As a result of her threats, as soon as I left, I made sure to send a copy of my diary straight to my friend who was a federal agent. *That's* how scared they made me.

"Anything happens to me, please make sure this gets into the hands of the media."

"Absolutely, I will."

That was the beauty about her. Not only was she a federal agent, she was close friends with reporters for major media and news sources. She was also former military.

My girl had my back.

Because I didn't know what else to do.

Instead of helping me to figure out how to get out from under their thumb with a realistic, logical plan, all they did was reassure me that this wasn't a normal bankruptcy and threatened me with retaliation.

Martha had said and I quote, "My finger is on the button. You do anything at all to displease us again and I will press it. Anything we don't like, and I will go Chapter 7 and you will lose everything."

All that did was reassure me that what they'd done to me was wrong and inappropriate. That they were all terrified of Dinky and that none of them were willing to help me get my life back into my hands.

That they didn't care if I was ever able to support myself again.

"You can get a job at Target." I still couldn't believe that Martha had said that to me.

*So can you, bitch.*

Well, maybe not. Target only hired people who had souls.

People who knew how to be kind and who wanted to help others. So, never mind. They weren't the U.S. Bankruptcy Court. You'd have to go get a job scraping up roadkill from the streets, like the vulture you were.

Maybe cleaning out the toilets I scrubbed to get Les the law degree he never used.

After all, that was what each of you deserved for what you'd done to my sons and me.

And at the end of it, no payment plan was proposed on how to get me back on my feet.

They merely told me that Martha had her finger on the button and was ready to push it if I displeased her or Newhouse in any way by saying or doing anything they didn't like, and that they would sell off my trademarks, copyrights and contracts, and make damn sure that I could never again support myself in this lifetime.

"I'll do it, too! You'll see."

She should have added, "and your little dog, too." And finished with a psychotic laugh.

So much for bankruptcy court trying to give someone a "fresh" start to make them able to get back on their feet.

These bastards were planning on turning me into a paraplegic and were giddy at the thought of it.

No apology at all from my attorney for betraying me.

Not a word.

Les's attorneys rallied around him like he was the Messiah and mine had left me abandoned like I was a leper during a St. Vitus Dance parade. After all the money I'd paid and knowing how much he'd wronged me.

And if that wasn't bad enough, while there, words that I'd spoken only to Melissa were also said back to me.

As a threat.

Which meant that Melissa was lying to me about violating attorney-client privilege, too.

Or there was still a bug in my home or on my phone, either by Les or the government. Because this was the third time that had happened. And since Melissa had told me that she'd forgotten we'd had the discussion, I presumed that leak wasn't from her.

I drove home in tears.

How could I tell my sons to pack up and get ready to live on the street, or out of their cars?

Something that had also caused ole Tom to panic during the meeting, by the way.

"You need to prepare for the future. When we throw you out, where are you going to live?"

"I'll find a place."

He'd rolled his eyes at me. "I'm serious. You have to make plans."

"I've already started packing."

They'd looked at me like I'd sacrificed an infant. "You've what!"

So, they wanted me to make plans for the future, but not make plans for the future? This was the kind of insane bullshit they kept doing to me. Every word out of my mouth and every action I took was greeted like a federal crime.

My God, I pity their children, and their poor significant others.

On the way home, I finally got a hold of Melissa.

"Sorry, I was sick last night. I just got up."

I'd been sick the night before, too. I hadn't slept and I was still sick. Was even sicker after my meeting. "Did you file the paperwork about the cabin?"

"I'm working on it, but Dinky isn't going to make him leave so that you can stay there."

Why should he? Wasn't like Les was actually using it given that all of his bills were in Georgia or that my business license was in Tennessee, and I needed to be in business where my license was located or anything.

*God forbid a judge do anything logical...*

Which was what the bankruptcy people had told me, too.

Dinky wasn't going to do anything for me.

I was screwed. He was corrupt, but I couldn't say the word. They'd acted like a bunch of vampires being sprayed with daylight whenever I dared say the "C" word during the meeting. They'd practically ducked and covered under the table. Ole Martha had clutched at her papers and cringed as if terrified the KGB was about to kick open the door and haul her off to the Gulag.

Then Melissa dropped the other bomb. "I hate to tell you this, but you lost your appeal."

"What?!"

"Yeah. They said that Dinky can do whatever he wants to in his courtroom."

"Are you fucking kidding me?" *I know, I keep saying this a lot, but you could see why.*

"Yeah, and where I said that he didn't have to give you the maximum sentence, they said that he didn't. He could have given you ten days *and* a fine of fifty dollars."

*Oh, okay. Because fifty dollars added to ten days in jail made so much difference.*

Now you saw the level of stupidity of the judges in Williamson County and Nashville. With that low-functioning intelligence, it was easy to see why our road system was such a screwed-up mess, and why no one in their right mind would ever willingly locate here.

Yeah. *Big* difference between paying fifty dollars and losing ten days of my life and putting my business in jeopardy (and probably ruining it) because your little buddy had a hissy fit and couldn't hold his temper because I said the word "pedophile" in his court to an actual pedophile.

My, my...

*Trigger word much, Dinky?* One must wonder why he'd reacted so violently to that word.

And why other judges would be so protective of him doing wrong to an innocent woman in his courtroom.

What was even more sickening was that when you read the transcript and my attorney tried to explain to him that I was a sole owner of my business and that I not only couldn't do my job in jail, I couldn't meet the outrageous deadline Judge Dipshit was setting for me.

"Take a laptop to her in jail to get it done!"

Oh, okay. Because they'd break those rules for me.

He was out of his fucking idiot mind.

"Don't worry. I'll appeal it to the supreme court. But… "

I already knew. My chances were slim to none.

Meanwhile, the pedophile who'd raped children, caused my sister-in-law to move to the farthest part of the country, sent Taylor to the grave and caused Les to lose his mind and turn on his own family because he was incapable of having any real emotions or feelings toward anyone would go free.

American Injustice.

I was wrongfully convicted and wrongfully sentenced.

For protecting my children.

All that happened before noon.

Even better? I went home to a rejection that was waiting for me in my email. Thus, proving what an idiot Martha was. I *could* write. Didn't mean they would buy anything from me after all the negative attacks they'd unleashed against me.

*Thanks to Les and his Hogg.*

As I kept telling the Dumb Fucks, I needed the trademarks and my contracts because any new series was likely to be rejected by publishers.

*Doubt me?* This was my rejection that I received that day, "This is quite a departure from what she's known for. We're not interested at this time."

*Thank you, Les for ruining my career.*

Then while I was reeling from all that, I was slapped with a frivolous defamation suit Les and Hogg had concocted. You know, the woman "not" his girlfriend.

Really? Then why were the two of them still together and filing lawsuits as a couple?

Against the rest of his family, that included his own sons?

At least I had to give Cisco credit, he knew to jump ship when he could and wasn't stupid enough to let them rope him in on their latest perjury and fraud.

And would you believe, so was Cockburn?

She'd turned down representation for that suit. Because she knew just what a liar Les was.

As my attorney told me, "She's done with it. She said that he was bat-shit crazy."

You had to love it. Another one of Les's get rich schemes.

And you were going to *love* this!

In 2005, Les set up my company, Mighty Balls, LLC. "We need it to protect our assets in case someone sues the website."

I thought it a little weird, but I hadn't gone to law school. "Okay."

Then, I hadn't thought anything more about it.

*Move forward thirteen years.*

Cockburn's pleading where she attacked me about the website and again put forth lies to the court that should have been sanctioned by the ever-ineffectual Tennessee Board of Professional Responsibility. "And it's a good thing they had insurance on their site or else Mrs. Manly would have lost everything."

Again, Cockburn lied to discredit me.

What really happened was that Getty Images came after me for images that my publisher had put on my book cover. But because my publisher had the rights and I didn't, the idiot Getty had hired to shake me down couldn't understand that I was allowed to put the book cover on my website, even though the license for the image wasn't in my name.

We went 'round and 'round about this.

It was annoying as shit.

Their attack dog kept issuing demands so Les contacted our insurance company and they slapped them down with the hand of God as I had every legal right to post my book cover on my site.

No money was paid to Getty. The insurance company, as well as my publisher, told them to go take a flying leap because they had no legitimate case and no legal claim.

> In light of the above, we must respectfully deny Getty Image's claim.
>
> If you have any questions or wish to provide us with additional information, please do not hesitate to

So again, Cockburn violated her oath of office and lied to the court by blatantly misstating facts and saying that we'd paid a claim that I could easily show we'd never paid by the statement above that came from the insurance company.

The last word on that claim came from Les himself:

> to me ▾
>
> Why couldn't our high dollar attorney have done this from the beginning.

For the record, Les was the one who'd hired that "high dollar" attorney.

Bitsy Dullard, again, refused to punish Cockburn for the bald-faced lies that she'd presented to the court.

I was so disgusted by this entire state and the judicial process that only tore down innocent citizens while lining the pockets of the corrupt lawyers and judges who harassed and broke us for their sick entertainment—this was the real *Hunger Games*, folks...

Apparently, that lie of Les's kicked off a reminder in their feeble little brains that I had a two-million-dollar policy on my website.

*Couple that with the fact that Tennessee was a triple award state.*

Vulture money for the vultures.

Didn't matter that they had no case.

Never mind the little bothersome fact that never once had I told a single lie against either Les or Hogg. Didn't have to. They really were that scummy and repellent.

No, honestly, they were worse. They wallowed in their loathsome repugnance and wore it like a diamond tiara.

Their "divine" thinking was that the insurance company would roll over and pay a settlement without arguing. Again, that was what Les had been told in regard to the Dumas case.

"It's what they do. They don't want to litigate because it's too expensive and they know that. I do it all the time. They'll just write a check to make it go away."

They had been wrong about Dumas. Just as I'd predicted.

However, Les was divorcing his brain—me—and was now stuck with the idiot Hogg who made him look like a rocket scientist.

But here was what I didn't get. Les wasn't suing *me* per se. He was suing Mighty Balls.

The company *he* had set up.

The company he had power of attorney over and that he was still the "operations manager" for as I was precluded by a court order from making changes to that part of the company. He was still in charge and was still claiming part ownership.

Here was the little exchange from 2011 where my accounting firm shoved me out a window and gave Dipshit control of my company without even asking me:

> **Sent:** Wednesday, February 10, 2010 6:27 AM
> **Subject:** RE: Jan financials

Is Terri correctly referred to as Owner, CEO, or President? What title am I supposed to use for her? Also, is she the only one who can be an officer since she is the only member? Can I be an Officer and Terri still be the only member?

The reason I ask is I want to make sure I am filling out all the forms correctly and I would like to be an Officer so that I can sign and submit all the forms on Terri's behalf.

The response back from my accountant:

Technically llc's don't have officers. Terri is the "managing member" of the llc but Les can sign forms as "operations manager", "financial manager" or any other appropriate title he desires. He can sign for Terri or sign for himself as "general mgr, op mgr, financial mgr" or any other title.

Didn't you love how Les was given control of my company without *anyone* consulting with me? Without my having any knowledge until I found the emails during the divorce?

And here was another nugget that no one would pay attention to. My company/LLC had been formed in 2005. If Les, as Cockburn had been lying to everyone, had quit his job as an attorney, and began in 2004 to work for my company, why did he wait six years to be asking those questions to my accountants?

Remember what I'd said about his bankruptcy cases and his law office I'd bought for him?

He had been a lawyer with his own law office and secretary until the fall of 2009, when my oldest boys were entering high school and my youngest was heading into middle school.

That email proved that he didn't do anything with my company until well into 2010.

Which meant he'd committed perjury and Cockburn had lied on absolutely everything she'd submitted to the court.

As had House and Commissioner Alaimo.

What that also meant since Les had made himself the "operations manager" for my company was that he had just filed a lawsuit against himself.

For his own bad acts.

For the insurance.

How was that not insurance fraud?

And he was going after that insurance money with the same employee he had hired illegally to work for him. The employee who, along with Les, had breached her employment contract and non-compete with a company that had sued Les.

*What?*

*Wait! It got better.* Remember that they were suing me for defamation *after* his own attorney had sent *her* personal friends and ex-husband over to my site and social media pages to attack me and my fans. They had instigated us to have to defend our reputations.

So, *his* primary attorney had set it up so that he could have a defamation suit against my insurance company.

And this wasn't illegal?

Was I the only person in the world who saw a problem with this?

Yet even more shocking were the claims by Hogg that she couldn't get out of bed for months because of the trauma I'd caused her when she was fired from being Nick's tutor.

Um... okay. While I knew she was an idiot, did both she and the moron attorney who'd filed the case somehow overlook the documents filed in the January 3, 2019 case where Hogg had written to my fan, bragging about how she'd been working as a tutor days after she'd claimed I'd fired her?

She bragged, in writing, to my fan that her firing from her tutoring job hadn't harmed her at all. Hogg was back at being a tutor and was doing fine, while libeling me and mocking my children (as well as the children and parents she was then tutoring days after losing her job that she'd lost because she violated her written contract, not because of what I'd said about her).

No one had known that she even existed until many, many months after the divorce had begun and after she'd started waging war on me.

In the beginning of it all, my fans hadn't even known I was in a divorce.

Not for months and months as I wasn't talking about it, and I kept thinking the idiot I'd married would settle and get out of my life.

*Ready for the big twist!*

Cockburn didn't file *this* lawsuit!

*Drum roll, please...*

Ladies and gentlemen, brand new from Williamson County... land of the corrupt and opportunistic attorneys who were barely trained, barely literate, and whose IQs were so small that not even a sub-atomic microscope could view them...

Place where we didn't have *the Seven Wonders of the World*, but rather the mass contenders for *Ripley's Believe It Or Not* because there was no fucking way *that* could ever happen in today's society...

*Let me introduce for your reading entertainment...*

The less than impressive, ever fatuous, and not to be outdone by Bonnie Jo Cockburn...

The one...

The only...

Miss Barbie "Dumbass" Borden!

This wide-eyed discarded kewpie doll on steroids who walked like one of Levin's *Stepford Wives* came out of left field. Born and raised in Williamson County, she proudly sported for her "professional" photograph an out-of-date hairstyle and looked like she should be standing beside Cockburn on an episode of *Williamson County's Lifestyles of the Idiots & Clueless*. Or *The Real Ex-Housewives of Nashville*.

Kind of. I mean, you could pretty much tell by looking at her that she was vapid from spending too much time in line trying to decide between her Frap or Latte, and that most of her brain cells went down the drain with her upper lip bleach, but still...

No, never mind.

I couldn't cut her any slack. She was so stupid, she made Cockburn look like a contender for Mensa. There honestly wasn't anything else to say. Yet another YMCA Night Law School graduate, because apparently you couldn't practice law in Nashville unless you had a degree from that non-ABA-accredited law school.

One would think the alarm bells would have rung from every corner of "Einsteinerella's" vacuous head that Cockburn and crew had passed on the defamation suit, especially given that Cockburn had been a good old-fashioned "dog bite" attorney who got off on fighting for no reason and making up any old lie to do it.

Not to mention the small fact that Cockburn had made hundreds of thousands of dollars off Les's idiocy. Seriously, when the Queen Bitch passed on an opportunity to be mean and make more money that God, you probably should have stopped and thought, "wait on a second... the lying whore is skittish of lying. Hmmm... maybe I shouldn't take this case?"

Instead, the Showing Too Much Upper Gum When I Smile Queen of Williamson County said, "Hey y'all, I want in on that perjury 'cause I ain't got no soul! I haven't had a chance to put forth my own lies to the court yet. I want to be a lying slag, too, and ruin an innocent person for the bum who refuses to work and who stole all the money from his sons! Cockburn shouldn't be allowed to have all the fun! That ain't right!"

And so it began. The only thing the bitch didn't lie about in the entire document...

She spelled my name correctly.

Kudos! She was a little brighter than Shovel-Face and Alaimo. I guess she'd managed to pass something in her night classes, 'cause God knew the kewpie doll had certainly bypassed the whole Ethics part of her law school curriculum.

Or maybe Nashville School of Law didn't offer *any* courses on that subject. Given my experience with their graduates, I couldn't imagine how they could. Or how any of them managed to pass those classes. Because I had yet to meet a single ethical lawyer from that school.

What killed me most?

I was charged for her time, too in that last eighty-thousand-dollar bill.

So that she could lie and defame me in her motion.

While I was in bankruptcy.

And even though I was not supposed to pay for her... Newhouse paid her anyway.

Illegally. As I was only required to pay for Les's "divorce" attorneys, and she wasn't one of them.

*Go, Barbie, go.* Guess you needed some renovations to your Malibu Beach House and an upgrade on your dream car. Lovely.

Reminded me of the old Devo song, *Speed Racer*:

> *I'm a Barbie doll but I got brains*
> *She's a Barbie doll but she's got brains...*
> *I like to drink and I like to kill*
> *Like to steal so here's your bill*

Anyway, no sooner had her complaint gone out than my bankruptcy attorney fired off his own return volley.

A contempt motion against her for violating my bankruptcy stay (for the record, I also had one in place in state court, too, signed by old creepy Dinky himself).

After all, they knew I was in bankruptcy, and they weren't supposed to be suing me until I could catch my breath from the unending frivolous SLAPP motions and suits that they had been bombarding me with since Les had walked out the door with his pockets lined with the money he'd stolen from our children.

And Barbie should have known better. Remember that her firm specialized in bankruptcies and was the same firm that had recommended I go to Leadwits as my bankruptcy attorney.

Which got back to, Commissioner Alaimo knew full well that I'd dropped my civil suit over the poisoning and collusion because I'd been forced to by my bankruptcy trustee.

He was talking constantly with Barbie. I had the bill to prove it. The bill that they'd saddled me with in violation of the court order they had written.

If that wasn't sickening enough (that I was being forced by Dinky and Newhouse to pay her to ruin my reputation and lie about me in violation of Dinky's own court order)... There wasn't a single word of truth in any of Barbie's lies, and I had more than enough documents to prove that Barbie should have gotten the smackdown of all time. Not to mention a thing I like to call reliable, professional witnesses.

Not the pedophile lowlifes that Les had dredged up for his side.

However, there was still a hiccup.

Bankruptcy attorney, Stefano Leadwits, had set the next trial date for February 11. Seventy-two hours before a response was needed to the complaint.

"Hello? I need money in order to hire a defamation lawyer to respond to the complaint!"

Newhouse refused to authorize it.

No response.

No permission to hire a defamation lawyer from the bankruptcy court, not even after they'd assured me in the "ambush" meeting that they would fund me to fight Les and his team of bullies. Because they were, after all, illegally funding Les and his team of assholes to keep coming after me and eroding my estate to the tune of hundreds of thousands of dollars over the period of a few weeks to harass and threaten me while my creditors went unpaid.

So much for the word of the U.S. Bankruptcy Court and the government. So much for them protecting my assets and best interests. Never mind my job. It was open warfare on me and my reputation, from the U.S. Government. They appeared just as eager to see me burn as Les was.

And why?

Because I was documenting their injustice like the head detective of Williamson County had told me to do.

Okay, then.

*Damned if you do and damned if you don't.*

Welcome to America 2020. Land of corruption.

*Get me out of this shithole.*

My worse fear? The rest of the country was as bad, if not worse. My God, what if this really was America? What if it wasn't just Williamson County?

*Is your county like this?*

We needed to know. Now! No one should ever go through this. No child or parent should have to go to bed at night, praying they didn't wake up because they were afraid of what new terror would be waiting for them in the morning.

From their own government and the legal system that was supposed to protect us.

No one should feel this betrayed by the people they were paying who were supposed to be protecting their rights.

What had happened to all those organizations that I'd given money to over the years? That I'd supported with my words and deeds?

They'd all disappointed me and betrayed me as much as Les had. None of them would return my calls or emails.

They turned their backs on me and my sons.

While still asking me to support them. With donations.

Oh, the bitter irony.

Especially when I got the call from my doctor and learned that in spite of everything, I was doing to improve my health, my kidneys were getting worse.

Not from hereditary. No one in my family had ever had any kind of kidney problem. Not ever. Not even kidney stones.

Not from any diet nor from any lifestyle choice I'd made.

There was only one thing that had damaged my kidneys, and everyone knew it.

Heavy metal poisoning.

*Thank you, Les.*

In spite of my best efforts, it was worsening. And I was beginning to have severe bone problems such as my broken foot that had taken two full years to heal. And it was still in a cast.

No one could tell me how to slow down the kidney disease because we had no idea what had caused it. Les wouldn't tell us what he'd been feeding me. So, while we knew some of the compounds, we didn't know everything. The tests didn't catch it all.

That was the most terrifying part of this nightmare. The one who could help me recover my health, refused. He was staying married to me because he knew that if I died while we were still married, he was the beneficiary in my will. He would inherit all the insurance policies because of the restraining order that he'd insisted be put in place.

If my kidneys gave out before this ended. He would get millions more from my life insurance policies.

My sons would be left out in the cold.

A race against time.

In spite of everything I was doing to get free of the monster who'd tormented me my entire adult life, I might not ever be free of him. He might succeed in killing me, after all.

And taking absolutely everything from my children. With the help of our courts and government.

God bless America.

How sick it made me. Literally and figuratively.

JANUARY 23

**T**HE HORROR OF THIS DAY actually started at ten o'clock the night before when I got an email from Newhouse's attorney, demanding that I pick out my twenty items that they may or may not allow me to keep, out of every single piece of jewelry owned by my deceased mother, father, grandmother, great-grandmother, niece and brother, along with my son's graduation watch and cuff links that they'd had no right to sell and that had been illegally taken from my home.

Not even the junk jewelry that I'd been given as a kid or my grandmother's fake brooches I'd played with as a girl.

They wouldn't even give me back my coat button. Or the awards I'd won as a writer. Never mind things such as my National League of American Pen Women pins or Dames necklace.

*Fucking bastards sent it at ten p.m.*

Apparently, I wasn't allowed any rest. Ever.

*No peace for the innocent.*

So, I sent an email off to my bankruptcy attorney to remind him that the trustee's threat of going Chapter 7 on me seemed stupid given that their fear was that this manuscript might be published. Because if they went to a Chapter 7, all my IP (intellectual property) would be sold off and that would include this manuscript that had scared them so badly that they'd decided to retaliate (they used the actual *retaliate* word in the meeting against me) by selling off all my personal family heirlooms that had no real monetary value.

To *punish* me.

Their words, not mine.

That was a confidential email between us.

How did he react?

Leadwits contacted the Tennessee Board of Professional Responsibility over it. That same Board that had refused to do anything to help me and that had continued to allow all those attorneys to break the very rules they had in place, gave him permission to withdraw as my counsel, even though he had violated the most sacred oath of all lawyers—attorney-client privilege.

*Yes, they did.*

And he filed a motion without speaking to me about it first. Publicly. Just to humiliate me because I hadn't been humiliated enough by arrogant pricks like him.

And he admitted that to a third-party witness. That and the fact that he was a *real* good friend of ole Bubba Dinky and Dinky's entire family.

Now it all made sense. His rabid defense of old Dinky and Dinky's family during our meeting.

Because it was always about protecting the corrupt judge in this town that everyone knew was being investigated for misconduct and who had been arrested in a prostitution sting. The same judge that everyone in town knew was unfair and biased.

But wait...

It got better.

At 4:45 that afternoon Stefano conferenced me and Melissa in on a call. Come to find out, he hadn't really meant it when he filed his motion to withdraw as my attorney. It was "a fire across your bow." A "warning shot to get your attention, Terri."

He said those words to me.

Why?

"Because in all my years as an attorney, I've never seen Martha get mad at anyone before. It has to be something *you're* doing to make everyone mad at you."

*Wait... what?*

*Stefano, you ignorant slut.*

*Are you getting Alzheimer's, old man? Do you really think her anger had nothing to do with that fact that you, Stefano, put into her hands a manuscript that threatened her job and her livelihood?*

That spilled the beans on what a corrupt piece of shit she was?

She'd said that, too, in the meeting as she stroked my manuscript in much the same way that Mike Meyers did his cat in the *Austin Powers* movies. A manuscript that had pointed out all the corruption in her county and her very own organization.

One that brought to light the fact that *you*, Stefano, along with Newhouse, and Martha, all told me to commit a felony and to destroy government property that I was under not one, but *two* court orders not to conceal or destroy? And this after all of you sat there for hours telling me over and over how none of you could go against any of Dinky's court orders to help me. Yet all of you could violate his order when it protected your own asses?

Hmm...

*You don't think for one iota of a second that* might *have been what had made her angry at me?*

Seriously? Even though she'd said, and I quote, "We're doing this as retaliation for your writing *this*, Terri. If you ever release *this*, it won't go well for you."

And that was right before all of you threatened Joan and told her that it would be in her best interest to go home and stay away from me. In other words, they were threatening her life because she was protecting me and being a witness for me against their misdeeds and abuse of my rights.

*Did you happen to sleep through that part of the whole meeting where you had me ambushed, Leadwits?*

It got even better. Old Stefano then required me to spend even more money that I didn't have to go get a counselor for "my own good."

I didn't have the money to spend on a coat to stay warm after they'd taken them all from me so that they could sell my coats to pay their bills (and none of my creditors). I'd been hassled that very day from the one-hundred-and-seventy-five dollar an hour accountant for routine bills that she'd known about again, and was being forced to spend money I didn't have while in bankruptcy because my bankruptcy attorney knew that he had fucked up and wanted to be able to make an accusation that I was crazy should I later file a well-deserved motion for malpractice on him.

Lovely. Just lovely.

Because he claimed that I was "acting out" in Dinky's courtroom when he'd never once been in one of my court sessions with Dinky.

For the record, never once had I shown any anger to them. Not even when Dinky had spent hours insulting me and my attorney or shaming us (which I recorded). Not even when Dinky had me arrested for *his* temper tantrum, and for confronting a pedophile who'd caused the death of Taylor and who had molested who knew how many innocent children. A pedophile Dinky, Commissioner Alaimo, and the Williamson County court system had protected to this day.

Even though Cockburn had acknowledged the molester in her own court documents.

*Sadness. Check.*

*Tears. Check.*

*Confusion. All the time.*

But never once had I shown anger.

Martha lost her temper at me because she was scared. And did so because Stefano had handed her a copy of my diary that he wasn't supposed to give her and had violated my trust, and attorney-client privilege.

What a guy. And instead of disbarring him and punishing him for his misdeeds, the Tennessee Board of Professional Responsibility hung *me* out to dry while rewarding him for his violation of his oath of office.

How was *that* for Tennessee corruption?

I was so fucking glad that I lived here, said no one in their right mind, ever. No wonder we had more bars and honky tonks and "peddle taverns" that careened down our city streets than Seattle had coffee shops. You'd have to be plastered out of your fucking mind to tolerate this hellhole of a city.

At least Stefano admitted that I had a right to be angry over the gross injustices being done to me.

*You think?* You, like everyone else in this town, blackmailed me, too. Betrayed my trust. Broke your oath of office and threatened me.

*Ready for the biggest kicker?*

Remember that defamation case against Les where ole Stefano was going to have them up for contempt for bringing it?

He decided to let them go.

Because I hadn't been screwed enough by everyone. And he was doing it "for my own good."

*Gee, Dad, I'm so glad all these people are looking out for my best interest. With overpaid friends like this, I didn't need enemies.*

Thank God, we had people like them who were licensed to practice law in this country. Whatever would *we* do without them to safeguard our rights?

"If I have proof on Monday that you have an appointment with a counselor, then I'll withdraw my withdrawal. It'll help. I've known Dinky for years, and his brother and father. They're good people." Yada, yada, yada.

Bullshit.

*Let us all frame Terri and steal every dime from her that we can.* This was truly a tale that not even Stephen King, Wes Craven or Clive Barker could write. *I challenge you, my compadres. I promise, your monsters have nothing on these bottom feeders.*

"Fine, I pick the therapist."

"Okay."

And when I did, I got a text from Melissa. "Why did you choose one out of state?"

My response?

Remember that I have friends who are counselors and psychologists? That means that I know for a fact that when you tell them your deep and dark secrets that they have as much discretion as an attorney. So, everything you say is likely to end up being told to their friends and family and used as a punchline at their next cocktail party, or in their speeches and classes or for the next paper they write. So long as they don't use your name, it's not an ethics breach. Having just been burned in an ethics breach by my attorney who pulled this little stunt to further humiliate me, I am not about to use a local therapist to spread more shit and lies about me in my local community.

Nor was I about to use a therapist who would have loyalty to their court system. I wasn't a fool.

Especially given the fact that old Newhouse's wife was a psychologist at Vanderbilt. Which meant that whoever I saw in town, would most likely come into contact with her, and she'd have access to them to "pick" their brain.

No wonder Newhouse was so gung-ho for me to see one even while he constantly threatened me with a Chapter 7 because, "you're running out of money, Terri!"

*You think?*

Newhouse was the one who kept recklessly spending it.

Not to mention, they'd already shown me what gossipy little bitches they all were and how they screwed the truth and lied to serve their own purposes. Worse than a bunch of old biddy school teachers. Really, they should have been embarrassed. I was embarrassed for them.

*A poisoned well.*

And still my creditors weren't being paid. More money being bled from my coffers so that Stefano could point a finger at me and have plausible deniability for his own deplorable actions that should have him disbarred.

*One of the most corrupt states in the union...*

And I was stuck in it with no way out.

JANUARY 30

**S**O CLOSE TO FINISHING OUT the month with no more drama... So damn close. Since Monday had held so very little bullshit in it, I'd made the mistake of taking a deep breath and thinking that maybe, just maybe, because Cockburn had finally realized Les was crazy and was tired of fighting that things might slow up.

*Haven't we all seen that horror movie enough to know better? That brief calm where the character pauses to rest and then...*

*Wham!*

*Off with her head!*

It reminded me of that time years ago when I was on a writer's panel with another author who'd arrogantly announced how we tortured our characters. "Because in real life that kind of thing just never happens! You never really have to worry about high stakes consequences in your daily routine."

I kept thinking, even though I was only twenty-five at the time, "you lucky middle-aged bitch that no one has ever done to you all the shit-things that had been done to me in my life" that had traumatized me even then.

Never mind the nightmare that had been my life ever since.

*Thank you, Les, for the horrendous memories I could have done without.*

And readers wondered why I put my characters through the wringer. As I'd so often said, it wasn't the fictional parts of my books that ought to scare people.

It was that parts that weren't.

Just as it wasn't the scars on a body that left the biggest nightmares. It was the ones on the soul.

And so that fetid Thursday began.

Of course, the day started off with the insipid questions that had been asked and re-asked a thousand times so that even my accountant was sick of answering them.

"Doesn't that woman keep any documents? I've looked back through your requests and the money she's saying you requested, you didn't. I can't figure out what she's even talking about."

"I know, Shelly. I know." I sighed at my accountant.

"And I know you've sent over these other receipts she's asking about. I wrote on the one about the microwave myself. Why's she asking about that one again?"

"No idea. I've sent it over, twice." Yet in the meeting where I'd been jumped, Newhouse had defended this woman he'd hired, claiming he'd had to talk her down to her one-hundred-and-seventy-five dollars an hour rate that I was being forced against my will to pay her for her grotesque incompetence.

She couldn't keep anything straight or read a single receipt (neither could Newhouse, for that matter). Never mind remember anything from one week to the next. So how her company, Scre-woff Advisors, could brag that they'd recovered X millions in debt and had saved jobs baffled me as this woman couldn't keep up with the most basic information when it was handed to her, even when someone wrote directly on the receipt what that receipt was for.

Wow.

Unless saving jobs meant creating them by ripping off people in bankruptcy when they inserted their people where they weren't needed and billed others for hours of work because their incompetent employees couldn't keep up with paperwork and kept harassing them with redundant questions.

Or Carol was doing it intentionally to get more money out of me and my estate. I mean, really, if they were as competent as they claimed, then the latter would be the go-to assumption. Because it had to be one or the other.

Either they were grossly incompetent and couldn't do shit, or they were extremely competent and intentionally ripping me off with the full backing of the U.S. government, and the endorsement of two federal trustees and their appointed attorney who rubber stamped their theft.

Then Shelly dropped the big bomb on me. "I ran the numbers for the attorneys. Who's Rose?"

"She works for me. Why?"

"Ah. You need to see this." Shelly emailed a sheet to me of the money I'd paid for Les's attorneys from July to December of 2019 (the dates of my bankruptcy).

The almost two hundred grand I'd paid them, I already knew about.

But it hurt a lot more to see it all laid out on a spreadsheet.

Ironic really. I'd been forced against my will to pay more during my bankruptcy while I had a trustee who was supposed to stop the waste and unnecessary spending for Cockburn, alone, to torture me, illegally search my home, illegally seize my property and illegally steal my sons' money, again, than I'd been allowed to pay for my own attorney and for two of my employees. Not to mention the giveaways for my fans at two different Comic Cons, Dragon Con, and for inventory to run my business.

Never mind the money they'd paid out of my pocket to Les's *other* attorneys to harass and humiliate me for Les's twisted and depraved entertainment.

*Are you as sick to your stomach as I was?*

And none of my creditors had been paid a single dime. No payment plan to get them paid had been put in place.

Six months had gone by while Newhouse jacked-off and handed out my money like a party favor to his buddies.

I was more broke than ever and there was no way out for me. Because my own attorney, Leadwits, had put an imbecile in place who had no problem giving away everything I owned to pay for Les's attorneys and his friends.

This was a perverted country that I no longer recognized. It wasn't the amber waves of grain with purple mountain majesties above some fruited plain. And my spacious skies weren't beautiful. They were filled with rain and thunderstorms that shot more lightning bolts at me than Zeus in a pissed off hissy fit.

Shelly was baffled by her findings, and even wrote to my trustee, Newhouse, to let him know how horrific it was. "This is ridiculous." Not that it mattered. As he'd said in the meeting where they'd ambushed me, as opposed to helping me find a way to get out of this madness, there was "nothing" he could do. He was under a court under from Judge Skeletor to pay out that ridiculous amount.

Because he, Newhouse, had negotiated with my terrorists to gut me financially and to give them more than I made and more than I had in liquid assets.

While my creditors went unpaid (I know I kept saying that, but damn, the horror of it all bore repeating).

Of course, Newhouse was also under a court order that said I couldn't "hide, conceal or destroy marital property" or "hide, conceal or destroy any property in my possession" that was of any "inherent value."

Hmm...

Did that include the copy that old Martha had fondled in the meeting, too? I should have asked for her to return it.

Yet I was supposed to believe that he and his boss were so afraid of the judge that they had refused to go before him to help me reset my case? Or before the federal judge to get some help with this travesty?

Sure.

They wouldn't follow the law to help me, but they were willing, in front of third-party witnesses, to order me to commit a crime to cover their asses. Funny how that always ended up being the case with people, wasn't it?

But that wasn't the only monkey wrench in the hour that flew at my head.

*Ready for the next blow?*

As I was reeling, up popped the next fun email.

Remember what I'd said about my newly pissed off bankruptcy attorney, Stefano Leadwits, selling me out? And to protect his own ass, he'd decided to let Les and crew go for their contempt motion?

Not only was he letting them go, he'd decided to join in on the boot party that up until then he'd claimed disgusted him, too.

Well, Leadwits had gone behind my back and filed to get himself some of my rapidly dwindling pie that they, the U.S. government and bankruptcy court was supposed to be helping to protect.

Instead, they were passing my pie around like a reverse collection plate for everyone to rob.

In fact, when I'd first gone into bankruptcy, my debt had been at one million. A staggering amount, I know. All of it for lawyers because of Les.

Thank you, Les, as we'd had absolutely no debt at all prior to his leaving. Every bit of that debt was a result of legal fees from his two lawsuits.

Dumas and the divorce.

*I know.* I married the dumbest fucking moron on the planet.

During the six months they'd brought in Newhouse, my debt had grown another half a million dollars. That was the next email I was hit with.

To my knowledge, or at least I hoped, I was the only person who'd ever filed bankruptcy and had their debt increased by fifty percent.

With no end to that growth in sight.

Then, if all that wasn't enough fun for one day, guess what came next...

The bill from Newhouse and our old friend, the lawyer he'd hired to "represent" him for the "bankruptcy." You know that attorney that when I'd filed, no one had warned me that I would have to pay for.

That same notice where they hit me with a small fortune they wanted from my diminishing assets said that I'd have not one, not two, but *three* separate hearings in downtown Nashville where it would cost me twenty-five dollars a day to park, because I needed another seventy-five dollars added on to my bankruptcy.

Out of the almost six hundred thousand dollars that Newhouse had been entrusted with in July, barely one hundred thousand dollars was left, and he was taking every dime of it to pay himself and his crew.

Barely one hundred thousand (that should have lasted me a year, instead it went to line their pockets).

And not one single creditor of mine had been paid out of it.

Not a one.

None.

Zilch.

Every fucking cent had gone to pay for Les's attorneys and Newhouse's friends. And this after Newhouse and Leadwits had told Oldham to make sure and pay himself with the cash he'd illegally seized from my home.

I had to take the word of a man who'd submitted perjury to the court and who had violated my civil and constitutional rights that what he said he'd taken was actually what he'd taken. Even though no third-party witness was there when he'd counted it.

Even though there was some unidentified kid running loose on my property while Les and Cockburn sat in the driveway with all my money unchaperoned.

Yeah...

None of that was suspicious at all.

And how much did Newhouse charge me out of those hundred thousand dollars I had left?

Brace yourself.

One hundred and eleven thousand dollars.

And yes, you read that correctly.

His bill would leave me with just enough to cover one last month before I was forced into that Chapter 7 they had been threatening me with like a group of interrogators during a waterboarding.

They were demanding the rest of my money to be paid to them immediately for their overrated, overinflated, redundant services that had allowed all the others to rape and pillage my estate.

Thus, guaranteeing that my creditors would never be paid.

Never in my life had I heard of anyone going into bankruptcy and having their debts doubled without any of their creditors being paid before.

I was never going to get out. These unconscionable bastards had stolen from my children everything I had spent my entire life working for only to give it to them and consign me to poverty for the rest of my meager years on this earth.

*What the actual fuck?* I thought the point of bankruptcy was to get someone out of trouble.

To give them "a fresh start."

Not rob them and double their debt to such a staggering, mind-boggling amount.

No one had ever told me that this would be a possibility. That the government would be adding on all these "employees" and hidden fees that I would be forced to pay while they threatened to turn me into a slave and arrest me at every turn.

Really, I'd rather have dealt with my creditors. They were far more humane and didn't have the ability to raid my home at will. Nor were they threatening to lock me up if I didn't work for free.

The terrorists that our government had hired with our own tax dollars were truly the most sadistic, twisted fucks ever unleashed on innocent citizens.

They were the American KGB, and I was certain that I wasn't the only citizen being terrorized by these sick bastards. That was what I found most disturbing.

How many more people were out there like me, being tortured and mentally broken by this power-hungry, drunk on their own authority monsters.

Remember, I had been promised that the bankruptcy would "stop" the divorce proceedings so that I could get caught up on my bills. And the federal court would take precedence over the state.

Not the other way around.

Instead, Les's attorneys had used it as a chance for them to pile drive me into the ground while they did "more" research on things they already had and refused to cooperate with my attorney at all.

No one had ever once told me that while I was in bankruptcy, I would be assigned a trustee who would force me to be responsible for Les's attorneys on top of what I was paying before the bankruptcy started, plus the new ungodly expensive ones Les had hired after I filed, and the additional bankruptcy staff that kept adding on to my expenses.

Whatever happened to full disclosure?

Whatever happened to telling the truth?

I guessed that it went the same way as attorney-client privilege and the ability to change judges and venue. Maybe that existed where *you* lived, but it was as common here in Williamson County or the state of Tennessee as a unicorn.

Or even conflict of interest. Which, by the way, during all this, I finally heard back from Ms. Dullard. She agreed that Les hiring ole Sal Tiller who'd represented Dumas during that suit was indeed a conflict.

However, the Tennessee Board of Professional Responsibility wasn't about to take any action to protect a Tennessee citizen. If I wanted justice, I'd have to take the matter before the corrupt judge who'd put me into this whole nightmare to begin with. The same judge I'd been telling her for months, and had shown her irrefutable proof, wasn't acting impartially or fairly.

Still, she passed the buck along.

*Don't believe it?*

Then you're like I used to be. Living in a fool's paradise and you'd been lucky so far that the reality of our modern-day court system hadn't caught up to you.

Yet.

I would say that I would pray it never happened to you, but honestly, I had stopped praying. My faith had been shattered by this nonsensical nightmare that refused to end.

At night, I was terrified to go to sleep, because there was no telling what new horror would come with the dawning day.

That was where I lived.

And there was no letup in sight.

EVERY TWO WEEKS, I was given the indignity of filling out a form to beg for my money from Newhouse to pay my bills, as if I hadn't been punished enough for daring to walk down the aisle.

Apparently, I, the one who'd earned all my money and who had crawled out of being a homeless mother to a millionaire while my useless husband couldn't be bothered to work, couldn't be trusted with the money I earned, and from whom I had to have permission to buy even a pair of socks.

Meanwhile, the trustee was handing it out, hand over fist. And Les was off without a care in the world, except for thoughts on how to further screw the family that had never done anything to him. The family that had to suffer his tantrums and abuse for decades.

While the only thought in his mind was coming up with new ways to steal more money he'd never earned from the sons who used to love him, in spite of the abuse he'd heaped on their precious heads.

And as I was scanning in the information, I opened the Annual Trustee's Report.

*Bad to worse.*

See, I was never allowed to know how much money they'd seized out of my accounts and taken from my children, which I still didn't understand how they could do that as my children were grown adults. My understanding was the with my children's names on those accounts, the court should not have been able to take it. After all, they weren't "new" accounts set up right before the bankruptcy. These were accounts that had been in place for years.

The same accounts they had threatened *me* with "perjury" because I kept saying that, "No, I hadn't transferred money to my children."

But since my name was on the account, they'd used that to illegally seize their funds, while trying to set me up for having done something improper when I hadn't.

*Good fucking job, you thieves.*

Yep, good ole U.S. Trustee, Martha Seaver, was trying to get me locked into a confession for Les for something I didn't do.

Now for the kicker...

You knew there had to be one.

What I learned from a legitimate attorney was that my bankruptcy application should have been refused from the get-go. Had the court and judge been doing what it was designed for, it would have denied my bankruptcy petition.

I didn't know that until this day. Because Newhouse had seized more money out of my accounts, once they were consolidated, to pay *all* my bills that were due when he took the money. In full.

And leave me with about one hundred thousand dollars in excess.

Yes, you read that correctly.

I would have been flush again, had I not had a trustee put over me by the court and the idiot Leadwits.

Instead, the U.S. government doubled my debt and took everything from me because their own trustees and judge had refused to do the job they were supposed to do.

As every single attorney in town kept saying, including the DAs my friends had approached on my behalf, I was being railroaded. And they all knew it and were talking about it, in droves.

Over and over, we were shouted down by Dinky and his little crew of henchmen.

Now the U.S. government was stepping in to take over that role. My entire life ruined by a pack of greedy, despicable dogs.

How I wish to God, I had never laid eyes on Williamson County, Tennessee or stepped one foot into Nashville.

Most revolting place in the world. At least I hoped so.

Because if other towns in our country were this corrupt, there was no help for any of us.

Meanwhile, I was spiraling toward welfare and homelessness again, and no one cared.

Just so long as they were able to get their last bite of my pie.

If there was a God, then I prayed for justice and for them to get exactly what they'd given me.

No mercy. Because unlike me, these bastards had earned their fate.

My worst mistake in life? Thinking for one minute that a lying sack of shit was worth something and not kicking him out the first time he'd bankrupted us in Mississippi.

*Oh, to have a time machine.*

Or at least the number for the Karma Delivery Service.

# FEBRUARY 5

**T**HE PLOT INVARIABLY THICKENED. But never in the way I thought. My sons had been talking about the posts their father had made on social media. Since I didn't care, I wasn't paying attention.

Until Nick made a comment about the horse stables.

My attention was immediately on high alert. "What?"

"He has a picture of the horse, at its stable."

The seven-thousand-dollar show pony I'd bought? That was intriguing. "Let me see this photo."

Nick pulled it up on his phone to show me.

Would you believe the stupid son-of-a-bitch was dumb enough to post the name of the stables where he was boarding the beast?

As I suspected, it was his sister's company.

But it got better.

Big Sister Annette (you know the one Les had claimed all those years that he hated and couldn't stand the sight of?) wasn't only keeping the horse for him, oh no, she was using the horse to make money with it.

*Say what?!*

Yep. After all Les's testimony, i.e. perjury, that he'd been unable to make any income at all and that he was completely dependent on me for his support, had been making an income with his big sister by renting out his horse at parties and for riding lessons.

Even at events. In fact, there were photos of "our" horse that they'd named after my stepmother, winning ribbons at numerous events since he'd bought her and sent her off to live with his sister who had set up a riding school for little kids while she lived next door to her pedophile father.

There were even photos of her mother at a party with those families.

It made my blood run cold and sickened me so that I couldn't eat for days thinking of that family of perverts and those kids.

Yet Les had been repeatedly testifying under oath and had filed another suit against me claiming that he was unable to make any money whatsoever because of what "I" had done to him.

Wow, just wow.

For a man who had once claimed that he was incapable of telling lies, he'd certainly learned to tell them with no problem whatsoever.

Even under oath, and at the risk of perjury (well, not while he had the judge in his pocket).

And now they were lying to the federal court. Still, old Newhouse refused to go after my half of the money the horse was making. Even though he threatened me constantly with a Chapter 7 because I wasn't making the kind of money he'd been told that I would make.

I was stunned. I had always been honest with him. The liars came out of Les's camp.

But then, what was a little perjury and tax fraud after you'd tried to kill your wife and son? After you'd murdered the family pet. Really? In the grand scheme of things, they were rather minor offenses. So, I supposed it made sense that Les wouldn't lose any sleep about tax fraud and perjury.

Once you'd reconciled yourself to murdering your spouse for an insurance payout, and stealing from your own children, anything else was simply icing on the cake.

His morality Band-Aid had been ripped off and for him, obviously, there was no going back.

If only the Williamson County court system or U.S. government would hold him accountable.

But I was living in a pipedream if I thought there was such a thing as justice in America. That only belonged inside the fiction books I wrote. It didn't exist in the real world where evil triumphed over good and good was punished at the whims of those who went unchecked by the crooked system we'd allowed to go too far.

# FEBRUARY 6

**N**O IDEA WHY I THOUGHT the fact that I was traveling on a cold, rainy Thursday would somehow cause the jackals to lay off me for one day. I must have hit my head in my sleep.

But for some reason, I kept hoping.

The day before had ended on a strange note. After keeping me torn up with news that they were planning to let Les go on the contempt charges, Martha had decided not to sign off on Stefano's motion to let them go.

So, the contempt trial was back on.

*What the fuck?*

Honestly, I was tired of this sick rollercoaster. *Make up your idiotic minds already. Are we going to trial or not?*

I'd grown up with a bipolar mother and it was painful to be slammed back into their bipolar madness that changed faster than the whims of a pubescent Gemini girl trying to decide what to wear for a date.

And they thought *I* needed therapy?

Seriously? I was willing to bet that there were saner people at a Lead-Paint Chewers Anonymous convention.

Anyway, there I sat in the airport when I stupidly thought it might be a good idea to check my email. Why? I have no idea, other than I must have eaten some paint chips as a kid, too.

Or I obviously didn't get beaten enough as a kid (keeping in mind that I came from a highly abusive childhood, so please read with all due sarcasm).

And we were off to the races (horse pun intended due to what I affectionately liked to call Pennygate). Up came Melissa with the deluge of complaints from the idiot Newhouse over the money I'd requested for the very therapy I didn't want or need that Leadwits had blackmailed me into. The same therapy that Newhouse had not only agreed to pay for but had thought "was a good idea."

*Are you fucking kidding me?*

"They need an invoice."

This, too, had started the day before.

"I requested it."

"Where is it?"

Was Melissa even dumber than they were?

"You know, I'm tired of them acting like they've never had a doctor's appointment or paid a fucking bill in their entire lives. I don't know what backwater closet facility they go to, but here in what I call the real world, I get a payment receipt from my doc and the invoice comes later with the full bill. Usually in about thirty days."

"He wants to know what the request is for."

Did they have amnesia or Alzheimer's? "The therapy they blackmailed me into."

"Why is it so much?"

This went on and on. Ad nauseum. Why Newhouse couldn't get it through his thick head that all medical facilities required payment "at the time services are rendered" was beyond me. I'd even taken photos at the offices to show him the signs they all had posted.

There was no way for me to put in two weeks in advance for a doctor's appointment I didn't know I'd have as, unlike my friend Tasha, I wasn't *that* psychic.

But because I'd sent over those photos as proof to them, I'd been called "difficult." Yet I was harassed and emailed, over and over, for the same information that I'd provided for them when I was doing exactly what they told me to do, for something I didn't want to do and didn't need and really couldn't afford.

*How ridiculous and difficult* were *they*?

But I was the one being difficult, according to my terrorists. Not the idiots who were refusing to do their jobs and who were recklessly running up my bills, harassing me and not going after those breaking the law and refusing to pay the government what they owed.

Okay.

We wondered why our government was in trouble. Because these were the nimrods being way overpaid to work for it, while they harassed and threatened the rest of us.

And refused to do their paperwork. Which was why my petition should have been denied. I had never given them a copy of my social security card that Old Les had stolen from my home.

Also, according to the U.S. Bankruptcy laws because of other paperwork not properly done, my case should have been dismissed.

Yet these bastards kept telling me that my case could *not* be dismissed in spite of all the laws and other legal articles and books I'd read.

Because they wanted to keep torturing me and stealing my money.

I finally got the invoice, but not before having my entire day wrecked before I arrived at a major event where I had to paint on a smile and interact with my fans as if everything was bright, and shiny and I had no problems in the world.

Meanwhile, I was being threatened with losing everything I had and being put in jail if I didn't agree to work for free once Newhouse and the bankruptcy court sold off all my contracts and gave over all my income to someone else while I was homeless.

That was a real threat, by the way.

Told to me, over and over again. In front of witnesses.

"Once we sell your contracts and royalties in a Chapter 7, you'll have to keep writing the books. If you refuse, we *will* put you in jail."

"I have no control over my publisher, who has told me that they'll cancel those contracts once you sell the trademarks to someone else. They won't have the rights to publish the books that are under contract. Nor will I have the rights to write the books under contract if you sell those trademarks."

"We will put you in jail if you don't write them."

Again, Newhouse and crew were ordering me to break the law. Why the lawyers couldn't understand that I could not publish a book with someone else's trademark on it if they sold my trademarks was beyond me.

How they could threaten me with jail if I didn't work without being paid was beyond me.

Yet here I was being threatened at every turn by Newhouse, Leadwits and Megan and the U.S. bankruptcy court.

*Fun fucking times.*

**FEBRUARY 11**

CHAPTER 7. THAT WAS HOW this day began. Melissa had sent over the "fee" schedule from Dipshit's attorneys after Newhouse had left me with less than eleven thousand dollars for the rest of the year to live on.

Writers only received residuals/royalties twice a year. What we really lived on were the "front list" titles, i.e. the books that we were currently writing. Our publishers paid us for those once we handed a book in, but that money wasn't given to us instantaneously.

It wasn't like a job where you worked two weeks and then pulled a paycheck.

While I'd handed a book in at Christmas, I hadn't received my editorial letter for it. In fact, my editor had written earlier in the week to say that she was sick and wouldn't get to me until the first of March.

Which meant that I wouldn't be paid for that book until July or August, after I had a chance to do the edits, hand the book in, and she had the chance to read it and then release my money.

Too late to save me.

Because of Les. And because of Martha and her threats, I couldn't sell the most marketable thing I had.

This little diary.

The third manuscript that my agent was shopping out was being systematically rejected by everyone.

Why?

*Brace yourself.*

Because of the lies that Les and Hogg had told about me. All that damage they'd done to my reputation and career, and that Cockburn had piled on with and helped them.

Anyway, being the imbeciles that they were, Les's crew of morons that included Dumas's attorney who'd originally helped send my career into a spiral, hit Newhouse up for roughly forty thousand more dollars.

Well, unlike those morons, I was pretty sure we were all capable of doing basic math skills. When you have 111,000-150,000 =...

Well, honestly, it equaled one broke motherfucker.

They put me forty thousand dollars in the negative. Which the jackals had been told would happen. Maybe they'd assumed that Newhouse had found a sense of humor up his stuffy, rigid ass?

I told Melissa to get Leadwits on the phone and to tell him to file a motion to get me out of bankruptcy ASAP, before they sold off my trademarks and contracts, as they were threatening to do. Since we now had irrefutable proof that no one would buy another series from me, there was no doubt that the federal government was about to put me on welfare.

Forever.

If I couldn't write the numerous series that had made me famous, I would never work again. Not in my mid-fifties.

Contrary to what the super stupid Martha thought, no one hired a woman less than ten years from retirement to work in the IT industry.

"Why not?" I can still see the stupid expression on her mousy little face. With those subpar deductive reasoning skills, I had to wonder who she'd been forced to blow to pass any of her college courses.

Including Basket Weaving 101.

"Because no one in the computer industry, especially web development, likes to hire what they call Boomers." Bitch. "They didn't like to hire old people back when I was in the field twenty-five years ago, and they won't do it now."

"Then you can go work at Target."

Which wouldn't pay my bills.

How this idiot had a bar license, never mind a cushy federal job, I had no idea.

But wait, you knew it had to get better.

Leadwits and Melissa argued.

"She can't do that. If she gets a dismissal, then Dinky will put the Receiver over her again." You remember him... I was still paying him because he was Newhouse's attorney. "And Dinky would just make it worse on her and be in charge."

WTF?

Had I missed a memo? We'd had a meeting with Newhouse, Martha, Leadwits, Joan and Bill Oldham. The one where they'd jumped me instead of helping me brainstorm how to get out of this nightmare.

Well, the other thing they'd made clear besides their threats to ruin me if I so much as looked at them wrongly or did and I quote, "anything that we don't like, at all," was the Judge Dinky and Les were in charge of my life and that I had no control over anything. "There's nothing we can do. We have to do what Dinky says. We have to follow all his orders. And Les can veto whatever we decide. He has the final say."

They had hammered home that they'd put my uber-controlling, sick in the head husband back in charge of my life.

A man who had so beaten me down and exerted so much control over me that my bank had sent a representative to my home to explain to me how my accounts worked and who told me, point blank, that what Les had done to be was spousal abuse.

Financial abuse.

They had firmly planted that monster back over me.

So, for Leadwits to act like Dinky being in charge was something new was suddenly the dumbest shit I'd heard and given the dumb shit you'd read thus far, you could imagine the look I'd worn on my face when Melissa conveyed this conversation to me.

Nashville really should petition to have their name legally changed to "The Twilight Zone."

"Fine," I'd told Melissa. "Tell him to do it. At least then I'd only have one asshole over me, and I'd only be paying one asshole to pillage my bank account." Better Oldham, alone, than him, Leadwits, Newhouse, Martha, the useless federal judge, the ungodly useless and expensive accountant Newhouse had forced on me at almost two-hundred dollars an hour, and Les's ungodly expensive bankruptcy attorney who also had admitted that Les was bat-shit crazy.

*Who in their right mind, which apparently no one in this state was, couldn't see the better choice?*

One asshole I had to pay. Or a crew of torturing assholes I had to pay.

Yet Newhouse refused to allow me to cut to the chase.

Refused to allow me to cut down the number one drain on my finances. That he had testified in court were draining my finances.

Again, they apparently failed to teach basic math skills in the state of Tennessee.

At least to lawyers who could only bill other people. No wonder they needed such expensive accountants. They obviously were incapable of doing any kind of arithmetic on their own.

Anyway, so Melissa called Newhouse. "Oh, she can't withdraw her bankruptcy. If she does, I'd be honor bound to protest it. Now, I don't want to. I'd like nothing better than to be done with this case, but there's no way I could, in good faith, allow Stefano to pull her out of bankruptcy."

*Excuse me?*

What happened to America, land of the free?

I had a right to deal with my creditors on my own, especially after all you motherfuckers had lied to me, threatened me and had done nothing but stolen money from me and my sons and failed to pay them.

I had never been ashamed of my country. I used to work in the government as a private contractor. We didn't have scummy pieces of shit like this in my department in Georgia.

So, I would like to think that this was a Tennessee thing and not a U.S. problem. But again, I was terrified that it wasn't.

What if this was nationwide?

We'd all heard the stories of corruption. I was seeing and living it firsthand as their hapless victim.

No divorce should cause someone to lose every last thing they'd worked for. It shouldn't leave their children out on the street and strip them of all their constitutional rights. Yet that was what they were doing to me.

And no one would help me.

No one.

They were all too busy holding out their hands for payment for me to reward them for abusing me and my sons.

All I could do was sit here and watch and wait for them to tear apart my life. As Newhouse had said, "There's nothing you can do, Terri. You need to get that through your head. We are in charge. You have no rights and no say about anything. We're going to do what we're going to do."

Newhouse even told that to my special needs sons.

He and Leadwits kept telling me that Melissa had to file to get me out of this nightmare and Melissa kept telling me that they had to file to get me out of this nightmare.

"The bankruptcy halted the divorce proceedings," Melissa kept telling me.

"Then why was I billed forty thousand dollars for Les's attorneys?" Obviously, they continued to work on the divorce.

"Newhouse said that they can proceed with research and such while they wait."

And I had to pay for it? Yet I wasn't allowed to do any research myself and I was the one who knew nothing about Les and what he'd been planning all those months and years before he hit me out of the blue with the divorce filing?

*Are you fucking kidding me?*

This was all true.

Everyone around me was aghast, including the attorneys I knew who weren't involved. No one had ever seen or heard of anything like this.

Appalled doesn't cover it.

I had been cast adrift, because no one wanted the taint of this on them. Or they were afraid of the judge and trustees, too.

After all, Joan had been threatened.

I was afraid for my boys. I was terrified for myself.

And while all of this was going on, I was packing up my sons' rooms and discovered yet another act of treachery. Les had even robbed their piggy banks.

What a bastard.

All their lives, we'd put any money they'd received for birthdays and holidays in their banks. The last time I'd counted it, Maddox had several thousand dollars in his.

There was thirty-five dollars in single dollar bills.

That was it. When I told Nick to check his, he shook his head. "Dad stole it the February before he left."

"What?"

"Yeah, I already knew. I'd found my Megaman wallet and it had six hundred dollars in it that you'd given me for Comic Con to spend for my birthday and Christmas presents, and I showed it to Dad. He immediately took the money and pocketed it. Then he grabbed the rest. Said I was irresponsible."

Oh, *Nick* was irresponsible. The man who was working two jobs while going to school, while Les had refused to work a single one. The man who took care of his cat and his brother's dog and watched over his mom. Nick was irresponsible. My son who'd gone online after his father had left him and devastated him to research schools to find a better and infinitely cheaper high school to finish out his diploma than the one Les had used that had cost more than most universities.

Not only had Les's school been excruciatingly expensive, he'd paid Hogg a fulltime salary to do the work and take the tests, and sit her corpulent ass in my home to make every one of us miserable while she abused my sons and poisoned me.

Not speculation, she'd documented the fact that she'd been "feeding" me and to the tune of fourteen hundred dollars for only two days of work.

Hmm...

Never mind the phone call to my aunt. "Terri needs to come home so we can feed her."

That wasn't suspicious at all. Who gets paid fourteen hundred dollars to feed someone two meals?

Especially when the person being fed was told that the person feeding them was going along for free because she was a "fan" and wanted to attend the event to have fun.

*Yeah, nothing dubious in that at all.*

*And these aren't the 'droids you're looking for, either.*

But Nick was the irresponsible one. Not Les who'd abandoned his family and then set out to single-handedly ruin them.

My how the stomach turned.

And still my nightmare continued, with absolutely no end in sight. No way out. My hope had dwindled to dust, and my heart was broken.

I didn't know what would become of me or my sons. Everything I'd worked for was being stolen from me. By soulless bastards who gloated about it.

While the government condoned it.

While the entire world watched it happen and no one said a word.

S O, I'D FOUND THE PIGGY BANKS the day before while going through my sons' rooms. Well, that wasn't all I found. Since the nightmare began, I'd been wondering why Les was so hellbent on getting back into the house.

I finally found at least one reason.

Aside from his favorite George Foreman grill he'd accidentally left stashed in the garage that was tucked under my workbench. I knew it must have pained him greatly to live without that. Hamburgers on that grill were the only thing the stupid bastard had ever learned to cook.

But that wasn't the point. Stashed in Nick's closet amidst thousands upon thousands of dollars of shit Les had insisted we buy that the kids had never wanted or played with was a half full tub of what appeared at first to be old Pokemon binders.

It wasn't.

I opened it up and lo and behold I found legal binders hidden underneath them.

This was no accident. How do I know?

It was evidence from the Dumas lawsuit. There was no way he'd have accidentally stashed these in the attic entrance and forgotten about it while we were in the middle of that lawsuit. Les would have torn the house down during those three years had he not been able to find that paperwork as it was critical for the case.

These were the original filings for all my trademarks. They were also copies of the Ceases & Desists that he'd sent out.

And it got better. Inside that binder was email after email that Les had forged, where he'd pretended to be me. Emails to attorneys and to the government.

Legal documents where Les had forged my signature. And you could tell that I hadn't written them. For one thing, he'd misspelled the name of the #1 bestselling series I wrote. And if there was one thing I knew how to spell, it was the series that had made me famous.

He also made the mistake of writing on the paper and my handwriting was very distinctive.

And illegible. Anyone who had ever attended one of my signings and who had seen my autographs could and would testify to the fact that no one could read my writing.

His wasn't. The fact that the words were legible proved that it wasn't my handwriting. As I said, my writing was very, very distinctive.

And about those trademarks. Many of them had been attained with improper proof. Newhouse was threatening to sell trademarks that I didn't have a legal right to claim. Really not sure how that was legal either as I thought selling something you didn't have a legal right to was fraud, but hey, I wasn't the attorney.

Apparently, the normal laws we were all told about didn't apply here in the state of Tennessee.

After all, Les had forged the paperwork and specimens to illegally get those trademarks.

And I'd just uncovered the truth.

Anyone else would be in jail for forgery and perjury. Last time I checked, forgery, perjury and impersonation, even when it was your spouse, was illegal. But not in Tennessee. Even when I'd shown the police the checks that Les had written on my personal checking account... not my business account or our joint account. My *personal* bank account that Les had no right to use, they had refused to do anything.

Again, I thought writing checks on an account you weren't authorized to use was illegal.

Welcome to Nashville.

Land of "I don't give a shit." I guess they were known as the Volunteer State not for helping people, but for voluntarily helping themselves to whatever it was they wanted of your personal assets and laughing at you and mocking you while they did it.

And here I'd thought the bully who shook us down for lunch money in grade school was bad.

At least I had the chance to beat the shit out of that kid after the bell rang and we left campus in the afternoon.

There was no recourse here.

All I could do was notify my attorney about the discovery and wait for her to tell me why the laws that applied to me and everyone else, and landed us in and under jail, wouldn't apply to Les.

HAPPY VALENTINE'S DAY! I supposed that I should be thrilled that at least this year I wasn't in court for the occasion as I'd been the year before.

What a disgusting thing I'd made the mistake of marrying. Just when I thought he couldn't possibly sink any lower, he found a new level to aspire to. Just when I thought that stealing from the kids' piggy banks was an all-time low, he'd managed to find one as close to that.

Remember the month before when they came and took my cars?

It had started the whole to-do about my diary and the threats they made against me and Joan, and this never-ending drama of intimidation from Leadwits and Newhouse, et al that culminated in them labeling me as a "national threat."

Well, since all my cars had been paid for and the only reason they were taking them was to "punish me" and because Newhouse was bitching over my insurance for them, I did what any normal human being would do who was in bankruptcy.

I called and canceled the insurance a couple of days after the cars were gone.

After all, I had signed over ownership of the cars. The auction house had taken possession of them. Newhouse had been taking a sick and twisted pleasure in reminding me constantly (and telling my sons) that I owned absolutely nothing anymore. That everything in the world I had earned with my twenty hours a day, seven days a week, three-hundred-and-sixty-five days a year for the entirety of my life with no vacations ever now belonged to the government. Even the air that I breathed. For all intents and purposes, I was a slave and had no rights and no property. I was at his mercy, and I wasn't legally entitled to a single cent that I earned.

All true.

While I was in a Chapter 11 bankruptcy that was supposed to leave me in charge of everything.

Martha reiterated the fact that I controlled nothing and had nothing, in front of witnesses.

They were sick bastards that way.

So, since I no longer owned the cars and they were no longer in my home or possession, and I had been bitched at for months over the insurance, which was the only money it was costing me to keep them, unlike the out-of-warranty piece of shit Newhouse had left me with that didn't run and that had cost me thousands of dollars to have repaired that I still couldn't drive (and that legally was a business vehicle I couldn't use for personal use unless I, like Les, wanted to commit tax fraud), I assumed he wanted me to cancel the only bill those cars were costing me. Right?

Wrong. Late at night on February 13th (because the bastards cannot allow me any peace, whatsoever), I received an email notifying me that the auction house did *not* have insurance for the cars.

*Are you fucking kidding me?*

*And am I really supposed to believe this bullshit from them?*

To which I immediately called out to my lawyer in email. Because they seemed to forget that I was a business owner in the state of Tennessee, and I knew that I was required to have insurance for my company here. Unless the state really was only picking on me and no one else and making up laws that only applied to me.

Which did seem to be the truth as every time something like this happened to me, everyone said without fail, "I've never heard of that happening to anyone before."

Just as I was required by state law to have insurance to cover all assets in my business, I assumed the auction house would be required to carry general liability insurance to cover their inventory against theft and fire.

Hell, I even had it against an act of terrorism.

Was I really to believe that a legitimate company operating didn't have insurance to cover my cars they had wrongfully taken?

As for the drivers...

The cars had no tags. I'd stripped them off before they took them as we were required to do by Tennessee law. So, no one should be driving the cars with no tags and even if they were doing so with dealer tags, their personal insurance should cover them.

There was no reason for me to continue coverage when I'd signed the cars over to someone else.

And if that was not the policy, then Newhouse should have told me this as he was the supposed "expert" on the matter. After all, I'd sold dozens and dozens of cars in the past, and every time I'd ever signed the title over and removed the tags, I was told to immediately cancel the insurance.

If that wasn't what I was legally required to do all of a sudden, then the fucking idiot lawyer/trustee the state had forced upon me against my will and made me pay over one hundred thousand dollars for while I was in bankruptcy should have told me that there was an unknown, new law they'd made up just for me to make my life hell.

Instead, I was being threatened again because I couldn't read his puny mind.

Well hell, assholes, for the money I'd wasted on all of you to torture me for you own personal amusement, I could have easily paid my way through law school.

Especially the Nashville YMCA Night School of Law. And obviously, as we'd seen from everyone's behavior, brains weren't required to graduate or to pass the Tennessee State Bar Exam.

But that wasn't the real kicker.

*Wait for it...*

Les, who had hauled me into court in August of 2018 for contempt when he'd refused to take his name off my bills and had cost me thousands and thousands of dollars to have my bills switched over into my name, had told the judge that *I* was refusing to have the bills switched over to my name.

Let me repeat that. Les was complaining that I had refused to have the bills switched over into my name, even though I had spent thousands of dollars to have the bills switched over into my name. Cockburn had, and this was on the transcripts, stood up in court and said, "Your Honor, all Mrs. Manly has to do is make a simple phone call and have her name put on the bills. She won't even do that much. It's a simple process that she's refusing to do."

*I* was the problem. Not Les who had screamed so badly at my banker when I'd tried to have my name taken off our joint account that I was so mortified, I'd attempted to switch banks as my banker would no longer talk to me after he attacked her because she simply asked him if I could leave the money in the account and remove my name from it. This was the same account he claimed I was taking money out of when I wasn't doing so (he was), which was why I wanted my name removed from it. If my name and access were removed from the account, then he couldn't haul me into court anymore to make false allegations against me over that account.

Since he knew he was lying, he refused to allow me to remove my name from the account, even though the judge had ordered him to separate all accounts from one another, and even though his own attorney had drawn up the orders for us to separate all our accounts.

This was the same stupid slag who'd then hauled me into court and attempted to extort twenty thousand dollars out of me for her insurance fraud scheme she'd concocted with him?

Yeah, *that* nightmare.

In spite of all that, which included a court order that demanded the name of the policy holder be changed, and everything I'd tried, I couldn't get my own insurance that I was paying tens of thousands of dollars to be put in *my* name. Asshole was required to call the agent and give "his" permission for the switch, even though he had never earned one single penny of the money that had ever paid for one item that was insured.

Les was too busy screaming that it was "his" account. Even though it also included one of "my" million-dollar life insurance policies. You know, those million-dollar life insurance policies he'd also forbidden me with a court order from changing the beneficiary on, so that Les would inherit all the money in the event something happened to me during the divorce.

Him.

Not our sons. The same sons he'd stolen the trust funds and inheritance from and recklessly spent on his girlfriend and horse and renovating my office.

After all, there was nothing suspicious about a man who'd stolen all of the couple's money and ripped off his own children after he'd tried to kill his wife refusing to allow her to change the beneficiary on her life insurance during a bitter divorce he started.

Hmmm...

No, the control freak could never give up control over my insurance policy that I was required to pay for every month, nor could he allow the bill I was responsible for to be delivered to my house.

Yes, you read that correctly.

The bill wasn't being delivered to my home and the idiot trustee wouldn't allow it to be auto drafted any longer from my account, which also cost more money for me (they offered a discount if you auto-drafted the money).

And because I wasn't getting the bills and it wasn't being auto-drafted, I was missing payments, which caused me to risk contempt orders. Every two weeks, I would have to remember to physically login to the insurance site and double check that I didn't have one of the ever-revolving insurance policies (we had a large number of them) coming due.

Because it wasn't like I didn't have a lot of other things that vied for my attention constantly, such as this blatant insurance/tag stupidity whereby Les's numerous attorneys were threatening my attorney with sanctions against her bar license.

*Are you fucking kidding me?*

I was about ready to print that on a t-shirt and wear it every time I appeared around them.

These were the same attorneys who'd violated the civil rights of my sons and done an illegal seizure of their property. Caused an illegal search of my home and had blatantly lied and violated countless codes of the Tennessee Board of Professional Conduct's rules.

And they dared to threaten Melissa.

Yeah...

Most corrupt state on the Union.

It sickened me.

Why wasn't Melissa fighting? She told me over and over again. She was afraid of losing her license.

After all, Dinky had declared war on two other attorneys in town. One for no reason other than Dinky "suspected" the attorney had outed his arrest for solicitation. Dinky had no evidence, but he was "sure" this attorney had done it.

For that suspicion and with no evidence, Dinky had caused the attorney to lose his license.

Likewise, my former attorney, Constance, had given that attorney a tape of Dinky bragging during a hearing that had nothing to do with that attorney about how he'd persecuted him.

As a result, Dinky had it in for her, too (which was one of the reasons I'd gone to Melissa).

No evidence was needed in Williamson County.

As for me?

Cah-ching. This battle raged on for twenty-four hours of agony as Dinky and crew set fire to what little money I had left.

*Happy Valentine's to me.*

But wait, there was more. Les was also stroking out over the fact that I had dared to remove the "tractor" off *his* policy.

"She had no right to do that! It's my policy, not hers!"

*First, you five-year-old twat, you should get a job and pay for something. Then you can claim it as yours.*

Secondly, it wasn't a tractor. It was a Gator. I grew up in the country and there was a big ass difference between a Gator and a tractor. A tractor was useful. A Gator was an ATV.

We'd never needed a Gator at my office, but Baby Huey had to have it because he wanted to joyride around my yard and yell at the landscapers. Les was too lazy to walk. He might develop a muscle that way.

That really was why I had one. He'd called me one day while I was trying to work.

"Terri, there's something I'm looking at. It's a small John Deere tractor... "

"We don't need a tractor."

"Well, it's not really a tractor. It's like a small truck you can haul things with."

"You mean a Gator?"

"How do you know what a Gator is?"

Had I rolled my eyes any farther back into my head at Les's stupid question, I would have gone blind. "I was raised on a farm." And I'm not your dumbass, ignorant mother who couldn't remember her own name. "You don't need a Gator."

He'd bought it anyway.

Last I'd seen it, two weeks before he'd filed for divorce, it'd been in three pieces in the garage of my office. Torn up. Rusted out. Not working.

I hadn't even known we'd had insurance on it. After all, it was fifteen years old and not worth the money it would take to repair it.

Why would anyone insure a piece of broken down shit that couldn't be driven?

Oh, that was right, Les! The man who couldn't save a penny for anything. Mr. "I love to spend the money I never earned"!

There he was, throwing his hissy fit because I was trying to save money to pay for his overabundance of attorneys before we lost everything I'd earned.

Including that piece of rusted out shit Gator. Why Newhouse hadn't seized it to add it to the auction instead of my cars, I had no idea. After all, it was just a glorified, supped-up golf cart that had no practical purpose for the cabin, other than to allow Les to run around and yell at people.

And it was mine.

Not Les's as he'd written it off as a business expense for my office.

But then, everything had always been about control when it came to Les. So why he filed for divorce, I had no idea. He couldn't stand the fact that he was no longer in control of our lives.

How sick was this control-freak-of-nature?

Because all the bills were going to him, they also sent him the refund from the insurance, and he wanted to know if he could cash the check and keep the money he hadn't paid to them.

What a guy!

Let me reiterate that his sons were working two jobs each to help out their mother and were buying groceries for me with money they earned from the sweat of their own brows (thank God they have my work ethic and not the lazy as shit Manly code of "take whatever you can grab"). And that lazy sack of shit refused to work a single job to pay a single bill.

Meanwhile, Les was allowed to spend seven thousand dollars on a horse that he kept in a state where he wasn't supposed to be living and was allowed to have his sister rent it out and make money from it while he lied to the court and claimed that he couldn't make any income at all.

And no one would punish him for his lies and perjury.

Now you know why my sons refused to have his name anymore. Why they were telling people that their father had died in a car wreck.

The worst was when my son said, "You know, I used to worry about how I would manage to give my kids the happy childhood that you gave me, Mom. Now, my worst fear is that I'll grow up and be the deadbeat bastard my father is."

"Hon, don't worry. He's set that bar so low, there's no way you could belly crawl under it. You'd have to be an ameba to be a worst dad. Really, it's a simple list to rise above the turd pool. Don't steal from your kids. Don't leave in the middle of the night. Don't poison them. Don't hire a disgusting pig to abuse them and don't abuse them yourself. It's really not a hard thing to be a better parent."

Basically, Maddox would have to set fire to his kids on purpose to outdo Les on the level of suckage and blowage.

And don't get me started on his pedophile grandfather.

After all, I felt bad for holding it against my dad that he'd once burned down my Barbie doll house in a fit of rage during one of his more stellar PTSD fits.

All my life, I'd thought that was one of the cruelest, meanest things a father could do.

Until Les had showed me what a real fucking monster looked like. I'd take my dad over him anytime. At least my father had a reason for his fit. He'd taken bullets in war, defending something he believed in. Protecting the soldiers in his unit.

Les was a lazy, greedy, jealous piece of shit who hated himself and couldn't find happiness. As his own best friend had so often said, "your biggest problem is that your self-esteem is so low, buddy, you'd never join any club that would have you as a member."

Sad, but true.

And the drama continued...

As if I needed any further proof of the corruption that existed, while Melissa was updating me on the latest threats being leveled at herself and me, I updated her on the binder I'd found hidden in Nick's closet.

"It's unbelievable."

I'd finally had a chance to really go through the paperwork.

It was much worse than I'd thought. And while Leadwits had blown it off, Melissa was listening.

"Yeah, that's identity fraud. I had a case where all the wife did was answer one of those credit card things that came in the mail for her husband and filled it out in his name. She got the card, while they were still married, and was only using it to buy fast food for their kids. But because it was in his name and she'd done it without his knowledge or permission, and even though she was paying for it herself, they arrested and convicted her for it. Here in Williamson County."

"Then why did Detective Lazy blow me off when I showed him proof that Les had written checks on my account without my permission or knowledge?"

"I have no idea."

"Why didn't he arrest Hogg for impersonating my sons when I showed him proof of what she'd done?"

"No idea. You'd have to ask the DA."

*Are you fucking kidding me?*

But then, I had to remember old Dinky's bragging in court. "Should any criminal charges be filed... that's up to me. I do it all."

But the worst came a few minutes later when Melissa told me that Les had been talking to old Detective Lazy, himself. Both him and his attorney.

Not because Les was a suspect.

Old Lynn had never bothered to even interview or talk to him about any of my allegations.

*Not a single one.*

But once Les and Barbie had wanted to come after me, then Lynn agreed to talk to them.

*What the actual fuck?*

So, Lynn? What happened to all your bullshit and emails about how the TBI was going to arrest Les once I had my expert witnesses? I had that in writing from the detective.

What about those cases where others were arrested for doing a whole lot less than Les and Hogg?

Why had I been arrested for nothing when I had so many actual crimes committed against me and my sons and no one in this town would even listen to us?

Instead, I was mocked, insulted and threatened at every turn by a corrupt judge who didn't even bother to hide his bias.

This was perverted justice at its finest.

And I was tired of being threatened.

I was sick to my stomach, especially when I learned that my cars, clothing and purses were being offered for "whatever fee they bring." No reserve.

Some as little as three dollars.

My beautiful perfectly restored Mustang that I had held onto for seventeen years because it reminded me of the car my older brother had and that my father had sold out from under me had a first offer of on it of only one dollar.

In the end, it was sold to pay the auctioneer for selling items that should *never* have been sold. Less than half of the value of the car and far less than what I'd paid for it.

I prayed to God that all of them burned in hell.

Especially Les, Megan and Newhouse. *May you rot and may God give you what you really, truly deserve as I've never done anything to deserve what you bastards did to me.*

*Did to my sons.*

I prayed that I lived to see Karma shit all over every last one of them.

If that wasn't bad enough, Newhouse had his name put right there on the auction along with a public announcement of my case for bankruptcy, in direct violation of Dinky's court order. After all his lectures and posturing about how he "could never, ever violate anything the judge says" to help me. But you could certainly violate old Dinky's orders to humiliate me.

Sick, twisted bastards all.

The only good to come out of it was that Leadwits had finally filed a protest against Newhouse's useless accountant.

One who was posting false information on my records to the court. And yes, that was the truth. With her overinflated salary, she was so stupid that she kept listing my IRS validated business expenses under personal.

Because neither she nor Newhouse could do the proper paperwork that they were charging me a fucking fortune to do.

They were that stupid and that lazy.

That greedy.

And of course, Leadwits had only done that after my insistence because of their gross incompetence.

I called Melissa. "Given what my items are bringing in the auction and what Newhouse filed for his fees, tell Leadwits to file to get me out of this bankruptcy."

"He said that if you make him do that he'll withdraw as your lawyer."

"I'm tired of being threatened by him." Last time I checked, a lawyer wasn't supposed to hold their client hostage. They were supposed to zealously protect their client. God knew that Les's attorneys had never failed to file the most made-up bullshit imaginable for him. Why couldn't I find an attorney who would simply be a decent human being for me?

Instead, I kept getting psychos.

"That's what he told me."

"Well, if I'm out of the bankruptcy, I don't need him. Do I have to have an attorney once it's filed? Can I speak to the judge myself?" I'd be fine with that. Personally, I'd prefer to speak so that I could tell her why I wanted out.

One, they'd threatened me.

Two, her U.S. Trustees had violated her own court orders and Dinky's and had told me to destroy a valuable piece of state property, and evidence, not to mention, marital property.

Three, that I was being extorted by them with their threats.

Four, that none of them had disclosed to me how expensive bankruptcy would be and that my debt, instead of going down would be doubled in only six months and that none of my creditors would have been paid, at all, during that time.

My God! I could have taken out a loan and had better rates than filing for bankruptcy had I known that would happen. There was no way I could continue to remain in bankruptcy if they were going to add over two hundred thousand dollars a year, plus, to my debt in bankruptcy attorney fees. Never mind the additional six-hundred-thousand dollars a year that Newhouse had obligated me to pay to Les and his attorneys.

That was bullshit.

And for the record, I didn't make enough after taxes to cover the bankruptcy attorney fees, alone.

*See my dilemma?*

If they refused to let me out, I was sunk. They weren't leaving me with anything.

I would be on welfare for the rest of my life.

And I was being threatened every single day.

No one should be forced to live under that kind of stress. A stress that was taking its toll on my health.

My blood pressure was out of control. When this started, I was on one single blood pressure table a day at twenty milligrams. Because of Newhouse and crew, my doctor added a second brand of blood pressure medicine.

Then they had me double the dose of the second blood pressure medicine.

On Valentine's Day, my doctor called after reviewing my latest report and had me double that, too, so that I was taking six doses of my medicine a day.

That was how high they were elevating my blood pressure with the constant stress and threats that they were putting me under. Never had it been higher, and I'd been on blood pressure medicine since my twenties. I went through three pregnancies. The death of my brother and parents with blood pressure issues.

I'd buried my niece and nephews.

Had been homeless with an infant.

Gone through the Dumas litigation.

Nothing had done this level of damage to my blood pressure. But the nonstop, constant assault by Les's team of bullies and the trustees who wouldn't stop picking at my corpse were more than my body could handle.

The only time in my life (aside from pregnancy) that I'd had any issues with my blood pressure had been when Les's poisoning had caused me to have anemia. The anemia thinned my blood to such a degree that my heart could barely pump it through my veins. That had caused an unnatural spike.

But once Les had left and the anemia miraculously was cured within a few months of no one spiking my food, my pressure had returned to normal.

Until this latest round of bullshit.

No wonder Les didn't want the beneficiary changed on my life insurance policies. People kept asking why Les would want to kill me.

There were millions of reasons for it.

And I had the policies to prove it.

FEBRUARY 19

JUST WHEN I THOUGHT NOTHING could get any more ridiculous in this travesty of a divorce, enter the FBI. And yes, you read that one correctly, too. Les, being the infinite cocktail party joke that he was, had to go and raise the bar on his stupidity and spitefulness. It wasn't enough that he had to make his own lawyers look like fools.

Now he was doing it to federal agencies, too.

Lovely.

Because "he" was getting death threats. What made this even more ridiculous? These were the same level and types of death threats that I had been getting during the Dumas lawsuit. Where fans of hers had been threatening to rape and kill me for all manner of things. Yet Les had blatantly dismissed those threats as "nothing to be concerned about" and had sent me out into the public where my schedule was posted for the entire world to see so if there had been a legitimate threat, the attacker would have known exactly where I was and when. *By all means, make it easy for them.* Never once had he called the authorities, such as the FBI in order to protect the mother of his children or his primary meal ticket.

I wasn't important.

"They're not going to do anything to you, Terri. You're being ridiculous. They're readers. All they're doing is sending you internet hate. You're overreacting."

*I* was overreacting.

Not Les who had called out the FBI because one of my fans posted a joke on a fan site where she said and I quote, "Someone should hire one of Terri's alien assassins to kick her ex's butt."

Okay.

As if one of my imaginary characters could leave their solar system and travel to ours to harm him.

And they called *me* delusional.

What galled me most was that Les wasn't even concerned when Lyra and I were accosted at a signing by an extremely large, tall fan in Los Angeles over the Dumas lawsuit.

Which proved he was trying to kill me and was hoping a fan would do it for him, so that he'd have an easy alibi.

Lyra, much like my son and cat, was cannon fodder. He really didn't care who was caught in the crossfire so long as he got rid of me.

Either that, or he was merely using the FBI as fodder for his bogus defamation suit. *You know...* "I was so afraid for my life, Your Honor, I had to call out the FBI. Now, give me triple damages in awards as punishment against her."

I guess the moron forgot the simple fact that *I* was in possession of the bipolar angry letters he'd written to our attorneys in the Dumas case. "Terri's getting death threats. You need to get off your asses and do something about it." Like somehow the lawyers were to blame for the threats that had been caused by Les's lawsuit.

Because back then, it'd been for them to do something, not my husband who was supposed to protect his family. *You know, being the head of the house, and all that.* Remember what I'd said about Les The Great Delegator? He could never do anything for himself. He always left it up to someone else.

In retrospect, I was amazed he'd never hired someone else to screw me in his place. He really was *that* lazy.

And worthless.

Which made me wonder who'd dialed the phone for the FBI? Hogg or his attorney?

Whoever it was hadn't hesitated to call out the FBI for a wild goose chase when none of my fans knew or cared where he lived. Because God knew, my sons and I had no clue if he was in Tennessee or Georgia, nor did we even care.

If you looked the loser up online, it would have sent them to my house, not his. And even if they had the address to my cabin, they wouldn't have been able to find it because it didn't have a mailbox or any kind of address marker on it.

Unless you knew where the cabin was, you couldn't find it. Not to mention the fact that the cabin had a mile and a half long driveway that was gated.

No one could get to him. Unlike my house that sat in a regular, ungated neighborhood.

And both he and his girlfriend had been the ones laughing all that time, and claiming that I didn't have any fans left, anyway. So there couldn't be any real "threat" to my safety.

Or his.

Except when it benefitted him in court.

His mental gymnastics should have won a gold medal as an Olympic event. Nadia Comăneci and Shannon Miller had nothing on this guy. His brain was so limber, it should have been leaking out his ears.

"We take these things seriously." That was what the FBI agent had told me.

"But the only threat I saw online was a fan who'd said she wished she could hire one of my Space Guild Assassins to beat him up. They're aliens. Some of them have gills and are green. They can't breathe in our atmosphere. I'm pretty sure it wasn't a serious threat as it would take my characters decades to get to the Milky Way galaxy from their fictional universe."

*Sadly, the FBI doesn't have a sense of humor.*

"He said that you might have hired a hitman."

*Okay, then.* It took a minute to stop laughing. "I'm in bankruptcy. As you can see—" I'd gestured at the messy house that I'd been packing up, alone and with no help, frenetically for over a week until every muscle in my body was cramped and aching for fear they'd have me locked up for obstruction of justice (a very real threat they kept leveling at me). "I'm in the middle of packing up my house that they're forcing me to sell to pay for his attorneys. Not my single attorney. Every dime I spend is monitored. Pretty sure they'd notice if one single penny went missing."

Especially since the trustee doled my money out to me to the very cent I needed to live on. And actually, overdrew my account repeatedly because of Newhouse's stupidity.

Not to mention, I'd been harassed relentlessly because I'd failed to provide a receipt for a

Coke I'd charged. Stupid me, I'd thought the fact that I charged the Coke *was* the receipt for it. It never dawned on me that I needed to hold on to the slip of paper to prove I spent two dollars on a Coke at an event I'd attended as it was on public record, I was at an event all day (I even had photographic evidence and had been interviewed for TV and newspapers). I had naturally assumed that a two hundred dollar an hour accountant would be brilliant enough to figure out that during the day, I'd need something to drink at least once while I was there for eight hours.

But no, I had to have proof and couldn't be trusted that I'd spent two dollars on a single Coke as I could have spent those two bucks on who knew what else!

Like tickets to...

Absolutely nothing.

Or hired a hitman if you worked for the FBI.

Therefore, I could imagine the look on old Newhouse's idiotic face should I ask for *this*. "Yo, can I have fifty grand in unmarked bills to knock off the hubster?"

The selfish bastard wouldn't even allow me money to buy boxes to pack up my house, or money to hire a cleaning lady or movers. I was pretty sure that Newhouse wouldn't okay a few thousand to clean the real mess out of my life.

After all, he was too busy approving my money be spent on his uber expensive accountant because he and this was a direct quote from his own lips, "Didn't have time to do the paperwork," nor did he "Want to."

And yes, he'd said those words to me.

In front of multiple witnesses.

I was being gouged because Newhouse didn't want to do his own job.

And billed for over one hundred thousand dollars for him and his two little buddies, alone, while I was in bankruptcy. Fees that no one had forewarned me about, even while I protested that I didn't want a fucking trustee put over me.

Yeah...

The government and my husband were allowed to financially gouge me at will and there was nothing I could do to stop it.

But that was neither here nor there.

Fact was that I would never hire a hitman for Les. I'd rather sit back, and watch Karma do the bastard in as Les deserved. In fact, I was living for the day when this would be over, and Les would be working at Wal-Mart.

And who had let the FBI into my home?

Les's own sons, including his favorite one that Les had so cherished and wanted back so desperately, and the eldest son that Les had been most proud of because he could brag that this was his Mensa-card-carrying son who'd graduated college in three years and traveled the world on his own, even though he had Autism.

Nick and Maddox.

The agent happened to pick the one single day that week that Maddox was off from his job in money management and finance. The day between his two thirteen-hour shifts.

Maddox was furious and horrified. He'd hated his father before, but not nearly as much as he did after that agent left. "The bastard threatened to come after me, but no one will take *that* threat seriously? The stupid cop wouldn't even talk to me about the deranged bastard screaming at me and threatening *my* life, and my brother's if we testified against him for what he did to us. He almost killed you and murdered my cat and no law enforcement agency will do a damn thing, but one fan makes a joke, and they spend thousands of tax dollars to harass my mom? What the fuck is wrong with this country?"

I had no answer for him.

After all, it was my seventy-year-old aunt who'd been threatened and terrorized in email by Les, and no one seemed to care about that either.

Welcome to America and our nightmare.

Where one insane lunatic could terrorize his entire family for years, and no one would stop him. Not even when his own attorneys were going around and telling everyone how crazy he was. He was allowed to call out the FBI with a false report and use them to harass his family and other innocent citizens.

With impunity.

I told the agent about what had been done to us, and the fact that Les's attorneys had called him crazy to my attorneys. I offered to show him my six hundred pages of evidence for judicial corruption. Of Les transferring money that wasn't his across state lines. Of his theft and everything else. Especially, the illegal search and seizure of my home.

And my tox reports that proved he'd tried to kill me. That he'd poisoned my son and cousin, and cats. Along with the letter I had from the Tennessee Bureau of Investigation that had promised me they'd arrest him if I had an expert who would corroborate the findings, and my emails from others who agreed it was poisoning.

"You'll have to submit a report online."

*Are you kidding me?*

"I've been doing that for two years. I was hoping my report was why you were here, today."

"When did you file the last one."

"In November."

"Have you called our offices?"

"Yes. Several times. I even tried to schedule an appointment to come in and show my evidence to an agent. But they brushed me off."

"When was the last time you called?"

"In November."

"Then you need to call again."

Awesome. My legitimate complaints fell on deaf ears, but Les could sit there and knowingly file false reports to harass us and they headed right on out.

Not just to harass me, but also my fans. They had gone to their homes over his lies and interviewed them, too.

Just so fucking awesome!

My tax dollars at work. Going to ruin my career and fanbase for someone so crazy that his own attorneys called him that. Constantly.

But my day had just started.

The next fun-filled adventure came when I received Newhouse's "plan".

You know... that thing that I'd been asking for since I'd filed for bankruptcy almost eight months earlier. I'd gone into bankruptcy with a plan already in my mind on what I needed to be done to pay off everything.

It'd been simple.

I couldn't consolidate all the accounts Les had opened up so that he could transfer and hide money and keep everyone confused about what he was doing (i.e. hiding money and stealing from our children and me) because every time I tried to do so in order to pay bills such as my IRS debt, they hauled me into court for contempt.

True story.

I had another contempt conviction that they had blackmailed me into pleading guilty on, as they were planning to put me into jail had I gone before the judge who'd been bragging he wanted to arrest me.

And every single attorney told me that. Even though I was innocent. "If you don't plead guilty to this, Dinky is going to put you in jail."

I even had the email where my attorney admitted that what they were doing was blackmail. Pure and simple.

So, I couldn't risk Dinky being an ass again for no reason as I knew he refused to hear my side of things, and everyone had told me the rotten corrupt bastard would put me in jail for it.

Including Newhouse.

Yes, Newhouse. The trustee had also admitted the judge was crooked and had it "in for" me.

Their lies and illegal actions were what had forced me into bankruptcy and what continued to have me hauled into court as Les's herd of jackals kept lining their pockets with my money while they beat me up for his amusement.

To the tune of hundreds of thousands of dollars.

A bigger idiot was never born.

All I'd needed bankruptcy for was to stop the jackals from hauling me into court every two weeks, literally, so that I could catch my breath and to stop them from bleeding my accounts dry. It was to allow me to be able to pay off my real creditors before they strip-mined every fucking dime I was making faster than I could make it.

I told Dipshit Newhouse from day one what I needed.

He refused to listen. Stupid bastard didn't like any of my answers.

Then once all that money was spent, months later, he would put my house up for sale.

"I'm not going to put Mr. Manly on the street." Those had been Dinky's actual words. He didn't care that he was throwing my sons (one of whom was still in high school) and pregnant daughter-in-law onto the street. Or that he was costing me hundreds of thousands of dollars in losses and shutting down my business.

I was out of everything I had ever worked for in my entire life, with no assets left.

Newhouse was *that* stupid. Just like when he'd told me, "I'll need a copy of all your contracts."

I was stunned by the stupidity of that request. "All?"

"Yes. All."

For thirty-five years? For thousands of books and short stories? With addendums?

*Any idea how many pages we were talking?*

To put it in perspective, I had six filing cabinets filled to the brim. And I didn't mean little ones. We were talking five-foot-tall cabinets.

When I tried to explain to Newhouse why it would be a bad idea, he called me impossible and said I was obstructing his job.

I took a photo and sent it to him. "I'll be glad to do it, but I need some time and money to have all these photocopied or do you want them digitized?"

Once he saw how much reading he'd have to do, he changed his mind about receiving that many pieces of paper or digital copies.

Newhouse, like the others, wanted everyone to think he was a lot smarter than he was. The problem was, he wouldn't shut up and listen to learn anything. He assumed he already knew it. Therefore, he'd kept bullishly charging forward with half information, while he insisted on doing it his way... which kept fucking up my business.

"What do you mean you don't get paid regularly?"

I really wanted to Gibbs slap him. "I get paid, but it's twice a year." He was completely unable to comprehend how an author's royalties worked. It was why I hadn't wanted a trustee to begin with.

This wasn't something a newbie could easily wrap their head around and I'd been in the business long enough to see that glassy-eyed stare from people whenever you tried to explain it to them. They didn't want to believe that it was the reality that writers dealt with. They'd been too exposed to Hollywood lies and misconceptions about us to even begin to fathom the reality of a real author's income and how we were treated and paid.

How I hated my bankruptcy attorney Stefano Leadwits. Another lazy POS who refused to listen. Who didn't want to do his job. Rather than do what he was paid to do, he shirked it off onto Newhouse and sold me down the river.

Leadwits said, "My loyalty isn't to you, Terri. It's to the bankruptcy court and trustees."

Really? That wasn't what the Tennessee Board of Professional Responsibility Ethic's code said.

But since they didn't bother to enforce their codes, who gave a shit, anyway?

Newhouse had jerked off for eight months and added more than half a million dollars to my debt with his grotesque incompetence and flagrant stupidity.

Or I supposed I should have said, he allowed Les's attorneys to pillage my estate for that in additional attorney fees, plus what Newhouse and his friends added to it with their unnecessary and redundant fees.

Therefore, my home was being sold. Along with my cars, my clothing, my family mementos, and he was threatening to put me on welfare for the rest of my life.

Along with his boss bitch.

Their fingers were "on the button" if I did anything at all to displease them.

Again, their exact words.

All he'd had to do was what I'd asked him to do that first day. That would have gotten me through without any problems, and without it having cost me everything I'd worked for.

Newhouse didn't want to do that. Even though "debtor in possession" was supposed to mean that I got to choose what was sold, not him because he wanted to "punish me".

To retaliate for the fact that I'd documented their abuse and illegal behavior.

This really was all about punishing an "uppity" woman. Just like Dinky, he couldn't stand a successful woman and it bled out of every part of him. I'll never forget the disdain in his voice the first time we spoke. "Don't think for one minute that you're going to continue traveling around the world with your entourage and staying in your five-star hotels with them.

Yeah. He'd said that to me. Newhouse was full of more shit that a manure factory and knew nothing about me or my business.

In all those months, he'd never bothered to learn anything about my business. Or me.

I didn't travel with an entourage. Because of my medical conditions and learning disabilities, I needed someone to go with me to help me. The others only traveled whenever we had the booth and I needed them to help staff it.

As for the hotels, I had never in my life stayed in a five-star hotel. The highest I'd ever gone was a four, and the majority of those had been paid for by my publisher.

Or Les had insisted on it because he was too snobby to stay somewhere else.

But that disdainful hatred from Newhouse had set the tone and he'd been punishing me and my sons from that moment forward over the lies he'd bought into.

Because he was too lazy to do his job (which he'd admitted). He didn't want to take five minutes to learn the truth.

This was someone I wouldn't have put in charge of a dog kennel of stuffed animals. He had mismanaged every bit of my estate.

And lied on court documents.

I was furious. And now they were all refusing to let me out of the bankruptcy.

Because when I got his "proposal" what I saw on it was that he'd taken enough money out of my joint accounts that he could have paid off my creditors within the first month of the bankruptcy, had he not been intent on paying off his "entourage" so handsomely.

No wonder he'd accused me of that.

Him and Les. They had a *lot* in common.

Funny how certain people loved to accuse others of their own conduct.

Newhouse had put me through a year of hell for no reason.

Other than to get a fat fucking paycheck off my back and to watch me and my sons bleed.

I was disgusted.

Even more so when I saw that one of my creditors was none other than my own son, Caleb, for sixty-three-*thousand* dollars.

*Are you fucking kidding me?*

Newhouse had put that on my bankruptcy bill. Why?

"I'll challenge it later." That was what he'd said.

*Excuse me?*

By law, he was not to include anything on my bankruptcy that wasn't legitimate.

That was his job. *You know, the one he didn't want to do?*

And he'd lied to federal court by putting something on my bill that he knew was bogus.

How did he know? Because he was the one who'd sold the car I was being billed for that he had no legal right to sell.

None. I was in a Chapter 11. A business reorganization and yet he was selling off personal property that had nothing to do with my business. Such as the car we'd bought my son for his graduation.

I wouldn't have had that debt added to my bill, or the one for my leased car that was near its end that would have cost me less money to keep it till the end than it was for him to terminate early.

Again, Newhouse kept racking up more debt on my account instead of helping me to eliminate.

Could someone please tell me how this was legal?

I knew for a fact that it was deplorable and wrong morally.

Even worse? Newhouse and crew (which included Les) had allowed my young son to commit a felony by claiming a debt on a federal court document that was clearly fraud, and a debt that I did not owe to him.

Cockburn and the team of jackals that she led had somehow coaxed my son into committing a felony. I knew this for a fact as I'd seen their records where they documented meeting and speaking with my child in preparation for my bankruptcy.

For Caleb to put forth a debt to the court, he was supposed to swear it was a legitimate claim on pain of perjury.

*On pain of perjury.*

They were using my Autistic son as a tool to further embarrass me, and they put his entire future at risk to further pillage my estate?

These were people who needed to be put beneath the jail system. What was wrong with these animals?

They had allowed my naïve child to commit perjury on a federal document? These were the same lying bastards who had come at me during the initial bankruptcy hearing to claim that I was committing perjury when I refused to say that I had transferred i.e. "given" money to my son because I had added my son's name to my account as payable on death?

Or put Nick's name on the brokerage certificate of deposit that he couldn't draw money out of? My name had been on those accounts, too. They were *my* accounts as well as my sons', so I had not transferred money "into hiding" as they'd attempted to insinuate.

If that was how it worked, then ole Les would never have been able to close out my children's accounts without their permission or knowledge as my sons would have owned those accounts.

And given that they were joint accounts, long established, Newhouse had no business closing them and taking the money as they should have had as much right as I did. As in Newhouse hadn't gone after my joint account with Les.

It was criminal all the way around, and a sick racket they were in on.

So, does this mean that Newhouse violated the law?

It thought it did and I believed that he owed my sons their money back as he had no right to close out those accounts.

If Boss Bitch Martha was accusing me of transferring money to my sons when I hadn't, then they broke the law and needed to give that money back to my boys. Why else would Newhouse have needed my sons present when we'd all learned that if I was a "joint" holder, then they didn't have to be there for me to clean out their accounts.

Someone was lying.

I knew it wasn't me.

Again, they'd been lying and trying set me up.

Allowing a boy to commit perjury so that Newhouse could later protest it and bill me for hours he worked while I was in bankruptcy. How was this not criminal?

*"I'll deny it later."* That was his answer for allowing my son to commit perjury after he'd lectured me against the seriousness of making perjurious statements, which I had not done.

But they had.

Repeatedly.

One that translated to: "I'll charge you more money to take care of a bullshit charge that I know is bullshit and that I allowed to be illegally submitted to the court so that I can continue to bill you my outrageous fees."

How did he know it was bullshit? Newhouse had seen the title when he'd sold Caleb's car. A title that bore Les's name on it because he'd been too big a dick to allow his son to have his own car when he turned twenty-one. Rather, Les was making sure that he "owned" it in the event I died from his poisoning. Why else not give the car title to his son?

It was the same title that I'd refused to sign for them to auction because I was disgusted by every single one of these lying pieces of shit I couldn't scrape off my shoes. Les had signed the title for Newhouse to sell my son's car in the bankruptcy.

I had refused to.

After all, my signature wasn't necessary for a legal transaction and yet Newhouse had forced me to sign anyway.

Sadistic, sick fucking bastard.

Yet I was the one Caleb was suing. Not his father who'd stolen and then sold the car out from under him.

Not his father who'd refused to sign it over to him before the divorce, or his father who'd been counting it as "marital property" since the night he'd snuck out of the house like the thief he was. Because Les had wanted me to buy that car again from him.

Okay.

And Newhouse was going along with the lie to charge me more money.

Ca-ching.

What repugnant creatures.

I immediately called Melissa. "Get me out of this bankruptcy."

"Stefano will withdraw as your counsel if you do that."

"I don't care. I'm tired of being threatened by them." I was also tired of being tortured.

Besides, Leadwits was putting in his petition to withdraw every four weeks anyway, and I was getting even sicker of that petulant, controlling bullshit.

This was terrorism. Pure and simple. No one should have to live under their constant threats.

*"Do what I say or else."*

First Les, then Megan. Then Newhouse. Now Leadwits.

It'd gotten old.

"Newhouse said it himself in his own document. The one problem I have with my finances is attorney fees. All my money is going to that. If they cancel the bankruptcy, that eliminates five of the attorneys right off the bat and it will allow the divorce to be settled."

*Let me repeat that.*

Because of Newhouse and Leadwits, I had *FIVE* high dollar attorneys, well technically *I* only had four, but at one-hundred-and-seventy-five dollars an hour, I was counting Newhouse's accountant in with them. So, *FIVE* high dollar bitches would be dumped out of my pocket immediately.

Plus, the cost of the bankruptcy.

They were looking for fat to trim... well, shit Shirley, that was a huge bulk and would have saved me about seventy thousand a month. Which was approximately what I was earning a year.

Wish I were joking.

No-brainer, right?

"Newhouse has said that he will protest it if you do it. He says that he doesn't want to, but that he'll be honor bound to do so."

"Fine. I don't care. Let him. I don't see how he can make a good faith argument to keep me in bankruptcy when his attorney fees are a huge bulk of what's bankrupting me."

And then I did what I should have done the day I walked out of that meeting with all of them.

I went to the FBI site and reported all of them for the threats they'd made against me.

Not that I thought for one minute that the FBI would do anything. They'd ignored me for all the other "tips" I'd sent in. But damn, I was tired of the shakedown. Tired of the threats.

No one should have to live like this. I was being terrorized on a daily basis, plain and simple.

And I was done with it.

# FEBRUARY 24

I**T WAS SAD TO WAKE UP AND** curse every day that you found yourself still alive. That was what they'd done to me. Every day when I came awake, it was with a lump of dread in my stomach for fear of what fresh hell would await me, because I had no way of knowing where or how they'd strike.

For the first time, I understood what my father had meant about living in a war zone. Waiting for the sound of the bombers to approach.

That was where I was living. And the strikes wouldn't stop coming.

Leadwits wouldn't email me directly. He was that big of a coward. Instead, everything was going through Melissa. I told him to protest the Newhouse's accountant's fees. Her nebulous job, as it had been told to me and my accountant, was supposed to only ensure that I was spending my money on what I was supposed to be spending it on.

Instead, that stupid slag had billed me for going over my expenditures for years, as well as phone calls to people in her company and other matters Newhouse hadn't cleared with me. Redundant expenditures that my accountant did.

And for filing incorrect information with the court. Information that could get me into trouble with the IRS.

I called the bullshit card on that.

Since I was in bankruptcy, I didn't need to be billed over forty thousand dollars for bullshit fees on a bitch I didn't need, while my own accountant who was less than half her fees went unpaid.

Bullshit.

Apparently, I wasn't the only person Newhouse wanted to enslave. In the government's mind, they should all be way overpaid, and we should all be working for free for them.

True statement.

And on this day, Leadwits put it in writing.

I had told him that I wanted out of the bankruptcy. I'd simply asked how to get out of it. This was his exact response:

Terri – your proposal is unrealistic.  Bankruptcies CANNOT BE DROPPED WITHOUT THE

CONSENT OF CREDITORS AND APPROVED BY THE JUDGE. Les Manly will never agree to the dismissal, especially after Newhouse has beaten him up over the remainder of the admin fees. So, lets move pass that point.

Are you begging for this case to be converted to a Chapter 7. Martha and Newhouse will do it in a heartbeat if I forward your email request to them.

This case is finally moving in the right direction. Do not screw this up because Dinky will have a field day on you if you try to dismiss (which will never happen) in this case.

How fucked up was this email? *Let me count the ways.*

First, he needed to proofread his bullshit.

Second, my attorney should have been helping me, not yelling at me. Why should Les not want to drop the bankruptcy as we were literally losing absolutely every single asset we owned (and I had email after email from him in the Dumas case where he'd told the attorneys that the last thing he wanted was to go broke)?

According to the plan Newhouse was putting forth, he wanted to sell my jewelry that included family heirlooms at less than one quarter of their value.

In other words, in direct violation of bankruptcy law, he was giving it away for pennies on the dollar.

He had sold off my Coach handbags that Les had bought at two hundred dollars for as little as three bucks.

Now I understood hating your spouse because let's face it, I was no fan of Les's, but losing every single dime of every single asset when you were unwilling to work seemed suicidal and beyond ridiculous.

Surely, not even Les could be *that* stupid. After all, I'd listened to him for three years screaming at his attorneys in the Dumas suit that we couldn't afford to go broke on attorney fees.

So what? Suddenly, he was okay with going broke on attorney fees in a divorce he couldn't win?

This was *War Games* at its finest.

Assured mutual destruction.

Was Leadwits telling me that a federal judge was so fucking stupid that she'd allowed one single, spiteful spouse to ruin another and use her court as a weapon?

Then again, seeing how brilliant they all were, why should I doubt that one?

He was probably right. The government wasn't known for employing the brightest bulbs on the tree.

As Leadwits had said, let's move past that point (unlike Leadwits, I actually knew grammar and could punctuate).

The second paragraph was my favorite as he admitted in it that he was in the meeting where Martha and Newhouse had threatened me in retaliation for keeping my diary. That they would indeed convert me to a Chapter 7 should I displease them and for no other reason. That Martha had her "finger on the button" and was "ready to push it" if I didn't make them happy.

Terrorism at its finest.

And there it was, in writing. Confirmed.

More than that was the third paragraph.

Dinky's impartiality.

Why would a state judge give a flying fuck about a bankruptcy? Shouldn't he be glad that we got it resolved and that we were moving forward with the divorce?

That last paragraph made no sense, other than to prove that Dinky had a vendetta out for me.

That he was constantly threatening to throw me in jail, even though I wasn't doing anything to warrant it.

And Leadwits should know. He was a personal friend of the Dinky family. Come to find out, he'd been the bankruptcy attorney for Daddy Dinky when he'd gotten into trouble and had helped him out.

He'd assured me when we first met that he'd be able to help me with Dinky in state court. At one point, he'd even tried to get me to fire my divorce attorney so that he could take over and "manage" things.

Now he'd turned against me and was siding with Dinky to threaten and intimidate me. Just like the others.

No one should have to live under these threats.

So, I sent a copy of this email to the FBI, too.

I wanted them to see what a legitimate threat looked like. One that was being made by people who had the authority to lock someone up for no reason and who were strip-mining my life out from under me.

Why?

Petty spite and jealousy.

Because of one fucked in the head spouse who wouldn't go away.

Better? This was all illegal in the state of Tennessee.

### T.C.A. 39-16-403. Official oppression.

(a)  A public servant acting under color of office or employment commits an offense who:

   (1)  Intentionally subjects another to *mistreatment or* to *arrest, detention,* stop, frisk, halt, *search, seizure, dispossession,* assessment or lien *when the public servant knows the conduct is unlawful; or*

   (2)  *Intentionally denies* or *impedes* another in the exercise or *enjoyment of any right,* privilege, power or immunity, when the public servant knows the conduct is unlawful.

(b)  For purposes of this section, a public servant acts under color of office or employment if the public servant acts, or purports to act, in an official capacity or takes advantage of the actual or purported capacity.

(c)  An offense under this section is a Class E felony.

(d)  Charges for official oppression may be brought only by indictment, presentment or criminal information; provided, that nothing in this section shall deny a person from pursuing other criminal charges by affidavit of complaint.

[Acts 1989, ch. 591, § 1; 1990, ch. 980, § 11.]

Why couldn't I get an indictment? Because Dinky had bragged that he was "in charge" of it all.

*How about the federal law?*

Extortion under color of official right involves the obtaining of property from another under color of official right. It is the wrongful taking by a public officer of money or property not due to him or his office with or without force, threats, or use of fear.

I was losing my life for no reason. I had done nothing wrong. My only mistake in life was marrying a psycho when I was twenty-four and being trapped in my marriage by our laws that protected pedophiles over victims.

No one would stand up for me. No one would help me.

Or my innocent sons.

My fans had put together a legal fund.

And where was my attorney?

She'd taken a vacation to the desert right when I needed her most.

W E HAD BUSTED OUR ASSES to get the house ready to be photographed for listing. Dipshit Newhouse refused to allow me to the money I needed for boxes.

Or to hire movers to help me.

My home was over eight thousand square feet, and I was told to have it packed up immediately.

Meanwhile, he was handing out my money like party favors to his idiot accountant who asked redundant, useless questions such as, "What's this Delta Dental bill? Do you have to pay it?"

Delta Dental was the largest dental insurance company in Tennessee. I was pretty sure that I wasn't the only one in town who used it and surely a two-hundred-dollar an hour accountant should have known that.

Yeah...

Better yet, Les was a hoarder, and I was under a court order that forbade me from throwing out anything. So, I had a decade's worth of trash to sort out in a matter of two weeks and get packed up, with a broken foot, two broken metatarsals, a bad back as in I have two compressed discs, a bad rotator cuff, a paralyzed hand, and severe arthritis that affects my knees, hands, shoulder and back.

*Go me!*

In other words, my entire life on my best day was pain management and because of the kidney and liver damage done to me thanks to Les's poisoning, I wasn't allowed any form of medication for pain management or to help my arthritis.

I lived in a state of constant agony.

And I had an entire eight thousand square foot house to pack up. Maddox wanted to help, but his job kept him working thirteen-hour shifts, six days a week. He was trying to make as much money as he could to save for his upcoming wedding and to help buy a place once we were thrown out on our asses.

Nick was doing the best he could, but he also had school and a job. Not to mention, his Autism was a lot worse, and he was freaking out over his room being dismantled—that was an added complication.

Newhouse had already spazed out over the fact that the house hadn't been ready by his first deadline that he'd sprung on me with no warning, while threatening me and running me through the wringer.

He'd also freaked because my money hadn't come in for the book I'd handed in at Christmas.

Which I had told the idiot repeatedly could happen as I had no control over when they cut a check and sent it.

I could hand a book in, but I couldn't force them to write a check. Every writer in the world knew this. Stephen King had even joked about that in his own book. "I can write a novel faster than a publisher can write a check."

True statement.

In my case, I could write two when I wasn't being threatened and under constant harassment.

So, here we were at the end of February and my check had yet to come. I wouldn't get paid until the publisher "accepted" my book. That wouldn't happen until I'd completed the revisions. I couldn't do the revisions until I got the revision letter that my editor had yet to send to me.

And even if she had sent it to me, it was really fucking hard to write a book while I packed up my home, with no money for boxes or movers.

And please keep in mind that COVID-19 was also starting in New York and that was causing major problems for my publisher.

Newhouse kept acting like I was intentionally being a problem when I couldn't stop a virus from shutting down a city.

While those bastards were picking on me and proved it with emails such as the one Leadwits had sent, that wasn't true in publishing. My publisher liked me. They naturally took their time doing their job as they liked to be thorough. We wanted only the best product we could have to give to the fans.

No wonder the federal attorneys couldn't get it through their heads. That whole projecting their sins onto us kept getting in the way.

Anyhow, the royalties had come in and as I'd kept telling Newhouse and crew in the fall, the royalties wouldn't be the amount Cockburn had said.

For one thing, they'd kept cancelling my appearances where I sold books.

"I don't see how this will help," had been Newhouse's redundant idiocy.

Both my agent and I had warned him that if I wasn't on the road to promote them that we'd be feeling it in February. Not to mention, the last book I'd released, Hogg had stopped dead in its tracks with her attacks. And I had the emails and texts to prove she was the ringleader.

So declining sales, meant declining royalties.

Duh!

There wasn't as much to milk now. What more could Newhouse sell? I was running out of assets to be strip-mined to pay for his overinflated salary. I supposed that was why, after almost a year, he'd finally come up with a plan.

Newhouse saw his little fun ending.

I wasn't amused given that he'd basically stolen a million dollars from me and handed it off to his friends.

Worse, we'd had two car wrecks trying to "declutter" the piece of shit house that Les had saddled me with.

Since I couldn't hire professionals to help me move as Lazy Les had done, and against court orders, stuck me with the bill, I was relying on my longtime friend Joan Hart, Rio and Rose to help whenever they could. It was killing us, especially since all of them came down with really nasty colds.

This was the beginning of COVID-19 and Rose was in her seventies.

*Ironic, right?* The entire time Les had been here, I'd never been well. I'd stayed sick for years, unable to get better. Yet they were coughing, wheezing and sneezing all over me and I didn't get so much as a sniffle. Even with the drastic changes in weather that I was in and out of.

Because I was no longer being poisoned.

We did get the house cleaned out and I could say beyond a shadow of a doubt that Les was a crazy motherfucker. There were no guns hidden in my house. Though I found the magazine clip for his Baretta in my downstairs safe.

Why? I had no idea. That gun was never kept there. He kept it in the upstairs gun safe.

Nor could I understand when it'd come to be in the downstairs safe. Why had it not been confiscated along with everything else when Oldham and House had raided my belongings?

For that matter, I'd been in the safe a number of times and couldn't recall seeing it.

Weird.

At any rate, I'd also found a couple of stray boxes of bullets Les had hidden throughout the house like an effing loon.

But no guns.

Other than my toy rifle I used at SF conventions.

Anyway, the realtor was amazed when he saw the house. "You really outdid yourself."

"Thanks. It wasn't easy."

My entire body had seized up. I could barely move, and I could no longer make a fist. I was lucky my friends were still talking to me.

And rather than being able to take a deep breath, Newhouse decided to salt my wounds.

How?

I finally, after more than a week of busting my ass for twenty-one hours a day, no exaggeration, sat down to answer emails.

"We need the title for the Mustang."

*Are you kidding me?*

Apparently, the stupid fucks had put my car up for auction without a clear and proper title. One would think that before they listed an item that they would want to make sure they had their paperwork in order.

But I forgot that I wasn't dealing with normal businesspeople.

I was dealing with the idiots of the universe who had worse entitlement issues than an uber rich, only-child on steroids.

For all of Newhouse's bravado and bullying bullshit of, "You don't own anything, Terri, get that through your head. We own it all. I am in charge. You have nothing and are nothing," that he'd been spouting off at me for months with a sick glee, he didn't have any rights without my cooperation.

Interesting.

They had to have me go get the title that I'd told them I didn't have for a car I didn't want them to sell.

This was all kinds of sick and twisted.

I included the auction house people in that statement. You weren't innocent either. *When you lie down with dogs, you get up with their fleas.* You knew what you were going to bed with. And you preyed on people, same as them.

I hope all of you get their syphilis because you were making money off other people's misery. I'd rather starve than earn a living that way. My parents raised me better than that.

Damn shame yours didn't do better by you.

I was harassed until eleven P.M. for a fifty-five-year-old car that under Tennessee law didn't need a title. Only a certificate of ownership, which I'd provided.

Wasn't good enough. With a broken foot and a body that was aching and during the COVID-

19 virus, I was to take even more time away from my job that was supposed to be earning money for all of them to swindle me out of and find the title office because they couldn't be bothered to harass the bastard who'd stolen the title out of my house when he left and had taken all the car titles.

The one who had no job and nothing better to do than torture me and his sons.

Okay.

Or better yet, since Mr. I-Am-In-Charge said that he owned everything, and I owned nothing and was too giddy to charge me out the ass, why couldn't Newhouse take his power of attorney and go get it? Newhouse apparently had nothing better to do with his useless life than bully me anyway and write dozens of emails ordering me around while charging me *three-hundred-and-ninety-five dollars an hour* just to harass me.

And yes, you read that correctly. The trustee was being paid *three-hundred-and-ninety-five dollars an hour* plus his attorney that I had protested was being paid *three-hundred-and-ninety-five dollars an hour*, which meant every time they were together, I was being charged *seven-hundred-and-ninety dollars* an hour *while in bankruptcy*.

And if they were with their bitch of an incompetent accountant, it was a grand total of *nine-hundred-sixty-five* dollars an hour.

What part of I was in bankruptcy did their itty-bitty brains not comprehend?

How could a bankruptcy court or judge approve such a sickening travesty?

It was as bad as the divorce judge who'd laughed while my attorney husband was surrounded by another six attorneys I was being forced to pay for while I was in bankruptcy.

There was nothing amusing about this as it tore my finances apart.

But that begged another question. If they were having trouble selling the Mustang and had listed it fraudulently without clear and proper title, what was going to happen when they did that with my mother's jewelry that my brother and sister owned?

It also got me to thinking about the trademarks Newhouse was so gung-ho to sell. While packing, I'd found the documentation where Les had fraudulently procured them. Where he'd forged my name and emails.

And I'd told Newhouse this. Which meant Newhouse intended to commit fraud.

Knowingly.

And if dealing with all this wasn't enough, I finally received the letter from my HOA about my dog that Les's old friend had been threatening me with.

My dog that seldom barked. The one we kept inside my home.

I found it interesting that no complaints about the dog began until after Les had started threatening Maddox to keep him from testifying about the poisoning. So, to hurt his son even more, he went after the one thing he knew his son loved.

His dog.

Wasn't it enough you murdered his cat, Les? That my baby came out of surgery, under the effects of anesthesia cursing you for the death of his beloved pet, but now you wanted to take another pet from him.

*How sick in the head are you?*

What was even worse was that I'd already been in touch with my HOA and had told them about the situation. That my neighbor had been accosting us. Told them about the three dogs next door that barked all the time and the dogs next door to them that also barked, day and night. The white dog three doors down that roamed the neighborhood at will. I even had video and audio recordings. Again, our pooch had always behaved, and we'd always monitored him.

Yet my neighbor accosted Joan so badly that the guy who'd come to pick up my cars had come back later that night to check on us.

And I had video and photos of Les's friend (my neighbor) behaving like an ass.

How much harassment was one person supposed to take? Especially from people who had direct ties back to my ex?

This was stalking and harassment at its purest form and no one would do anything to stop it or help me and my sons.

If Les had been the victim he claimed, then he'd have been like us and would have wanted out of the nightmare as fast as possible.

All my sons and I had ever wanted was to get Les out of our lives.

To be left alone so that we could live in peace.

But there was no way to get him gone.

He wouldn't let us go and the email from Leadwits proved it. Les was intent on control and abuse. He had no real desire to get out of our lives.

And the government, at the highest levels, was backing and aiding him in that abuse.

Not even the Attorney General's office would help. "We don't do anything for individuals. You'll have to report them to the Tennessee Board of Professional Responsibility."

The same Board that had continually refused to do anything. Because they wanted me to report him to the judge who was so clearly in their pockets.

That was the problem with how our government was set up. It was a game of *Hot Potato*. Each organization was too busy passing it along to the next with some bullshit reason as to why their organization didn't have responsibility over it.

It reminded me of the old movie, *Gotcha*, where the guy was trying to get papers to return home from East Berlin. The woman looked at him and said, "Visa?"

He handed it over.

"This is expired! You cannot leave with this."

"Where do I go to get it renewed?"

"Next window!"

He goes to the window and the same exact woman then moved over. "Yes?"

He just stared at her in disbelief.

"What do you need?"

Exasperated, he handed her his Visa. "I need a renewal."

Then she forced him to the other window for it to be stamped. We mocked that in the 1980s, but that was America in the first quarter of the twenty-first century.

Pushed from pillar to post, and each one of them said the same thing to me.

"I've never seen or heard of anything like this! It's awful!"

But no one was willing to help.

**FEBRUARY 27**

AGAIN NEWHOUSE CONTINUED TO harass me over the title to my vintage Mustang that I hadn't wanted sold.

All day long.

Even though I was trying to get my house ready to be listed with a broken foot, while trying to do my actual job that all the fucking leeches were draining my life over, while they threatened to lock me in jail if I didn't work because I wasn't able to focus on a happy-ending novel with their constant threats coming at me, night and day.

Literally.

They emailed me from morning, to noon, to as late as midnight with their threats.

"I don't understand why you can't write a *romance* novel!"

*Well, Dipshits, it's a little hard to concentrate when I'm answering all your bullshit emails, all day long, and you keep me in a state of constant turmoil. Not to mention, I really don't feel like writing a fucking romance with a happily-ever-after when my Prince Charming tried to kill me, robbed my children, killed my cat and you bastards are helping him to continue to abuse us all.*

That dog don't bark. And the fact that none of them could understand that, made me seriously weep for their families and doubt their own mental conditions.

I wasn't insane. They were.

Not to mention their ability to reason and function in society.

Especially, the idiot known as Martha. How she'd ever become a U.S. Trustee lent credence to all those jokes people made about government workers and their exceptionally low I.Q.s. Having been a government employee, I used to take offense to that.

But then, Les was a former government employee, too, and now, having dealt with Martha, Newhouse and crew, well...

Sometimes stereotypes existed for a reason. That was all I was going to say on that point.

Anyway, I received the lovely news from Melissa that Cockburn was no longer speaking to her as she was now furious that Melissa had dared to question her outrageous attorney fees that she'd charged me that month (again, while I was in bankruptcy and after I'd just paid them two hundred thousand dollars). After all, Cockburn had refused to allow us to depose Dipshit for the divorce.

"With the bankruptcy going on, you can't proceed with any of the divorce. It's stalled."

Yet that bitch had dared to bill me another forty grand for proceeding to do divorce research, subpoenas and such on my case, while denying *us* discovery.

*How does that work, bitch?* Especially when I was the one paying everyone's salary?

The blatant robbery of them all was the most galling and disgusting display of miscarried justice that I'd ever seen.

But who would stop them?

Certainly not Bitsy Dullard who kept telling me to take it up with the corrupt judge who always sided with them because they were his former business partners.

And we now know how corrupt he was after Leadwits put it in writing.

Do not screw this up because Dinky will have field day on you if you try to dismiss (which will never happen) in this case.

I was a special case. For Dinky and all of them. Not paranoia.

Fact.

They made no bones about it. They had no love for me, which was fine as it was a mutual hate-fest going on. Especially given the fact that I was being raked over coals. I was done with their cruelty and mismanagement of my property.

Didn't help when I saw the paperwork where Newhouse had claimed that I owed *seventy-four-thousand dollars* on a lease that Dipshit Newhouse had forced me to break. And yes, you read that correctly, too. I'd only owed a couple more payments for the SUV I'd been forced to lease when the other Dipshit (Les) had stolen the family car from us, and the idiot judge had allowed the parent with no children who would speak to him to keep the family car.

Yet the parent who had a high school student and who needed to buy groceries and run a business was left with one vintage car that wasn't road-worthy and one two-seater.

So instead of allowing me to keep the car I needed, Dipshit Newhouse thought it would be smarter to break the lease and add another *seventy-four-thousand dollars* to my debt than to let me pay out a couple thousand dollars and have a car for that interim.

That was how stupid and vindictive that bastard was. And the federal and state judges (and Trustee Martha who'd "hand-picked" him as my trustee) were all good with his idiocy.

Because the judges in Williamson County, Tennessee were all absolute fucking morons who wouldn't listen to both sides of any case. They were too busy running their idiotic mouths and proving the old adage that it was far better to be quiet and allow people to think you're stupid than to open your mouth and remove all doubt.

They constantly removed all doubt.

*How do I know?*

Aside from the horrible miscarriage of justice delivered to me by multiple judges, I was talking to my accountant who had been talking to a woman in her accounting firm, a former legal assistant in a prominent Williamson County law firm.

Her friend said, "The Manly case isn't so bad. I've seen a whole lot worse while I worked for those lawyers."

I was stunned by those words. "Are you fucking kidding me!"

"That's what she said. They are famous for tearing apart lives. Sucking people into a vortex so bad that they were forced to walk away with absolutely nothing but the clothes on their backs and start over without so much as a car."

She wasn't kidding. I knew of a case where one of the judges here had forced a woman to live out of her car. *Google it.*

It was a real case that really happened.

Our judges were famous for their cruelty and nonsensical rulings. They were power hungry and out of control.

No one should have that kind of power over someone else's lives. I was sickened by it.

My sons couldn't have hated their father more.

Something proven when Nick received a text message from Caleb. "Heard you were being thrown out of the house. Dad said you could come live with him at the cabin."

Nick was livid. "I'd rather live in a sack with you, Mom. Fuck that bastard. And fuck Caleb."

Those words broke my heart. I'd spent their whole lives trying to keep my boys from fighting. In one fell swoop, Les had broken them apart.

"That's what Les is good at." Maddox no longer called him Dad. Neither did Nick. "He'd play us off each other."

Joan, who'd returned from Georgia to help us pack up the house had scowled at them over dinner. "I don't understand why you didn't stand up to him while he was here."

Maddox scoffed. "We didn't know. He accused me constantly of being a parasite. Get out, you worthless bastard! You're a bad example for Nick. You've graduated college. Get out! Even though I had a job and was writing my novel and posting to my online comic. He accused me every day of doing nothing. Then, when he and Hogg ran me out and I was leaving for Japan, he started crying every day. 'Don't leave me! You can't leave me! I want to go with you.' The fucker's psycho."

I snorted. "He's not kidding. He did the same thing with me. 'You have to need me. I want you to need me.' Then he'd start screaming at me that it was too much pressure because he didn't want to be needed all the time for everything."

"Yeah." Nick let out a growl. "It infuriated me. He wouldn't let us do shit. He'd hide stuff so that we couldn't do anything without him and then curse us because we had to ask him for it. Or make us use tutors when we didn't want them."

"Oh my God, yeah!" Maddox came around the counter. "That made me insane. 'Use all your resources. Why would you do it yourself when you can hire someone else? You have the money to have them do it!' He never would let us learn how to do anything and then he'd curse us for being stupid and useless after he'd made us useless."

I shook my head. "And I was too sick to know what was going on. They didn't tell me."

"Because he told us not to bother you. 'Mom's making money and she doesn't have time for you." Nick sighed. "I was so destroyed by him and Hogg that I locked myself in my room and never came out. I couldn't stand the sight of that bitch. It made me so sick to my stomach that I thought I had an ulcer."

Maddox nodded. "Me, too. I hated her. If I came out, she'd be in my face, yelling at me. Les wouldn't do anything, except take up for his slut. And Mom looked so bad that I didn't want to tell her anything because it was obvious that she was too sick to fight him. I thought she was going to die. She looked awful."

"Yeah." Joan sighed. "I remember. None of us thought she'd live through another year."

That included me.

But I wanted to lighten the mood. So, I looked over to Nick. "Are you going to move in with your dad?"

He glared at me. "When hell freezes over."

"What did you tell your brother?"

"I'm not answering that prick. Even with all this going on, I'm happy. Last thing I want is them back in my life, tearing it apart."

"Yeah." Maddox grinned. "You don't open your doors to vampires. They'll suck you dry."

The only problem was, I couldn't drive them out of our lives. They were circling me like the vultures they were.

Nothing and no one could get them off me. Apparently, there wasn't enough garlic in the universe to get them gone.

What would it take to make Les get a life? He'd left us and now, years later, he was still torturing us.

What would it take to get *us* out of this vortex?

# MARCH 2

**W**ELL AT LEAST MY ATTORNEY was no longer in the desert. Sad when that had become a highlight to my pathetic life. But it was a hectic day of fretting about my eldest being able to bring his fiancée over.

Something that shouldn't have been a problem at all since my son only needed to prove he had a minimum of seventeen thousand dollars of assets.

My son whose father had stolen almost two hundred thousand dollars out of his trust fund the night he'd put him on a plane for Japan after looking him straight in the eye. "Don't worry, son. Everything will be fine. Nothing's going to happen. I'll hold down the fort while you're away."

Lying fucking bastard knew at the time he'd spoken those words that he'd already stolen his son's money from him.

Then after Maddox had returned, he'd stood by and allowed an illegal search and seizure of our home, where they'd confiscated Maddox's last sixty thousand dollars out of his bank account.

*May you all rot in hell.*

*Especially you, Tom Newhouse. You are a special lowlife, barely surpassed by the fuck-up I married.*

How his own wife and children could ever trust him, I had no idea. It made my skin crawl to be in the same room with him, as he was such a two-faced back-biting little shit. The kind of smarmy character they used in Hollywood to betray their best friends and allies.

Power hungry and too stupid to ever pull off anything effectively. He liked to exert what little authority he had. And on this day, I got a full dose of how stupid he actually was.

After having made me jump through all his hoops, Melissa texted to let me know I could "drop the insurance on the cars."

So, after wasting thousands and thousands of dollars of my time and that of insurance adjuster's, as well as having run up another good ten thousand dollars or more in attorney fees while I was in bankruptcy over something completely stupid since the auction house had liability insurance to cover the inventory they sold, I now got to drop it.

*Stupid, thy name is truly Tom Newhouse.*

Really, if you needed a job, apply to the government. Actual brain functioning was obviously not required.

Zombies welcomed.

The truly stupid seemed to be a sought after species for them.

And it got even better. While speaking to the guy from the auction house who had to come all the way back to my home (because Newhouse insisted on it) to have me sign the titles, which wasn't legally necessary as they'd already been signed by Les, we discovered that Les, the lawyer, hadn't signed them in the proper place.

Les had intentionally signed them improperly.

And I knew he'd done that on purpose. How?

Remember Princess Drama from years ago and her mother, Psycho Drama? The pair Les had gone to visit in Georgia to dig up dirt on me so that they could lie for him?

Well, if you recall part of their original drama had been Les repossessing Princess Drama's car from her after she'd failed to make payments to us for it.

Les had learned a whole lot about car titles in the state of Tennessee, especially after Psycho Drama had tried to have him locked up for car theft. The judge had publicly ridiculed Les for being an idiot and a lawyer when Les had said he didn't know such-and-such about titles and contracts.

"Well, you're a lawyer, aren't you?"

And at that time, Les *was* a practicing lawyer. He still had his law office and an actual legal secretary, not Hogg passing her stupid self off as one.

Believe me, it wasn't a lesson that ole Les forgot. In fact, it was one he continued to rant about up until the night he walked out of my house and stole from his children.

He'd obsessively taught himself all about car titles after that.

So, it was with certainty that I could say that he knew exactly what he'd been doing when he signed in the wrong place. Another game he played with everyone.

But then, that was what Les did best.

And the Passive-Aggressive bitch known as Newhouse deserved to have to deal with it given his own little powerplays that he constantly did to others.

Two little sick in the head peas in a pod. Sadly, I was trapped between the dueling penises as they warred with each other, and I couldn't get away.

Not to mention, I'd heard from another attorney in town who said that they had a conflict and couldn't represent me for the bankruptcy.

Had Les gone to every fucking attorney in town and put up a retainer to keep me from using them? This was ridiculous.

I wanted out of this hick, inbred town and away from these corrupt bastards who twisted the law and threatened me every single hour of the day. But I knew they weren't going to let me go until they'd drained every last cent from my accounts and left me with nothing.

The only real question was why was Les so willing to let them do it, if he had no intention of ever working, and wanted to live off my money for the rest of his life?

What did he stand to gain by allowing them to ruin me?

As stupid as he was, even he had to see that ruining me was the worst thing he could do. Yet he was gleefully allowing his team to run us into the ground and strip away every cent I'd ever earned at the end of our lives when we wouldn't be able to rebuild.

*Who does that?*

Why would a judge allow this to happen?

Why were there no stop gaps to protect an innocent party or the children?

That was the most sickening part. That my children had no say and no advocate.

Where was that Hollywood Tom Cruise character to ride in and save the day?

Sadly, this was reality and there wasn't one. All I had was a circle of vultures who needed to lose their bar licenses. A bunch of soulless bastards and outdated laws that served no purpose.

And the only thing I heard in my head was the litany of my accountant telling me that I wasn't alone.

"It happens all the time in this town. Once you get in that vortex, you had to lose everything and start over with nothing."

But I was almost sixty years old. No one should have to lose a lifetime of their hard work because of one fucking idiot who needed mental help.

And because he'd been able to fall in with a pack of conscienceless jackals who'd all admitted he was crazy.

*All of them.*

How could this be allowed to continue when his own lawyers knew he was unhinged? Yet they were all too willing to prey on me?

Shame on the entire Board of Professional Responsibility and on the entire State of Tennessee that all of you would allow this to happen. And especially Judge Dinky and every Dinky out there for ruining a family.

For destroying my sons' futures.

Karma would come for all of you. I believed that in my heart and soul. For what you'd allowed to happen, there would have to be an accounting. If not in this life, then in the next. For no one should be allowed to do this to so many and get away with it.

And the worst, most sickening thought was the knowledge that I wasn't the only one.

That by turning to my government for help, I had only been abused more. Instead of helping me, they'd taken it as a chance to stick their hands in and take even more, while knowing I couldn't do anything to defend myself.

While threatening my freedom and to put me in jail if I dared to tell others how they were abusing me and my children. That they were stealing from us and ordering me to break the law.

They had the audacity to tell me that I should be grateful to them for their abuse. Like all good abusers, because they'd handpicked Newhouse as my abuser.

"We could have given you someone much worse." Those had been Martha's exact words. A woman with a Department of Justice email.

*Thank you, Martha, for your kindness.*

What was it with abusers that while they hurt and tore through their victims that they always believed we should be grateful to them for hurting us? Les had done me the same way, too.

The mental gymnastics that it took for them to cast themselves in that light had always baffled me. Was that what allowed them to be the villains they were?

"I'm tearing your life apart and I'm doing this in retaliation for you pissing me off. I'm hurting you for your own good or because you're making me hurt you. Now say, thank you!"

*Fuck you.*

*Take your retaliation and stick it straight up your skinny little ass, Martha. I won't say thank you for retaliating against me.*

And she used the word *retaliation*.

Not to mention, it got better.

By this time, they had almost doubled my debt. Even after selling off my assets that included my clothing, my reliable transportation, etc. Items being systematically picked off because Newhouse wanted to punish me (he had said those words on more than one occasion).

The only asset I had left was my home.

Because they wanted to "punish" me.

Newhouse needed to lose his job because no one should be that incompetent or cruel. I wouldn't trust this bitch to run a shit show. He was too stupid even for that.

So, no Martha, I felt no gratitude. She didn't really want to know what I felt toward them. *Vengeance is mine sayeth the Lord, I shall repay.*

I expected the Big Guy to deliver on that promise. It was the only thing that kept me going. That and the fact that my children had no one else in this world to watch after them. Their worst fear was being left alone with that bastard.

Something made worse by Les's invitation. While Nick had left earlier that day on a road trip with friends to Ohio, he was terrified that he'd be stuck with his dad.

"Don't leave me with Les, Mom. I need you."

He kept checking in with me every few hours. Like he was afraid I'd vanish on him while he was gone the way his pathetic father had.

"I'm right here, Boo. Not going anywhere."

But I didn't know where we would be living once the house sold. I couldn't get Melissa to file the papers with the court to overturn that decision.

Worse?

Because I was in bankruptcy and Newhouse refused to let me out of it, I couldn't pull a credit report and rent someplace to live.

That meant that I would be homeless again.

With my kids.

And no one seemed to give shit out of all the attorneys I was paying hundreds of thousands of dollars to that I wasn't allowed to keep a single cent of.

Welcome to America.

Home of the corrupt.

**B**ECAUSE I WAS NEVER allowed a single moment of peace; the next bomb was dropped at 5:09 in the evening. After everyone was gone and I couldn't get a hold of an attorney or anyone else. Not that it would have mattered. The asshole in charge, Newhouse, who'd started it, was out on vacation.

As they all kept doing.

In order to prolong my agony and in what seemed like an intentional effort to frustrate me, one of them was always out on vacation, usually right after they'd taken a huge chunk of my money from me.

*Funny how that worked.*

The day had started out with a reminder from my decent, reasonably priced accountant that today was the day we had to put together the bills to go beg Newhouse and his overpriced moron for money to live on and run my business. The business that all these motherfuckers were draining dry and expecting me to pay everyone's bills out of.

So, I frantically pulled all the bills together while needing to vacate my home from the snotty, pretentious couple who wanted to come look at it.

A woman who was so much like my mother-in-law that she should have been sterilized at birth. Over and over again, she kept making comments about her five kids and how she didn't want them at home, not even the one who came home from college to visit. Some people, such as Les and his family, should never spawn. Having been raised by parents who had no business bringing kids into the world, trust me when I've said we'd be better off if these people were sterilized. You had to have a license to drive and fish, or even hunt. For that matter, it was harder to take home a stray cat or dog. But in this country, we'd let any arbitrary asshole walk out of the hospital with a baby because why?

Two people screwed each other for less than five minutes under who knew what circumstances.

They may not have even been sober or remembered the occasion.

No parenting class required. "Here, folks, take this, the most helpless creature on the planet that can grow up to become a serial killer if you fail as a parent, and good luck! You don't need any instructions or common sense. Just wing it!"

I will never forget the day I was finally able to bring my eldest home from the hospital after all the weeks he'd spent in NICU. Immediately, I'd called my mother while I was in a panic. "Mom, what do I do? He's so tiny and frail. I'm scared to death I might hurt him by accident."

"Oh, don't worry, Terri. They're hard to kill."

Which pretty much said it all about my childhood and what my mother thought about raising children. As I'd so often said, my hard-ass drill sergeant father who took mercy on none was my sympathetic parent.

The man who was famous for saying, "Ah hell, Terri, I went to war to get peace from your mother." And the ever-eternal phrase that rang in my ears whenever I felt like crying. "Shut-up, Terri. I've gutted men you whined less than you!"

Anyway, I'd been forced out of my home with my employees for most of the day. We'd finally been able to get back to work when I opened my email to this:

> Tom cannot figure out a way that to fund Comic Con and pay your regular living expenses at this time *(Please keep in mind that I had been telling him about the expense and they had been nagging me about this since December and the bastard had just sold all my personal property, so he had a massive infusion of cash)*. The February income was well less than everyone expected, and we have this hearing next week to determine if Tom has to pay the attorney fees or not. He's told all of the attorneys he cannot pay any more fees and he is trying very hard to keep the administrative fees down, but he is afraid you will not have enough money for living expenses and this will have to go to Chapter 7.
>
> I understand you feel strongly that Comic Con is critical to your career. If that's the case, the only one that may be able to influence him is Bob *(my agent)*...
>
> I talked with Leadwits and unfortunately, the bankruptcy stay does not affect the criminal contempt matter, and so I do need to continue drafting this application. It's a lot of work and I will warn you that the Supreme Court only agrees to hear 7% of the applications- so if I am going to do this it needs to be my focus this week. I've got the outline going and am still researching some caselaw. I'll let you know when I have a draft for you.

*Fun times, eh?* I had the threat of jail looming over me because of Dinky's tantrum. The state might have to pay to incarcerate me for a full ten days because I dared to call a pedophile a pedophile and Dinky allowed the pedophile to go free. To this day, his grotesque outburst in court needed to be questioned. No one had that virulent an outburst and went on the attack against an innocent person for no reason.

Everyone who'd witnessed it that day (including the bailiffs) had agreed that Dinky went way beyond the pale. The fact that he'd allowed me out of jail proved that he knew it, too. Rather than commute my sentence or pardon me during COVID when Dinky was letting real criminals out so as to "protect" the criminals, they were recklessly pursuing this.

Against an innocent law-abiding citizen.

While under a state mandate from the Supreme Court to let *any* and all nonviolent offenders out of jail.

Dinky was insisting I go to jail.

To protect a pedophile and judge that everyone in town knew was under investigation for his own wrongdoings.

Why?

Because Tennessee was the third most corrupt state in the country and Nashville was its crown jewel of corruption.

And I'd been caught in the middle of this fucking nightmare because of one selfish, greedy monster who decided to walk out during the half an hour I dared to sleep after I put my baby on a plane to another country.

The reason my income was down? Both my agent and I had told Dumb Fuck Newhouse and crew repeatedly that when he made me cancel New York Comic Con and my London event, among others, that it would seriously impact my future income and royalties. That my royalties were dependent upon my appearances as my appearances drove my sales.

Same for Les and his pack of jackals who had insisted that I cancel events prior to the bankruptcy as they'd deemed them "unnecessary." This from Les who had written countless emails to my attorneys in the Dumas case to tell them how vital my appearances were.

Funny how every year we'd attended Comic Con New York, I had a number one bestselling book. When we stopped going, I slid out of the number one slot. Could it have anything to do with the fact that I lost massive exposure at one single event?

Never mind all the other revenue streams and major connections that came to me during those events, such as my movie deal. And my deal with Bradford Exchange.

And we won't even talk about how I would cancel an event and then Newhouse, once it was too late to put it back in place, would then call up and say, "Can you still go?"

*No, stupid fuck.* This wasn't like grounding your daughter from her friend's party. You couldn't wait until fifteen minutes before the party and then say, "Sorry, honey, but if you promise to behave, I'll let you go."

It took months of planning for an event, and they had strict deadlines that had to be met. Once a deadline passed, it passed. You couldn't get hotel rooms. You couldn't book flights. You couldn't ship your merchandise to reach the show in time.

And this was the stupid shit-stain they had put in charge of my business who couldn't understand the most basic fact of how any business ran.

Him or his way overpriced accountant who was part of that more than one hundred-thousand-dollar administrative fee he was "trying so hard to cut back on."

My accounting didn't cost thirty-one thousand dollars a year, never mind for four months.

And as I'd said repeatedly, I'd grown sick of having the Chapter 7 threat thrown at me every waking minute of the day when it wasn't even feasible. I didn't meet the Means Test. Yet that they assured me they would put me in it, regardless of the law.

Apparently, the laws of the country and of bankruptcy didn't apply to Tennessee trustees any more than the laws applied to old Dinky.

"I don't care what the law is."

That motto went from the state to the federal court of Tennessee. Because those trustees seemed mighty sure that the judge was going to rubber stamp whatever nonsense they put before her. And Melissa agreed.

"She will trust them and not question it."

Was this true of all our courts in every state?

None of the innocent could be trusted? Only the lying lawyers?

We were fucked, people. God have mercy on us.

Every time I asked a question or made a comment.

Boom!

There it was. A new, terrifying threat. Now I couldn't even ask for money to run my business without the threat of being ruined.

Not to mention, I should never have been forced to pay for Les's attorneys given that he'd robbed me, and my children and I had a court order saying that he had to pay for his portion of the divorce himself.

The only reason I was in that mess was because Newhouse had fucked up his only job and, contrary to the warnings of my attorney, had allowed them to pillage my estate. She had fore-warned him what Les's team of jackals was going to do and rather than do his job to protect my estate, he'd given them open access to write a blank check for however much money they wanted out of my accounts.

Yet now half a million more dollars had gone to Les and his jackals, and I was being threatened again.

All because of the incompetent U.S. Trustee who was threatening me while strip mining everything I'd ever worked for or acquired in my entire life, including the little rock ring my son had made for me for in grade school.

Because they wanted to punish me for daring to question their illegal activities and threats. I prayed that Newhouse burned in hell alongside Les and the rest of them. His own daughter wanted to be a writer. God help her, for I saw the future her own father was guaranteeing for her.

For the record, this was my response:

> I'm ccing Bob in here as he will be calling you later to discuss. What you saw in February was exactly what Bob and I warned you about when we began canceling events last year. I tried my best to explain to you, as did Bob, how my industry worked. Interest in my work and book sales are dependent upon my appearance at these events. While I may not make a ton of money at them, or any at times, the fans see me at them, and we hand out free samples and books there which then drives the sales of other books and generates revenue for my work.

> New York was a massive hit to my revenue when you made me cancel it. Bob and I warned you last year that we would feel that impact and we have. The same was true for London that you also made me cancel and for Australia and other events Cockburn and crew made me cancel. We're in Nashville, I'm sure you're all familiar with No-Show Jones. Not showing up to events when you've been booked for them is catastrophic for us and it harms our bottom line and reputations with the fans.

> It took me thirteen years to get my booth space at Comic Con San Diego and if I lose it, they will never allow me to have it back. That event has helped to build me a lot of fans and has been instrumental in getting me other deals such as the movie deal Les destroyed, and other revenue streams such as the coloring books, dolls and countless other offers that have come in over the years.

> It is critical that I be there.

> As for my revenue, it would be a lot easier to keep it going if I was able to focus on my work and not have me and my staff constantly pulled off it to answer questions that I've answered a hundred times, look for paperwork that I've already submitted after I've submitted it, etc. Now we're having to be uprooted and constantly leave the house instead of filling orders and we can't plan ahead, nor have we had any kind of budget to order new merchandise. Instead, I've been repeatedly questioned and second-guessed whenever I've tried to order merchandise and store supplies. These constant and redundant hoops have made it impossible for us to focus on running the business and make money.

> Just as it's been making it impossible for me to focus on my primary job of writing while I answer the same questions repeatedly and am worried constantly over the same matters that never seem to get resolved. I don't understand why a Chapter 7 should still be looming given how much money was just made in the auction and how much money just came in. And more

will be on the way once my editor finishes her editorial letter and I am given my edits, provided I am given time to do the edits once I have them.

The store is still making money. However, it is impossible to create and continue to do my job when every time I ask for the bare minimum to run my business I am met not only with resistance, but threats of personal and financial disaster that everyone here is well aware will put me on welfare for the rest of my life and prevent me from having a way to support myself or my family and staff in the future. No one should be expected to live under constant and unrelenting threats of ruin.

This isn't a frivolous expense. If you expect me to stay in business, then I need the money to run my business. Not allowing me to go to Comic Con is the same as refusing to provide fuel to a trucking company. While the gas costs money and doesn't seem to make any money back, the trucks can't deliver any goods to any stores unless that gas goes in the tank. Comic Con is my fuel.

I don't have a book out this year. If I'm not out in the public, I won't have ANY royalties come this August. It is more critical than ever that I am in the public eye and hand-pushing my books to the readers. Those books will not move unless I am there to sell them face-to-face. That is how we find our new readers.

Failing to provide me with the money now will only worsen the situation. As we have told you in the past, this is how my money is made. I am in this situation because none of you have listened to me while I have been hammered by unrelenting attorney fees no human being should be strangled with and all of the lawyers have interfered with my business while expecting to get ninety-nine percent of all the profits from it. Les didn't build the business. I did. If you want my company to generate revenue, then you need to listen to me and provide me with the means I need to run it properly and not interfere with it.

All of my past success was a direct result of what I have done and how I very wisely managed my money. I am only here today because of inexcusable lawyer fees caused by Les and his actions.

If you will give me what I need to make money, I will make money. As my sons say, give Mom a dollar and she will turn it into twenty. Give Dad a twenty and it's gone.

Of course, no one responded, other than my agent who said he would call me in the morning, and the autoresponder that told me Newhouse was on vacation.

Again.

Meanwhile, what was I looking forward to? Leaving my house all day the next day while people came to criticize it and throw me out, onto the street.

My bright spot was that my son had been approved for a loan through his job and so I was going with him and his brother to find a condo for them. They would at least have a roof over their heads.

I would be homeless, but my sons wouldn't. That was all that mattered.

Nick came home from his trip where he and his friend had gone to pick up a dog for his friend's girl, just before midnight and hugged me. "I love you so much, Mom. Thank you for everything you've done for us."

I had no idea why he'd said that. "Love you, too, Boo."

Maddox followed him into my office. "I got the approval for immigration. Will you go with me to sign the papers tomorrow?"

"Of course, baby. I'm so happy for you! You did a great job getting all that together on your own."

"Nah. My girl did most of the paperwork and you found my lawyer for me."

But he'd paid for his lawyer, himself.

"I'm still proud of you."

"I couldn't have done it without you, Mom. Thank you."

Those words made me smile. It was something in all the decades I'd been married that his father had never once said to me. Not even when he got his law degree that I and my father had paid for. That I had helped him study for and had written papers for him that he'd turned in.

His law degree was more mine than his.

Yet never once had Les ever said, "Thank you, Terri."

Not once.

But that was okay. Unlike the worthless Snooty, I'd succeeded in raising men. Not snotty little crybabies.

I guess I had a lot to thank my father for, after all.

What I wouldn't give to put the whole lot of these jackals up against my family. They wouldn't last a day.

But then they knew nothing of the integrity and honor that my family had instilled in me. While my family hadn't been perfect, they had been moral and decent.

They weren't thieves.

And I was tired of being abused and being told to be grateful to those who were abusing me. It was sick that now even my own attorney was telling me to be grateful to my abusers.

"He's only trying to help." It was the same sickening litany that Les had used with Hogg while she sat there and shattered my Nick. While they both sat there and poisoned us.

Why was there no one here to help?

And how and when would this hell end?

MARCH 6

ANYONE WHO HAS RAISED a child with Autism knows the special challenges that were a part of that diagnosis. Having grown up with a very low-functioning sister with Cerebral Palsy, I was very much aware of how much worse my fate could have been. Unlike my sister, my sons could at least speak, hear, see and bathe themselves.

Because I grew up with a Down Syndrome cousin and Cerebral Palsy sister and other special needs children around me, I always counted myself very lucky with my boys. Unlike Les who only focused on what they were lacking and on how difficult they could be.

Such as when Les had left in the middle of the night without a word of warning.

The one thing that marked Autism was that we all have trouble with transitions. We don't like for anything to cause a disturbance to our routines. We had to be adequately prepared for the coming change.

So, I'd been doing my best to warn the boys about the move. Had been keeping them abreast as best I could.

This was also one of the things Newhouse and I had gotten crossed up over a few months earlier when I'd wanted Nick in a meeting.

"I wouldn't let one of my children attend this. It'll disturb him."

*How nice for you that you have "normal" children.* But Autistic children, and I was one of them, can't process information the same way other people do. We don't get emotional unless we're unprepared for something.

As long as we knew what to expect, even if that something was chaos, we were alright. Remarkably so.

What was difficult for us were the so-called "normal" people of the world who refused to be flexible enough to tolerate our differences and to not judge us.

If something caught us off-guard, we needed a moment to catch our breath and process it. Not because we were emotional or difficult, but because we needed time to understand why things weren't working the way they were supposed to. Why the system had broken down and failed us.

That was what we had a hard time dealing with. The prime order had failed, and we needed to understand why. There was a system, and it was always supposed to work.

A good example of this was when Maddox was in third grade. Being the room mother, I planned their class party, as I'd done for all my sons' classes. I'd made up little gift bags for every child there and a couple of extras in case someone had a brother or sister at the party I didn't know about.

Maddox insisted that he hand out all the bags. But when we got to the six leftover bags, he started over, handing them out.

"Baby, you can't do that."

"Why? They're supposed to be handed out."

"We don't have enough to give everyone two."

"But they're supposed to be handed out."

The fact that it was unfair and that the unfairness of his "favorite" classmates having two bags to others having only one didn't register over the fact that the bags were supposed to be given out. That was their purpose. It was the natural order.

My natural order was the "fairness" of everyone only getting one bag and to ensure everyone had their one bag. So, we had a clash of what our "prime" directives were.

When I refused to allow him to hand out the extra bags, he had a full-on nuclear meltdown in his classroom.

Because my prime order overrode his.

On this day, it happened again. Because we were on the verge of losing the house and I was being threatened with being homeless and on the street every second, I couldn't sleep.

I knew Maddox was about to get married and that Nick was still in high school. While Nick had a part-time job, Maddox was making good money, working in finance. He had more than enough money to pay for an apartment (they had decided against a condo), and with his fiancée on the brink of coming into the country, it was time to get them someplace to live.

Maddox, being the stubborn go-getter, ran out without consulting me and grabbed up the first place he could find.

It was terrifying. There were burglar bars on apartment doors. And shattered glass in a space in the parking lot where someone's car had been broken into the night before. Having been raised on the wrong side of town, in a similar place and having birthed Maddox and Caleb while living in unsafe apartments of this nature, I was well versed in what kind of life my son was about to step into.

He wasn't.

And I hadn't crawled out of the gutter and busted my ass for over three decades to watch my sons crawl back into that same hellhole that I'd scrimped and saved to get them out of.

This was that squalor that my babies had lived in:

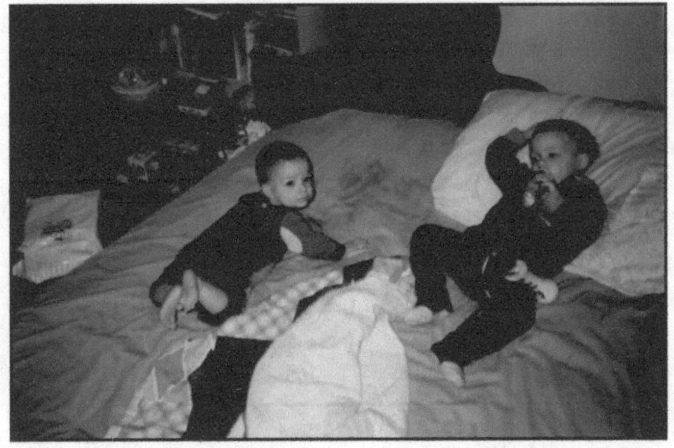

*Our apartment at that time.*

Never in my life had I hated anyone as much as I hated Les. You fucking evil monster that you'd stolen the money I had set aside for them that would have bought them a house in a safe place. The cabin that you had sworn to both of them would be theirs once they were old enough that you had stolen out from under them.

It broke my heart that anyone should have to live like that anywhere in the world. Every day of my life that I'd spent living in a place like that, afraid of becoming a victim to that environment had been impressed hard on my soul.

I was scarred from it. Below was the house I grew up in.

*Our stove/oven didn't work*

And in that moment, I held every last one of the vultures who'd done this to me accountable. The judges, the attorneys, particularly Cockburn, the trustees and especially Les and Hogg.

Monsters every one.

*May you all get what you deserve and more.*

My sons thought I was being ridiculous.

Maddox was angry. "This is why I didn't want you to come. I knew you wouldn't like it."

"No mother would like *this*. You can't live here."

"It's all I can afford!"

"Did you look around?"

"Of course, I did!"

Bull. Shit. I knew it for a fact. My baby was terribly stubborn. And it didn't help that he had his Autistic best friend with him.

"Did you try Iron Horse?" It was another set of apartments, in a safer environment.

His best friend, Ashton spoke up. "Those are over three thousand dollars a month."

"No. They're not. Apartments are roughly the same in this area." So, I drove them over to them.

I was right and they were wrong.

And Maddox was furious at me for being right. Because I had messed up his plan. He wanted to be the savior.

But their safety came first.

We argued for two days.

I finally found them a safe apartment.

Then, Maddox got the brilliant idea to go get a new car.

My head felt as if it would explode. "You can't do that."

"It's what credit is for."

Oh. My. God! "You don't need the stress of being under that kind of commitment. Do not tie-up every cent of your check. Your car is paid for."

"You can pay me back, Mom."

Could I? Not at the rate we were going. This fucking divorce and bankruptcy appeared to be endless. "Maddox, I can't have that stress on me right now. Please. Do not take out another loan. You can't use your current car as a down payment. I'm under a court order that forbids me from selling your car, and an idiot fucking judge who would love to put me in jail for violating a court order."

We were still in the middle of this fight.

Meanwhile, I was trying to prepare myself and them for the fact that I might be headed to jail to serve out Dinky's ridiculous sentence. My attorney had called to tell me that she was trying, but it wasn't looking good. I'd sent off my papers to the governor and corrections department, begging for clemency, but honestly, didn't hold out a lot of hope given that Tennessee was the most backwards, corrupt shithole I'd ever seen.

Why not lock up a hard-working citizen for two weeks because a judge refused to do his job and couldn't hold his own temper. Last time I checked, they were supposed to only rule on facts. Not on their own prejudices and assumptions.

You know the three main judicial rules that all judges were supposed to follow:

*A Judge Should Uphold the Integrity and Independence of the Judiciary.*

*A Judge Should Avoid Impropriety and the Appearance of Impropriety in All Activities.*

*A Judge Should Perform the Duties of the Office* Fairly, Impartially and Diligently.

That last one was the one that stuck in my craw as it was the one that Dinky couldn't follow at all, and yet Williamson County kept him on the bench. Again, he was under an order from the Tennessee Supreme Court to release criminals from jail to protect their health, but he was more than willing to put an innocent citizen in jail because of his own hissy fit.

The Judiciary Board of Review refused to act on the fact that they had a madman on the bench that everyone agreed was out of control.

Yeah. Three rules so simple even a child could follow, yet this one sadistic bastard couldn't because he was too busy insulting me every time I walked into his courtroom.

*For the record, Dinky, I wasn't the monster. You were.*

Monsters were the creatures who destroyed people's lives with no regard for what they were doing. No care. No conscience.

That has never been me.

That, Lord Skeletor, was you and your whole crew of jackals that you had chosen to surround yourself with.

And on that day, I received news from Melissa that I'd have to be back in court on Monday, at nine, to face him and them again.

Yee-fucking-haw.

Just what I wanted to do. Just what I needed, especially on the day when I'd also received news that my editor was still sick and hadn't had time to get to my latest book that I'd handed in at Christmas.

No editorial letter. No pay.

No pay. No hope of ending my nightmare.

Even better? On this day, I received an email from the realtor telling me that that two couples wanted my house and that he was expecting an offer.

Good and bad. Bad because it meant I was about to be homeless.

Good because it might put me one step closer to getting out of the bankruptcy.

However, I was furious. I had been less than three hundred thousand dollars in debt when it all began.

That meant that Newhouse had more than doubled the rest of my debt and the house was listed at twice what I owed on it.

The sale of the house would have covered every single dime of what I owed (thanks to Les and his legal fees) and left me enough money to find another home somewhere else, free and clear.

Newhouse hadn't needed to threaten and belittle me for all those months. He hadn't needed to sell my clothing or my only means of transportation. To humiliate me.

No, in his words, "to punish me." Or in the words of Martha, "to retaliate for having written" the book exposing their corruption.

Or to steal my mother's jewelry or my class rings. Or the only ring my deceased father had ever given me when I was a little girl. A tiny blue zircon ring for my birthday because it was my birth stone.

The ring wasn't worth fifty dollars, but it was all I had from my dad.

My deceased brother's and his deceased daughter's jewelry. The pair of earrings that my mother had used to have her ears pierced when she'd been a girl.

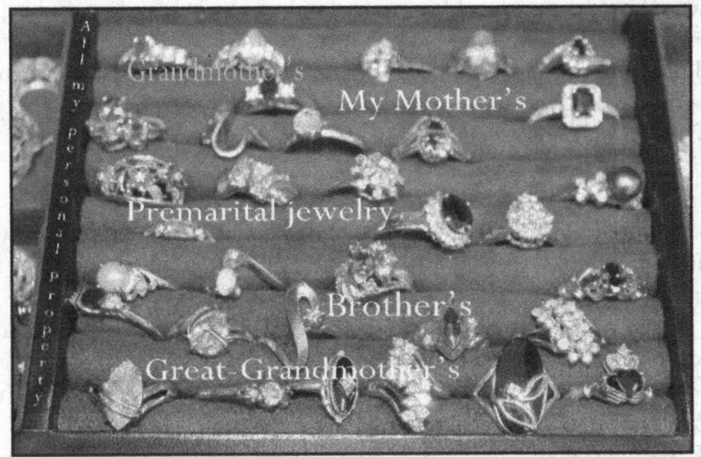


All lost because of these fucking monsters. And over a Chapter 11 where they had absolutely no legal authority over my personal property. None.

For no reason other than absolute greed and cruelty. This was a sick and twisted travesty. The U.S. Trustee who'd been appointed by the federal government with a Department of Justice email had no interest in protecting my estate or doing the right thing.

Or even following the law.

The fucking government had come into my home and plundered my hard work after all the years of bending me over a barrel with taxes. Of taking more than half of what I'd made every year.

What little I'd managed to hold on to that hadn't been ripped out of my hands by my greedy husband and a government that had let me, the daughter of a decorated war hero, go hungry with small babies (I had been denied government services while we were in poverty in Mississippi and I couldn't feed my babies—the caseworker had not only mocked me for applying while I was homeless, but had made a racial slur against me) had not only refused to help, but worse, had come in and victimized me again.

I'd been born into poverty. I had crawled up into that category that everyone craved and had been slapped right back down into poverty by one idiot spouse and a pack of greedy, sadistic lawyers.

By a Department of Justice bitch.

And my only crime had been to get married to a man I stupidly thought loved me.

Les had wiped out a ten-million-dollar estate in less than two years.

With the help of the United States government and the trustees who'd been put in place to help pay back other hard-working businesspeople.

Only instead of paying them back, they made sure that they took the money, and then they went out and screwed my creditors out of theirs.

That was Newhouse's great plan.

Take every dollar "I" earned, while denying the claims of all my other creditors.

Never had I been more ashamed of the country that my father bled for. This wasn't the government he'd taught me to respect. These weren't the laws he'd given his life for.

I didn't recognize this place, and I was horrified by what I saw. Honestly, I wanted to go back to living in ignorance.

But it wasn't possible.

This was the American truth.

Our judges were beyond corrupt. Our courtrooms were not a system of justice, but a three-ring circus where we might as well go back to trial by combat because at least then, if you lost your case you'd have the satisfaction of beating the shit out of your opponent and you wouldn't lose everything you'd spent your life working for on a bunch of greedy monsters who didn't care about justice. They cared about stealing money out of your pocket.

*Veritas et Aequitas?*

Bullshit!

The legal motto shouldn't be truth and justice. It needed to be the mock law firm that was used in all the legal textbooks: Dewey, Cheatum and Howe (*for real—pick up any legal textbook and you'd see that firm used*).

Because that was all they cared about. Truth and justice be damned. Their code of ethics was a joke. Why had they even bothered to create one when the only time it was enforced was when a lawyer ran afoul of a judge who wanted to put them out of business? Like they'd done with my attorney Constance and Brian Manookian.

And how sick that all the attorneys joked about their sadistic trick of dropping a notice on a client at five o'clock on Friday to let them stew all weekend under the stress of it.

Or better yet, when Les had been in law school, the assholes who'd bragged in his class that they could get anyone convicted. All they had to do was drop a kilo of coke on their table and look at it, then look at whoever they had on trial. "We don't even have to enter it into evidence. Just having it there, and having the jury see it in the room with the person on trial, they make the connection, and they'll give you the conviction every time."

It was sickening. They were proud of it.

Fuck evidence? Fuck a fair trial?

This was not how law was supposed to work.

That alone should call for the disbarment and disbandment of the entire legal profession.

Sick motherfuckers. To do that to another human being, and to think that it was funny, to mentally torture someone when they couldn't get help, said it all.

If we needed such an antiquated form of justice, then as I said, let's go back to one that was at least the fairest of them all.

Trial by combat. Sell tickets and let the combatants split the proceeds. Quick justice and instead of going broke, at least both parties would get something out of it.

*Fair is fair.*

And there was nothing fair about what had been done to me. Contrary to the lies that had been told by those who'd stolen from me over the years and my enemies, I'd never done anything to deserve this. This wasn't Karma paying me back for being a bad person.

I had never taken anything from anyone. Nor had I ever sought harm against another. The one thing anyone who knew anything about me was that I had always given. In business, friendships and charity. That when I'd been robbed, I had never spoken ill of my robbers.

Even when someone did me wrong, I rarely, if ever mentioned it or their names again.

Rather, I moved on and kept my eyes on the future and my thoughts on positive things.

I'd only ever defended myself when I'd been forced to. And I'd allowed others to go when I shouldn't have. Others who'd come back to cause me harm that had then forced me into actions that I would have much rather never been forced to take because they refused to move on with their lives.

Like Les and his crew that would not go away. He was the one who was always obsessed over things.

Hogg and her vile shit where she kept coming back, over and over, to attack me and my sons.

Because they were broken people who, after attacking someone, weren't content to just leave, they had to keep trying to break someone. Because they had no life, and they couldn't be happy unless they were making someone else miserable.

I'd spent my entire life trying my best to stay away from these rotten souls.

Les had brought so many of them into my life and now he, the biggest one of all, wouldn't go away.

I was trapped and I was tired.

Every day, I woke up baffled as to how this had become my life when I'd done nothing to deserve it. If I had, then I could accept my fate. But my biggest mistake was trusting people who were untrustworthy. Was thinking that my government followed the laws that were written. That people entrusted with power were honorable and wouldn't abuse that trust.

And that if they did, there were checks and balances in place to handle their misconduct.

I couldn't have been more wrong.

And everyone around me kept telling me to bow my head down, curl into a ball and let them beat me into the ground.

"Don't fight it. Just let them take what they want and do what they will. You'll come through it and then you can rebuild."

What kind of sick, fucked-up logic was that?

That was what had allowed these abusers to abuse for so long and believe themselves untouchable. And if I didn't cry foul and let the world know, then I would be personally responsible for everyone after me that they did this to.

So, this was the warning for the rest of this country. If you choose to ignore it, that was *your* choice.

But I warned you. Unlike me, you wouldn't be able to say that you'd never heard of this happening to someone.

Because every single word of this was true. I had witnesses galore who'd suffered with me.

Some suffered more.

No more blindfolds for Themis. That bitch needed to see, and justice should serve everyone. Not just those who were lucky enough to go to law school and who had learned to twist words to confuse others and corrupt our laws so that they could get rich while destroying lives.

That night, my friend texted me to say, "Yah! We made it to Friday!"

Yet the last thing I felt was victorious. I was sick to my stomach, and I went to bed that night praying to God that I wouldn't wake up in the morning.

**M**AYBE, JUST MAYBE THERE WAS some kind of Karma in the universe. As I said, given the unbelievable hell that I'd been put through on Friday for no reason, I'd begun to have serious doubts about it.

Until I woke up on Saturday to learn that the publisher who'd done me so incredibly wrong over the Dumas matter was suddenly being put on the auction block.

Why?

Lack of profitability and viability. Maybe if they'd actually paid the true creators instead of conniving ways to steal property out of their hands, they might have done a lot better.

I'd also like to think that funding lawsuits to protect their guilty parties had cut into their profit margins. They'd been so brazen with me that I knew I couldn't be the only one they'd done this to.

So maybe, just maybe, Karma was starting to wake up and do her business.

One hoped and prayed. After all, I hadn't slept the night before. The worry of what would be waiting for me come Monday weighed heavy on my mind.

As did the growing COVID-19 threat.

Last thing I wanted was to step another foot into that courtroom with Lord Skeletor of the Irritable Bowel Syndrome. There was no telling what he'd hurl at me. He couldn't look at me that he wasn't thrown into apoplexy.

Melissa had assured me that I wouldn't be required to testify, but I'd been promised that before, and had been lied to. It ranked up there with the old, "Don't worry! No one gets arrested in a civil trial!"

Yeah, right. Hard to reassure someone who'd been arrested for *complying* with the judge's orders. In all my life, I was the only one I'd ever known who got in trouble for following the rules.

All because of one stupid bastard.

And a lying bitch.

Who kept lying about every single thing.

Well, he couldn't lie about the state of the book industry anymore. It was now frontpage news that my income was on the decline, along with everyone else's.

COVID-19 was shutting down New York and putting people out of work, right and left.

There was no way to stick it to me for alimony based on my past wages, given that my entire industry was going down in flames, and now everyone knew that. It would be like basing alimony on the income of someone who manufactured videotapes in 2010 by saying, "Your Honor, they furnish videotapes to Blockbuster!"

So, what?

Blockbuster may have been the biggest thing on the block for decades, but by 2010, like me, they were in bankruptcy. Their product a thing of the past.

That was what was happening to books.

Baby Huey had picked the worst time in history to leave me, and he'd firebombed my income on his way out the door.

Now we'd only had four publishers left.

*Good job, Nimrod.*

And my reputation was in tatters. Because of him and the Hogg he'd brought home.

Les had always said that he had bad timing in all things. He should have remembered that before he started another lawsuit he couldn't win.

In all my life, I'd never seen anyone dumber.

Except maybe me for having married the loser and not kicking him to the curb during the first year of our marriage when he'd decided to quit work to go back to school.

*Live and learn.*

When I'd started this business, there had been dozens and dozens of New York publishers. We were now down to four.

It was a scary world I was facing, but for Les, it had gotten a lot more frightening. And the biggest difference was that he was too stupid to know it.

If he wasn't so vicious and hadn't caused so much damage to everyone, I'd almost feel sorry for him.

But I hoped and prayed that Karma was awake and that she would deliver to him and all the other malicious bastards he'd led into my life exactly what they deserved.

MARCH 9

ANOTHER AWESOME DAY IN watching Lord Skeletor hold court, as if he were something to be admired. God, how I wished he could see what a repugnant piece of shit he appeared to the rest of the world. How unjust and biased his decisions were. *Shame on you, Tennessee, that you have allowed this mockery of the law to dispense such gross miscarriages of justice in your name.*

Even more sickening than having to look at him was the fact that right before my case was a poor woman who'd demonstrated in no uncertain terms that the nightmare my accountant's office friend had told her about was all too true.

My case wasn't unusual.

Oh. My. God.

This poor woman had been trapped in her divorce for over five years and she was before Skeletor literally in tears, begging him for help while he mocked and ridiculed her. Talked to her like she was a dog.

If that wasn't enough, there was the case of this woman who was about to lose her house to creditors because she'd won a case against her ex who was refusing to pay what he owed. Instead of going off on one of his long lectures to the husband about how he needed to nut-up and pay what he owed, Skeletor had the nerve to tell the woman that she had to be "responsible" and "live in the real world" where she "had to pay" her "own bills."

*Wait? What?*

Yes, you read that correctly. He'd humiliated and lectured this woman about paying her way, but not the deadbeat husband who was there in the courtroom who owed her money and wouldn't pay it.

Just like he refused to tell Les the attorney to go get a fucking job and support the son he'd run out on while my baby was still in high school.

Or better yet...

Support himself with the law degree and MBA I'd bought for him.

Yet Dinky lectured the women.

Never the men.

It was repulsive.

Just like when he'd taken the side of a father who was abusing his child and the key witness was a psychologist. Oh, but Skeletor must protect the father's rights, even though there had been bruises on the child.

"She could be lying. Children lie all the time."

And so did shitbag men, such as Les, and Dinky whom I was quite certain had never told his wife he was out cruising prostitutes before he was arrested for it.

Because everyone in the world knew that child abusers always told the truth about their abuse. By all means, Lord Skeletor, err on the side of protecting the father and his rights.

Child protection be damned. After all, you'd left my sons in the courtroom with a pedophile while you'd had their mother hauled out in handcuffs.

Forget the little girl's rights to not be afraid in her own home. Maybe that was the reason she was acting out in school and having other problems.

Given that I was one of those children, I knew the signs of what that poor baby was going through, and I wanted to scream.

Most of all, I wanted Dinky yanked from that bench and thrown into jail where monsters belonged.

Because unconscionable bastards like him were what had kept me trapped in my marriage. Rather than protecting the child, they were all too quick to put that baby in harm's way.

*Because the child might be lying.*

Yeah. *Adults never lied.*

Remember this juicy tidbit from Skeletor's repugnant lips? "I'm not even going to hear this matter. There's no need in damaging a good attorney's reputation."

Oh, okay. So, perjury in Williamson County was fine by everyone, including the Judiciary Board of Review who gave their judges a pass on that, along with the, "I don't care what the law is," comment.

*Made sense, right?* Third most corrupt state in the Union. One of the most corrupt cities in America.

I wept for every drop of blood my father had shed in defense of this sham court and the disgusting piece of shit sitting on that bench. No wonder the robe he wore was black.

For the first time in my life, I understood why.

Shit should be black. That way, there was no mistaking Dinky and his ilk for what they really were.

A massive shit-stain on the Constitution and laws that so many men and women in uniform had given their lives to protect.

But the real kicker came when I realized that half the courtroom happened to be Les's disgusting attorneys that I was being forced to pay for, including the blond troll he'd found to come at me and who, under Dinky's own court order, I wasn't obligated to pay. Only she looked nothing like the photos on her company website. While Cockburn always came to court dressed like the two-bit floozy coming home from a walk of shame, this one looked like the local bag lady who'd crawled out from beneath a hobo in order to appear in court.

Everyone kept asking me who she was because she was sitting with Hogg.

"I don't know." All I knew was that she couldn't be a friend because Hogg had no real friends. Just the other two Stygian bitches who'd helped her rob me.

I never dreamed the hobo shopping for shoes on her phone the entire time court was in session was the idiot who'd committed contempt to come at me. But then, that explained it all, didn't it? Les was paying her extravagant wages with my money to sit there in court beside Cockburn and Hogg so that she could shoe shop with my money.

He was always a loser. If only he knew what a real fucking joke he was to the rest of the world.

Like Dinky.

So, this was the moron he'd hired who had illegally filed the defamation suit that was filled with their lies. Lies the bimbo hadn't even bothered to do a modicum of fact checking before she put it forth to the court.

Par for the course in Williamson County.

My favorite being that Les's father wasn't a pedophile. I couldn't wait for those witnesses to come forward and bury the bastard. One in particular, I knew was more than eager to watch him burn and was salivating for her chance to testify.

Couldn't wait to see the look on Hobo Barbie's face when that day came, and I got to countersue her clients.

And of course, Hogg saying that she hadn't done all the things I had in writing, with her own email headers on them, that she'd done. Not to mention the witnesses I had who were willing to come forward and testify in person against her, too.

So, why this bitch kept giving me dirty looks in court astounded me. Surely as stupid as these idiot bitches were, even they could figure out that the parent the grown sons were standing by and sitting next to in court was the parent in the right.

Then again, they were *that* stupid.

Wow. We might have a contender for Cockburn's crown of idiocy.

And all I could think about was how Skeletor had torn up my attorney when I brought Melissa in to represent me that first day in April 2019. He'd called me names, on record, while publicly shaming her so badly for daring to take me on as a client that Melissa had sat down, shaking.

"I'm so sorry, Terri. I didn't know what to say for fear of making it worse on you. I've never seen anything like that in my life."

Instead of reprimanding this new bitch from Les's kennel for flagrantly disregarding the law and for asking the court for money she wasn't entitled to by the judge's own order, Dinky applauded her for her breach of law and ethics.

"You did nothing wrong, honey. Don't let anyone tell you differently. I'd have done the same thing."

Of course, he would.

*Flagrantly disregard the law? We know, Skeletor.* You preferred ignoring the law. It was why you were arrested for prostitution and yet you managed to be put on a bench.

'Cause Williamson County was that big of a disgrace.

And he was a shit-stain on that bench. The black robe gave him away.

Just like the disgusting Hogg that was in the room along with Les. How anyone could deny the fact at this point that they were fucking was beyond me. Why else would she still be hanging around him all these years later? She was *his* highly overpaid employee. Not a friend. He'd mocked her endlessly while he lived at home with his family.

"People are starting to think she's my wife, Terri. It's embarrassing. I don't want anyone to think that, and I don't want to be seen in public with her. You have to come out with me."

Yet now he had no compunctions about being seen in public with her while the Hogg was gussied up?

Even my former attorney who was there had noticed it and texted me.

"What the hell is Hogg doing here?"

"Told you they were having an affair."

"Yeah. I see that. She's all dressed up and even did her hair and makeup."

Which was code for the fact that she looked like a painted-up clown. *Honey, blue eye shadow went out in the seventies. It hasn't come back, and it didn't make your eyes pop. It made you look like Pennywise.*

All she needed was a red balloon.

Seriously, if I had, for two solid years, shown up with a man at my side to my court hearings, no matter how repugnant he might appear, no one would let me get away with saying, "We're just friends."

After all, Les had accused me of fucking every man I'd ever spoken to. Married or not. Didn't matter what they looked like or their age.

He accused me of it constantly.

Even women.

Yet because all the men around us shuddered at Hogg's foul form, they wanted to give him a free pass on the fact that he was flaunting his paramour in the courtroom.

Even Nick was repulsed. "Gah, can you imagine how bad it must stink to be that close to her? How can he stand it?" He was right. We'd been forced to fumigate the room where she'd slept and worked in my home. And it'd taken weeks to get the stink out.

"He's probably lost all ability to smell by now."

I'm surprised Dinky didn't have us arrested for Nick's laughter.

Then, even after Newhouse had told Dinky that he didn't want to pay the bill for the confederacy of idiots Les had hired to represent him as it would throw me into a Chapter 7, Dinky didn't care. "Well, no one wants that. But lawyers gotta be paid."

Yes, but no one needed six attorneys to my one. If only Les knew what a joke he appeared to everyone as he sat up there, surrounded by all those unnecessary, overpaid idiots in a state where the law gave him half automatically.

My mother was right. That level of stupid should be terminal. And I couldn't believe that I'd voluntarily allowed those genes into my family tree.

Maddox was right. I should be ashamed that I'd bred with that imbecile.

And as Dinky went on, I shook my head. What happened to the state law that said it was prohibited for a spouse to waste marital funds? To the court order that said Les couldn't waste our money on excess and that I was only to pay for his *divorce* attorneys? Not his own personal frivolous suit that had been illegally filed.

Oh yeah, that probably went alongside with the fact that over and over, Dinky admitted he never read anything put in front of him. He couldn't recall "seeing" anything that had been filed for him to read. Not just in my case.

All cases. He was the least prepared judge that I'd ever seen in my life.

And embarrassment to the state.

If that number of attorneys wasn't excessive for a man *with* a law degree, please tell me what was?

Not to mention, there sat ole Sal Tiller, Dumas's former lawyer, among the mix. At least I finally got to see what the bean pole looked like.

He did look as incompetent and decrepit as Les had called him every single day of the Dumas litigation.

Guess Tiller got the last laugh because now the man who'd mocked him for all those years was currently overpaying him for work he'd already done in that litigation with my money.

And Dinky was okay with this.

How was that supposed work?

The attorney that everyone, including the Tennessee Board of Professional Responsibility had told me had no business on my case, representing Les after he'd been our opponent less than a year ago. That it was a gross breach of ethics.

Yet Dinky paid him, too, in spite of all the legal and moral reasons why this bastard should have been kicked out of the courtroom.

Sickening and disgraceful.

And Dinky refused to pay *my* attorney.

Yes, you heard that correctly. When it got to Melissa's pay, "Well, we don't want to go back."

This from the bastard who had made me pay Les's attorney's two hundred thousand dollars of back payment that Les hadn't paid them while I was in bankruptcy?

*Are you fucking kidding me?*

He was denying Melissa her money?

And at the end of it, I at least got to show Melissa what an absolute and total liar Newhouse was as we went over all the other lies that had been leveled at me during the hearing.

Still, Newhouse had balked. "I've got your emails."

*So, do I, asshole.* And they all refuted every lie out of Newhouse's mouth.

My God, Les had nothing on his gaslighting techniques. I pitied his wife and children. One would think that a psychologist would have broken him of it.

Guess not.

Newhouse also affirmed that I had an offer on my home large enough that had he done that instead of selling off everything else, the bankruptcy would have ended before I lost my clothes, cars and my mother's and grandmother's jewelry.

Before he put me half a million dollars more in debt. "Uh, I testified in ignorance, Your Honor. I didn't understand the value of the property or how Ms. Manly got paid."

Because he refused to listen to me. Rather, Newhouse had bought into the lies of Cockburn and crew, and now he was trying to hold me accountable for the fact that he had refused, time and again, to listen to me or my agent when we'd tried to correct him.

*This was all your fault, Newhouse.* You had botched your fucking job and jeopardized my entire life.

You, and Leadwits who had insisted that your stupid ass be put over me, when Newhouse wouldn't take five minutes to listen because he magically knew everything.

Much like Emma Swan, he thought he had the superpower of telling when someone, i.e. me, was lying to him. Only problem was, I was the only one telling him the truth.

He didn't like it.

All this for nothing.

Not true. All this *for greed*.

For all of them.

Especially Newhouse who wanted to bleed more money from me.

And with every single lie that dripped out of Cockburn's overly painted, whorish lips I could tell that they had no intention of ending my nightmare. Why?

Dinky, again, told them to go write their own checks for whatever amount they wanted out of my account.

Free rein.

"You can do all the discovery you want."

What a total piece of shit. How was that preserving the marital estate?

I guess he absolved himself by his numerous comments of, "No one wants a Chapter 7."

Obviously, Les wanted one, as he wouldn't stop his stupidity.

Meanwhile, Cockburn kept lying about my income. Apparently, the ignorant slut had spent tens of thousands of my dollars to hire someone to tally up all the money I'd ever made.

*All of it.* As if my accountant couldn't have done that for free. Or simply any imbecile with my tax returns.

Then the arrogant, brainless bitch went on to say that it was the total value of my IP.

Currently.

*Um, Jane, you ignorant slut.* Les spent that money while we were married. Just because I had a thousand dollars in my bank account ten years ago didn't mean that he was entitled to five hundred dollars of it today after it'd been spent on his "lavish" lifestyle that he'd insisted on.

My God, how had she ever passed a law school class?

The only income you needed, and the value of my IP was what it was worth *today*. Just because you bought a car for forty thousand dollars six years ago, it didn't mean it was worth that now.

Especially after Cockburn and crew had gone out of their way to beat it up and post lies about it in public.

Oh. My. God! Her stupendously sad logic made my head ache.

On and on she went with her lies.

And Dinky ate it up like gospel.

He even went back for seconds.

*But wait, it got better.* Cockburn then brought up the fact that my beloved fans had come together to start a Gofundme so that they could help me keep my trademarks and contracts that Newhouse and crew kept threatening to sell and put me out of business.

Forever.

"It's not right, Your Honor! She's getting money from her fans to pay for *her* legal fees!"

Excuse me? Not right was the fact that I was having to foot the bill for six fucking attorneys to torture me and couldn't afford to pay for my one to keep my own work that I'd spent a lifetime building because Les was too lazy to work. That I'd started writing before I ever met that fucking loser who wouldn't leave.

Melissa even told Judge Twat this. "Your Honor, I've put my bills aside."

"Well, we can't go back in the past." I.E. after Skeletor had forced me to pay over two hundred thousand dollars for back pay to Les's attorneys while I was in bankruptcy for the bills Les had refused to pay (he was months in arrears), he was now telling my attorney to eat it?

*What the fuck?*

Really, I kept waiting for Rod Serling's voice over. How could this be legal?

What a piece of shit-sucking scum.

Of course, this was also the King Moron judge who thought that his little iota of power in Tennessee gave him authority over my fans who were in New Hampshire and the rest of the country.

Newsflash, Nimrod. You aren't omnipotent.

*You cannot dictate what fans in other states did from your tiny little corner of Williamson County. Get over yourself, you worthless footnote of a footnote.*

However, my all-time favorite fatuous moment out of the twat's mouth was... "She voluntarily put herself into bankruptcy, Your Honor!"

Now, I suspected that Cockburn had most likely sucked so much cock in her lifetime that she'd suffered irreversible brain damage from oxygen dep, but...

Seriously?

Almost all bankruptcies I'd ever heard of in my entire life were "voluntary." Most people "put themselves" into it.

And I definitely hadn't wanted to go into it, at all. I'd fought against it with everything I had.

Yet no one, except maybe Bill Gates or Besos, could keep taking the hits to their income I was getting hit with every month because of Queen Twat and stay afloat. Those tens of thousands of dollars she, alone, was costing me in attorney fees had bankrupted me.

She was a sickening piece of work.

Never mind the little fact that every time I had to transfer money from a savings account into a checking account to pay for something like my taxes that I was legally obligated to pay, Thundercunt would come screaming out of the woodwork with yet another motion to drag me into court for contempt where she was threatening to throw me into jail because I dared merge enough money from one account to another to pay my bills and not overdraw my account.

*God forbid!*

Right hand on the bible, that was what had happened. Over and over. This was the actual emails exchanged:

In reality, I think he will pay the attorneys whatever their invoices state, which is the same amount that was on the proposed Agreed Order that I forwarded yesterday.

Mika House is going to add the language regarding their agreement that they will not set a contempt hearing on the issues of the transfer of funds that had been made, or any other issue mentioned in their motion to lift the stay. They will reserve those issues for the final trial.

But he doesn't want to take the time to add that paragraph if we are not going to agree to the order anyway.

So in short, look at the attached order. If we agree to let Judge Dinky fill in the blanks, they will add the paragraph about not setting a contempt hearing.

If we don't agree, they will file the order as it was announced at the hearing- basically like it is and without the language regarding the contempt issue.

Take a look and let me know. I need to get back with them soon.

My response:

So what I'm hearing is extortion in its most purest form of the legal definition under all law statutes. Is that correct? Unless I pay them off, they are going to drag me into court for contempt and make my life utter hell with unreasonable and frivolous motions they know aren't valid and continue to breach the very ethics they took an oath not to? This is what you just said. I want to make sure I have this documented because that is exactly what Mika House has just said.

And I want it added in that I have to agree for it to be a BLANK check for them to write out whatever amount I am to pay them for them to submit to the judge, THEIR FORMER PARTNER, for whatever fees they want to rob me of so that they can continue to harass and stalk me for frivolous motions and information they already have and to lie and have me arrested for things I didn't do. I have to agree to that to have them put an ethics paragraph in a motion that they agreed to put in the motion a week ago or they won't do it. They are holding me hostage. and they are refusing to do this order that I agreed to after they changed the terms I agreed to and jacked up the rates by already violating what I agreed to. I just want this documented.

Her response:

So, I agree with you. Those motions would be frivolous. And if they set them, I don't think they'd be very successful. It was just something we added that we wanted because I think Judge Dinky will give them their attorney fees anyway.

I expected Cockburn, John and Mika to have some hefty invoices. My understanding was that Les owed Cockburn $55k, Mika and John were owed $37k. But the balance must be the bankruptcy attorney's invoice, which seems unreasonable to me.

But the only option we have here is to leave the numbers blank and let Judge Dinky look at the

> invoices and write a figure he thinks is reasonable. I'm pretty confident he will give them what their invoices are for. But that doesn't mean we can be successful at trial in showing the totality of Les's legal fees were exorbitant. Especially when Les is a freaking bankruptcy attorney.

My response:

> I don't see how this isn't a bar complaint on the whole lot of them. I want to talk to Leadwits in the morning and I still don't see how this isn't illegal. I'm disgusted.

> Am I wrong or is this not blackmail? They're threatening to take me before the judge, their former business partner, who has already illegally convicted me for something I didn't do and without due cause, if I don't pay them whatever outrageous fees they demand? And they're writing themselves a blank check? I'm not even allowed to see what their fees are before I pay and they've already broken the terms we pre agreed to on the order? Is this not them holding me hostage?

Her response:

> I get ya. And I think they should have to show us their invoices before we blindly agree to pay their fees

And for the record, Newhouse was cc'd on this entire exchange and signed off on the entirety of it. He agreed with Les's little blackmail crew and allowed them to pillage my estate.

More than that, he jumped in on allowing them to settle that contempt for whatever outrageous demand she'd made because, "Dinky's going to throw you in jail again. You don't want to go in front of him. He's just aching to put you there."

Yes, Newhouse used those exact words against me and joined the boot party. "The last thing you need or want is to go in front of Dinky. He hates you. Cockburn hates you. She has a personal grudge against you."

Newhouse admitted and warned me that Dinky would grant them attorney fees for harassing me with their illegal and unconscionable frivolous motions that tied up the court and wasted my marital assets.

After all, it wasn't like Dinky hadn't stated it on open record that he was aching to put me in jail. "Give me one single reason." That was a direct quote from his mouth, on record. "I'll do it, too."

How was that impartial? How could the Judiciary Board give him a pass on that level of intimidation and bullying when I'd done nothing wrong? When I was being asked for paperwork that I could prove Les had as it was on the computer he'd taken with him and I had the emails to prove it.

More than that, that Les was living in my office where my business files were kept, and his own fucking attorney had charged me thousands and thousands of dollars to scan and copy files that Les had already paid hundreds of thousands of dollars to be scanned and copied in the Dumas suit.

Files no one had provided me a copy of?

Didn't matter. Dinky wanted *me* in jail. Because I was everything he hated.

A successful woman he couldn't buy.

Everyone from Newhouse to Leadwits used that fact to bully me. "If you don't behave, little girl, Dinky will throw you under the jail. You better do what we say, or he'll put you in there."

I couldn't protest anything.

No one would help me.

Even the Receiver had admitted what he'd done was wrong. "I didn't have the court order or papers, but I didn't dare say anything. Normally, we wait on the papers, and I wasn't prepared for this. But I wasn't about to say no to Dinky. I had no choice."

Yeah, right. Remember Nuremburg? The old, "I was just following orders, even though they were unconscionable and wrong?" Remember what it got those guys?

Hanged.

Legally, doing something you knew was wrong didn't absolve you from guilt. In fact, it made it worse, and juries never took that into consideration. It made them madder.

As well it should.

This was the same thing.

And they had *all* participated in it. Gleefully.

Remember that the Receiver had charged me thirty-five thousand dollars for violating my Constitutional Rights that he admitted was wrong.

Yet there Cockburn and Dinky sat and lied, "No one protested."

*Yeah, bitches, I did. Over and over again.*

But because my attorneys were afraid of you and your unreasonable temper, no one would file it for me.

As Newhouse had said, I had the emails to prove it.

And Cockburn's ridiculous motions against me that in any normal state would have had this moron disbarred were what had driven me into the poorhouse. Worse, they were about to land me in a Chapter 7.

Where was Nemesis and Themis when you needed them?

How much lying and corruption could one town hold? It was sickening that this was the norm, and no one would do anything to stop it.

I wasn't alone.

Dinky was abusing countless others. I'd witnessed his abuse again, myself, that morning against a number of other poor citizens who'd been hauled before him.

If that wasn't bad enough, Newhouse yelled at me over the fact that he was refusing to give me the money that I needed to run my business that all of the leeches, including him, wanted to bleed out of me.

"Don't you dare blame me for what's happened in your career!"

Was he delusional? Were the little Green Men in his head on acid? Dude, it *was* all your fault. I had told you what was going to happen. My agent had told you. My editors.

*Everyone.*

*You* refused to listen. That had been Newhouse's problem from the get-go. If he, the U.S. Trustee didn't like an answer, he ignored it or rewrote it. His little mind refused to accept the truth. He kept buying into the lies of the liars.

Such as when I'd told him that I didn't get paid until after I handed something in and then my editor had to read it and write the editorial letter.

Once I had her edits, I had to then go in and rewrite the book. After that was finished, I sent it back and waited for her to read it again. If she was happy with my changes, she released the money. If she wasn't, we'd go through another round of edits and revisions.

"But you said the money would be in this February."

"I said that when I normally handed a book in at Christmas, as I did, that I usually got paid in February and that I was expecting payment, because you wouldn't accept the real answer when I told you that I had no fucking idea when it would come in and that I had no control over when the checks were written."

Him and his idiot boss, much like my four-year-old son who'd thrown a fit for a toy in Target when I told him we couldn't afford it had looked at me and said, "Well, go write another book!"

Which said that they had the same intellect and basic understanding as a four-year-old toddler.

After all, Melissa had been working on a four-page document for three weeks.

Obviously, writing a book took a little longer. Why they couldn't get that one through their thick skulls, I had no idea. And that was when I wasn't being mentally abused by a herd of losers every single day.

Being told to pack up my house. Having to try and find a place to live with no money and no credit, and no car that I could drive.

*Hmmm... see the problem?* Under that stress, most people couldn't work a normal job. Never mind one that required me to write about a couple who find ever-lasting love.

Nimrod Les hadn't thought that one through and why none of these grossly overpaid morons couldn't get it through their heads that I was incapable of writing a romance at that point, I couldn't understand.

*Are you all fucking stupid or crazy?*

"That's not what you said!"

Uh, yeah, dumbass, it was. Repeatedly. "I drew you a diagram of how I got paid. And showed you and the receiver and Melissa exactly how complicated it was. How much time it took. I told you that I could write a book faster than they could write a check." I had said those exact words to him.

On more than one occasion.

"She did," Joan said, sitting across from my attorney. "I was there when she drew it for you and the other trustee."

"Then when are you going to get paid?"

I'd never wanted to Gibbs's slap anyone more in my life. By now, you could probably answer him for me.

"I don't know."

Should we play the game, "Repeat after me... I don't know."

That was what I felt like saying. Instead, "My editor has been sick since January and she's still out. Because of the Coronavirus, they have put her on leave until she's healed. Manhattan is currently on lockdown over this. She'll get to it when she gets to it. I can't make her read it while she's out of work. I have her email right here where she says that. And I can't make Manhattan go back to work during a pandemic. I don't have those powers."

"You said you'd be paid in February!"

Oh my God! What part of Force Majeure had he missed?

It was a struggle not to roll my eyes. "I didn't know my editor would get sick or that a pandemic would break out and start shutting down businesses. Normally, we're on a crunch because I have a September or August release." As I had told him and the others repeatedly. "Thanks to Les and Hogg, I don't have that this year. My publisher," contrary to more lies in court that Cockburn had told to the judge, "will not release another publication because of the attacks Hogg has been doing to my last releases. I cannot force them to publish it."

Again, in spite of everyone's effing lies, I had no control over my schedule. No traditionally published author did.

I had told them this. My agent had told them that.

Newhouse hadn't liked that answer at all. Somehow, the whole idiot brigade thought I had complete control over my entire career even though they'd read through thousands of emails with me complaining to my agent about how I had no control over anything and would like to have some control over something.

Over how I'd been forced to buy a book back less than six months before Les had left because my publisher wouldn't bring it out when they'd promised me, and I didn't want to disappoint my fans. I had given them my word that the book would be out that fall and so, at great harm to myself, I'd bought the book back and self-published it because my publisher wouldn't bring it out on the date I'd promised my readers.

It was also a book Hogg had attacked, and then lied to a fan that she'd "copy-edited."

Cockburn *knew* this. Had read it and stood before Skeletor and told a blatant lie.

And still Newhouse hammered me about how he wasn't going to be responsible for the damage that he, himself, had done to my career. Even though he was the one who had single-handedly made the dumbest effing decisions with me and my agent telling him not to do it.

"It is going to seriously harm my career."

"I don't see how. You have to do what I say. *I'm* in charge."

He'd said that so often that I'd begun to wonder if his wife didn't have some kind of sick control of him at home. Why was he so obsessed with exerting his control over everyone else?

How could the government put someone in his position so mentally stunted that the basic concept of business eluded him? In order to make money, one has to spend money on the company. One has to buy inventory to have inventory to sell. In order to sell books to fans, I needed to meet the fans.

Again, if you didn't buy gas for the trucks that ran your shipping company, you had no company.

It was really a very basic principle.

Like last fall when I had a new release and he'd screamed at me about not having it in my store. "Why didn't you sell it?"

"I needed two thousand dollars to buy the inventory and you wouldn't get back to me or release the funds." Since I didn't have the money in my account to buy the books, I couldn't buy the books without overdrawing my account.

Fucking duh!

Books have a lead time of three to four weeks in advance that they have to be ordered by in order to get them on the release date so that they can be shipped to the fans on the day of release.

By the time he'd finally gotten around to authorizing my money to purchase that inventory, I'd missed the initial rush of orders that we always had the first two weeks.

So, my customers went to other stores and not mine.

Any businessperson would say that had seriously impeded my bottom line and sales. *This* was what the government had saddled me with?

Okay...

Dumbass for the loss.

That made Newhouse the third dumbest moron on the planet. Third behind Les and Cockburn. Maybe fourth if you counted Judge Skeletor.

What made it so bad was that Newhouse had his office on Music Row. Land of Country Music. So why he couldn't comprehend the basic concept that acts needed to travel to meet their fans in order to grow their fanbase and keep selling their product was astonishing. Better still, his accomplice, Bill Oldham, shared office space *with* one of my publishers.

Yes, you read that currently. One of my publishers had a Franklin office in the same building, on the same floor as Newhouse's accomplice. Why they couldn't ask a single question of their elevator buddy, I had no idea.

And spoke of an intelligence level so low that I'm sure there were amoebas who questioned his sorry intellect. In fact, they probably had a saying. "Yeah, I'm stupid, but I'm not *Newhouse* stupid."

By the time I was done with court, I was done with court, and had I been forced to endure one more lecture by Skeletor where he thought he was dispensing wisdom, but instead just showed the world how idiotic and petty he was, I might have vomited.

Yet again, Dinky had sat there lecturing me about needing to preserve money while wasting thousands of my dollars by tying up over a dozen lawyers I was having to pay for, while in bankruptcy.

And my fave was Skeletor's sick look as he swept his gaze over the attorneys. "Hmm... who should I pick to write up the order?"

*Way to go, Lord Moron.*

The fact you had a choice should have made your little pea brain click on that this was morally wrong and a waste of my marital funds.

And the only thing that kept going through my mind the entire time as I stared at all those idiots in front of me was that Les had absolutely no intention of ending this torture.

Ever.

Not from that goofy, vacuous smile pasted on his face. Was he drunk?

Or high?

I didn't know. But for a man who wanted away from me, he wasn't willing to leave. And these jackals weren't going to leave while there was so much as a single crumb on the table.

How stupid could one effing idiot be?

They were going to strip us of every last dollar. Les had understood that in the Dumas case. Yet every single brain cell he'd once possessed had somehow vanished.

Why he was set on this total annihilation, I had no idea.

But there was no way out.

No end.

We had a fucking imbecile at the helm, and no one was going to help me find a safe harbor.

My sons and I were screwed and no one was going to have any mercy on us.

THE DAY STARTED OFF WITH another unexpected accusation. As I'd said repeatedly, one of the biggest problems with my nightmare was that I never knew what bizarre, psycho attack the ex-lunatic would come up with.

The FBI stunt was a shocker, but this one was an all-time low. Keep in mind that Joan had had two wrecks only a few days before in the company car. So, I sat down to write, stupidly thinking that I could focus that morning on my job that paid the bills for all of Dipshit's vultures who kept circling.

Nope.

I should have known better. How dare I think that they'd leave me alone to do my job. Not like Newhouse had been nagging me, in person, just the day before to "go write a book."

Yeah. This was his email that Melissa forwarded:

> The Chevy Traverse is NOT currently covered on the auto insurance policy. Was it removed by Terri? Either way, it needs to be instated immediately.

Newhouse kept proudly telling me that he was, "holding back in my emails whenever I deal with you because I understand the pressure and difficulties that you're under." Well, I also kept assuring him that I, too, was holding back in mine. Because to quote my mother, *I do not suffer idiots lightly.*

And I don't count ignorance and arrogance in the same category any more than I do stupid. Ignorance was those who didn't know better. I had infinite patience for those who didn't know something as there are so many things I was ignorant of myself.

In fact, I'd been praised the whole of my life for that fact that I was very slow to anger and that I was unshakable in a crisis and while under pressure. Remember that I was raised in a home with a Cerebral Palsy sister. That my niece was mentally retarded. That my cousin had Down Syndrome. I've been around a lot of small children. My sons were born Autistic and with Asperger's.

So, I have held my temper at times when others would scream. Like in court while Dinky spent two hours yelling to the point he should have had a stroke and died while he called me every name imaginable.

Anyway, all that being said, I admitted that when it came to the special level of stupid that these people functioned at, my trigger was at a hair level.

For one reason. I was being gouged. Once I had told you something five hundred times and especially while I was being billed almost a thousand dollars an hour against my will for your blatant and flagrant stupidity and you can't get it right or keep it straight, I could become hostile.

*Extremely hostile.*

I owned that. Because I didn't want to deal with you in the first place. I shouldn't have to deal with you and if you dared to charge and gouge at that arrogant price, then by God, buddy, you damn well better be functioning at that rate, or charge at an acceptable rate like the kind soul at Walmart or Burger King who made my life pleasant. Not the fucking arrogant asshole who was currently making my life hell.

Because here was the one thing about me. I would never, ever in a million years take my frustration out on the kind soul working for minimum wage no matter how bad my day had been. But if you were the top of the food chain, arrogantly gouging the piss out of me while flaunting what you thought was your superior intellect and fucking up on a daily basis and taking *that* snotty tone with me.

Brother, it was on.

*You better keep your shit straight.* Don't tell me that I should be grateful you were *only* charging two hundred dollars an hour against my will while you continued to fuck up and accuse me of shit because you were a fucking, overpaid imbecile.

That was the same as waving the red cape at a charging group of bulls at Pamplona. You better get out of my way.

*Because you know the old adage that there's no such thing as a stupid question?*

*Let's revisit this one:*

> The Chevy Traverse is NOT currently covered on the auto insurance policy. Was it removed by
> Terri? Either way, it needs to be instated immediately.

Remember that this jackass was gouging me for his overinflated salary. Was he so stupid that he thought I'd remove my company car off my insurance when I had had an employee who'd wrecked the fucking car twice in one week?

While he might be so stupid as to put may-pop tires on his own daughter's car and brag about the fact that he held no love in his heart for his child, I was not that flagrant a moron.

The sense-formerly-known-as-common should have told King Moron that since Les had gone in and added his fifteen year old gator that I'd removed off it because the damn thing wasn't running and we didn't need insurance on something that was a garage decoration (and Les had again changed the billing address to his, as opposed to say the one who was actually paying the bills, me) that should have clued Anti-Einstein into the fact that Les, not me, had changed the insurance.

Christ Almighty, and Newhouse dared to say that he was the one "holding back" his temper in emails.

Dude, you don't want to know what thoughts were going through my head every time you opened your mouth and let out the whole slew of stupid. How your wife tolerated a simple conversation with you, I had no idea.

Oh, and the "instated" wasn't a typo. That was what he'd typed. So, you see what *I* was holding back? This from someone who'd just billed me, while I was in bankruptcy, over one hundred thousand dollars for his stellar abilities.

Because and I wanted to make sure that I captured this little nugget verbatim, "I was misled, Your Honor, about how much was in the estate when I took over. So, I paid out the attorneys before I knew what money was actually there."

Motherfucker, wasn't your job to do some research before you spent a penny?

*To find out basic information?*

And I wasn't the one who'd lied to you. I was more than honest. Ironically, the receiver had been more honest. He'd told Newhouse, same as me, that the jewelry would never bring at an auction what it was insured for. The insurance was the replacement cost. I thought everyone in the free world would know that. The only ones lying were the jackals and they were the ones he'd listened to.

*How dare you lie to the fucking judge while you tried to save your own ass.* You'd made a very bad call while you raided my estate and paid off all your little legal buddies.

When I tried to tell that to his boss, rather than listen to me, Martha's answer was to threaten me and to retaliate by selling off "all" my jewelry. Why?

Because Martha didn't want to jeopardize *his* bond.

Direct quote from Martha.

It was okay to destroy my life and my future, to put me on welfare for the rest of my life and to single-handedly annihilate a lifetime of work.

But I better not harm Newhouse's trustee bond.

*Are you fucking kidding me?*

And this bitch worked for the Department of Justice?

*Yeah, okay.*

To call me appalled was an understatement.

That was how my day started.

Guess how it ended...

You won't guess. How could you? Again, after I ran around, jumping through their hoops and staying all torn up all day, needless to say, no writing was done.

But at eight that evening, after thirteen hours of bullshit, I stupidly thought, they'd been home for hours, surely, I could get some writing done now.

Of course, there was an email from Melissa that was about an hour old.

My idiocy thought that it might pertain to the house and that it might be a response to our counteroffer. So, like a fool, I opened it.

*When will I learn?*

> I received 2 checks from Terri in the mail today – one is from Cason Cross- Account: Dutiful Duchess ($60.72) and the other is from Sid & Shyster ($338.43). I need supporting documentation so I know how to code them in the system and what they are for. Thanks.

This was another award-winning act of fatuousness.

Let's play another round of "How Fucking Dumb Was Newhouse?" Hmm... Aside from the fact that this wasn't the first time I'd sent these residuals to him, keep in mind that months had gone by where we'd been playing this game.

But here we go.

I was a writer.

Writers were paid royalties for their work. *Easy enough, yes?*

From reading this book, we all knew the Sid & Schyster was one of my publishers. We doubly knew this because they were the publisher in the Dumas case. Not like that was hidden in any way, and as my trustee, old Newhouse had heard about them a lot.

Okay, then.

What on earth could that effing check be?

Especially as it came in during February and what came in during February and August?

C'mon, Newhouse, you had just reamed my ass about it the very day before.

"You lied to me about how much money was going to come in, in February with your royalties."

*No, motherfucker, I hadn't. I'd told you the truth and you hadn't wanted to hear it.*

Again, I pitied his wife and children. No wonder she'd gone into psychology. I could only imagine how many times a day she had to go into a room to tap on herself to calm down from a five second conversation with this man.

And I thought Les could be frustrating. Now I remembered why I'd married my loser.

But back to the point. That, Anti-Einstein, was the royalty check. Obviously.

The other, the one that held the title of a book I'd written, would obviously be the royalty from *that* book. Because what always came in during February?

Royalties.

What had old Cockburn stood up in front of Dinky and lied about the day before. "She's received two hundred thousand dollars in royalties, Your Honor. We've had to hire a professional to track down every one of her short stories that she's written and novels. There are over two hundred of them. And they have a market value of fifteen million dollars!"

*I fucking wish.*

If they were worth that, I'd have bought a private island and my own team of lawyers.

As you could plainly see by those stellar amounts, Cockburn was a fucking liar, and I had the check stubs to prove it. That was what had gotten Newhouse into trouble. He had listened to the liars and not me. His greed had given him the boner from hell, and he thought he'd just stumbled into the Rockefeller estate and that he could go buy a new Tesla off my royalties, only to realize that I'd gone into bankruptcy because I didn't make the money the stupid lying whore was telling everyone that I made.

That she was lying to get her client money that didn't exist.

Unless we were counting the money in our Monopoly game in the closet.

Because of Les's idiocy prior to leaving, I'd had to take the bulk of my savings to buy back several contracts.

That was why Les had stolen money from my children. I was broke because of a massive multimillion dollar lawsuit he'd started and refused to finish that had caused me to spend another almost million dollars to buy back contracts to keep from having my book release dates pushed back.

Which he knew. That meant that every time Cockburn got up there and said that I had control over my release dates, she knew she was lying as I'd been forced to buy back my books in order to have that control.

Yet no one would discipline her for it.

My head throbbed from this. Not to mention that I couldn't understand why the accountant bitch Newhouse had forced upon me at two hundred dollars an hour couldn't figure out how to "key it in" when my eighty-dollar-an-hour-accountant had never once had to ask me what a royalty check was. Somehow, she'd miraculously known that my income came from royalties and entered it in as such without wasting my valuable time with moronic questions so that she could bill me more time by asking that question over and over. Not to mention that he sent those questions through my attorney, which then caused me to spend more money as she had to forward me the question and then forward the answer back to him.

Ca-ching. Ca-ching.

So much for looking out for my estate while in bankruptcy, yeah?

He was really good at his job. *Please read with all due sarcasm.*

Oh, and about that "documentation." Dumbass had been told until I was blue in the face that all royalty checks came with a single piece of paper:

Statements will be provided separately. Please detach check before deposit.

That was it. Ergo, I didn't include that tiny piece of paper as I didn't feel it was worth his charging me the time to rip it off, as it provided no additional information as my publishers gave us the benefit of the doubt that we were smart enough to know these were our royalty checks.

Because we weren't "Newhouse stupid." We were only "author stupid."

But the biggest humdinger of this was the anthology check.

*Get ready for your head to explode.*

Let us revisit Cockburn's rant to the judge about those tens of thousands of dollars that she wasted going after my "anthology" i.e. short story money with Dumas's lawyer.

Because Les was demanding every single crumb of money.

Okay. Here was the problem with that. They had stipulated from the beginning that Les was my "business manager" who ran every facet of "our" family business.

*Wait. Give me a second. My eyes had to roll so far back in my head on that one that I can't see. I have to wait for them to roll back into place before I can continue...*

All right. Then why the fuck was my "short story" check for sixty dollars still going to our old house?

The house I hadn't lived in for almost a decade?

See, that little nugget came in with a fan letter. It was very sweet. The man who'd bought my old house was kind enough to tell me that he'd received mail for me, "all the time." However, he normally threw it away.

Unfortunately, he'd opened this one piece by accident, and it happened to be a check. So, he kindly forwarded it to my home with a sweet letter explaining it to me and telling me how much he loved my books.

*Thank you, sweetie for your kindness.*

But where do I even begin to unpack the problems with this? Had Les never gone to the post office and had our mail forwarded?

Oh my God! How many checks had I lost over the years?

The problem with royalties was that they got smaller until they dried up. That was a tiny residual and if it was still going to the old address, then the larger checks had never been received.

Or had they?

The only one who would know would be Les.

Who never kept track of anything.

Yet here they were acting like *I* was the problem.

Yeah. I was disgusted on a level unimaginable at this point.

Newhouse was backing the wrong horse. He kept believing them while acting like I was the enemy.

How much evidence would I have to give him before he'd remove his head out of his ass to see the truth? For one thing, he'd have been a lot less embarrassed before Dinky and his boss had he listened to me from the beginning and not let his greed lead him around by his penis.

He'd come into my case with the preconceived notion that I must be in the wrong because I was the one in bankruptcy. Obviously, I didn't know how to manage money. Rather than believe me when I'd told him the truth. I was there because I was being hammered by irrational, lying assholes who kept dragging me into court every two weeks and charging me a fortune for the misery.

Again, no one's checkbook could sustain attorney fees of thirty-five to fifty thousand dollars *a month* unless they were a member of the Walton family (owners of Walmart). While I'd made a good wage as a writer (thank you, fans), I had never made so much that I could sustain those kinds of bills.

Very few people in this country could.

That was what had forced me into bankruptcy.

Instead of helping me get out of it, Newhouse had turned into an even bigger threat than Les and his team of imbeciles combined.

All because of arrogance and greed.

And rampant stupidity.

Now here I was. Still trapped. No answer about the house. Caught in limbo and with no idea if, or when, my nightmare would ever end.

# MARCH 11

**H**OW SICK OF THE BULLSHIT was I? Let me count the ways...

This lovely gem of a day had begun with emails asking about the very "valuable" silver that I had in my house that Newhouse should come seize.

*Are you fucking kidding me?*

At this point, I was ready to stick that phrase on a coffee mug and mail it to all the imbeciles that I had to deal with.

To which I replied, "Are you referring to the fucking silver set that I reported to the police and every attorney I've spoken to that Les stole on his way out the door? Along with my Reed & Barton Tarpley silver chest, that in and of itself was worth about a thousand dollars?

"Why don't you get a court order, go to the fucking cabin, and get my silver back?"

After all, it'd been my twenty-fifth wedding anniversary present. And the bastard had stolen it on his way out the door.

What I had left was a "nice" set of stainless-steel cutlery I'd inherited from my mother. On the back, it was clearly stamped 18/10, which any moron (I know, I know, that meant they had no clue) knew was the chromium to nickel ratio for stainless-steel.

*C'mon, Newhouse. You're my age.* That meant that like any Gen Xer, you'd been around when Billy Joel's *Allentown* had been ruthlessly played into the ground by every radio station in the country and MTV.

This was before the age of satellite, YouTube and Wifi.

> *No, they never taught us what was real*
>
> *Iron and coke*
>
> Chromium steel

So, you had no excuse not to understand that 18/10 ratio that was stamped on the back of the fork that I sent you. And why could Terri never have any nice silver in her marriage?

Because Les had been so effing lazy that he would have stuck it in the dishwasher and tore it up. Les was horrible that way. I had an entire collection of clothing and dishes that he'd ruined because he refused to do anything the right way.

This included my grandmother's cast iron skillet she'd inherited from her mother that he'd rusted out and I still hadn't been able to re-season properly to my expensive Le Creuset pot he'd absolutely annihilated because he couldn't give me the time to clean it and he'd stuck it in the dishwasher while I was on a phone call.

The three-hundred-dollar pot was reduced to this sticky, horrific nightmare.

Because he was too lazy to do anything properly.

Or worse, he'd laughed and admitted he tore it up on purpose so that he wouldn't be asked to do anything again. "Remember the Bill Cosby skit, Cake for Breakfast?" Then he'd get this stupid grin and laugh about it. He even backed into my brand-new Mustang because he was angry at me and tore the whole back end off it. And he'd scraped the whole nose off the front end of my baby sports car.

He was that jealous a bastard.

His philosophy was, if I fucked it up badly enough, I'd never be asked to do it again. "I could go back to bed and sleep, which was what I'd wanted to do in the first place."

This was what he had proudly done to my mother's limited-edition Paul Revere Copper pot.

He melted the copper right off the pan one night in a hissy fit.

Oh, but that wasn't the last of it, then came the emails, again, about the jewelry, which I thought had been sold in "retaliation" as Martha and Newhouse had told me they were going to do in January.

"Terri has it!"

Remember that this was the jewelry that had been illegally confiscated out of my home. I had nothing left. They'd taken everything from me, except the little black studs where I'd had my ears re-pierced that had been in my ears at the time they came into my house. I was amazed they hadn't forced me to hand them over, too.

After all, they'd even taken the button from my coat that had been in my safe.

And the rock ring my son had made for me in elementary school, and the one my boys had bought for me out of a bubble gum machine.

Fucking bastards.

"Check what she had on her in jail. They would have written it down when they booked her!"

*Proud of that, are you, you sacks of shit?*

Wow. Just wow. Only something as low as Cockburn and Les would continually bring up with pride the fact that they'd had Dinky violate my Constitutional Rights and lock up the mother of his sons who was trying to protect his sons from the known pedophile that was his father he'd sworn for thirty years that he hated because of the sexual abuse he'd suffered as a boy.

And there was no need to even bring it up as I'd been arrested the week before they'd raided my house, so it didn't matter what I was wearing then.

They loved to bring up their illegal actions that violated my civil rights and dignity.

Needless to say, at this point, I was disgusted. Having read the daily chronicle of bullshit, I think you could see why.

So, I called up my attorney. "Tell those idiots that I'm done. They are either to come to terms with this divorce by Friday and stop running up my bills for bullshit or at five o'clock on Friday afternoon, I'm calling Newhouse and we're going to a Chapter 7."

*Not a threat. A promise.*

My attorney didn't believe me.

"I'm not kidding, Melissa. They have until Friday, and I'm nuking this shit. Make him aware that he won't get half of anything. He will only have one quarter. Because whatever is left, he only gets half of that. And I have the word from on high that when they sell those contracts and royalties, my publisher will cancel them and pull the books out of print."

"Why would they do that?"

Why couldn't any of them retain anything I said? "Because they will not risk a lawsuit from the new trademark owner. Or any other legal bullshit. They don't know what legal tangles could come from it. So, for them, it's cheaper and easier to pulp it all. Which means Dipshit won't have shit. Make that clear to them. I have told this to Newhouse and so has my agent. Repeatedly. But at this point, I no longer give a flying fuck. I am done paying to be harassed by all of you. I won't do it another day. And if Newhouse refuses, I will publish this book that he's terrified of and force Martha to uphold her threat."

*Let's play some Russian Roulette, shall we?*

I knew I was good to my word.

Were they?

Either way, I was finished. I was done being held at the figurative gunpoint. It was more than any human should have to bear.

At the rate he was going, I was going to lose it all anyway. The only question was when.

I wasn't going to keep working and paying for his herd of hyenas to keep coming at my throat and dragging me in front of Skeletor.

To hell with it.

There was nothing more I could do to make that bastard hate me, including set fire to a baby in his courtroom.

They had flipped my "fuck-it" switch. All that mattered was that I didn't spend another day of my life being needlessly tormented over bullshit that was irrelevant.

The bastard had left me. Either he wanted a divorce, or he didn't.

This was beyond ridiculous and cruel. The fact that the court was not only allowing, but gleefully (Skeletor laughed about my abuse) participating in it should be criminal. This was wife and child abuse. Sickening mental abuse that no one should be put through because they'd loved someone and had wanted to take care of them.

Maybe it would have been different had I cheated on him or done something to him. But I and my children had been the ones abused by this sick fuck for years.

And the judge signed off on his madness.

This was the real Confederacy of Dunces.

Welcome to Williamson County, Tennessee 2020. Land of the sick and twisted.

AFTER WORKING FOR WEEKS, Melissa sent over the appeal for the Supreme Court she was filing. My first thought was, "Wow. It's taken you all this time, and all you produced was ten pages."

Yet all of them thought I should be able to shit out a book in a week and get paid for it.

*Tell me again how that works?*

I guessed they were "special."

In that document, she called Dinky out for his abuse. That I had followed his orders and remained calm while he'd exploded over the fact that I'd followed his orders.

Entrapment 101.

That was the truth of what happened that day. Not the lies that had been spread by Les and his crew of flesh-eating jackals or even the stupid bitch known as Lily Ships. The one thing I'd always hated about the media was their sloppy research and lazy reporting. She was the Queen Bee of lies and defamation.

Or a hired hack.

They could deny the truth all they wanted, but truth was truth and Les's sister had been more than open about what they'd done to her.

After my sons were born, Les had spent hours and hours venting his own hatred for his parents over his own sexual abuse, and Cockburn herself had put it in her April 2018 motion to the court.

My boys were also willing to testify. *Shame on you, Les, for the fact that you were willing to betray your sons and leave them out to hang the same way you'd abandoned your sister when she'd asked you to back her.*

The way you'd abandoned Taylor.

You were and would always be a coward. Contrary to the lies you'd told others; I was never the one who emasculated you. I tried to prop you up and bolster your ego, which apparently was one of my biggest mistakes next to not leaving you years ago.

But then blaming others for your own actions was what you were always good at. Even Melissa had finally caught on as we were talking about the silver you had stolen from our home.

"Sounds like he's trying to get you in trouble and blaming you for what he did."

"Yes, ma'am. It's what he always did." That and he took credit for things he never did, either.

Such as my son's comic.

My son going off to Japan.

And my career that I, myself, built while he mocked and belittled me. The career I had to steal a stamp out of his wallet to get because he'd doled those stamps out to me only when I "deserved" them.

I was the abused spouse.

And the Tennessee courts kept heaping even more abuse on top of me.

All I wanted was out. I wanted it to stop. I'd spent my entire childhood under the fist of my grandparents and the emotional turmoil of a bipolar mother. I went from that horror show to living with the madness of Les and his repulsive, lying Stepfordesque family.

Why was I, the woman who'd spent her entire life seeking peace, caught in such never-ending drama?

*Please, God, end this nightmare, one way or another, and get me out of this hellhole state.* Why Josh Whedon had set *Buffy* in California, I had no idea. The real Hell Mouth was in middle Tennessee.

And the face of the devil was the judge on the bench that everyone in town knew was corrupt, but no one would speak up against him. They only whispered about it behind closed doors.

MARCH 14

**I** HAD NO IDEA WHERE I STOOD. How fun was that? I'd tried all day yesterday to get a hold of Melissa. I didn't know if that meant she was on another vacation or what as she'd never bothered to return a text, email or call. I was left completely hanging.

Not like this was important, as in my life was on the line or anything.

Really, I'd never understood lawyers.

The only thing I knew for certain was that she wasn't in court as all court sessions had been suspended due to the Coronavirus. Too bad they hadn't done that on Monday. They could have saved me tens of thousands of dollars in Les and Cockburn's fees as they had ramped it up since Monday on harassing me again, now that Cockburn and crew knew that Dinky would okay whatever amount they wanted to gouge me for.

He'd told them that. "While other judges might not agree with me in this case, I'm not going to have lawyers working for free."

*Yee-fucking-haw.*

Another boot party was on.

My other fave moment had been at the end when ole Dinky looked out upon that vast and repugnant number of Les's attorneys and instead of telling him it was a waste of marital assets and that he needed to cull the herd, he'd laughed and said, "Hmmm... I don't know who to assign this order to for them to write it."

Then he played eenie-meenie-minie-moe with *my* money for him to pick his favorite he wanted to give more of my money to.

If that wasn't blatant partiality, please tell me what was?

Where the fuck was the D.A. and the Department of Justice or FBI for this disgusting display of corruption and blight on our judicial system?

It ranked right up there with when I was talking to Rose later that night, and she said that she'd been speaking with her friend who moved out of Williamson County to Lewis because of the corruption. "I asked him if he knew Dinky, and he said, 'Oh yeah. That bastard is one of the worst of the worst. I've got stories about him you wouldn't believe.'" According to her friend, Dinky had even lost his bar license at one point, and somehow had gotten it reinstated, but no one was sure who'd pulled what strings as it'd all been covered up.

Number three in the country for most corrupt states. Nashville, one of the most corrupt cities. *Yah! Me!*

And what chafed me most was that my only contact with my attorney that day came as another harassment email. You knew it would. After all these months of Newhouse's overpaid bitch breathing down my neck about the two-thousand-dollar deposit for Comic Con, it'd gone through.

But of course, there was a snag.

Caused by Dipshit. He'd stood in the courtroom, telling me to get "someone else" to pay for Comic Con. I kept trying to tell Dipshit that Comic Con had rules and that it didn't work the way he "thought" it should work (much like the courts in Middle Tennessee didn't follow the laws they were supposed to). While he had this delusion he was God Almighty and kept saying that he could "break contracts" and do all this other shit that had proven false, I kept assuring him that to the God of Comic Con he was a turd who had no authority.

We were all peons out there.

And I was well aware of it. So, the only way to secure our rooms was with a single credit card. Which I couldn't do as Dipshit refused to allow me to have the extra two grand I needed, even though I had to have it to run my business.

Oh, he'd pay the bastards torturing me and that overpaid bitch of his that we didn't need, but God forbid I have some money to run my company.

Okay.

Well, I was authorized for two thousand which I'd spent on the rooms as I was supposed to and that I had permission to do (keeping in mind that when I didn't spend the money they'd allotted me on the exact item I was supposed to spend it on, they also chewed me out).

One would think I'd sacrificed a fucking goat on my church altar at Easter for doing what they'd told me I could do.

At that point, I told Melissa, "Put me in a Chapter 7. I am done with being harassed over every single business decision by an imbecile I wouldn't put in charge of a herd of stuffed animals."

*Damned if I do and damned if I don't.*

Enough!

No one could live under this constant bullshit, especially since I had to take two hours away from *my* job to go to a notary to do *more* bullshit paperwork on the cars that didn't have to be sold had Newhouse not been an incompetent jerk-off.

Paperwork to certify the odometer reading on a car I never drove that the I-refuse-to-work-Les could have done since he had nothing better to do with his useless life other than harass me and cost me tens of thousands of dollars he'd never earned to be paid out to fucking jackals I couldn't stand. But no, by all means, let us pull the only person working that we're all leeching off of to stop her productivity for something stupid and then demand later, "why haven't you finished your book?"

"Um, because I needed time to work, and you kept interfering with that time for bullshit *you* fucked up and didn't do right the first time?"

How was that for an answer?

And what killed me most was that Newhouse kept telling me that I should be grateful to him for his harassment because the other trustees *were worse*. Wow. Was there a course where abusers were trained for that shit?

"Don't make me slap you again, Terri! This is for you own good. I wouldn't beat you if you'd just do what I say. I know I keep changing the rules on you and you have to read my mind, and I'm irrational, but damn bitch! Catch a clue and stop making me hurt my hand when I smack you!"

Seriously. I was done being his whipping girl. *Go home, asshole, beat your own wife and kids if that was what you got off on. Leave me alone.*

So, on that morning I went and did what I knew was futile, but futility had become my middle name. I filed another complaint with another government agency who had ignored me in the past, adding more facts since they'd done more shit since I'd filed my last complaint. Want to see it?

Here you go (this one went to the Department of Justice in Washington):

I was told by my local police department to document the gross breach of due process, threats of retaliation, gross mismanagement by bankruptcy trustees, and judicial misconduct, as well as the violation of my civil rights that has been going on in Middle Tennessee for the last two years. After the U.S. Trustee was appointed, against my protests, he came in and hired his friends, and almost doubled my debt while none of my original creditors have been paid, nor has a plan been entered for their repayment. Almost a year has gone by and more than enough of my personal belongings and assets have been sold to satisfy all my debt and then some, yet he and his boss, as well as the judge have made it clear that they intend to ruin me and force me onto welfare. They have said, repeatedly, that if I refuse to work for absolutely no payment whatsoever for my work, they will put me in jail.

I'm a #1 *New York Times* bestselling author. So I began documenting their abuse and threats in a diary, and my bankruptcy attorney, against my wishes, gave a copy to the U.S. Trustee who then hauled me in for a meeting and threatened my liberty and property, and then made direct threats against my childhood friend. Both trustees used the word "retaliation" and have said that my property that had been illegally seized from my home was to be sold "to punish me" and that there was nothing I could do about it. That I was to go write more books to get myself out of bankruptcy but that if the book that documented what was happening to me and all their wrongdoings should ever be sold, that I would regret it and that they would ruin me financially and put me in jail for it.

Since that day in January, they have made my life a living hell and are about to put me out on the street. They have ordered me to break the law. They have put me in jail when I did nothing wrong, and I have witnesses who will verify this. I was sentenced to ten days while I was complying with the judge's orders. And they have used that to bully and intimidate me into paying whatever outrageous fees they demand of me, while I'm in bankruptcy. Their actions have almost doubled the debt I was in. In less than five months, the bankruptcy trustee has charged me over $100,000 in fees which is approximately 1/3 of the debt I started with. They have committed perjury, done illegal searches and seizures of not only my property, but that of my grown sons' property and my sons are not part of this bankruptcy.

I have their extortion documented in emails. They haven't even tried to hide the fact that they are threatening and intimidating me, and intend to leave me on welfare and with no means of support after they've plundered my entire estate. Please help me.

These are the people who were in the meeting on January 16, 2020 who threatened retaliation against my illegally seized property:

Martha Seaver, US Trustee
Tom Newhouse, US Trustee
Bill Oldham, Attorney of US Trustee

Stefano Leadwits, Bankruptcy Attorney
Joan Hart (personal friend)
Terri Woods (me)

These are the parties involved in the illegal search and seizure of my home on June 19, 2019 and Bill Oldham has admitted it was improperly done, as has my best friend who is a Marshall.

My property was removed from my home, including cash and no receipt was left for it. It was taken to an undisclosed location. Bank accounts, including my son's personal accounts were seized without there being a proper court order and the divorce court had no jurisdiction over my 19-year-old son's property or that of my 24-year-old son whose property was also seized. We were illegally held in my home by an officer, Bruce Meyer, who will also testify it was improperly done.

Judge Bubba Dinky (presiding judge who threatened and intimidated my friends- he told them that he was "watching them" and followed them to their cars) has refused to hold a hearing on my property or return it to me, or my sons.

My accountants Valorie Plum, Nancy Harrison and Meg Beech will also testify that I am being gouged by Tom Newhouse for services and while he is failing to do his job. When I tried to report his activities to his boss, Martha Seaver, she threatened me and my friend Joan. I cannot stress that enough. She told me that my "book" was never to see the light of day or that she would ruin me. Her exact words were "My finger is on the button. If you do anything to displease us, anything at all, I will push it and you will be ruined. Do you understand?" There is no mistaking that threat and Attorney Leadwits has since put that threat in writing, in emails, on several occasions. It is well documented. No one should be threatened and humiliated and robbed by the government the way I have. I went to them for help, not to be treated this way. Please help me, and please protect my family and friends.

I seriously doubted they would do anything other than ignore me as they'd done in the past, but I was hoping. After all, the FBI had jumped for Les and gone out to harass my fans and come to my house for a false report he'd given them. Maybe, just maybe, someone in the Justice Department might actually give a shit about justice.

# MARCH 14

**T**HIS WAS A SATURDAY, ERGO one would think that I'd have a day off from the never-ending harassment to focus on writing the book that absolutely everyone kept nagging me to write so that I could earn money.

One would be catastrophically wrong.

The day opened with old Newhouse back, lying as he did so much that he was giving old Cockburn a run for her money. Damn. I didn't think anyone could lie more than that bitch.

I was wrong.

Just like when he'd shouted in the conference room of the courthouse, "I have emails!" Meaning he was lying.

Not to mention, the stupid bastard had told us in that January 19 meeting where they'd ambushed me, "I don't even read the emails you send me."

*So, which was it, Pinocchio?* Did you read those emails or not?

What was it with liars that they never could keep their lies straight?

Since Dipshit was lying about the contents, I would say that he'd lied Monday, March 9 to both me and the judge, in court, and told the truth in January when he'd said that he didn't read my emails because he didn't have time or inclination to read them.

Same reason he'd hired his overpaid bitch of an accountant. He was simply too lazy to do his job.

Careful, Newhouse, I have an incredibly scary recall, especially when I was under attack. They had called me Memorex my entire life.

So, when he began this lie, I knew we were in for a day of drama:

> Not true. It was initially authorized a long time ago when I had no idea she would be in the financial condition she is in now. Then we kept asking why the check had not cleared and to give us proof that the check was mailed. She said she had not sent it. Eventually we started telling her over many funding requests it was no longer authorized since she could no longer afford to go to comic cons. She was notified that comic cons were not being funded well before and during our Monday March 9 meeting at the courthouse. Why would she do that if she knew she could not afford to go to comic cons? She needs to reverse that charge.

First, I kept telling Dipshit that it wasn't a check. It would be a credit card transaction. That was how stupid he and his overpriced Alzheimer's accountant were.

Ready for the proof of what kind of fucking liar I was dealing with on a daily basis? Here was the last notice I was sent the day before that hearing:

| Comic Con 2020 | 2,000 | Booth rental; Trustee is following up with MM to determine which comic con this is for, whether the debtor is still attenting and if a stop payment should be issued if the debtor is not attending |
|---|---|---|

I don't know about you, but that doesn't look like an "order" to me. I read it like a question. *Was I still attending?*

Um, Newhouse, for an attorney and trustee, you had a stunning lack of reading comprehension.

Also, there was only one Comic Con that I'd paid for, and the idiots should have known that.

Never mind that this was his two hundred dollar an hour escapee from the senile farm who, months later and after dozens and dozens of corrections by both me and my much more reasonably priced accountant, couldn't remember that I had told them both repeatedly that the booth was paid for. That the two thousand dollars was for the hotel room reservation. That I needed the money way in advance because of the way Comic Con did their reservations. Vendors were required to put in hotel requests, but we didn't actually know what hotel we'd end up with until a later date. Those were assigned by the powers that be.

Once the assignments were sent out, we were given just a matter of days to put the money down on them or lose them forever. Since Dipshit couldn't be bothered with my financial needs and would only deal with me every two weeks, I couldn't make an emergency request for funds should something like this come up. So, I had to make early requests for things in anticipation of them.

Which had led to them yelling at me constantly as I tried to run a business while playing Nostradamus.

Something that was a big problem with Comic Con, because if you didn't get your room when it was sent out, then you had no hotel for the duration of the event as Comic Con in San Diego takes every single hotel room in the city, and you would be shit out of luck. I had told them this, on repeat.

Even on the phone.

That was how stupid they were.

And now you have the proof as to what kind of liars and morons I was dealing with.

Let me pick apart the rest of his lie. He hadn't spoken to me at all prior to March 9. About anything. He was going through others, so if he had issued those orders, his lackeys had failed to forward them to me. That was on him and his lackeys.

Maybe he should have spent my money on cheaper and better lackeys.

He had sold my clothing, my cars and my pocketbooks out of spite and he'd admitted as much in front of witnesses. In front of the judge, he'd admitted that he'd mismanaged my estate from the beginning. His exact words were that he'd been misled about the value of my property.

Not by me, mind you, but by Cockburn and crew who were continuing to lie to the judge who feasted on those lies like a professional wrestler at an all-you-can-eat buffet. And rather than correct the lies that Cockburn continued to tell the judge as he was required to do to protect my estate, Newhouse had stood there and let her go on and on instead of speaking up.

He was as worthless as they came.

The reason my finances were bad, and he admitted this too, to the judge was because he had taken money from my children that he was not entitled to take. I didn't realize it then because they kept threatening to put me in jail and telling me not to rock the boat.

Well, I was rocking it now.

God had sent me another angel. Nan.

She was a new friend of my brother's, an attorney who specialized in bankruptcy and divorce.

Best of all, she was an appellate attorney, and when I told her what was being done to me, she didn't believe.

"Terri, that's not how the law or court work."

Then I sent her my evidence, emails, transcripts, recording and court orders.

"Oh my God! I live in Podunk, Alabama and I have never seen or heard of anything this corrupt! How is this possible?"

I had no idea, +and it was why I'd wanted to speak to her.

But with her, I learned a lot about the law, fast.

Most of all, I learned how crooked Williamson County and my trustees were.

Now, I was done being lied to and lied about while my business was being destroyed by these animals who had no business in their jobs. They weren't fit to tie shoes at a shoeshine booth.

I told Dufus Newhouse when he came on board that I was only paid twice a year and that my money had to stretch. Rather than believe me, he listened to the idiot brigade who'd told him that every time one of my books sold in the country, I got a check for it.

Yeah, they were that stupid.

So much for Les being the manager of my business, eh? Thirty years and the imbecile sill had no idea how royalties worked.

That Monday, Newhouse had told the judge that he'd handed out all my money to the jackals and left me with nothing to run my business or to do what I needed to do to make more money.

Like go to Comic Con.

Last fall, when the idiot had sold me out and paid off the attorneys and given them blank checks to pay themselves whatever obscene amounts they wanted, Newhouse had started making me cancel events.

"Why do you need to go to them? You don't have a book out."

Stupid, why do you think bands travel when they don't have a new album?

That was how we kept our names out there and built-up new readers. I thought everyone over the age of four knew this. I damn sure would have thought someone they put over a business would understand the basic precepts of business and how one worked.

No. I got stuck with the dumbest motherfucker on the planet. One too arrogant to listen to anyone.

And I really resented his overpaid bitch calling me "the debtor." Let me tell you something, you overpriced slag, I was not "the debtor." I was dragged into a nightmare against my will, and I could guarantee you, bitch, that you could not handle what I'd been given to deal with, nor could you pay the bills that were lobbed at me because of an idiot I made the mistake of marrying.

I prayed and hoped to God that each and every one of them got a dose of what they were shoving down my throat.

They deserved it. I did not.

I was so pissed off that I finally did what my attorney should have done. I went to the Tennessee legal case site and found all the cases that Les had worked on as, wait for it...

A bankruptcy attorney.

Nearly one hundred of them.

In Tennessee alone.

It also proved that he and Cockburn had again committed perjury and lied in documents and to the judge. Those records showed that Les had practiced law and was the lead attorney on cases from 1995 until 2009.

2009.

Years after Cockburn had lied about him "giving up" his practice to raise our sons.

Remember that my sons had graduated in 2013 and 2014.

In 2009, they were both in high school.

Who raised my sons?

I did.

Alone while Daddy sat on the couch, flipping channels and complaining about how the world had done him wrong, and saying that he "didn't have time to mess with those kids." While he drank his Scotch.

For that matter, I still had this little nugget that old Les had sent to his attorneys right before he left my home to file for divorce:

> I don't think it is appropriate to depose me. I serve as Terri's attorney on a daily basis. Another factor that separates me from Dumas's husband is the fact that I do not co-author books with my wife.

So, Mr. "I can't work because I have no skills" was lying his ass off, as was his attorney, who was committing a bar violation every time she opened her mouth. Obviously, he was a working attorney and I had it from his own email account, multiple times and now from the Tennessee Court System to show how many cases he'd worked.

And then the kicker came about nine that night when Melissa emailed me that I'd sold the house.

I was done.

Come Monday, I was going to do what Nan had told me I was legally able to do. Fire my bankruptcy attorney and force this bankruptcy to be dismissed before Newhouse spent every last dollar of my house money on those jackals.

I prayed that for once, God would be with me. Because I knew I was in for one hell of a fight.

But I was ready. My loins were girded. I was taking my life back and one way or another, I would get these jackals out of my life if it was the last thing I did.

**W**ELL, IT WAS DONE. I'D fired my bankruptcy attorney. After the email was sent, I kept thinking, "Is this what it feels like after you hit the button to launch a nuke?" Because you knew in your gut that there would be some kind of fall-out and devastation. That the person you'd just launched against was going to retaliate.

Just didn't know how or when.

Or how bad the return strike would be.

And there was nothing to do but sit and wait for their reaction.

It was a bad feeling. Similar to the ones we'd had as kids whenever we approached the door to our home, not knowing the mood our mom would be in when we walked through it. If it was a good day, we'd be facing June Cleaver. All smiles and happiness.

If it was one of her bad days, we'd be facing June with a cleaver. And she'd be aiming for our heads and hearts.

That never-ending game of uncertainty. It'd sucked as a child and I'd sworn to myself then that if I survived that childhood that no one would ever make me walk on eggshells like that again.

Especially not in my own home.

*Thank you, Les.*

And as I waited for the hell that I knew would invariably come, my mind kept thinking back and wondering what had gone through Baby Huey's head when he'd been planning all of this.

Forget the fact that he'd poisoned me.

I kept trying to understand the sickness of his mind that he'd listened to Hogg and whomever when they'd told him, "Screw over, Terri. Do you your worst and everything will be fine!"

Because at the end of the day, he had shown his sons the absolute worst of his personality. As bad as he'd claimed that he hated Dumas, he hadn't gone after her with as much passion. Nor his parents who'd allowed him to be raped as a child and then forced him to sit at the table with his rapist and pretend everything was fine.

Never mind the fact that he'd welcomed into his home the father responsible for the molestation other family members.

Over and over, for years, I'd listened to him rail against both his mother and father. Yet he'd never once attacked them.

Not the way he had the wife who had done nothing but love him and take care of his every need. With a lavish lifestyle he'd never dreamed was possible.

Instead, he'd turned all that malice he'd held back against the people who'd done him wrong loose onto the mother of his own children. The woman who had protected and cared for him. The one *he'd* abused and treated like crap, in front of his sons.

Sons who knew the absolute truth. That their mother had never done anything to their father to warrant this level of hatred.

What sickness had possessed his mind that he believed for one second those sons who knew the truth would side with a monster?

Just because he'd turned rabid for no reason, didn't mean they would.

And why would they? He'd shown them his true face. That at the end of the day, it didn't matter how much you loved or cared for him, for no reason whatsoever and out of the blue, he could turn on you and go for your throat.

How could his sons ever trust him again?

Didn't matter how many years he might have built a bond of trust with those kids. Even if he hadn't been abusive toward them, they would never have trusted him again.

Not after witnessing his brutal attacks on innocent people.

In one fell swoop, Les had shown his true colors and his sons had been horrified by the level of undeserved cruelty where he'd lashed out at them and their mother.

The level of betrayal was such that they could never forgive or forget. And the worst part was that they now had a fear in their heart that because they carried his genes, they could awaken every bit the monster he was.

So was Maddox's wife. She lived in terror that her husband could become like his father.

For no reason.

I kept assuring them that they were good men. That I'd raised them to be *much* better. I wasn't Snooty. I would never allow my sons to do this to my grandkids or my daughters-in-law.

But then, I could never in good faith harbor a pedophile. Snooty had proven herself sick in the head for years, which was why I'd never wanted her in my home.

Not after Les had confessed to me who and what they were.

My flesh still crawled at the thought of them being in the same room with me. Of them being near my children.

The only comforting thought was that my boys would make sure that my grandbabies were never put in harm's way.

And still the clock ticked by as I waited.

All I could think about was Leadwits's irrational, over-the-top response on February 24, 2020 when I'd asked if there was any way I could get the bankruptcy dismissed.

Rather than answering my question with a civil email, here was his response:

Terri – your proposal is unrealistic. Bankruptcies CANNOT BE DROPPED WITHOUT THE CONSENT OF CREDITORS AND APPROVED BY THE JUDGE. Les Manly will never agree to the dismissal, especially after Tom has beaten him up over the remainder of the admin fees. So, lets move pass that point.

Are you begging for this case to be converted to a Chapter 7. Martha and Tom will do it in a heartbeat if I forward your email request to them.

This case is finally moving in the right direction. Do not screw this up because Dinky will have field day on you if you try to dismiss (which will never happen) in this case.

What did admin fees have to do with anything? And why was Les a party to my *business* bankruptcy? None of it made sense.

But in one email, Leadwits had referenced everything. The fact that the judge was biased and "punishing" me and that the trustees were abusing their power and threatening me, constantly.

That was the state that I was being forced to live in. With an attorney who had told me that his loyalty was with them and not with me. "They are the ones I have to deal with for all my cases. Their relationship is the one I value most."

At least, Leadwits had been honest on that point that he was willing to feed me to them.

And for the record, that had been his response when I'd asked him on January 19 why he'd breached attorney-client privilege and given them things that I'd told him and shown him in confidence.

"My loyalty is to the court and them, not my client."

Rule 501 of the Tennessee Code of Ethics for attorneys:

T.C.A. § 23-3-105. ATTORNEY-CLIENT PRIVILEGE

No attorney, solicitor or counselor shall be permitted, in giving testimony against a client, or person who consulted the attorney, solicitor or counselor professionally, to disclose any communication made to the attorney, solicitor or counselor as such by such person, during the pendency of the suit, before or afterwards, to the person's injury.

T.C.A. § 23-3-107. SAME

Any attorney offering to give testimony in any of the cases provided for in T.C.A. § 23-3-105... shall be rejected by the court, and such attorney commits a Class C misdemeanor, for which, on conviction, the attorney shall also be stricken from the rolls, if a practicing attorney.

Leadwits had handed me his bar license and instead of helping me, kept threatening me more on their behalf.

Maybe they thought they had beaten down so many people over the years who were defeated by poverty and such that they didn't realize some of us were Weebuls. We didn't bow down no matter how much we were beaten. My child abuse and marriage had Troxlered me. I was used to it.

So, this was the email that I'd sent to Leadwits that morning:

In lieu of past events and after much soul-searching, I think it best if you file your motion to withdraw as my counsel in this bankruptcy.

I trust that in the future you will abide by attorney-client privilege and hold it with all the due respect that relationship is supposed to carry.

Thank you,
Terri

Civil and to the point, especially as they'd breached it and had been threatening me with ruination on a daily basis. And using their threats to control me such as when Leadwits sent this email on January 28:

I continued it for 4 weeks and so long as you tell me that she is counseling, then I will stay on the case.

He had even gotten Newhouse to approve enough money for that "therapy" that I didn't need or want that I could have paid the reservation for my Comic Con room that they'd kept harassing me over.

For that matter, Newhouse had spent more money protesting Comic Con than the two-thousand-dollar deposit I had put down on it.

Even then, after I'd jumped through all their hoops, they continued to harass me. When I submitted the bill for the "counseling" I didn't want or need, Newhouse immediately jumped my shit again. This from the moron who kept telling me to "cut back" on my employee hours and shut down my business, then kept complaining that I wasn't making the money I had been because I'd cut back everything.

Even dumber, he was running all of this through my attorney and driving up my legal costs constantly over utter bullshit.

Case in point this little nugget had cost me twice as much as the counseling sessions Newhouse was protesting that I hadn't wanted or needed, but had been blackmailed into by these bastards:

> Tom wants to protect your privacy and so does not want to ask your accountant about this.

> Have you gotten an invoice yet?  Why did you pay an additional $850- is that for another test?

> He wants to know the details so that he can decide if the charges are reasonable or not.

> I understand why you feel this is harassing, but I also understand his point of view.

> He did agree to counseling, but these fees are at least 10 times higher than he would've expected. He expected an expense of 100 - 200 every few weeks or so. I have to say that that is what I would've expected also.

Well, had Newhouse been a grown up and asked himself, he would have learned that it was for multiple sessions and an intake fee. I didn't have an invoice as they hadn't mailed it out yet. And what aggravated me then and still aggravates me now was that he always questioned everyone's rates except his own outrageous and ungodly fees.

And those of his "friends."

As if thirty-five thousand dollars for his idiot accountant wasn't ten times more than I was used to paying my accounting firm. In fact, that was more than what I paid them for a year's service.

And that was only for a couple of months while she'd charged such incredible amounts as almost nine hundred dollars for a single phone call to her boss?

No, that was not a lie or misstatement. The bankruptcy bitch had charged me nine hundred fucking dollars for a single phone call.

Now I ask, whose rates were ridiculous?

Don't even get me started on the tens of thousands of dollars that the auction house had charged.

Or Newhouse's stupidity in adding *over seventy thousand dollars* to my debt because he'd broken a lease that didn't need breaking.

His reason? "I don't want to see you in something so flashy."

*Are you fucking kidding me?*

But *those* ungodly fees old Newhouse didn't flinch over or question at all.

It was sickening.

So, given all these unrelenting threats that Leadwits could walk with Newhouse's blessing at any time, I didn't think firing the betrayer would be that a big a deal.

Here was the response:

> Terri and Melissa – My phone has been buzzing from Tom, Bill, and Martha since the word got

out that I was terminated. I got a telephone call from Tom Newhouse asking me my opinion of whether Terri would have any stream of income if the case gets converted to a Chapter 7. He said my departure would the trigger the UST to file a motion to convert and that I was the buffer keeping the case in Chapter 11. He went on to say that you (Terri) have found authority where the Court could dismiss the case.

Martha called and asked if you were freaking crazy. She said that Tom as Trustee would intercept all of your income, and that you would not even have the monies to buy food or gasoline. She told me to give you the heads up that she is filing an expedited motion to convert the case to a Chapter 7 by the middle of the week.

My responses to both were that I have been relieved of duties in the case. Tom all but begged me to send out this email saying that he would try to claim all Etsy sales and royalties if the case was converted. And you would not be pleased with the results if this case was a Chapter 7 bankruptcy. I told Martha and Tom that I will convey the messages.

As I have stated in several emails, you are not going to get this case dismissed. You do not have an absolute right to dismiss. Candidly, this is your case and your call. You do not need to handle this case pro se as Bill Oldham has suggested that you are planning to do. And frankly, without having an attorney to calm everyone down, your motion to dismiss will be denied, and the case will in all likelihood will be converted to a Chapter 7.

Since you have terminated me as counsel, you need to find new counsel as soon as possible. And you need to figure out how to compensate that attorney. Tom will not release any money to pay for new bankruptcy counsel. And I am not sure that Melissa will want those duties knowing that it is unlikely that she will be paid for the bankruptcy side of the case.

I have conveyed the message from Martha and Tom.

Wow, there was so much corruption to unpack in that email.

Aside from the fact that the U.S. Trustee had threatened to leave me and my special needs sons with no money for food and no gas (or money for the medicine my life depended on, which they'd been doing), and please keep in mind that this was during the height of COVID and that at the time these threats were made, I'd had a fever of 99.9-101.8 for four days. That I had a cough rattling in my throat and was extremely sick and under quarantine.

Here they were threatening me with all kinds of malice to "punish me" for standing up for myself.

Not trying to help me or work things out. They were proving that they had allowed Leadwits to bully and intimidate me with an empty threat as none of them had intended for Leadwits to leave.

All that money I'd been forced to waste and that misery all of them had heaped on me and now they dared to protest the fact that I told him to walk, after he'd held me hostage for months with his threat that if I didn't behave and do what they said he'd walk.

*Are you kidding me?*

More than that, they were telling me that, again, I would be refused my Constitutional Rights to defend myself in court. To have access to the money I had earned.

And this was only seven days after Newhouse had stood in that courtroom beside Cockburn and allowed her to tell Judge Dinky that I "had voluntarily put myself in bankruptcy, Your Honor." And had allowed them to beat me up for the hell that Newhouse and company were putting me in. Cockburn acted as if I were being protected and had done this as a shield when the truth was, I was being financially pillaged and threatened on a daily basis.

Yet Newhouse had stood there with that smug smirk I wanted someone to slap off his face.

And he, according to Martha's own words, was their "compassionate" trustee. He'd been "hand chosen" for my case because he, unlike the others, had a heart?

If this was an example of having a heart, I would hate to meet any of the others.

My God, what were these people unleashing on us?

And this was the Department of Justice?

Seriously?

Well, I didn't respond. Didn't know what to say to the pack of liars. They were out of control. Power hungry and drunk on authority.

How could anyone fight that?

So, I did what I knew would be futile, I sent another letter to the Tennessee Board of Professional Responsibility.

This was what it I sent:

> Hi Ms. Dullard,
>
> By now, I know you know that I'm in the middle of a bitterly contested divorce that drove me into bankruptcy in July 2019. I went to Stefano Leadwits to represent me, and he told me that he'd contacted your office, but I am sure that he left out some important details that I now wish to address and supply evidence for so that you can see the extreme abuse of power, intimidation and threats that the three of them have subjected me to for months now.
>
> Back in the fall of 2018, I was told by the chief of detectives of Williamson County to document everything that was being done and occurring in the divorce. He told me that it was my responsibility to document everything and I have two witnesses to this conversation. Because I'm a writer, I've written it in prose, as diary entries and have been meticulously documenting everything that has transpired.
>
> When I filed for bankruptcy, Stefano Leadwits was dishonest with me about what to expect and he misled me about how bankruptcy works. He assured me that my trademarks, copyrights and contracts would never be under threat. Furthermore, he assured me that the federal court would take over and dispense with the nonsense going on in state court and that I'd no longer have to deal with it. He also assured me that no trustee or receiver would be put over me. He lied. The federal judge immediately kicked the case back to the state and my condition was made a lot worse, rather than better as Stefano had promised.
>
> Once he had me signed up, Stefano immediately filed to have Tom Newhouse put in as my trustee, even against my protests and against his own assurances prior to my filing bankruptcy and paying him money that he would not do this. Even Judge Harriett asked him if he was sure about doing it as it was apparently unheard of in cases like mine.
>
> Stefano never explained to me that I would not only be responsible for paying Newhouse's excruciating salary while I was in bankruptcy, but also that of Newhouse's attorney and an accountant that Tom hired at $175 an hour because Tom said and I quote, "I have neither the time nor inclination to do the paperwork." He steadfastly refused to use my CPA or bookkeeper who charges a reasonable rate of $80 an hour and who is more than capable of doing the work.
>
> When I tried to get Stefano to protest their outrageous fees, he told me to shut up or they would put me in a Chapter 7, even though I don't meet the Means Test, and that I would lose

everything, including my trademarks, contracts and royalties. He did finally protest, but then dropped the protest against my wishes and after telling me that if I continued to protest the outrageous amount, they would put me into a Chapter 7. When I told him that would ruin me and put me on welfare as I would have no income now or in the future and that my publisher would cancel those contracts, Stefano told me that if my publisher exercised their right to cancel, I would be put in jail. Likewise, Tom told me that if he sold those and I refused to write my books under contract for free, and please keep in mind that it takes a year of hard labor to write a novel, that he would put me in jail—that I had no choice except to work twenty-hour days for no compensation if he sold my contracts. Those threats and their bullying were immediately taken up by attorney, Martha Seaver and have been unrelenting ever since. Aside from emails, I have multiple witnesses to their threats and abuse of power.

By January 2020, half a year later, Tom had so mishandled my business and assets that he had left me with no car to drive and had almost doubled my debt without paying a single dollar to my creditors or even entering a plan to get me out of bankruptcy. A lien had been put on my home by a disgruntled creditor. I had a plan for the bankruptcy the minute I filed, yet Tom refused to implement my plan or even discuss it. Rather he, and he admitted this to Judge Dinky, in state court, mismanaged my estate and entered into agreements with my husband's attorneys to pay them and Tom's staff over half a million dollars of my money. Even though the laws I have read say that those attorneys should not have taken precedence over any of my creditors, especially since they were not my attorneys. They should have been entered on the bankruptcy as "creditors" and weren't.

Meanwhile, my attorney was told that she'd have to wait on her payment. Stefano, for the record, told Tom's attorney to pay himself with the cash that had been taken from my home during an illegal search and seizure where no receipt for that cash had been left, nor had the cash been counted. To this day, I don't know exactly how much money and property was actually taken from my home. Months after it was seized, Tom and his attorney began hounding me for property that was photographed as being in their possession, telling me that if I didn't produce the property that his attorney had removed from my home and had, weeks after the fact, given me pictures of, that Tom would report it to the insurance agency and collect on it. Which is fraud, given that I had proof it was removed from my home by them and that at least at one point, had been in their possession. Even so, Tom hounded me relentlessly over the jewelry that he'd been told by his attorney and me wasn't worth what I was being charged, for him to waste everyone's time. Tom also admitted that to Judge Dinky—that the jewelry wasn't worth what my husband's team of attorneys had led him to believe, and that Tom had acted in error on their misrepresentation of facts. That Tom's error in judgement, alone, was what had put my finances in such a horrendous state that I was teetering on a Chapter 7.

Stefano knew I was chronicling the events and kept asking to see the diary. "This is going to be your best seller yet."

In January, I sent him a copy in confidence and asked for a meeting with U.S. Trustee and attorney, Martha Seaver to talk about how Tom had been mismanaging my account, and the unrelenting threats he'd been making against me.

Unbeknownst to me and in strict violation of attorney-client privilege, Stefano sent a copy of my diary to Tom Newhouse, Bill Oldham and others, and to Martha. What I walked into on January 19 was an ambush where Martha and Tom, with Stefano present (along with a third-party witness that they threatened), told me to "destroy that novel. Make sure all copies are burned and that this never sees the light of day." Martha went further to say, "if you ever let another soul see this, I will immediately file an expedited Chapter 7 on you and ruin you. My finger is on the button and I will push it. Give me one reason. If you displease us as in any way, or make Tom upset at all, we will ruin you. And because you did this, we are going to punish you and sell all of your jewelry." This included the fake bubble gum machine ring my sons gave me in grade school and a ring my son made for me when he was a Scout. It's also the jewelry that belonged to my deceased parents, brother and niece that I lost long ago and is all I have left of them. Martha told me that it was being done and she used the words, "for retaliation." Not for any other reason.

The moment they said they would sell my jewelry, Stefano asked if he could bid on it.

When I asked Stefano why he'd betrayed me so, he said and I quote, "my loyalty is to Martha, Tom and the bankruptcy court. It's not to you." I was stunned as that was not what I'd been told. My understanding was that attorneys were to hold their clients first and to advise them accordingly, not to do things that they knew would jeopardize and harm their client.

But what stunned me most was that Martha Seaver's orders that day and those of Tom Newhouse's violated two court orders. One from Judge Dinky in Williamson County that says I "cannot destroy any of my IP as it's considered marital property." And given that I'm a #1 New York Times bestselling author, my diary has an inherent value. Likewise, I have a federal court order while in bankruptcy that says I cannot conceal, hide or destroy any property, including my IP, that could be considered valuable. Yet they both told me to destroy a diary that I can legally sell and make money with.

So did Stefano. They all ordered me to commit a crime. Never mind the fact that I was logging evidence for the Williamson County police department in an ongoing investigation that the chief had told me to log.

Their threats didn't end there. Since that day, they have been on a continuous onslaught against me. Stefano, knowing he'd breached his attorney-client privilege with me and once he saw that they were retaliating against me, immediately contacted your department to withdraw as my counsel. I can only assume that he did such in an effort to extricate himself from the mess he knew he'd created.

On January 23, 2020 at 4:45 PM, Stefano conferenced me in on a call with my divorce attorney, Melissa Magillicutty, where he admitted that they'd threatened me and told us that he was "firing a warning shot across my bow" to get my attention by filing his motion to withdraw as my counsel because I dared protest how Tom and Martha had outrageously threatened me in our meeting—Martha went so far as to call me a threat to national security. He said that so long as I did what they wanted and made no waves, he'd remain as my attorney, but that every two weeks he would file the motion to withdraw and only withdraw that motion so long as I kept my mouth shut and did everything they told me to do.

No one should live with the unrelenting threats and bullying that I've been subjected to by these people. Every time I ask a simple question, the answer comes back, "Do you want Martha and Tom to file a Chapter 7? They'll do it. You'll be sorry." Basically, they tell me to sit down, shut up and let them take from me whatever they want while they ruin my career and life, and charge outrageous fees to me to do it.

After court last week where I witnessed Tom Newhouse tell lies to the judge and mislead him, I'd had enough of their threats, intimidation and abuse of power while they wasted all my money. So today, I very politely told Stefano to go ahead and file his withdrawal as he's been doing.

This was their response: (I then pasted the two responses you'd read earlier).

Because of his actions, Stefano has put my entire welfare and those of my children at risk. He has created an impossible situation between me and my trustees who have made no bones about the fact that they are "punishing me" because I displeased them. Joan Hart witnessed those threats, and they threatened her, too.

I am in a very scary situation and have no idea where to turn. Please tell me that you will take this seriously and finally do something. No one should ever be put in harm's way because they trusted their attorney and he betrayed them.

    Thank you for your time,
    Terri

Since I refused to rehire Stefano, and they were refusing me the money to hire a new attorney, all I could do was wait for Wednesday and for Martha to file her Chapter 7 on me, even though she had no right to do so, so that Tom and crew could come in and lock up all my money and assets.

Which I found to be a funny threat as they'd already done that, right down to the Etsy money they were threatening me over. I had absolutely no access to that account at all. Didn't even know what bank it was at. Couldn't see it or anything.

Were they that stupid that they'd forgotten the fact that they'd seized it on Day One? Which I still didn't understand how that was legal given that the store belonged to my son, and he wasn't part of this.

Still, they'd seized it and continued to threaten me. And threatening someone who'd grown up in poverty that you were going to put them back there wasn't much of a threat. I supposed in their rich, white-bred world, it was horrible and the worst thing imaginable.

But there were a lot of things worse, such as selling your soul and humanity to make money.

From experience, I knew that I could easily go three days with no food before it began to bother me. I knew how to make spaghetti sauce from the free ketchup packets in restaurants. And I could exist on ten crackers and water a day if I had to.

Sadly, there had been many times in my life when I'd had to, which was why I knew those facts.

I'd even been homeless, so that wasn't much of a threat. I knew how to find shelter.

But what sickened me was that I'd gone to these people for help, and they'd turned out to be sick abusers, too, who threatened me at every turn and then told me that I should be thanking them for their abuse and that I should be grateful they weren't making it worse for me.

If this was the norm, then why hadn't others complained about it? How could our government allow people like this to preside over others and torture them?

Cockburn was right. No one cared.

I was shouting into a hurricane and there was no one to hear it.

For me and my sons, there would be no mercy.

All I could do was ride out the storm and try to make a fire later out of whatever debris remained.

Because there was no justice in this country. No hope left for me. At that point, on that day, my only thought was that it would be better to have a Chapter 7 and get it over with than have to deal with these power-crazed lunatics for another two to five years.

I had done no crime, yet I'd been sentenced to hell.

## MARCH 17

HAPPY ST. PATRICK'S DAY! Before my nightmare had begun, I would have spent that day promoting my books and the Irish Night-Seekers in my series. I would have done some giveaways and had a fairly pleasant day.

Thanks to Les and his grotesque stupidity, pleasant days had become a thing of the past. All I prayed for was a boring day. One day where no one yelled at me or started shit.

Like when I was a child. I'd grown up in the war zone. Had hated it then and really hated it now.

Maddox had called first thing in the morning to check on me.

Since I'd taken ill and with all the COVID scare going on, he was petrified that I'd succumb, and he'd be left with his brother to deal with that "monster man" as they called their father.

"We only have one parent who loves us and who cares what happens to us. You're the only one whoever took care of us. We can't lose you!"

Nick had been so paranoid that he'd come and stayed with me every afternoon, even though I didn't want to make him sick.

I kept reassuring them. "Trust me, God doesn't love me enough to kill me and put me out of my misery. He intends to leave me here to suffer as much as possible."

Sad part was that I believed it.

So, I waited for the continuation of the day before.

As expected, the law firm I'd called to meet with called me back and canceled, then recommended me to another firm in town.

With a reluctant sigh, I called the new firm and left a message.

Hours went by and when I finally talked to the attorney, he confirmed that everyone in town knew about my case. "I've been following it from the sidelines."

Great. Thank you, Les, for turning us into a side freak show. I'd spent my entire life guarding my reputation and causing no drama.

In less than a handful of years, this poisonous bastard had turned us both into laughingstocks. He thought it was just me they were laughing at as he did his best to discredit me.

But he was the greater fool, and everyone knew it. They laughed all the harder at him.

Including his own attorneys.

Why?

Well, when it came time to sign the papers on the house, the moron refused.

He wanted my teacups and dolls, among other ridiculous property out of the house that obviously wasn't his.

"What kind of man wants a teacup?" Melissa asked and she wasn't the first one to make that comment or laugh at Les.

To which I responded, "He took what he wanted when he left. He had five full days to raid my house while I was at work with my son. And he did." He'd even taken furniture out of my house. And Woodruff had sat there, so smugly, and denied me the equal chance to get my things out of my office that was my work product and furniture.

"What's good for the goose is good for the gander."

Well, the goose had spent five days raiding my home and a year or more planning his betrayal against me and my sons.

The gander hadn't been treated fairly at any point in this circus tent system they called Williamson County court.

"When he returns the millions of dollars in cash that he walked out of here with, then we can talk about other items." I was standing firm on that.

He deserved nothing but our hatred. And with that, he was a rich man, indeed.

And when I finally heard back from old Newhouse and crew, it was Melissa telling me that after all their bullshit lies, threats and horror that they'd been putting me through for months, "Tom said that he'd put the sale of the house through and then you'd be released from the bankruptcy."

After their fucking lies of telling me that it was an impossible thing I'd asked.

That they would convert my case.

After stealing so much of my money to line their pockets, while making my life hell, I was told that the very thing I'd wanted was doable.

Seldom in my life had I been angrier.

Contrary to Cockburn's lies, I hadn't entered bankruptcy voluntarily. Between Les's Dumas lawsuit and her antics on his behalf, Les had left me holding the bill for almost a million dollars in legal fees.

I'd always heard that the bankruptcy court would stop harassing phone calls and that it took power and precedence over state court.

Again, they lied. Trust me, the harassing phone calls from creditors were nothing compared to these power-drunk bastards. At least creditors had to follow the law.

These dick-swinging troglodytes were the law and made sure that you knew it. "We can do anything we want."

That was their threat and their belief system. They weren't here to help us in our hours of need. They were here to pillage and plunder and take whatever they could grab before they flushed everything a person had ever worked for down the toilet.

"We don't care what happens to you later. Bye!"

While relieved, I was furious. They'd put me through so much, so needlessly.

All the lies and threats.

But at least, I now had an end date, and it wasn't years from now, while I was in my sixties.

I only had to make it to Maddox's birthday.

Seven weeks. In seven weeks, at least this portion of my nightmare should be over.

Seven weeks.

"Please, God, end this horror and give me my life back!" That had been my prayer for years.

It was all I wanted. An end to the abuse and to never lay eyes on my abusers again.

But I had seven weeks to get through. Only God knew what bullshit they'd throw at me between now and then.

I was terrified. Because the one thing the crazy bastards had taught me was that they never hit what you thought they would.

And you never saw them coming.

*Cowards strike from the back, between your shoulders where they could reach your heart without you seeing them approach.*

There wasn't a brave soul in the bunch. Which meant I had another day to face, and I was sick to my stomach with what new hell they'd unleash on me.

Mostly because I knew that I'd acted on the presumption that they were going to carry out their threats, as they'd been doing.

Again, they were talking to someone who'd been thrown in jail for cooperating with the judge and doing what he'd asked.

These were a sick bunch of fucks to threaten and bully someone they knew had been so abused, especially Newhouse whose wife was a psychologist. So, he knew better.

My only certainty was that I had reported the whole jolly crew to every single agency I could. The Office of Inspector General, Department of Justice, Attorney General, FBI and the Tennessee Board of Professional Responsibility.

While the other departments could take years to process my complaint (as Newhouse and crew had laughed about to my face), I knew Ms. Dullard wouldn't.

Those complaints were processed in six weeks or less.

So close to my being out of here, and yet...

She might act on the fact that they'd retaliated, and she would take action against Leadwits for his breach.

If I was lucky, she'd do so after I was clear of their hands.

But I wasn't lucky, and fate had never been with me. She was a wicked bitch, and I was usually her favorite punchline.

Shit. If they were mad now, they would be extra furious when that inquiry hit their desks...

But there was nothing I could do. Their threats had set it into motion. I'd only told the truth and I would stand by the reports I'd filed.

From the beginning, I'd told Newhouse not to threaten me. That it wouldn't cow me and that I would stand my ground. That I would take those threats as gospel and react as if they were promises. Because with my parents, they *were* guarantees, so I assumed the rest of the world operated that way, too.

He and Martha had threatened to put me on the street while I was under quarantine and to make sure that I didn't have enough money for food or gas. Never mind the fact that I needed a thousand dollars in medication a month to live on or I would die. I had life-threatening medical conditions that would kill me if they cut off my money.

And my income was too high to qualify for social services. While I might not have access to it because the pirates were taking it from me and I wasn't even allowed to see how much they were funneling off, I still made a fair living wage that should have supported me if they, including the bankruptcy court, weren't charging ridiculous rates to harass me.

Martha, Newhouse et al had literally threatened to kill me by threatening to take away my medication and food.

There was no mistaking that. It was a real threat that both Martha and Newhouse had told Leadwits to convey to me because they wanted me scared and compliant to their whims and merciless cruelty.

And they expected me, at that time, to be under that amount of duress for years and still earn a living while they continued to threaten and harass me.

*Please keep in mind that Newhouse's wife was a psychologist. If anyone knew better than to treat a human like this, it should have been him.*

Yet they'd kept hammering me.

With no let up.

I had no idea how this would end.

But I had seven more weeks of hell to endure. *Please God, could you show me a modicum of mercy?*

**MARCH 18**

J UST WHEN I THOUGHT MY life couldn't get any more farcical or bizarre, fate kept screwing with me. Out would trot a whole other level of "what the fuck" that forever had me shaking my head, wondering if the Big Guy upstairs was freebasing.

Or bored.

Surely, with everything else going on in the world such as COVID-19 and a war, God had better things to do than pick on me, right?

Apparently not.

So, as I set about trying to work and pack up my house while waiting for the hammer to fall, it was an off day anyway. The grocery store shelves were so bare, we'd dubbed it "shopocalypse." It was surreal to be in the supermarket now. Like being part of some zombie movie.

"Hey! I scored dried beans and a can of soup!" I started on one side of the grocery store while Joan would start on the other.

We'd meet in the middle to see who got what.

Yeah, COVID-19 was messing with everyone. And I was trying to stock up not from the virus scare, but because at any moment, I was in fear that Newhouse and Martha would cut me off and starve me out like they'd been threatening to do.

I even picked up more medicine, because that was the most terrifying part of their threats.

My medication wasn't an option. Due to the stress they kept me under, I was now taking six doses of two difference kinds of blood pressure medicine a day, and my pressure was still high.

It hadn't been this out of control since I'd been pregnant and was losing my home while my father had cancer and lay dying. While my stepmother had a court order barring us from visiting him or calling.

How pathetic was that?

These bastards were supposed to alleviate my stress and were supposed to be helping me. Instead, they were piling on so harshly that it was about to kill me, and they were threatening to take away the medication that my life depended on.

Why?

Because I'd dared to question their abuse. Because Newhouse had screwed up and had admitted it to the judge, and he was petrified of being caught.

No one's life should be ruined by people abusing their authority. Especially not by a bitch who worked for the Department of Justice.

I honestly thought that no one cared.

Until I received the email late that afternoon from the Office of the Inspector General. Of course, it was the usual, "we don't handle this." Apparently, they could only take complaints that involved a private trustee who lied on their application to become a private trustee, not on their misconduct once they became a trustee.

How screwed up was our government?

But they told me that they did forward it on to the Department of Justice for me.

In four days.

That was a record. Normally, I heard nothing back from anyone. So at least someone had read it and thought enough of the matter that they'd fired it up the ladder, instead of telling me to go file my own complaint with another department.

That was a first.

Even so, I had to wonder if anything would come of it. After all, Martha had already told me that she'd spoken to her "bosses" in Washington who had told her to blackmail me and instructed me to violate my court orders.

I would assume that the office the OIG was forwarding my complaint to was the same "bosses" who'd given those orders to Martha.

Which meant that if Martha had been telling the truth, I was screwed as they'd all be coming after me now for whistleblowing.

But I kept praying. Hoping.

Surely the government couldn't be this corrupt. Could it?

We would find out.

Seven more weeks. Would I make it to the end?

**T**HEY SAY THE DEFINITION OF stupid was repeating the same thing over and over and expecting a different result. If that definition was true, then Newhouse really was the dumbest motherfucker alive.

After Les.

My phone rang with Melissa's number, and I knew it wouldn't be a good call.

I would say I'm psychic, but really, you'd read enough by now to know what I did. They weren't about to let me have a moment's peace.

This day was no different.

The irony? It was Newhouse calling Melissa to waste more high dollar money to tell her that "I" needed to cut back on my expenses. Keeping in mind that this imbecile was gouging me eight hundred an hour (because everything was between him and his buddy) and she was charging two-fifty. So, a thirty-minute conversation between them was over a thousand dollars.

*Over one thousand dollars an hour.*

He had spent more than two hours on the phone with her bitching, which equated to more money than my Comic Con advance that he'd "ordered" me to cancel after he'd approved it.

More than the payroll that ran my store for *two weeks* of work for *five* people.

To clarify that, if Newhouse spent two and a half hours arguing a matter with Melissa, which he routinely did, then he spent my *entire* payroll for two weeks.

He was a fucking financial genius, wasn't he?

And weren't you glad this idiot wasn't in charge of *your* money?

That stupid bastard had spent more money than it took for me to pay five people to operate my store for an entire year. In fact, he'd spent more money than that year's payroll in less than four months on his single, idiotic accountant.

My entire payroll for a year for the people who ran my boards, answered fan questions and emails and who ran my online store and the booths at events.

My *necessary* support staff that my company was dependent upon.

Not the redundant unnecessary accountant hired because Newhouse said and I quote, that he had neither time nor inclination to do my paperwork.

How cavalier of him with my money.

Dear God, he was Les, Jr.

And he was calling, again, to tell Melissa that I needed to cut back *my* expenses because *I* was the problem?

*Are you kidding?*

Then he went on to tell her that I had to get a "handle" on my expenses. This after he'd stood up in court, in front of Judge Dinky and lied. "The store never brought in the money I was told it did, Your Honor. The sales from the store don't even cover payroll."

Really?

We did, in fact, cover payroll.

And that was with it having been closed for half of March.

While math wasn't my best subject, even I could tell that if you subtracted what we made by what I paid out, the store covered my employees' payroll.

Who was the liar, Newhouse?

Oh yeah, *you* were.

And my store had made a whole lot more than that before he came on board and got in the way. I had the proof that he'd destroyed my income.

Single-handedly.

I also knew how to trim fat, starting with what he had in his head that he thought was a brain.

But first, I needed to explain this nightmare of stupidity that the government had saddled me with.

When Newhouse came in, I expressly told him that the ungodly legal fees that were running thirty to seventy thousand dollars a month had to go.

So, what did Newhouse do?

Ignore me and bitch and run up those fees even more.

He immediately went after every asset I had as if I were in a Chapter 7. He sold my clothing and cars that were paid off and cost me nothing sitting in my closets and garage. Better still, he sold the cars that were still under warranty and left me with the one that cost me thousands of dollars to get running again. The one that was older than dirt and had no warranty whatsoever.

Wasn't he the awesome money manager?

How he ran his household (other than into the ground), I had no idea. I didn't even understand how he was still in business. He couldn't make a decent business decision to save his life.

Hence the intelligence he had when he surrendered my lease that got me sued for over seventy-four thousand dollars.

'Cause that made all the sense in the world, said no one ever. *I swear Dave Ramsey just had a heart attack.*

*Thank you, D.O.J. for hiring someone who shouldn't be in charge of collecting cans for charity.*

That was how I ended up in twice the debt I started out with in less than a year and had this jerk-off screaming at my attorney, running up my bills even more, while telling me to cut back on the very things that were making money.

Not spending it, like him and his zoo crew of morons.

Yeah. Now we know why our government runs at such a horrific deficit.

If that wasn't bad enough, I found out who old Dinky had "chosen" to write the order.

Our good friend Cockburn.

Who couldn't remember anything from the hearing.

I found it interesting that he'd chosen *her* to get the bonus pay. Guess we could tell who Dinky's favorite was. And of course, she was trying to pull a fast one and lie about his orders.

As she always did.

Thank you, Ms. Dullard for not disciplining that embarrassment to the legal profession. This disaster, who wore clothing that would shame a prostitute, should never have been allowed to walk a courtroom floor. Nor should she be allowed to continue to milk my estate for money.

If Newhouse wanted to cut back the waste, then he should have been a man and faced down Dinky in court and told him where the waste was.

The stupid bitch who should have her bar license suspended. Which begged the question, was Newhouse in on the scam along with them? Why was he okay with Cockburn and crew milking me? Why hadn't he stood up there and seen them disciplined for lying to him and to the judge?

Newhouse claimed he couldn't tolerate anyone lying to him and yet he gave them all a free pass.

Just like Dinky did.

But then that was the definition of a bully coward. Newhouse shriveled up around anyone who had any kind of authority over him and then came down like a ton of bricks on those he had authority over.

His kind sickened me.

Indeed, he laughed and cut up with Cockburn and crew like they were his lifelong friends, knowing what liars they all were.

Meanwhile, my children and I were sold out and abandoned.

In his own words, he "threw us under the bus."

I was so mad at myself that I had ever allowed something so despicable as Les into my life. How could I have ever loved such a wretched, horrible, soulless snake?

My heart was broken. *This* was what my father had died to protect? A system ruled by spineless, greedy cowards.

*I'm sorry, Dad. I'm glad you aren't here to see what they've done to your daughter, your grandsons, and the country you were so proud of, that you bled for.*

And if that wasn't bad enough, then the weirdest thing of all happened. Someone had put broken bottles, leaves and dangerous trash in my trashcans and left them for us to clean out.

I received the note from my trash collection company that we had to clean them. One of the boxes was for a chainsaw which I didn't own and didn't have.

It was as strange as finding my gate opened again, after the rainstorm a few nights before. Remember what I'd said about my neighbor who was Les's old friend who'd been making a stink over Maddox's dog?

Well, Maddox had moved into his apartment and taken his dog with him.

No sooner was Rex out of my yard than my gate was left open, again. For the first time in a year.

Really? What were the odds?

Now someone had put dangerous trash in my bins?

This was ridiculous. And I was done with the childish antics of all of them.

Seven more weeks.

That was what I kept telling myself. I had to survive seven more weeks of this torture.

*Please, God, help me make it.*

MARCH 20

**H**ERE WE WENT AGAIN. I was being harassed by Newhouse to cut spending. *So, let me show you his frugality, shall I?* And what I was being billed an excruciating amount of money for.

I'd handed in my "expenses," i.e. the galling list where I had to beg Dipshit for my own money to pay my bills and run my business. That list was always met with the idiotic questions that came every two weeks. Idiotic because they asked the same thing over and over, and I'd told them what they were for, usually at the time the request was made.

To give you an idea of what I'd been forced to deal with, here was what was sent this week to me by my reasonably priced accountant (which meant that Newhouse and his idiot had already gouged me their exorbitant fees and then sent it to her anyway—anything they could do to drive up the cost of my bankruptcy):

*Here are a few questions from this weeks funding. What are these for?* (Typos left in as they were theirs. Please note that my accountant said that these were only a *few* of the redundant questions. They had ceased sending them directly to me as I had begun to call them out on their ridiculous waste of my funds with their combined idiocy when it was obvious that they weren't reading my responses or if they were, they "forgot" them on purpose two weeks later so that they could charge me again to ask the same exact questions about the same fees).

*IncSub $199 paid via paypal* (they had been told repeatedly, for nine months at this point, that these were autopays for the apps that ran my WordPress website. Since I was sure that I wasn't the only one in the world who used WordPress for my site, a $200 an hour accountant should know what these were and why they were necessary).

*Property payment $100* (I was supposed to be paying for my son's online classes, but he'd paid for them, thinking to help me out. Then, because of COVID-19, he'd been laid off and didn't have the money for his apartment. I paid his apartment fees, which were actually cheaper, so I saved money by helping out my Boo.)

*Property Payment $250* (Again, I was helping my Boo pay as he'd saved me money.)

*Web Book $12 paid via paypal (they had been told repeatedly, for nine months at this point, that these were autopays for the apps that ran my WordPress website).*

*Next Gen $67 (I think we discussed this but I am at home and don't have my files.) (Again, an app for my site that they knew about).*

*Which car is on the $120 Farm Bureau insurance policy?*

That last one was my favorite because it truly showed the depth of their stupidity and willingness to waste my time and money.

Please keep in mind that at the time this was sent to me, I'd been working to make money and so had been pulled off my job for an hour to deal with their idiocy.

Again.

And Newhouse kept hounding me on why my work wasn't getting done. Because apparently, Anti-Einstein couldn't figure out that I had to stop my job to attend his imbecilic requests that I'd answered a thousand times in emails that he'd admitted he never read.

Emails he'd lied about in court and thrown in my face. "I have it in emails!"

The ones you'd told me, in front of witnesses, you never read?

Which lie of yours, Newhouse, was the truth?

One way or another, he was a liar.

Anyway, back to the stupidity of the moment. That last little nugget. Remember the week before when he'd called with his hissy fit that accused me of having a car removed from my insurance and all that trauma and drama I'd been forced to deal with?

Apparently, Lord Senile couldn't remember it. Though how he could forget, I had no idea.

And remember that this was the fucking idiot who'd wanted my writing contracts of all types so that he could read them, and what? Absorb them when he couldn't remember a redundant charge that occurred every two weeks?

All hundred thousand of my contracts (slight exaggeration).

Yet he couldn't recall the single car policy that he'd supposedly read, or my handful of insurance policies that had been sent to him.

Nor could he recall the week before when he'd thrown a tantrum for days on end demanding that I add a car back to that policy because "somehow" the car had been removed.

And he'd accused me of removing the car, even though I'd had no idea the car was off the policy.

Well, be that as it may, I guessed Lord Imbecile assumed that while he and his greedy accomplices were paid a thousand times what they're worth, the rest of us must work for free. After all that was his threat and attitude.

"If you don't work for free, we'll put you in jail."

Or in his other words, "You own nothing. Get used to it. We're putting you out on the street. But I care about you, by the way," said every abusive asshole ever.

However, Farm Bureau, like most places, expected payment whenever they rendered services. So, when I'd called to add the car back, guess what they wanted?

Fair payment.

Not lawyer wages.

*Fair* payment.

But I guess old Newhouse and crew had to drive up their exorbitant, ungodly fees for those of us in bankruptcy by hounding us with these idiotic questions so that he could stand in court so sanctimoniously. "I have to ride her on her expenditures to keep her in line!"

Really?

Because I knew how to trim a shitload of fat from my budget.

I could have saved myself over ONE HUNDRED THOUSAND DOLLARS by getting rid of him and his useless accountant, and biddy buddy lawyer.

And if that wasn't the worst news of the day, I got the another.

My buyer wanted more time.

Sixty days.

I wanted to cry. Here, I'd almost seen the end of my torture and in one fell swoop, it'd been ripped away.

Sixty days might not seem like much to some people, but two minutes in hell was an eternity.

And my fear was that it wouldn't end.

Because of COVID (while we were under a shelter-in-place federal mandate that should have forbidden them selling my home and throwing us out), they kept moving the closing date back until there was nothing left. I mean, I understood. They wanted a conventional loan over the VA, which made sense. VA loans were tough, and they made everyone jump through hoops. Plus, with everything going on with COVID and the economy, it was a guarantee that the FED would drop interest rates on home loans to stimulate the economy. *Smart move on the buyer's part.*

However, I received the email from Dipshit saying he wanted a meeting at 1:30.

Okay.

He opened it with, "The buyer backed out."

And that said it all about how stupid Newhouse was.

"They didn't back out."

"Yes, they did. They don't want to buy it. It's their way of getting out of it."

Wow. He really understood nothing about saving money. Damn. Poster child for idiocy. I couldn't believe that they'd put him in charge of bankruptcies.

And for once, Melissa got to see him in all his glory as he launched into a screaming fit that we taped. He didn't hold back. He admitted that Cockburn "hated" me and had a personal dislike. Duh, shit.

Really?

Besides being highly unprofessional of him to tell me something I already knew, so? What was he trying to prove with that? My enemy hated my guts. It had nothing to do with me. She'd acted that way with her first attack before she'd ever laid eyes upon me.

Why? I don't know.

That bitch was psycho. She was also the woman who'd set up a vet and drove him out of the country. There was something fundamentally wrong with her. The fact that she sent her ex to my publisher owned site to insult my fans, said it all.

I was honestly glad that this psycho didn't like me. I would take that as a victory.

Was Dipshit trying to make me cry because he thought I might give a shit what a psycho bitch thought? Seriously?

But he went on from there. He told me to "fire all my employees." Even though the government at that time was telling all employers not to do that.

"You know that's how I make money. Right?"

"I don't care."

Really?

"What about your accountant? If we get Les to agree—"

Newhouse blew a gasket. "I don't care if he agrees or not, at this point. I'm not about to let her go. I need her to do my paperwork!"

Ah, so we were back to retaliation. His imbecile could be way overpaid by my money, even though one hour of her time was the same amount as two weeks of pay for my employees?

One hour = two weeks' pay.

How in the world was that fair?

They made my life easier and helped my fans and ran my store.

His bitch harassed and bullied me and kept me from working.

*Are you serious?*

This was beyond sick and twisted. I was being gouged to make *his* life easier? My business was being run into the ground so that he wouldn't have do to paperwork?

"I need my employees."

"No, you don't. You have to cut back."

I needed the money the store brought in. My writing, because he wouldn't give me time to write and because all of New York was shut down, wasn't bringing in anything.

Now I didn't know where the fuck he lived, but in my world, that was money I needed.

*Let me repeat: I needed the money my staff and store brought in.*

Never, ever file for bankruptcy. That was all I could say to anyone. Better to deal with your creditors yourself. These bastards were crazy.

Not to mention, he launched into his insanity. "Do you understand what Chapter 7 means? I will take every dime of your money from you. You won't have a cent for groceries or gas or anything else!" I.E. the medication that I needed to live on. "What will you do then?"

I guessed that I would die as I needed food and my meds to live on. Most people did.

"You better listen to me!"

Wow. Was I his teenage daughter?

He was as bad as Les, screaming at me like a lunatic, trying to bully and intimidate. I was embarrassed for him.

"You need to be reasonable and settle this divorce!"

Like I hadn't been trying to do that since the day the other Dipshit had walked out.

Melissa finally spoke up. "She has been. They won't come to the table. She's not the unreasonable party."

"Well, if they don't get this settled this week, I'm filing a Chapter 7."

"Go ahead." I was done with the threats.

"I mean it!"

"I do, too."

But what sickened me most was that up until this meeting, I'd respected Bill Oldham even though he'd done the illegal search and seizure on my home.

In spite of those actions where I'd assumed he was too afraid of the judge to stand up to Dinky, I had thought he was an honorable man.

Until he lied.

I mean, I knew he'd committed perjury when he'd put forth a document to the court saying I owned my son's company and that had pissed me off. He really should lose his bar license for that, but I'd let it slide.

Then he had to go and lie for his friend.

Newhouse had to scream out, "I have your emails!"

"Thought you didn't read them. Which is it?"

"What?"

"You said in the January meeting that you never read my emails."

"I didn't say that!"

"Yes, you did."

Bill spoke up. "I didn't hear him say that."

"Yes, Bill, you did. You even nodded in agreement. I saw you. You were there. Leadwits and Martha were there. Joan was there. He said it. Don't lie."

I couldn't stand a fucking liar.

It was why Newhouse always accused everyone of lying, such as when he began screaming about the Comic Con money. "You need to get that back."

"I can't."

"You didn't even try."

*Not until you get rid of your bitch, I won't.* "You approved it."

"And I sent you an email telling you that I'd unapproved it."

"No, you didn't."

"I sent it to your accountant."

"I didn't get it."

"Are you telling me that she didn't send it to you?"

"I didn't get it."

"Are you calling her a liar?"

"I'm calling you a liar, Newhouse."

That set him off like a rocket. But I refused to back down. I had the emails I'd been sent, and that I'd sent them to Melissa. As Newhouse had said, I could prove it.

He was the one acting like a screaming banshee and who was out of control.

It was horrible.

Over an hour, and a thousand dollars spent so that he could scream at me like I was his errant teenage daughter.

Nothing productive. He was a fucking imbecile who needed to be fired and never given another client again.

My God.

This was my life. I had no say and no control.

Only threatened by everyone around me.

And how did my day end?

My baby spent six hours in the emergency room because of the stress of trying to work thirteen-hour days, seven days a week to help out his mother. Because he was so terrified of losing the only parent he had who was being threatened that she was about to be turned out with no money for food or gas.

Or medication.

Because he wanted the vultures to leave us alone and there was nothing we could do to drive them away.

They just kept coming.

I wasn't even allowed inside the hospital with him. Thanks to the COVID-19 outbreak, I was relegated to staying in the car in the hospital parking lot the entire time, while texting him, worried sick.

And the whole time I prayed for him, I kept thinking that this was how his life had begun. Us living out of a broken down, piece of shit car in a hospital parking lot while he was in and out of the ER.

*Please God, don't let this be how it ended.*

And all because I'd married a worthless piece of shit who refused to work.

Then and now.

Not one happy memory of being with Les. He'd ruined my entire life. How I wished to God that I'd never met him.

For the second time in my life, God had taken everything from me, and I was left unable to get to my baby while he was hooked to monitors. I hated that feeling. He'd been two weeks old before I'd been allowed to see him. I'd been too sick myself to get to him when he'd been born.

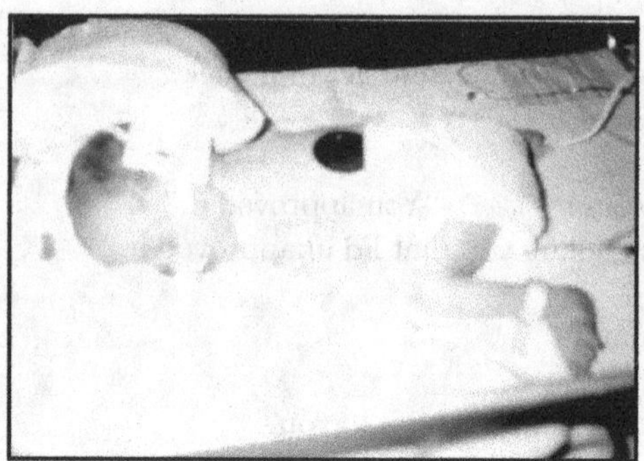

I'd made a pact with God, twenty-five years ago that he could take anything from me he wanted: my career, my house, my life, just not my son.

It was a bargain he'd accepted.

That night, my bargain was for him to take Les's worthless life and leave my son alone. We'd suffered enough because of that piece of shit. I'd already lost everything else.

It was time for Les to pay the piper. Surely, there would be some Karma somewhere.

**T**HE ANNIVERSARY OF THE DAY I lost my mom. This was always a hard day for me. Not to mention, I figured Les would do something horrible as he always seemed to come up with some way to turn the knife in my back on this week.

But much to my surprise, I received a letter from Bitsy Dullard, my nemesis at the Tennessee Board of Professional Responsibility.

I was so used to my complaints being ignored that the letter had come in two days earlier and I'd laid it aside.

On this day, I opened it.

For once, it wasn't a curt dismissal. She wanted individual complaints against Newhouse, Seaver, Leadwits and Oldham.

I couldn't believe it! Could it be possible that after all this time they might have *finally* crossed the line?

What the hell? They'd committed how many crimes against me? Starting with disseminating my "book" which we know from this familiar warning was illegal:

FBI Anti-Piracy Warning: The unauthorized reproduction or distribution of a copyrighted work is illegal. Criminal copyright infringement, including infringement without monetary gain, is investigated by the FBI and is punishable by up to five years in federal prison and a fine of $250,000.

I should think an attorney who worked for the Department of Justice should be well aware that by accepting and sending my "manuscript" to her "bosses" in Washington that she'd broken that law. Never mind her order for me to destroy property that I was court ordered not to destroy, etc.

My heart pounded with hope, especially after that ugly, nasty phone call on Friday where Newhouse had hammered me with threats.

Maybe, just maybe Dullard would finally come through for me.

*Please, God, please.* Let there be justice! If not for me and my children, then for the other victims who were out there. These people didn't need to be in control of anything. They shouldn't have bar licenses.

They needed to be out on the road scraping up roadkill.

As Seaver had said to me, "You can go work at Target." Only I hoped that Target employed far kinder and better people than her.

**T**HE ANNIVERSARY OF THE DAY I buried my mother. And the anniversary of the day that Les, with full knowledge of how emotional it was for me and knowing that I'd spent the night before in the ER because of my heart condition he'd brought on with his poisoning of me and stress, had filed for divorce.

Which meant that I knew he'd pull some kind of sick stunt. He always did. Even when we'd been married, he'd cruelly done shit on this day. As if he couldn't bear to share my attention for even a moment.

He was the biggest brat I'd been forced to babysit. *I know, my fault.* I should never have dated him, and when he'd called to tell me how much he "loved" me, I should have told him to take a flying fuck off the nearest skyscraper.

Hindsight.

So, what was his stunt that he pulled this day?

Cockburn, after two years, finally got around to sending over his "demands."

I knew it'd be bad from the opening line Melissa sent:

> Here it is.  Take a deep breath and know that they do not expect to get this.  The first thing I would do in any counter is eliminate the alimony.  Read it, think about how you want to respond and once you're done seeing flames, we can discuss our response.
>
> If we are going to get this done, it needs to be done by the end of the week.

I wasn't angry. I actually laughed at how pathetic and stupid each and every party was who'd signed off on that document. Beginning with Cockburn and the trustee who was supposed to watch out for my estate.

Her opening line was, "Husband will be granted a divorce on the grounds of irreconcilable differences."

*Are you fucking kidding me?*

This from the slut who'd come out two years ago accusing me, the woman who'd been too sick to walk across a room without help, of abusing her husband? A woman who couldn't breathe and who was forced to suck incessantly on an inhaler because of what they'd done to me? I couldn't yell for help, never mind yell at the bastard who'd almost killed me.

Had Thundercunt put *that* mild statement in the original divorce decree, everything would have gone a lot differently. But the stupid bitch who should never have been granted a bar license had decided to make ludicrous, sick allegations without any evidence or proof so that she could ruin my reputation and career.

Then drive me into bankruptcy.

Now she wanted irreconcilable differences.

For that alone, the bitch should be slapped and lose her bar license over the sick cruelty of her actions. *You don't tear up someone else's life so needlessly with so many lies as she did.* There should be some form of repercussion against someone this sick in the head.

But I supposed that they didn't teach intelligence or the ability to think ahead in her part-time night law classes. That was what sickened me most about divorce attorneys and why they needed to be banned from practicing law. None of them thought about the fact that after this, people with children would need to get along for the sake of those children. Instead of forcing parents to take parenting courses, the state and federal government should require all divorce attorneys to take sensitivity training and to donate pro bono time to abuse shelters for their sick and twisted cruelty that they heaped on people in the name of greed.

Case on point, Thundercunt opened her letter with this:

> This letter represents Mr. Manly's offer of a global settlement to bring to an end the two year of acrimony between the parties. It would serve everyone's interest to bring this to a swift close as to continue is proving too costly to both of our parties. Despite each of their positions in attempting to get their day in court, they are both losing everything to get there. In an attempt to save what is left and get on with left this is Mr. Manly's proposal. It is more than fair.

That typo was her stupidity, not mine and left to show what a brat she really was. Now that she'd sucked out all my money, she wanted to settle.

*Too late stupid bitch.* Everything I'd loved, aside from my children had been taken from me.

Unlike Les, I had tried on Day One to settle this. I'd offered him everything we owned, except my car, my computers and the rights to my books. All he had to do was split the money in the bank.

In other words, he would have owned four cars, two homes (all paid for), and would have walked out the door as a millionaire.

The only furniture I wanted was my computers, office chairs and my dining room. Everything else had been offered to him.

Everything.

They had refused.

Les had wanted a fight and had refused any and all of my efforts to settle.

He'd had one purpose, to drive me into the ground and destroy me.

The courts and lawyers had only been too happy to assist him.

Honestly, poverty didn't scare me. Her level of cruelty and stupidity did. The fact that slags like this were allowed to function in our society and go unpunished, scared the absolute hell out of me.

Oh, for the days when they'd put a bitch like her in the stockade and left her there to rot.

And how fair were they being? They were leaving me the house that had already been sold to pay for all of Les's debts and Cockburn's income.

He was to be given my office that he'd promised to his sons free and clear. Likewise, he was to be given the newest SUV and I was left with nothing worth a damn after my decent cars had been sold to pay for his attorneys.

After my winter coats and purses had been sold to pay for his ridiculous attorney fees.

He was to keep the contents of my office, including my office furniture that had been written off as tax deductions and I wasn't to be allowed anything from it, while he had a list of almost one hundred items he wanted out of the marital home that he and his Hogg had raided for months and then had his goon squad come in and raid again.

Meanwhile, I had never been allowed to step foot in my office after he squatted his lazy, worthless ass in it while his son and I were working at a convention.

He was "graciously" awarding my jewelry that had been given to me as gifts, mostly from my sons for Christmas, Mother's Day and my birthday. But remember that my jewelry had been confiscated by the rat bastard trustee and I'd been told that all of it would be sold to pay for Les's bills and attorney fees. So, he was planning to leave me with nothing while he walked away with almost one-hundred thousand dollars in watches, and several of the extremely expensive pieces of *my* jewelry that they were demanding the trustee hand over to him before the sale.

Then the kicker, he was expecting me to pay more than twelve thousand dollars a month to him for fifteen years. Non-modifiable, while also demanding forty percent of all my royalties.

Now, let me explain what a fucking kick in the teeth that was for just a second.

They wanted forty percent off all *gross* income and to have someone put over me to intercept all my income. In other words, the controlling freak wanted someone else in charge of my life.

Forever.

And another woman was agreeing to this.

*Even sicker?*

My attorney was agreeing to this and telling me to be a businesswoman and sign it.

Oh okay. Then why, as a businesswoman, was I the only one capable of doing the math?

First, I got paid the *net*, not the gross. I earned eight to ten percent of the cover price of my books. 8.99-27.99.

That was it.

Out of that, my agents took twenty percent right off the top. One they'd taken their share, Uncle Sam took fifty percent to pay for my self-employment and regular taxes *(I verified this percentage with my accountant. It's real).* On top of Uncle Sam and my agent taking their cuts, they were asking me to give Les thirty percent of my backlist and forty percent of all future books that I sold on new contracts?

Am I the only one who realized that I would be working at a deficit?

I would be in the red and wouldn't have a fucking cent to live on? Instead, I would be paying that worthless bastard for the honor of working?

Not to mention, he wanted forty percent of any and all books or anything else I sold based on characters and series that I had created before I ever met the sorry piece of snail shit.

And they dared to call me unreasonable.

I supposed all of them, including my own attorney, were planning to turn me into a slave for this stupid, worthless son of a whore.

Then, they wanted me to stand up and commit perjury. Don't you love how this stupid prat kept trying to get me to do that? Cockburn wanted me to swear, under oath, that all works not yet published were written during the time of marriage.

*Are you fucking kidding me?*

Again, I had to wonder how much brain damage she'd suffered from oxygen dep while giving blowjobs. Obviously, she lacked any capacity to think.

I couldn't believe that this was to be my life. My reward for being a good person and working my ass off for my family. For taking care of a worthless piece of shit, son and grandson of pedophiles.

For all the years I'd loved my children and dedicated my life to raising them. For all the years I'd worked so incredibly hard to get out of poverty and build a life and career.

That the laws of this land would put me right back into poverty with no way out.

None. Why?

Here you go. The email from my attorney to me:

> Before I send this, I wanted to take one last attempt to change your position on some of these responses. I do not see how this ends anything with Les. I am afraid that if anything, it will only drag it out. He is likely to be awarded a portion of your royalties as a division of the marital assets. Heck, he could be awarded all of them. I think it is likely that Judge Dinky will rule that you are voluntarily under "employed" and order you to pay alimony also. I think there is a good chance Les could end up with assets and alimony and you will end up with nothing. I only have your best interests at heart. I am able to make a much less emotional and unbiased view of your case than you are. This should be business transaction at this point.

*Are you fucking kidding me?*

Underemployed during the Covid-19 crisis where one third of the country had lost its job and the entire state where I made my money was shut down?

Underemployed after he had spent three years going after another author in a lawsuit where my reputation had been torn apart? Where my sales had tanked as a result of his stupidity and I had the emails that he, himself, had written to other attorneys, my attorneys, screaming at them over the fact that my sales had plummeted because of Les's actions.

Then, because of Les's actions and the idiot lawyers he'd hired, I'd spent two more years with them dragging me through the mud, telling the world I was crazy to keep their client, Les, out of jail for attempted murder. Even though Les, during this last round, had sent a photograph showing items out of my house he "wanted."

Let me show you two of the photographs that he'd taken in his own words "as he left" that weekend while Nick and I were at an event in another state. These were made at approximately five P.M. We knew this as he also took video and captured a clock in the background.

Which also showed that when he'd sent me those emails telling me to settle the lawsuit he'd started so that we could be "walking hand-in-hand" in Williamsburg, he'd been lying. Just has he had been when he'd left the roses for me saying, "I love you, please call me." He had no intention of saving this marriage or coming back. It'd all been a setup and in any other state, he'd be in jail for handing over evidence of intentionally and maliciously hiding marital property and stealing money out of the accounts of his grown sons.

Welcome to Tennessee most corrupt state in the union. How we're number three, I have no idea. I can't imagine any state worse.

Anyway, here was the first one that left me gaping.

Notice anything weird? Like the fact that it was his office and there was no computer on the desk? See the printer? There was another printer that used to rest beside it. But all of that was wiped clean. Why was this important?

Here's an excerpt from the court transcript a couple of weeks after this photograph was made.

Cockburn: You have made one large purchase for a computer, is that correct?

Les:  Yes, that's right.

Cockburn: Would you please inform the Court, approximately, how much you spent on said computer and why you felt you need a new computer?

Les: I spent about $2000 on a computer because I needed something. I had not returned to the –I had not returned to the house. My wife had told me, do not come home. And I purchased a computer to conduct work, communication, take care of business.

Now do you see the problem? Obviously, he'd committed perjury. He'd been back to my home. He'd raided it.

He'd had a computer long before he'd spent that two grand as we'd been emailing back and forth.

So, why did he need a new computer when he was holed up in my office that was filled with, what?

Computers.

In fact, I had a brand-new computer in that cabin, too.

Why would he need to buy a computer after taking the one from my house?

Only the imbeciles in the Williamson County Police Department couldn't figure out that he'd taken that computer and destroyed it because it held evidence on it that would prove he'd tried to kill his wife.

Nothing else makes any sense. And his attorney helped him to cover it up and smear me at the same time.

It was sickening.

And his attorney handed over the evidence that proved his guilt.

Even better, was this little nugget.

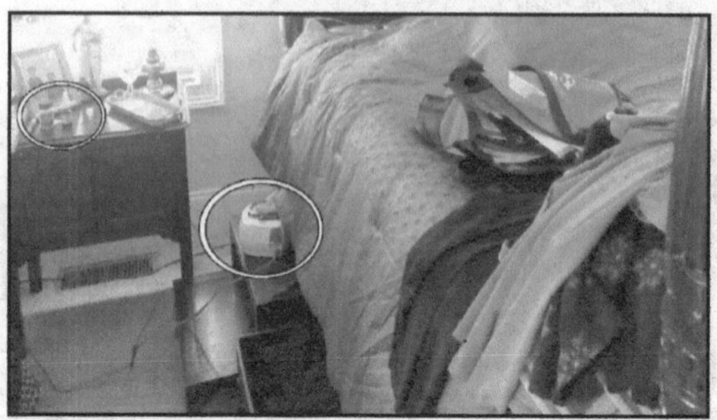

Why was this one important? Well, those weren't my clothes on the bed. Remember, I was out of town, working, with my son. Mr. I-always-took-care-of-the-kids-so-I-deserve-half had run out on our child in the middle of his senior year and left my Autistic child in a bad way. Without even telling him that he was planning to destroy my baby's senior year.

And unless Les wanted to confess to crossdressing, those weren't Les's clothes on the bed.

They were Hogg's. A *lot* of Hogg's clothes. They were next to a bag of hers, that was actually a bag of mine she'd stolen, piled full of files of mine that she wasn't supposed to be stealing. In the color photo, you could see that plainly. But the real kicker is the CPAP machine I circled. I don't have a CPAP and neither does Les. That's Hogg's that she wears at night when she sleeps.

An unmarried woman was spending the night in my marital home, alone, with my husband while I and my son were out of town, working. And my husband was the one who'd taken the photo and sent it to the attorneys. Yet everyone kept telling me that I was crazy and that they weren't having an affair.

But wait, it got even better.

Look up on the nightstand. There was an empty wine glass that you could barely see in this photo, but it was quite plain in the color photo. And next to the wine glass were two kinds of supplements that are sold in the Vitamin Shoppe.

Not anything I'd ever taken.

But I couldn't help wondering what they were. Could those have been some of what they used to poison me with?

My brother argued that one of them could be nose drops. But I'd been on every kind of nose drop and while the bottle was similar, it wasn't any kind I'd ever seen or that we could find online. It looked more like supplement bottles. Even it was drops, don't forget that people have poisoned and murdered their spouses with the same brand of eye drops that Les uses.

And they did it in the state where Hogg used to live at a time when Hogg lived there and would have seen it on the news.

Interestingly enough, my symptoms were eerily similar to that kind of poisoning, too.

We still don't know what exactly they were tainting my food with, but these photographs were damning.

Anywhere else, I would have some form of justice.

But not in Tennessee.

Instead, I was being put on welfare and told that I was going to have to support this bastard for the rest of my life and that I would have to work for nothing.

And that I should be grateful.

After all, it was for my own good. My attorney even had the nerve to say to me, "Look, this is what's been done to men for decades."

No, it wasn't. See, if I'd had a wife, she would have done actual housework. She would have baked cookies and done the parties for the kids. She would have planned the family vacations, bought the presents, been the room mom, etc.

All the billion and one things that I had done on top of being the primary breadwinner.

While Les sat on my couch, drunk, abusing me and my children, refusing to work, and I couldn't get rid of him for fear of his pedophile father raping my sons.

There was a big fucking difference.

All I'd asked was that the cabin and cars be sold and split evenly. That he would be given the same amount of royalties that I made, ten percent and that he was only to be paid for the books sold during our marriage. I was even willing to give in and let him be paid for the books I'd written prior to meeting him.

He would have those royalties for the rest of his life. Ten percent.

That was fair. No royalties on anything after he'd cruelly stolen from my sons and willfully left on March 7, 2018.

But because of a biased judge that I was told refused to recuse himself, I was supposed to give up everything I'd ever earned or would earn again to him for the rest of my life.

And even though he had a court order that had forbidden him to spend the money he'd stolen from my children, that I wanted him to pay back to them, I was told that I was being unreasonable.

That the corrupt judge was going to give him those unfair royalties plus alimony, which would have me paying him to work.

At that point, I knew I had no choice.

I sent the email to the trustee.

"File a Chapter 7."

I had to commend my future to God. I might as well go on welfare now and stop writing. There was no need to work so hard just so that I'd be forced to go into debt to pay the man who'd abused me. Who'd broken my son's arm and been such a coward that he'd left my baby in pain for two days before he'd told me that Caleb had "fallen" so hard that he'd fractured his collarbone.

If only I'd had proof. I would have contacted a divorce lawyer then to ask if I could divorce him because I'd known that he'd broken my son's arm. But at eighteen months old Caleb had been too little to speak. And I had no proof.

His word against mine.

Two days, he'd left my son suffering. "He has colic."

Les Manly. Biggest coward on the planet. And I was being punished for having married him.

Where was the justice in this world?

There wasn't any.

This was my reward for being a good wife to an absolute piece of shit, son of scum.

And this was how my career was going to end. Not in my happy old age, after hundreds of bestsellers.

Cut short because of one man's cruel greed. His final blow to take away absolutely everything from me.

Because the law allowed it and there was nothing I could do. I had no advocate. Everyone in this town was that afraid of the judge.

My ultimatum had been given. All I could do now was sit back and wait.
And pray for a miracle.

# MARCH 24

**I**NSULT TO INJURY. OR THE hits just kept coming. I should be used to it by now, but what the hell? The day had begun with a phone call for ole Les on my business line. They wanted to talk to him as an attorney.

Yeah. For someone who "couldn't" work or find a job, how weird that a local company was calling him to get him to advertise his "law business" in our grocery stores?

But that didn't count.

*Right...*

He got calls all the time for him as an attorney. He was more than able to work. As always, Les was scamming the system. And no one would call him on it.

After all, he was a bankruptcy attorney. The one job that was currently in demand.

Oh, the bitter irony.

If that wasn't annoying enough, I received the call from my insurance company.

Les had committed another act of insurance fraud by illegally reporting my jewelry (that had either been stolen by him when he left or taken in the illegal search and seizure that he had caused) as missing.

I supposed that after he'd heard ole Newhouse testify in court that they couldn't get anything for the jewelry, Les had decided to report it missing so that he could get the inflated value for it. After all, with the downturned market, he knew he couldn't sell whatever he'd stolen and get anything for it. So, what was his next great plan?

Scam the insurance company.

I was appalled.

At first, I thought Newhouse was in on it given that he'd been threatening for months to call them, until Melissa told me that he wasn't.

"He's furious at Les. He told him not to do it."

Then it dawned on me why.

Because Newhouse's little buddy Bill would be in all kinds of trouble for having left no receipt during their dubious seizure of my property. The insurance company might do something over the way it'd been taken and how they'd behaved.

Last thing cockroaches wanted was a light shined on their activities.

After all, there were two people in this life that I have never, ever messed with.

And never would.

The IRS and insurance adjusters. Neither had a sense of humor. My older brother had once been a Claims Investigator for Farm Bureau. Having heard his stories as a kid, I never, ever wanted to go up against an insurance company.

Les, however, was a greedy idiot.

What was doubly annoying, was that they refused to tell me what he'd claimed was "missing." They wanted me to fill out forms when I had no idea what they were even talking about.

Although I couldn't understand how Les could even claim the jewelry was gone given that we knew it was in one of two places. The cubby hole that Les had paid to have made in my cabin office.

Or in Bill's dubious custody.

How do I know? Here was the sloppy ass work they had charged me hundreds of thousands of dollars for and harassed me over. Remember the almost forty items Bill and Newhouse had sent and claimed was missing from my collection?

Here was a couple of them:

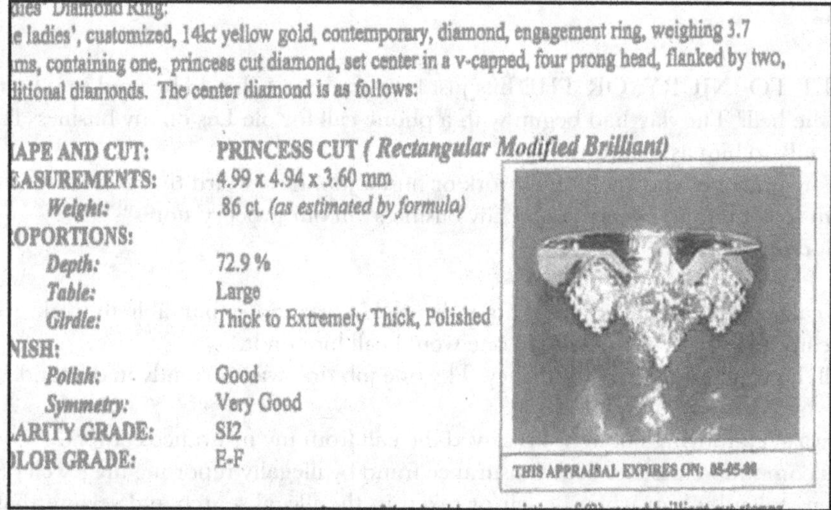

ies' Diamond Ring.

e ladies', customized, 14kt yellow gold, contemporary, diamond, engagement ring, weighing 3.7 ms, containing one, princess cut diamond, set center in a v-capped, four prong head, flanked by two, ditional diamonds. The center diamond is as follows:

| | |
|---|---|
| APE AND CUT: | PRINCESS CUT ( *Rectangular Modified Brilliant*) |
| EASUREMENTS: | 4.99 x 4.94 x 3.60 mm |
| Weight: | .86 ct. (as estimated by formula) |
| OPORTIONS: | |
| Depth: | 72.9 % |
| Table: | Large |
| Girdle: | Thick to Extremely Thick, Polished |
| NISH: | |
| Polish: | Good |
| Symmetry: | Very Good |
| ARITY GRADE: | SI2 |
| LOR GRADE: | E-F |

THIS APPRAISAL EXPIRES ON: 05-05-08

And this was the photo Stupid Bill had provided me weeks after he'd done his improper seizure:

Obviously, sitting next to my mother's anniversary band was my wedding set. The engagement ring Dipshit Newhouse had had a stroke over and claimed was missing. It was clearly present in the photos Oldham had sent over. And it was a unique, custom setting so there was no way to miss it or mistake it.

Another example was my great-grandmother's ring from the 1800's:

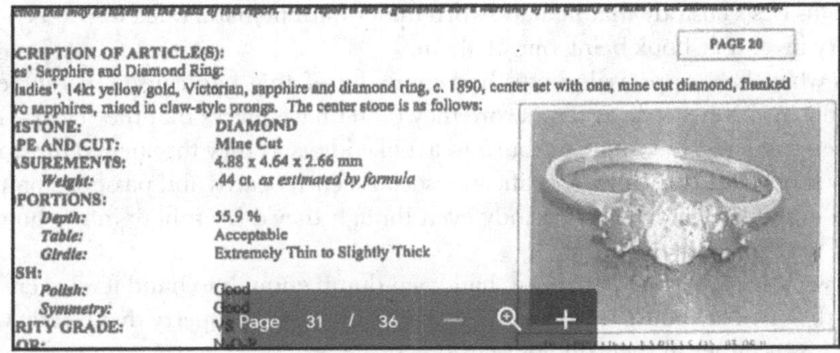

Here was another photograph Bill had sent weeks after the seizure:

There it was nestled right next to my mother's synthetic "pink ice" ring and the pink ice ring she'd given me when I was eighteen that were each worth about fifty bucks a piece. And next to my college class ring that had my name engraved in. Never mind the little cheap ring my mother had bought for me in junior high that was worth less than fifty dollars, because it had a synthetic stone, too, and was gold-plated.

All pieces these sick fucks had told me they were going to sell for "retaliation" and to punish me for having documented their cruelty and bad acts.

This showed and proved the sloppy, shitty work that both Oldham and Newhouse had billed me roughly eight hundred dollars an hour for while the two of them sat in Oldham's office and "went through" my jewelry with an inventory book that Les had stolen from my home.

The same book that Les had committed perjury over when he'd said that he had not *removed* it from my home (his attorney had also testified to that fact in front of the judge and had written it up in her motions).

All this while they were hauling me into court for contempt every two weeks. One of the things they'd kept demanding was that I produce those records for my jewelry that Les had "mysteriously" found after Oldham had improperly and illegally seized it all.

I kept telling them that Les had stolen my records when he left the house.

Cockburn had emphatically denied it, while knowing they had the records. At one point, while denying they had them, she'd even produced some of them.

You'd seen the transcript where Les had been under oath and claimed that he hadn't been back to my house and that he'd taken "nothing" with him.

He lied under oath. Perjury plain and simple.

Well, lo and behold, the minute old Bill had seized my property, suddenly a lot of things had "turned up" in Les's custody that he had sworn under oath he hadn't taken.

My jewelry inventory book being one of them.

That was what those appraisal photos had come out of that had caused me endless harassment from Bill and Newhouse as they swore they didn't have pieces that they clearly had.

Which then triggered Les and Cockburn to act like idiots as they threatened me, too.

It, like my sons' class rings, birth certificates, social security cards and passport, had "mysteriously" been found by Les in Les's custody even though they'd been here in my home and/or safe prior to his leaving.

And his own idiot attorney, Cockburn, had been dumb enough to hand it all over.

Yet I was the one Newhouse was screaming at over the "lost" property that clearly wasn't lost.

As I said, it was either in their dubious custody or Les's.

The question was who was scamming whom?

I could no longer tell who the bigger liar was. Les or the attorney they'd hired as a receiver that Newhouse had taken over as his attorney to "represent" him in my business bankruptcy. Which really made no sense. After all, Newhouse was an attorney and bonded. Why did he need another attorney? Wasn't that the point of his being an attorney and bonded?

The bankruptcy court had the biggest racket going. Especially as they were allowing them to raid and liquidate personal property for a *business* bankruptcy where they had no authority to do away with my *personal* property.

How do I know? Let me show you what ole Newhouse was charging:

| Expense | Estimated Amount |
|---|---|
| Trustee's Estimated Unpaid Commission (if all admin expenses and priority claims approved) | $14,484.25 |
| Trustee's Expenses | $132.50 |
| Attorney Fees and Expenses for Thompson Burton, PLLC | $20,105.30 |
| Commission owed to McLemore Auction | $25,262.89 |
| Financial Advisor Fees | $10,972.50 |
| TOTAL | $70,957.44 |

This came in *less* than a month after he had taken *over* one hundred thousand dollars of my personal money for their pay.

Let's take a gander at the party they were having with my jewelry that a business bankruptcy gave them no authority over, and remember that this was only the fees that Oldham was charging me. So, the cost I was being billed would need to be *doubled* for each session:

| 02/04/20] | | 395.00 | 5.2 | 2,054.00 |

collect and send information regarding jewelry to appraiser (0.5); inventory jewelry in order to find "missing" pieces (0.5)

| 02/05/20] | Work on jewelry | 395.00 | 0.7 | 276.50 |

inventory

| 02/12/20] | Review email from | 395.00 | 0.3 | 118.50 |

jewelry expert (0.1); r

| 03/04/20] # | | 395.00 | 0.4 | 158.00 |

1); emails to jewelry expert (0.1)

| | | 395.00 | 2.8 | 1,106.00 |

(0.6); email to jewelry auctioneer (0.1); r

So, for the two of them to have a party over my jewelry for this one month, alone, (and in a Chapter 11 business bankruptcy where they had no authority over my personal jewelry) was almost ten grand that I was being charged. That meant that every single ring from my childhood that you saw (plus a lot more) was being sold to cover their bills for their stupidity in a business bankruptcy where they were not supposed to touch my personal assets. Because they obviously couldn't match up the book to the pieces they had, and were determined to steal every last item I had ever been given, earned or inherited.

I wasn't allowed in to do it for them as they didn't *trust me*. Nor, according to them, would the other side allow me to show them what pieces were what. Even though the other side had sat outside in the driveway of my home (in violation of a court order), unsupervised, for hours with my jewelry, while I'd been held hostage, along with my sons and friends, at my kitchen table.

And what difference did it make if they had an "expert" look the jewelry over? This was the most flagrant waste of my money.

Not only did we have the appraisals that showed the value of my jewelry, but I was a certified gemologist from the GIA and have been for years. The one thing I knew, was the value of jewelry, especially my own.

I told Dipshit when it was seized that though the replacement cost for everything might be one amount, you'd never get that at an auction. And that was before the economy took a header with COVID-19.

Oldham said the same exact thing sitting in Melissa's office.

So, when Newhouse had stood in front of the judge and said that we'd misrepresented the value of the jewelry, he'd lied to the Court. Just as he lied again in the motion he would put in a few days after this to the bankruptcy court.

No one had ever misrepped the value of the jewelry, except Newhouse.

Jewelry, like my copyrights, was a complicated matter and if this fucking idiot didn't get that, then he had no business as a trustee.

None of them did.

They had wasted tens of thousands of my dollars chasing after something I had hundreds of emails telling him not to do because it wouldn't be worth it. A large portion of what he was hoping to get at auction had already been spent by him and his "friends" talking about selling my jewelry.

I was sick to my stomach over the unnecessary waste and expense.

All of this caused by Les and his selfish greed.

His twisted cruelty.

All of *their* sadistic cruelty.

This was what the government had put over the lives of innocent people to bully and harass us.

How was this even possible?

And then, when we were at our financial lowest, to gouge us when we could least afford it.

This should be criminal.

And they had the nerve to ask me for a release against *them* for their bad acts?

*Are you fucking kidding me?*

Anyway, I was extremely upset when the investigator called to further harass me about the jewelry that wouldn't have been missing had it been left in my home.

I told him the full story.

By the end, he was as appalled with Les as we were. Furthermore, I told him that I owned the jewelry (until it was sold) and that I didn't authorize them to investigate anything, unless it was Les for fraud.

Les had no business reporting my jewelry missing. He didn't own my jewelry. Nor had he paid a dime of the policy.

But the kicker came when I got the paperwork and saw what ole idiot Les had said. He'd reported a "mysterious disappearance."

Yeah, he must have been drunk. There was nothing mysterious about having a Receiver, a Williamson County deputy, my attorney, and Les's attorney walk my jewelry out of my home without a proper warrant and without proper cause having been shown to the court for that seizure.

An action I had on video, by the way.

While Les sat in my driveway with Cockburn.

How would it end? I had no idea. All I could do was pray for justice.

*THE PRIVACY OF TERRI MANLY is highly valued and you shall make each and every possible effort to maintain confidentiality with respect to all information and other material of every kind whatsoever concerning Terri Manly, including but not limited to documents, recordings, and pictures, however coming into your possession or otherwise discovered by you (individually and collectively, "Manly Material"), expressly excluding information intentionally publicly disclosed directly by Terri Manly. You acknowledge that due to the particular nature of the entertainment industry, any disclosure or dissemination, whether or not inadvertently, of the Manly Material without Terri Manly's express written approval will cause severe and irreparable financial and other harm to Terri Manly. Accordingly, you hereby agree that you shall not at any time use or disclose, directly or indirectly, to anyone other than to Terri Manly or her legal representatives, any of the Manly Material and you further agree to keep all such information strictly confidential, private, secret and sensitive. All Manly Material, and all other documents, pictures, recordings, records, documents, business contacts (business associates), client contacts, readership lists or other materials in any way relating to Terri Manly, however coming into your possession, is and shall forever be Terri Manly's sole and exclusive property, and you shall not retain, copy and/or disclose any of them without Terri Manly's prior written consent, but shall at Terri Manly's written request, immediately deliver to her any and all Manly Material which may come into your possession.*

*In addition, I expressly grant and assign to Terri Manly any and all monies or other benefits whatsoever received by or payable to me (or any designee or representative of mine) in connection with any use, dissemination, or exploitation of the Manly Material or any other information or material described in this agreement. **Any such monies received by me, or on my behalf shall be held in trust for immediate payment over to Terri Manly.***

That was an excerpt from the Non-Disclosure that ole Les had forced absolutely everyone to sign when they came to work for us. It was the same NDA that ole Les had agreed to uphold and sign himself.

In fact, here was the email that Les had written to our attorney in the Dumas suit:

Thu, May 26, 2016, 10:45 AM

Yes, sorry for the delay. Mighty Balls, LLC is all I can think of right now. As you know this is a small at home business. The website, employees and marketing functions are under Mighty Balls. Robert Sullivan, Loeb and Loeb, suggested this arrangement since the writing functions always carry a personal guarantee with the publisher.

Bobby Brewster at Bass, Berry and Sims files the paperwork for the LLC. On insurance for Mighty Balls, we always get personal riders to cover Terri and me.

Karen Hogg is an independent contractor. If you need an NDA on her, I can ask. Maybe others on Terri's witness list like her agent, Bob, need NDAs. You can get an NDA on me as well as a representation agreement. That's probably a good idea.

Les Manly

There were so many juicy details in this one itty bitty email. First, Les had said in this that he agreed, of his own free will and with full knowledge of what that meant, to be bound by the NDA that he'd written and executed with all the people he'd hired around us.

Also, that Hogg was not my employee as she and Les had continued to lie about with everyone. That Les was still my attorney as he'd lied under oath and said that he was not working as one. Obviously, he couldn't have a "representation agreement" with me if he wasn't my attorney. Which meant that he had been violating his own attorney-client privilege with me all throughout the divorce.

The fact that he knew he'd also breached an NDA with me and that he'd allowed his Hogg to do the same. That he'd induced others to breach those NDAs in the *Vulture* article to cause irreparable harm to my career. A career he wanted to suck off and have support him for the rest of his life.

As if that made any sense whatsoever.

And why hadn't he forced Hogg to sign an NDA prior to this? At the point he'd sent that email, she had been working for him for about three years. One of them as his legal secretary.

He'd always been so anal about anyone and everyone signing those NDAs the moment they walked into our home, especially the tutors. Why was she an exception?

That in and of itself was peculiar.

But my favorite had to be the admission of the personal rider on our insurance policy that he had set up.

It was insurance he'd put in place, that his attorneys had court ordered me to maintain while those attorneys baited me and my staff and forced us to defend my reputation with comments such as this:

That would make you a mouth-breathing sycophant.

I bet she has a hard time writing because she'd ran out of Japanese source material to plagiarize.

She needs a strait jacket.

Remember ole Cockburn had admitted that was indeed her ex who had posted those comments on my site and who had threatened and insulted me and my fans. Not speculation. She admitted it to my attorney.

She had sicced her people onto my publisher-owned social media site to attack and defame me and my fans.

They had baited us and forced us to respond so that they could set up a lawsuit for Les to go after my insurance policy for a company that he was a managing officer in.

Insurance Fraud 101.

Not to mention, given that I had not only the actual signed NDA, but an email where Les had admitted that he'd agreed to be covered by the very NDA he had drafted and executed countless times against others, then maliciously and willfully breached to do excruciating mental and financial harm to me. How could he receive a dime of alimony or any proceeds from my contracts given what the NDA said?

To me, it was cut and dry. He had breached his own agreement and induced others to do it.

It clearly said:

> In addition, I expressly grant and assign to Terri Manly any and all monies or other benefits whatsoever received by or payable to me (or any designee or representative of mine) in connection with any use, dissemination, or exploitation of the Terri Manly Material or any other information or material described in this agreement. **Any such monies received by me, or on my behalf shall be held in trust for immediate payment over to Terri Manly.**

That meant that Les could not profit from what he'd done to me in the divorce and that he wasn't entitled to anything. For that matter, his attorneys owed me a refund for all the harm they had done.

It was as plain as the nose on his hideous face.

My attorney agreed, but didn't want to make the argument since, in her opinion, it would elongate the divorce.

Right. Like it wasn't already elongated. Cockburn had no interest in cutting off her revenue stream.

On this day, they backed out of all negotiations.

Cockburn had told my attorney that we were "too far apart." Why? Because I refused to be his slave.

The only thing I was standing firm on was that he would never receive a dime from anything I did in the future. He wasn't entitled. And that our remaining homes and cars would be sold and evenly split.

Fair was fair.

But he didn't want fair. He'd taken his half when he'd left, and now he wanted it all.

*Baby, it was time you swallowed your bitter pill and realized that you were going to have to get a fucking job like everyone else in the world. There was no such thing a free ride.*

And we were about to be absolutely broke.

Thanks to him.

NEWHOUSE HAD YET TO FILE that Chapter 7. It'd been eerily silent since Cockburn backed out. Each day had passed with reports on the COVID-19 outbreak worsening and me waiting for the other shoe to drop.

I knew stupid would have something planned. He always did. Stupid in this case meant both Les and Newhouse.

I didn't know which direction they'd come from. The word from Melissa was that Newhouse was holding off to see if Les would come back to the table.

I knew better.

What I did learn on this day was that Newhouse's two hundred dollar an hour moron was listing my business expenses as "personal" on the paperwork she was filing with the court.

That was how incompetent she was. She had no idea what she was doing. Yet he stood by her and allowed her to continue to waste my money.

It was sickening.

Also sickening? My son's car had broken down and I was going to pick him up from work. As I pulled to the end of my driveway, there was a black truck blocking my exit.

A large man got out. By his stance and demeanor, I could tell he was ex-military. There was a certain air about them that anyone who'd been raised around military families could pick up on immediately. The way they stood and carried themselves.

I'd never seen him before.

"Ms. Manly?"

"Yes?"

"I'm Brad Allen. I do your yard, and I wanted to talk to you about the money you owe me."

I let out a tired sigh. "I don't know if you've heard, but I'm in bankruptcy. I've been trying to get you paid." For months while Newhouse pillaged my estate to pay for his buddies and refused to pay for hardworking vets like this man in front of me.

I was furious. Anyone who knew me knew that there were certain things I was always highly protective of. My family. My work. And anyone in the military and their families.

Having been raised at Ft. Benning and having seen the way those soldiers were when they returned from Vietnam, and how my father and other family members had been treated, I would do anything to help a brother or sister in uniform.

Current or former.

My daddy taught me a deep and abiding love and respect for those who put their lives on the line for us.

And it infuriated me that Les and Newhouse had lied and deprived this man of his payment. A payment that didn't amount to one fucking phone call between Newhouse and the asshole attorney buddy he'd forced on me against my will.

What was worse? Brad told me that Les had been lying to him. "He said you'd changed your phone number and that he had no way to get in touch with you."

Bullshit.

I have had the same number since we moved to this godforsaken hellhole of a state.

Les had changed his number and his email.

Because I had to work for a living, I couldn't randomly change mine. It was too much of a hassle to change them as I had too many important contacts and didn't have time to run them all down for such petty bullshit.

But why would Les play that game? Why not give him my contact information or that of the bankruptcy attorney? It wasn't like Les didn't know it or had anything better to do with his useless, endless nonworking time. He'd contacted them on his own constantly.

For his own selfish interests.

But he'd left Brad, the man who'd been cutting our lawn for years, out in the cold.

A real veteran, not the fake vet that Les was. Someone who had actually served his country in Afghanistan with honor and distinction. Not stayed at home and hid while he was too afraid yet used the fact that he'd played at being a soldier in college to get money and to gain sympathy with a judge.

That wasn't all Brad had to say to me. "He told me that you'd been poisoned and were sick." *Say what?*

You read that correctly. Les had admitted to Brad that I'd been poisoned and that it had made me sick.

Free and clear.

He'd omitted the fact that he'd been the one who'd done it. So Les knew I was poisoned. He wasn't denying it.

More than that, he was the one spreading the "defamation" in public.

Not me.

So, his whole illegal lawsuit that he'd filed while I was in bankruptcy had been another fabrication. And the kicker? *The fact that when you signed off on that suit at the time you'd filed it, punkin', it had the clause "under penalty of perjury."*

Les had committed more perjury.

The lies just kept coming.

I was floored.

More than that, I was determined. "I will get you paid. Whatever it takes, I will make sure you get every cent you are due. I've never in my life cheated anyone and I have no intention of starting now."

So, I got his name and number and stayed in touch with him.

My mind reeled at everything Brad had let out. And still, I was waiting for the shoe to drop because it was being too quiet.

I knew they were planning something. I just didn't know what.

APRIL 1

**T**HIS WAS MY SISTER'S BIRTHDAY. On the day she'd been born, my father had been out on maneuvers. Because she was early and it was April Fool's, my dad had assumed that it was a prank of my mom's when she'd called to tell him she was in labor.

My mother was a terrible prankster.

Sadly for him, it hadn't been a joke. She'd been in labor and my sister was born while my dad was at work. To the day he'd died, he never heard the end of *that*.

My mother wasn't someone you wanted to piss off.

So, I'd always been leery of April Fool's pranks. On this day, I received notice that Newhouse had filed that expedited notice to Dismiss my bankruptcy or Convert to a Chapter 7.

Our hearing would be less than a week away.

While the courts were closed due to COVID-19.

I didn't even know how to respond or where to begin with this latest fucked up act. First, there were so many misrepresentations of facts in the order that it again appalled me. How could they keep lying like that with no repercussions?

But the most galling was the fact that after all these many, many months of telling me that we could *not under any circumstances* have my case dismissed, have my case suddenly dismissed after Newhouse and crew had robbed me of over a million dollars of my assets and not paid off a single creditor?

They had robbed me of more money than I had owed when I filed. Millions more than what I'd owed.

How was this even possible?

And what killed me was that, even though I did not legally qualify for the Means Test to have my case converted to a Chapter 7, the bastard was asking for it to be converted anyway.

Really?

Had he had a head injury?

Fine, if he wanted a war, I was girded up and ready.

As Martha had said when she'd fondled my diary in her conference room, "This looks like it's in a publishable state. It appears that you could print it out and make a book from it, right now."

*Yeah, bitch, I can.*

And I was planning to. Hadn't planned it until all the threats began, but the world needed to know what the trustees were really like.

Especially now when so many people were on the brink of bankruptcy.

*People, please don't do it!*

And this biggest kicker? My attorney had said that the reason Newhouse had agreed to finally to let me out was because I could get forty thousand dollars of free money from the government over the COVID-19 relief for small businesses.

However, he was billing me for forty-three-thousand dollars in bills.

Three thousand more than I could get in help.

Wasn't he a gem?

He wanted me to get money from the government just to pay him.

My jaw hadn't left the floor. The gall of this bastard knew no boundaries.

Even more stunning? Cockburn and crew agreed with me about him.

They really did.

I was floored. They held the same opinion that I did. That Newhouse had botched the case and had intentionally bled me dry. Even though he'd been paying them and only them the entire time.

Not my creditors.

But they omitted the fact that he'd done so with their help and at their behest. As Newhouse would say, they were "throwing him under the bus".

His attorney, too. The same attorney that old Cockburn had picked, herself, to illegally seize the property from my home.

However, that wasn't the end of her galactic stupidity.

Oh no.

Since the bankruptcy looked to be ending, Cockburn now wanted all of the money to be handed over to another Receiver and for the jewelry to be kept with Oldham, the man she'd just insulted.

*Are you fucking kidding me?*

Those outrageous fees and the milking of my estate was what had caused all this to begin with.

The definition of stupid: Repeating the same thing over and over and expecting a different result.

*Stupidity thy name is Cockburn.*

Not only that, but in October old Dinky had overturned his previous order and released all my property that had been seized. Thundercunt ought to know that as her team wrote that up so that they could write themselves a blank check with my money and have old Newhouse pay them.

Under the law and the way bankruptcy normally went, they had no authority to withhold my property or money from me once the case was dismissed.

No cause had ever been shown or given for it.

However, I didn't have a bankruptcy attorney and Newhouse knew it. He was trying to get this done before I had anyone in place who could stop him.

Or so he thought.

Enter my baby brother, Esteban.

"I might know someone."

What?

Sure enough, yet again, the baby Caboose who'd saved my butt all those years ago in Mississippi and so many times that I couldn't count, knew of a savior.

Someone who'd been doing bankruptcy and divorce law for over twenty-three years.

*Enter Nanette Savior!*

Nan knew her stuff! And she was the first to tell me that everything they'd done had been utter bullshit. That nothing in my case had gone the way it should have.

It was indeed the travesty I knew it to be.

God love her, but she wrote up a response for me so that I could send it off to Newhouse and demand what needed to be done.

What *should* have been done.

And for them to give me my life back and to get out of the bankruptcy nightmare for once and for all.

I sent it off to them on Saturday night, April 4.

Now all I could do was wait.

And hope.

And pray.

Maybe, just maybe there might be some form of law and order in Williamson County, Tennessee.

APRIL 7

**T**HERE WAS NO SUCH THING as law and order in Williamson County, Tennessee or Davidson County, either. The bankruptcy court was a Davidson County, federal court matter.

And it was just as sick as Williamson.

Oh, the bullshit lies Judge Harriet let them get away with. I was sickened by it all. So sick, I wasn't even sure where to begin. First, holding court on an open phone line was such a joke. But at least I didn't have to stare at Cockburn's hyena face this time.

She was there, even though she had no business in federal court.

The lies that were told.

Under oath.

*Oh perjury, let me count the ways.*

First, Newhouse swore he'd paid my creditors. If that was true, explain to my why every single creditor I had was now demanding payment from me?

*C'mon, Newhouse. Show me one fucking creditor you paid in almost nine months of bankruptcy. I dare you.*

He couldn't because he hadn't.

One count of perjury down.

Newhouse again lied and said he'd been "misled" about the value of my property. No one misled him. He was given the appraisals by the hired authorities. Common fucking sense would have told him that what a piece of jewelry was bought for and what you could get for it if you sold it/pawned it were vastly different. Everyone with an IQ over five knew this.

Which said it all about his IQ level.

Not to mention, I have countless emails where I'd told him that the jewelry was worthless in an auction.

Oldham had told him it wasn't worth selling.

The only one arguing to sell it was Cockburn, the whore, who wanted to deprive me of everything I owned.

Out of spite.

Same for my house. How could I mislead him about the value of my home when I'm not a realtor? But you know who was?

Cockburn.

We'd had three appraisals done on my home.

Three.

If they were wrong, how would I know? I was an author, not an appraiser.

But they must not be too off as another offer for my house came in that day.

Suck it, Newhouse, you lying sack of shit. And this time it was under oath.

However, the biggest kicker came when he went off on his long diatribe about *my four-hundred-page book* that I'd published. *Yeah,* this *book.*

He went on to tell the judge that it was necessary for her to strip me of my rights to sue him and his cohorts because I had their dubious activities and threats well documented.

"It would result in a Rule 11 sanction, Your Honor."

He actually said those words. Not that it "might" or "could." It *would.*

I supposed that confession was good for his soul.

Even if the judge was so lax in her position that she didn't clue into the fact that he needed to be disbarred, and that she should have stepped in a long, long time ago and done her job.

Finally, I was given a chance to speak. "Your honor, my jewelry consists of inherited pieces and gifts. Ninety percent of it is not marital property and doesn't fall under the purview of the state court. It needs to be remanded back into my custody, where it belongs." And actually, I was being kind. One hundred percent was not marital property, but I knew Les would argue.

Enter the lying bitch. "Your Honor, that's not true. We had a full hearing about the jewelry with Judge Dinky and he ruled on it. It is not ninety percent marital property. It's all marital property."

Really? We had had a hearing?

Want to tell me when, you lying cunt?

Dinky had refused over and over to have a hearing on this matter. He didn't want to know about the fact that he'd broken the law and seized property he had no jurisdiction over.

Then we'd have grounds to go after him (not that we didn't already).

But let me clarify this for a moment. Out of *five-hundred-and-fifty pieces* only six weren't mine.

Six.

Of those six, two were Les's. The rest belonged to my son, Maddox. They took his cufflinks that were a gift. His graduation watch. Crusader cross and a ring he'd bought when he was in middle school.

The rest were inarguably all mine.

Over five hundred pieces had been stolen from my home.

And out of those, over four hundred pieces belonged to my family or me before I was married.

Most of those pieces were fake and a number of them had been given to me by my fans over the years.

Cockburn couldn't keep herself from lying. Even when she had no business being in my bankruptcy hearing as she didn't practice in that arena.

And of course, relying on nothing more than their lies and refusing to see any evidence, the judge sided with the liars and again deprived me of property that the state court had no jurisdiction over and that I had been tortured over for a year.

Let's hear it for American Injustice.

And the wastefulness of our tax dollars on these overpaid troglodytes who were so busy rimming each other that they couldn't be bothered with legalities, morality or even doing the right thing.

The decent thing.

Again, we know why a judge's robe was black.

Shit-stain on the American Constitution and on the American people.

The judge also refused, even though the law required my funds to be returned to where they'd come from (the sale of my personal property) to return my money to me.

So old Newhouse made good on his threat.

He left me with no money to buy food, medicine or gas, in the middle of the COVID epidemic. All my money was sent to the Chancery Court, which was why my store orders couldn't be shipped out to my fans that week.

I didn't have the money to pay for postage as it had all been confiscated by our court system.

They had taken the money that had been paid by the American public and then refused to give it to me so that I could fulfill those prepaid orders.

During a financial crisis.

The judge and court had committed fraud on the public, and there was nothing I could do.

Thank you, Cockburn, Newhouse, Oldham and the Department of Justice employee, Martha Seaver.

Oh, how proud she was to announce to the judge that she worked for the DOJ.

"Your Honor, since Mr. Newhouse brought up my book, I want it noted that I was documenting their severe threats against me. I never made any threats toward them." Up until that point, Newhouse and Oldham had both lied to the court by saying I had threatened them.

I never knew telling the truth was a threat.

Wow.

But then, I supposed if you were violating someone else's rights, not doing your job and doing all manner of unconscionable and illegal things to another human being, and that person was a public figure capable of letting the public know about your bad acts...

Okay, I supposed that could be construed as threatening. Cockroaches usually scurried away whenever someone turned on a light.

"But the court should note that I have reported them to the Office of the Inspector General, the Department of Justice and the Tennessee Board of Professional Responsibility."

Martha was real quick to jump in. "Your Honor, I work for the Department of Justice and I'm unaware of any complaints that have been filed."

*Lying much, bitch?* First, I attempted to report them to you and *your* answer, Martha, was to threaten me and my friend.

Repeatedly.

And to threaten me with retaliation.

Remember the old, "You better destroy every single copy of this book. I have my finger on the button. You give me any reason or do anything at all that displeases me, or Tom, and I will press it. My bosses in Washington have told me to make sure that you never say a word in public about this."

Yeah.

So, she was well aware of my reporting their bad acts.

But I guess when I went over her head to her bosses in Washington and reported her there, as well as to the OIG who had promised me that they were reporting it to the DOJ, too, they weren't telling the people they were investigating that they were investigating them.

Made sense I supposed.

Or, what I truly suspected, neither department gave a shit that their people were breaking the law and terrorizing innocent victims.

Because Martha and crew were all smirking about it. You could hear it in their tones.

*She who laughs last...*

After the judge sided with them and left me with no money and again took my personal property that they had no right to, and then deprived me of my right to sue these animals for putting my son in the ER from the viciousness of their threats (the judge actually made me take an oath in federal court that I wouldn't sue them—another illegal act), I got the best call of my life.

"Stefano got a bar complaint today. He's furious."

My heart sang when Melissa told me the news.

Finally! Finally, Dullard had come through for me and had done the right thing. If I'd been able to with my broken feet, I'd have turned a cartwheel.

I couldn't believe that after all this time that maybe, just maybe one of them might get what they deserved. That maybe one of the organizations charged with protecting the public might make sure that no one else was abused the way they'd done me and my sons.

It wasn't a guarantee, but as Leadwits had written to me in his last email, "It was a step in the right direction."

But that happiness didn't last long. As I was pulling emails for the Tennessee Board of Professional Responsibility, I happened upon this little gem from the early days of my bankruptcy that I'd completely forgotten about:

> Tuesday is Les's motion for relief from stay at 9. Call me when you can - I am uploading my Pretrial statement, and I wanted to tell you what I am writing.
>
> As for Tom, he is a newbie Trustee and this is his first big case. He is overly cautious because he is scared.
>
> As for fees, the UST is only allows Tom a percentage of disbursements, not an hourly, but keep that to yourself.

Too bad Newhouse's fear hadn't lasted long before his arrogance had overridden it and his greed had overridden his common sense.

And that was why Newhouse had been so gung-ho to sell me out to my husband's attorneys to get them paid. Why he had "negotiated" against me to allow them to write themselves a blank check. The more of my money he handed out, and the more of my items he sold off, the more money he was paid.

*Are you fucking kidding me?*

That was how his office worked and how they screwed over the American people when they were at their lowest.

I was sick to my stomach. Given that he was paid a percentage of how much of my money he irrationally handed out, he shouldn't have even been allowed in the meeting to negotiate with Les's attorneys. Especially given that he benefitted financially from the outcome, and that he had the power to force me into a settlement.

At the very least, he should have been forced to disclose that fact to me. Because I'd been under the assumption that as my trustee, his job was to protect my assets and all my income. I had assumed he was being paid a flat rate from the government to do his job.

Not a percentage to sell me out.

To sell out everyone going through a bankruptcy and get rid of everything they'd worked for. Just think about it. This lying bastard had passed my money around like a party favor because the more of our assets they sell off and the more of our hard-earned money they give away to people other than our creditors they're supposed to be paying, the more money they make personally.

*What the ever-loving fuck?*

No wonder he'd threatened me with jail if I didn't agree to their outrageous extortion. And it was extortion. Remember the emails I'd copied from Melissa where I'd outlined their blackmail? And she had agreed completely that they were blackmailing me.

Newhouse's own words, "You can't go in front of Dinky. He hates you and you'll be sent to jail again. You have to take this deal. It's for your own good."

No, Newhouse. It'd been for *your* own good. You had raided my estate like a fucking bandit to pay yourself and your friends.

"Well, it's how they get paid and it's legal." That had been Melissa's explanation for it.

A bad law didn't make something right.

It made the lies all the more nauseating.

And if that wasn't bad enough, I was at the bank to meet with a friend to notarize my paperwork for the Tennessee Board of Professional Responsibility when I met a friend there whose wife just happened to be a court reporter. Ironically, in all the years I'd known him, I'd never realized what his wife did for a living.

I told him about the problem I'd had with some of the transcripts having been tampered with.

"Girl, that happens all the time. Everyone knows it. My wife's company won't do it, but others in this town... "

Constance had been righter than she'd known. Like all the other corruption in this town, no one bothered to keep that a secret either.

Wow.

Just wow.

But at least I had the name of a court reporter I could trust who couldn't be bullied or bought. One who wouldn't tamper with the transcripts.

And now I had another court date. Because no sooner had the bankruptcy ended than old Cockburn was up to her tricks to bleed me dry.

Yee-haw. I was going back to being hauled into court every single week again.

Because rather than move this toward a conclusion, she wanted another Receiver put over me.

Which meant that she and Les were in it for the long haul. If they'd really wanted this ended, why waste the time and money for a Receiver?

We should be filing motions to end this travesty. Go to mediation or anything to end this fucking joke divorce.

Not pay off more of Cockburn's friends when I needed to be paying off the creditors that Newhouse had refused to pay.

And Les needed to go get a fucking job so that he could do something other than torment me and his children.

Oh, but wait...

Fate wasn't done with me. Guess what other little nugget I found. My son had told me about the Zelle app on the banking site. So out of curiosity, I opened it.

Guess who ole Les had been wiring my money to?

His pedophile father. The one that old Cockburn had stood up in court and proclaimed as "rich and wealthy." So why would Les need to give Pedophile Dad any of my money?

Hiding marital assets. Of course, what else.

"But it's legal to send money and give gifts to relatives while you're married."

I wanted to throw my shoe at Melissa. "It was also legal to deny women the right to vote. But again, it doesn't make it right."

And every piece of law that I'd seen said that if you knew you intended to divorce your spouse and you began to conceal and transfer property in preparation for the divorce, it was a crime.

Tennessee Code Annotated § 36-4-106(d) sets forth as follows:

(1)(A)  An injunction restraining and enjoining both parties from transferring, assigning, borrowing against, concealing or in any way dissipating or disposing, without the consent of the other party or an order of the court, of any marital property.  Nothing herein is intended to preclude either of the parties from seeking broader injunctive relief from the court.

(B)  Expenditures from current income to maintain the marital standard of living and the usual and ordinary costs of operating a business are not restricted by this injunction.  Each party shall maintain records of all expenditures, copies of which shall be available to the other party upon request.

(2)  An injunction restraining and enjoining both parties from voluntarily canceling, modifying, terminating, assigning, or allowing to lapse for nonpayment of premiums, any insurance policy, including, but not limited to, life, health, disability, homeowners, renters, and automobile, where such insurance policy provides coverage to either of the parties or the children, or that names either of the parties or the children as beneficiaries without the consent of the other party or an order of the court.  "Modifying" includes any change in beneficiary status.

*The intent of the statute is to impose a freeze on the status quo being for the most part preservation of the marital estate that will be divided by the court.  Dissipation of marital assets unlawfully interferes with the court's ability to fairly divide the marital estate.*

In dividing marital property, the court is to consider whether either party has dissipated any of the marital assets. Tenn. Code Ann. § 36-4-121(c)(5)(A). Dissipation of assets requires a showing of intentional, purposeful, and wasteful conduct. Altman v. Altman, 181 S.W.3d 676, 682 (Tenn. Ct. App. 2005).

The factors that courts most frequently consider when determining whether a particular expenditure or transaction amounts to dissipation include:

(1)  whether the expenditure benefitted the marriage or was made for a purpose entirely unrelated to the marriage;

(2)  whether the expenditure or transaction occurred when the parties were experiencing marital difficulties or *were contemplating divorce*;

(3)  whether the expenditure was excessive or de minimis; and

(4)  whether the dissipating party intended to hide, deplete, or divert a marital asset.

See Halkiades v. Halkiades, No. W2004-00226-COA-R3-CV, 2004 WL 3021092, at *4 (Tenn. Ct.App. Dec.29, 2004).

The statutory definition for dissipation of marital property is prescribed at Tenn. Code Ann. § 36-4-121(c)(5)(B) which states: For purposes of this subdivision (c)(5), dissipation of assets means wasteful expenditures which reduce the marital property available for equitable distributions and which are made for a purpose contrary to the marriage either before or after a complaint for divorce or legal separation has been filed.

Well, that was pretty cut and dry.

They had all aided him in breaking Tennessee law code, including the two judges, who hadn't batted an eyelash when Les had admitted in court that he'd concealed marital property out of state.

Again, what could be more proof that Les had knowingly and willfully concealed marital property from me than he transferred over half a million dollars of my sons' money into an out of state bank account in his name only? Transferred another hundred-and-fifty thousand dollars into his own account in another bank that I didn't know about? Sold off my koi fish. Stole our gold and took my store cash, then I find out that he'd wired money to the father he once took a shit on the desk of because the bastard was a pedophile.

Seriously?

In what alternate universe was this okay?

I prayed to God that only Williamson County, Tennessee could be this corrupt and fucked up. Because if this was normal and acceptable, God help us all.

**B**ECAUSE LESS WAS A SICK and twisted fuck, this was my son's birthday and of course, being a special day, he had to make sure I was hauled into court for the third year in a row. Since the bankruptcy was over, it was now time to play "Let's Haul Terri Into Court Every One To Two Weeks" again.

Not an exaggeration, before this court session ended, they made sure to put the next court date for me on the books and it really was in two fucking weeks.

Because, as Skeletor said, "Lawyers gotta get paid." Especially the smirking, sick bastards who were his former business partners. He had to make sure they took as much of my money as was possible before it was all gone.

And even though it was a video phone conference because of COVID-19, Skeletor had to show up dressed in his black bathrobe to remind us all that he was a shit stain on the American justice system. Not that there was any doubt, as he removed any we might have had the moment he began to speak.

Oh, and what was one of his first stimulating comments?

"Uh, I see there's a Terri here. Who's that?"

Wow. Just wow. Einstein didn't even know the name of the party he was presiding over for the last two years. Guess he had the same level of brain damage as Cockburn.

*I won't bore you with the whole detail, but the highlights?* The shit stain enslaved me.

No, really.

And threw my son and I out onto the street.

He actually did.

As promised, he put another receiver over me at $400 dollars an hour, which was more expensive than either Newhouse or Oldham and this bastard was out of state who would take my money and dole it out to me if I behaved.

I was to be given whatever amount old Shit Stain determined I was worth.

Wish I were making that up, but no, that was what he said because, "I don't think she's changed her habits or ways." Yeah, you read that correctly. My behavior was being questioned and I was being lectured to by the judge who had been arrested for buying and selling women for his sick pleasure.

I shuddered as I typed this word in application to him, *man* (sorry, I just threw up a little in my mouth) who had a daughter and a wife and thought so little of them that he went out cruising someone else's daughter to buy her because he's all about how much power he could wield over a woman's life.

This sick and twisted fuck should never have been given a bar license, never mind free reign in an American court system. He was so bad a judge that his decisions were constantly being overturned.

Just not the ones he made to ruin my life because my attorney was too afraid of him to fight.

No, really, she said that.

Repeatedly and in front of witnesses.

I was told that we couldn't even appeal this one because guess who got to hear the appeal on how wrong his decision was?

Skeletor.

How was that for American Justice? In Tennessee, you appealed a bad decision to the same shit stain who'd made it.

Oh, okay. That made all the sense in the world said no one with a functioning brain.

Welcome to Williamson County and I prayed to God that it wasn't like that everywhere. Because if it was, then this shit needed to be changed.

This wasn't justice. It was sick and twisted torture.

For some other screwed up reason, Les's bankruptcy attorney, also an asshole buddy of the Shit Stain, was there and Skeletor made sure everyone knew what good friends they were. "Your honor, she set up shell companies and transferred hundreds of thousands of dollars to her sons."

*No, fuck, I hadn't. And of course, he had no evidence as such to Cockburn's and Alaimo's claims that I had done this as I'd never done it.*

Besides, had I "transferred hundreds of thousands of dollars" to my sons, Newhouse would have had me put under the jail.

But in Williamson County, Tennessee, hearsay was par for the course. Anyone who was a friend of the judge could say anything they wanted to, evidence be damned, and it would be held as truth because if the judge kissed your ass, it was all he needed.

Truth be damned.

*I* had never set up a shell company, but I did have proof that Les had. Just as I had proof he'd sent money to his pedophile father.

Money I had earned.

But for that, Skeletor decided to rob me of my non marital property.

Illegally as he had absolutely no authority over it. And as you'd seen from the previous law code, he wasn't supposed to be interrupting or interfering with my business, either.

The sick and demented bankruptcy attorney, Dreg Roberts, (who had no business in that room as his services should have ended with the bankruptcy) knew nothing about the subjects he was speaking on (and his Code of Ethics was supposed to prevent him from giving testimony in court). Yet Dumbass Roberts gave testimony as if he were a Baptist preacher on Sunday talking to his congregation about how Jesus had moved him in the supermarket to pick out pears over strawberries.

And for the record, Skeletor had no jurisdiction over my family property that I'd inherited or that Dipshit didn't give me—that is Tennessee law. He had no right to deprive me of it without a hearing. He didn't know what property he was depriving me of, such as my high school and college class rings that were engraved with my maiden name. Clearly not marital property.

Dinky was that sick and fucked in the head to "punish me" because I was the one thing he hated. A successful woman with a brain who looked at him like the absolute disgusting piece of shit he was.

The county commissioner was also there, telling more lies. "Your honor, she's opened another account." He made it sound like I'd done something wrong instead of the truth.

Newhouse had told me to set up a brand-new account so that we wouldn't have a joint one anymore.

It was the fucking law.

For the record, here was how much money I had in it:

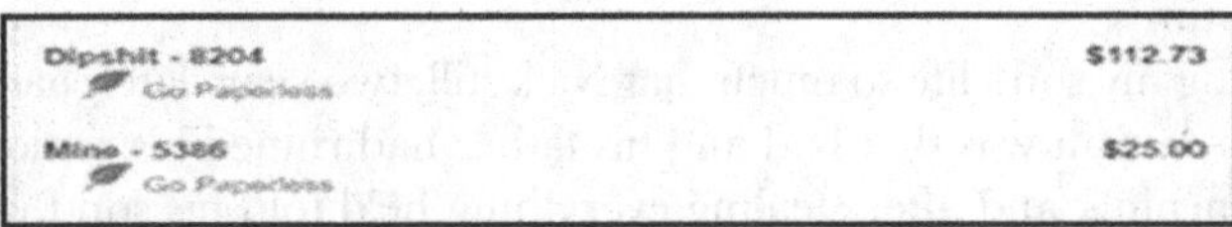


The Dipshit account was the one I shared with Newhouse.

As you could plainly see, Newhouse hadn't closed the other and that was all the fucking money they'd left me with for an entire month.

Because they had taken my money, I'd been off my blood pressure medicine for a dangerous amount of time.

They were all trying to kill me. There was your proof. Newhouse knew that cost of my BP medicine was two-hundred dollars. More than I had in my account for the month.

Newhouse had promised to leave me with no food, gas or medication and as you can see, he did just that.

And now the judge was depriving me of that little bit of money that had been made by them selling off my personal items, not Les's. That was all that was left of what I had earned and worked my entire life for, to upkeep a lawyer who refused to work.

The same lawyer who had written this:

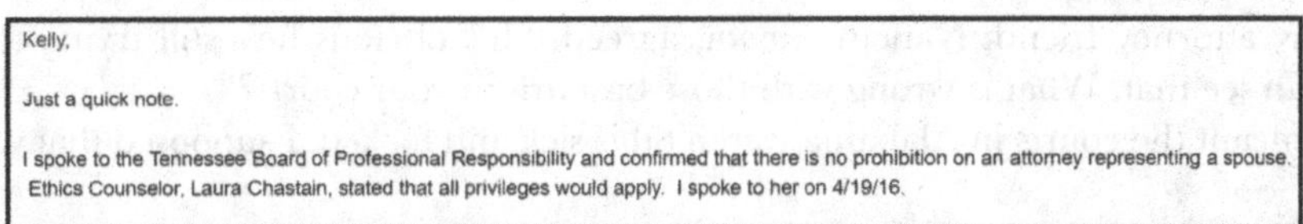


Which meant that Les had been working as my attorney on the Dumas suit as of April 26, 2016 and had committed perjury under oath and in front of Skeletor. That little old Cockburn had been lying for over two years by claiming that Les couldn't work as he had no job skills.

Really? He'd been an IP attorney on the case that had netted the largest payout in trademark history.

And he had no skills?

More than that, it also meant that Les had violated the Tennessee Board of Professional Responsibilities code of ethics when he breached:

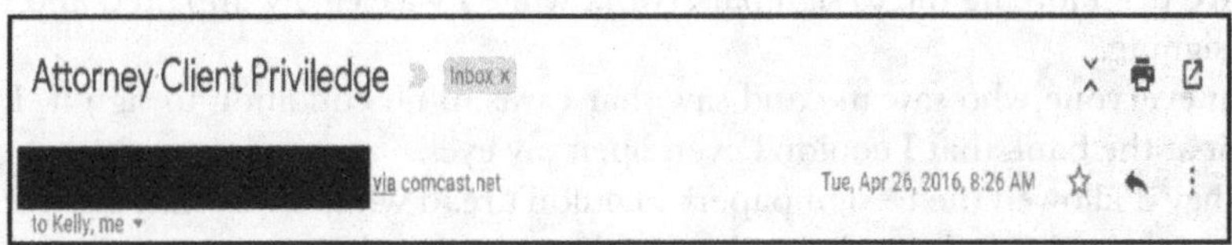


That was the heading for the email he'd sent. Attorney-Client Privilege. Misspelled because he was that stupid, but nonetheless, he'd put in there that he was my attorney. Just as in a separate email he'd told my attorney that he would abide by the NDA he'd forced everyone to sign.

That email ranked with up with this email he'd sent:

> Thank you. This is a tremendous help. Can you generate an invoice to Terri Manly and then identify it as performed at the direction of Les Manly, Attorney at Law?

Yet he claimed that he hadn't worked as an attorney since my youngest was in diapers. Meanwhile those had been sent months before he walked out the door with every dime I'd put aside for my children's futures.

And after wrecking my son's life so much that Nick still, two years later, hadn't graduated high school. Because his Autism was that bad and his father had ruined his senior year when he left without word or warning, and after stealing everything he'd told his son that he could depend on for his future.

That was how twisted Les was. The mind games he played with everyone, even those on his team.

Those he claimed were his "favorite."

This was what Skeletor was backing against an honest, hard-working mother who was trying to protect her children from the pedophile family that had murdered other family members. Caused a cousin to walk herself out into interstate traffic to escape the nightmare of this family and their sick head games. And remember that his own grandmother had also driven herself into traffic in an attempt to kill herself to escape the horror of the Manly family.

Instead, she'd killed her pedophile husband in that wreck.

They had driven the only sister-in-law I loved and who wasn't part of their sickness all the way to Hawaii to escape their twisted hands.

Because, like me, she wanted nothing to do with them.

But at least she got away.

He refused to let us go.

Even my attorney friend, Nanette Savior, agreed, "It's obvious he's still trying to kill you. Anyone can see that. What is wrong with those bastards in your courts?"

Which meant the courts in Alabama weren't this sick and fucked. I supposed that was a good thing?

Except I wasn't in Alabama.

And how demented was Les? Here was another email he'd sent to a realtor days before he'd run out in the middle of night on his family:

> I've shared this information with my wife. Can you act as a buyer's agent to help us find other homes she might like? We want to be walking distance to CW. We are downsizing as our youngest starts college next year, but we still want 4 bedrooms or 3 and an office. A garage is preferred. We like the look and feel of the historic cottages rather than contemporary.

He'd been leading me on that we were moving to Virginia and that everything was normal. So that he could bash me in the head and rob me and our sons blind. At the same time he'd sent that, he'd been forcing me to sign paperwork while I was legally impaired and had no idea what I was signing.

Shame on everyone who saw me and saw that I was in no condition to sign it. I was so sick and out of it at the bank that I couldn't even open my eyes.

And yet they'd allowed me to sign papers I couldn't read while I was slurring words and was obviously incapacitated. Because I was there with my husband.

Yeah...

It was a fucked up place where I lived.

I had witnesses aplenty to show he'd robbed us, but the judicial system was too busy helping the robbers escape and to victimize my sons and I than it was in helping us get justice.

Or even what was fair.

Because my Autistic son and I were being thrown out onto the street so that Les could pay his lawyer while he lived in my cabin that had been my office and refused to work. While he sat in front of Skeletor and committed perjury I could prove.

But Skeletor refused to hear it because he didn't want to "ruin a good attorney's reputation." And the Judiciary Board refused to discipline him because "a judge can do whatever he wants. It sounds to us like you didn't like his opinion."

Failure to do your job wasn't an opinion.

It was fact.

*Welcome to my nightmare.*

I was being forced to sell my home even after my attorney told them that I had no credit or money to buy another. During one of the worst weeks of COVID-19.

"Well, I'm sure she knew she'd have to move and has been making plans for it."

"Your honor, she wasn't allowed to pull her credit scores or make any plans." (Newhouse had forbidden it).

"Well, the house has been up for sale for a while… "

Uh, no, Skeletor it hadn't. And how would you know unless you were talking to the other side off record? No evidence had ever been presented to you about the house going up for sale. None.

It wasn't like Skeletor didn't have a history of speaking to his former business partners off record and those complaints hadn't been brought against him by others.

He was that fucked.

Had Skeletor bothered to get information instead of listening to the voices in his head (the same ones that told him he was good-looking and not a creepy old fuck that gave normal people the heebie-jeebies), he would have known that my house went on the market one week before we'd been ordered to quarantine. Which was one month from when we were holding court this day.

Now, I realized that he lived in a special place of stupidity, but surely even in his exceptionally challenging realm, the judge had to know that meant that I had had no chance at all to look for any place to live.

Nor had I been able to prepare anything.

I had no money to move (as you saw from my stellar bank account), and thanks to all of them, my credit score was 502.

It'd been 820 when this nightmare began. That was what they'd done to me.

Melissa tried. "Your Honor, her creditors will be wanting payment. She needs her money."

"The receiver can give it out. I don't think it makes sense for her to have it."

Oh, okay. It made no sense for the person earning the money to have access to the money. The person Les had been lauding just weeks before he left for her business acumen.

But by all means let us pay some other asshole like the judge and his cronies four hundred dollars an hour to dole out my money like we weren't in the middle of a fucking crisis.

After all, it wasn't like the entire state of New York where my money was earned had been shut down or anything.

Like millions upon millions of people weren't out of work.

Or that my income had been sliced to one-tenth of what it'd been the year before.

One-tenth.

No lie. No exaggeration. It was the same income I had earned at the turn of the century.

Twenty years ago. And I still had bills to pay. Newhouse had only paid lawyers.

Not a single creditor.

I was in debt because of Les.

And I had dozens of emails to prove the debt was all his.

Skeletor wouldn't listen to that either.

It was about punishing the woman. He even said that. "Have you learned your lesson yet? I don't think you have."

What fucking lesson?

That they were corrupt?

That they were liars and thieves? In collusion with each other?

Oh, I knew that all too well.

I'd sat through enough of his court sessions to know that I wasn't the only one he did this to. He was an embarrassment to the entire judicial state.

Or if he wasn't, then God help us. And maybe he was normal. That would explain why they kept protecting him. Why no one would remove him.

If this was how it worked, well...

I was terrified for every man, woman and child living in their realm of fantasy that we had any form of justice in this country.

We had nothing. And we were one heartbeat from losing everything because of unethical vultures who had no pity or regard for humanity or the laws of our country.

I was so sick when it was over that I called Melissa. "Get me out of this shit!" I caved and offered Les what he'd been asking for. More money than I made off my books.

That my agent made who worked for a living.

Les didn't take it.

He refused the very offer he'd made to me already.

This wasn't about money. This was about him trying to kill me, and by refusing the very terms he'd wanted, he proved it.

Only problem was no one was listening.

The court was too busy assisting him in my torture.

I had no way out and no hope.

Even my insurance company was assisting him. Three times during the week I'd been contacted with them wanting me to give them information about my "missing" jewelry. To swear under penalty of perjury as to what was "missing."

I told them repeatedly that nothing was missing. Les had stolen part of it when he'd left and took it to Georgia. He'd testified to that under oath, twice. The rest had been illegally confiscated from my home and was being held by a judge who had no legal jurisdiction over it.

If anything was missing, they needed to arrest either Les, Bill Oldham, or Judge Dinky. Because guess what else had come out during that hearing?

Old Bill had put my jewelry in a suitcase and had bought a ticket to New York, planning to sell it.

Funny how no one on my side knew that, but Les's attorneys did.

That wasn't suspicious at all. Bill had knowingly violated the terms of my insurance policy and no further inventory had been given to me. Les was trying to milk my policy for money.

Who had stolen my jewelry?

No one would give me an updated inventory. I had no idea what was still there.

If anything.

This was state and federal sanctioned theft.

But no one would help me. Instead, the FBI was too busy harassing innocent citizens for prank phone calls from Les and his team of bullies that they refused to investigate serious judicial corruption that victimized us all.

And I had no way out.

Les was calling the shots and they were all laughing at me. I had it on video how they were here for no other purpose than to punish me for being a woman.

My attorney had been right. "This is Williamson County and you're a woman. Don't expect justice here."

And my favorite part about all of this? When Melissa called up to tell me that Cockburn had "receipts for all the jewelry purchases to show that they were made during your marriage."

First, another lie. I could guarantee that my 1984 class ring was not purchased during my marriage, especially since it was two years before I met the sick asshole.

Same for my University of Georgia class ring that had been purchased before I married that sonofabitch.

Secondly...

"Good. I want a copy of every single receipt. That will prove that Les committed Friendly Fraud and used my credit card that he was not an authorized user on, and that he did so without my knowledge. More than that, it will prove that Cockburn, again, got in front of the fucking judge and lied, which was what had gotten my jewelry confiscated. The whore claimed that I'd charged tens of thousands of dollars on my card. I hadn't. Les did it when he bought that jewelry, and they are holding the evidence I need to prove that I was railroaded."

They were also holding the evidence that I had been dragged into court, repeatedly, and chastised by the judge and punished for contempt over not handing them the receipts this bitch just admitted she had in her custody all along.

*Are you fucking kidding me?*

This was the game they were playing. The lies Cockburn kept telling that the judge refused to sanction her over.

What was more, I had witnesses willing to testify that Les had purchased the jewelry illegally and that it was gifts not from him, but from my sons.

And not just my sons. The store manager who had hand- delivered it to my house. The jewelry reps who'd heard Les mock me behind my back. "She's not worthy of this."

Oh, okay. I wasn't worthy of the jewelry he was buying me with the money I earned while he sat drunk on my couch, abusing my children.

I supposed I deserved this for not kicking him out, but I'd been trapped like Cloris Leachman in the *Twilight Episode, It's a Good life.* The poor, bedraggled housewife trying to placate Bill Mumy and keep him calm so that he wouldn't plant me out in a cornfield.

Just like he'd always promised me he would.

"You can't leave. I'm going to be buried on top of you." How sick and twisted was that threat that he'd made to me so many times?

Now he was proving it with everything he said and did. Just what a demented bastard I had been forced to endure for thirty years.

Just what a fucked up judicial system we had in place in this country that allowed this to happen to decent people.

As my agent said, "If you had a normal judge."

But I disagreed. The problem wasn't the corrupt judge. It was also that slag, Cockburn, with no soul or conscience. God have mercy on the brood of children she'd spawned.

They weren't learning any form of decency or compassion from the Whore of Babylon who needed to be disbarred and cast out to scrape up roadkill from the street like the vulture she was.

And of course, the brain damaged Les who thought this was funny and who had nothing better to do with his useless life than torture his wife and children. While the state looked on and laughed about it.

Worse, the state participated in it.

Even the realtor.

I had emailed him twice to let him know that things had broken in my house and that I needed to update my disclosure items for the listing.

Apparently, like everyone else in this fucked up town, he didn't mind being dishonest, either. He refused to allow me to disclose that I'd discovered black mold. That my pool had stopped working.

That there was rot in the bathroom that we'd found while packing up.

Buyer beware, indeed. But then Cockburn was a realtor. Now we know why she was a failed realtor who had to go to law school. How many times had she failed to disclose something she knew was wrong?

The scariest part? This bitch was going to be a builder here in town. God have mercy on whomever bought a house from her because you'd be stuck with it and if you tried to sue her for whatever piece of shit she dumped on you, you would be FUBAR (fucked up beyond all recognition).

Yeah, this wasn't Mayberry paradise. Franklin, Tennessee was hell on earth and the devil looked like Skeletor.

*Want to see the biggest joke of all?*

This was written in Les's own handwriting and done days before he robbed his children and left me. These were notes he'd made while talking to Peggy about taking over the Dumas case:

> 4. Protect business interest & reputation.
>
> #5. Not go broke.

Guess the joke was on me that he'd wanted to protect my business interest and reputation.

Then why had he fired off that angry bullshit and lies just a matter of days later, accusing me of witchcraft and other stuff so laughable that I cannot imagine any lawyer other than Cockburn being dumb enough to put it on paper.

Not to mention the fact that he'd violated attorney-client privilege.

But the best part?

*Not go broke* and yet he was the one who'd single-handedly driven me into bankruptcy. And Newhouse had testified to that in court that it wasn't anything I did or my business acumen.

"Your Honor, it's all the legal fees. The estate simply cannot absorb all the extensive legal bills that keep coming in."

That was why none of my creditors had been paid off.

And so, what had Skeletor done? Saddled me with an entire office down in Georgia to support, in addition to Les's team of attorneys.

So much for thinning the herd.

My attorney was using five more attorneys to come after me.

Skeletor was okay with that.

Yeah, I was watching everything I had earned and worked for in my life be set on fire.

And there was nowhere to turn and no one willing to help.

My dad had been right. "You come into this world alone, and get spanked on your ass, and the world keeps kicking it until you draw your last breath."

There was no end to my boot party.

What sickened me even more was my attorney sending me an article about how "artists" divided their estates.

But I had a serious problem with the stupidity of the article. Songwriters and artists create something that can be sold independent of them. Anyone can record the song. Anyone can sell the painting.

Fiction books aren't the same.

No one else can slap their name on our book and sell it. That book was an extension of us. Everyone knew this.

If the author failed to support the book by hand-promoting it, then the book had no value of its own.

People read books based solely on the reputation of the author.

That wasn't property. That was an extension of a human life. What she was proposing and what the law did was circumvent the constitution to enslave authors.

After all, the average author only made five thousand a year or less. Barely enough to support themselves. Our jobs required us to plunge a significant portion of our income back into our careers.

Yet we were now to go out and give away a portion of our souls? A life form that was wholly dependent on our support of it to have any value at all?

That wasn't right.

"Well, it's the law."

Yes, and it used to be the law that women couldn't vote. Just because something was the law it didn't make it right.

Bad laws had been around for a long time.

This one needed to be changed. It was time someone stood up and said, "Bullshit!"

It violated our constitutional rights.

If what they said about my books was true, then I had as much right to his law degree, more so since I was the one who'd written his papers for him, as he had to any of my writing. More so since he could have never gone to law school or finished it without me.

He had contributed nothing to my writing career.

He'd been too lazy to even order pizzas.

And now all I could do was vomit. There was nothing left.

Especially not any hope.

EVERYONE WHO KNEW me was aware that this was the day when my older brother was born. A sacred day that I have mourned every year since the day my brother was taken from me when I was only twenty-one. Hank wasn't just my brother; he was my best friend. My number one champion.

April 17th is also the day I was at a conference in Richmond, Virginia while we lived in Jackson, Mississippi. My father, right before he'd died, had been kind enough to pay for the plane ticket so that I could meet my new editor who'd purchased my first fiction novel. Another book that I'd written in college.

I was ecstatic. Except all weekend long, my editor, Diane Smalley, had been avoiding me.

I didn't know why.

Not until that Sunday, on my brother's birthday, when that bitch sat me down. I'd always promised everyone that I'd tell the whole story of what happened early in my career.

*Brace yourself.*

With her hair in a tight bun and looking much like Ball-Breaker in *Porkey's,* Diane sat there eyeballing me. "There's a problem with your book."

I had just turned twenty-four and had no idea what she was talking about. "Problem?"

When I'd received the contract from her, Les had immediately snatched it from my hands and started changing things. After all, he was in law school on my dime and thought he was some brilliant negotiator, even though he had no real-world experience and was the same age I was. "It's a contract. It's all negotiable."

"I don't think we should touch it. Just let me sign it." Especially given that the advance was only five hundred bucks. That alone told me what my publisher thought of me.

Expendable.

Last thing I wanted to do was piss off my first publisher for a trivial amount on a pulp fiction book.

Les refused to listen. He made changes to it anyway.

With no choice except to do what he said or suffer his wrath, I'd called my editor to tell her that we had changes to the contract.

"Just send it back!" I could tell by her tone that she was furious.

With a knot in my stomach, I returned it with all the changes Les had made, carefully highlighted and with a note that explained each and every one.

One section had said that they could withhold all my money if they were ever to receive any threat of a plagiarism. Not only for the book that they were currently buying, but for any and all fiction books I might publish with them in the future.

That wouldn't be so bad except that I had a friend back then who was currently suing this particular publisher because "someone" they had refused to name had placed a call on one of her books, accusing her of plagiarism and they were withholding her royalties for every book she'd ever written for them.

"Couldn't they have at least waited until someone actually filed a suit to tie up all my money?" She had a valid point as they had been withholding her money for years and no one had ever done anything more than supposedly make a phone call.

They wouldn't even tell her who had called. So, needless to say, there was a lot of doubt whether or not anyone had actually called.

I should never have told Les that story. But then, I'd had no idea at the time that I might be published with them in the near future.

The next clause Les changed allowed them to hold the rights on my book for twenty-one years after the book went out of print. Most publishers back then only wanted the rights until the book went out of print for a few months to a year. Then, the writer could ask for their rights back.

Twenty-one years when you were in your early twenties was a lifetime. I agreed with that change. It seemed excessive given what the normal amount of time was with other publishers.

The last clause Les changed said that they could take up to two years to render a decision on whether or not they wanted my option book. That was unheard of in the industry where they normally only allowed six weeks to a couple of months. Because what that would do was tie up your next book so that you couldn't send it out to another publisher.

Very carefully, I explained to my editor why those three things seemed excessive and sent the contract back in.

Months went by with no word from her.

Until April 17th.

"Mmmm. Seems that I got a call from someone who says you judged them in a contest, and they think you stole this book from them."

*What the ever-loving fuck?*

I had never in my life judged a contest.

For anything.

Because my book was in a genre that hadn't been created yet in the industry, there was no contest for me to enter my book into. And because I was unpublished in novels, no legitimate contest back then would have allowed me to judge it.

For that matter, the only people who'd even seen the contents of my novel were my childhood friends who'd read it when we were kids, and my critique group who helped me with grammar.

No one else.

Ever.

So how could anyone claim that I had taken their material when literally only eight people had ever read it?

And again, this was before any genre for the book had been created so there was nothing in it that had been around. This was that book back in 1986 that I had typed up on a borrowed typewriter from my brother.

The irony, right?

I had been writing this book since I was a kid.

Not to mention, my critique partner said, and I quote, "You plagiarize? That would mean you'd have to actually like a book and respect the author enough to want to take their stuff." Then she'd broken off into a cackle.

Sadly, she was right. In my early twenties, I was a harsh critic. Worse, I was a paid one.

Though to be fair, I did my best not to let my venom out in my reviews as I kept reminding myself that this was someone's baby and no author ever set out to write a shitty book. Like me, they put their hearts and souls into it. So, it wouldn't be right to tear them apart in public.

In private, however, I was rather fierce with my opinions. I was in my early twenties, after all.

Without a doubt, I knew Diane was lying her ass off. The only way that call could have been made was if one of my critique partners did it out of spite. They were the only ones who knew who to call about the book or who had read it.

While our sessions could get heated at times, I didn't think I'd ever inspired actual hatred from them. They always seemed sweet and pleasant when we met. So, I was rather certain she was lying.

Especially when she refused to name the person who'd called.

"I don't want to get into the middle of that. It doesn't matter."

Oh, but it did.

And when they agreed to publish the book provided, I fall in line, I knew for a fact that the bitch was lying. Back then, there was no way in hell any publisher or editor would have touched a novel they thought might be plagiarized. No legitimate publisher would run that risk.

Especially for one they'd paid so little for. One letter to a lawyer would have been more than their profits off a first, small run romance novel.

What a fucking bitch.

Why do that to me? I had no idea.

Other than Les had destroyed my early career because he wouldn't listen. Smalley spent years bad-mouthing me in the industry. I was destitute in Columbus, Mississippi when my new agent called.

"Do you know Diane Smalley?"

"Yeah. Why?"

"I just met her at a conference and pitched her your historical. She told me that she'd had a call on your first book about plagiarism?"

*Are you fucking kidding me?*

For a second, I wondered if she'd been telling the truth. Until I told my agent that she'd refused to name the author who had supposedly called her.

My agent had snorted. "She told me it was the agent who called her."

"She's lying." Liars were notorious for changing their stories. "I have people who read that book when we were twelve years old and who will verify it. I have notes in my old year books where my friends talked about that book. One of my friends even has a copy of it that is still sealed with the postage from where I mailed it to her in the mid 1980s. Not to mention, if it was the truth, then why did they release the book two years ago? And no one has come forward with a claim against it!"

That settled the matter and proved what a liar Smalley had been.

Yet it had been damning for me. Because of Les's stupidity, my career had been set back half a decade.

No one would touch me for five years.

Not until Diane was fired because I wasn't the only one she'd played sick head games with.

And it took a sick bitch to dump that on me on my brother's birthday after I'd spoken about it on a panel she'd attended. To tell me such of horrific thing, knowing that I had a four-and-a-half-hour plane ride to get home.

Alone.

Sadly, this world was filled with way too many twisted people who loved to see others suffer. I was never one of them. I couldn't stand to see someone in pain.

Ever.

Through a miracle and raw determination, I'd survived that nightmare to rebuild my career for Les to destroy it all again.

Enter my current nightmare.

On this day, after my rights had been stripped from me while I'd been banned from attending the court session...

*All true.*

Judge Dinky had intentionally blocked my email access to court so that I could neither hear nor see what they were doing with my life while they used lies told against me and, as usual, with no evidence being presented...

After my family's jewelry had been reseized by the divorce court that had absolutely no jurisdiction over it, at all, I was told that my Autistic sons and I were to be thrown out of our home.

In the middle of the COVID pandemic while the laws were requiring everyone to "shelter in place."

Yeah, you read that correctly, too. Because they'd refused to remove my home from the market after the bankruptcy as I requested, an offer came in for it.

Lowball.

My home had been appraised at more than twice what we paid for it. One million, four hundred and fifty thousand dollars. A lot of money, but we'd made substantial improvements to it over the years.

However, the buyers were only wanting to pay slightly more than we had paid when we'd purchased it almost a decade ago.

I'd rejected their offer immediately and asked for my home to be taken off the market.

The buyers had come back with a slightly higher offer. Before I could counter or say anything, Cockburn, a former realtor, insisted we take it. This after saying that the housing market hadn't cooled off and that we should take an offer that was a quarter and half million dollars less than the listing price.

With my personal items thrown in there.

*Are you fucking kidding me?*

"Your Honor, she agreed to the sale of her home."

No, bitch, I hadn't.

As Newhouse had loved to tell me and my sons so many times, "Your mother owns nothing and has no say in anything. We're going to do what we're going to do and there's nothing she can say or do about it."

That included listing my house for a *business* bankruptcy.

So again, they lied to Skeletor who lapped it up like a dog at his water bowl after a three-mile run.

Didn't matter to Skeletor that after we paid off the HELOC that the trustee, in a year, had failed to pay anything on and had refused to pay off with the money he'd illegally taken from my sons (it would have paid it in full) that I'd barely have enough money left to relocate.

"She can pay up to a full year's rent." That was Skeletor's response when my attorney reminded him that I was coming out of bankruptcy and had a 502 credit score.

In the middle of the COVID "shelter in place" order.

How cavalier he was with my money. Well, a year's worth of a lease was a significant chunk of the money my house would net. Then came the cost of relocating, another twenty to thirty grand as I had a lot of books and a pool table, which I knew from previous moves was extremely expensive to relocate. My last move a decade ago had been twenty-five thousand dollars and we'd only moved ten miles away.

For that matter, Les had moved two hundred boxes from my office to my home and they'd charged me two thousand dollars to move that tiny bit three miles. It cost six hundred dollars for less than two hours, to move a few boxes from one storage unit to the next after Newhouse had ordered me to condense them (a fee I should add that would have kept my storage unit for four months, which was longer than that bankruptcy had lasted after he gave his stupid, time-consuming command).

No shit.

I had an eight thousand square foot home with its furniture, inside and out, and my store inventory Les had dumped on me from the cabin. There was no way I'd find another eight thousand square foot home to rent on what they were allowing me. In fact, I'd barely have enough for a twelve hundred square foot apartment.

Which meant I'd have to rent storage units to hold the property I was under a court order not to sell, hide, giveaway, etc.

Rent plus storage, alone, would be more than my HELOC payments if I'd just stayed in my home. Never mind the cost of moving.

And I had specific requirements. Remember that I ran a business out of my home and according to the laws of my county, I had to have a minimum of two acres for my company. On any given day, we shipped out two hundred packages, or more.

Most neighborhoods and all apartments would have a little bit of a problem with all the mail that came and went from my address. It used to make Les insane to the point he'd throw giant tantrums over it.

I have a nice long gash in the foyer of my home where he'd had one of his more stellar hissy fits.

And since New York was closed for business due to COVID, my store was the only income I had at present.

Not to mention, a large dog that every rental I knew about forbade a tenant to have.

In spite of all logic, common sense and intelligence, Idiot Skeletor refused to allow me to move back into my office that Les wasn't actually living in because he was spending most of his time in Georgia. And was forcing me to spend more money to relocate.

Out of spite and retaliation.

Just like when the trustees had ordered all of my coats sold in the dead of winter that then caused me to have to spend more than one of the coats sold for to get a new one I could wear.

Weren't these awesome business advisors? No wonder Skeletor's dad had gone bankrupt.

I had been forced into my bankruptcy by a bunch of sick lawyers who wouldn't stop over-charging me and their twisted judge-buddy who gave them free rein with my pocketbook.

Just as he was doing now.

And there was nothing I could do. My attorney flat-out refused to file an appeal (as she had every time before). I had less than four weeks to find a home with no one allowing me to see properties. The country was in quarantine, and I had less than $150 in the bank.

Yeah. How was I supposed to even apply for a rental contract as all of them requested a submission fee?

This was my nightmare and there was no letup in sight. Les had turned down every offer of settlement. Even when I'd agreed to give him everything I earned in royalties just to make him go away.

He refused.

If that didn't convince the judge and everyone else that he was insane and bent on my death, what would? No normal person would do this to their children.

To a wife who'd done nothing to him other than to lavish him in gifts while he wallowed drunk on my couch and insulted me and my children. While he beat my sons who were too afraid of him to tell me the truth until he was gone from our lives.

He and his lawyers were going to strip me of every single dollar I had, and no one would stop them.

I was alone. The sole protector of my sons and I didn't know what to tell them. My faith in everything, even God, was shattered.

Holding on by a hair, I had nowhere to turn. The only member of my family I had was my little brother who was having financial troubles because of COVID, and an elderly aunt.

Where was my champion?

*Anyone who would help me?*

Oh, I forgot. They only lived in my books. This was real life, and it took pity on no one.

*God will repay each person according to what they have done.*
*Romans 2:6*

*Beware of the teachers of the law. They like to walk around in flowing robes and love to be greeted with respect in the marketplaces and have the most important seats in the synagogues and the places of honor at banquets. They devour widows' houses and for a show make lengthy prayers. These men will be punished most severely.*
*Luke 20:46-47*

Where was this vengeful God that my grandfather had assured me would come to smite the wicked? My brother kept telling me it was the devil, but I still said that the devil wouldn't do anything unless God stood out of the way to let it happen.

I clung to my faith but had no idea why. How could I believe in a just God who took no mercy on me. I was so tired of this world and all I'd been put through.

For no reason.

But at least I had one thing. My precious Boo said, "I'd rather live with you in a cardboard box on the street than in a mansion with that thing that donated his sperm to me."

For them, I had to hang on. While my sons were great and wonderful men, they weren't strong enough to fight the sickness of their father and his unfounded malice. I'd heard him threaten them both.

"I'm coming after you! There will be consequences!"

Having dealt with unstable minds my entire life, I'd done my best to shield them from it. I was all they had.

And I wouldn't fail them.

So bring it, you fucked up unconscionable monsters. And I will meet you at that battle. Like David before Goliath.

One finger. One fist. I'd come into this world on my own two feet, fighting against it and covered in someone else's blood.

That appeared to be my destiny.

So be it.

*Buckle up, bitches. It was about to be one hell of a fight.*

# T

**T**HE HITS JUST KEPT ON COMING. Why not? The vultures had a body to pick clean and they were salivating at the prospect of it. My attorney, Melissa, was being overrun with their dirty tactics, and they were determined to aid my ex in killing me.

A little dramatic?

No.

Truth.

As old Newhouse had promised, I was now over a month without the medication that my life depended on, and they knew it. While they could go in front of the judge in less than twenty-four hours to steal my house out from under me and threaten me, they couldn't do it to get the money I needed for my blood pressure medicine.

So, this was the email that I sent to my doctor first thing this Monday morning:

> I just wanted a note made of this that for the last four weeks Les's attorneys have left me without the money to buy my BP medicine and I've been without any. This is what my blood pressure has been running.
>
> 163/111
> 167/123
> 174/120
> 167/93
> 134/92
> 167/120
> 164/100
>
> Thanks!

This was the email I sent my attorney:

> I have notified my doctor and my brother, along with my sons that my blood pressure has been running:
>
> 163/111

167/123
174/120
167/93
134/92
167/120
164/100

I need my blood pressure medicine. ASAP. They better release my money to me by noon or they are liable for this. I have a BAD family history of stroke at my age. Heart attack is what killed my niece at 24. My father had two of them before he was my age and my uncle died of one two years younger than I am. I also have a heart condition that has three times now required me to wear a heart monitor. I need $800 to pick up the meds that my life depends on and that have been waiting at Publix since Newhouse decided to get cute and wrongfully withhold my money from me after making threats, in writing, to leave me penniless.

I don't care that the judge said I couldn't sue him. If I die, my kids and brother have a lawsuit against them all for wrongful death. This is their warning. They are tampering with my life and putting it at risk. This not a joke.

Their response?

Melissa,

I will let David know and see if this needs to come as an AO from the bankruptcy court or if we are getting the check cut from Chancery Court if the funds have been transferred.

David, what is the status on the funds being held by trustee? We need to get a check cut to Mrs. Manly.

As you can clearly see, they were in no hurry to get my money to me to save my life. They were dicking around while every minute, my life was at risk.

So, this was what I sent my attorney:

When I have a stroke, my brother and sons are going to sue them blind. They better hope I die because Cockburn set my net worth at 15 million dollars, and they are ALL liable for it. Whether I'm left dead or alive, they will have a hefty amount to pay if I have a stroke.

After all, those sorry bastards knew that sick and demented example every instructor used in law school with future lawyers: *If you come across someone in an elevator shaft and they're hanging onto the edge by their fingertips, then you'd better step on their fingers and make sure they die. Because a dead body is worth a lot less in a lawsuit than a living paraplegic.*

That was how fucked in the head lawyers were.

It was a real example. Google it. They trained those bastards to think that way.

As I've said, we need to go back to the melee. It was a far better system of justice than the joke America uses today.

But at least if I did die or was left like my uncle and in a state where for the last forty years of my life I wouldn't be able to speak and would need a caretaker, I had it notated and these bastards would have to pay for it.

Because it wasn't enough that they knew this, they kept adding more and more stress to me.

How that wasn't considered attempted murder, I had no idea. Because these were my blood pressure readings for this day:

168/107

158/107
163/111
167/104

What a beautiful site, right? And for those who were unaware of what a normal blood pressure reading is, 120/80.

At 140, you were at risk for a stroke. Something that goes up if you had kidney disease, which thanks to Les, I had.

High blood pressure could also give you:

Stroke
Loss of consciousness
Memory loss
Heart attack
Damage to the eyes and kidneys
Loss of kidney function
Aortic dissection
Angina (unstable chest pain)
Pulmonary edema (fluid backup in the lungs)
Eclampsia
Severe Headache
Shortness of Breath
Nosebleed
Severe Anxiety

So, every day that they left me with this, they were running the risk of doing more damage to my kidneys.

Or heart.

They were playing Russian Roulette with my life, and everyone seemed good with that.

Including Judge Dinky.

Oh, and Hypertensive "crisis" was 180/120 and as you could see, they'd pushed me into that on a number of occasions. That was whenever either number hit that high, and they were setting my blood pressure off to where both were riding dangerously close to that critical level.

On purpose. They couldn't plead ignorance. They weren't *that* stupid.

Because these were some of my other emails that I received that day.

I was told that I had to get out of my house for the inspection.

For hours.

Now remember that this was in the height of "shelter in place" where nothing was open. No restaurants. No malls. No parks.

No theaters.

Yet I was sent this email from the effing realtor:

Hi Melissa,

The inspector's policy is that no one is to attend the inspection except the inspectors due to COVID-19 compliance.

If she is not able to do this, please advise the other attorney immediately and we can call the inspection off.

Now remember that I was under a court order by Psycho Bitch that if I interfered in any way or delayed the closing in any way that she could call out Judge Skeletor on me and have me thrown in jail again for contempt. And given that I had a taped recording of Skeletor screaming at me for two hours telling me that he was "dying to put me in jail. Just give me a reason," I knew these morons would do it.

But where the fuck could I go as there was no place for me to go? Not to mention, having these assholes traipsing through my home was exposing me and my family to germs.

*Thank you for putting me and my sons at risk.*

Want to tell me again that the Williamson County court system wasn't trying to kill us?

Here was what my attorney sent back:

> She is not sick and from their own email, it sounds like it's not a problem for her to be there. Since everything is closed, she literally has no other place to go.

His response:

> Hi Melissa,
>
> When we spoke with the judge on the zoom hearing, I thought his instructions were for her not to be there.
>
> Please advise if we need to cancel the appointment.

And her last word:

> No. The Order says she won't interfere. And she won't.

Not to be outdone, Thundercunt came back with this:

> Melissa, we need you to stress to Mrs. Manly and her family to please vacate the property during the inspection. Her interference will not be tolerated during this inspection or transaction.
>
> Any purposeful destruction to the property is only going to take money out of her pockets from the proceeds when the sellers have to make repairs.

Wow. Every time that bitch opened her mouth, she told on herself. What a petty fucking whore. Now we knew exactly what kind of person Cockburn was and the dirty tricks she traded in as that had never entered our minds. As my grandma used to say, "the guilty dog barks."

At least my attorney knew that:

> Considering the amount of work it took her to get the house in selling shape while Mr. Manly continues to live a life of leisure, I think she would find this extremely insulting.
>
> She wants to sell the house, she is just reasonably concerned about her ability to find somewhere else to live and the immediate costs of moving furniture and items from an 8000 sq. ft. house in such a short timeframe and during this epidemic.
>
> As usual, Mr. Manly has rushed to Court to assert his wishes without consideration of all of the costs and consequences.

Failure to think ahead. That had always been Les's number one problem in life. He'd lost many a job for that reason. He was an effing moron when it came to that. He rushed off, half-cocked and didn't think it through.

Besides, he was too giddy at watching me be beaten up by the bullies. And all these bastards, including the realtor who had breached his own ethics at this point wanted to put me in jail and were trying hard to do it.

After all, money was always more important than a human life.

That was the one thing I could honestly say, never once in my life had I ever put profit over someone else.

But here in Williamson County, there was no compassion. They were all bloodsucking savages.

I was so happy I had reported this bastard to the Tennessee Real Estate Commission for his part in getting a court order to ban me from filling out that disclosure. I only hoped that they did their part and yanked his license over it.

Because I had no intention of interfering, I pulled my lawn chair into my driveway and sat there, hour after hour, while they did whatever they did and infected my house with their germs against the rules of the governor and every health agency in the world.

And all because Cockburn thought she was smart.

What a fucking idiot. She'd just screwed her own client in so many ways and Les was the true moron who didn't comprehend that she was taking him to the cleaners.

He was losing half a million dollars out of the house because they were selling it below market value during a severe downturn and they had court ordered me not to negotiate for more money.

All so Cockburn could take the money we had in equity and line her pocketbook with it.

I knew he was stupid, but dayam!

Crown that man. King Idiot of All Time.

The only one who came close was old Leadwits who popped back up on this day.

Because God was apparently bored and as a result, I received his response to my complaint in the mail.

I won't bore you with all the details, but rather just simply post the letter I wrote to Ms. Dullard in response to it as it said it all:

> I have received Mr. Leadwit's response and it seems that there is a systemic and most disturbing trend among every Nashville lawyer I've had the misfortune of dealing with and that is that they all practice deception and half-truths even though that is clearly against your own rules. That they all misrepresent facts and withhold evidence, which is contradictory to RULE 3.3. The very email that Mr. Leadwits provided to you where I said, "You can share this one with Martha" only demonstrates that we had earlier conversations where I had told him explicitly "not" to share my material with Trustee Martha Seaver. I was so emphatic that he not share that on January 5, when he first asked and I said no, "I thought so," was his response.

> It was only after Mr. Leadwits kept on nagging me about sharing my diary with Ms. Seaver that I allowed him to do so because I trusted him and assumed that he had my best interest at heart. That he was abiding by Attorney-Client Privilege and that because I had asked for a meeting with her to report the bad acts of Mr. Tom Newhouse et al, that he wanted it to show her my evidence. I assumed that he would have forewarned me of any possible negative consequences that could come from her review of it given the nature of Attorney-Client Privilege and his due diligence. Instead, he knowingly led me into an ambush where Ms. Seaver, Mr. Newhouse and Mr. Oldham made no bones about the fact that they were retaliating and punishing me for trusting in my attorney. He allowed them to continue their abuse of me and their threats against me for months.

> Rather than try to mitigate the damage he had done, Mr. Leadwits only sought to serve himself, and to add more harm to my anguish. In fact, when Ms. Seaver said that she would be selling my family jewelry for "retaliation," he had the nerve to ask if he could bid on it.

After the meeting, when I asked him why he'd done such a thing, Mr. Leadwits said and I quote, "My loyalty is to the US Bankruptcy court and to Martha."

His actions have cost me over a million dollars in monetary losses, and immeasurable mental anguish. For me and my sons. What is worse, he admits to sharing my IP with those I gave him no permission to share it with, and that, too, is illegal.

Title 18, U.S. Code, Sections 2319, 2319A, and 2319B. The unauthorized reproduction or distribution of a copyrighted work is illegal. Criminal copyright infringement, including infringement without monetary gain, is investigated by the FBI and is punishable by up to five years in federal prison and a fine of $250,000.

There is no mistaking that law, and he has admitted to sharing it with people I did not authorize him to share it with.

I have been horribly abused by the court system of this state, and I implore you for your aid so that no one else has to be so abused by those who refuse to abide by the codes that were put in place to protect the public. No one should have to endure the legal travesty I have suffered.

Likewise, Mr. Leadwits is well aware that my diary was written on proprietary software that makes everything I write appear in a book form. He was told this repeatedly. That "ISBN" he references, is a dummy number much like the Latin texts that appear in any template software. I assure you that 123456789 is not a legal ISBN as all ISBNs are 10 or 13 number sequences and they appear like this inside a real book:

ISBN 978-1-250-04298-9 (hardcover)
ISBN 978-1-4668-4096-6 (e-book)

As for the copyright, "all" works are copyrighted the moment they are put on paper by law. It's why my software automatically affixes a (C) to them with the date. However, Mr. Leadwits again misled and misrepresented facts in that I never applied with the USPTO for a copyright from them as he asserted. That process takes months and cannot be completed until after something is "published" and made available to the public. Not to mention, it's costly and Mr. Newhouse would never have approved the funding of that process for me. A USPTO assigned copyright is not a completed process until the "final" version of a book, music, art, etc. is on file with their office. An attorney should know that. No application for a copyright or ISBN for my diary has been made to date.

As I said, he, like every lawyer I've dealt with in this town, specializes in presenting misrepresentations of facts, if not outright lies to the court or to others, and I am really, really tired of it. I pray that you will hold him accountable to the standard he is supposed to be held to.

Thank you for your time.

But I will give Donothing credit, he did throw his compatriots under the bus:

The first hiccup in the case that that the Trustee did not understand or want to follow the business model that Ms. Manly had laid out. A writer, in order to be as successful as Terri, has to network with her audience. There are many venues which required her personal appearances and contact, and the Trustee did not grasp the necessity of that.

The second hiccup was a hearing in the state divorce proceeding which resulted in order that all Les Manly's legal fees were in the nature of alimony, without any oversight. I could not believe that ruling and expressed my frustration, especially that it was never appealed by Ms. Manly's divorce counsel nor the Trustee. Alimony is a top tier creditor in the order of priority in a bankruptcy proceedings. Les Manly's attorneys were granted by that ruling a blank check to plunder the assets in the bankruptcy to the detriment of Ms. Manly's creditors. And Les Manly's attorneys were able to obtain for their services staggering legal fees. The bankruptcy estate was hemorrhaging its assets at an amazing pace. The Trustee was concerned that the bankruptcy estate was becoming administratively insolvent.

And my favorite part of his letter:

I, for one, do believe her story something was done by Les Manly to her personally.

There it was. Vindication. I was being unethically hammered by these bastards and no one would stand up to them.

Where was my hero?

But what really, truly broke my heart were the two letters that my sons wrote about their father and sent to me simply so they could get this turmoil off their shoulders.

The first one I received was from Maddox:

To whom it may concern,

The relationship between Karen Hogg and my father, Lester Manly, according to him was strictly professional of an employer and his employee.

But my own experiences will testify to the contrary. I don't remember everything that happened between the two, but fortunately I don't have to remember much to be able to testify to obvious signs of infidelity between the two. Just the few months before I left to go to Japan, and he initiated this divorce I remember the following:

- Him repeatedly caring about Hogg's employment status over the mental well-being of his own sons. Despite constant verbal abuse from Hogg at my brother and me, and our constant pleas to get her out of our house and out of our lives he instead invited her to stay with us and did nothing when she insulted us. She called me unimportant and worthless, while calling Nick lazy, stupid, a spoiled brat, and also worthless. Despite witnessing this himself he said we were thin-skinned and that we were bullying her by being so upset by these things. Even now, he will put Hogg, strictly his employee in his own words, above his own family at every opportunity.

- His hatred towards women and relationships. When I was worried that my girlfriend may be cheating on me, he told me "When the cats are away, the mice will play." Needless to say, those words didn't make me feel any better. I was bitter over the failure of my first relationship, and my father did me no favors by urging me down a hateful path by casting blame on women as a whole and how they couldn't be trusted on without a proper man guiding them. A sentiment I have outgrown, but I'm afraid he hasn't.

- Him attempting to sever the relationship between my mother and me. I loved my father, but I couldn't confide in him anymore because he would always side with Hogg over me. He gave bad advice and even worse comfort. Instead, I was forced to go to my mother for advice or even just basic support when I felt exhausted. At some point he thought I relied on my mother too much for support, especially once I started talking to her about how Hogg was treating all of us. He then started telling me that mom was too busy for me and that I shouldn't bother her anymore. He also added that I was simply not to talk to anyone about the way we were being treated. He told me that "shit rolls downhill, and if your mom gets mad at me, it'll get around to you."

- The two of them roleplaying together. My father decided it would be a great idea to invite Hogg to live with us during this time. He said it was for Nick's tutoring, but Hogg spent most of the time cooking, sleeping, and pretending to be our mother. When she moved in, she started making rules for how the house worked and tried to tell me, a grown man, my bedtime on my days off and how much sugar I was allowed to have in a day. She was comfortable she would roam through the house in her underwear while my mom wasn't home. She started talking to us about how our school days were, like our mom used to do when we were little and treating us like we were her kids. Our father kept telling us when we thought it was creepy that we would warm up to her in time like a teenager accepting his new stepmother. He told his kids our mom didn't love us anymore and may never return home. When we called her on the phone, she said a completely different truth. Our mother was on a business trip but I could understand why she might not want to rush back to a house that had another woman in it while her husband made zero effort to get someone who was making everyone, including himself, miserable.

- Him giving Hogg unprecedented control over our lives. At every opportunity our father would tell us to work with Hogg for school, advice, writing, relationships, and everything in-between. He constantly wanted us to interact with her for everything. My little brother had no choice, but once I made the mistake of accepting her offer. I wanted her to proofread an essay for me. It was for a history class I had. I couldn't think of a more Faustian deal. Before I knew it, her being able to proofread my paper, ended with her having access to all of my emails and passwords. She started sending emails on my behalf and speaking for me. The access my father gave her for a simple history paper lasted until I was looking for jobs overseas, and she even locked me out of my own emails bypass coding them that she sent between me and my possible future employer. While I struggled to retain access to my own passport and was refused to be given my social security by him he more than eagerly gave over to her. He gave Hogg, an employee, more control and access to my information than me. My little brother Nick can attest to the same experience. It wasn't an issue of trust, but an issue of control. He wanted Hogg to have more control over our lives than us with our own.

These are just some of the incidences I can remember personally. I know between my family and me the amount of indiscretions we can remember are countless. These are just some of the big ones I can remember after the two years he left the house. According to his own mouth, their relationship was a professional one, but these incidences show a wildly inappropriate affair. The rift he has created in this family for her sake will never be fixed and his willingness to destroy us for her is disgusting. Even now, by his own choice he has more of a relationship with her than his own children.

I attest, these are my words. I have spoken the truth and nothing but the truth, and with God as my witness I hope that justice is done. Maddox Manly.

That broke my heart. What they had done to my baby was criminal and I wanted them held accountable. But as chilling as that was, it was nothing compared to Nick's:

To whom it may concern,

The period of high school at Independence for me was by far the worst of my life so far, even surpassing my parents' divorce and the collapse of the once family, which by most logical accounts should've been worse. While I have tried to forget most of it really, the period of my life was so impactful it would be hard not to recall most of it, and at the heart of the headache was Karen Hogg, and the forcefulness my father, Les Manly, had with putting her on top of me.

I recall repeatedly hating my time with Hogg, and despite my constant protest with her, my father would always insist on keeping her. While I've had several tutors before Hogg, they were nothing like Hogg. I remember fighting with her nonstop on several occasions, and despite this, my father told me constantly that I would never be able to get A's without her. Considering he was my dad, I listened to him, but now that I have hindsight I know I would go on to make A's with the next tutor I had, Adam, and even on my own as I currently have been working on school by myself, proving this was not the case.

After constantly fighting with her, day after day, my energy began to quickly drop, and my anxiety began to skyrocket through the roof. Countlessly, they would gaslight me, call me dumb, and make me second guess myself. To prove that, I was once renowned for my mathematics in school, literally sleeping without a care and constantly scoring no grade less than a 97 and scoring in the top 1% of mathematics in the country. Having done this, I had developed a few odd or unusual methods in order to calculate, the most iconic being that instead of showing my work I would just dump random numbers on the page until I got the answer and circled it. Most teachers I had would eventually recognize this and not care, or the ones that did I would just go back and show my work after it. Same thing with my tutors. But with Hogg she would always say I just got lucky, and that I was doing it wrong. Or if I argued with her that it worked, she would call me a brat or tell me her way was better. And at the end she would win the argument by saying this is what the teacher wanted. I went from soaring in math to barely scraping by with an A in 9th grade. Even my 9th grade math teacher noticed this and commented later in the year about how I always did my work and now I never turned any of my work in, to which I had told her I was tired. Which was really true. And a side note, I remember always sleeping in school from boredom in years past, and yet 9th grade was the first time in school I would just collapse from pure exhaustion. I tried constantly to stay awake in my 9th grade teacher's class because I actually liked her a lot, both because she was the only real teacher who seemed to notice me struggling in that grade emotionally, and because she had a really good relationship with my older brother Caleb who she helped get through his math when he was struggling on top of being a really pleasant person. Where my other teachers just recommended me for honors or AP because of my grades, she actually recommended me for standard geometry because of how exhausted I was. And that was because as my grades started to dip and my energy faded, my dad's solution was to elongate the hours Hogg was at the house, so much that it was the USUAL for her to show up at 4 and stay until 11 o'clock at night or later, to where she would force me to go to bed after we were done, and called me lazy, and would yell at me from downstairs when I was playing the piano or anything to go to sleep, or would yell at other people to tell me to go to sleep. which is also weird because that meant she was staying even after I was supposed to be going to sleep. and when we were doing our tutoring sessions, if anyone else showed up she would always tell them they were a distraction and to go away. Everyone, except my dad of course, who she would suddenly swap personalities hard and suddenly act so friendly and jovial around me.

Something I told my dad about countlessly, but he ignored me. This meant my life became wake up at 6 am, scramble and get ready for school, collapse because I had 7 hours of sleep if not less, inch my way home arriving about 3, where I would just go to my bed and nap for the 1 hour I had before Hogg would come from 4 to 11 again, and again, and again, and again 5 days a week, every week, Sunday through Thursday, staying for 7 hours, just as long as school, with no interaction but the occasion my mother came up, my brother came down, cat dropped by, or my dad came. It was so awful to the point I would just stay upstairs for an extra hour or two, just because they liberation of an hour or two more of sleep, or just finally getting to play a game for a couple of minutes after getting home was worth getting yelled at. Before 9th grade I was able to do both art lessons, music lessons, hang out with friends, and do tutoring to get As, and was much happier for it and still had time do whatever else I wanted to like a normal schoolboy, but high school? No, that was now my life. sunrise, sunset. Hogg and school.

Eventually, I had a school assignment, I don't even recall what it was, but I wanted to write a paper about "gods are aliens," because I was watching a bunch of ancient aliens and thought it would be cool to talk about, but she set her foot down, and said he had to be "gods are real, and that they were aliens," because gods are not inherently considered fact. We fought so badly over this that my dad actually just paid her to do this for me, and I just threw my hands up because I was tired of fighting. I also remember around this time, Hogg staying all the time after my schoolwork to help my dad with the Dumas lawsuit, alone with my dad after I would finish, staying until 2 am or later some nights. my dad famously called her "1 more thing, Hogg." My dad saw us constantly fighting, and yet I remember one day he paid her to spend the whole day playing chess with me, which I don't really remember the details of besides a few off-handed comments she made while we were playing. Although when we did tutoring sessions, I usually would drink coke, but 1 she would tell me I've had too much caffeine for a day and would forbid me from having anymore. Given that she was my tutor and not my parent, and my parents were fine with it I would just get up and grab myself another coke in frustration, where she would do things like physically grab it or hide it from me. And when I would just go and get more when she did this, she would just call me a spoiled brat. I actually had forgotten about that until writing this just now, but I vaguely remember her constantly taking things from me and refusing to hand them to me. Actually like, all the time. I don't even remember what they were now it's been so long.

But I digress, eventually summer came, and it was nice, but when sophomore year hit, I pleaded with my dad to not bring Hogg back, to which he didn't.... for two weeks. but when I didn't kick off with an immediate bang after 8 months of hell and only a 2 month break, he came to me and said she gets me the As, even if I hate her, no one else does. I said sure as long as he doesn't become what it was last time, but well, hey we know how that ends.

By this point, I had gone a full year with almost no social interaction with anyone my own age. I never had friends over aside from a single hand's count for a year, and my social skills fell through the floor. I recall one day cracking after class and asking my teacher how I could drop out of school just because I was so tired of this endless cycle that had returned. I began to become afraid of talking to people because the only person I talked to day after day was Hogg, who is one of the most frustrating people I'd ever talked to. If you say a fact, she would pin you for a source, and if she didn't like your answer she would just keep asking questions until eventually you ran out of things you knew, and then would say I should do more research before speaking. Or she would constantly cut me off mid-sentence to fix my word choice, such as if I dare say who instead of whom she made sure to point it out. God, I remember one time I used the wrong too in a sentence for an English paper, and instead of saying hey you messed this up, or hey could you fix it she instead said, putting her hands against her face how she could not believe I didn't know the difference between toos like that was the problem. She constantly ridiculed me, my humor, my knowledge, my structure. God, it's no wonder I hate English so much as a school subject, if I dare mistype anything Hogg was there to make SURE I knew. and she would. and she would smile while insulting you while she did it. All of her compliments were backhanded. They were all belittling, she would only applaud me on basic things like signing my name on a paper. but if I dared do my own homework without her, zero-zip nothing. Just more critiques.

Fast-forwarding a bit, AP became so paralytic of writing I would have actual heart palpitations and anxiety attacks from writing English papers, subjecting Adam to that lovely byproduct. I feel really bad for that man having to deal with that mess Hogg had created. Obviously, that's gone away given I'm writing this. Although anger is also a good motivator, I suppose. I, of course, complained about this to my dad, but he told me about how when he was young, his parents had a friend that he just could not stand to be around, even just looking at the them made his stomach sick, but you have to do what you have to. "When the going gets tough, the tough get going." After all.

There's not much more to really say about sophomore year except that I can validate that there was no one home except me, my mother who was downstairs in her office and always told to go back down because she was a distraction, and my dad who lived at the house at this time. So, whenever I was sent to go to bed, my dad was indeed alone plenty of hours with just him and Hogg, because my room was directly above the dining room where we could hear each other more or less. Something Hogg made sure to remind me of by screaming to go to bed if I dared even get on my computer or play my piano after we finished. One very distinct memory I have is a friend of mine was at a party across the street from my house and I wanted to go, but I had Hogg again like every night before, but I asked my dad if I could go and just blow off Hogg this night, and he snapped and called me lazy and said if I wanted to go ahead and ruin my own life then fine before storming off and leaving me alone with Hogg. I didn't go to the party.

Fast forward to junior year, you know how this story begins. It was August 2016 by this point, and I don't even remember how I got here but something had snapped in me by this point. I've always been hesitant with things and gotten stressed, but not only was junior year the first year I would need to leave to go to the bathroom to take a break from class, I would have to do it nonstop in several classes having full blown hyperventilating in the bathroom. It was honestly insane, and even surreal now thinking back that that was my life just 4 years ago nearly. Time really does fly doesn't it? My test anxiety had gone through the roof to the point I literally could not finish a test. I was so browbeaten I would literally freeze on tests and panic, and it only got worse if I ever got a grade back that wasn't a 100. Sure, I was hesitant and cared about my grades before, but I was never so scared before. Like the world would end and all this struggling would be for naught. It was so bad it had hit November, and I had a test from august that I still just could not do, and my homework had gained such a massive backlog because I just could not work with Hogg anymore. I was so tired of her and everything I remember going to school one day asking if I could get in school suspension just so i could be alone in a room for a day to just do some homework alone to catch up without her in the room. I had completely, and honestly just shutdown at this point to where i literally could no longer do schoolwork. it really was insane and I can't explain it. I got PTSD, from school of all things. School gave me PTSD, thanks to Hogg and my dad's complete and utter refusal to get rid of her. But eventually, EVENTUALLY on thanksgiving break, when it became impossible to get me to do work, only then, did my dad do anything about it. It was so bad at this point even Caleb, my older brother, had gone to my dad on his own accord and told him he should get a new tutor for me. I'm pretty sure it was Caleb who recommended Adam for me to begin with. And Caleb, and Adam, I remember it clear as day, had taken me aside to his room and talked to me about how awful Hogg was, and how even he hated her and that he thought it would be a good idea to find someone new for me. I was probably on because of Caleb pitching Adam to my dad and the fact i just could not move forward that he would finally gave up on having Hogg as my tutor. But the damage was already done, and by this point my dad had to swap me to online school so i could reset my junior year so my grades didn't explode from all fs from how backed up everything was. I begged my dad to give me a month, or at least just a few weeks to recuperate and destress from everything, but nope. In just as few days, despite my protest, he threw Adam on me and we began tutoring immediately, leaving Adam with having to deal with my broken mess of a self. Keep in mind i had i swapped to online classes which were self-paced, so yes, i could have waited. But don't worry, as you already know this wasn't the last of Hogg. Despite no longer being my tutor, my dad had decided to keep her by hiring her as an employee even though my mom said no over and over again, so she was still constantly around believe you me no matter how much we protested. This is when Maddox comes back into the picture as December 2016 is when he graduates and also moves back into our home.

On top of all of that, my father took note of how bad my anxiety was and had become, and even though I pleaded with him to not, saying that if I was going to go to therapy I would at least like to go to one where I could talk to someone, although I really didn't want to do that either. But instead he ignored both of those and decided to take me to neurofeedback where they just run a machine that's supposed to help. Something I really hated doing then and have only become angrier as time went on. But despite bringing up how much i hated this, he told me about how expensive it was and how it should help, and that only a fool wouldn't use all the tools available to him.

On top of that, the last few months I was with my dad, we would bicker and fight all the time. On the drives to neurofeedback we would argue when talking, and on the way back we would stop by and see Hogg on the other side of town while she was at work. My dad left me in the car for hours while he talked to her and never told my mom about it. I remember going in there and seeing it after it had flooded. I also remember in one of our arguments, I in the heat of the moment stated how nobody likes Hogg, not even Adam liked her. He swung his head, baffled, and then said, "what do you mean no one likes her? she likes everyone, that's a real shame. She really likes Adam too." This is really the last few things I remember about my dad before March 7th, 2018. Other than him moving Hogg into our home so that she could torture me night and day.

It's funny, my dad once told me his biggest fear in life would be helping everyone, and then finding out he only hurt them instead and having them resent him for it. And ironically, that's exactly what he ended up doing, although given he mentioned to me means this isn't the first time this has happened to him. And although it took me awhile, I think I know why. His problem is he would go to everyone else to ask them for their ideas on how to help you instead of ever talking to you or listening to you on what you think would be the best for you. Because no one knows you better than everyone else. I had constantly successfully communicated what i would have wanted, but he never once trusted me and just listened to everyone else.

I used to consider myself very close to my dad, even when we would fight. But when he left, I was surprised to find myself happier, and that's the part that's hit me the hardest. I lost my dad, but I gained my sanity. Slowly, but I did, and even now as I'm back in school with no tutors at all, I'm not having any difficulty at all, and haven't frozen yet.

And even after this divorce, I had visited my dad a few times the first few months, and it was surreal but his whole demeanor had changed from when I knew him before. And even through all this time, he is still constantly spending time with Hogg, even having her sit on the bench with him every time he's come to court.

I wanted to find a way to transition to this, but I suppose just a throw away paragraph works too, and that's that my father will tell you repeatedly that I don't talk to him anymore and will tell you have I never reach out to him anymore. But what I know he won't tell you is the fact that when this divorce first broke out, I told him I wanted to stay neutral and keep both my parents. But despite this, he would constantly use anything I would say to help him in the lawsuit, even lying about things i know he knew wasn't why. When i had called him on the phone to talk, he stopped me before I hung up, and asked me if I wanted to him to have the white cat. I paused, because I knew exactly what he was asking it for, and eventually because he was so insist I give an answer, I did, reminding him I wanted to stay neutral in the divorce. But and you can check the court records to see. When he mentioned this to his lawyer, he said I froze because I was afraid of what my mother might do, despite me having told him in the conversation why I froze. On top of this, When I met up with him again much later, I told him how I got into Harvard like a proud son, and he looked me dead in the eyes and said over dinner, "you know you didn't really get into Harvard right?" and then later that dinner, I had showed him my credit card to show him the business I had started and how proud I was, only for him to turn around after that meal and sue me, forcing me to close my business.

That made me sick to my stomach to read. All the years I'd listened to Les bitch and moan about his own parents, and he was so much worse than they'd ever been. All that was missing was the pedophilia.

How pathetic that the pedophile and the worthless bitch who'd helped him get victims had been better parents than he had.

Said it all, didn't it?

How anyone could keep that cruelty hidden was chilling. The whole Dr. Jekyll, Mr. Hyde.

Just like Hogg. "I'm putting on my pastor hat."

It sickened me to think that these people were in our society, masquerading as normal. That people passed them on our streets without ever knowing the black hole that functioned as their hearts.

That they had no compunction about tearing down someone else's life.

Not even that of their own children.

What hope did any of us have? My life had become its own episode of *Fatal Vows*.

And I couldn't change the channel. Couldn't stop the production. There was something seriously wrong in this country that it allowed a sub sentient life form to weaponize our judicial system against the wife who'd once made the mistake of loving him and his own children.

Where were those checks and balances that we'd been promised? Who would ride herd on these people?

The FBI had come out for his bogus complaint. I had email after email from attorneys that verified I had a corrupt judge. Articles about his corruption in the *USA Today* and no one would investigate it.

How many lives would be ruined while everyone sat on the sidelines?

Just how chilling and how much of a cautionary tale would this become?

Worse? Nanette Savior had looked it over and was aghast. "My God, Terri. Two years in and you're not even through Discovery? Christ, your divorce has just started."

Never in my life had I wanted to cry more and given my life and past, that said it all.

**T**HE MOST GALLING PART was filling out a financial report to file with the court so that I could beg to have "some" of my paycheck that I'd earned. Which, by the way, was a violation of the law.

Fair Labor Standards Act (FLSA). What was the Fair Labor Standards Act? It was a federal law that established the minimum wage, overtime pay eligibility, recordkeeping, and child labor standards affecting full-time and part-time workers in the private sector and in federal, state, and local governments. Their posters were all over workplaces as all employers were required by law to post them because of FLSA.

Yet in direct violation of the law, this entire team of lawyers and my husband who used to work for the EEOC (Equal Employment Opportunity Commission) and Judge Dinky were willfully and maliciously violating the law.

All to teach me a lesson.

Dinky said that on record. "Has she learned her lesson yet? I don't think she has."

*No, bitch. I haven't.* I don't believe a woman should have to kowtow to a man. Especially not for the money she earned.

That shit went out when we were given the vote. Sorry you missed the memo while you were cruising prostitutes.

But this was a new millennium and women weren't playthings for you.

So that morning, I began hammering again everyone I could think of with this email:

> I am writing about a most egregious matter. For the last two years, I have been caught in a bitter divorce with my husband who is an attorney and who hired the former business partners of the judge assigned to our case. Rather than recuse himself, the judge has stayed and shown blatant favoritism that everyone from the bailiffs to attorneys who aren't a part of my case have been appalled by. I even have it in writing from federal attorneys that the judge is over the top. His latest actions are now life-threatening.
>
> Because the judge ordered me to pay for my husband's attorneys and gave them a blank check, something unheard of, I was forced into bankruptcy last year. That was dismissed earlier this month. But rather than allow me to have possession of my money that I earn from my busi-

ness, as is required by law, the judge, has kept my money tied up in limbo and I have not been paid since April 1. I run a small business and my employees have not been paid either for the work they have done. This is illegal.

I own a store and merchandise that has been bought and paid for cannot be shipped to the people who have paid for it because of the judge's illegal actions. More than that, I cannot buy the medication that my life depends on, and I have now been out of it for weeks.

This is a most serious matter as I am being told that they won't hold a hearing about paying my employees for another week. That means that my staff will have to go a month, during this horrible time, with no pay, because a Williamson County judge has a God Complex and wants to "teach me a lesson." He said that on record. In fact, he has called me a monster and a buzz saw and I have him recorded where he spent over an hour insulting me and my attorney for no reason whatsoever and threatening to put me in jail over paperwork my husband already had because the judge had awarded him my office where my paperwork he was demanding I hand over was kept. That is how unreasonable this judge has been. I have two years of evidence against him. When I tried to bring a case of perjury against my husband, the judge refused to hear it on the basis that he didn't want to damage a "good lawyer's reputation." And he has made the comment on record that he "doesn't care what the law is."

I have reported him to the Judiciary Board of Review, and they have failed to take action against him. That resulted in an illegal search and seizure of my home. Now I am being deprived of my income and my employees are going unpaid. And he is now throwing me and my special needs son out of our home for no reason and in the middle of a pandemic when he knows that I cannot find adequate shelter because I am coming out of bankruptcy and have no credit and no money. I am imploring you for your help. This persecution needs to stop. It was bad enough that my husband's attorney accused me of witchcraft in her first filing, but seriously? This is ridiculous for a modern court. Can you please help me to get my employees paid and to force this judge to recuse himself so that I can get a fair trial as I am guaranteed by the Constitution?

> Thank you for your time,
> Terri Manly

The first response came back from the governor:

Dear Terri:

Thank you for contacting me concerning the issues you are having related to the court system. I appreciate you sharing this information.

Unfortunately, the situation you face is a matter that must be addressed by the court system. As Governor, I have no jurisdiction or control over the Judicial Branch of our state government. If you have a complaint about a particular judge, you may wish to contact the Administrative Office of the Courts:

Administrative Office of the Courts
511 Union Street, Suite 600
Nashville, Tennessee 37219.

I genuinely hope that you find an appropriate resolution of this situation. Please accept my best wishes, and I look forward to working with you and all Tennesseans to make our great state an even better place to live, work, and raise a family.

Warmest regards,

Bill Lee

Needless to say, Governor Lee not only lost my vote, but he just made me a staunch supporter and advocate for whomever ran against him in the next campaign. Because if judicial corruption and failure to pay employees during the COVID epidemic didn't get him off his ass to do something to protect his citizens, this bastard had no business in office. After all, I wasn't so stupid that I didn't know he could call in an investigation. He did have those powers.

He was simply too lazy to use them.

And it wasn't like this was the first letter I'd sent him, either. I also sent it to the Tennessee Department of Labor, the U.S. Department of Labor and every Small Business and Women's Business Organization I could think of. Not that I expected them to care anymore than the governor did.

Apathy was the name of this game. But I felt like I needed to warn people. No one had warned me that this kind of corruption went on. I'd been blindsided.

The last thing I wanted was to be responsible for this happening to someone after me. The least you could say was that I had warned you.

Caveat Emptor.

Had I been forewarned by anyone that this could happen, I would never have married. I'd have never put my copyrights in jeopardy.

Had I known my in-laws were pedophiles, I would never have had children.

So many things that I hadn't known then that I should have been told about before it was too late.

Just like the bankruptcy. They lured you in with lies and then when you were given the truth, it was too late. My accountant had been right, you were caught in this vortex from which there was no escape.

It was why I'd refused to let my buyers walk into this house without knowing what was going on. At no time in my life have I ever put a single cent over the value of a human life. I won't be that person. There was nothing more sacred to me than a human being. And no amount of money would ever mean more to me than someone else.

My integrity and my soul weren't for sale.

Which apparently had pissed off the realtor as that afternoon I received this email:

> The repair proposal and inspection report have been attached. Please be advised that WIN Home Inspection would like to pick up the Radon test on Friday. They request an hour window on both sides of 11 am on Friday (4/24). How would you like to proceed with the proposal?

> Please confirm that the mold found in the inspection report is the same mold referenced by Mrs. Manly in her email to me on April 17th at 7:05 am, which was also read aloud in the recorded hearing with Judge Dinky on April 17th at 1 pm, and in Mrs. Manly complaint filed against me with the Tennessee Real Estate Commission that included pictures of mold.

> Also, if necessary, please have Mrs. Manly complete the update to the Tennessee Property Condition Disclosure on form RF202 provided to her on April 17th at 10:38 am to include specific information regarding the structural and mold issues stated in her email on April 17th she referenced that have been found. Additionally, provide any and all supporting documentation regarding the structural and mold issues.

I wasn't making any friends, but I didn't care. Reporting this whole jolly crew of assholes had become my only form of entertainment. As you could see from that, he'd read my emails to the judge in an effort to get me into trouble and to make it appear as if I'd done something wrong during the hearing they had locked me out of so that I couldn't defend myself when all I'd been trying to do was what I was required to do under the law. Something Cockburn knew I was required to do under the law as Thundercunt was a former realtor herself.

Instead, they'd used my good intentions to smear my reputation and good name.

I was tired of it. And if they were going to play dirty, then I was going to report them for their underhanded tricks. At least one, of the million and two agencies I'd reported them to, had finally said something. It was about time.

And boy, had that inspection come back with a whole lot more than I'd known about. So had the jackass allowed me to report the three things I'd tried to tell them about, no one would have been in trouble.

Instead, Newhouse had screamed at me, and they'd smeared me for things that came out anyway.

It was ridiculous.

And how did stupid Les react?

"At that price, the house is to be sold 'as is'".

Which meant he knew he was giving away my home. So how much money had this bastard stolen from me and our children that he could be so cavalier with giving away our biggest investment that I had paid for?

Remember that this was the same asshole who'd written in his own hand:

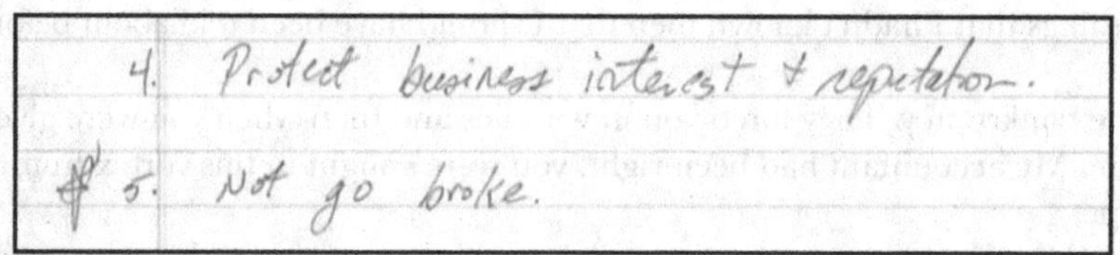


Yet he was systematically driving us into the ground while letting it be known that he had no intention of working.

Ever.

Because he'd also called off all attempts at settlement, while having his team of hyenas work, night and day, against me.

He was determined that I was going to pay him, contrary to the law, for all my future earnings.

And I'd see him in hell before I did that. He left me for a cow-faced, heinous piece of shit who had tortured my children. That did not entitle me to work for him for the rest of my life and have him take one-third to one-half of my profits for the rest of my life.

Fuck him.

He could get a job like everyone else in the world. What kind of man, and I used that term loosely, could look at himself in the mirror and have any kind of self-respect? How could I have ever deluded myself that I could have loved such a worthless, repugnant piece of shit?

They were right, I had been delusional. I'd convinced myself that this sub-sentient bottom feeder had been worth something.

For thirty years, I'd given up my happiness to live with that monster. I wasn't going to give up my future for him.

Goddamn the fucking laws of this country that they allowed the ongoing torture of innocent people by such insane monsters. How could there not be someone to oversee this?

I had no end in sight.

No way out.

How could this be? There was no one in charge of the asylum. The inmates were in charge, and I was trapped in hell.

# APRIL 27

S TILL NO MONEY AND WE were almost to the end of the month. The bastards had made good on their threats, and no one cared. No one would do a damn thing. How sickening was that? I'd reported them to the FBI, Department of Justice, TN Department of Labor, the governor, U.S. Department of Labor, Attorney General and every state and U.S. congressman and rep that I could think of.

Nada.

My attorney had assured me that she'd expected a check the week before, but nope.

Even though I'd agreed to give Les a cut of all my future earnings.

He'd still refused, which meant that he had no interest in getting divorced.

I couldn't understand why the courts didn't demand that if it was a no-fault divorce that it had to be finished within three to six months. Or that if it was a "fault" divorce that the one bringing it had to establish their case, like any other trial, or drop it. It wasn't right for the innocent party to be tortured and to have no way out. That a life could be torn apart and dragged through the mud for years by an abusive asshole simply because he was bored and had nothing better to do with his useless life.

This was why women in abusive relationships couldn't get out of them. Why we didn't dare leave. Because our court systems backed our abusers and the judges piled on to help them torture us.

No agency or anyone else would help us end our nightmares. The same thing had happened to me as a child.

Damn that caseworker to hell. The bitch had almost gotten me killed. To this this day, I hated her for what she'd done to me and then walked away to live her life in peace while leaving me behind to deal with the nuclear fallout she'd caused.

For what? So she could feel good? So that she could sleep at night, thinking she'd made a difference?

Yeah, bitch, you made a difference. You got a little girl beaten so severely that she'd barely survived it. That she'd been black and blue for weeks. A beating that had forced her to crawl, shaking, on her hands and knees into her room where she'd prayed to God to let her die because she couldn't bear the pain of her life anymore.

That little girl, forty years later, still had scars on her body from it.

*Thank you for your kindness. I've never forgotten it.*

And here I was, trapped again, with my children. In an apathetic, vicious court system that only served those who violated us because it made them feel big to beat down those around them.

*Were you happy, Les?* Was this what it took to finally make you feel like a man?

Newsflash, Mommy Snooty still wasn't proud of you. And I could assure you that this wasn't making you look any more like a man than sitting drunk on my couch had done for all those years.

The only people who'd every held you in any regard had been your sons and I, and you'd lost every bit of respect any of us ever had for you.

Instead of blaming me for your life, you should have been thanking me.

Your jackals knew it as much as I did. They were just too greedy to care.

And your Hogg didn't care, either. Her "friends" had contacted me to tell me that you were another in a long line of others she'd done this to. Because you were her sport. This was how the hideous beast who felt betrayed by God for the fact that she looked like she did and was trapped in her own pathetic life got back at people.

She destroyed their happy homes.

Then she went on her merry way to the next one.

All these years that you warned me about bringing trash in, Les's words, because you feared that they would talk smack about you and come between us. That they would "destroy" what we'd built, and you were the one who let it in and fell victim to a common con artist who didn't even care about you. One who was only using you and doing this because she was jealous.

You really were the dumbest motherfucker on the planet.

Sooner or later, I knew God would remove you from my life and I would carry on. Over, under, around or through. There was always a way.

You were just another obstacle in my way. And I was determined to get past you, no matter what. You'd been my albatross for too many years, and I wasn't about to let you hold me back any longer.

*Get thee behind me, bitch.*

Life was short and I had too much to do to waste time with shitholes like you and your vultures. I had sons who had futures I had to help them with, and you were not going to be the anchor to drag any of us down.

By hook or by crook, we were going to cut you loose. *Go wallow with your Hogg and get out of our way.*

So, that morning, I finished off my letter for the Tennessee Board of Professional Responsibility. Not that I expected much. Ms. Dullard had let me down so many times in the past. But this was what I'd prepared for her:

Dear Ms. Dullard and Mr. Leadwits:

I am writing in regard to Mr. Leadwits's letter dated April 15, 2020. After careful consideration of his letter and all facts, I sincerely urge the Tennessee Board of Professional Responsibility to offer no mercy or leniency toward Mr. Leadwits, as he has shown no remorse or apology for his actions. Mr. Leadwits needs to understand the seriousness of what he has done and the sanctity of attorney-client privilege so that he will never again betray his innocent clients, and will understand why such a relationship should be preserved at all costs and held as sacrosanct.

He was given every opportunity to do the right thing and to rectify his actions, and instead of helping his client, he willfully chose to worsen my situation and to look after only his own narrow self-interests, while allowing his client to suffer worsening conditions brought on as a direct result of his breach and failure to render aid. Something that clearly violates T.C.A. § 23-3-105 and from the Rule 8 Preamble:

[22] In reliance on the attorney-client privilege, clients are entitled to expect that communications within the scope of the privilege will be protected against compelled disclosure. The attorney-client privilege is that of the client and not of the lawyer. The fact that in exceptional situations the lawyer under the Rules has a limited discretion to disclose a client confidence does not vitiate the proposition that, as a general matter, the client has a reasonable expectation that information relating to the client will not be voluntarily disclosed.

By his own words and admission, Mr. Leadwits  clearly and willfully betrayed this sacred pact when he shared my diary with Misty Spicer without my permission or knowledge. He also violated the well-known copyright laws that protect all intellectual property:

Title 18, U.S. Code, Sections 2319, 2319A, and 2319B. The unauthorized reproduction or distribution of a copyrighted work is illegal. Criminal copyright infringement, including infringement without monetary gain, is investigated by the FBI and is punishable by up to five years in federal prison and a fine of $250,000.

Mr. Leadwits even attached a standard copy of that legal notice from the template of my diary in his own letter that he provided to the Tennessee Board of Professional Responsibility:



Therefore, he was well-aware that he should not be disseminating my intellectual property to anyone for any reason, without my explicit written permission, and he knew he was violating the law.

If what Mr. Leadwits is saying to the Board is correct, that he feared anyone else seeing or reading my material, then he should have counseled me to that fact, and have never shared it with anyone, including Ms. Spicer. That would have been the prudent and correct behavior for any conscientious federal attorney.

Instead and in spite of Ms. Spicer's warning that the material should not be disclosed (his own words in his own letter), Mr. Leadwits baited me into taking an action that he has admitted to the Board he knew for a fact was detrimental to my best interests, and that clearly violates the Rules set forth by your Board that govern proper attorney behavior.

While my case has been going on and with the full knowledge that I am a #1 *New*

*York Times* bestselling author with millions of fans the world over, all the attorneys involved in my case, including Mr. Leadwits have joked about what a great book my life story would make when this travesty they have intentionally and willfully created is over. That was why I originally shared my diary with Mr. Leadwits. And for the record, he wasn't horrified by it as he claims. He called me up, laughing, to say that he thought it was a brilliant piece of work and that he enjoyed it immensely.

Contrary to what he stipulates in his letter to you, I had been asking for a meeting with Ms. Seaver for weeks to discuss Mr. Newhouse's incompetence that Mr. Leadwits notes in his response. She didn't ask for the meeting after she'd read the diary. That meeting was already in place before he gave her a copy of my material and he led me to believe that he wanted her to see the diary to help her understand my situation before the meeting was held, which was why I'd finally agreed to let her see it, even though I had empathically told him not to share it with her all the other times he'd asked me if he could do such.

The one and only email he shared with the Board also shows that we'd had prior discussions and emails about my diary that he failed to share with the Board where I told him implicitly *not* to share my material with Martha Seaver:

You can share this one with Martha.

It is a gross misrepresentation of fact that Mr. Leadwits is using with the Board to try and get himself out of trouble when he attached that one, single email that indicts him, and shows just how corrupt an attorney he has become in his dealings with others. And that no one can rely on him to tell the truth in any matter. Clearly, we'd had other communications prior to that email where I had told him not to share copies of my diary with Ms. Seaver. Otherwise, the email wouldn't have been phrased the way it is.

It was because he continued to ask me about sharing it with Ms. Seaver that I, due to the inherent nature of attorney-client privilege, assumed he had my best interests in mind. Why else would my attorney continue to want the U.S. Trustee, a member of the Department of Justice, to see it?

Since we were heading into a meeting he fraudulently led me to believe was being held to report on the gross misconduct of another trustee, Tom Newhouse, I naturally assumed he wanted my diary because it held the evidence of the trustee's bad behavior and actions against me. Actions and behavior that Mr. Leadwits admitted occurred in his letter to the Board. Instead, that meeting was an ambush where I and my friend were threatened, harassed and intimidated by members of the Department of Justice and licensed federal attorneys while Mr. Leadwits did nothing to help us.

I had every legal and moral right to assume my own attorney would have counseled me prior to releasing my material to Ms. Seaver of any negative consequences that might ensue from Mr. Leadwits's handing it over, especially if he had the severe misgivings he claims in his letter to the Board. He never gave me those warnings. Instead, he laughed and told me he thought the "book was brilliant."

Once Ms. Seaver overreacted so vehemently and began threatening me with retaliation in a manner that is barred by the rules of the Board and by her own office, as Mr. Leadwits also acknowledges, he abandoned me with more lies instead of helping me through the very situation and turmoil he'd caused by his unconscionable breach where I was stripped of my personal property in retaliation for his deliberate actions.

Rather than turning on his own client and seeking to leave me with no counsel at all, Mr. Leadwits should have aided me in turning the trustees in to the appropriate authorities and helping me to safeguard my rights and property that they then continued to threaten while I was helpless under their authority. Instead, he chose to again misrepresent facts to the Board so that he could withhold his representation from me as another threat against me to get me to comply with their outrageous demands, which were not in my best interest.

As he said on his call with me and my attorney, Melissa Magillicutty, he only filed his motion to withdraw as my counsel to "get your attention. It was a warning shot across your bow." No attorney should weaponize the Tennessee Board of Professional Responsibility against their own client so that they can silence their client into complacency while the client's assets and their lifetime of hard work are plundered by unscrupulous attorneys, trustees, judges and their associates who have no problem flaunting their oaths of office or willfully violating their Rules of Professional Conduct. While the client is being threatened and harassed on a daily basis by an out-of-control trustee who has been given the authority by an unscrupulous member of the Department of Justice to put the client in a Chapter 7 bankruptcy regardless of law, and whether the client meets the Means Test or not. As Seaver said in front of multiple witnesses and as I have documented in writing, "if you do anything to displease us, we will convert your case at a moment's notice. My finger is on the button. If you do one thing that upsets Tom, we will liquidate everything you own, including your books and trademarks. You better destroy every copy of your book, or we will convert your case. If it ever sees the light of day, we will convert your case." She went on to say that, "We weren't going to sell your jewelry, but after this, we're selling off every piece of it in retaliation." That included selling off the twenty-five-cent bubble gum machine ring my sons purchased as a Mother's Day present and a little rock ring my baby made for me.

Furthermore, Mr. Leadwits is also deliberately lying to the Board about the Defamation suit that was filed. That suit was filed *after* Mr. Leadwits had released my diary into the hands of the U.S. Trustee who then liberally disseminated copies to others, and I hold him personally accountable for Seaver's illegal actions, especially after he admits that he knew better than to give her a copy and did so against his own reservations and against the advice of another attorney in his own office. It is my belief that the suit was filed as a direct result of Mr. Leadwits's releasing my diary and because of his breach of attorney-client privilege. Our meeting was held January 16th and I was served with the suit the very next day on January 17th after Ms. Seaver had threatened me, and after others had told me that they had seen and read the diary, too, days after Leadwits had given his copy to Seaver and she had acknowledged that she'd sent copies as far and wide as Washington, D.C. Something very easy to prove as the lawsuit is on record, as is the meeting where we had third-party witnesses to her statements.

Thus proving my point that Mr. Leadwits has no compunctions about misrepresenting facts to the Board or anyone else, which is also a breach of your own rules for attorney behavior:

## RULE 3.3: CANDOR TOWARD THE TRIBUNAL

(a)  A lawyer shall not knowingly:

(1) make a false statement of fact or law to a tribunal; or

(b)  A lawyer shall not offer evidence the lawyer knows to be false...

(c)  A lawyer shall not affirm the validity of, or otherwise use, any evidence the lawyer knows to be false.

There are circumstances where failure to make a disclosure is the equivalent of an affirmative misrepresentation. The obligation prescribed in RPC 1.2(d) not to counsel a client to commit, or assist the client in committing a fraud, applies in litigation. Regarding compliance with RPC 1.2(d), see the Comment to that Rule and also Comments [1] and [7] to RPC 8.4.

## RULE 4.1: TRUTHFULNESS IN STATEMENTS TO OTHERS

(a)  In the course of representing a client, a lawyer shall not knowingly make a false statement of material fact or law to a third person.

## RULE 8.4: MISCONDUCT

It is professional misconduct for a lawyer to:

(a)  violate or attempt to violate the Rules of Professional Conduct, knowingly assist or induce another to do so, or do so through the acts of another;

(c)  engage in conduct involving dishonesty, fraud, deceit, or misrepresentation;

Comment

[5] Paragraph (c) prohibits lawyers from engaging in conduct involving dishonesty, fraud, deceit, or misrepresentation. Such conduct reflects adversely on the lawyer's fitness to practice law.

Other facts that Mr. Leadwits knowingly presents to the Board that are wrong is where he claims that I had purchased an ISBN (International Standard Book Number) and presents facts as if he's an expert. Then he uses a dummy number that was generated in my template (which he knew I wrote in as he'd been told about my template on numerous occasions, including during the January meeting with Seaver) so that he could make a false claim to the Board that I was planning to publish my diary. His assertion that 123456789 is a purchased, legitimate ISBN is clearly a wilful and intentional misrepresentation of fact to the Board.

A simple internet search shows that all ISBNs are ten digits long if assigned before 2007, and thirteen digits long if assigned on or after 1 January 2007, not the nine digits that are set in my writing program as dummy/template numbers. And they look like this:

ISBN 978-1-250-10269-0

He also lied and said that I had copyrighted the book when I have not. Any working attorney should know that all works are copyrighted the moment they are committed to paper or digital form, but that is not a "legal" copyright. My writing program automatically applies a copyright symbol to my work and keeps a record of it. That is not the same thing as filing with the U.S. Copyright Office and filing for a copyright as he is asserting to the Board. Something any attorney should know cannot be completed until after a work is finished and published, and a copy of the final manuscript is sent to the Copyright Office. Since the diary has never been published to the public, I cannot legally file a copyright for it. Not to mention the fact that Mr. Leadwits is well aware of the fact that due to his egregious acts against me, I was forced to endure Tom Newhouse's Draconian rule where I had to beg to buy even a stick of gum and had to wait for Newhouse's approval for every expenditure I made, no matter how big or small. Ergo, Newhouse would never have approved my spending the $79.95 to file for a copyright or the $125 for an ISBN (all of which would have been put on public record had I made those purchases due to my bankruptcy filing). Mr. Leadwits's entire argument is moot and one made just to show how willing he is to lie to anyone for his own benefit and to throw his clients under a bus.

I was well aware that my diary was property of the bankruptcy estate which is what I counselled Mr. Leadwits to remind Newhouse and Seaver of when they, *against the law*, ordered me to destroy it in front of him (and others) and he didn't report them for their unconscionable acts and threats against me and my property, as the Rules of Professional Conduct compel him to do whenever he sees a fellow attorney breach their oaths and misuse their legal degrees to bully, harass and intimidate others. It was that very email I'd sent to him that he lied about to the Board so that he could gain permission to withdraw as my counsel, or in his own words, "fire a warning shot across" my bow to get my attention. In that email, I told him to remind them that they were ordering me to commit a crime against the U.S. government. I'm very happy that he admits in his letter that it was, indeed, federal property the *two* Department of Justice representatives ordered me to destroy against federal and state court orders and the law, and that he was complicit in their orders for me to violate state and federal court orders. Which I believe is another infraction as attorneys are not to instruct their clients to commit a crime or to breach a court order.

18 U.S.C. § 1361: This section prohibits actual physical damage or destruction of both real and personal property, but mere adverse possession of that property without physical harm is insufficient to violate the law. United States v. Jenkins, supra, 554 F.2d at 785. Section 1361 is a specific intent crime, see United States v. Jones, 607 F.2d 269, 273-74 (9th Cir. 1979), cert. denied, 444 U.S. 1085 (1980), and the government must prove that the defendant acted willfully; that is intentionally, with knowledge that he/she is violating a law. United States v. Simpson, 460 F.2d 515, 518 (9th Cir. 1972); United States v. Moylan, 417 F.2d 1002, 1004 (4th Cir. 1969), cert. denied, 397 U.S. 910 (1970). The government is not required to prove that defendant knew the property belonged to the government, because government ownership

is "merely a 'jurisdictional fact'." United States v. LaPorta, 46 F.3d 152, 158 (2d Cir. 1994), quoting United States v. Feola, 420 U.S. 671 (1975). In fact, title or possession by the United States is not a necessary element of this offense, if the property in question was being made for the United States. The government must present evidence establishing value of damage. United States v. Seaman, 18 F.3d 649, 651 (9th Cir. 1994). The penalties for violations of this section are tied to the extent of the property damage. As amended on September 13, 1994, if the damage exceeds $100, the defendant is subject to a fine of up to **$250,000, ten years imprisonment, or both**. See Violent Crime Control and Law Enforcement Act of 1994, Pub. L. 103-322, § 330016, 108 Stat. 1796, 2146-47 (1994). When property damage does not exceed $100, the offense is a misdemeanor punishable by a fine of up to $100,000, one year imprisonment, or both. See 18 U.S.C. § 3559(a), 3571.

Given that Seaver loves to flaunt her Department of Justice title and that Newhouse is a U.S. Bankruptcy trustee, and that they both made me swear under oath that all my property and belongings, including my intellectual property were property of the United States government, I think it's safe to say they knew that it was, indeed, valuable federal property that they ordered me to destroy and thereby commit a felony. Just as Newhouse and Seaver are aware of how much one of my books is worth as Seaver ordered me during that same meeting to "go write another book" to get myself out of bankruptcy. Everyone in that room was well aware that the value for any of my books would exceed the $100 mark. Mr. Leadwits, as well as the trustees and Bill Oldham were very much aware of the fact that they were ordering me to commit a crime on January 16, 2020 and threatening my future livelihood if I failed to do so at their direct behest and under their threats to do harm to my future earnings, while holding my property as hostage if I failed to comply with their orders. All of which, among many other actions they have taken against me, clearly violate TN Code § 39-17-308 (2016).

Mr. Leadwits then betrays a strategy that he never advised me he was planning to implement prior to signing me up for bankruptcy when he says and I quote, "My strategy was simple. File a Chapter 11 for Ms. Manly; seek the appointment of a Chapter 11 Trustee who would *liquidate* all of the assets to pay Ms. Manly's creditors, and the balance would then be divvied up in the state court divorce proceedings."

Mr. Leadwits is not King Solomon nor is he a judge. That decision was never his to make with my entire life's work hinging on his greed and lust for my property as was evidenced in the meeting with Seaver when she told me that she would be selling off all my jewelry, including items that belonged to my deceased mother, brother and niece, "in retaliation" for my having written diary that documented their bad acts. Mr. Leadwits immediately asked her if he and his sister could bid upon my property, which also shows just how self-serving he is and his utter lack of remorse, and regard for his own clients. This ranks right up there when I asked if I could have Christmas lights for my house and he replied, "You are asking a nice Jewish boy if you should have Christmas lights?" Then he went on to say, "Let me answer it as follows:  Here is how to say NO in 110 different languages:"

Had Mr. Leadwits ever told me of his insidious plan to divest me of all my hard-earned property that included thirty years of novels, contracts and trademarks, I would never have entered bankruptcy as his suggestion was the horror that became my life under their Torquemadic threats. Rather, he told me that the bankruptcy would allow me to consolidate my multiple bank accounts and stop the state proceedings in divorce court long enough for me to pay off the massive legal bills my husband had run up so that I could catch my breath and begin the divorce proceedings again. All I needed to do when the bankruptcy started was combine my accounts without the threat of a frivolous contempt motion being made against me.

Mr. Leadwits's defiant actions of putting a trustee, his attorney and all the other players over me against my wishes are what added another million dollars of debt to my bill and resulted in absolutely no creditors being paid. I have now lost my personal clothing, my purses, my cars and my home as a direct result of his intentional deception and lies.

Mr. Leadwits, against my direct wishes and under my virulent protests, put a trustee that he and Martha Seaver hand-picked (her words) over my estate to liquidate all my personal assets while I protested every single sale which under a Chapter 11, I, not they, should have had final say about. Meanwhile, they all threatened me at every turn and in direct violation of the law to sell all my intellectual property which included all my writing contracts and trademarks that I need in order to make a living and that is not part of the bankruptcy code and is in fact, in direct contradiction of it. Only an absolute imbecile with no regard for his client would have conceived of doing such a thing. The purpose of bankruptcy is to give someone a "fresh start," not cut their legs off so that they can never again stand on their own feet. Especially as all my debts could have been paid off by simply merging my accounts together which I couldn't do because of a state court order that was in place last summer that my divorce attorney couldn't get overturned. That was why I needed a Chapter 11 reorganization, and I only needed it for a few weeks to access my funds that the state had blocked me from in order to pay off my debt. I should have been out of my bankruptcy in a matter of weeks.

Instead, Mr. Leadwits allowed his friends to plunder my estate for their own personal gain, all the while Mr. Leadwits lied to me. Furthermore, they refused to allow me to dismiss my bankruptcy and he is grossly misstating facts when he says that you cannot dismiss a voluntary bankruptcy, even a Chapter 11. I have since spoken to other bankruptcy attorneys who will testify if you need them to. None of my creditors were ever paid during the bankruptcy, only the attorneys who have been colluding against me to line their own pockets. All of my creditors were willing to stop the bankruptcy as they wanted payment and Newhouse continued to refuse to pay them while Newhouse and Leadwits both refused to dismiss my case for no good reason, and while Leadwits knew full well that Newhouse was being paid a percentage of my money he had agreed to pay to my husband's attorneys without any supervision. Or more to the point as this email shows:

> As for fees, the UST is only allowing Tom a percentage of disbursements,
> not an hourly rate, but keep that to yourself.

In other words, Mr. Leadwits failed in his fiduciary duties when he allowed Newhouse to negotiate unsupervised and without Mr. Leadwits being present with my husband's attorneys while knowing that Judge Bubba Dinky (a longtime family friend of Leadwits's), as Leadwits has stated in multiple emails you have seen, is prejudiced against me and is a former business partner of my husband's attorneys who always finds in their favor against me. Knowing this, he allowed Newhouse to give those unscrupulous attorneys unfettered access to my bank account, while I was in bankruptcy, and for the trustee to pay himself a percentage of whatever money he dispensed to them from my account, as Leadwits admitted in his letter. Thus allowing attorneys Mika House, John Alaimo, Bonnie Cockburn, Tim Woods, Sal Tiller, Dim Roberts and Barbie Borden to write their own checks for whatever amount they saw fit at my expense while they, with the full backing of Judge Dinky, denied my attorney the right to file motions during my bankruptcy, or as you saw in the emails I have provided you, to allow me to have additional counsel to assist my attorney against that ungodly team that outnumbers her that I am still being forced to pay for by an unscrupulous judge.

Instead, they repeatedly threatened to convert me to a Chapter 7 unless "I behaved"; a threat they knew would put me on welfare for the rest of my life, and leave me with no money for food, gas or the medication I need to live. A threat they have since made good on.

This is the exact level of threats, bullying, insults, collusion, and intimidation that they have subjected me, my friends and family to for months. You can see it for yourself in writing in this email that Mr. Leadwits sent to me and my attorney after I told me not to withdraw his next motion to withdraw as my counsel that he kept putting forth to the court for no other reason than to publicly embarrass and humiliate me and to control me:

> Terri and Melissa – My phone has been buzzing from Tom, Bill, and Martha since the word got out that I was terminated. I got a telephone call from Tom Newhouse asking me my opinion of whether Terri would have any stream of income if the case gets converted to a Chapter 7. He said my departure would the trigger the UST to file a motion to convert and that I was the buffer keeping the case in Chapter 11. He went on to say that you (Terri) have found authority where the Court could dismiss the case.

> Martha called and asked if you were freaking crazy. She said that Tom as Trustee would intercept all of your income, and that you would not even have the monies to buy food or gasoline. She told me to give you the heads up that she is filing an expedited motion to convert the case to a Chapter 7 by the middle of the week.

> My responses to both were that I have been relieved of duties in the case. Tom all but begged me to send out this email saying that he would try to claim all Etsy sales and royalties if the case was converted. And you would not be pleased with the results if this case was a Chapter 7 bankruptcy. I told Martha and Tom that I will convey the messages.

> As I have stated in several emails, you are not going to get this case dismissed. You do not have an absolute right to dismiss. Candidly, this is your case and your call. You do not need to handle this case pro se as Bill Oldham has suggested that you are planning to do. And frankly, without having an attorney to calm everyone down, your motion to dismiss will be denied, and the case will in all likelihood will be converted to a Chapter 7.

> Since you have terminated me as counsel, you need to find new counsel as soon as possible. And you need to figure out how to compensate that attorney. Tom will not release any money to pay for new bankruptcy counsel. And I am not sure that Melissa will want those duties knowing that it is unlikely that she will be paid for the bankruptcy side of the case.

I have conveyed the message from Martha and Tom.

As I have shown the Board in previous emails and motions that I've submitted, I was harassed, embarrassed and threatened by Leadwits and the trustees as they made themselves at home with my money and assets, and threatened me if I spoke up against their egregious threats and actions.

In fact, that is why my case was finally dismissed. Not because Newhouse was benevolent as Mr. Leadwits again misrepresents at the end of his letter. Newhouse wasn't trying to get the case dismissed. If you read the transcript and his court filing, it is more than obvious that Oldham and Newhouse, aside from the perjury both committed under oath, not only betrayed the fact that Mr. Leadwits gave them additional information about me that he shouldn't have, committing more breaches of attorney-client privilege, but that they were pushing the judge toward a conversion to Chapter 7, rather than a dismissal. The very thing they had threatened me with for months, in writing, and the option Mr. Leadwits claims he'd wanted them to do for my estate, even though I didn't meet the Means Test, and even though Newhouse had paid enough out to himself, his friends and my husband's lawyers that he could have cleared my estate of all debt without selling off any of my assets or clothing.

Newhouse went out of his way during that hearing to ensure Judge Harriett and all those present were well aware of my diary, thus exposing its contents, and to let the judge know that if my diary was ever "brought to light" that he was sure he, Martha Seaver and Bill Oldham would be subject to sanctions by the Tennessee Board of Professional Responsibility under Rule 11. He didn't say "if" to the judge, he "was positive" in his sworn testimony that they "would be subjected to Rule 11 sanctions" (his exact words).

After that public admission to their wrongdoing, Newhouse then had the judge order my legal right to pursue actions against him, Seaver and Oldham for their parts in raiding my estate and inflicting emotional harm on me and my family be taken away from me, because he knew that they were indeed liable and culpable for their bad acts, (which Mr. Leadwits acknowledges in his own letter).

Even during that hearing when I told the judge that I had reported them for their bad acts to the Tennessee Board of Professional Responsibility and Department of Justice, and even after their admission of wrongdoing, Seaver had the audacity to mock me to the judge in an attempt to discredit me with her misrepresentation of facts. "I'm with the Department of Justice, Your Honor, and I know nothing of any reports or complaints having been filed with any department." I think it's safe to say, Ms. Dullard, that you are well aware of the fact that I will not hesitate to report someone for their wrongdoing, to any and all agencies.

Had Newhouse truly wanted to help as Mr. Donothing misrepresents in his letter, he wouldn't have waited so long to request the dismissal that I had been begging them for months to file, nor would he and Oldham have argued so virulently during the hearing for a conversion. Even worse? By delaying me with their stalling tactics they kept me from being able to apply for the CARES Act for so long that by the time I was able to do so, the program was out of money.

For that matter, Newhouse didn't need to dismiss my case, nor did he have to sell any of my property. Rather, he could have used the CARES Act to cover all my debt and free me of their threats and lies.

The one thing he couldn't have done under the CARES Act was misappropriate my funds for himself and others as that money would have been carefully scrutinized by the government and its agents.

Not to mention that the above Act went into effect in February, and my case was dismissed on April 6, which proves that they intentionally delayed dismissing my case or taking any action to help me and did everything they could to willfully and intentionally cause me more financial harm to their betterment. And for the record, during all the months I was in bankruptcy (July 2019-April 2020) no one ever filed a payment plan with the court for me to pay my creditors, even though I'd gone into bankruptcy with a full plan on what needed to be done to repay my creditors that would have had me out of bankruptcy by September 2019.

It is my honest belief that Newhouse gave his true motivation for the dismissal away to the judge during his sworn testimony during the hearing. There was nothing more left in my estate of any real value that they could easily sell.

Because of their direct actions and explicit threats, Newhouse, Oldham, Seaver and Leadwits are currently in violation of the FSLA laws that have kept my employees from being paid since the first of April. Just as they had threatened to do on so many occasions, including in writing, they tied up all my money and have left me with none whatsoever. As a direct result of their actions and threats, all my money for payroll has been tied up for two pay periods, in contradiction of current Bankruptcy Code 11U.S.C. §1326(a)(1)(A) and 1 U.S.C. §503(b). As you are well aware, it is illegal to withhold wages from employees. The Tennessee Department of Labor & Commerce has told me that it has filed a complaint with the Tennessee Judiciary Board of Review over the fact that two judges, at the behest and insistence of Oldham, Seaver and Newhouse, and in spite of the bankruptcy laws that clearly stipulate that my money and property should have been returned to me, knowingly and intentionally entered a ruling to deprive me of my property and money, and my employees of their pay.

The Bankruptcy Code is explicit, 11U.S.C. §1326(a)(1)(A) and 1 U.S.C. §503(b), they were required to return to debtor, all remaining property and funds in the possession of the trustee. Yet they, along with attorney, Bonnie Jo Cockburn, who clearly violated T.C.A. § 23-3-10 when she made an appearance in federal court, willfully circumvented this Code to deprive me of my property and money without due process. Over and over, they have lied, misrepresented facts, and colluded to line their pockets, which is clearly against the Board's Rules of Professional Conduct.

I am now weeks without my necessary blood pressure medication and my blood pressure remains at stroke level. They have knowingly and intentionally put my life at risk as one of the major effects of untreated high blood pressure is kidney disease and all parties involved are well aware that I already suffer from kidney disease:

So that you are not blindsided, I now have liver disease in addition to my kidney disease that is not improving and is moving toward stage 4. When I get home, they will need additional blood work and tests and I have no idea what that will cost. But this is life-threatening and must be done.

This is all being documented, and they have all knowingly and willfully put my life at risk, after they threatened me for months that they were going to do this if I displeased them. That is how little regard these people have for others.

Because of this and the fact that they have shown no remorse for their actions, I beg the Board to hold all of them accountable for their cruelty and their multiple violations. Violations that Newhouse admitted to the Court under oath that should result in Rule 11 sanctions against them all. No one should be put through the horrors and degradations my family and I have suffered at their hands.

As it says in the Preamble of Rule 8:

[6] A lawyer's conduct should conform to the requirements of the law, both in professional service to clients and in the lawyer's business and personal affairs. A lawyer should use the law's procedures only for legitimate purposes and not to harass or intimidate others. A lawyer should demonstrate respect for the legal system and for those who serve it, including judges, other lawyers, and public officials. While it is a lawyer's duty, when necessary, to challenge the rectitude of official action, it is also a lawyer's duty to uphold legal process.

None of them have shown this and they have sought to deprive me of due process and my rights. In fact, Newhouse has shared other confidences I'd told Mr. Leadwits in private at both the January meeting with Seaver, and while he was under oath at my dismissal hearing, as did my husband's attorneys. Facts that only Mr. Leadwits knew that came back to me through not only them, but attorney Bob Harvest, and Mr. Harvest can testify to the fact that Mr. Leadwits violated attorney-client privilege then, too.

Mr. Leadwits cannot be trusted to serve his clients with candour and discretion. He has caused me and my family irreparable financial and emotional harm.

I think one of the worst indictments against him came after the January 16 meeting when I asked him, in front of a third-party witness, why he had allowed Ms. Seaver to see my diary given her vicious threats to retaliate against me, he said and I quote, "My loyalty is to the bankruptcy court and the trustees. I have to preserve my relationship with them." That very statement flies in the face of T.C.A. § 23-3-105 and from the Rule 8 Preamble:

[22] In reliance on the attorney-client privilege, clients are entitled to expect that communications within the scope of the privilege will be protected against compelled disclosure. The attorney-client privilege is that of the client and not of the lawyer. The fact that in exceptional situations the lawyer under the Rules has a limited discretion to disclose a client confidence does not vitiate the proposition that, as a general matter, the client has a reasonable expectation that information relating to the client will not be voluntarily disclosed.

If Mr. Leadwits truly believed that my diary was harmful as he, himself has asserted to the Board, then his fiduciary responsibility was to tell me such and to withhold it at all costs from Martha Seaver and Ms. Spicer. The fact that he baited me into harm cannot and should not allow him to be forgiven for his unconscionable actions, nor should it go unpunished. As he said, he valued his relationship with Seaver over that of his client and he proved it with his actions that have caused extreme financial and emotional harm to his client.

As one bankruptcy attorney told me after I consulted with her, "if my clients aren't better off after they come to me, then I've failed them."

Mr. Leadwits more than failed me. He has put me more than a million dollars more in debt and sold off a lifetime worth of assets I cannot replace, and my son and I are about to be homeless because of his unconscionable actions. Actions that continue to cause me financial harm and extreme duress. As such, I implore the Board to please do its duty and ensure that he doesn't harm another innocent client who makes the mistake of putting his or her faith in such an unscrupulous attorney who thinks so little of our lives, our families, our lifetimes of hard work and the laws that he's supposed to enforce and represent.

Thank you for your time.

Sincerely, Terri Manly

That was the letter I sent. Would it make a difference? I had no idea, but I had to try.

And in the name of fairness, let me put here the letter from Leadwits since I referenced it so many times in my own:

The complaint in this matter can be divided in three parts. The first one is the release of the "diary" that Ms. Manly wrote which she said violated the attorney-client privilege. I disagree with that assessment and statement of the facts. When I received the manuscript, I read it cover to cover and was terrified that if the contents were made known generally, it would subject her to liability and extensive litigation for libel.

Ms. Manly already had one claim for libel being asserted against her resulting from claims made by her former husband, Lester Manly (note that the domestic proceedings are still continuing in Williamson County Court). I was terrified that Ms. Manly was going to release the book, which would escalate matters out of proportion. I asked Misty Spicer, an attorney in my office, to read the book for a second opinion. She concurred in my assessment – this book should never be released.

On page 5 of the manuscript, the following legend was listed:

*NIGHTMARE IN WILLIAMSON COUNTY,* Copyright © 2019.

All rights reserved. Printed in the United States of America. No part of this book may be used or reproduced in any manner whatsoever without written permission except in the case of brief quotations embodied in critical articles or reviews.

This book is a work of fictions. Names, characters, businesses, organizations, places, events and incidents either are the product of the author's imagination or are used factiously. Any

Book and Cover design by Shutterstock
ISBN: 123456789
First Edition: January 2019

I was concerned from my initial read of the manuscript about the attorney-client privilege. Once the book was copyrighted and had a specific ISBN number. The International Standard Book Number (ISBN) is a numeric commercial book identifier which is intended to be unique. Publishers purchase ISBNs from the affiliate of the International ISBN Agency. Since Ms. Manly had both copyrighted the book and obtained an ISBN number, the book, in my opinion was property of the bankruptcy estate.

Property of the bankruptcy estate is defined by Section 541(a) of the Bankruptcy Code, which is stated as follows:

The commencements of a case under section 301, 302, or 303 of this title creates an estate. Such estate is comprised of all the following property, wherever located and by whomever held:

Except as provided in subsections (b) and (c)(2) of this section, all legal or equitable interests of the debtor in property as of the commencement of this case.

All interests of the debtor and the debtor's spouse in community property as of the commencement of the case that is—

Under the sole, equal, or joint management and control of the debtor; or

Liable for an allowable claim against the debtor, or for both an allowable claim against the debot and an allowable claim against the debtor's spouse, to the extent that such interest is so liable.

Any interest in property that the trustee recovers under section 329(b), 363(n), 543, 550, 553, 723 of this title.

Any interest in property preserved for the benefit of or ordered transferred to the estate under section 510(c) of this title.

Any interest in property that would have been property of the estate if such interest had been interest of the debtor on the date of the filing of the petition, and that the debtor acquires or becomes entitled to acquire within 180 days after such date—

By bequest, devise, or inheritance;

As a result of a property settlement agreement with the debtor's spouse, or or an interlocutory or final divorce decree; or

As a beneficiary of a life insurance policy or of a death benefit plan.

Proceeds, product, offspring, rents or profits of or from property of the estate, except such as are earning from services performed by an individual after the commencement of the case.

Any interest in property that the estate acquires after the commencement of the case.

Based on the above definition, had Thomas Newhouse, as the Chapter 11 Trustee, demanded the turnover of the book, I would have been obligated to do so based on my reading of the law. However, out of an abundance of precaution, I declined to release the book without the permission of Ms. Manly.

In order to protect Ms. Manly's interests, I asked for her permission to show the book to Martha Seaver, an attorney with the office of the United States Trustee. The United States Trustee Program is a component of the Department of Justice responsible for overseeing the administration of bankruptcy cases and private trustees. Attached is an email from Ms. Manly allowing me to show the book to Ms. Seaver, as well as the title page and the legend of the book.

I then forwarded a copy of the book to Ms. Seaver. After she read the book, a meeting was set up with Ms. Seaver, and Ms. Manly where everyone strongly encouraged that the book not be disseminated further. I have not and will not release the book other than what I have stated in this response. If third parties had read or heard snippets of the manuscript, they have not gotten it from me.

The second portion of the complaint deals with my assistance with the administration of the bankruptcy estate. Pre-bankruptcy, the divorce in Williamson County had appointed a receiver. Ms. Manly is a nationally recognized author with millions of books that have been purchased by her followers. The receivership had to be terminated. The order appointing a receiver was poorly drafted, and there was really no way that Ms. Manly's business being an author could thrive under the state court receivership order.

My strategy was simple. File a Chapter 11 for Ms. Manly; seek the appointment of a Chapter 11 Trustee who would liquidate all of the assets to pay Ms. Manly's creditors, and the balance would then be divvied up in the state court divorce proceedings. Unfortunately, the case did not go as expected.

Once a Chapter 11 Trustee is appointed, my role as counsel for the Debtor is a reorganization case becomes limited. My responsibilities are to assist Ms. Manly to comply with her duties as defined by Section 521 of the Bankruptcy Code, to wit:

(a)  The debtor shall—

(1)  file—

(A)  a list of creditors; and

(B)  unless the court orders otherwise—

(i)  a schedule of assets and liabilities

(ii)  a schedule of current income and current expenditures

(iii)  a statement of the debtor's financial affairs and, if section 342(b) applies, a certificate—of an attorney whose name is indicated on the petition as the attorney for the debtor, or a bankruptcy petition preparer signing the petition under section 110(b)(1), indicating that such attorney of the bankruptcy petition preparer delivered to the debtor the notice required by section 342(b); or if no attorney is so indicated, and no bankruptcy petition preparer signed the petition of the debtor that such notice was received and read by the debtor; copied of all payment advices or other evidence of payment received within 60 days before the date of filing of the petition, by the debtor from any employer of the debtor; a statement of monthly net income, itemized to show how the amount is calculated; and a statement disclosing any reasonably anticipated increase income or expenditures over the 12 month period following the date of the filing of the petition;

(2) If an individual debtor's schedule of assets and liabilities includes debts which are secured by property of the estate—

(A) within thirty days after the date of the filing of a petition under Chapter 7 of this title or on or before the date of the meeting of creditors, which is earlier, or within such additional time as the court, for cause, within such period fixes, file with the clerk a if applicable, specifying that such property is claimed as exempt, that the debtor intend to redeem such property, or that the debtor intends to reaffirm debts secured by such property; and

(B) within 30 days after the first date set for the meeting of creditors under section 341 (a), or within such additional time as the court, for cause, within such 30 day period fixes, perform his intention with respect to such property, as specified by subparagraph (a)of this paragraph; except that nothing in subparagraph (A) and (B) of this paragraph shall alter the debtor's or the trustee's rights with regard to such property under this title, except as provided in section 362(h);

(3) if a trustee is serving the case or an auditor is serving under section 586(f) of the title 28, cooperate with the trustee as necessary to enable the trustee to perform the trustee's duties under this title;

(4) if a trustee is serving the case or an auditor is serving under section 586(f) of title 28, surrender to the trustee all property of the estate and any recorded information, including books, documents, and papers, relating to property of the estate, whether or not immunity is granted under section 344 of this title;

(5) appear at the hearing require under section 524(d) of this title;

(6) in a case under chapter 7 of this title in which the debtor is an individual, not retain possession of personal property as to which a creditor has an allowed claim for the purchase price secured in whole or in part by an interest in such personal property unless the debtor, not later than 45 days after the first meeting of creditors under section 341(a), either—

(A) enters into an agreement with the creditor pursuant to section 524(c) with respect to the claim secured by such property; or

(B) redeems such property from the security interest pursuant to section 722; and

(7) unless a trustee is serving in the case, continue to perform the obligations required of the administrator (as defined in section 3 of the Employee Retirement Income Security Act of 1974) of an employee benefit plan if at the time of the commencement of the case the debtor (or any entity designated by the debtor) served as such administrator.

If the debtor fails to so act within the 45-day period referred to in paragraph (6), the stay under section 362(a) is terminated with respect to the personal property of the estate or of the debtor which is affected, such property shall no longer be property of the estate, and the creditor may take whatever action as to such property as is permitted by applicable nonbankruptcy law, unless the court determines on the motion of the trustee filed before the expiration of such 45-day period, and after notice and a hearing, that such property is of consequential value or benefit to the estate, orders appropriate adequate protection of the creditor's interest, and orders the debtor to deliver any collateral in the debtor's possession to the trustee.

(b) In addition to the requirements under subsection (a), a debtor who is an individual shall file with the court—

(1) a certificate from the approved nonprofit budget and credit counseling agency that provided the debtor services under section 109(h) describing the services provided to the debtor; and

(2) a copy of the debt repayment plan, if any, developed under section 109(h) through the approved nonprofit budget and credit counseling agency referred to in paragraph (1).

(c) In addition to meeting the requirements under subsection (a), a debtor shall file with the court a record of any interest that a debtor has in an education individual retirement account (as defined in section 530(b)(1) of the Internal Revenue Code of 1986), an interest in an account in a qualified ABLE program (as defined in section 529A(b) of such Code,[1] or under a qualified State tuition program (as defined in section 529(b)(1) of such Code).

(d) If the debtor fails timely to take the action specified in subsection (a)(6) of this section, or in paragraphs (1) and (2) of section 362(h), with respect to property which a lessor or bailor owns and has leased, rented, or bailed to the debtor or as to which a creditor holds a security interest not otherwise voidable under section 522(f), 544, 545, 547, 548, or 549, nothing in this title shall prevent or limit the operation of a provision in the underlying lease or agreement that has the effect of placing the debtor in default under such lease or agreement by reason of the occurrence, pendency, or existence of a proceeding under this title or the insolvency of the debtor. Nothing in this subsection shall be deemed to justify limiting such a provision in any other circumstance.

(e)(1) If the debtor in a case under chapter 7 or 13 is an individual and if a creditor files with the court at any time a request to receive a copy of the petition, schedules, and statement of financial affairs filed by the debtor, then the court shall make such petition, such schedules, and such statement available to such creditor.

(2)(A) The debtor shall provide—

(i) not later than 7 days before the date first set for the first meeting of creditors, to the trustee a copy of the Federal income tax return required under applicable law (or at the election of the debtor, a transcript of such return) for the most recent tax year ending immediately before the commencement of the case and for which a Federal income tax return was filed; and

(ii) at the same time the debtor complies with clause (i), a copy of such return (or if elected under clause (i), such transcript) to any creditor that timely requests such copy.

(B) If the debtor fails to comply with clause (i) or (ii) of subparagraph (A), the court shall dismiss the case unless the debtor demonstrates that the failure to so comply is due to circumstances beyond the control of the debtor.

(C) If a creditor requests a copy of such tax return or such transcript and if the debtor fails to provide a copy of such tax return or such transcript to such creditor at the time the debtor provides such tax return or such transcript to the trustee, then the court shall dismiss the case unless the debtor demonstrates that the failure to provide a copy of such tax return or such transcript is due to circumstances beyond the control of the debtor.

(3) If a creditor in a case under chapter 13 files with the court at any time a request to receive a copy of the plan filed by the debtor, then the court shall make available to such creditor a copy of the plan—

(A) at a reasonable cost; and

(B) not later than 7 days after such request is filed.

(f) the request of the court, the United States trustee, or any party in interest in a case under chapter 7, 11, or 13, a debtor who is an individual shall file with the court—

(1) at the same time filed with the taxing authority, a copy of each Federal income tax return required under applicable law (or at the election of the debtor, a transcript of such tax return) with respect to each tax year of the debtor ending while the case is pending under such chapter;

(2) at the same time filed with the taxing authority, each Federal income tax return required under applicable law (or at the election of the debtor, a transcript of such tax return) that had not been filed with such authority as of the date of the commencement of the case and that was subsequently filed for any tax year of the debtor ending in the 3-year period ending on the date of the commencement of the case;

(3) a copy of each amendment to any Federal income tax return or transcript filed with the court under paragraph (1) or (2); and

(4) in a case under chapter 13—

(A) on the date that is either 90 days after the end of such tax year or 1 year after the date of the commencement of the case, whichever is later, if a plan is not confirmed before such later date; and

(B) annually after the plan is confirmed and until the case is closed, not later than the date that is 45 days before the anniversary of the confirmation of the plan;

a statement, under penalty of perjury, of the income and expenditures of the debtor during the tax year of the debtor most recently concluded before such statement is filed under this paragraph, and of the monthly income of the debtor, that shows how income, expenditures, and monthly income are calculated.

(g)(1) A statement referred to in subsection (f)(4) shall disclose—

(A) the amount and sources of the income of the debtor;

(B) the identity of any person responsible with the debtor for the support of any dependent of the debtor; and

(C) the identity of any person who contributed, and the amount contributed, to the household in which the debtor resides.

(2) The tax returns, amendments, and statement of income and expenditures described in subsections (e)(2)(A) and (f) shall be available to the United States trustee (or the bankruptcy administrator, if any), the trustee, and any party in interest for inspection and copying, subject to the requirements of section 315(c) of the Bankruptcy Abuse Prevention and Consumer Protection Act of 2005.

(h) If requested by the United States trustee or by the trustee, the debtor shall provide—

(1) a document that establishes the identity of the debtor, including a driver's license, passport, or other document that contains a photograph of the debtor; or

(2) such other personal identifying information relating to the debtor that establishes the identity of the debtor.

(i)(1) Subject to paragraphs (2) and (4) and notwithstanding section 707(a), if an individual debtor in a voluntary case under chapter 7 or 13 fails to file all of the information required under subsection (a)(1) within 45 days after the date of the filing of the petition, the case shall be automatically dismissed effective on the 46th day after the date of the filing of the petition.

(2) Subject to paragraph (4) and with respect to a case described in paragraph (1), any party in interest may request the court to enter an order dismissing the case. If requested, the court shall enter an order of dismissal not later than 7 days after such request.

(3) Subject to paragraph (4) and upon request of the debtor made within 45 days after the date of the filing of the petition described in paragraph (1), the court may allow the debtor an additional period of not to exceed 45 days to file the information required under subsection (a)(1) if the court finds justification for extending the period for the filing.

(4) Notwithstanding any other provision of this subsection, on the motion of the trustee filed before the expiration of the applicable period of time specified in paragraph (1), (2), or (3), and after notice and a hearing, the court may decline to dismiss the case if the court finds that the debtor attempted in good faith to file all the information required by subsection (a)(1)(B)(iv) and that the best interests of creditors would be served by administration of the case.

(j)(1) Notwithstanding any other provision of this title, if the debtor fails to file a tax return that becomes due after the commencement of the case or to properly obtain an extension of the due date for filing such return, the taxing authority may request that the court enter an order converting or dismissing the case.

(2) If the debtor does not file the required return or obtain the extension referred to in paragraph (1) within 90 days after a request is filed by the taxing authority under that paragraph, the court shall convert or dismiss the case, whichever is in the best interests of creditors and the estate.

Under the devised strategy, an application of a Chapter 11 Trustee was filed and shortly after the case commenced. Thomas Newhouse was appointed Trustee, and my office and staff worked with Ms. Manly and the Trustee to comply with section 521 requirements/Mr. Newhouse reviewed the schedules and was working with Ms. Manly.

The first hiccup in the case was that the Trustee did not understand or wanted to follow the business model that Ms. Manly had laid out. A writer, in order to be as successful as Terri, has to network with her audience. There are many venues which required her personal appearances and contact and the Trustee did not grasp the necessity of that.

The second hiccup was a hearing in the state divorce proceeding which resulted in order that all of Lester Manly's legal fees were in the nature of alimony, without any oversight. I could not believe that ruling and expressed my frustration, especially that it was never appealed by Ms. Manly's divorce counsel nor the Trustee. Alimony is a top tier creditor in the order of priority in a bankruptcy proceedings. Lester Manly's attorneys were granted by that ruling a blank check to plunder the assets in the bankruptcy to detriment of Ms. Manly's creditors.

And Lester Manly's attorneys were able to obtain for their services staggering legal fees. The bankruptcy estate was hemorrhaging its assets at an amazing page. The Trustee was concerned that the bankruptcy estate was becoming administratively insolvent.

If the bankruptcy estate became insolvent, then the only recourse would be for the Chapter 11 Trustee to convert the case to a Chapter 7 proceedings. Such an event would have been devastating for Ms. Manly. A Chapter 7 bankruptcy, by definition, is a liquidation bankruptcy. All of her assets would be liquidated, including her intellectual property. Mrs. Manly has spent a career protecting her brand, including the characters that she has developed. If a malevolent third party obtained rights to this information, including the internal bible of the characters, havoc would be on Terri's brand, including theatrical rights.

Ms. Manly then terminated me as counsel, and I forthwith filed a motion to withdraw. In early April 2020, the Trustee filed an expedited motion to dismiss or convert the case. A hearing was conducted April 7, 2020 and the case was dismissed under a structured dismissal. I casually spoke to the Trustee on unrelated matters, and he mentioned that he could have converted the case to a Chapter 7 proceedings but was doing Terri a favor. By dismissal, she could take advantage of relief afforded under the Cares Act while at the same time preserving the remaining assets to be administered by a state court receiver. In essence, the Trustee did what I, as counsel for Ms. Manly, was unable to do.

I wish Ms. Manly the best of luck in her endeavors. I, for one, do believe that something was done by Lester Manly to her personally (this is the action that the libel claim has been asserted). I also regret that she believed that I had released any part of her manuscript without her permission. While I would never have done that, she never asked me if I did. Throughout my involvement in this case, I have only had her best interest at heart. I hope after reading this response that she realizes that I did nothing unethical or in any way violated the Canon of Ethics and Professional Responsibility.

Was it any wonder that his words induced anger in my heart? All the lies and omissions. Such as the fact that when he'd lied to the Board to get their permission to withdraw as my counsel without my knowledge or permission that he'd had a hearing on that within seventy-two hours and had used it to blackmail me and force me to spend money I didn't have to spend.

But then when I'd told him that I no longer wanted him to represent me, to get the fuck out of my life, it'd taken him a month to withdraw.

Seriously.

And I particularly loved how he threw my attorney under the bus by saying she didn't appeal the decision. Why?

She really couldn't. One thing, it hadn't been a ruling. That had been an agreement that Newhouse had made, himself, between the lawyers so that Newhouse would get paid. Hubby's bankruptcy attorney had been there for that meeting.

Leadwits should have gotten off his lazy ass and been there since it was part of my case that he was in charge of, and he knew the trustee was new and needed guidance.

Secondly, the way appeals worked in Tennessee, the attorney had to go before the judge who made the ruling in order to appeal the ruling. So basically, you had to ask the judge if he would change his or her mind and admit they made a mistake.

*Well, it doesn't take a rocket scientist to figure out how often that works.*

As my attorney so often said whenever I asked her for an interlocutory appeal, "Hon, it's just a waste of time and money. Dinky hates you and he's not going to do it."

Given that Leadwits was a personal friend of the judge, he knew that, too, so he was throwing that in there and knew it for a lie as we'd discussed that in the meeting and he'd agreed that Dinky would never, ever reverse his own decisions and that we'd just waste money trying to do it.

Wow.

And my favorite part had to be where he lied to Dullard about ole Newhouse's benevolence. "He could have converted it, but out of the goodness of his heart, yada yada yada." How I wish you could have been in that hearing to listen in on the way those bastards had torn into me. They'd been like hungry lions in the den with Christians, tearing at me, begging the judge to convert. I was stunned that she hadn't.

And then Leadwits was stupid enough to say that "preserving the remaining assets to be administered by a state court receiver" right after he'd written "The order appointing a receiver was poorly drafted, and there was really no way that Ms. Manly's business being an author could thrive under the state court receivership order."

Dude, I realized that you were old, but damn. You really did need to retire if you were so senile that you couldn't catch that fallacy of logic while proof-reading. Obviously, no one was doing me any favors.

You were all colluding to screw me over.

It also proved the lie that he'd ended with. He'd never had my best interests at heart. As I'd said repeatedly, he told whatever lie needed to try and make himself look good.

Clients be damned.

That was the fair wind he tried to sail under.

And I was tired of being held down by these self-serving assholes who had no business preying on everyone around them. Nashville was eaten up with these people. As I'd told Ms. Dullard, this was a systemic problem in this town.

It was a hell of a day. One finished off when the Tennessee Department of Labor called me. Have to say the lady was very kind who spoke to me.

Well, not at first. At first, she'd called to get me into trouble for not paying my employees.

But once I explained to her that my money had been seized by Lord Skeletor and that I hadn't been given any of the money I'd earned since the first of the month and that this lovely email had come in that very morning from my attorney:

> I called a bit ago and they still do not have the order from Judge Dinky. I will call his assistant again and see if she can push him to get it done.

The woman was appalled. And well she should be. The judge, himself, was putting my life at risk. He was withholding pay from my employees in defiance of the law during a time of crisis and no one would hold him accountable. While she said there was nothing she could do, she promised me that she'd make a few calls and see if someone in her department might know someone who could help us.

All I could do was pray.

And hope.

I had no idea why God and fate was doing this to me. My friend had a theory. "Maybe you're their Karma. Because you're strong enough to survive them. Maybe you were put in their path to stop them from doing this to others."

But I was getting tired. I'd been fighting tyrants and assholes my whole life. Even the mightiest oak could be brought down in a hurricane. And this storm kept battering me with no sign of letup.

I just wanted one single day of peace. One hour without some kind of trauma.

It'd been so long since I last saw daylight that I could no longer remember what it felt like to walk with those rays on my cheeks. To smell the scent of a calm sea.

All I heard these days was the sound of a typhoon rushing in my ears. My sons' weariness whenever they spoke. I kept trying to reassure them. To promise them the very things that I no longer really believed myself.

That brighter days were ahead. That the storm would break soon, and we'd be okay.

Because the truth was, I didn't know. I'd lost my horizon. My north star was covered by a cloud so dark that no light could penetrate it. Everywhere I turned, there was another demon intent on dragging me down and laughing while I suffered.

Whenever I reached out for a hand, I was slapped down so hard that I was scared to even try.

And as I sent out more letters that day to more organizations that I knew would ignore me or give me an excuse as to why they couldn't help me, I knew I had no choice.

It was fight or die.

Losing was a given, I figured.

But I wasn't going out without a fight. To my last breath and with everything I had. Kick. Scream. Bite. Whatever it took.

No, Skeletor, I hadn't learned my lesson and I never would. I would not be oppressed. Not by some maggot like you. I would not kowtow to a bastard who bought and sold women for his sick, perverted pleasure, and who mocked the laws my honorable father had fought to preserve.

*Fuck you, you shit stain on humanity.*

I would not dishonor those in uniform who had put their lives on the line for their beliefs. *We are here and we matter. Every life. We are important.*

*Maggots like you who think you're superior, you are the ones who should be scraping roadkill from the streets. And I will not let you break me.*

Not today.

Not tomorrow.

Never.

*I am not a survivor.*

*I am a warrior.*

Battle-tested. Strong and determined. I was going to stay this course and see this through. Not for me, but for my sons.

For my characters.

For my fans.

I was all they had, and I owed them everything.

This was the Splatterdome.

And I was determined to win.

No motherfucker like you was going to defeat me. And no piece of shit like Les would steal from my children. Not on my watch.

Over, under, around or through.

I was going to be here, and I was going to stand my ground.

The blood of conquerors ran in my veins. The blood of Vikings and Native American warriors. I could hear their battle-cries in my ears, ringing down through the centuries.

*Bring it, you bitches.* Give me your worst and I will deliver unto you my best and show you the pride of my father and mother. Those who taught me to act with honor, decency and nobility. Not to be the lying sacks of shit who would sell out anyone in the name of greed. You were all the worst of humanity, and you would be seen for who and what you really were.

All of you. I was here to make sure of it.

Sully my name. But nothing in the dark could be hidden for long. I intended to drag you into the light and let the world see all of you for who and what you really were.

And I prayed to God for the world to show you the same lack of mercy that you'd shown my children.

WHERE DO I EVEN BEGIN with this day? I had no idea. Honestly, I felt like I was living in a war zone. Like bombs kept falling on top of me, every day. There was no place to take shelter and no end in sight. I was absolutely dizzy from it.

Every night, I dreaded going to sleep because I knew come morning, it would only begin again.

And I didn't know from which direction the bombing would start.

This one...

Yeah. To begin with, Baby Huey was still refusing to hand over his expenses. Which meant that he was wasting my money and wasn't where he was supposed to be.

No brainer there. He'd been on vacation for two years and buying such necessary things as a horse in Georgia. Hair salon treatments for his girlfriends, and mani-pedis. Along with visiting women in other cities.

He was having the time of his life while they were forcing me to pay for his attorneys to torture me and my sons.

But something interesting happened today.

Today, because I'd reported the realtor for his underhanded dealings with old Cockburn and crew, he responded to my report to the Real Estate Commission.

*And guess what cat he let out of the bag?*

Oh, you'll never guess how in cahoots they all were or how deep their little racket ran. Because while I knew these little incestuous assholes were tied together, even I was shocked by this one:

> Dick, please see the attached emergency motion we have filed regarding the offer on the house. We really would need you to be on the call for this hearing and I would be able to let you know when that would be set. We have high hopes that we could at least have a phone call with the judge's office today. Is this a possibility for you?
>
> Also I have copied my co-counsel who will be handling the motion on this so that you can communicate directly with him. His name is John Alaimo. It is imperative that the perspective buyers not be told that John is involved in this case whatsoever as the potential buyer was involved as a defendant in one of John's prior cases.

*How do I even begin to unpack this one?* Aside from the fact that Cockburn was barely literate, and that I was barred from that hearing, literally, they'd blocked my emails account and prohibited me from attending the meeting where they threw me out of my house.

How illegal was that action?

But here they were conspiring behind my back even more with ex parte communications. Well, I looked up that case and sure enough, they'd fucked over my buyer just as they had me.

In his divorce, that had been going on right as Les had started mine.

What were the odds?

My first thought was, dude, why would you *ever* get remarried?

God knew I would never, ever make this mistake again. Not in a million years and not in this fucked up, hellhole of a town.

But who was I to judge?

And yeah, they had royally screwed him. He'd been denied his rights and wrongfully accused of raping his wife. They had torn his life apart.

No criminal charges had been filed, but they had gone out to the papers, even though he was a prominent businessman and made his humiliation public. This at the same exact time they were appearing in court and claiming I was damaging Mr. "I can't work because she hurt my reputation."

*Are you kidding me?*

Barry Hunt had just purchased my home. Obviously, his business and his reputation hadn't been harmed at all and they had viciously accused him of rape.

Talk about a "deplorable" accusation.

Yet they hadn't arrested his wife and put her in jail for ten days over making such an "outrageous" accusation. And she didn't have the additional witnesses that I had.

Oh, and it got even better. She'd told her ex-hubby that she was going to make that allegation if he refused to pay her off.

And the best part? They'd denied Barry discovery so that he could prove his innocence.

Granted it wasn't Skeletor in his case.

Guess who it was!

Skeletor's ole business buddy and the daddy of Cisco's attorney: Robert E. Lee, Senior.

*Swear to God on a stack of bibles.*

It always came back to that same corrupt law firm where they'd all worked together, and that same piece of shit unaccredited law school. What were the odds that the man buying my home would be someone who'd had the misfortune of running up against these bastards?

Well, given how much they seemed to run this town? I was beginning to think pretty good.

Because they seemed to have their fingers in everyone's pie, and what sickened me most was that Alaimo flaunted his SAR (Sons of the American Revolution) membership as a badge of honor.

You, piece of shit, spat on their sacrifice and graves every time you opened your mouth. You were an abomination for every drop of blood they'd shed and every ideal they'd had. This was not what our patriots had in mind when they'd set out to create America.

You were the tyrant they'd fought against.

They would be ashamed of you and being a member of the Daughters of the American Revolution, I can honestly say that you, Alaimo, needed to be stripped of your membership, and tarred and feathered.

When my great-great-great-great-grand uncle had ridden the Mecklenburg Constitution that had been written in his father's tavern to the Continental Congress and risked his life and my family for it, it was to stand up against people like you.

You were the worst sort of embarrassment to everything our organizations and those patriots had stood for, and it disgusted me to think that your name was on the same rolls as that of my sons.

The fact that you would deny due process to someone. To anyone...

You were a disgrace to humanity. Shame on you!

And he held a political office. It just got better and better.

How many more of us were there that you'd shit all over and denied inalienable rights to? I now knew of a doctor, and two lawyers they'd persecuted (one of those lawyers had been disbarred). The wife of a country music singer. Now a prominent businessman.

And me.

They'd run another prominent businesswoman out of the state and an Army veteran out of the country.

Wow.

Just wow.

And the governor seemed to be okay with this. Didn't mind that Tennessee kept losing tax dollars and citizens because of their corrupt behavior.

He'd gotten back to me and said there was nothing he could or would do. Thank you, Governor Lee.

It was obvious you didn't care about anyone or any kind of political corruption. You didn't even care that a young mother, my employee, wasn't being paid in violation of federal law while she lived in your state, and we were under COVID restrictions.

You couldn't be bothered.

So, I told her to go file unemployment. Maybe then, she might get something.

Not a single politician cared that they were violating any of the laws, federal or state.

It seemed they were fine with the fact that I wasn't being paid. My employees weren't being paid.

No money had come to me since April 1.

But Les was getting his, and his attorneys were being paid to torment me and my children.

Wow.

And we were being forcibly kicked out of our home while the government had told the banks that they couldn't kick people out of their residences.

Welcome to Tennessee where the laws of the U.S. and human decency never applied.

Never, ever move here.

Personally, I wouldn't even visit. Given Governor Lee's apathy, I would say that this state didn't need anyone's money. They had plenty.

S TILL NO MONEY. THEY WERE trying to starve me out and it was obvious. How this was legal was anyone's guess. Actually, we all knew it wasn't. The last word from Melissa was that the state had run out of money (guess ole Governor Lee should have cared a little more that the judges in his richest county were fucking over his businesspeople) and that they'd have to wait to process my money today.

But honestly, none of what she said made any sense to me. How could the state be out of "my" money it was holding and be unable to turn my money over to me? Had it given my money to someone else?

That was a whole other problem, wasn't it? I certainly hadn't loaned my money to the fucking state for them to give it to other people. They should have had all my money in their account and should have had it readily available for me when I needed it.

I had a major problem with this.

Even better? The bastards weren't planning to have a hearing on releasing my money until May 21 (keeping in mind that I had to be completely out of my house by June 1) so that I could pay my employees and bills. However, they could haul me into court in a matter of hours to take my money away from me and force me out of my house at the whims of a bitch who used to work in the judge's law firm, but were planning to make me go two months without my money?

Money, I had fucking earned?

*Are you fucking kidding me?*

And, yes that apparently was legal. Because I'd been dragged into a divorce I hadn't been consulted on or wanted. Or forewarned about.

Divorce, according to my attorney, deprived citizens of their natural and constitutional rights. It had a separate set of laws that the rest of us didn't know existed.

Laws that weren't posted or talked about until you were sucked into their vortex.

Normally, courts couldn't deprive you of your inalienable rights.

Unless you were stupid enough to get married.

Why had no one ever told us this?

Well, I was telling you now.

This was utter bullshit. I hadn't surrendered my constitutional rights at the door. No one had told me when, at twenty-four, I put my name on a marriage certificate that I was allowing the government to do illegal searches and seizures of my home. That I would be allowing Uncle Sam to take my pay for no reason and put me under home arrest and turn me into a slave for a piece of shit who refused to work and who'd stolen my children's futures.

This was utter insanity.

Where the fuck had been my disclaimer for that marriage license? We were required by law to have disclaimers for everything else.

My God, every single county marriage office in the land should be required to have a massive divorce disclaimer at the door to inform every couple coming in for a marriage license of the rights that they'd be giving up in a divorce, especially given the divorce rate in this country.

Before you married, every couple should be required to attend a divorce class. Seriously.

For your own good. Everyone should be made aware of their rights and what they would lose.

The law required we have a fishing license, and we were required to pass a test in order to drive.

This should be required for marriage. No one should be allowed to walk into this blindly.

Not when you could lose so much of your life. This wasn't right.

Damn you, America, for doing this to your citizens, in the name of Greed.

I knew Les had said he'd wanted a Squaw when he found out from my uncle, Carlos, that we had Native American blood in us, but I was sick of it, and my ancestral blood was boiling at the prospect of what had been done to us. I could hear my great-great-great aunt who'd been forced from her home and business during the Trail of Tears screaming in my ears, cursing those who'd stolen her life from her without any due process and for no reason, other than greed (she had cursed an entire town in Alabama into obscurity over it). All my family members who'd had the government seize their farms and force them west with no just compensation.

And it was happening again.

I was being displaced and forced to leave, while the government stole my money, my home and took my earnings from me for a lazy man who refused to work.

And this was 2020.

What kind of screwed up ancestral Karma was this? They were feeding him like a king off my back and taking my money to feed who knew whom else.

While leaving me and my children to starve.

And this was legal.

In the middle of COVID. And they weren't planning to have a hearing on this for three more weeks.

Three more weeks.

Provided the judge was prepared for it and felt up to it.

Think I was kidding? This was the actual email I was sent from the judge's assistant:

> Judge Dinky requested income and expense statements from both parties and has not yet received Husband's income and expense statement.
>
> Once Judge Dinky receives all of the necessary information, including but not limited to, the income and expense statements; all exhibits and other information from any witnesses who may be testifying, including accountants; he will review all of the information; then, will determine when to conduct a Zoom video conference.
>
> Once a Zoom video conference is scheduled, all information necessary must be forwarded to Judge Dinky at least four (4) days in advance of the scheduled Zoom video conference for Judge Dinky's review and consideration. Judge Dinky simply will not have sufficient time to review

**any information filed at the last minute, even the day before the Zoom video conference, to properly prepare for the scheduled hearing.**

**Hoping each of you and your families are well and safe.**
**Take care.**

I particularly loved that last little bit. Keeping in mind that Skeletor and crew were well aware of the fact that I had no money at all as they were in possession of every single penny of my money while they dragged their asses. And that this was sent after a full year and a half of Skeletor screaming at me every two weeks for not handing over inconsequential, bullshit information such as how many books I had published that Les already knew (because it was public information) and had at my office they had awarded him and on the computer Les had stolen out of my house and taken with him that Skeletor had held me in contempt for not handing over because Les already had the records and I couldn't hand over what was in his possession.

Yeah. Skeletor had put me through more than a year and a half of listening to him apologize to Les for the fact that I hadn't handed in paperwork Les already had. Listening to him berate, insult and belittle me over the fact that I hadn't handed in paperwork Les had and was demanding I give him that I couldn't because I had no way to get it as I had a court order preventing me from accessing my office Skeletor had given Les, yet now Skeletor was giving them a free pass on allowing Les and crew to starve me and my children.

Better still, Skeletor had screamed at me for two recorded hours and threatened to put me in jail, in front of my sons, for paperwork Les already had.

Yet not a word was being said over the fact that Les was committing contempt because Skeletor had told them to have that paperwork in more than two weeks before that email had been sent.

Skeletor knew they were committing contempt and not a single insult or threat.

Yet I had a two-hour session of being screamed at and threatened over it, for paperwork Les already had.

How was *that* for sexual discrimination?

And here Dinky had said that I needed to be taught a lesson (also on tape).

But what could anyone expect from a family of pedophiles and a judge who gave that family a free pass to walk among society?

My God, these people were sick in the head.

And no one would call them out.

Every last one of them. Because they all knew it. Including the secretary who wrote that letter. I could have never served such a sick, pathetic bastard. I had walked out of jobs in the past because my boss was too disgusting to work for.

True statement.

I refused to be around people that toxic.

The entire time of my marriage, I had forbidden Les to have his parents around my children and had done my best to stay away from them. I had never spoken to my in-laws on the phone. Wouldn't visit their home. My children could easily verify this. I had been coldly, grudgingly polite on the handful of occasions I'd been forced to endure their presence.

Had I known of the demon that lived inside Les, I would have kicked him out and made sure that he had been banned from my children years ago.

It sickened me that I hadn't seen the devil inside him. The fact that his Hogg had unleashed a monster that I had been ignorant of. How had I not seen it? That was what bothered me the most. I'd always thought that I was a better judge of character than that. Yet he'd sucked me right in.

I hated myself for being so stupid. For allowing him to deceive me so.

And at times I hated God for not giving me a way out of this nightmare. No matter what I tried, I couldn't get away. Les would take no settlement. I had no access to my money.

I was supposed to be moving in four weeks and yet I had nothing with which to move.

No credit cards. No money.

How did they expect me to close on a house when I had no funds, and they weren't allowing me any access to them?

The moving company told me they needed two weeks.

Last time Skeletor had done this, it'd taken the receiver three weeks to get us groceries. Hell, it'd been almost four weeks now, after they'd threatened to leave me with no money for food, groceries or medicine.

And I was supposed to have all my belongings out of an eight thousand square foot home, along with my sons and pets in four weeks.

By myself.

Yeah.

How could this be modern day America? How could we, as a nation, allow this to happen to a citizen? How could there really be absolutely no organization or government group out there to not help someone caught in this kind of torture and abuse?

No one listened and no one gave a shit.

I was being abused every single day, in front of the entire world. With millions of people watching it happen.

Everyone saw it.

No one stopped it.

This was my nightmare.

And it was public.

*What the absolute fuck?*

W HERE TO EVEN START? Funny how many days had begun that way since Dipshit had stolen our kids' trust funds and left without warning. How many times a week, I'd asked myself how this had become my life. How one human being could become so screwed in the head that he'd go off and wreck his entire family for absolutely no reason.

I guess it all went back to that one text that Hogg had sent:

> *When the divorce is over and Terri loses her shit...*

They were blatantly trying to drive me crazy, and the idiot judge was all too willing to help.

The fact that the Tennessee Board of Professional Responsibility, in spite of having rules that forbade attorneys from that very behavior, signed off on it...

More sickening.

But on this day, I met the other poor soul that Alaimo had tortured for profit for two years. He was incredibly sweet. Everything I'd stupidly thought I'd married. Doting on his new wife and her kids from a previous marriage. Even her parents while they toured around the house and took measurements

They were so nice, and I wished them well. I really did hope that the house was kinder to them than it'd been to us.

Most of all, I prayed that Commissioner Alaimo and his group of vipers got exactly what they deserved for preying on people like us.

The entire time they were here, all I kept hearing in my head were the words that had been printed in the paper from Alaimo's own client:

> What she thought would take a month dragged out for two and a half years. She and her ex-
> husband's case was finally dismissed earlier this month with an agreed order.
>
> "I felt like I was being held hostage." As the case wore on, she would hesitate to call her attor-
> ney, "because it was costing me money."

If that wasn't an indictment against Alaimo and his firm, as well as the judges in this town who not only allowed their travesties to go unanswered, but participated in them, I didn't know what was.

Even their own clients hated them. All anyone had to do was look at the reviews for their firm and it indicted them. Yet the state refused to protect its citizens. It was open season on the people of Williamson County.

*Third most corrupt state in the Union. One of the most corrupt cities in the nation.*

Yes, it was. And they were so proud of it. No one could deny it.

We even had our county commissioners boldly participating in scams and immoral behavior.

If that wasn't the icing on the cake, an old friend called. Another professional, here in town.

Bet you'd never guess what she had to say.

Her husband had tried to poison her, too.

My jaw hit the floor. Apparently, when I'd gone to the lab to get my blood tested and the tech had made the comment that it happened more than anyone thought, she hadn't been kidding. Nashville seemed to be the place to go if you wanted to off your spouse and not get into trouble for it.

She, too, had been threatened. So much so, that she couldn't even get an attorney for a divorce. There had been no way out for her, either.

"If you're a successful woman in this county, it's open season on you. They hate you." She'd been terrified of having a divorce case heard here.

A direct quote from her lips.

How pathetic was that?

But because this was where her business was located, she didn't have the ability to just pick up and leave. She'd spent a lifetime building her connections and she was too old to start new somewhere else without a client base.

My heart broke for her.

"I knew something was up with Les."

"What do you mean?"

"The last time I saw you. He said that I was low class and that you didn't need me hanging around."

*Are you fucking kidding me?*

My jaw hit the floor. Especially given the low-rent attorney he'd hired. She looked like she should be walking the red-light district.

Never mind the Hogg he kept galivanting around town with. What I found hilarious was the way he used to mock Kiki for her weight and her clothing choices. "She looks like she shops at Walmart. It doesn't reflect well on you, Terri. You need someone of a higher caliber to be your assistant."

Yet now, he was flaunting his Hogg whose clothes looked like they'd been pulled out of a hobo's cart and smelled like a real hog had rolled around in shit for three days.

So, his change in attitude was baffling. All the years he'd mocked me for my weight...

Had talked about his own mother's "fat ass."

It didn't make sense.

While I couldn't care less what someone weighed, he was the one who'd always said that "you can't trust anyone whose ass is wider than their shoulders."

It made me wonder if Hogg wasn't poisoning him, too. Something was wrong. People didn't change like that, did they?

Not that I cared what was going on inside his lizard brain. That was now someone else's problem.

"I'm sorry I didn't tell you, Terri. I didn't want to criticize your husband or make you mad."

That seemed to be the consensus of all my friends and my sons. Yet if they had spoken up, I would have seen the pattern in time to stop this.

"Don't feel bad," Joan had reassured her. "He did that to all of us. Made us feel like it was Terri pushing us to the side."

Like the master manipulator he'd turned out to be, he'd run off all my friends.

Right around the same time.

Right before I'd begun to get sick...

Bastard! How anyone could do that to another person was beyond me. How he could sit there, day after day, and watch me suffer.

But then, that was what he was doing with the divorce. He had no intention of ending it. He only wanted to torture me and watch me suffer.

And for what? Because I'd loved him? Had given him children and everything he'd ever wanted?

They all knew his behavior was wrong and it killed me that they weren't being held accountable for it.

Just like his mother who should have been held accountable for all the children she'd brought around his father to be molested, knowing who and what he was.

Like his grandmother who'd brought children around his grandfather. How could these people find so many willing to help them?

I didn't understand it, any more than I could understand why no one would help me do the right thing and stop them.

**The only thing necessary for the triumph of evil is for good men to do nothing.**

Edmund Burke had hit that on the head. Evil was running rampant. All I wanted was out. My boys and I were tired of being held hostage. Of being tormented.

I dreaded tomorrow. The new lies. The new torment.

Why couldn't God throw me at least one lifeline?

**H**OISTED BY HIS OWN PETARD. There was a phrase that just wasn't used enough in modern society. But in this case... Well, I'd like for it to be even more apropos.

I had almost made it through the day without Les's bullshit.

Almost.

I should have known better. After all, I never made it through a day without some sort of nuclear level bullshit from the jackals. They couldn't let me have any peace.

This day was no different.

Today's drama came in the form of Cockburn's hissy over the fact that Les hadn't been paid his almost eight-thousand-dollar check for spousal support (remember that she got paid separately).

*Well, no shit, stupid whore.*

*Guess you should have thought of that when you were sucking off the judge and lying your ass off to him and getting all my money taken away from me. That's what happens when you burn out all your brain cells from oxygen dep from blow jobs.*

Really, she should take a breather and come up for air once in a while and save the last three brain cells she had.

At any rate, it took her five days into the month to realize that since all my money had been confiscated and that she hadn't set the next hearing until the twenty-first that there was no one to pay her idiot client.

She wanted me to sign off on getting him paid.

Really, had she lost her last three brain cells?

"Tell her to go fuck herself." That was my exact quote to my attorney. "And remind her that she's kicking me out of my home, along with my son and I need money to hire movers. I'm supposed to be out of here in twenty-five days. I have to have the movers on the schedule, or I won't be able to leave."

"She'll want to know where you're moving to."

"Fuck her." I couldn't believe Melissa would ask that. "Remember her husband issued a terroristic threat against me. Cockburn doesn't need to know shit about where I'm going and neither does Les. He tried to kill me and has issued threats against my aunt and my sons. They can all fuck themselves until they walk bow-legged."

"What do you want me to tell them?"

"What I just said."

I really wasn't kidding. I had no problem with a verbatim quote. "I've sent you all the information. Hand it over to them."

"What about the two-thousand-dollar fuel charge?"

"What about it?"

"They'll want to know what that is."

"Then ask the movers. I have no idea." Why did Melissa play five hundred questions with me over every little thing, but she was okay with their stupidity.

Such as Les finally handing in his expenses once he realized that he needed to have them in order to get paid.

*Want to see them?*

*Here you go:*

| MONTHLY INCOME: | | |
|---|---|---|
| 1. Williams-Sonc | | $615.71 |
| Deductions: Fed | | -$2.54 |
| FICA | | -$38.18 |
| Medicare | | -$8.93 |
| 2. Family Support | | $7,382.00 |
| **TOTAL NET MONTHLY INCOME** | | **$7,948.06** |
| MONTHLY EXPENSES AND PAYMENTS: | | |
| A. General Expenses | | |
| 1 Residence - Maintenance/landscaping/furnishings | | $4,493.02 |
| 2 Utilities | | $476.66 |
| 3 Auto/Gas | | $246.18 |
| 4 Insurance | | $945.86 |
| **TOTAL "A"** | | **$6,161.72** |
| B. Personal Expenses | **Myself** | |
| 1. Groceries | $483.46 | |
| 2 Dinning out | $474.82 | |
| 3 Household Supplies - Amazon | $426.11 | |
| 4 Household Supplies | $48.38 | |
| Real Estate Taxes | $203.00 | |
| 5 Medical/Dental | $1,075.91 | |
| 6 Personal care | $1,114.41 | |
| 7 Entertainment/Electronics | $395.54 | |
| 8 Phone | $61.93 | |
| 9 Paypal | $65.79 | |
| 10 Business Expenses | $33.42 | |
| 11 Travel | $308.20 | |
| 12 Taxes | $36.36 | |
| 13 Veterinarian/Pet Expenses | $61.01 | |
| 14 Attorney Fees | | |
| 16 Miscellaneous Expenses | $479.18 | |
| **TOTAL "B"** | **$5,731.09** | **$5,731.09** |
| C. Installment Payments on Debts: | | |
| **TOTAL OF A, B** | | **$11,892.81** |
| **TOTAL MONTHLY INCOME MINUS MONTHLY EXPENSES** | | **-$4,907.74** |

Now read that first item and take a second. "Family support." Seriously? He had no kid willing to talk to him. At all. That is just for one idiot man, too worthless to work.

The landscaping fee and remember that I was forced to sell the home my sons and I lived in because the landscaping fees were almost half of what he was claiming he needed for my office.

Half.

And his idiot attorneys had argued to the judge that it was "outrageous" for me to pay that a month in landscaping.

Yet now they were claiming he needed more than that a month himself?

*Are you fucking kidding me?*

Now, it was okay to charge even more? Just so long as Les was the one who was living there. And for a yard that was a pittance of the size. Want to see?

It was a tiny postage stamp of a yard. But wait, it got even better. I had even more proof that he was lying. God love the meticulous bastard. He'd left evidence at my home that he was lying.

*Want to see?*

Cabin Thompson Station Rd

IN ACCOUNT WITH
Chuck Fly
2156 Lee Rd
SH, TN 37174

| Month | | | Amount |
| --- | --- | --- | --- |
| April | 8, 15, 29 | | 140 00 |
| May | 8, 15, 23, 29 | | 220 00 |
| June | 3, 10, 17, 26 | | 220 00 |
| July | 1, 10, 17, 24, 31 | | 275 00 |
| Aug. | 6, 13, 21, 28 | | 220 00 |
| Sept | 4, 11, 18 mth, 25 mth | | 270 00 |
| Oct | 2, mth, 9 mth, 15 mth, 22 mth, 29 mth | | 400 00 |
| Nov. | 6 Leaves, 11 mth | | 135 00 |
| Dec. | 4 mth, 18 Leaves | | 135 00 |

| CURRENT | OVER 30 DAYS | OVER 60 DAYS | TOTAL AMOUNT | 2015 00 |

Chuck Fly
1.1.01
Cabin Thompson Station Rd

27
2/26/17
$ 2015.
DOLLARS

So, for the entire year, it was less than half of what he was claiming for the month. And even better, the check that you can see tucked under that? That was written on my own private account by Les that he wasn't authorized to use. I'd shown that check to ole detective, Lynn Lazy, along with others, and he'd refused to arrest him for writing checks on an account that he wasn't authorized to use.

Uh-huh...

And for that matter, eighty plus dollars a month in vet bills? We were in the middle of COVID where everyone should remember that the veterinarian offices were all closed, so obviously he was lying and hadn't been to a vet clinic with the cat in a long, long time, but how about this little doozy from the files he'd left behind?

| Date | Type | Staff | History |
|---|---|---|---|
| | | | Special orders: D+ since depto injection, p has not seen a vet since 2009, o is ok to do rabies if we need to, o wants to leave here till d+ is gone<br>- 1/2/2018 11:00 AM marked Completed by 76 Rachel L. Crutcher |
| 1/2/2018 | B | 2 | 1.00 EXAMINATION RECHECK (2381) by 000 |
| 1/2/2018 | B | 2 | .50 ounce of METRONIDAZOLE ORAL SUSPENSION (07010) by 000 |
| 1/2/2018 | B | 9 | 1.00 BOARDING (FELINE)/NIGHT (6515) by 000 |
| 1/2/2018 | B | 9 | 1.00 [None] of Your Technician Today was Rachel (RC) by 000 |
| 1/2/2018 | B | 9 | 1.00 Your Doctor today was, Dr. Jim Russell (JR) by 000 |

Please note what the vet said at the very top of this: *Patient has not seen a vet since 2009.* 2009 being the date when she was purchased. So for nine years, my cat that he'd poisoned, had not been taken to a vet.

Wow.

Just wow.

All that made a mockery of this little statement appended at the end of what he'd submitted to the court, didn't it?

> I make oath that the foregoing entries for my income and debts are true and correct to the best of my knowledge, information and belief and that the general and personal expenses are good estimates for the next three (3) months based on averages from the last twelve (12) months and/or other information.

Yeah... So much for having that puppy notarized. Yet again they were lying to the court. Blatantly. And as you could see by the dates, all that had happened just a matter of weeks before ole Les had abandoned the marital home.

Which meant that those fees for my office and our cabin were current. Or at least no more than a year old, and given that Mr. Fly billed us yearly as I had his bills all the way back to 2012 and could prove that, too...

And I was most certain that he hadn't changed his lazy habits and had suddenly become a conscientious pet owner overnight as he was still the lazy piece of shit he'd always been. After all, he couldn't get any facts correct or do his own accounting.

I knew from my sons that he was having his lackeys do his grocery shopping.

Which meant that *sworn* statement showed as always that Les, Cockburn, Alaimo and crew were again presenting false evidence to Lord Skeletor. And that Judge Dinky couldn't care less that he was being lied to and made to look like a fool.

Just as Dinky wasn't apologizing to me because Les was dragging his ass on his paperwork and refusing to hand it over.

That I was being lectured to by Skeletor and told that the cost of upkeep on my huge yard was so much that they had to sell my home, while Les claimed four and a half thousand dollars a month. But that was okay! He didn't have to sell his property, but my sons and I were to be put out on the street.

In the middle of an epidemic with a stay-at-home order in place.

They should all be ashamed.

Just as I'd happened upon this in Les's desk drawer while I'd been packing:

**Confirmation of Address Change**

Dear Client,

This letter is to confirm that we updated your address effective 03/21/2018 to the following mailing address:

Note the date. It was two days before he'd filed for divorce.

The same exact day that he'd sent me this email:

I love you and I keep telling you that. I needed to clear my head of the chaos. I told you where I was going and when I would be back.

Which showed the exact kind of sick head games that he'd played and what a liar he was. And for the record, he'd also already paid a deposit to Cockburn for the divorce at the same time he'd written me that email where he was toying with my emotions.

Obviously, he didn't love me, or his sons, and never had. Because no one could do the things he'd done to us if they loved us.

Lying. Stealing. Cheating. Without any remorse? Having me arrested for no reason while the pedophile who ruined his childhood and that of his sisters went unpunished?

Watching me turn blue in front of him while I choked on the poison he'd fed me?

If that was love, he could keep it.

Yeah. He was some prince, wasn't he?

This was what the judge was endorsing, while "teaching me a lesson."

If that was the type of judge that Williamson County wanted to enforce their laws and protect them, then I wanted out and I never wanted back in. In fact, I didn't even want to fly over the state of Tennessee ever again.

This was beyond the pale of acceptability.

All the lies that they kept letting him get away with while I and my sons were being punished for having loved him.

My sons and I were being persecuted.

I was going through the Labors of Hercules. Only there were a lot more than twelve and for me, there was no end. No appeasement for the gods.

And the way things were going, when they threw me out of my house, my son and I would be forced to leave with only what we could carry.

Nick and I didn't know what to do.

Twenty-five more days.

We needed a miracle, and God wasn't listening.

**F**UTILITY, THY NAME IS Terri. I'd started the day with another complaint. Why not? It'd been sent to me by the Judiciary Board. That was a first. I had assumed that the other agencies had complained, as they said they would. And as a result, the Judiciary Board sent the complaint to me, wanting my side of things.

As if they'd listen. Not like I had anything to lose at this point. I honestly believed that ole Skeletor couldn't hate me anymore if I'd set fire to a baby on an altar.

Or a kitten.

So here was what I prepared:

I'm not sure why I'm bothering to try again to bring this matter to your attention since it is a well-known fact in this town that Judge Bubba Dinky needs to be removed from the bench and my complaints were summarily dismissed out of hand the last time I contacted you. But since this time the Department of Justice and Tennessee Department of Labor are also reporting him with me, maybe this time my complaints might be taken a little more seriously.

I suppose the best way to open my complaint is with the direct quote from my bankruptcy attorney, who said, and I quote, "normally Dinky at least makes an attempt to hide his prejudice with people. With you, he doesn't even make a pretense of it."

As you are aware from my previous complaints, Judge Dinky violated my constitutional rights and had property illegally seized from my home while my sons, friends and I were held hostage, first in his courtroom, then my driveway and later in my kitchen by an armed officer. This was done in divorce court by Dinky's former business partners, Mika House and John Alaimo, along with attorney Bill Oldham, who came into my home and took my company's operating cash which they refused to count in my presence, inherited jewelry and my sons' jewelry and other jewelry that is not part of my divorce. Nor was any receipt left for it at the time they took it, which is also a gross procedural violation.

Jewelry I might add that has not been fully inventoried to this day. That was June 19, 2019.

It is now May 7, 2020 and Judge Dinky has still refused to have a hearing on that jewelry or to return it to me. He has no authority over my family's jewelry or that which I inherited and had no reason to seize it. I have him on record from two weeks ago, refusing to hold a hearing on my jewelry that he is planning to send to the state of Georgia for a receiver to hold, even though I can't afford it and most of the jewelry isn't worth the cost of sending it to Georgia.

More than that, he has thrown my special needs son and I out of my home while I am the sole support of my family (and I run my business out of my home so he is effectively putting me out of work) while refusing to make my attorney husband get a job and allowing him to live free and clear in my office that is a secondary home in Thompson's Station. He has given his former business partners 100% free rein with my checkbook, allowing them to pay themselves whatever outrageous attorney fees they want out of my pocket, and I have to pay it or go to jail, which has driven me into bankruptcy and as a result, I don't have any credit or any means to get another place to live because of the bankruptcy. And he has refused to allow my son and I a decent place to live. More than that, because he has seized all my money, I have absolutely no money with which to move.

At all.

When this was pointed out to Dinky, he said on record and I have it recorded, "Has she learned her lesson yet? I don't think she has." That is blatant sex discrimination. And that isn't the only time he has uttered such phrases. "We need to protect her from herself." Or "this little lady." I am a grown woman who has run her own business since I was in my teens. I am highly offended by his obsessive need to put me in my place.

Just as I have it recorded when John Alaimo, Dinky's former business partner, smirked and joked about his bill that he would be sending me in my indigent state that they have driven me into, to pay.

I have Dinky recorded where he has screamed at me for over two hours and has called me a "monster" and a "buzz saw" for no reason. Where he threatened to put me in jail for paperwork that my husband already had in his possession and I can prove that as my husband is on record as being my attorney. And as I mentioned, he gave my husband sole custody of my office where I kept all my paperwork, as well as photos of my husband preparing that paperwork right before he left me and emails of my husband referencing the records days before he filed for divorce. Then Dinky went on to shame my attorney for daring to represent me.

But the absolute worst part of all this is the fact that Dinky has left me now for three pay periods without the ability to run my payroll for my employees, and that is a direct violation of FSLA. And you cannot argue this fact, nor can you let him off for that. He knowingly violated federal law. This was pointed out to him and he flat out ignored it. Dinky flagrantly disregarded federal law and has refused to give me my money that I earned so that I can pay my employees the money they have earned.

He has violated Federal Law. No if, ands or buts. He knew that at the time he took my money from me without due process. He refused to allow me, my attorney or my accountants to have any say in this matter. The only ones he allowed to speak were his former business partners who lied and misrepresented facts. No evidence of my mishandling money was ever presented to him, nor were we ever allowed to refute or dispute the lies presented to him. Lies that included his old friend telling him I had made purchases that were actually illegal transactions done by my husband on my credit card without my authorization, and one transfer between my bank accounts I had made to pay the IRS for my taxes. God forbid! Something that could have easily been shown had Dinky allowed either my accountant or CPA, who were both in his courtroom that day to testify. But as always, he refused to allow anyone from my side to say a word on my behalf. He has never allowed anyone on my side to testify for me. I wish I were making that up.

He wouldn't even listen when the U.S. Trustee told him that the whole reason I was in bankruptcy was because of the outrageous legal fees that were being charged to me by my husband's attorneys who had been given free rein of my pocketbook by Dinky, himself, without any restraint or restrictions. Meanwhile, Dinky is refusing to pay my attorney all of her attorney fees.

Are you really going to tell me that that is impartial?

Any more than it's right or decent that I am supposed to be moved out of my house on June 1 and he has yet to release a single dime of my money for me to hire movers? We're supposed to have a hearing on May 21.

He is setting me up for contempt. Dinky likes to do that. I have had three out-of-state attorneys look at my case and they are appalled by it, as you should be, too. No one who looks at this case and the transcripts or who takes the time to hear the recordings can believe it. This includes a fourteen-year veteran of the Davidson County police department. "In all my years on the force, I've never heard a judge talk to someone like that. You expect a certain level of decorum in a courtroom. That is ridiculous."

I am not a felon. I am a #1 *New York Times* bestselling author who has never been in trouble with the law. I'm an international motivational speaker. No one should be subjected to the degradations I've had to suffer at this man's hands when I've barely spoken a word in his courtroom. No mother should be screamed at by a madman with a God Complex and lectured to with condescension by someone who has no concept about the things he thinks he knows.

Your own Williamson County deputy, after I was wrongfully and horrifically arrested for no reason, in front of my children and my brother who is a former police officer, was also horrified by Dinky's actions. "We were led to believe a wildcat was coming in and instead this tiny little thing stepped out of the car. You were so composed and quiet. We were stunned."

I don't know why Dinky has decided to persecute me or why he does this to others, but I am not alone. Sit in his courtroom for one day and you will be stunned at his inappropriate behavior, I promise you.

And, in my case, his behavior is extremely over the top and it is well documented.

For well over a year now, I have been threatened and bullied by this man. For months they have told me that I would be left with no money for food, gas or the medication that my life is dependent upon. And here, during this crisis, that is exactly what he has done. Dinky intentionally left me and my son with no money for over a month. He knowingly and willfully put my life at risk.

Please see the attached emails from my attorneys who have used him to threaten me while I was in bankruptcy. They have all verified the fact that Dinky is out to get me and that he is highly biased in my case.

My accountant will verify the fact that he has refused to pay my employees.

He has knowingly and willfully allowed perjury to be conducted in his courtroom time and again, and when I attempted to bring cause against his former business partners and my husband he refused to hear it, not for any legal reason, but because he said, and I showed you proof in my last complaint when I handed you the transcript where he said, "I don't want to ruin a good lawyer's reputation." That is not a matter of my not "liking his opinion." That is not a judge basing his dismissal on a matter of law. That is a judge refusing to do his job.

Let me repeat, "I don't want to ruin a good lawyer's reputation" is not a legal reason for a judge to refuse to hear a case. That is a judge covering for his friend. And I have to wonder why the Judiciary Board would refuse to discipline a judge over something that serious.

Just as you failed to discipline him over the comment I showed you last time where he said on the transcript I submitted, "I don't care what the law is."

Again, that is not a matter of my not liking his opinion as you suggested when you dismissed my complaint out of hand. A judge who makes an open statement on record that he doesn't care what the law is when my attorney brings a legitimate matter to his attention, is a problem. Just as it was a problem for you to ignore my earlier complaint.

As a result, his behavior toward me has grown more and more extreme, and threatening, and has resulted in a gross miscarriage of justice for me and my sons. I have lost my freedom and property as a direct result of your failure to act. My constitutional and inalienable rights have been violated.

Is this really the court system you wish to endorse? A place where a hardworking citizen isn't allowed to speak? A place where there is absolutely no due process? Where citizens are subject to the whims of one single human being and their capricious nature? Where a person can lose their freedom, a lifetime of their savings, their home, their clothing and cars and be threatened and held hostage because of one out-of-control judge who has it in for them and who will not follow the law? Because he says on record that he's "teaching them a lesson" when they've done no crime or committed no act to be taught a lesson over?

I cannot get a fair trial or even get a trial, at all. This is a nightmare that no one will help me escape.

For whatever reason, Dinky is on a vengeance quest against me. He has accused me of bribing *the USA Today* without any evidence and just goes for my throat and is now throwing me out on the street, violating federal laws and is punishing my innocent child in the process.

I realize that you don't care and that most likely you'll do as before and dismiss this out of hand, but you should know that my home is being purchased by another victim of the same group. It's a shame that you've allowed this kind of conduct in this town. We should be allowed to live in a land where law reigns. Where our rights are protected, and the legal system works the way it's supposed to. My father gave his life for this country and served it with honor and distinction. Because of his service, I spent most of my life without him. And I come from a family of lawyers, judges and law officers. Never have I been more ashamed, and I know that this is not the way the legal system is supposed to work. That judges are not supposed to behave the way he has done. I am not reporting him lightly and I urge you to take this matter grievously and to act accordingly.

Even if you refuse to act for me, would you please at least act on behalf of my employees and make sure that they get the pay they have worked hard to earn?

Thank you.

As I'd said, I wasn't expecting them to do shit. They hadn't done anything the last time, except mock me. That was what I expected them to do again.

But at least I'd sort of be heard.

And Melissa was going to finally file a motion against Les.

That only took forever. I couldn't believe it. But while I'd spoken to her, I'd heard the fear in her voice. At first, I'd thought I was imagining it.

Until Joan concurred.

"She's afraid of something. I think they threatened her."

That wasn't comforting. While I'd thought it, it didn't help to hear Joan voice it out loud.

But this was what Melissa filed:

---

### MOTION TO LIST REAL PROPERTY FOR SALE

---

**COMES NOW** the Defendant/Wife, Terri Woods Manly (hereinafter "Wife") by and through counsel of record, and moves the Court to compel the Plaintiff/Husband, Lester Manly (hereinafter "Husband") to list the following property for sale. For grounds, Wife would show as follows:

1. The parties jointly own real estate located at XXX, Thompsons Station, Tennessee.

2. The estimated value of the property is approximately $625,000.

3. There is no mortgage on the property. However, Husband's recent Income and Expense Statement, Husband indicates he is spending $4,696 monthly for property maintenance.

4. That Wife's career has encountered setbacks over the last twenty-four months and her income has been significantly reduced.

5. The parties are in financial distress and can no longer afford the maintenance and upkeep on the property.

6. Furthermore, the parties need funds a sale of the property would provide to pay creditors, for Wife's moving and rent expenses, for Wife's critical business expenses, as well as husband's excessive legal fees.

7. That despite the statutory injunction contained in Tenn. Code Ann. § 36-4-106(d), Husband spends money frivolously, purchasing over $75,000 in antiques and furniture, as well as a horse, among other expenses.

8. That Husband lives alone in the 3700 sq. ft. cabin, although his financial records indicate he spends significant time at a location in Georgia.

9. Wife submits that it is in both parties' best interests to list her former office for sale.

10. Wife submits that the parties have used real estate agent, Eleanor Peirs, in previous transactions.

---

**WHEREFORE, PREMISES CONSIDERED**, Wife moves the Court to:

---

1. Compel Husband to fully cooperate in good faith in listing her former office for sale;

2. Designate real estate agent, Eleanor Piers, as the listing agent to sell the property and advise the parties as to sale price;

3. Compel Husband to cooperate fully and in good faith in negotiating the sales terms of the office.

4. Compel Husband to cooperate fully with all real estate agents who wish to show the office and keep the office clean and in a good state for display for potential buyers.

5. Award Wife any such further general or special relief this Court deems appropriate, including, but not limited to, attorney's fees, expenses, and costs for this motion.

Oh, to be the fly on the wall when Les got that. I could hear the scream. I knew that angry shout. But fair was fair. I couldn't afford to keep him up, especially with the expense sheet he'd sent in. How stupid could he be?

It wasn't right to throw me and Nick into the street and leave him in lavish comfort.

We'd suffered enough.

He was the one who'd chosen to leave and destroy us. I was tired of watching my sons suffer. Of seeing them cry and ask how their father could do this to them. While he laughed about it and lived off the money I had earned for them, not him.

He was supposed to help me support his sons, not steal it out of their mouths.

I had to constantly remind myself that his parents were pedophiles. Because I kept thinking, how could grandparents allow their son to do this to their grandchildren? But then when I remembered that this was a mother who'd allowed her own daughters to be raped and her son to be raped so that she could live a lavish lifestyle...

I was asking too much to expect her to take her son to task for stealing from his own kids.

What Les had done to my children was so very mild compared to what she'd allowed to happen to hers.

They were soulless animals.

And this proved it.

All my boys had in this world was me. I had to hold on and hope that against all odds and all evil that somehow, some way, good would find us. That maybe God would remember we were here.

My hope was fading more every day. I was down to holding on to the edge by one finger and all I could do was pray that someone didn't come along and step on it because truthfully, I didn't know how much longer I could hold on.

Enough was enough.

The façade I kept up for everyone around me was wearing thinner by the heartbeat. My body was wearing down from taking all the shrapnel.

Every night I prayed for God to send me a rowboat. But it just kept raining.

And raining.

I needed the flood to stop. My little dingy was taking on more water than I could bail out.

But I would be here, bailing until the bitter end. It was all I knew to do. I couldn't guarantee a happy ending. All I knew was that if I stopped, I would definitely do down.

*Fight or die.*

Like my dad used to say, "I could have laid down in that field and bled out. Or I could belly crawl over the bodies of the men I called friends and get to the medics I needed to save my life. No, it wasn't easy, and I was scared. But I had no choice. I had a family at home that needed me to live. Life ain't easy. But you do what you gotta do."

"You're right, Dad." No one was shooting bullets at me. At least, not yet.

My kids were safe. That was all that mattered.

So long as they were safe, I was okay. I could do this.

One breath at a time.

Over. Under. Around or through.

I would find a way.

*I am my father's daughter.*

I was the daughter of the woman who'd flipped off God the day they told her she had terminal cancer. She hadn't cried. She'd answered with a defiant snarl, "I ain't got time for this shit. Next!"

One finger. One fist.

Standing on my own two feet.

Not a survivor. A warrior.

And I had sons I had to protect. No one would ever threaten my boys. They had to have me here because they had no one else.

I couldn't leave them the way my parents had left me.

The way their father had left them.

*Deep breath. One more day. It would end.*

All things did.

## MAY 8

**T**HE ZOO CREW MADE NO response to our motion. At all. Instead, the imbeciles came back, hammering me with two of their own.

Because they were *that* stupid. You know, the kind of stupid where you watch them like a zoo animal in a cage. Not because it's pretty, but because you were thinking, how do you survive in the wild and not get eaten?

*That* level of stupid.

Their first motion that they thought was "brilliant" made me laugh my ass off. Oh my God! My mind was so boggled that I just couldn't believe Les had found attorneys dumber than he was.

Surely, this was a record? Where the hell was Guiness?

*Okay, let me explain this grotesque waste of brain cells...*

No, wait. I can't. Really. They were *that* stupid.

I supposed that the best way to explain would be simply to put responses to their idiocy here and then get to the *really* good stuff that we uncovered about the jackals:

---

### WIFE'S RESPONSE MOTION ACCEPTANCE OF RECEIVER REPLACEMENT

---

**COMES NOW** the Defendant/Wife, Terri Woods Manly (hereinafter "Wife") by and through counsel of record, in response to Husband's Motion for Scheduling Order. In support, Wife would state and show as follows:

1. While the hearing was indeed extensive, Wife and her Counsel were never once allowed to offer any evidence to refute the lies and misrepresentations of Husband and his team of attorneys who have a proven background for boldly lying and misrepresenting facts to the Court. Evidence A, B, C and U. Nor were Wife's witnesses, who

were present that day, allowed any opportunity to speak on Wife's behalf or to refute the lies and misrepresentations given to the Court by Opposing Counsel. Ergo, a Receiver was wrongfully placed over Wife, due to erroneous and prejudicial information being given to the Court while Wife was denied her right to refute Husband's lies. Those actions on the part of Husband and his Counsel, and the catastrophic resulting bill from them and the appointed Receiver whose first bill, alone, was in excess of thirty-five thousand ($35,000.00) dollars are what forced Wife into Bankruptcy.

2. Again, on April 16, 2020, Wife was denied her right to have a witness or any refuting evidence be presented to the Court to show the lies and misrepresentations of Husband and his legal team, as well as denied a chance to show the Receiver, whose billing is identical to the one being proposed was what drove Wife into Bankruptcy and therefore a new Receiver will obtain a similar result as Wife's finances are worse off today than they were almost a year ago, due to the irresponsible and unconscionable actions of Husband and his Counsel. Court refused to hear further evidence and testimony, even though Wife has never been allowed to show her evidence or speak in defense of herself. Wife was even blocked from attending the hearing when the marital home where she and her sons reside, was Court Ordered to be sold out from under them in order to pay for Husband and his attorneys. Furthermore, Husband's bankruptcy attorney, presented erroneous information and hearsay during his presentation to the Court. He spoke about matters of which he had no knowledge, direct or indirect, and of facts that had been greatly misrepresented to him, further prejudicing the Court against Wife.

3. Husband's insistence on a Receiver, which was never needed, and to which no real evidence was ever presented has caused catastrophic and irreparable harm to the marital estate. Opposing Counsels' entire argument to have one appointed hinged on prejudicial private emails Wife had sent to her publicist that Counsel lied to the Court about and said Wife had made public while Counsel intentionally, willfully and maliciously withheld the follow up emails from the Court that showed Wife had never released emails to the public in order to get the ruling they desired. This is in direct violation of RPC 3.3[4]. Furthermore, they had their own "expert" witness present testimony to the Court about transactions Husband had applied to Wife's business American Express account without her permission or knowledge, which is in violation of Tenn. Code § 39-14-119, and lay the blame for those excessive charges to Wife, as well as use a bank transfer Wife had made between her Savings Account to her Checking Account so that she could pay for IRS bill as "evidence" without allowing Wife or her CPA or Accountant to explain those transactions. Again, no evidence of Wife's misconduct was ever presented to the Court. Wife, who has successfully run her own business since she was eighteen years old, has no need of Receiver to further deplete the rapidly dwindling marital resources that even the Trustee testified was a direct result of Opposing Counsels' misconduct and gross waste on behalf of Husband.

4. Again, as has been noted in Evidence U, Opposing Counsel is deliberately, willfully and maliciously misrepresenting facts to the court. Wife had warned the Bankruptcy Trustee that he was requesting an inordinate amount of information from her and that it would deluge his email. Trustee was insistent, due to the lies and misrepresentations of Husband and his legal team about Wife. He insisted that she send over all documents in her possession. Wife had no choice other than to comply with Trustee's instructions, caused by Husband's attorneys who knew they were setting up Wife,

which resulted in 100s of emails to the Trustee. It was, in fact, Husband's contact, and that of his own legal team that drove up the cost of Wife's bankruptcy to such an extent that none of their creditors were paid. Instead, Wife left her bankruptcy with twice the debt she'd entered into it with. As the Trustee, himself, testified to in court, all her money and personal property sales went to pay Husband's Counsel in direct violation of RPC 1.5. Likewise, Husband's attorneys have been such a nuisance to Wife's publisher, agent and other business associates that they have now put her entire business in jeopardy and have caused her publishing schedule to be pushed back as a direct result of their unceasing harassment of those they have been told not to contact, except through Wife's Counsel. Therefore, Wife requests that should a Receiver be appointed, neither Husband nor his Counsel have any contact whatsoever with Receiver and that the Receiver be chosen by Wife and not Opposing Counsel as they have shown themselves to lack any restraint or composure whatsoever. The trustee commented multiple times throughout the Bankruptcy that Husband's Counsel was out of control and lacked professional comportment. Indeed, Husband's own bankruptcy attorney said that Husband was crazy. Therefore, to cutdown on the outrageous bills that Husband and his Counsel have already caused that have devastated the marital estate, all communication is to go solely through Wife's counsel.

5. Because of Husband's erratic and thoughtless actions, as of June 1, all insurance on Wife's jewelry that is currently being held by Receiver will expire and cannot be renewed as it is tied exclusively to the Homeowner's Insurance. The Court ordered Wife to sell the marital home that her jewelry is tied to and that coverage will cease upon the sale of the home. Since Wife is no longer in possession of her jewelry that was removed from her home in June 2019, Husband, acting blatantly and defiantly, against the direct orders of the Bankruptcy trustee, has filed an insurance claim with his insurance company so that he can be reimbursed for the what the Trustee called an "inflated value" of Wife's jewelry. As Court no doubt recalls, Husband and his Counsel dispossessed Wife of her own personal property on June 19, 2019 without presenting any evidence whatsoever to the Court that Wife had ever made any attempts or had any intentions of ever selling her personal or family property, and had her jewelry put into State custody. Not only was Wife's jewelry improperly taken from her home, but also jewelry belonging to her children and other property that clearly is not part of the martial estate, such as Wife's coat button and son's graduation watch. As a direct result of Husband's outrageous actions, no insurance company will provide coverage for Wife's jewelry. Especially since Trustee and Receiver have failed upon numerous requests by Wife to provide her with a full inventory of what was improperly removed from her home by an armed Williamson County deputy and the Receiver who failed at the time of their seizure to leave a receipt with Wife for all the property and cash that they removed from her home. More than a month went by before Wife was given any information on her seized property, and never was it a complete record of what was taken, as the Receiver said while sitting in the office of Wife's Counsel. As a direct result of that improper search and seizure of Wife's home under the direction and participation of Husband's Counsel, no insurance company will cover Wife's jewelry unless Wife's jewelry is in her custody at the time of coverage, especially given that Wife has no idea where her jewelry currently is or where it's been kept since June 19, 2019 and especially after hearing testimony that the last Receiver had placed "all of the jewelry" in a suitcase and was headed to New York to sell it without informing Wife or anyone else. Something Wife finds greatly disturbing that Husband's Counsel

was notified of their intentions while Wife, the proper owner of said jewelry, was never told this, nor was her Counsel. Given all their dubious actions, and the fact that Husband has a highly suspicious insurance claim for reimbursement filed against her current insurance company for Wife's jewelry, Wife prays that the current and future Receiver has enough insurance for all the pieces that have been seized as the current insurance policy doesn't list every piece of jewelry that was improperly seized from Wife's home on June 19, 2019. Any future coverage so long as Husband is involved with Wife's jewelry and it remains outside of her custody is highly unlikely.

**WHEREFORE, PREMISES CONSIDERED**, Wife moves the Court to:

1. Remove the order for a Receiver as no proper hearing or evidence was ever conducted or given;

2. If the Court continues to insist on a Receiver being placed without proper evidence being given, that Wife be given time to find an appropriate, more cost effective alternative so as not to further harm marital resources;

3. Husband and his Counsel be restrained from any and all contact with the new Receiver so as to keep the cost as low as possible;

4. To sanction Husband's attorneys under Rule 11 for their egregious and outlandish actions against Wife and the marital estate.

5. To return all jewelry to Wife forthwith so that she can inventory it and get new appraisals as will be demanded since her current ones have all expired to put appropriate insurance coverage in place when the current insurance ceases on June 1.

6. Any and all such further compensation and relief to which Wife may be entitled.

That was Round One. Round Two?

**WIFE'S RESPONSE MOTION TO SCHEDULING ORDER**

**COMES NOW** the Defendant/Wife, Terri Woods Manly (hereinafter "Wife") by and through counsel of record, in response to Husband's Motion for Scheduling Order. In support, Wife would state and show as follows:

1. Husband's obscenely expensive legal team is well aware of the fact that Wife never filed a Chapter 7 Bankruptcy. The insistence on repeatedly filing false and misleading statements to the Court about material facts regarding Wife and her character in order to mislead the Court about Wife's character and prejudice it against her needs to stop and be disciplined. Clearly Opposing Counsel is maliciously, willfully, and knowingly violating RPC 3.3. Furthermore, it was the Opposing Counsel's egregious, outrageous and unnecessary actions against Wife that they took where they presented no real evidence to the Court, but again offered only dubious, prejudicial evidence

without allowing Wife or Wife's Counsel an opportunity to speak in her defense that forced Wife to file for a Chapter 11 Bankruptcy. And it should be noted that while Wife was in her Chapter 11 Bankruptcy, again, due to the nefarious, unrelenting actions of Husband and his Counsel, Wife was never able or allowed to pay any creditors other than Husband's attorneys. As was noted repeatedly by trustee, even under oath, Husband's attorneys, and their reckless disregard for their client's marital estate, are what forced Wife into Bankruptcy. Husband's Counsel even went so far as to force the sale of Wife's and Son's personal property to pay for their own fees while Wife's and Husband's creditors went unpaid and remain unpaid to this day. The Trustee, himself, gave testimony before the Court that it was Husband's excessive legal fees, alone, that clearly violate RPC 1.5 that had made Wife's estate "administratively insolvent" and that was continuing to devastate the marital estate.

2.  The delays in this case have been the direct result of a succession of frivolous and unnecessary motions put forth by Husband and his Counsel, who have repeatedly dragged Wife into court for information and documents that Wife had already provided to them, or for information Husband already had in his possession in a blatant attempt to prejudice the Court against Wife. Information that was more than sufficient and yet Husband's Counsel intentionally, maliciously and willfully kept telling the Court that it didn't meet their "needs" or was "insufficient," while refusing to specify how it was insufficient. Then, after multiple costly hearings on the matter, Opposing Counsel would tell Wife's Counsel said information wasn't necessary and that they didn't need it. Thus proving beyond all reasonable doubt that they had wasted the Court's valuable time and Wife's hard-earned money on frivolous motions and hearings. All the while attorney-Husband, who was working as an attorney right up until he abandoned his family, has stubbornly remained unemployed or willfully underemployed as a retail clerk, working less than part-time hours. For the last two years, Opposing Counsel has filed frivolous and unnecessary motions to not only prejudice the Court against the Wife, but to inflate unnecessary fees for themselves, which clearly violates sections RPC 1.5, 3.4 (d)(1)(2), 5.2 (1). As proof that this is their modus operandi with all their clients, see exhibits A, B, C and U.

3.  Again, Husband and his Counsel are presenting facts to the Court that are false and prejudicial, as attorney, John Alaimo willfully and maliciously did to the local news and other media outlets in August 2019 when he publicly defamed Wife by saying she dropped her civil case against Husband and his cohorts because she didn't want to "face a jury of her peers" while knowing full well at that time that the Opposing Counsel willfully and intentionally drove her into Bankruptcy to keep her from pursuing her legitimate claims against their client and denying her the justice to which she was entitled (RPC 1.5, 3.4 (d)(1)(2), 5.2 (1)). Husband and Opposing Counsel are well aware that the trustee, not Wife, dropped Wife's civil suit against husband because of her bankruptcy. RPC 4.1. That trustee denied Wife the funds and Counsel she needed during the Bankruptcy to pursue Husband for his willful and malicious actions against Wife and their sons.

4.  As has been stated, those motions to compel Wife were all done for no other reason than to prejudice the Court and to defame Wife as Opposing Counsel has done from the beginning and as a matter of strategy they employ in direct violation of RPC 1.5, 3.4 (d)(1)(2), 5.2 (1) and that is well documented by others. See Evidence A, B, C and U. Counsel is well aware that Wife cannot meet their outrageous scheduling demand as

she no longer has the money to pay for ten (10) depositions or a weeklong trial, thanks to their ravenous depletion of the marital estate as was testified to by the trustee. In order to pay for their already outrageous legal fees that violate RPC 1.5, Opposing Counsel forced Wife to sell her own personal possessions, as well as those of her children, which includes the marital home where Wife and her sons reside. Wife has even been billed for Opposing Counsel to research where to sell her personal items to pay for their excessive fees that clearly and unquestionably violate RPC 1.5. As a result of their unconscionable actions, Wife is left without the financial means for a fair trial or with enough money to secure any experts for her side.

5. Wife has attempted repeatedly to settle this matter and has agreed more than once to all of Husband's outrageous demands. Rather than meet Wife for the settlement terms he proposed, Husband and his Counsel have walked away from all good faith offers of settlement for no reason whatsoever, thereby lengthening the duration of this divorce and driving up the ghastly cost to both parties unnecessarily as is referenced in Evidence A and U as their common practice to inflate their fees and gouge their clients. RPC 1.5, 3.4 (d)(1)(2), 5.2 (1)3.

6. Being an attorney himself, and one in charge of the depositions of the Dumas lawsuit Husband (Evidence K) was overseeing and paying for with Wife's money (Evidence M-O) from her own personal checking account that he wasn't authorized to use prior to abandoning his family right before filing for divorce and stranding Wife at the end of the Dumas lawsuit he'd coerced Wife into filing, Husband is well aware that Wife lacks the funds to hold ten (10) depositions. In his own handwritten notes that Husband prepared and left in the marital home just days before he abandoned his family before dawn while they were sleeping (Evidence L), Husband wrote for his co-counsel in the Dumas case that he was forbidding Wife to go to trial in that case because he didn't want to "go broke" on lawyers, and yet he has driven Wife into Bankruptcy with his divorce that he filed because he told his son and others that he felt like he was "losing control" of Wife and her money. Likewise, please note that Husband also wrote it was his intent to "protect" Wife's "business interest and reputation" and yet he has done everything from the date of his initial filing to defame Wife and to abuse and sully her good name and business reputation with the public and the Court. Husband's own counsel has not only noted his erratic and unpredictable behavior, they have willfully, maliciously and intentionally participated in ruining Wife's business interests. Husband's Counsel has even gone so far as to seek out the media to make false statements against Wife as has been noted above and to have their own friends and family repeatedly post injurious and false statements, threats, attacks and such against Wife, her business and fans. Evidence D-I, P-Q. Husband has even gone so far as to knowingly make a false report to the FBI so that they would harass Wife, their sons, and her fans on his behalf. In direct contradiction to his own orders to prior counsel in the Dumas lawsuit to protect Wife's business interest and reputation, Husband has, during this divorce, gone on an all-out smear campaign which has been devastating to Wife's career and the marital estate, which Husband was well aware would happen given the Non Disclosures attorney-Husband drafted and forced all employees and contractors they employed during their marriage to sign that clearly states: "due to the particular nature of the entertainment industry, any disclosure or dissemination, whether or not inadvertently, of the Manly material without (Terri) Manly's express written approval will cause severe and irreparable financial and other harm to Manly." Evidence R and

S. This is an NDA that Husband, himself agreed to abide by and yet upon his first filing with this court, he willfully, intentionally and with all malfeasance breached. Evidence T. As he well knew and wrote in the NDAs that he demanded all sign and that he, himself, enforced and agreed to be bound under, Husband's willful, malicious and counter-intuitive actions have devastated and irreparably harmed the marital estate and Wife's career, as well as all her future earning potential.

7. Husband and his Counsel are well aware that Wife only gets paid twice a year and that due to their outrageous behavior, excessive fees, and defamation against her that her career has suffered catastrophic losses. As a direct result of Husband and Counsel's attacks where Husband's attorney, Bonnie Jo Cockburn, went so far as to have her own ex-husband and others accuse Wife of plagiarism on her fan social media pages (a fact Ms. Cockburn later admitted to, to Wife's Counsel), see Evidence D-K, among other accusations, threats and insults, along with Husband's former assistant who has led boycotts against Wife's novels during the divorce proceedings, see Evidence K, Wife cannot afford the schedule Opposing Counsel is proposing as they have completely devastated her finances.

   a. Wife cannot meet a June 1, 2020 deadline as Court and Husband have forced her to sell her home and it doesn't leave her time to move her sons and herself to a new location. Such a deadline is unfair to Wife who has a business to run and is the sole caregiver for the sons that Husband has abandoned while Husband is willfully underemployed at a part-time job where he has not been working.

   b. Wife cannot afford depositions by this time as the relocation move that Husband forced on her to pay for his excessive legal fees and support will consume the majority of the home's equity, if not all of it.

   c. Wife cannot afford depositions by this time as the relocation move that Husband forced on her to pay for his excessive legal fees and support will consume the majority of the home's equity, if not all of it.

   d. Wife cannot afford trial by this time as the relocation move that Husband forced on her to pay for his excessive legal fees and support will consume the majority of the home's equity, if not all of it.

---

**WHEREFORE, PREMISES CONSIDERED**, Wife moves the Court to:

---

1. Compel Husband to an emergency mediation within ten (10) days so as to finalize this divorce and allow Wife to get on with her life before Husband consumes the last of their marital resources with his reckless disregard for his family or allows the antics of his attorneys and employees to further damage Wife's career;

2. Husband to reduce the number of his Counsel to one to level the playing field and reduce the unwarranted financial devastation being placed on the marital estate;

3. Require Husband to work his job and stop receiving any financial support from Wife.

4. To pay for his own legal counsel going forward as he was the one who hid a vast fortune in marital assets from Wife as he testified to, under oath, in April 2018;

5.  Should mediation fail, for the Court to compel a second mediation within five (5) days in lieu of a trial as Wife cannot meet the financial burdens of a trial at this time or any time in the foreseeable future due to Husband and his Counsel's unconscionable and destructive actions against the marital estate.

6.  To sanction Husband's attorneys under Rule 11 for their actions against Wife and the marital estate.

7.  Any and all such further compensation and relief to which Wife may be entitled.

The only question was whether or not Melissa would have the backbone to file those motions. Why would I think or say that? Because the evidence that had come into light had placed her in a *very* compromising position.

What had we learned?

When Melissa had moved two blocks up into her new office, ole Bobby Lee's wife (the mother of Cisco's attorney) just happened to work there. More than that, her office mate was in with the circle of vipers and was part of their network.

Yeah. I'd just stumbled into John Grisham novel without realizing it.

*Thank you, Les.* Where the hell had my incompetent goober found these lowlife sick fucks?

I couldn't have been more stunned had I learned my sons were running a Meth Lab in my writing chair.

*Don't believe me?* Here was the evidence for those motions and that we'd uncovered.

*That* level of stupid.

Their first motion that they thought was "brilliant" made me laugh my ass off. Oh my God! My mind was boggled.

This was an email sent to me by the man who'd bought my home—a previous victim of Alaimo's where the buyer mentions Melissa's new office mate as being in on their collusion.

> Just to be honest, we almost did not offer a second time on the house when I discovered he was your husband's attorney.
>
> There is a group of business owners who reached out to me last week to go over my dealings with him and the Judge, Robert E. Lee Williams, who is also in the same law firm. In my opinion what they are doing is morally wrong and borders on being illegal. There is now a state senator involved in looking into these guys along with Judge Dinky. I wish i had advice for you but I really do not. They are part of the "old guard" and they seem to get away with whatever they want to. They will keep you guys fighting and spending money until they can't get any more then they will walk away or suggest that the two of you settle. That is their history.
>
> There is an app these attorneys use where they put in the vocation of the spouses and it tells them how much they should be able to make on your case. If they get wind of large money, they keep going back to court so they can keep billing hours.  My ex-wife's bill to Jenny Novel was over 17k and mine was only $5,600.00. She runs with Alaimo, Dinky and Williams and Williams' wife is a paralegal in Jenny Novel's office.

That was the email I'd received from my buyer when I'd reached out to him with this:

> Please forgive me for emailing you out of the blue like this, but I am under extreme fire at the moment, and I don't know where else to turn, because no one else has been able to give us an answer. How did you EVER get John Alaimo off your back when the judge is his old business partner? My attorney is getting hammered by these rats and we cannot catch our breaths or

a break.

If you don't wish to write back, I understand. I need help and I don't know where to turn. I know about your situation because of an email from the realtor where they told him not to let you know that John is representing my husband in the divorce. But I don't like underhanded moves.

Anyway, thanks for at least listening. I'm trying to get as much fixed in the house as I can before you guys get here. My son's fianceé is staying with me and we're working hard to get it cleaned and straightened out for you guys.

When I sent that email to my buyer, the last thing I'd ever expected was for him to come back to me with the tidbit that old Bobby Lee's wife was the paralegal in the office where my attorney had decided to take up residence *during* my divorce.

This town wasn't *that* small. But it was beginning to be *that* crooked.

And it explained why Ms. Novel had declined representing or even talking to me. Her paralegal was the mother of the prick who'd been representing Cisco.

*What the actual fuck?*

How was that *not* a conflict with my attorney?

If that wasn't enough, he sent over a follow-up email:

I have researched some of their cases. Normally when they see the money gone, they let go. One family had done the same thing you have done and they left them basically standing in the courtroom to basically defend themselves.

John Alaimo lied to two of my attorneys and both attorneys and myself debated on filing a complaint with the bar. Whatever he tells your attorney it needs to be documented because if it is not, he will say it never transpired.

The thing that saved me was that Williams was so egregious in his original rulings - I could call no witnesses, one being the female detective in the case, and we were given limited discovery an hour before the hearing. The appeals court seemed to be shocked at the behavior of Williams and ordered a new hearing to allow me to call witnesses and get the discovery we wanted. Once the judge was forced by the appeals court to do the right things, my ex wanted to settle the case. It was always about money. The good news is John had to work out a deal with my ex to get his money because the appeals court and the Tennessee Supreme Court ruled in our favor.

There are at least 7 other business owners who have had highly contested cases in front of Williams and Dinky where their firms' attorneys have appeared before them and have made what most legal minds believe are outrageous rulings. Some have fought back and won at the appellate level and some have just walked away. There are numerous attorneys in Williamson County that simply will not take a case and who drop cases that are going before Williams and Dinky as they know the results are predetermined.

*Is your jaw hanging open as much as mine was the day I opened that?*

I was stunned at the level of corruption. No wonder the trustees had dove under the table.

And of course, I immediately fired off another letter to my "friend" Ms. Dullard. Not that I expected her to do anything. But damn.

Just damn.

Didn't anyone give a shit that Nashville was one of the most crooked cities in America or that

Tennessee ranked at number three in the nation?

*Hell, no! Let's exploit that!*

Un-friggin-belieavable.

Yeah. That one email from Hunt said it all. Didn't it? That was just how corrupt this town was and if you ever wanted to see how repulsive Nashville was or if you'd doubted my case, look up Danny Tate. They did the same to him as what they've done to me, and that was a decade ago.

An even bigger celebrity. With more contacts.

Dottie West was another, and the same players had been involved. Only in Dottie's case, they'd succeeded in killing her.

This was why they were so cocky. Because no one would stop them.

They were untouchable.

Welcome to America. Land of the lies. We were the dupes of a corrupt government and every citizen who was asleep at the wheel was one heartbeat away from their own nightmare where they could lose absolute control of their life because one of these greedy unconscionable bastards got their claws into you.

That was the unholy terror that stalked all of us.

And only a tiny handful of us knew about it.

Because there was no way out. I'd talked to countless legal "experts" in my state and outside it.

No one knew how to help me.

Why?

Because while talking to the buyer of my house, the worst news yet was dropped on me.

My own attorney was compromised.

**M**Y SON'S BIRTHDAY. A DAY that should have been one of peace and celebration. But as you've seen, there was no peace for us.

This day, I found a subpoena taped to my front door.

They couldn't even give me a Saturday.

Not one fucking Saturday. And of course, my attorney was nowhere to be found. It wasn't like it was the weekend or that Mother's Day was the next day or anything...

Please be advised that I have been named by your insurance company, the Tennessee Farmers Mutual Insurance Company, to ask you questions under oath regarding the above identified loss. I will be asking you a series of questions about the loss as part of the Tennessee Farmers Mutual Insurance Company's investigation of this claim. You will be placed under oath and your statement will be transcribed by a certified court reporter. You may also be videotaped as provided by your policy.

Your examination has been scheduled for **11:00 a.m. on Wednesday, June 3, 2020,** at the Columbia Regional Claims office for the Tennessee Farmers Mutual Insurance Company located at 181 Theta Pike, Suite A, Columbia, Tennessee 38401, in the downstairs conference room (Room B).

In addition to giving an examination under oath, you will need to provide the following items in advance:

1. any photographs of the personal property taken prior to the loss;
2. a copy of the loss report or incident prepared as a result of your notifying law enforcement of this theft;
3. a list of all creditors and debts that you owe. Include the name of the creditor, the amount owed, the term of the loan, note, or agreement, and how much the installments are for each debt;

> 4.     photocopies of your personal Federal Income tax returns for the years 2015, 2016, 2017 and 2018; and
>
> 5.     all receipts, invoices, warranty booklets, and other proofs of purchase that relate to any personal property which you claim was taken in the theft.
>
> Please forward these items to my attention at the Murfreesboro address above so that I receive them no later than Monday, June 1, 2020. If you incur any expense in securing the requested materials, please bring proof of payment with you so that you may be reimbursed.
>
> Please be advised that the taking of this statement is in no way to be construed as a waiver of any policy terms, conditions, or defenses of the Tennessee Farmers Mutual Insurance Company. If you have an attorney representing you regarding this matter or retain one for this matter, please have that person notify me of their representation and to advise whether they intend to be present.
>
> I look forward to meeting you on Wednesday, June 3rd at 11:00 a.m. at the Columbia Regional Claims Center.
>
>                 Sincerely,

Where do I even start on this spectacular level of stupid? To begin with, I was being thrown out of my home by a court order because Les was too stupid to live. Guess what that meant? The jewelry he'd reported as "mysteriously missing" that he'd had illegally stolen from my home and then was trying to scam the insurance agency into paying for would no longer be covered.

Since I was coming out of bankruptcy and lacked all means and credit with which to purchase a new home, and since all of my jewelry had been illegally snatched from my hands a year before then and had been given over to who knew who, no one in their right fucking mind would provide coverage for it. Especially as I had no idea who had it, or where it was being kept. For that matter, Les had a current claim saying part of it was missing. The trustee and receiver had refused, again and again, to ever let me see the jewelry. The receiver had refused, again and again, to hand over a full receipt of everything taken. He'd refused to give me a receipt on the day he'd removed my property.

Les and crew had never, ever allowed me to see the jewelry while it was being taken or after they'd removed it.

Last I knew, the idiot receiver had placed it, unattended, in his car while Les and Cockburn had been left, unattended, in my driveway with an unidentified third party.

Then, according to Les's idiot bankruptcy attorney, at some point the receiver had crammed it all in his suitcase and "was about to board a plane to New York to sell it."

And this same receiver had been so afraid that he, along with the trustee, had made the federal judge issue an order, against my Constitutional Rights, to prohibit me from suing either of them for any reason.

Such as them stealing my jewelry?

How much more suspicious could any of these bastards look? Especially the trustee who had a hissy fit when Les, for whatever reason, had reported the jewelry he'd ordered seized as missing when I had been forbidden to see it.

Had they allowed Les to see it, while telling me that I couldn't? To my knowledge, every piece was in their custody.

What did Les know that I didn't?

This sounded like some masquerade where the partners in cahoots had betrayed each other.

Meanwhile, I had nothing to say in this deposition as I didn't have the jewelry, hadn't seen the jewelry and had no documentation. They had been told this and I was sick and tired of being harassed by everyone at Les's insistence, including the FBI.

Why was everyone so willing to dance to his command and no one would help me?

Seriously? No one would listen to me and yet he kept making all these insane claims and no one doubted his lies.

I was telling the truth and had everything documented and no one would take a second look.

This was heartbreaking.

And disturbing.

Was this really what our society was about? Protect the trash and torment the innocent?

When had we sank so low?

One thing was sure. I was the one who made the money and when this nightmare was over, I knew which insurance company I would never use again. They might dance to Les's command, but they'd lost my endorsement and my money once this was over.

I T WAS OFFICIAL. MELISSA WAS in with Skeletor and crew. Not sure why that surprised me. Why anything surprised me. But it did. I'd texted her early that morning to call me when she had a minute.

She texted back that she'd call on her way in to work.

"I'm so pissed off."

She'd laughed. "About which part?" Melissa had a valid point.

"All of it really." And as I'd gone into all the dirty shit they were pulling, we started talking about my buyers and what they said. "I know that you share an office with Novel and Williams' wife."

She'd grown eerily quiet at that point.

A bad feeling settled in my gut. "You're compromised in that office, aren't you? It's why you're always calling me from your car and from home."

"Uh... It's a small office. I know they can hear things."

That was an understatement. It also explained why she refused to file appeals and motions that I had begged her to file. Motions and appeals my other attorney friends from out of state had been confused as to why she'd failed to file them.

Why she'd said to a friend, "Well, he needs the money from her books to support himself later."

No, he didn't. Les needed to get a fucking job like the rest of the world and support himself.

I was stunned.

Worse? I was trapped. They'd taken all my money. Had it tied up so that I couldn't hire an attorney. Couldn't live. I still couldn't even pay my employees.

I was completely in their hands and had no way out.

Now, my attorney was part of it.

For the rest of the day, she refused to answer anything. I was alone and now I knew the truth.

They really did control this town.

And they controlled me.

O NCE AGAIN, I WAS WRESTLING with futility and had no idea why. At this point, it was a reflexive as breathing. *Get up, write a complaint, make breakfast.*

Wish I were joking.

But since this time Judiciary Board of Review had sent me the form to fill out, what the hell? Right? Might as well try.

What a fucking joke. The only light in my day was that Cockburn and crew were having a hissy over the fact that Baby Huey hadn't been paid his "support."

As if I cared. I had a simple solution. Release my money and I could pay him. They were that stupid.

Or settle it. Then he could go on with his life and not be begging for money like the bastard he was.

Oh and of course, there was the birthday card that came for Maddox.

Not from his father. From the one Maddox termed "Satan" i.e. his grandmother.

Wow. Sad that she had to ask because she had no idea how old her grandson was. Couldn't even get him a card that said "Grandson." But wait, it got better:

Hope you have a great birthday! We don't have to count them in "dog years" but pray that they keep coming! I will be 80 in September and happy to be in remission from cancer. I love you—Grand-Mama

What. The. Fuck? First, in dog years, Maddox would only be three. Second, it came a week after his birthday, which given that she only had four grandsons, the stupid bitch should be able to keep up with it. Then, don't you love how the Narcissist hijacks his birthday and makes it about her?

Yet another year and no present from Grandma. Not that we expected one. However, this was his response to her:

Eighty years, Grandma. Wish in all that time that you had spent five minutes teaching your son not to steal and especially not to steal from his own sons. Know what would have been an awesome birthday gift? You to tell your son to leave my mom alone or to give us back the money he stole from us. That would be nice.

Me and Nick want him to go away and stop bothering our mom. Like he used to tell us, he needs to get a real job and stop living off our mom. Could you tell him that? He needs to grow up and support himself and be a man, not a parasite. That's what he called me. For once in his useless life he needs to do the right thing. Aren't you ashamed of him. I am. It's why me and Nick are changing our names. We no longer will be Manlys.

Out of the mouth of babes. But my heart was broken. I would die if my grandson felt that way about me. Of course, I would never, ever do that and it warmed my heart that Maddox was aware of it. It wasn't in me to sit by and watch my family suffer.

I wasn't Snooty. She was a cold-hearted, self-absorbed bitch. As Maddox had noted, we'd all listened to Les whine and complain about how much he hated her and why.

Even to the end, she was worthless.

Just like the sack of shit she'd raised.

Parasites all.

But not my sons. They were amazing and they were good men.

And I was still fighting, even though it was futile. So, I sent out another complaint that morning, hoping for the best, knowing it was useless.

Would it work? I doubted it. The system was broken. The judges were corrupt.

I didn't know how this would end. All I could do was put one foot in front of the other and keep going.

And praying God and/or Karma would get off their ass and do something.

W E WERE LIVING IN A WAR zone. That was what it felt like. Every day, we woke up to a whole, unforeseen nightmare that wouldn't end. We never could even begin to contemplate what trauma would hit us with the dawning light.

This day came with a DEA raid.

Not kidding. I wasn't there for it. Joan was. It was sick and twisted, and it damn near killed her. That was how fucked in the head these bastards were.

And no one would stop them.

It also came with another hearing where I wasn't allowed to attend. My attorney refused to provide me with the link to the hearing. They were deciding my fate and I wasn't allowed any say in the matter.

My illegally seized property was being sent out of state, even though the asshole judge had no authority over it, and everyone knew it.

I had corroboration from my friend who was a police officer. It was called theft:

**39-14-103. Theft of property.**

A person commits theft of property if, with intent to deprive the owner of property, the person knowingly obtains or exercises control over the property without the owner's effective consent.

What could be clearer than that? They had taken my personal jewelry that they had no right to take, out of my home, without a warrant and were refusing to return it to me.

The judge continued to refuse to have a hearing on the matter because he wanted to teach me a lesson.

That made him a thief as much as they were.

And how was my attorney handling this?

I understand you want to file an appeal of Judge Dinky's Order to appoint a receiver. That Order was entered April 24. Per T.R.A.P 9, that needs to be filed and delivered to opposing counsel within 30 days of entry of the order. Due to the weekend and holiday, I would have to file it by Tuesday.

Here are my issues with filing it. First, I will have to draft and file the motion with the trial court and set it for a hearing. Under the local rules, I cannot set it any closer than 2 weeks from the time of filing. At that point, opposing counsel will have the opportunity to ask for another date if they are not available the date I choose. I am certain Judge Dinky deny my motion and so we will have to fie another one with the appeals court. Per the rule, filing a TRAP 9 appeal does not stay the current order. So, the receiver goes in place until an appeal is won.

Then, it could take months for the appellate court to decide if they will accept the appeal or not. They deny 99% of these. Our chances of them even agreeing to take up the matter are nil. Especially since it is a very fact-based argument and left mostly to the trial court's discretion.

By the time we get a response from the Appellate Court, several months are likely to pass, and by then, it is likely that we would have mediated this case already.

There are obvious costs involved in filing these motions and attending the hearing(s). I fully expect Judge Dinky to deny our Motion and the Appellate Court to deny our request to hear this matter.

I don't care what the buyers say. His case is not yours. Having gone through one case does not make him an expert.

I do not advise filing this Motion. It's a waste of time and money.

The fastest way to get rid of the receiver is to settle this matter. We were not that far apart in our settlement negotiations. At some point, you are spending more money fighting than the money you are fighting over. I strongly advise that you spend your time an energy on drafting a reasonable, organized settlement offer.

They asked for 30% of the royalties after your agents get their cut. Then and additional 20% of springing royalties (again, after your agent gets his cut). They also wanted alimony. I think we have a good argument against that; he can live just fine on what he earns from the royalties, especially if he gets the any other assets such as the cabin or even any cash from the sale of the cabin. Plus he can supplement his own income by getting a damn J.O.B.. But it's worth considering offering him a small amount of transitional alimony for one year to get this settled. The offer needs to be as simple as possible, but also include what happens with the jewelry and cabin.

I don't want to talk about this with you by phone or text today. If you insist on me filing an appeal, you can email me back after you consider what I have said, and I will draft it over the weekend.

If I'd had any doubts before that my attorney was in their pockets, that email quickly told me that she was fully aligned with them. This stupid bitch was giving away everything I had made and leaving me with nothing. She was forgetting everything they'd taken from me already.

That my clothing had been sold to pay these animals. That the bastard had stolen EVERYTHING from his own children.

That I had proof and had shown her the proof that the greedy animal had taken out a mortgage on our home days before he left, and even right after he'd filed for divorce, in violation of his own court order to the very penny of his half of the value of our marital home, intending that I'd have to pay him for it twice.

To screw me and his sons.

So that he could "benevolently" give me the marital home with a mortgage that he'd pocketed the cash from while he took my office free and clear.

She knew that.

And for the record, twenty percent of my royalties was what my agent made, and he worked hard for those royalties. That would leave me with less than thirty after taxes.

How sick were these fucks?

And on top of that I was supposed to pay him alimony out of the money I was already giving him so that he could sit on his fucking ass as he'd done my entire marriage and not do a damn thing?

*Are you kidding me?*

And this was *my* attorney. Why wasn't she fighting for me with half the enthusiasm his psychos fought for him? I was disgusted.

Which meant I'd already begun the bar complaint against her, too.

I was done. I couldn't understand this world where so many were willing for fight for evil and I was left alone to fight for what was right. What had happened to the John Wayne ideal? To the place I'd told my sons about where right won the day and evil was trounced?

At least my sons made me feel better.

"You're the most important person in the world to me, Mom. Please don't give up."

As if I ever could. I knew they had no one else. Because I had no one. The one thing that had become so incredibly clear to me was that we were alone. Others might say they felt bad, but no one was willing to put their neck out or stand up and fight.

The only defender my boys had was the person who'd brought them into this world.

Unlike their piece of shit sperm donor, I wasn't about to run out in the middle of the night and leave them hanging.

But it was so hard to keep putting that foot in front of the other.

Melissa wasn't fighting. "The receiver will drive up Monday."

Fucking awesome. At four-hundred-and-fifty dollars an hour, that meant that I'd be charged four thousand dollars just for his travel time, alone. Never mind the time to actually do his illegal shit and for him to spend the night.

I was certain at this point that he'd hit me with a thirty-five-thousand-dollar bill, same as the last one.

He must have been a giddy son of a bitch when they called and said they had another live one for him. No wonder he didn't mind taking possession of jewelry that wasn't insured. That Dipshit had a fraudulent claim against.

And that I couldn't get insurance on as my new company wanted me to bring in every piece in order to get it reinsured.

Not that it mattered. See, there was this clause in the receiver's contract that said he could sell any and all my property at his discretion to pay Les's attorneys.

That was why they kept talking about selling it during the hearing. I told this to Melissa. "They won't do that."

Yeah, she was in on it.

Because not even she could be *that* stupid. I saw this train wreck coming, and I knew where it was heading.

Straight for me and all I could do was sit on the tracks with my foot wedged on the rails and wait for it to run right over me.

**S**O MUCH FOR MY HEARING that was supposed to give me the money I needed to move. Keep in mind that this was a Friday, and I was supposed to be moved completely out of my home by the following Friday.

Seven days.

And rather than hold the hearing to get me the money I needed to pack my house and move, the judge decided to move it to the following week.

"Are you available on Wednesday?"

I literally took off Melissa's head over the stupidity of that question. Whoever said there was no such thing as a stupid question had never once met an attorney.

Lawyers took stupid and ran with it across field goals, spiked the ball and danced a jig with it.

In fact, they took pride in asking the stupidest fucking questions of all time.

Was I busy... ?

"I have an eight thousand square foot house that has to be vacated in less than forty-eight hours from that court date. Are you out of your fucking mind?"

Apparently, she was. "Well, that's the date."

Wow. Just wow. They'd forced me to sell my home against my will, and now they were expecting me to move without a single dime to move my furniture.

In a small car.

Okay, then.

"Well can't she pack the boxes?" That was the question from Cockburn and crew.

"Unlike her fucked in the head client, we have been packing since February. But I have a job. My sons have jobs, unlike her fucked in the head client. I also have two broken feet. A bad back and a busted rotator cuff. Not to mention, kidney and liver disease from the poisoning. How the fuck do you expect us to get moved out of here?"

It was a three-story house, with a slate top pool table. Never mind all the other things, such as the beds, that I had no clue on how to take apart.

To say I was offended was a mild understatement. This generated another complaint to my old friend, Ms. Dullard:

I'm sorry to bother you again, but this case is so far out of hand, and I don't know where else to turn. I need help and these attorneys, and the judge are beyond the pale of acceptability.

At the beginning of this month, Bonnie Cockburn, John Alaimo and Mika House had their former business partner, Judge Dinky order me to sell my home to pay for their attorney fees, leaving me and my sons homeless. They also put an order in place that I wasn't to interfere with the sale. They also had Dinky seize all my money illegally, as you know, and without any due process. To date, no real hearing has ever been held about withholding my money from me. Dinky said on record he was doing it to teach me my place.

That has left me with no ability to hire a mover or to sign a lease or do anything. I have to be out of my home by June 1 in order to close or they are threatening me to have Dinky put me in jail for contempt. But they are withholding the hearing from me, as well as the money I have earned (and the legal pay from my employees in violation of FSLA). We were supposed to have the hearing today and they have now moved it to next Wednesday. I am supposed to be completely moved out on Friday.

My attorney, Melissa Magillicutty, has admitted to me that she is compromised and that they are threatening her. She cannot file a motion to help me as Dinky will harm her if she does so. She's so afraid that she won't even call me in her office because she works with someone who has close ties to the judge. That is how serious this situation is.

Please help me. I cannot move an 8000 square foot home on my own in two days, especially when I don't have money for a new lease because they refuse to give me the money I have legally earned. No human being should be put in this position. I was again locked out of the hearing on Thursday (yesterday) that they held where they put a Georgia receiver over me, and they are going to take the money they are keeping from me to pay him to drive up here on Monday at an ungodly amount to seize my property again. Last time they did this, it cost me thirty-five thousand dollars. And because of their actions, I have thousands of dollars in jewelry he is illegally seizing that the judge does NOT have jurisdiction over as it is NOT marital property. My insurance for the jewelry is a rider on my homeowner policy. Once I sell my home, the insurance stops and no insurance company will renew it unless it's in my possession. I have the emails to prove this. The court has NO authority over my personal non marital property, and again, no hearing over my jewelry has ever been held. Dinky refused to hear testimony on it, twice. And this receiver is about to carry it out of state with no insurance on it.

How is this legal? And how can you stand for it to take place in your state when you are charged with overseeing them?

I beg and implore you to take action on my behalf. I am being threatened and bullied on a daily basis by these people. I am not a criminal. This is supposed to be a divorce, not a fight for my life where I lose everything I've spent my entire lifetime working for and where my children and I are put out on the street because a judge and four lawyers are out of control.

Please help me. This has gone to a criminal level and I am not their only victim. Please tell me that you aren't going to stand by and continue to let them get away with this. I implore you for help.

But I knew I was shouting into the wind. Dullard, like all the rest, had failed me, time and again. The system was completely broken down.

Worse than when my brother had been killed and they'd let his killer walk on a technicality.

Protect the criminals. That was what America was based on.

Better a criminal go free.

That was the mindset. But the problem was, the innocent woman was being tormented without any due process. All my rights were stripped, and I had no legal recourse.

There was no advocacy group. No white knight.

All those lies we'd been told. The truth was simple.

No one gave a shit. And all I could do was wonder how many more people were out there, like me, being trampled over. Because these bastards were so bold and blatant. I wasn't their first victim. I knew that for a fact.

Because they knew there was nothing in place to stop them from preying on us.

All of us.

God, how I wish I could go back to that girl and slap her when she'd said yes to that marriage proposal. I have become the heroine in the *Twilight Zone* episode, *Spur of the Moment*. A ghost trying to catch myself before I made the worst mistake of my life because I married someone I loved.

Because I put faith in a lazy, cruel piece of shit.

If only he'd put as much effort into building my career as he'd put into tearing it apart. Or as much effort into our marriage as he'd put into the divorce.

Damn, Les, you finally found some motivation to get off the couch. Only instead of getting a hobby and doing something smart and productive, you ruined all our lives.

Especially your own.

What a fucked up idiot.

No, I was the bigger idiot. I'd married that sick bastard and had taken care of him. This one was all on me for not kicking him to the curb like my friends and family had told me to do through the years.

He was as worthless as they'd all told me. I should have listened. I guessed I deserved this.

Les deserved to be victimized by the crew who laughed at him behind his back while they stripped him of every dime I'd ever made. He was going to be left as homeless as I currently was.

Only he was too stupid to see it.

But in the meantime, my boys and I were in grave danger. I had no doubt that Dinky would lock me up. Especially when this email came through from the realtor:

> Hello All,
>
> The buyer has received an email from Mrs. Manly at 5:12 this evening that she cannot close on June 1st. She states the court refused to have her hearing today and that it its delayed until next Wednesday. She says the court has all her money tied in their hands. And that she cannot get her furniture out by June 1st and says she is open for suggestions.
>
> What do you suggest?

Don't you just love how the pathetic bastard was trying to get me in trouble again with Cockburn and crew? Especially given that he'd left off this part of my conversation with the buyers:

> We can't close on June 1. They refused to have the hearing today and they have now delayed it until next Wed and they have all my money tied in their hands. I cannot get my furniture out of here by June 1. I don't know what to do. I'm open to any suggestions you have.
>
> I'm doing everything I can do get out of here. But as usual, John and crew are doing everything they can to be impossible and to make this has hard as they can on us all. We're moving out by the carload. But the rain is making it all the harder on us. They have been refusing to give me

the money for my moving company for this since the beginning of the month. This is the most sickening mess they've caused.

*Context makes all the difference, doesn't it?*

But that was how they rolled. On lies and half-truths that they distorted. As I'd said from the beginning, truth doesn't scare me. *When you live a life of integrity, you have nothing to fear.* They were the rats who scurried in the darkness, terrified whenever someone shined a light on them. All feeding from me while trying to tear me down.

How could this be allowed? They weren't even sentient creatures. They were the lowest bottom feeders ever known. Worse than mullets.

They were the tick-turds of the universe.

If only someone would stand up to them and say, "enough!" But I was fighting alone, and I knew it.

I didn't even have my attorney on my side.

The betrayal stung deep, and I felt like my mother that day in the doctor's office when they'd told her she had cancer and she flipped off God. "Seriously? After all the shit in my life? Are you fucking kidding me? I don't have time for this shit! Next!" And she'd stormed out.

One finger. One fist.

To the bitter end.

Alone.

That seemed to be the curse of my family.

And here I would stand, while the wolves were surrounding me, salivating and nipping at my heels, hands and heart.

I was the only thing keeping them from my children. So long as I stood, they couldn't get to my boys.

That was what I had to stay focused on. One breath at a time. One heartbeat. I had to get through this.

But I knew they were trying to get me locked up. For the crime of being married.

The crime of not dying when my husband had poisoned me.

No, for the crime of being a successful woman in Williamson County, Tennessee. One of the most corrupt cities in America that prided itself on its corruption.

Six days...

Could I make it out of here?

God, please help us. No one else would.

MEMORIAL DAY. WHEN I WAS a girl, this day had been sacred to my veteran father. A day to remember all the soldiers like him who had sacrificed and bled for this country and our rights. It was the third one since Les had walked out of door without warning. The third since my civil and inalienable rights, and those of my sons, had been violated.

For the first time ever, I was glad my father was dead. Glad he couldn't see these bastards spitting on his sacrifice or that of all the men and women who'd bled for the rights that were being denied to our citizens in the name of greed and personal power.

People like Dinky and Williams and their cohorts who thought themselves above the law, because they *were* the law.

And I had the texts to prove it.

From another lawyer in town who'd been put in jail by them, whose license had been suspended because she'd stood up to them:

> Ellen Slater is in with their group and outrageously expensive. And she will force the mediation down your throat.

That was in response to the mediator that Melissa had suggested I use for our case. I hated to be so suspicious of my attorney, but both mediators she'd pitched to me had been part of their inner circle.

Not to mention, her words about my taking care of Les. Of paying him more than I was making. What the fuck was I supposed to live on?

No, she wasn't on my side. Not anymore. They'd gotten to her.

And the more I read from the other attorney, the more I began to believe it.

"Do you know of a mediator I can use?"

> Bobby Deal. Bobby was a judge and basically got pushed off the bench by the Williams/Dinky henchmen. I don't think he has any love loss for them because Williams, who served as Woodly's treasurer, was out raising money for the Woodly and raised like $300k for Woodly.
>
> Deal did not have the trove to best that.

Honestly, I think some of the Woodly money came from Dinky's leftover campaign money.

That was about the size of it. Political and judicial corruption at its finest. And the FBI wouldn't talk to me.

They could trot themselves out for a fake call any day of the week.

But they couldn't check into a legitimate call about a terrorist plot before 911 nor could they be bothered to look into real corruption of this magnitude that was affecting thousands of people a year.

Because I met four more victims that week.

All here in Williamson County. An electrician who came to take down my fan in my office and three painters who'd been hired by my buyers.

Average people. Victimized by these bastards who didn't care about anything, least of all their oaths of offices or their clients.

They'd sold their souls to the god of Greed.

That was the reason why old Cockburn was getting out of this after only six years. It made sense, right? Why else would she have spent three years and all that "debt" to go to law school if she only intended to practice for just under six years?

No one did that, unless they were Les and they happened to marry well.

After all, Cockburn was a "Super" lawyer. She bragged on her site that she was one of the best. Her old alma mater, laughable though it was, wrote articles about how impressive she and her sister were.

Yet they were throwing in the towel after barely getting started?

And what was she planning to do?

Go into a profession where she was guaranteed to lose her ass faster than Les.

Yeah, that made no sense at all.

Until you factored in that she knew Dinky was being investigated. Anyone with a brain would have to know that given what they were doing to the innocent residents of Nashville, it would only be a matter of time before that crow would come home to roost. If she had an actual brain cell (which I doubted most days), then this would be a good time to get out before it nested in that hideous thing she called a hairdo.

Poor Les. His attorney was about to jump ship and he was her last victim. The last take before she sailed off into the sunset with her ill-gotten gains.

His worst fears in life had always been to be alone and to be made a fool. To be taken to the cleaners by a scam artist.

And he had dragged the whole rotten crew to our doors to clean us out.

Not me.

He'd run off all my friends and family because they were what he'd termed "white trash" who were using us.

That included Kiki whom he saw as nothing but a low-bred trailer whore (his exact words) who was too lazy to work. "They're just using you, Terri."

And now he was surrounded by the very things he'd once accused me of courting.

Yet I was broke and sinking, and my real friends were rallying to help me.

His vultures were only helping to further sink him more. They were attacking me and watching him burn.

And laughing at him while they did it. Cockburn called him crazy behind his back. As did the bankruptcy fool she'd hired.

Alaimo had said that he was an idiot and that his law degree wasn't worth the paper it was written on.

Mika House bragged to everyone that they were in control and that Les was a puppet in their hands.

Meanwhile, Hogg treated him like an imbecile. and I'd heard her mock him to his face. "Here, Les, let me do it. It's too hard for you. You sit down and don't worry about it."

She'd called him stupid to his face and mocked him twice as much behind his back. "How did he ever get a law degree?"

And never mind what Cisco said about him. "Why did you ever marry someone that sorry? Christ! He's an idiot! How can you stand him?"

I knew what each and every one of the jackals actually thought of Les. Not to mention all the times that Les had called me, crying, because his mother had wanted him gone from her home. "Why doesn't she love me, Terri?"

And now he had deluded himself into believing that she did.

How stupid could anyone be?

She didn't love him. She loved my money that he'd stolen. That he was lavishing on her.

As the old Styx song went, "I have all the friends that money can buy."

And his fun was about to end because those funds were quickly running out.

Broke and alone.

His worst nightmare.

Unlike me, he'd brought this on himself. My only mistake was that I'd married someone I loved, and I'd spoiled his pathetic, treacherous ass. That I had assumed he loved me as much as I'd once loved him. That he wouldn't harm his children or steal from them.

That he'd never try to kill me.

I had nurtured a viper at my bosom.

How ironic really. Les used to chastise me all the time about my sons. "God, Terri! What's wrong with you? You have no expectations for the boys!"

"You're right, Les. All I ask is that they don't do drugs. Stay out of jail. And be happy. That's all I want." I didn't even ask that they love me. Only that they obey the law and have a happy life.

That was all I wanted for my sons.

Even sadder?

All I'd asked of Les was that he not cheat on me or hit me.

Or try to kill me.

For that, he was free to do whatever he wanted, whenever he wanted to do it. He had unrestricted access to millions of dollars, and I never questioned anything. He didn't even have to work.

Really, really, low bar. And he couldn't even rise to that pathetically low level.

*How sorry a human being are you?*

Again, because of my childhood, I never asked to be loved. I figured that my own parents had never managed to do it, so why should anyone else? I only asked not to be abused.

I have never expected much from people.

It was so sad that given how little I asked of others that they kept disappointing me.

So here we were. Four days to go and I would be out of this godforsaken county.

Four days. And if I could hit that fucking line, I was never, ever coming back. My intent was to bypass this state for the rest of my life. I had no intention of even flying in a plane over it. I'd spent the rest of my life plotting paths that took me anywhere, except over or through this hellhole of a state.

Just four more precious days.

I prayed I would make it.

MAY 27

I SWEAR I HEAR THE THEME *music from the* Twilight Zone. All I needed was Rod Serling's voiceover. Yeah, it was that bad. You know, because everyone needed to hold a hearing right in the middle of a major out-of-state move. And it wasn't like all the dipshits didn't know what I was doing.

Except for Judge Dipshit who had ordered the move a couple of weeks ago and had since held two more hearings after that.

Of course, he was so fucking stupid that three times during this one hearing he had to be told that, "No. Ms. Manly's payroll doesn't include her pay."

*Are you fucking kidding me?*

To begin with Skeletor, my pay rate is higher than yours. Back when I was a programmer and instructor, they billed my hours at $1,800-$3,000 per hour.

So, believe me when I said if they were paying my hourly rate, Skeletor would drop a serious load.

And where was old Skelly?

On the fucking beach. So much for COVID. Too bad it didn't target the assholes we needed to have removed from our gene pool.

Of course, Les had to show up with two people to speak for him on my money.

Which caused old Skelly to launch into this whole diatribe, "Now I know some people want to have judges recused... "

*You fucking think?*

Maybe if one of the Williamson County Judicial Mafia might abide by the law and their code of ethics, the rest of us wouldn't keep trying to have you bastards removed from our cases. Sadly, everyone who got hauled into court who didn't hire one of the members from your old firm or who took the boating and beach trips with you got screwed.

Les always said he wanted a judge he could bribe...

True story, that. He made that comment almost every day of the Dumas trial.

Anyway, Skeletor allowed my attorney to speak this time. We were both stunned.

I was thinking he might have caught wind about some of the people I'd been speaking to. Some of the people my buyers had been speaking to.

Could it be that he might be running scared?

Or was he simply that oblivious? Because he went into an expensive opine about how well he knew Les's witness. "Why I've had cases with him and against him. I'm just putting that out there. We haven't always been on the same team."

Yeah, but you were buddies just the same. The affection in your tone was obvious. He wasn't ass-kissing this asshole. He was rimming it.

Which meant Skelly was giving undue consideration to the lies out of this overpaid asshole's mouth. As he'd done previously. This was the same bastard who'd said that I was "making mysterious transfers between accounts" because he was too damn stupid to read an accounting sheet where it clearly showed I was paying my taxes.

Or worse, he had read it and willfully committed perjury because he knew his "buddy" Lord Skeletor would never hold him accountable for it.

*I vote for the latter.*

Which meant that they both broke the law and should go to jail.

*What's good for gander is good for the goose.*

And the gander was tired for being the only one getting cooked by these crooked bastards.

All this, while I was supposed to be packed up and out of my house in three days.

Oh, and that...

"She has two people living with her, Your Honor, that she supports."

Those are called children, Commissioner Alaimo. Mr. "I'm a Republican who ran my campaign on family values." I guessed the concept of having a family and being responsible for them was an alien concept to you.

Someone better tell his wife about this, soon. *Honey, move out of Williamson County and hire yourself a damn good lawyer and take that sick bastard to divorce court before you spawn his evil to another generation.*

*You're doomed.*

Anyway, the last time I checked, support didn't end the minute they turned eighteen. After all, I had been forced to endure over thirty years of listening to Les rant his hatred about his parents kicking him out the door at eighteen and then never again giving a shit about him, until Old Les was near death and Snooty decided she wanted to travel the world on my money with the son she'd never had five minutes for prior to Old Les's cancer treatments that cramped her lifestyle.

Yeah. True story.

Why this was my hell, I had no idea. I kept asking God why I was being punished when the only bad thing I'd ever done in my life was marry this sick son of a pedophile.

In the end, they violated federal law. Judge Dinky did not approve for me to pay my employees.

"But the lawyers gotta be paid and Mr. Lie My Ass Off, old buddy of mine." *He* got paid.

All the assholes stealing from me, they got their cut. But the ones who were trying to keep my business going that Les wanted to live off...

The judge screwed them.

Yeah, they were that stupid. No matter what my attorney argued, he couldn't figure out that in order to make money, you had to pay your employees.

"I just don't get it. She made fifty thousand dollars and spent thirty. That doesn't seem reasonable to me."

*Because you're an idiot, Skeletor.*

Most businesses operated at a one to two percent profit margin. That was normal. I had to pay my people. Pay rent, web site, conferences and let us not forget that DragonCon and Comic Con were very expensive undertakings. But if I didn't do them, then I wouldn't make anything. The authors who didn't pay that kind of fee from their royalties had other jobs they had to work and made less than two grand a year writing.

I wish I were making that up.

More than that, I wished authors were paid for the time we put into our books. But when you factored in the twenty-hour days, seven days a week, three-hundred-and-sixty-five days a year, it was heartbreaking how little return we got back for our labor.

We loved what we did, otherwise we'd go do something that paid better and where we didn't get filleted for fun every day of our lives by some asshole with an opinion who wanted to build their rep by tearing us down.

Believe me, the one thing in life that I could handle was being criticized. It was an Olympic sport in the house where I grew up.

Or worse, the "critique" was put out there by someone who was rallying supporters to attack you in order to harm you. I wasn't alone and Hogg wasn't the only one to ever do that.

> However, if the group makes a determined effort to start posting comments and bombard the page with as many as possible (after midnight or 1 am Eastern time) and continue commenting for a number of days, it will have some kind of effect.
>
> It might also be good for some of those 'box' comments to go on the Etsy site. I'm not sure if she modified the settings and is getting every email again or not. I had changed it because she didn't need to see every little comment and sale. If not, the comments will last. I also don't remember how much control stores have over what shows, they may not be able to block any. [Etsy does have rules, i.e. only posts from purchasers and they can't be bully posts. The real frustrated fans wouldn't do that anyway. ]

> These things would be better than just making negative whining comments on Amazon or B&N.

Didn't you just love her comment about "real frustrated fans," which weren't her orchestrated "fake" fans that she'd unleashed on me?

That was only one of a number of such emails and texts Hogg had sent out to my readers. And don't you love how she said that she "changed it" to hide sales and other information from me?

She went on in the next sentence to say:

> One thing you can all be assured of:
> She makes all decisions and runs her own business.

If I ran my own business, then how was she able to change my sales info and hide it from me? Yeah, she outed herself right then and there and showed that they were in control and doing all sorts of illegal and unethical acts behind my back.

Or how about some of these digs?

> Yes, she would enjoy that panel and be a good participant. I woke her up to confirm. :) but it was worth it. __I think. I'm not in the house, so maybe time will tell_ )

> Oh - an SUV, please. :)   (Too many costume events in the evening and indecisive women make for lots of luggage!)

That latter one went to my publisher, and it was for an event where I took no costumes at all. She wanted the SUV, and I was hauling promotional and giveaway items for my fan.

I literally had hundreds of emails and texts from Hogg where she made comments like that to belittle and undermine me to my fans and publishers.

If she had to wake me up, it was because they'd drugged me. Anyone who knew me, knew that I didn't sleep much at all, and I had the emails at all hours to prove it.

Better yet, check my medical files. My insomnia was legendary.

And well-documented.

Hogg had never awakened me for anything. But notice, too, she mentions "not" being at my house. For the record, she'd documented living in my home with us.

Tennessee... one of the most corrupt states in the union.

And I was now being put on an allowance that Skeletor knew wouldn't run my business so that he could ensure his former business partners could raid my estate of whatever amount they wanted while I lived on a pittance of what I earned and wasn't allowed to reinvest it.

There was a reason why my income took a hit.

Les and Hogg.

Yee-fucking-haw.

MAY 29

STILL NO MONEY. NONE. How much stress could they put on me? The movers had told me that if they didn't have a check or credit card that they would take my furniture and keep it, then start charging me storage fees and cranking up the fees at such a rate that I'd never get my items back.

No one, other than me, seemed to care.

Melissa wouldn't even return my calls. She was too busy telling me how much she was being threatened by them and trying to placate them,

I was left out to hang.

The excuse du jour was that the judge was in juvenile court, as if he hadn't known he'd be in that all day and couldn't take five fucking minutes to sign the order that he'd approved two days before to get the money to me that I needed since they were throwing me out of my house.

Yeah.

That was the kind of country we all lived in. A hardworking woman and her children were being thrown out of the home she'd been forced to pay four times what it was worth, without due process, by a corrupt judge who couldn't do his job. This was beyond cruel and unusual punishment.

Instead of doing his job, which was to protect the marital estate, the judge was too busy helping them to destroy it. At this point, it was so obvious Skeletor had to be on the take that only someone with Skeletor's IQ would doubt it.

No other judge would allow a set of morons to waste this much court time on their docket. No one else would continue to allow their frivolous and silly motions to keep cycling through his court, or to set aside entire days for them.

Nor would he be so willing to go over the time limit allotted to them.

Yeah. They weren't even hiding it.

How sick was I? I couldn't count the ways.

Not that it mattered. The world was on fire. The TV was running 24/7 about injustice and yet no one addressed this one.

This was allowed to go on without a single news reporter giving a shit. Anyone in the country could find themselves at the mercy of jackals and be ruined.

Killed.
No one cared.
No one was listening.
I even received another email from Ms. Dullard.

We are sorry to hear of the continuing huge difficulties you are experiencing.

Our office has no power to intervene in a case. We are not permitted to represent individuals. We also have no authority over Judge Dinky, since he is regulated by the Board of Judicial Conduct. We have no power to order any judge to recuse himself, if being a former business partner has played a part in Judge Dinky's decisions. Incorrect judgments can be appealed to a higher court.

If your own attorney is "compromised", you may want to seek counsel from an experienced attorney without the ties and fears of your current one. Public or official corruption can be reported to the FBI, if you believe, backed by good evidence, that such corruption is occurring, and you are not able to get state help. www.usdoj.us .

We hope this information is helpful.

How unhelpful was that? Not like I hadn't already reported it to everyone and their brother. Yet no one cared. Just like her, they all told me why it wasn't their problem and why they wouldn't do anything to help me.

That was why these bastards were so bold. They'd found the loophole and it was open season on us.

We were fucked. And everyone lived in their happy bubble not knowing that this was out there, just waiting to snag them.

How I wished I was still ignorant. But I'd been the idiot who'd married a crazy, fucked in the head bastard who was intent on destroying me and my career.

There was no way to get the money I'd earned.

Only criminals got help.

The rest of us...

We were screwed.

Welcome to America. Home of the fucked.

I HAD TO MAX OUT ALL OF my son's credit cards and borrow money from every friend I had to pay the movers. Worse? All my items didn't fit in my storage units. I ended up forced to rent two more units in order to fit everything in them. So much for saving money. Skeletor had cost me so much more money than it would have had they simply left me in my home.

But this wasn't about preserving the marital estate any more than it was about getting divorced.

This was all about punishing me. And they were all in on it.

Oh, but it got better. The new owners, who'd been burned by the same attorneys, had to come and make it all the worse.

First, they'd hired the asshole pool company who'd kept getting in the way the entire week while my movers were there. Which also added to my bill that they knew I couldn't afford.

Yeah. Way to go, Hunt. Not like you hadn't cheated me out of my home and bought it at half its price, which you knew. That pissed me off enough.

Then, they ran up my water bill as they'd drained the pool. All the while knowing I couldn't afford this.

I felt like the town bike. Everyone was piling on.

Though what I'd ever done for this shit, I had no idea.

Yeah, okay, that was my stupidity I was paying for. I should never have trusted the son of a pedophile. Never have made the mistake of thinking I loved a snake.

Never turned my back on a piece of shit.

Anyway, we rolled out to what I prayed would be something better and I left the items Baby Huey had been hounding me for at the house for him to pick up.

You know what happened?

*I'm sure you do.*

"I can't get them by myself!"

*Are you fucking kidding me?*

After all the shit they'd given me. Why couldn't a full-grown man rent a truck like they'd said we could do? He had a man living in my cabin. He claimed he had friends. Couldn't some of them lend him a hand?

I was an old woman with other old women, and we'd moved most of the furniture and house without any help in the back of my son's Jeep and a shitty minivan.

Why he couldn't move his "armoire" he'd given me hell over and a chandelier and a desk was beyond me. Three hours would have gotten everything I'd left in a small U-Haul.

Yeah. So much for Les being a man and having friends. Then again, we'd all known the truth long before this.

But the weirdest thing was the fact that the realtor, Dick, had shown up.

Wanting to know where I'd gone.

As if that was any of his business.

"Is she local?"

What do you care? How was that any of his business?

Unlike Les, I had friends, and they didn't rat me out to him. It was sick.

And creepy.

Meanwhile, Melissa still hadn't received my moving money or done anything more than bitch at me on their behalf.

Seriously. I was beginning to think that she was more his attorney than mine.

Heartbroken, I headed home to Georgia. Not knowing what the future would hold and praying to God for something good to happen.

NOTHING GOOD. JUST MORE CRAP. At this point, I had nothing but disgust over the entire ordeal. As noon came and went, I was beside myself with the fact that the judge had yet to sign off and get my money to me. This was beyond ridiculous.

Melissa's sole concern seemed to be to get support for Les and not me. I kept telling her to appeal the order and get my money.

She finally did, at 3:30. Less than half an hour before the banks closed.

"What do I do with the check?"

"Drive it to the bank." Duh! What did Melissa expect? I was out of state. Had she wanted me to deposit it, she should have gotten it to me on Friday while I was still there.

This was beyond ridiculous.

I was beyond frustrated. And Melissa was hounding me for information I couldn't lay hands to as everything I owned was currently packed up and my computer wasn't set up yet.

What part of I'd just been forced out of my home had she missed?

"They want to see your statements."

"I want to see Les's." My statements, contrary to their lies to the judge, had been public records. And contrary to Alaimo's blatant lie to the court, the trustee hadn't given me whatever amount I asked for. I'd been forced to beg for it like a kid wanting ice cream.

More than that, I'd had to show him cause for every single dime, and by the time he'd approved it, it'd usually been too late.

Which had caused my business to rapidly decline. Because in business, timing was everything and if you missed an opportunity, you missed it.

They had forced me to miss a lot of them.

And were holding me accountable for their incompetence.

Yeah, that was the vicious cycle I was living in.

If only there was some letup in sight.

# JUNE 5

I *JUST GOT OUT OF A HEARING...*
Those words rang in my ears as I read them from Melissa. Now, they were not only locking me out of hearings, they were holding them without even telling me they were having them.

*Are you fucking kidding me?*

My entire life was being turned upside down and rulings granted while I was unaware that anything was being held about it?

How was this legal?

How was this possible?

What country did I live in that this could happen and there was nothing I could do? I was being forced to pay for things and an out of control, corrupt judge and his former business associates were able to completely steal my money and property, illegally, from me and I couldn't even attend. There were no laws and no organizations in place that would stop their robbery.

I was flabbergasted.

Worse?

Melissa had put forth perjury to the court because she'd filed a motion without even consulting me. I couldn't believe it. These bastards were gunning for us and instead of checking with me and dotting her I's and crossing all T's, she'd fucked up so royally that all I could think about was the fact that they'd locked me up for doing nothing wrong. What would the crazy bastards do now that she'd done something they could hold us accountable for?

I was terrified.

Over and over, she'd told me how they'd been threatening her. How many times Shovel Face had told her he was going to get sanctions against her.

But she wouldn't return my calls.

Nan admitted when she read the order that Melissa had fucked up royally. "Did she read that order before she signed it?"

"I don't know."

"I can't believe she signed that order. I'd have *never* signed an order like that. Those idiots are blaming you, but it makes Melissa look bad because she was the one who was supposed to do that, not you.”

“I know. They pull that shit all the time and they’re lying, anyway.”

It was all bullshit. But Dinky always allowed them to write the orders so that they could pad their overinflated salaries and protect him. It was so obvious. Otherwise, he’d allow Melissa to write one once in a while.

But he never did.

Favoritism at its best.

Nan was as appalled as I was. “What are you going to do?”

“I don’t know.” And I didn’t. I was being homecooked, and Melissa was getting more and more afraid.

She wouldn’t take my calls. She’d admitted it on the phone. They’d placed her in a no-win situation.

Worse?

She kept trying to strong-arm me into a ridiculous settlement. To keep Les up in a better situation than I was. To pay him more than I earned.

I was not going to pay him more than I earned. That was bullshit. He’d already taken his half of our property.

“Dinky is going to give it to him at trial.”

“Then we will appeal it.”

She wouldn’t commit on that.

I was so frustrated.

“I’m going to draft a settlement.”

“Fine, but I will not sign off on springing rights.” Not after the rank bastard had sold my house out from under me. I had developed all my series before I’d ever met that fucking bastard and he would never again get a single dime from anything I did after he’d walked out.

Divorce meant that he left and never came back.

He was no longer entitled to me or to anything I did. Why they couldn’t get that through their heads, I had no idea. But he was not entitled to a fucking dime of my future contracts.

I meant that and I was standing firm on it.

Fair was fair and this was all utter bullshit.

MELISSA DIDN'T LISTEN. Her email came in and she'd done exactly what I told her not to. She'd wanted me to give him as much in royalties as I earned. Seven years of alimony that was more than I was currently earning and that I couldn't guarantee I'd make given the vicious attacks he, his attorneys, and Hogg had made on my books and on me, personally. More than that, she wanted me to sign over the cabin free and clear and give him almost half of all my future earnings.

When I refused, do you know what she did?

"It is obvious that I can no longer represent you."

Yeah. At 10 P.M. on a Sunday night, while knowing no one else in Nashville would represent me and that Dinky held all my money and was refusing to even pay my bills, Melissa quit.

Because I refused to sign over everything to him after the bastard had tried to kill me and my son.

My cousin.

I was supposed to give him everything.

And be left with absolutely nothing. That meant that my fans would never have a conclusion to any series because I couldn't write my books for free.

Last time I checked that was against the law and constitution.

Except in Tennessee where they proudly had a statue of Nathan Bedford Forrest on the side of the interstate and in their courthouse.

And in the office of Judge Robert E. Lee.

They loved their backwards thinking. It was why they called themselves the "Athens of the South." In ancient Athens, women had been denied the right to vote. They couldn't even purchase food for themselves. Not without a male relative being with them so that the male could buy it for the woman. Women were denied all rights.

Welcome to Tennessee 2020.

Women still had no rights and were treated like third class citizens. As my attorney had said, "This is Williamson County and you're a woman. Don't expect justice here."

They were proud of their backward ways. Bragged about them, in fact.

Now I had no legal representation and no money to find anyone else. Not that it mattered. I'd contacted enough attorneys in the past to know that no one else would take my case. Everyone in town knew about it and refused to touch it.

The jackals had seen to that.

Dinky had seen to it.

I was alone and they were out to ruin me.

This was how it was going to end.

No one cared.

That was the saddest part. This was happening right in front of the world, and no one spoke up to help.

**M**ELISSA CAME BACK. But there was even more fear in her now. I couldn't place the source and there was no denying it. Something had happened. I knew it sounded paranoid, but it bled from her pores and shook her voice.

At least it did if she'd answer my calls.

That was the worst part. She was now dodging me. No longer answering email or texts. She wouldn't speak to me at all.

Not even my attorney bud, Nan, could get her on the phone. What was worse was the fact that Melissa refused any help Nan tried to give her. She wouldn't file the papers for Nan to assist her in Tennessee.

Nan wrote motions and she refused to file them.

*What the fuck?*

Why was Melissa so willing to sell me out? It didn't make sense. Of course, it would help if she'd talk to me and tell me what was happening.

Nothing.

I was screaming into a void and not even my echo came back at me.

W ELL, I FOUND OUT WHY Melissa wasn't talking to me. The dipshit brigade had fucked us over again. With their lies and stupidity.

Again, I was completely blocked from the hearing and not allowed to attend. Dinky made sure of that. Last thing he wanted was for someone to be able to defend themselves in his court against the pack of jackals he was paying to torture me.

After the hearing where Dinky refused our appeal for a receiver, County Commissioner John Alaimo then put in an order that lied about what the judge said.

According to this new order, that Melissa obviously didn't bother reading before she signed, all my money was now called my husband's "legal fund."

*Did your jaw hit the floor?*

You heard that correctly. Every single dollar I had earned, and every single dollar made on the sale of my home, was being reserved to pay his attorneys.

They were calling it a "legal fund."

I was left, in the middle of COVID, without a cent to my name.

No way to pay bills or run my business.

If I spent even a single dollar of that designated "legal fund" that was every penny I had, then I would have to pay it back to the legal fund.

Yeah, you read that correctly, too.

At two different hearings where I wasn't allowed to attend, I was being forced to pay my tormenters to torture and humiliate me.

Welcome to Williamson County. God help us all.

Worse? My jewelry that no one had a right to take and that had been illegally seized out of my home was now moved into another state and into the hands I was having to pay four-hundred-and-fifty dollars an hour for.

Yeah.

Are you as disgusted as I was?

Deprived of my rights, my voice and my property.

Fuck the Constitution. Apparently, it wasn't worth the paper it was written on.

All they did was use it to wipe their asses while they laughed at the rest of us and stole at their leisure.

Meanwhile Americans were protesting wearing masks because they thought *that* infringed on their civil liberty.

Yeah, those fools wouldn't last a day in my shoes. This shit had been going on for a year and I was still being tortured.

In front of the world.

None of them could bother to protest a real violation of their rights. One that could assault them at any moment.

Because again, I had committed no crime. All I'd done was get married, provide for my family and pay my bills and taxes.

*God forbid.*

"Did Melissa read this order before she put her name on this shit?"

I was as appalled as Nan was. "I don't think she could have."

"They keep saying you didn't do it, but it was her responsibility, not yours."

"I know."

"How can they do this?"

I scoffed. "You're the attorney, Nan, you tell me."

"This is bullshit! No one in any of our courts would ever stand for shit like this! Oh my God!"

While I appreciated her indignation, it didn't help. Melissa wouldn't fight.

And Nan had been correct. She'd allowed them to set her up like a massive patsy and embarrass the shit out of her in front of the court. I had no idea what was wrong with her.

She'd told me that she was compromised, but damn! Some fight was better than nothing.

Nothing was all I was getting. So many mistakes.

So many heartbreaks.

My goose was getting cooked, and no one cared. The world was on fire, and everyone was so worried about protesting the encroachment of their freedom over wearing a fucking mask. They thought *that* was the nightmare.

Imagine what they'd do if their home was illegally invaded, and they were held hostage in their own kitchen while every family heirloom and piece of plastic ring their children had given them was seized and hauled from their homes. By a corrupt, power-drunk judge who had absolutely no authority over their property.

A fucking idiot who had them jailed over a lie.

They had no clue how little rights they had and that a king was waiting to pass judgement on them.

And no one could or would stop it.

I was soul sick and told over and over again that there was nothing to be done.

This was how America ran. And no one gave a single shit.

At this point, I offered Les one hundred percent of my royalties if he'd go the fuck away.

I thought we had a deal.

This sick bastard walked away, ever intent to punish the woman he'd tried to murder. A normal, mentally sound judge would have long put a stop to their torment.

Instead, Judge Drunk-On-My-Own-Power Dinky had my jewelry that he had no authority over, moved to Georgia. All my money seized with an illegal order that infringed on the rights of every member of my family, employee and friends. It allowed the receiver to sell off any and everything I owned without a court order and at his discretion to pay for my tormentors.

The homes of my family, friends and employees could be searched at will.

I wish I were joking.

What the fucking morons didn't even bother to realize? They had just breached every publishing contract I'd ever written.

Now those weren't worth the paper they were written on.

THIS WAS SUPPOSED TO BE the hearing about selling off my former office, "the cabin." Melissa had told me that the Dipshit Crew hadn't bothered to write a response to her motion.

Weird, right?

So, we waited as the hearing was set for 2:30 in the afternoon.

At noon, Melissa called to tell me that Judge Skeletor's juvenile docket was running over.

He really did do it all, which I found preposterous. Williamson County, alone, was more than half the size of the population of the city of Atlanta. They also had jurisdiction over Hickman, Lewis, and Perry Counties.

That meant that four fucking idiots presided over and decided the fates of hundreds of thousands of people. Four morons who were civil, criminal, juvenile and adult. To quote ole Dinky during one of his insane rants, "I do it all!"

Yet Fayette County, Georgia had ten for less than half the number of people that Williamson County "served."

And no one judge "did it all."

Their judges were assigned to one type of law and certain types of cases. Unlike Williamson-Fuck-You County where they let their judges get away with everything. "I don't care what the law is."

They proved that time and again.

My friend who is a private investigator said it best. "I've been speaking and networking with police and bail agents throughout the twenty-first district (legal district). It is incredible the stories I am hearing—but victims are terrified to come forward and do anything."

Another round of confirmation. Everyone knew how corrupt and scummy these bastards were and no one would put a stop to it.

Where were those alpha heroes?

Oh, I forgot. I only wrote about them in my novels. In real life, they didn't exist.

"Sorry, Terri. The hearing has been postponed to July 2."

"Are you kidding me?"

"There's nothing we can do."

And that was the whole gist of my frustration. They just kept coming and there was no end in sight.

JUNE 25

OUT OF THE BLUE, TANYA called. Tanya was the former store manager at Jared's who'd sold Les my jewelry. She was also the one who'd gift wrapped it and written on the notes that every single piece of my jewelry was from my sons and Dipshit.

Which, under Tennessee law, meant that Les wasn't entitled to a single piece of it.

Not a damn bit.

Melissa had even found the case law. Which meant that Dinky had knowingly come into my home without a warrant, for no reason whatsoever, and seized not only the personal property of my family.

He took mine, too.

His jurisdiction was only over marital property. He had none whatsoever over my personal property.

Dinky had not only violated my civil rights, but he had also robbed me. And for over a year, he'd refused to return a single piece of my property to me.

Of course, Les had his. Dinky had made sure to return it to him.

Yeah.

"Terri, you won't believe who just called me."

"Les?"

"Yes! Oh my God! Would you believe he asked if I would testify for him?"

Of course, I would. The man had poisoned me, my son and my cousin along with my cats. How far he'd go to cover his illegal activities would never surprise me.

"What did you say?"

"That the last thing he wanted was for me to testify. That he would not like what I had to say."

Awesome.

Then my phone rang again with Shelly, my LeVian rep who'd sold the bulk of that jewelry to Les. "You won't believe—"

"Yeah, I would. I just got off the phone with Tanya."

Shelly immediately wrote me a letter to use against them that proved my jewelry was all bought during holidays.

I thought the matter was settled.

Yeah, I was an idiot. Of course, I was an idiot. I married a monster.

JULY 2

O NCE AGAIN I WAS locked completely out of the hearing. Old Dinky wasn't about to let me in to hear their next insidious move.

But this time, Melissa was prepared, and she'd called me so that I could listen in on the Zoom meeting. We had my agent and our realtor standing by to counter their lies.

Or so I thought.

Somehow, I'd forgotten that the law doesn't matter in Williamson County, Tennessee. It wasn't even a suggestion.

On this day, Dinky was in rare form. He'd not only shushed my agent when he went in to talk, he refused to let my realtor or even the court reporter in.

That was how you knew how dirty he was being. He didn't want any record of it.

But the one thing about the state of Tennessee, it was a one-party consent state. Which meant I could record the session by audio so long as I was present during it.

So, I did.

Rolling my eyes, I listened to the idiot brigade.

"I don't know how she's paid—"

"Your Honor, I can—"

"Who are you?"

"Her agent."

Dinky then shushed him with a bullshit, made-up rule that had never once been implemented in any of our hearings.

Remember when his old buddy came in and... I can't say testified because he'd lied like a fucking criminal. Remember how I protested his speaking, but old Dinky spoke up about how he'd known his good buddy for all those years, and he trusted him.

I protested harder.

And Dinky had let him testify anyway.

Well, now I couldn't have a witness unless Cockburn agreed to let him speak.

That wasn't the law. My agent was there to refute Cockburn's lies and explain to the judge how I was paid as Dinky continually lamented that he didn't understand my industry.

Yet Cockburn and Dinky went on and on in a well-rehearsed speech.

"You have to give three days notice to have a witness."

Melissa scoffed. "Your Honor, I wasn't given their response until two days ago."

Literally at ten p.m., long after the court had closed so that Melissa could put in a witness' name. Or file a reply since Cockburn had added new complaints and new information.

For the first time in over three years, Dinky and Cockburn brought up a rule that no one had heard of...

Well, here was Melissa's response:

> I have combed through the rules and asked everyone here *(which included the wife of Dinky's old partner, Robert E. Lee)*. There is no three day rule. Total Bullshit.

It doesn't get more cut and dry. She went through the rule book and asked her colleagues. For the record, these weren't newbie lawyers. They were some of the "best" in this godforsaken hellhole.

But what Dinky and Cockburn revealed that day was a lot more damning.

They were having ex parte discussions about my case outside of court.

That was illegal.

How do I know?

Let's step back in time for a second. *Remember this email from Cockburn to ole Dick, my realtor?*

> Please see the attached emergency motion we have filed regarding the offer on the house... We have high hopes that we could at least have a phone call with the judges office today. Is this a possibility for you?

I had been so focused on the latter part of the email where she indicted John Alaimo about his part in screwing my buyer that I had missed this crucial piece of evidence.

*We have high hopes that we could at least have a phone call with the judges office today. Is this a possibility for you?*

The important thing to note here was that no attorney wanted to speak to a judge. There was no reason for Cockburn to call up Dinky's office with a witness, unless they were talking about my case outside of court.

My attorney knew *nothing* about this phone call and told me that she wasn't present for it.

Ex parte.

This was so dirty a three-day laundry cycle couldn't clean it.

"Were you on that call?" I asked Melissa later.

"No. I don't know anything about it."

*There you go.*

A rigged hearing. At my expense.

During that hearing, Dinky let it be known that he would not put Les out on the street, even though he'd done that to me and my two sons.

How was that for bias?

More than that, Dinky reiterated that all my money was to be held to pay off his friends, Les's attorneys, and that if I took any money from their "legal fund" that I had earned and spent it on my groceries, living expenses or the medication my life depended on, then I would have to pay it back. Should any additional funds be needed for the legal fund, they would begin selling off my personal property and not Les's.

Yeah. That was said.

Truth.

Cockburn had the order written up in less than an hour after the hearing, which means she already had it ready to go.

More proof they had cooked this up and that she already knew the judge's orders before he'd stated them.

It was sickening.

And I learned something else in that hearing. I had a mediation no one had told me about. Seriously. I supposed they'd intended to hold that, too, without my being present for it. My attorney friends who lived out of state were livid. But there was nothing to be done. Williamson County, one of the most corrupt places in this godforsaken country.

**E**VERYONE KEPT TELLING ME to give Les whatever he wanted and just get this done. The only thing I refused was to give him a cut of my future contracts. That wasn't the law, and the rotten, murderous bastard had no right to anything I earned after the divorce.

What did I agree to?

Forty percent royalties, *eighty thousand* dollars in cash from the sale of my home, and to let him keep the cabin and his car, show pony and gator free and clear. *Get the fuck out of my life, you deadbeat bastard.*

He walked.

No lie. I conceded everything and he *still* wouldn't take it.

The mediator, Ellen Roberts, had started the day off disgusted with them.

"Cockburn showed me two binders filled with complaints you've lodged against her with the Tennessee Board of Professional Responsibility."

I didn't even blink. "Does she have the two new ones I filed this week? Her binders probably need updating."

What had she expected me to say? Did she think I'd lie or stammer?

Hell, no.

It wasn't an indictment against me, but against the lying slag whore Les had hired who had no soul. No conscience.

No human decency.

"Well," Ellen sighed, "it had to be hard on her. Being the only woman in an all-male law firm."

I arched a brow. "Seriously? I was a woman in IT for twenty years where I was the sole female. That doesn't turn you into a bitch. Trust me."

Nothing was more misogynistic than IT in the eighties and nineties. Every time a guy saw me in the office, they told me what kind of coffee they wanted.

Or to hold their calls.

My satisfaction? The look on their faces when they were introduced to me as the director of the department.

Anyway, I learned quite a few personal tidbits about the whore. None of them good.

Too bad Cockburn had no idea what a walking embarrassment she was.

Melissa cleared her throat. "So, who is in there with him?"

"Cockburn and Sal Tiller."

My jaw went slack. "Are you kidding me?"

Ellen appeared confused. "Is there a problem?"

"You know the Dumas suit, right?"

"That the one over plagiarism?"

"Yeah... that bastard, Sal? That was her attorney that Les sued. The one he said was a flaming moron for four years. The one who is now charged with enforcing the settlement against *all Manly personnel and parties.* Les was a party to that, and I have a letter from the Tennessee Board of Professional Responsibility saying that it's a conflict."

If only Dinky had enforced it.

Now Ellen gaped. "Oh no! He has to go!" She promptly got up and went to tell Tiller the news.

He wasn't welcomed to be a part of this negotiation, which made my lip curl. "Why did he bring an IP attorney to this?"

Melissa shrugged. "I have no idea."

"Does he need him?"

"No."

*Anyone want to tell me that old Dumas wasn't behind this somehow?* Maybe I was wrong, but damn. Hell of a coincidence, eh? Remember that Nashville was the home of Country Music. You couldn't toss a pebble without hitting ten IP attorneys in this town.

And out of all the firms and all the lawyers, they just happened to get the same one as Dumas. *Yeah. Uh-huh...*

"My God, Terri!" Ellen fell down in the chair in front of me. "How could you stay married to that idiot for thirty years?" *Direct quote.*

So much for mediators being impartial. "I have never, in forty years of practice seen a more indecisive person! I'm surprised you didn't strangle him." *Also, a direct quote.*

She would spend five to fifteen minutes with us and then two and a half hours with them. *No lie.*

At the end of the day, she sighed. "I'm going to be honest. In forty years, I've never seen a woman separated from her jewelry in any court. I told them that. But you're dealing with Dinky, and he clearly doesn't like you. So, let me be blunt. Doesn't matter what the law is or what it says. Dinky will do whatever it is he wants and that means you can kiss that jewelry goodbye."

Those words still rang in my ears.

Another person admitting that Dinky was crooked.

Another person failing to stand up for the law and for what was right.

Awesome.

Meanwhile, after wasting ten hours of my day and a ride from Georgia to Tennessee, Baby Huey slinked out of the office and held his hand up to shield his face from his son as he passed by him in the lobby.

Cockburn waved like the lunatic she was.

Maddox just stared after them, dumbfounded. "I didn't even recognize him at first. Not until he held his hand up to shield his eyes. Then I knew the weasel."

I prayed to God that my children never said or thought that about me.

Worse? Ellen had told Les that Maddox's wife was expecting his first grandchild.

Les's response? "After I get that bitch jailed, I'm going to put you in prison. Then they'll deport your girlfriend back to her third world country, and she can have your kid there." Then after saying that to my son, he texted Maddox, "I hope you have the same joy bringing your child into the world that your mom and I had."

*Are you kidding me?*

We had lost everything when Maddox was born. We were homeless and starving and we'd almost lost my son.

That was what you wished on him? You sick, twisted son of a pedophile whore.

To quote my brother, "Jesus, Terri, he's too stupid to even be a good bigot."

It was true. Japan was far from a third world country.

What had happened to him? This was a man who had voted for Jesse Jackson when I married him.

Now, he was some racist lunatic no one recognized.

"His reputation is important to him." That was what Ellen had told me.

"And mine isn't to me? I've told the truth about him. They have accused me of everything from witchcraft to spouse abuse."

"Well, I could understand the spouse abuse," Ellen had whispered under her breath.

Too bad it was a lie. I seldom even raised my voice to Les.

What a total piece of shit.

Even so, my boys tried to talk him into meeting with them.

"We're going to get this settled, Mom. Enough is enough."

I prayed Maddox and Nick could do it. Because he was right. Enough was enough.

MADDOX CALLED TO TELL me he was meeting his father for lunch.

"You sure about this?"

"Yeah, Ma. I'm done. I want to get on with my life."

Me, too. For over two years for Maddox and six with me, that bastard had kept us in utter chaos and limbo. First with the Dumas case and then with this.

I just wanted them gone and out! Stick a fork in me and serve me already.

Then I checked my email.

"I hate to be the bearer of bad tidings... "

My appeal against Dinky's bullshit conviction where Cockburn had lied had been denied.

"You're out of appeals. Dinky has ordered you to serve ten days and you have to report on July 30."

*What the fuck?* I'd already served one of those days.

So, he was giving me a longer sentence than he was entitled to by law.

Welcome to Williamson Fucking County. Where the shit stains ruled, and the Constitution wasn't fit to be toilet paper to wipe our asses.

Wow.

I immediately called Nan. "Is this true?"

"No. You can appeal again. Ask for a rehearing." She called Melissa.

Guess what she learned?

Melissa had known about it and had deliberately withheld that information from me. She had sat there, all day, in mediation, and not said a word. She knew that one of my best friends was an appellate attorney and rather than ask her for help, Melissa had deliberately waited until it was past the time that I could file a motion or appeal on it.

So much for being compromised.

I was beginning to think she was on the take.

Or worse, as I learned from Nan, she'd been threatened by Dinky and was terrified.

Yeah, you heard that right, too. Dinky had called her about my case, at home, on the weekend, and threatened her. Then when Melissa made the mistake of telling a friend, that friend went to another attorney and told them what had happened.

"Oh, that must have been Dinky."

That was absolutely one hundred percent true. Dinky was so corrupt that it was normal water cooler gossip.

And of course, that rat ran straight to Dinky to tell him that Melissa had contacted that attorney and asked him what she should do. During Melissa's next hearing (the one I wasn't told about), Dinky had shamed her in court, over the phone call where he'd threatened her.

That was why she'd been so terrified and mousy over the last few weeks.

Had it also been why she'd waited to ensure I had no appeals?

That I could do nothing, except go to jail?

Well, they couldn't take my fingers. I immediately started my next newsletter.

Then Maddox called. "That fucker cancelled lunch! No reason. I guess he was embarrassed that he walked away from the settlement you agreed to."

"No, baby. He knows that I have to go to jail for his lies."

Now Maddox, who was there and had witnessed the lies, was furious. The fact that Dinky could continue to lie on his reports was even more sickening.

Pull the footage and listen to the tapes. I was the only person in the world who the judge had to yell at three times for them to speak up because I was so cowed before him. That was some outburst, huh?

"I can't hear you!"

Three times he shouted that at me.

"I know you're deaf! Speak up!"

And yet I was the one sent to jail, and I wasn't the one having a fit or losing control.

It was so bad, even the police who were present apologized to me for his behavior.

My son immediately began calling his own lawyers. "I've had it. That bastard abused us, treated you like shit and now this?"

I was terrified. "Stay out of it. I don't want them arresting you." These soulless bastards were insane, and no one would stop them.

But I still had the senators I was talking to and my fanbase.

Maybe one of them could help.

M Y FANS WERE RALLYING. They were the one thing, besides my sons, I could count on. Les and his crew had begun their bullshit counterattacks.

*She's a plagiarist!* They accused *me* of "ripping off" one of the authors Les had been trying to sue for years.

And they accused me of "cutting and pasting" material.

Yeah. They were the ones who needed new ideas since they couldn't come up with anything original to insult me over.

Right down to the ole, "I pulled the transcripts and read them."

Really? During COVID when everyone was out of work and needing money, you paid five hundred dollars for a transcript?

And received it, even though the courthouse was shut down and no one was working, there?

How did that happen?

And how did you find out which transcript was the right one since I was constantly in and out of court? Especially as they'd been hauling me into court every other day, literally. So, you happened to pick the right day and the right transcript.

Or you bought every one of them to the tune of thousands and thousands of dollars.

Sure.

And they thought I wrote fiction.

Not to mention, I knew it was a lie. The transcript only said, "Ms. Manly left the room."

There was nothing there about my "storming out" or any of the other bullshit Dinky had lied about in his court report. If I had called the whore a "fucking liar" loud enough for the entire first row to hear, I was rather sure the court reporter would have notated it.

Yeah. They were all liars, but it was the voices in their lizard brains that were calling them that.

Anyway, I knew the contempt motion would be coming. What I never expected was this utter bullshit:

> 3.     Upon filing of each accounting under this Order, Wife shall submit to the Court an order for approval of disbursement if necessary for the difference of her monthly income received and $22,382.00. If necessary for the payment of Wife's spousal support obligation for Husband, this order shall direct the Clerk to make disbursement of whatever shortfall owed by Wife of Husband's support payment directly to Husband rather than to Wife.

Yeah. They had illegally confiscated every single dime I'd ever made in my life. Then directed all my publishers and agents to pay it to the asshole they'd picked out, not me, and ordered me to pay that douche-nozzle four hundred and fifty dollars an hour to keep my money and property.

Now I was being held in contempt for the fact that the very ass-wipe Cockburn and crew had put over me, who was ripping me off, wasn't paying *them*.

*Are you fucking kidding me?*

Then, after knowing I was being sent to jail for their lies and bullshit, they added this:

> 3.     The Court order Wife imprisoned until purged of contempt pursuant to Tenn.
>
> ode Ann. § 29-9-104 & 105 and complies with all violations outlined herein;

Violations? How the fuck could I be violating their order when they'd taken all the money out of my hands and put it in the hands of their own people and the fucking county clerk?

The court clerk held one half of my money and their monkey held the rest.

Yeah. They were that fucked in the head.

And now putting their threats to jail, in writing.

Because I was being held in contempt for their stupidity and greed.

And they were intending to keep me in jail until they decided when to pay themselves out of my money they had illegally confiscated.

Now, in a normal court with a normal, fair judge, this wouldn't be a problem. A normal judge would slap them and laugh them out to the street.

But we weren't dealing with normal or fair.

We were dealing with Bubba Dinky.

Corrupt piece of shit. In their pocket. "I will do whatever you want." More to the point, "I don't care what the law is."

Welcome to America. Land of the severely disenfranchised. Where a judge who was arrested for prostitution and let go (his charges purged) by his buddy who was then put in jail for attempting to frame a woman.

They were publicly extorting me, and he was the judge so there was nothing I could do.

*Are you sitting down?*

*Or did you fall over?*

I hadn't told you about the real kicker yet.

*Are you ready?*

Dinky had personally picked out the date that I, an at-risk woman with severe health issues, was to go to jail.

At the time he signed that, he was signing orders to let real criminals out of jail so as not to infect them with COVID.

Truth.

He was under orders from his superiors to release any "nonviolent" offenders out of jail.

While he was ordering me to serve time because he'd had a tantrum and couldn't control himself.

Then, Dumbass Dinky assigned for this new bullshit motion to be heard at the same exact time he was telling me to report to jail to make sure that I could not refute their lies and be heard. Because I would be in jail.

I.E., they could now find me guilty without my being present to defend myself and be thrown in jail for no real crime to never again be let out.

Just what they'd been threatening. They intended to lock me away for no reason.

I wouldn't be let out until Dinky determined that I "had learned my lesson."

Stupid me, I'd thought the days of doing this to a woman who'd displeased her husband had ended in the Victorian Era.

Oh wait, this was Nashville, the Athens of the South. Yeah. I forgot. Nashville: land of Nathan Bedford Forrest. Where a judge could hang that on his wall, and no one blinked.

They were that sick.

And I was that screwed.

**M**ELISSA WAS AS USELESS as tits on a boar hog. No, really. Forget the fact that she'd sat on that Appellate decision until the time for me to file another appeal had run out and allowed Dinky to resentence me for his temper tantrum.

We had less than four days to go and I couldn't get the stupid bitch to file anything to mitigate the sentence.

Dinky had threatened her well. She was so scared she wouldn't do anything.

"Get this shit settled!" she screamed at me. "You'll still have to serve the ten days."

"I didn't do anything!" I couldn't believe that I was going to have to serve time for a judge who'd committed a crime, but because his criminal friend had let him off and expunged his record, he was allowed to be a judge and punish women.

Dinky was a sick in the head fuck! He was allowed to lie, and no one would stop him. I had proof he was a liar. I could prove he'd lied on his court report. It didn't even match the transcript.

*Are you fucking kidding me?*

A judge was not allowed to embarrass or disparage the court system. To cause the public to lose faith in the integrity of the system.

This bastard was wiping his ass with our Constitution, and no one cared.

In fact, they were helping him.

Nan was the only one on my side. "I wrote a motion for Melissa to file. He should, given COVID and the fact that the Supreme Court is telling judges to let all nonviolent offenders out, allow you to pay a fine and go."

But it was Dinky and Melissa blaming me.

As if I did something. Melissa hadn't even been present when it happened. Constance had been my attorney at the time.

Not that it mattered. Everyone seemed to forget the fact that my sons had been told by their brother that I was going to jail that day.

That all of that had been preplanned. That a fan had emailed my aunt to tell her that Les and crew were going to set me up that day to make sure I went to jail.

Dinky was in on it.

There had been nothing I could do.

No one got ten days for calling a pedophile a pedophile. Especially when the judge knew the Manlys had pedophiles in their family because Cockburn had already admitted it and told Dinky it was why Les was so fucked in his head. The molestation of his childhood had made him a monster.

Why he took that out on me and his sons, I had no idea. No one did. He was crueler to us than to the ones who'd molested him. Why he'd transferred his hatred to us, I didn't know.

Stockholm Syndrome was real. He'd always wanted his mother's approval.

Too many years of wanting a "perfect" life. He'd resented his sons for having safety and a loving mother.

I knew it sounded sick, but it was the truth. He'd made so many comments about that. "I wish I was a Manly kid."

Unlike me. I'd suffered abuse and I'd wanted better for my children. I'd never resented them. My job had been to protect them. To shield them.

I would never understand Les's cruelty.

My only hope was that hell was real and that he'd spend eternity there, roasting.

Alongside the monsters he'd brought into our world.

How could I be facing ten days for no crime? All because of a criminal judge while the rest of the world remained silent?

No news agency would say a word.

How was this not news?

The county yelling at a woman to repaint her rainbow house. *That* was news. But not a woman and her sons having their home invaded and their private property seized by a judge who had no jurisdiction over it.

A judge seizing a woman's money and making her an indentured servant.

That was okay, too.

Along with jailing a mother during COVID for no reason. Sure. Welcome to America. Land of the vapid and selfish.

*If anyone thinks for one minute that this couldn't happen to you or a loved one, think again.*

All my rights and property had been seized.

I was poisoned in front of hundreds of thousands of fans and witnesses.

No one said a word.

*So, tell me, who would stand up for you?*

N O WORD FROM THE magpies. So much for the "we'll have something to her on Saturday" lie. But then that was all they'd done since they started this nightmare. Lie about everything.

There was no way out. How could I settle a divorce with a collection of sadistic psychos that the law had allowed to abuse the public with no oversight?

No one had seen or heard of anything like this. Normally, someone in a divorce had a brain and/or a conscience. Either the judge or at least one attorney on the other side.

There was nothing to be done when all of them were fucking crazy and possessed of absolute greed.

Meanwhile, Nan finally convinced Melissa to file Nan's emergency motion requesting Skelator to either commute my sentence to "house arrest" or to drop it.

At the last minute.

Because, at this point, Melissa was determined to see me go to jail.

Not speculation. Truth.

Nan had been forced to strong-arm her into doing the right thing. Melissa was that afraid of Dinky.

Her motion covered everything, right up to the fact that Dinky, himself, had been releasing actual criminals while he demanded that a hard-working mother of three be jailed during COVID for his hissy fit.

The only thing Nan had left off was the mention of my liver and kidney disease that had been caused by Les poisoning me. My asthma that I'd had since childhood and my bronchial spasms that had left me with a prescription for a nebulizer.

Not to mention, the GURD and stomach issues and high blood pressure that required thirty dollars worth of medications a day.

When I mentioned that to Nan, she laughed and said that the judge would require proof.

"He has my medical records. He knows I have all that. It's more than well-established. He even has the test results, and X-rays. Along with the two kidney stone surgeries I've had in the last year and the fact that he knows he is denying me the critical medical care I need by refusing to allow me to go to my doctors." Because Dinky was that sadistic an asshole.

With no regard whatsoever for anyone's life.

"It's all business," he claimed, which often left me wondering if he was a paid hitman for the other side. That was the only reason I could conceive that he could have so little regard for someone's life and consider it "business."

After all, even an idiot as stupid as he was had to know that you couldn't deprive a woman of the medication her life depended on and the medical care she needed for two years and it not have devastating consequences.

"I'm not from the AG's office. I was a practicing attorney. You can't BS me!" That was his lunatic answer to everything. As if being a regular idiot attorney imbued him with magic omniscience. But given the stupidity of the rest of the attorneys at the Cheatum & Howe firm he'd founded, I wouldn't be bragging.

The attorney generals I'd met had all been intelligent and, contrary to Dinky's mad ravings, had practiced real law and not the made-up bullshit that came out of his mouth. At least they knew what the law was and made a pretense of following it.

Unlike Lord Skeletor.

But then he'd been invested with unlimited powers by the state of Tennessee that refused to ride herd on the monster they'd unleashed on the public.

And I couldn't understand why no AG would listen to my tale and see what an unbridled monster he was.

He's going to give Les everything."

The mediator had made it worse. "You created the monster when you let him stay at home and not work."

I still wanted to claw her eyes out for her mocking stupidity. It wasn't my fault. I had tried my best to get that bastard off my couch. But the laws of the land would have thrown my babies into the hands of a pedophile.

I'd been trapped. And for protecting my children and not being selfish, I was going to spend the rest of my life paying for it.

How could this happen?

All I could think about was that day when Cockburn had stood before Woodly, an ex-Army Ranger who should be ashamed of himself for the rest of his life, and said, "As soon as she reads this, Your Honor, she'll want to settle."

He'd let that bitch blackmail me and hadn't say a word.

And they'd allowed her to continue to do it every day since.

To torture me and my children.

I had offered them absolutely everything to stop this madness.

"They think it's a trick." That had been Melissa's text to me.

Of course, they thought that. They were so crooked and dirty, it defied believability. Everything they did was a trick. They couldn't conceive of anyone doing anything above board.

Good faith and decency were as alien a concept for them as their level of malevolence was to me.

Beware anyone who ever tried to buy a home from Cockburn Construction. That was the dirty, underhanded bitch who owned it and ran it.

You would be screwed.

Caveat emptor to the extreme as you'd be locked in the same court system that she controlled if you ever had a problem with her products.

"That's the problem when you don't have a unified court system." Nan had been as disgusted as I was. "It lends itself to this level of corruption. Honestly, I thought we'd done away with it. But what do I know? I live in Po-dunk Alabama. But damn, I'll take that any day over the made-up bullshit that passes for laws and court up in Tennessee. That's some fucked up shit you got there."

She wasn't alone in thinking that.

And their failure to get back to me after I'd made yet another attempt to give the fucking idiot one hundred percent of my royalties and all the cash and property we had left, showed that he really, truly had no intention of settling this. That he didn't want a divorce.

They only wanted to continue to abuse me for as long as possible.

This had never been about divorcing me. Only about humiliating and destroying me.

As he'd said to my sons.

All I could think was that I'd hoped Dumas had paid him handsomely. It was the only thing that made sense. Why else would her attorney be embroiled in this?

Why would he have forced me to stop that lawsuit, then start this madness to destroy me when the entire time we'd be in that earlier suit his whole concern had been to "not go broke on attorney fees" and to "protect Terri's reputation at all costs."

Yet if he really meant to continue to live off my writing, then why would he be so hellbent on ruining my career?

As Arthur Conan Doyle so often wrote, "Whenever you remove all possibilities, whatever remains, no matter how improbable, must be the truth."

Nothing else remained.

So here I was. Caught in a vortex with no way out.

And just how ridiculous was the level of stupidity I had to contend with?

This was the email my attorney sent to me:

> Melissa,
>
> I hope you are doing well and had a nice vacation. Welcome back! My associate, Carly, is going through the financial records and confirming various amounts. One thing we are missing is the log in credentials for the Etsy store. Is that something you have or can obtain? Mr. Manly did not have it.
>
> George Murrey

*Are you fucking kidding me?*

Now since this was a divorce what would make the idiot known as George Murrey think for one second that my do-nothing, lazy sack-of-shit husband would have the login information for my store?

And who above the age of five in this day and age was so fucking stupid they'd be idiotic enough to ask for anyone's login information for their store account?

*Can we say data breach?*

*Can we say invasion of privacy?*

*Can we say major fucking lawsuit?*

*I think we can.*

And my idiot attorney was stupid enough to ask me to hand it over without a second thought, knowing Les's idiot barracuda was in on this chain.

Know what else was in that store? The evidence that proved Hogg was contacting my fans and disparaging me and my business.

More than that was the evidence that she was lying to customs and committing felonies (and stealing from my company). And these fucking morons wanted me to put that evidence into the hands of people who had shown absolutely no regard for the law or my rights.

Okay, sure.

As if the lying whore known as Cockburn wasn't above going into my system and deleting whatever she wanted or going through my purchase history to see where I'd bought a birthday present for a friend so that she could declare, "Look! Manly's a witch! She bought a Voodoo doll, right here!"

God forbid I buy my friends presents or how about the anniversary present Les had bought me that was a Shaman rod. Now those very purchases he'd made in my account could be held against me.

Just as they'd lied about his illegal charges on my credit cards.

My attorney was stupid enough to tell me to let them in.

*Anyone else still in doubt that she hadn't been threatened?*

*Or worse, that she might be in on that take, too?*

After all, she'd told my friend Nan what good friends she was with the jackals and how they hung out together. I was sick to my stomach.

My own attorney was selling me down the river. No wonder she'd helped carry my personal property out of my home and in over a year hadn't asked to get any of it back. Nor had she ever filed an appeal on any of their egregious acts.

She had to be in on it, too.

They had plundered everything. Meanwhile, Melissa was complicit to let me go to jail from now on so that they could mock me again. Post my mugshot and covers all over the internet while knowing I'd have no access to stop them.

And how could I run my business if I was behind bars? How was that protecting the marital estate?

If ever there was a judge that needed to come off the bench, Bubba Dinky, whoremonger, was it. Yet no one said a word. They were all too busy attacking me.

The worst part? Because I stood up for my fans and their right to privacy, because I was protecting their credit card information and home addresses, I knew I'd have another contempt charge leveled at me.

And more jail time added.

For nothing more than following the laws that forbade me from handing over the private information of my fans to a hostile third-party.

JULY 30

T**O CALL THIS DAY A SHIT** show was an insult to shit shows the world over.

After I survived this day, we needed a better term. Like shit shower. Shit typhoon.

*The shitter dome.*

Something, because this was the Mother of All Shit Shows.

It began with the near miss the day before where the judge had shown a modicum of common sense.

Or so I thought.

Then he'd decided to double down by forcing me to appear in public.

During the height of COVID.

Rather than help me as she was supposed to do, my attorney who'd been practically packing my bags for me to go to jail, refused to do anything.

"You have to be there."

This said to me after 5:00 PM EST. She refused to budge even though she'd told me repeatedly that I didn't have to be there and that it would be a Zoom hearing.

Now, Melissa was telling me something different.

How was I supposed to be there when it was a four and a half car hour ride and the last time I'd made it, my car had broken down and stranded me?

*Ever try to get roadside assistance in the middle of a pandemic?* It wasn't fun.

Nor was it easy.

Most everything was shut down.

Not to mention, they'd withheld my money from me that they'd illegally seized, I had no money to get a hotel room. No reliable transportation.

And my attorney had shrugged it off, unlike the fucking barracudas my husband had hired.

Then God sent me another angel.

Nine o'clock that night, my former attorney, Constance, called to check on me. I must have really broken down because by the end of the call, she'd agreed to take me on again as her client.

I was sobbing, I admit it. I felt as if my attorney had not only thrown in the towel, she was using it to strangle me.

Constance, unlike Melissa, told me that I could continue it, which really pissed me off as I had asked Melissa to do this repeatedly and she'd refused.

Even Nan had told her to do it.

"Why?"

Oh gee, because your client was supposed to be in jail, and it was a motion to keep her there and she wouldn't be there to defend herself? Where the fuck was your head?

*Oh yeah, up her ass.*

More to the point, where was her heart or any semblance of compassion? The last thing any human being needed was to have another contempt charge being thrown on them while they were about to go to jail for ten days.

See, I'd thought that I was supposed to report directly to jail. Come to find out, Melissa knew I was supposed to go to court first, before they locked me up with an additional bullshit contempt charge for however many days.

Or weeks.

Or months.

Was she trying to kill me, too?

Who the hell did this? Had any of them read the Constitution? Did they not teach that in the shoddy night school Cockburn had attended?

> The Eighth Amendment to the U.S. Constitution prohibits the federal government from imposing cruel and unusual punishment for crimes. The amendment states, "Excessive bail shall not be required, nor excessive fines imposed, nor cruel and unusual punishment inflicted." The due process clause of the Fourteenth Amendment to the U.S. Constitution bars the states from inflicting such punishment for state crimes, and most state constitutions also prohibit the infliction of cruel and unusual punishment.

> In attempting to define cruel and unusual punishment, federal and state courts have generally analyzed two aspects of punishment: the method and the amount. The U.S. Supreme Court held that the Eighth Amendment had been contravened when prison officials had disciplined an inmate for disruptive behavior by handcuffing him to a "hitching post", once for two hours and once for seven hours, depriving the inmate of his shirt, exposing him to the sun, denying his requests for hydration, and refusing to allow him the opportunity to use the bathroom. *(Hmmm, so when Dinky had put me in jail for having to go to the restroom for my kidney disease, this would definitely fall under this doctrine, yes?)*

> However, a defendant need not suffer actual physical injury or pain before a punishment will be declared cruel and unusual. In Trop v. Dulles, 356 U.S. 86, 78 S. Ct. 590, 2 L. Ed. 2d 630 (1958), the U.S. Supreme Court held that "[t]here may be involved no physical mistreatment, no primitive torture. There is instead the total destruction of the individual's status in organized society. It is a form of punishment more primitive than torture, for it destroys for the individual the political existence that was centuries in the development." The Court also opined that the Eighth Amendment must "draw its meaning from the evolving standards of decency that mark the progress of a maturing society."

But wait, it gets better:

> In Solem v. Helm, 463 U.S. 277 (1983), the Supreme Court held that a sentence may not be disproportionate to the crime committed, regardless of whether the crime is a felony or a misdemeanor. To measure proportionality, the court must look at several factors. These factors

include the severity of the offense, the harshness of the penalty, the sentences imposed on others within the same jurisdiction, and the sentences imposed on others in different jurisdictions. *(Ten days for going to the bathroom for a proven medical condition and calling a known pedophile that the opposing counsel had even admitted was a pedophile was beyond extreme).*

The Supreme Court owed me an apology, and so did the state of Tennessee.

They had seriously violated my constitutional rights.

Not that anyone gave a flying fuck.

Morality and the law apparently had no place in the great state of Tennessee.

At any rate, Constance wrote me a quick continuance and told me how to file it with the court first thing that morning:

> I, Terri Manly, received notice after 5 PM EST on July 29, 2020 that the Motion for Civil Contempt was an "in person" court hearing on July 30, 2020. For the last four months, we've had only Zoom hearings. Naturally, I assumed that would be the format for this one as well as no one had informed me otherwise.

> I particularly assumed my presence wasn't required as I'd been ordered to report to jail on July 30, 2020 at the same exact time as the hearing, as there was no feasible way for me to be in two places at once. Not to mention that I had been told repeatedly by my attorney that my presence wasn't required for this hearing. Given that and since I was told that my report date had been moved 60 days and with the recent rapid resurgence of COVID, I naturally assumed there would be no need for travel as most states are again quarantining and my attorney told me it would be a Zoom meeting.

> Trying to appear in person at this point and with so little notice being given to me is an impossibility. At this time, I am living four and a half hours away because my home was ordered by the Court to be sold and I was given very little time to find new housing for my circumstances. The only car I have left in my possession is a 2015 Chevy Traverse. This vehicle needs repairs that I have been unable to complete due to the financial limitations imposed by the Court and it broke down recently when I had to travel to Nashville for mediation.

> I know that this is the first time this is set on the docket and due to my extenuating circumstances, I am respectfully requesting that this be continued until I can arrange to be in Franklin with my counsel.

> Thank you for this consideration.

How simple was that? Why couldn't Melissa do it?

I thought everything was fine until Nan told me they could order my arrest anyway.

*Are you fucking kidding me?*

Now I had Melissa screaming at me, too.

"Trust me." Constance was calm in the middle of my shit storm.

I did what she'd told me, and Melissa went wild over it. "You can't do this! I'm withdrawing as your attorney!"

Awesome. Now she was taking ques from the bankruptcy dipshit.

*Bail when the heat got hot.*

At this point I was thinking that she was like the tour bus driver we'd had who couldn't read a map or follow GPS.

*Dude, you need another career.*

Obviously, you were ill equipped for law if you didn't like conflict.

*And how did it go?*

Well old Dink was up to his tricks. He started it off with a senile tirade against me. "Tell your client to stop her social media posts where she's accusing me of having an affair with Cockburn!"

Excuse me?

While I had alluded to it and questioned it many times in private because of their weird actions in public and court, I had never, ever posted about it on any of my social media sites. Especially not one owned by my publisher.

Were those the scary voices in his head again?

I would have thought Schizophrenia should preclude a judge from having a seat on that bench.

But then it got even better. "And tell her not to post that I've been following her into parking decks!"

All right, you senile old goat, I knew where that stupidity came from. Apparently, he'd gotten around to finally reading one of my complaints against him that I'd filed with the Judiciary Board of Review.

But I never said "I" was the one he'd stalked.

It was my friends Rio and Rose he'd followed to their cars in a parking lot. They would both testify to those facts as that had happened and he was guilty of it.

If that was an example of his ability to read and comprehend facts or to recall them, then I had an even better reason why this stupid bastard had no place on a bench.

And it naturally spawned another complaint from me to the Judiciary Board of Review:

> Dear Board,
>
> Yet again, I am writing to you about Judge Bubba Dinky and his egregious behavior on the bench.
>
> On July 30, 2020, after I'd sent the enclosed request for a simple continuance, Judge Dinky decided to take that opportunity to shame me in court, and accuse me of actions I haven't taken, with absolutely no evidence whatsoever.
>
> These are acts that are wholly unbecoming of a judge and that clearly violate his rules of judicial conduct. Rather than simply grant my motion, the judge spiraled off into an incoherent rant to my attorney instructing her to tell me to refrain from my social media posts where he claimed that I'd accused him of having sex with attorney Bonnie Cockburn.
>
> I have never once posted that to any social media site, and I am appalled that any judge would level such an appalling and graphic accusation in open court without any evidence. Not only is it defamation against me, but it had to be shocking and embarrassing for Ms. Cockburn who was also present.
>
> More than that, he went on to say that I was not to post about his "stalking me" in parking decks. Again, I have never made such a post, nor have I made such an allegation. I can only assume Judge Dinky read that in one of my earlier complaints to you about his egregious actions on June 19, 2019 where he followed two of my witnesses into a parking lot to intimidate them and they both felt threatened by his actions. They will gladly testify to this fact as it left them both unsettled, and one of them reported his actions to a Lewis County detective because she was so unsettled by it.

The fact that this judge cannot keep the facts straight should appall, concern and offend you as much as it does me. If this is an example of his reading comprehension, recollection of facts and deductive reasoning, he needs to be removed immediately from the bench for the sake of everyone in Williamson County.

And please remember that this is a judge who gave me ten days in jail for saying in court that a known pedophile was a pedophile. He had me arrested over that one word by saying, "That's a deplorable allegation." Yet at that time he held in his hands the motions where not only my attorney, but Ms. Cockburn had verified the fact that the man was a pedophile. So, I find it absolutely "deplorable" that he would make such unfounded accusations in open court against me without any evidence whatsoever and use his position as a judge to threaten, intimidate and bully me while attempting to deprive me of my First Amendment rights after he'd already violated my Eighth Amendment rights.

Never mind the fact that his comments are, again, blatant sexual harassment against me and the rest of the women present, and the language he used was shocking and chosen to illicit graphic images unbecoming in a court of law, and in particular from the mouth of a judge.

How many times is this judge going to breach the Judicial Code of Conduct before you take action?

Canon 1: A Judge Should Uphold the Integrity and Independence of the Judiciary

Canon 2: A Judge Should Avoid Impropriety and the Appearance of Impropriety in All Activities

Canon 3: A Judge Should Perform the Duties of the Office Fairly, Impartially and Diligently

Again, there was no reason for him to single me out and reprimand me in court for specific acts I have never taken, and to use such graphic, shocking language that has been deemed inappropriate by human resources. This shows a clear bias for this judge against me, which undeniably violates the third canon.

I beseech you, again, to exercise the authority you have been given to protect the citizens of Williamson County. Please remove this menace from the courtroom so that he can no longer act as if he is a king, and it is his own private kingdom. The laws are in place to protect us and a judge is charged with enforcing them. Not mocking them and ignoring them while he randomly picks on citizens for his own personal and sick satisfaction.

Thank you.

Did I really expect anything from them?

No.

They had completely destroyed my ability to believe in the American court system. It was a bigger joke than confessions gathered by tying someone to a rack.

And at least those victims died and weren't caught in the never-ending nightmare that my life had become. The endless threats of jail for things I hadn't done.

This level of bullying was so far beyond the pale of acceptability that no one around me could believe it.

Joan told me that every day she came to work she expected to find my corpse. "I walk through the house with a sick lump in my stomach, wondering if today is the day you couldn't take it anymore."

This was a woman who'd known me almost the entirety of my life. A woman who'd witnessed the abuse of my childhood. The fact that even she was waiting for me to throw in the towel said it all about what they were doing to me.

And the fact that Hogg was right. They *were* trying to kill me.

The court was assisting them in it.

No, was a willing participant in it, and no one would stop them from their murder.

The whole world was watching.

When it was over, I got a text from Melissa. "You lucked out. The judge granted your motion." I lucked out.

Those were her exact words. Lucked out that the judge had followed the law? Seriously? That was exactly how sorry Williamson County was.

How corrupt.

That a person was "lucky" on the day a judge decided to do his job and obey the law.

Wow. Just wow.

The only reason why Dinky had done that was the fact that the motion had been written by Nan. A twenty-year veteran of appellate law.

Dinky had recognized the fact that it was written so that it could have been immediately filed with the Appellate Court. Nan had already prepared that motion too, to be filed in the event Dinky did what we'd expected him to...

Deny it.

But his common sense must have made a rare appearance.

I wanted to take a victory lap, but I knew better. I'd have to be in court, again, in two weeks. Because the jackals had to bleed my estate and prey on a sick man who was too stupid to stop them.

And I had no way out. I couldn't buy them off or get them off my back.

The torture continued with no end in sight.

TODAY STARTED OFF with another bar complaint. As I'd said, this was becoming a game. How many times would I report them? How many times would the Tennessee Board of Professional Responsibility refuse to do anything?

The number appeared to be infinite.

At any rate, here was what I filed:

Dear Board,

Yet again, I am writing to request your intervention against Bonnie Cockburn, John Alamo and Mika House for their illegal and immoral actions against me and their own client, Lester Manly. These are three attorneys who have no business with a bar license and who need to be disciplined and removed from the legal profession.

As you can see from the attached files, my attorney had done, for the fourth time, all the paperwork those three demanded and refused to accept for no good or legitimate reason, and had filed it with the court. Yet after those three took an illegal action to have all my income seized by a judge who is their former business associate and without showing one iota of evidence to the judge for any misdeed or misconduct on my part, they are now holding all my money and refusing to allow a single cent of it to be given to either me or their own client for us to pay our bills. Rather that money is being earmarked as their "legal fund." So to ensure they can keep as much of it as possible for themselves, they are now filing frivolous motion after frivolous motion to drive up their cost while both their client and I are being forced to go month after month without a penny.

Do not even begin to tell me that this is okay with you. My attorney, Melissa Magillicutty, has attempted to negotiate with them, but the only way they will drop their frivolous motion and allow their client to be paid is if, in direct violation of the judge's orders, I agree to pay their client and do without the money they illegally seized from me that I legally earned that I need to pay my bills and for the medication my life depends on (money the judge said I was entitled to be paid every month that they, not I or my attorney, have stopped the payment of for no legal or moral reason). Otherwise, they are going to put me in jail for no legitimate reason.

The legal definition of extortion:

Obtaining money or property by threat to a victim's property or loved ones, intimidation, or false claim of a right. It is a felony in all states, except that a direct threat to harm the victim is usually treated as the crime of robbery.

Under that legal definition, they are guilty of robbing both me and my husband, their client. This is absurd that they are allowed to practice law in this manner, and that you are okay with it.

Likewise, rather than call my attorney about the insurance in this matter, they tacked on another frivolous claim for no other purpose than to enrich themselves. As you can plainly see from my other attachments, I have ample coverage, which they also knew I had as that had been filed with the court and they had a copy of it at the time they filed this frivolous motion to enrich themselves. What expired was a redundant policy that I chose to replace with another company. I am allowed, under my court order, to do that as that falls within the confines of "running my business" even though I've had it run into the ground because of their tortious interference with it by filing needless motion after needless motion to enrich their own pockets and utterly destroy our marital estate.

Even more egregious, they are preventing their client from seeing his own children and will not allow him to accept any settlement offer I have made, including one where I offered him everything just to stop this three-ring circus they are headlining. Rather, the minute I agree to all their terms, they walk away and refuse to let us settle this divorce. Ask our mediator. I was willing to concede and give in to everything they asked for and rather than write up the MDA, they filed more frivolous motions against me to again drive up their income.

Three times now, those attorneys have told us that they'd draft the MDA for me to sign and have refused to do so, so that we can end this travesty and go on with our lives. And none of this is helping their client as you well know. Rather, they are holding us hostage until they deplete every dime we have.

Yes, I have taken this to the judge, but as noted and as you well know, he is a former business associate of theirs and is refusing to discipline them. You have the authority to stop attorneys from preying on their clients. Nothing is clearer than these three intentionally, willfully and maliciously refusing to get the money their client needs and wants because they are too busy collecting billable hours at our expense, while threatening my freedom, health and wellbeing in order to get what they want.

This is criminal behavior in its purest form.

Because of their actions, I am on my third month without the high blood pressure and stomach medication my life depends on, and they are aware of this. They are very much aware that they are putting my life at serious risk. These attorneys are threatening my life, my liberty and are knowingly violating laws and acting in an egregious manner that is against every single code in the Tennessee Board of Professional Responsibility's ethics doctrine. How you can allow them to continue to bully, threaten and rob people is beyond me. I, again, implore you to exert the power you have been given and stop them from menacing the public. We are not their only victims and I have given you proof of this, time and again.

Please do something.

Sadly, I expected this to fall on the same deaf ears and for them to come back to me with yet another sorry excuse for why they refused to take action and put a stop to the monsters they were charged with wrangling.

How many complaints would it take before they did their job? I'd lost count. There was a box in my office filled with their lame excuses to absolve themselves of any responsibility.

That was why the jackals were so confident and proud to prey on everyone around them.

My friend Nan said it best, "Tennessee's legal system is set up to foster corruption without oversight."

*Third most corrupt state in America.*

*Nashville, one of the most corrupt cities.*

And I was at ground zero for it.

This was beyond ridiculous. No one should have their life threatened because of a divorce. And it wasn't even my spouse trying to kill me at this point.

His own attorneys were now willfully and deliberately aiding and abetting him. They were playing Russian Roulette with my life and with my family history of stroke and heart attack. Deliberately pushing my blood pressure higher and higher and causing as much stress as possible while denying me the medication I needed to regulate it.

They were assassins.

And still they continued their brutality.

# TODAY'S COMPLAINT:

Dear Board,

As an addendum to my complaint, I want it noted that they are continuing to persecute me for a well-known, highly protected ADA acknowledged disability, and are asking for me to be jailed over it.

> 3. The DOJ did add a reference to dyslexia as an example of learning disabilities. The phrase used in the final rule is, "dyslexia and other specific learning disabilities."

That means that they are not allowed to hold me accountable for something I cannot physically do or to make it a criterion for my getting paid or to withhold the money I need to live on and that my life depends on due to a well-documented disability I have had since birth. Making me responsible for accounting is like telling a paraplegic that they cannot have the money they've earned and are legally entitled to until they have walked or climbed to the fourth story of a building with no elevator or ramp. Those lawyers and the court cannot legally make this a requirement for me, and those attorneys are violating my rights by harassing me with their frivolous motions to deny me my rights and the money I have earned so that they can have more billable hours.

Yet those unconscionable attorneys, Bonnie Cockburn, John Alaimo and Mika House, are trying to put me in contempt for not producing accounting when everyone knows that I cannot even write out a check or do a tip. My sons have had to do that for me in restaurants.

This is a serious condition I have, and I've been asked to write forwards in nonfiction books and to give lectures at schools and to teachers about it for decades. It was diagnosed while I was in school, and I have videos of me messing up in public while trying to read. The attorneys know this as they have mocked me about it in court, during our hearings, which also violates my Title II protections.

By ADA law, they cannot put me in jail for something I cannot physically do or continue to ask for it to be made a criterion for me to be paid the money I have legally earned while I have a legal diagnosis for my condition.

They need to be held accountable for their cruelty and for their continued interference with my life and my business with their frivolous and unnecessary motions. Not to mention the undue stress and suffering they are putting on me and my family through with their sadistic cruelty for no other reason than to increase their profit, which violates your own code of ethics.

Google me and dyslexia, and you will find dozens of articles and interviews to prove that my condition is well known and well documented. They are violating my rights and the law and need to be sanctioned for it. Since the judge won't do it, I expect you to.

# AUGUST 13

**T**O CALL THE DAYS LEADING up to this day a nightmare would like comparing Hurricane Andrew to a spring shower. If the intent of the bastards had been to emotionally cripple someone, they'd succeeded.

The level of cruelty went unsurpassed. Three motions made for no other reason other than legal greed and the love of a bully to feel large while exerting power over someone they knew couldn't fight back.

It was horrifying.

More so by the fact that the judge was in on it.

So was my attorney.

Had I had any doubts, they were squashed the moment Constance returned to the case after my crying for two days on the phone with her and telling her everything that had happened.

"Why didn't Melissa file this motion?"

"I don't know. She won't file anything to help me."

And it got worse. Apparently, we had another motion on the thirteenth that Melissa hadn't even bothered to tell me about. Constance found it on the docket.

When I contacted Melissa, her answer was bone-chilling. "I thought the judge already ruled on this."

On a motion for contempt the stupid little bitch hadn't even bothered to mention?

"Well, I don't know how to defend it." She put that shit in writing.

*I'm sorry, bitch, that is your job.*

If you couldn't defend your client, then you needed to surrender your license at the door. Especially since you'd sat there, taking hundreds of thousands of dollars from me while they defended a sick son of a bitch who'd stolen money from his family while they slept.

And protected a fucking pedophile, and a man who'd attempted to kill his wife and son.

But *she* could think of nothing to protect an innocent person. When she'd told me she was compromised, what she should have said was that she was in on it.

Something confirmed that morning when I saw Shovel-Face walk past her with a knowing smirk and she nodded at him.

Yeah. I wasn't the only one who saw it.

Sick fucking bastards. Corrupt through and through.

So, knowing I live out of state with a crap car that had stranded me the last time I'd driven it up there, and that I still had a broken foot, the idiot judge insisted that I show.

In person.

While we sat there, hour after hour, with my money draining out the door for them to look like the lumps of shit they were, Judge Dipshit took call after call, proving that the only reason I was there was for him to mock and ridicule me in person.

Yeah. Truth.

While we waited, I went out to the hallway, thus proving that the only reason Skeletor had arrested me was pure spite. He said nothing about my going to the bathroom this time.

But as I was in the hallway, guess who came out of the men's room?

Not Les.

Nope.

Ole Cockburn herself. In a cheap, painted on spandex dress that looked like she'd been walking the red-light district. Boobs hanging from her cheap ass bra that had given up under duress from too many years of trying to give the hopeless bitch some semblance of dignity.

*Hmmm...*

Had my case not been about to start, I would have waited to see who followed her out.

Anyway, there I was when Shovel-Face dropped a subpoena down on Joan and my son.

My son that they had testified to and knew suffered from severe anxiety. Cockburn had done her damnedest to have him thrown out of the courtroom in the beginning over that very issue.

And they dared to cruelly aggravate it.

There had to be a special place in hell for these monsters. Because it was utter and complete bullshit. They were asking him for documents he didn't have and even his high school diploma.

*Fuck them.*

I wanted to see *their* transcripts. What school would graduate pieces of shit like this?

How could they?

The only moment of satisfaction was the look on Skeletor's face when he saw Constance back at my table.

"Uh, what are *you* doing here?"

"I filed my notice of appearance yesterday, Your Honor."

*So much for reading all the documents, you lying shit stain.*

Her presence didn't just quell Skeletor. The "squirt" team took a step back, too.

Because they all knew that Constance was recording them.

That she was the one who was out to get them.

"Your Honor, we don't really want her to go to jail."

My jaw dropped. Seriously? Then why, for a year, had they filed motion after motion, demanding I be locked up?

For that extortion alone, they should have been put in jail.

Instead of protecting me, the judge had aided and abetted.

"I just want her to swear that she won't sue me from Georgia." Those were the actual words from Shovel-Face's mouth.

So, I now knew his deep-seated fear.

An unbiased judge. Actual justice in a courtroom.

Wow.

And Dinky made me swear an oath that I wouldn't sue the bastards over the extremely legitimate bill that I'd sent them.

"It's ridiculous!" Skeletor had sneered.

Really? Had he overlooked the ridiculous bills his "friends" had filed month after month that he'd made me pay?

But this was the bastard who then went on to say, "When the money's gone, this will end."

Whether we were divorced or not.

Idiot Les sat there with that stupid grin on his face. Unaware.

While everything I'd ever worked for in my life was being stolen from me.

And him.

*Idiot supreme.*

If that wasn't bad enough, the judge then began to testify for Les.

"Well, you can't really expect him to find a job! Law firms are downsizing everywhere!"

Constance cleared her throat. "He can hang out a shingle, Your Honor."

The judge said, "It's not that easy. It takes money to open a firm!"

As in the million dollars of cash he'd stolen from us and had squandered over the last two years on such "useful" things as his show pony and clothing and purses for another woman?

Constance didn't miss a beat. "This is Nashville, home of Nashville Law School where fifty-year-old attorneys graduate every day and work out of the trunks of their cars." Not to mention he was currently living in my office that had been a fully functional office before he'd spent hundreds of thousands of dollars renovating and redecorating it.

Yeah.

Like Cockburn who lived only a mile away from the cabin and who worked out of her house that was in a residential neighborhood.

Judge didn't care. He was too busy insulting me and mocking my disabilities.

"She doesn't do what she's told! I know she won't obey!"

Excuse me? First, you stupid motherfucker, you forgot that this wasn't Communist America. My father gave his life, as did those before him, so that I, and the rest of this country would be free.

I didn't have to obey stupidity just because it came out of the mouth of an idiot. That was also my constitutional right.

However, I had been handing over everything they'd asked and had abided by the court orders far more than any of them had.

Yet I was the one insulted and degraded.

The one who was paying for all of them.

Then Skeletor dropped the bomb. "You will hand over your login for your store."

Pardon?

Constance stood up. "Your Honor, she has information in that store that is evidence for this case."

"I'm sure they won't do anything with it."

Because what? They'd been so trustworthy since the beginning?

A bitch attorney who lied every time she spoke?

A snake who'd robbed his own family?

Yeah.

Skelator had turned red. "I don't care what you say! In a divorce, I'd have her hand over her banking login if they asked for it."

Well, we all knew what motion would be hitting me next week.

*If that wasn't bad enough, after this travesty of a kangaroo court ended, guess what was said in the hallway?*

Cockburn and the receiver were laughing. "I'll interview the FBI."

Did they mean the same FBI who had already gone out to harass my fans at their homes over the bullshit lies they'd filed, knowing the claims were fraudulent?

How did I know that it was fraudulent?

One of the things Les had to file with the court was a list of all the places he'd applied to for jobs.

If he'd really been so terrified of my fans that he'd felt the need to call out the FBI on them, then why was he applying at bookstores, publishers and for other publishing related jobs?

That would be the same as saying you were terrified Faith Hill's fans were going to harm you and then getting a job at the Grand Ole Opry.

Liars to the end.

Now they wanted to destroy evidence and harass the rest of my fanbase.

Because the judge had also testified against me about the poisoning.

*What?*

Yeah, he did. Dinky who had never seen a single piece of evidence or heard the testimony from a single witness.

The same exact judge who'd said in January 2019, "should any criminal charges ever be filed, I'd be the one to decide that."

Cockburn had stood up in court. "Your Honor, the poisoning case has been closed."

Really? No one had told me that. In fact, I had the email from the detective promising me prosecution.

I had been in recent contact with him, and he'd told me that it was still open.

Then Skeletor said, "That's because it was ridiculous and without merit."

*I beg your fucking pardon?*

Whatever happened to actually hearing a case before rendering a judicial decision?

So much for impartiality in an American court.

*Are you as sick to your stomach as I was?*

Yeah, my bankruptcy attorney had been right. In my case, Skeletor didn't even try to hide his bias.

And the Judiciary Board refused to act on his blatant discrimination and bias. Even though they were required to.

This was corruption on a grand scale.

No one gave a shit about their citizens.

They were too busy handing out citations for mask violators to worry about a corrupt judge helping his buddies steal from innocent citizens.

Yeah.

At least I wasn't sent to jail. How sorry was Williamson County that I had to use that as my only sign of victory?

That I, a woman who hadn't had a speeding ticket or ever broken any law, wasn't put in jail by these sick in the head bastards?

Oh, but I had forgotten the best part. Skeletor had a brief moment of sanity where the zoo crew was demanding I hand over information to them.

"Has she been given a list of what you want?"

"No, Your Honor."

"But you filed a motion of contempt on her demanding it?"

"Yes, Your Honor."

"Well, how about you make a list and give it to her so that she can get you that information before you file a complaint? Let's start there."

Holy shit! Half a brain had finally made an appearance. I was stunned.

The other "brilliant" part of that contempt was over my insurance policy. That played out like an episode of *Who's on First.*

"She has insurance?"

"Yes."

"Life?"

"No, it's her company policy."

"Term?"

What part of a company liability insurance could Skeletor not wrap his senile head around?" I swore it lasted twenty minutes to explain to Numb Nuts, who had a copy of the policy in front of him, that I had a general liability for my company that covered me and my workers.

"Oh, okay!"

"We just want to make sure that it's in place with the same coverage so that we can sue her, Your Honor."

*Thanks for telling me your game plan.*

The judge laughed as if it were funny, instead of punishing Les for planning another fraudulent claim.

Remember the fraudulent claim he'd put in for my jewelry against the orders of the trustee?

That was claim one.

Claim two had occurred on my ride in when the same insurance company had called about a damaged "water box" at my cabin.

Now I had no idea what a water box was as we didn't have one there at the time I'd owned it.

So, Les had spent more money on something and then was putting in for it to be repaired.

Anything to steal a dollar from someone.

Now he was planning to file another fraudulent claim.

Yeah.

And the judge was good with that. He was too busy insulting and belittling me to say a word to someone who was actually breaking the law.

Sure.

But at least in the end, he did agree to pay me one-third of my money that was due to me that they'd illegally taken from me and were withholding from me for no reason.

*One-third.*

So, I could finally buy medication and pay rent.

However, they couldn't release it to me that day.

Oh, no! He had to make sure and gouge me more by making me wait to the next day so that Melissa, at two-hundred-and-fifty dollars an hour could go collect my money and take it to the bank.

What was the best part of all this?

When Melissa went to the courthouse the next morning, this was the actual sign on the door:

CLOSED FOR POSITIVED

COVID-19 CASES

Check website for updates www.williamsoncounty-tn.gov

They couldn't even spell.

And because of their vicious stupidity and need to yell at me to my face and drop a subpoena on my anxiety-ridden son, we had all been exposed to COVID.

My pregnant daughter-in-law and Joan's elderly mother were all put at risk over these heartless, soulless, selfish pieces of shit.

And for what? The mighty dollar.

They were garbage. And no one would help me put them on the street where they belonged. Rather the entire system was set up like the one person in a firing squad who had the blank.

"It's not my fault she's dead. I'm sure I have the blank and couldn't possibly have been the one that killed her."

Plausible deniability.

Pass the buck.

"That's not my job and here's my bullshit reason why I can shrug it off or hand it over to someone else who will lie to you and do the same."

Williamson County, Tennessee. One of the most corrupt places in the country.

Now we knew why.

I WASN'T IN JAIL. IT was sad that I who wasn't a career criminal, a woman who hadn't had a speeding or parking ticket and who didn't even drive the wrong way in a parking lot, was having to count every day I didn't go to jail for bullshit as a victory. Meanwhile the bastard who had murdered my cat and poisoned three people and stolen from us was free to ruin as many lives as he could.

Without any fear of repercussion for his illegal acts.

How could this be my life?

They hit me with three more bullshit motions this day.

Every single minute of my life was a screaming nightmare that I couldn't wake up from. And they were using the money I had spent my life earning to tear my life apart.

How could one corrupt judge do this, and it be allowed?

And the record was in...

My income for 2019 had been *negative* five hundred thousand dollars.

Les had spent more on lawyers than I had made.

*Negative* half a million dollars.

So much for all the times his asshole jackals had stood before Lord Skeletor and lied, "She went into voluntary bankruptcy, Your Honor!"

That didn't sound voluntary to me. Especially given I was still paying those same jackals almost one hundred thousand dollars every two months.

No one could keep up with those kinds of financial losses for long. Not while they kept hauling me into court every two weeks and kept me so torn up that I couldn't work.

For two and a half years.

Threatening to put me in jail.

Here was the latest threat:

**Author Jailed For Protecting Fans**
**Williamson County, TN.**

Ω#1 *New York Times* bestselling author, Terri Manly, has been jailed by Williamson County Judge, Bubba Dinky for protecting hundreds of thousands of fans by refusing to publicly disclose their private home addresses, emails, shopping habits and other personal and private information that the judge has demanded the author hand over to her hostile husband and his agents or be held in contempt of court.

In a most abusive act against the bestselling author after her husband filed fraudulent charges with the FBI where he claimed her fans were hiring her fictional race of space aliens to beat him up that had federal agents turning up on her doorstep and that of her fans, Williamson County Judge, Bubba Dinky, against Tennessee law and common sense, has ordered the author to hand over her personal logins for her online store, her websites and her newsletter where the author holds the private and personal information and communications for hundreds of thousands of fans all over the globe.

"You're still married," said Judge Dinky as he sneered at the author in divorce court. "I'll have you handover your banking logins if he (husband) asks for it." The judge was incensed when Ms. Manly's attorney dared to point out to the judge how invasive and ridiculous his demand was, especially given the sensitivity of online privacy and her fans' right to have their personal identifying information held in trust and not be placed into the hands of an unnamed hostile third party, or put on public record.

Even so, Judge Dinky recklessly dismissed the attorney's objections and told the fifty-four year old Ms. Manly who is an at risk person for COVID that if she failed to hand over and expose the personal and private information for her international fanbase, in violation of current privacy and internet laws, that he would put her in jail for contempt until such a time as she complied with his order that completely disregards the privacy rights of all her fans and customers, as well as the terms of service for her sites and services that she has used to build her #1 international bestselling brand.

"I was stunned by the order," said Ms. Manly. "I worked IT for over twenty years and the one rule everyone knows: you never, ever, under any circumstance give out your own personal login to any site. Never mind logins that jeopardize other people's privacy or their personal information. Who would even ask for it?"

Yet they did. Not that the author should be surprised. Ms. Manly has been persecuted for over two years since her fifty-five year old husband, Lester Manly, first filed for divorce, alleging witchcraft among other ludicrous charges after tampering with his wife's food, all to discredit the author and harass her fans in an attempt to distract the court and the world from his own dubious conduct, that includes abandoning Ms. Manly and her sons while they were sleeping, after stealing money from Ms. Manly's business and their joint accounts, and all the money from their sons' trust funds.

Other nefarious actions have included the friends and family of his own attorney, Bonnie Cockburn, posting insults and taunts to Ms. Manly's fans on her publisher owned social media site, and hiring a known reporter to take out a hit piece on Ms. Manly so that they could discredit Ms. Manly with those fans who have remained loyal to Ms. Manly while her husband and his team have done their best to ruin her reputation and good name.

That loyalty flows both ways as Ms. Manly is willing to go to jail for an unspecified amount of time in the middle of COVID where her life will be at risk due to her age and elevated health risks, in order to protect her fans who have been abused and harassed by Mr. Manly and his agents. Something that seems unreal at a time when the Tennessee Supreme Court, along with other courts across America, have urged all judges to release any nonviolent offenders out of jail so as not to risk their lives from the pandemic.

"I was on the brink of a nervous breakdown," said Sheila Brown, one of the fans who'd been harassed by Mr. Manly's known associates after he filed for divorce. Ms. Brown is terrified of Mr. Manly or one of his representatives regaining access to any of her private information, especially her home address or email.

"I won't have my fans abused, or my customers," said Ms. Manly. "It's one thing for the judge and my husband to abuse and insult me. I'm a grown woman, and I've been taking their abuse for years. But I will not allow them to stalk my fans and customers. My job is to protect them the same way I've always protected my children and family."

Given the judge's past disparate and harsh treatment of the author, there's no telling how long a sentence she will have to serve as the current contempt order says that she will be forced to reside in jail until such a time as she willingly releases fan and customer information to a hostile third party. The judge, contrary to normal sentencing procedures for the county, already sentenced the bestselling author to ten days in jail when she complied last year with his questions.

Having grown used to the injustice she's been served by the Tennessee courts where they have threatened repeatedly to strip her of all her book series, novels and copyrights, including those she wrote before she married, Ms. Manly is only concerned about the welfare of her children, fans and customers. "We are strong. We will get through this abuse, too. I can't let my fans, family or customers suffer any more harm. I will do what I have to, to protect them."

That was what I was up against. An insane judge making insane rulings with no regards for anyone other than his "buddies."

I'd never heard or seen such.

Neither had anyone else.

My head reeled daily from it all. We were all overwhelmed trying to keep our heads above water.

But at least I finally got through to the FBI.

In spite of the lies on their website and what their own agent had told me while sitting in my home, the agent on the phone told me that they didn't investigate judicial corruption. "You'll have to take that up with the judiciary board."

"They have no authority to arrest him."

"Well, we don't investigate that."

"So let me get this straight... you will waste tax payer dollars to go out to the homes of innocent people because a lunatic calls in and tells you that he's in fear of his life from a race of fictional space aliens that someone's fan said she wished would go kick his ass, but refuse to investigate a group of malicious thieves who are being protected by a corrupt judge who had no authority to seize a woman's property and have it taken across state lines?"

The agent turned silent and stopped typing. The only satisfaction I had was knowing that our conversation was recorded.

Not that it'd done me any good.

My friend who was a Marshall was right. The FBI was a worthless organization.

Space aliens they'd go after. Real criminals? Forget it. No wonder our country was in the mess it was in.

But then my friend who was an attorney explained it to me. I couldn't go after the judge because Les's attorneys had been the ones who told him to take my jewelry and all he'd done was act on their lies.

*What?*

And I couldn't go after them because the judge had been the one who'd placed the order, even though the judge in a divorce court had no legal authority over my private jewelry.

Since no one oversaw the judge and he was God almighty of his courtroom, I was fucked.

Sovereign Immunity.

When the Supreme Court had said that no man was above the law, what they meant was that no man other than those of us in bathrobes were above the law. *We can do whatever the fuck we want. Ha. Ha.*

It was disgusting.

"That's the way it's always been."

I scoffed at Nan's glib answer. "And it was illegal for women to vote at one time. When kids could be paddled in school for any reason. Just because it's a bad law that's been around for a long time doesn't mean it's right."

Nor did it mean it was permanent.

The world was on fire and my life had been nuked.

Change was brewing and it was time for people to say, "Enough!"

REMEMBER THOSE DOLLS from childhood that if you squeezed their bellies, their eyes, ears, and nose would pop out? That was how I felt.

The jackals kept coming. I was beginning to have PTSD any time I saw an email from my attorney, or my phone rang.

Then, the phone rang.

I sighed before answering it.

It wasn't my attorney. It was one of the other people who'd been fucked by Dinky and his crew. "You feel up to a class action suit?"

I laughed bitterly. "I've had my horses hitched to the wagon that's stockpiled with pitchforks and torches. Where the hell have you been?"

Was I ready to start shit?

Shit was my middle name. *Ring the bell and summon the villagers.* "Burn the Bitches!" To the ground and beyond.

He was amused. "I found another one. Started with Dinky and got transferred to Woodly." The opposite of what had happened with me.

"Yeah?"

"Yeah. She's had two attorneys and is now pro se. They've been eating her alive and abusing her, just like you. I'm sad to say this, but it's these old judges going after women. I'm the rare exception as a man, but they are predominantly taking their misogyny out on you guys."

"I know."

"Who all do we have?"

"Ex of an NBA player, the ex of a country music star, doctor, lawyer, three more, and you."

I kept hearing that song from *Hamilton* in my head. *Today there are four of us...*
*Tomorrow there will be more of us.*

I clenched my teeth. "Start the fire."

"So, you're in?"

"My father fought in two wars for this country. He said over and over that he put that uniform on to fight so that his kids wouldn't have to. I would never do any less for my own. Nor would I spit on my father's memory by being any less than what he raised me to be."

God. Country. Family. Honor.

*When we are called, we answer.*

And that answer was never "wait a second."

"Let's do this."

"All right," he said. "I'll be in touch."

I only hoped that for me, it wouldn't be too late. Dinky had said at the last hearing that once my money he'd put into their "legal fund" was gone that it would be over.

So would I. I had nothing left to fight with. My publisher had already cancelled all my releases. Les had made it clear that he was going to continue suing me and ruining me.

*What the ever lovin' hell?*

All I'd ever done was try to take care of my family and write books. I'd never set out to harm anyone.

Yet the entire world was now coming for me.

And all I'd ever wanted was to be left alone, secluded from the world to play with my fictional people.

Now I was being drawn into a fight to stop corruption.

Life, it was never what we thought, and it forever took us places we didn't want to go.

It'd taken my father all over the world to fight in bloody battles and it was dragging me into the trenches here at home.

All because of one fucking psycho who refused to move on with his life.

**SEPTEMBER 1**

**I**'D SPOKEN TO A REAL JUDGE. Not to the loser masquerading as one. A longtime friend of mine, and a fellow author happened to be in a critique group with a Superbowl Champion of judges.

The conversation was and wasn't helpful. While it confirmed everything I already knew (that Dinky was a crook and that Williamson County was a joke), she also told me that until the Judiciary Board decided to get off their ass and do something, I was trapped.

The system where I lived was broken.

Constance also confirmed this. She sent over a link of a friend of hers, John Gentry. A man running for the senate and who intended to run on an Independent ticket in 2022 for Tennessee governor. Unlike the bastards in place, he had a conscience and a heart and was as sick of Tennessee being a joke as I was.

He knew of the conspiracy and robbery and instead of turning a blind eye, he and others were trying to make a difference.

Publicly.

God, how I wished he could.

But the jackals were coming for him, too. They were determined to see him fail. Just as they'd defeated Byron Bush, another victim of the Williamson County judicial mafia, who'd had the temerity to stand up to them and then who'd run for office in an effort to clean up that town.

Bush even had the guts to run ads during the Superbowl, calling them out by name.

I admired them and I wished them luck.

But we were fighting a losing battle.

We all knew it.

Meanwhile, Nan and Constance were fighting night and day to try and keep me out of jail while the jackals, with Dinky's backing, continued to rob me and blackmail me.

Melissa withdrew as my counsel. "If you bring Constance back in, I can't represent you."

"Why?"

"You know her reputation. I can't work with her."

Yeah, I knew her reputation. She was fearless and wouldn't kowtow to Dinky.

They'd persecuted her relentlessly and even thrown her in jail.

Better still, she recorded every single session, and they knew it. So, when they lied and altered transcripts, she had proof that they lied and altered transcripts.

Funny how the moment she came back into the picture, they'd stopped dragging me into court every two weeks.

Constance, alone, had quelled a degree of their insanity.

But only a little.

Their Georgia asshole receiver, Murrey was in rare form.

"She has to turn over all her logins. For everything."

My other judge—the sane one from out of state, had also verified that illegality of that, too. "What judge in their right mind would ask for that?"

Well, we were dealing with Dinky. He didn't have a right mind. Only a twisted, sick one.

At least I had corroboration that he was wrong and that a real judge would never back him in his madness.

Constance tried to argue how illegal it was.

Still, they kept demanding.

And I prepared myself for jail.

But at least I finally had a set of attorneys who weren't telling me to pack my bags and go.

I had attorneys I knew would fight for me and do everything they could to keep me out of jail.

And my fans were behind me.

*Thank you, God, for that.* I could feel their support every time I logged onto my accounts. That was why I'd never give them up. Why I was willing to face jail or whatever the bastards threw at me. I wasn't about to let them harass or bully the only people I had on my side.

Not today. Not tomorrow.

Not ever.

It was on and I was willing to fight.

**SEPTEMBER 3**

**T**HEY SERVED MADDOX AT WORK. How utterly humiliating. My boy was at the window, helping out when he was handed the subpoena in front of all his coworkers. Shameless. Monstrous.

Les blamed me for the fact that his sons hated him. *No, punkin'*. It was unnecessary actions like this that you'd done to them that had made them hate you.

Since the divorce had started, Maddox had been begging to give his deposition. When he'd been home from Japan the first year, he'd tried to give one.

Cockburn had been too "busy" to take it. She'd passed with some made up bullshit. Because she'd been terrified of putting on record what a monster her client was.

Now she was humiliating my son and putting his job at risk for shits and giggles.

They thought it was funny.

It wasn't.

That level of cruelty went unsurpassed. They had scheduled it for the prenatal appointment where my son was needed as he and his wife had just learned that his son had complications. That appointment was to determine if his son would live or die.

Yeah, they were that fucking sick.

What was worse? The new receiver and his imp, Sissy, were lying to the judge. They kept claiming that I wasn't handing in all my receipts.

They claimed my bookkeeper had told them this.

Yeah, they were that stupid and that malicious. They who were supposed to be impartial and who were living off my dole, too.

My bookkeeper was livid. "That wasn't what I told that bitch."

"I know, but here's the email where she lied."

Did they really think my accountant and bookkeeper wouldn't tell the truth?

But then, did it matter?

After all, Dinky believed whatever bullshit lie they made up. As I'd said, they could tell no lie and we could tell no truth.

It was old and tiresome.

Worse, Cockburn had put in a motion to sell off pieces of my jewelry.

That had brought out the lion in Nan. "Oh, hell no! I'll make that sonofabitch judge crawl through every single piece for three days and rule on every piece, including the coat button. So help me, God! I'm going to show what a piece of shit he is. He has no idea what he seized, but by the time I finish, I'll make sure he sanctions the whole fucking giddy crew of them."

"Dinky said that he could rule on all of it in a matter of hours."

Nan had scoffed. "He's fucking crazy and if he does, then I'll appeal it." That was what Nan specialized in. She was an appellate attorney and unlike Melissa, she wasn't afraid to take them on. Nan liked the fact that when she showed up in court, the Empire theme from *Star Wars* was played.

Of course, Cockburn, again, lied about the value of my jewelry. She claimed it was worth two million even though we had records from the former hyena she'd hired that said it wasn't worth even five thousand dollars (including the coat button). Remember that the trustee had stood up in both State and Federal Court to testify that he'd been "misled about the value of the estate's property."

I wasn't the liar on that. Cockburn was.

And she still was going.

Gah, how could anyone be so shameless?

And if the auction house took their usual twenty-five percent, we wouldn't make enough selling all my jewelry to cover the day in court for the hearing to sell it.

Weren't they awesome at math?

And Les claimed he'd been my business manager. Well, that explained why we'd gone bankrupt and homeless in Mississippi and why, once I took over household management from him and started running my business after he'd run us into the ground, he finally had a pot to piss in.

Until he decided to take over again.

Then we were back in bankruptcy.

*Good job, Baby Huey. Good job.*

You were just as worthless and stupid as your parents had said you were.

SEPTEMBER 15

**D**EPOSITIONS FOR LES AND I were scheduled to begin on September 21.

Nick's twenty-first birthday.

That was what a total piece of shit Les and his attorneys were.

"He won't go through with it." That was what I kept telling everyone. "He's a fucking coward. His worst fear, for whatever reason, is being put on record." Probably because he'd had brain damage as a child.

I wasn't being mean. Due to his mother's coldness, he'd suffered oxygen dep that had left him with brain damage that didn't allow him to remember things.

That was why he couldn't have made it through law school without me. He had no short-term memory.

And he knew what a liar he was. It was why he'd fled in the Dumas case. He'd been absolutely terrified of being deposed.

I saw the end coming.

Especially since I was hiring the expert Les had hired in the Dumas case to testify against him in the divorce.

That scared them, too.

Because now I had Les's own expert to verify that they were lying about the value of my estate.

"Uh, she can buy him out for seven million dollars."

"Fuck off. For that, he can buy me out and I'll go sit on a beach." Not true, I'd go write another series.

But I wasn't about to pay the loser that amount of money.

Ever.

So they came back with a counter offer.

"Fine. Les will buy her out for 1.5 million."

"Okay. I'll take it." After all, everyone, including Constance had told me that Dinky was going to give them whatever they wanted and more.

And that there was nothing I could do to stop them.

Last thing I wanted was tainted IP that Hogg and Les had ruined with their lies.

I could go on and write other things. I'd already run it past my publisher, and I knew they weren't happy, but they were less happy with the jackals and wanted this over.

"What can he do with your property?" Constance had asked.

"Not a damn thing. My publisher will cancel the contract immediately. If they'd take five minutes to read one, they'd see that no one, other than me, can write the books."

One of them must have read a contract because suddenly, they were no longer going to hire a ghostwriter.

"The deal's off."

"Fine. I'll see them in court. But tell him that I no longer want the IP. I want the cabin. If we go to trial, he will be forced to buy me out."

The moment they refused to take my IP after years of torturing me over it, I had learned his Achilles' Heel and I was going to make him choke on it.

C AN NICK PICK UP THE files at Melissa's office and bring them to mine?"

I was stunned that the jackals were still being so stupid. "They are aware that as of Monday, I am flat broke, right?"

The only reason I was able to have a hotel room for the depositions was because I'd had so many points that I could trade them in.

"I know."

"So, what are they thinking?"

Constance sighed. "No idea. But I need the files to prepare for his deposition."

Because Melissa, during all those years, had never bothered. That was, by the way, why Constance had agreed to take me on again as a client. When she'd spoken to Melissa and realized that Melissa had made no plans to defend me.

At all.

That she had lined up no experts and had no strategy whatsoever, other than to sell me out.

And Melissa had dared to tell me that I needed to get rid of Constance.

Yeah, she was in on it.

Or they had threatened her to the brink of insanity.

I had Nick swing by and pick up the files and transport them to Constance's office.

Of course, the jackals were also working night and day to wring every last penny from us.

And Les was stupid enough to let them.

"He wants a list of all your titles."

Something I kept on my website, and that he already had from the Dumas case.

"If they insist on this, they will buy me out. I am not having them pull me into court for the rest of my life. They are going to get out of my life and never have a single way back into it. I mean it, Constance. I'm done. No alimony. Nothing. They either take what I'm willing to give or they take it all. No negotiations." I was done.

And the clock for Doomsday was ticking.

W E SHOULD HAVE BEEN celebrating Nick's twenty-first birthday. Just like we'd done for his brothers. A weeklong celebration to make him feel loved and to know that the world was his oyster.

Instead, we had to report at nine a.m. to Constance's office to sit and wait for his father to grow up.

Poor Nick.

He looked as tired as I felt, and I didn't know what to say to him. We'd had a small party the night before in my hotel room.

Cupcakes instead of a real cake. A tiny wallet and a card.

*Damn you, Les, you rotten piece of shit.*

Les had given him nothing. Unless you counted the subpoena.

And the ulcer.

Our depositions were to begin the next day.

I showed up in order to prepare.

Constance was still trying to negotiate a settlement. "I think we're close."

"I don't care." And I meant it. They'd lied and walked out so many times that I was done. "Unless they guarantee that I don't have to serve any jail time, it's off the table."

"We can do that."

Really? Because Melissa had lied and said it couldn't be done.

I cocked a brow at Constance.

"I was a prosecutor. We made deals like that all the time. It'd serve no purpose to put you in jail for Contempt once the divorce is over. Dinky can sign off on it."

"He better or I won't settle. We are broke. I have nothing to lose at this point and my satisfaction will be to see Les on the street like he's done us."

It began at nine a.m. in the morning.

All day long, they hammered us with utter and complete bullshit. Remember that I had offered them one hundred percent of my royalties.

Hell, I'd offered him everything to let me go.

For years, they had made my life hell by telling me that he'd end up with alimony and all this bullshit.

By the end of the day, they'd confessed to Constance and Nan that they were afraid of Les, themselves. "Look, we know he's unhinged. We don't want him to sue us for malpractice. We need to get this settled today with language he'll accept. Could you please help us out?"

*Help you out? Shovel-Face, had you lost your fucking mind?*

You wanted mercy when you'd shown me none? I hoped and prayed that Les did wake up and sue you blind.

You deserved it.

More than that, you'd earned it.

Worse, they knew they deserved to be sued. It was why there was real fear in his voice.

My sons sat with me the whole day. And my best friends. They held my hand while we hammered them.

In the end, Les walked away with a fraction of what he would have had had he simply asked me for a divorce and never involved the Whore of Babylon he'd dredged out from whatever hobo she'd been sucking on.

He'd lost his family. His dignity and a fortune that he hadn't earned.

Most of all, he'd lost the respect of his sons who would never speak to him again.

Sons who would never again bear his last name.

Nor would his grandson.

The legacy that he'd been so determined to keep, and build was destroyed.

*Hoisted by his own petard.*

I was financially broke. They'd left me with less than seven thousand dollars to my name.

Not even enough to cover the legal bills from that day that ended at eleven thirty that night.

"We can't allow them to go home without this being signed. We know Terri will change her mind." That was the lie Shovel-Face told Constance.

He knew it was a lie. I had never once backed out of a settlement.

Only Les had.

They had made us drive to their sickening office that was covered with offensive art and sit there while they finalized the agreements.

I was again, surrounded by my friends and my family.

Les was alone.

The man who couldn't stand to be alone, had no one. The one who'd made me sit with him while he studied, who'd told people that he was divorcing me because he was lonely.

*Yeah, buddy, you chose badly.*

No one in their right mind would have you now. Not after everything you'd done to the people who'd loved you.

The truth always came out.

As quickly as it'd started, it ended on my baby's twenty-first birthday.

"I guess this is his present to you."

Nan had scoffed. "Nah. The bastard ended it thinking he wouldn't have to pay child support." She winked at me.

I laughed nervously, because I knew she was right.

But deep in my soul, I knew it wasn't over. They would be back.

Like Jason Voorhees or Freddy Krueger. Monsters like them never went away. Not as long as they had a foothold anywhere near you.

They'd always come back.

I would be ready.

As Sal Tiller had said at the end of the Dumas suit, "one thing we know about Terri, she will fight."

Yes, I would, motherfucker.

Because honestly, I didn't know how my story would end...

*Well not true.*

Ultimately, I did know how it would all end. With my death. *But until then, buckle up, bitches. Buckle up.*

**M**ORE THAN A FULL WEEK after the divorce was final, and the order entered into record, Bill Oldham and crew still refused to release my family jewelry back to me.

All my attempts to contact them were ignored.

With no other recourse, I hired an off-duty police officer to accompany me and Joan to Oldham's law firm, with a copy of the court order that said they were to release the property that should have never been taken.

They refused.

"Then I am going straight to the police department and issue a warrant for your arrest. You are illegally holding my personal property against the law and committing Conversion. Theft by taking."

The receptionist had stammered. "Um, give me until after lunch to get that for you."

"Fine. I'll be back in two hours and my jewelry better be here."

Two hours later, after having lunch with the officer who was the investigator for a DA, I learned exactly how illegal their actions had been.

That included Dinky's.

When we returned, I found that they had defiled my mother's jewelry box. She had been the last person to touch the contents that were now in plastic baggies as if they were junk.

When my mother had died, the mortician had returned a synthetic ruby ring that had been on her hand to my brother (it'd been my grandmother's ring my grandfather had given her as an anniversary present). Unable to cope, my brother had placed that ring in tissue paper, and put the ring in her jewelry box.

Those animals had removed the tissue and never returned it.

On the way home, the officer again stated that what had been done to me was immoral, wrong and illegal.

It would be another week before I'd have to make another trip to Franklin in order to get my last seven thousand dollars from the county clerk.

She acted as if I had put her out and she, too, made me wait hours before she'd release the money to me that should have never been taken from me, while knowing I had a five-hour drive home.

While there, this was the sign those bastards had in their window for everyone to see:

*Work with me people. I am sooooo not listening.*

They were really proud servants of the public, weren't they? Advertising to the world just how apathetic they were to the suffering of everyone around them.

As I left there, with my meager check to start a new life, all I could think was that I would never, ever step foot in this god-forsaken county again.

I was going to put it behind me and never look back. But I felt sorry for all the innocent people who would be victimized after me. So many ruined lives.

And for what?

Power? Infamy?

Or pure greed.

Honestly, I felt sorry for those jackals as this was the legacy they'd leave behind. A trail of broken families and lives. Of people who hated them.

The one thing that I cherished most (aside from my children) was when a reader came up to me and took my hand. "You have no idea how hard my life has been, but your books helped me. Thank you."

Sadly, I knew all too well how they felt. Books had been my sole comfort and light through the darkest hours of my life.

Even my Nick had said, "You're a good person, Mom. You don't deserve this. I don't know why this is happening to you, but I'm so glad you're my mom."

I cried every time I thought about that. Authors and books had saved my life. I'd never gone into this intending to make money. My only reason for writing had been to slay the evil monsters in my life. To gain a little control when I had none.

And I wanted to pay forward the kindness of all those authors who'd helped me make it one more day.

The fact that my readers and fans still come and tell me that something I wrote helped them... that was all I asked in life.

All I'd ever hoped for.

To make the world a better place and to help those who needed it.

My heart had been shattered and my life torn apart. My only hope was that one day soon, I'd hear the voices of those characters I'd worked so hard to keep, speaking to me again.

Just like the years following the death of my brother, they'd gone quiet.

Every day I woke up without them talking to me was an even worse hell.

But even though my life had been torn asunder by monsters, I had faith that one day my characters would return to me, just as they'd on that cold day in Richmond after the death of my brother.

Then they would be loud and demanding that I type their words onto paper.

So, I'd wait and hope.

And pray.

Pray that they returned to me and that no one else ever had to endure the nightmare of Williamson County.

**M**AYBE KARMA DECIDED to wake up.

God knew that this wasn't exactly where I thought I'd be at this place and time in my life.

But as I'd always said in my books, sometimes things had to go wrong in order to go right.

Or as one of my best friends had told me right before she'd passed away from cancer, "Sometimes, Terri, God has to clear the snakes out of your garden so that good things can grow."

I received a call in from my psychic bud. "Did you hear the news?"

"I don't know. What news?"

"The FBI invaded the homes of three Tennessee legislators, including the ones you wrote who ignored you. They're suspected of bribery."

*Are you kidding me?*

Of course, she wasn't. For once, the FBI had left their offices for something other than little green men suspected of being hired as a joke to kick someone's butt.

Wow. I was stunned.

But that wasn't the big kicker.

*Wait for it...*

That one came a couple of weeks later.

Our old friend Bubba Dinky hit the news.

Again.

Yes, he finally got the ear-ringing slap the little bitch deserved for the unwarranted persecution he'd launched against the attorney I had mentioned earlier.

*Want to see it?*

*I know you do.*

A trial court (*legal-speak for Bubba Dinky*) held two attorneys in contempt, assessing damages and sanctions against them. Shortly before another hearing in which the court was to consider a supplemental award of attorney's fees, the judge of the trial court made comments in an unrelated case about one of the attorneys held in contempt. That attorney moved to recuse based, in part, on the judge's comments. The trial court denied the motion to recuse and later entered a supplemental order of damages against the attorneys. Because the judge's comments provide a reasonable basis for questioning his impartiality, we reverse the denial of the motion to recuse. And because retroactive recusal is appropriate, we also vacate the contempt and damages orders.

### Tenn. R. App. P. 3 Appeal as of Right;
### Judgment of the Circuit Court Vacated

## OPINION
### I.
### A.

In this consolidated appeal, we review the trial court's denial of a motion to recuse and its orders holding in contempt and sanctioning two attorneys, and their respective law firms. The orders on appeal arise from, but have little to do with, a case filed by "Plaintiff" against multiple defendants. Mr. M and Mr. H represented several of the defendants. Purportedly to defeat an element of the malicious prosecution claim brought by Plaintiff and to prove Plaintiff had not suffered reputational harm, Mr. M subpoenaed individuals and entities that were not parties to the case. The non-parties included Plaintiff's parents; and entities to which Plaintiff had some connection. Mr. M also sought deposition testimony from Plaintiff's parents.

Wanting to protect confidential information, (collectively, "Petitioners") proposed an agreed protective order before responding to the subpoenas or submitting to the depositions. And, after negotiations, counsel reached an agreement on the terms of the protective order. Among other things, the proposed order defined confidential information, provided methods for both designating information as "confidential" and challenging such designations, and restricted the indiscriminate or mass designation of information as "confidential".

Counsel for Petitioners then proposed that the document production could proceed provided that Mr. M would agree that the production was subject to the protective order despite it not being entered by the court. Mr. M responded: "I agree that the Order is binding on me and my clients at the time it is signed with permission as opposed to entered by the Court." So counsel for Petitioners filed the proposed agreed protective order with the court. The same day, Petitioners produced over 78,000 pages of documents in response to the subpoenas. Petitioners designated all of the documents as "confidential" under the proposed agreed protective order. In a cover letter, counsel for Petitioners stated that, while they "realize[d] that the Protective Order cautioned against mass designation of documents as 'confidential'... it would have been unduly burdensome upon our clients to review each of the... documents...." Counsel for Petitioners offered to conduct a page-by-page review if Mr. M's clients would pay for it. Counsel alternatively suggested that Mr. M's clients could challenge any "confidential" designation to a specific document or documents.

Mr. M objected to the mass designation and, in a filing with the court, withdrew his consent to the proposed agreed protective order. But, a few days later, he made another filing requesting that the court enter the proposed agreed protective order. Petitioners then filed a motion requesting the entry of a protective order and that the court sustain its confidentiality designations. They set the motion for hearing on October 30, 2015.

Before the hearing took place, Mr. M filed documents and excerpts from the deposition transcripts of case, all of which had been designated as "confidential," in response to a motion filed by Plaintiff. Counsel for Petitioners appeared at an October 20, 2015 hearing on Plaintiff's motion and made an oral motion. Counsel requested that the court treat as confidential all documents already produced by Petitioners, as well as the deposition testimony. Counsel also requested that the response filed by Mr. M, including the exhibits, be kept under seal. The court granted the oral motion.

At the October 30, 2015 hearing, the court again ruled in favor of Petitioners and ordered that "all pleadings or documents containing, attaching, or referencing documents, testimony, or information designated as confidential... were to be filed under seal." And the court "adopted," 2 with modifications, the proposed agreed protective order. The court ordered that documents designated as "confidential" be protected consistent with the terms of the agreed protective order. The court's oral rulings at the October 20 and October 30 hearings were reflected in written orders entered on November 7, 2015, and November 6, 2015, respectively.

**B.**

On February 25, 2016, Plaintiffs moved for sanctions. They claimed that, on February 3, 2016, confidential materials were featured on two television news broadcasts and were also published online. And other media outlets had published stories using the same materials.

While the motion did not specifically allege that either Mr. M or Mr. H provided the confidential materials to the media, it blamed the pair for use of confidential documents in separate litigation they had filed on behalf of another client. The motion asked the court to identify who had violated its previous orders and to hold those parties or counsel in contempt and award costs, attorney's fees, and other expenses.

Following a hearing on the motion for sanctions, the court entered an order identifying four attorneys "whose actions in this matter strongly indicate violations of Tennessee Rule of Civil Procedure 37.02 and possible contempt of the orders of th[e] Court" *(even though Dinky refused to do this against the hyenas when they violated those same rules in my case, and I handed him the evidence).* The court granted leave to those "affected by alleged violations of Tennessee Rule of Civil Procedure 37.02 and violations of the corresponding Court Orders [to] file appropriate pleadings for sanctions, listing specifically each violation alleged to have occurred and the specific injury inflicted upon each party". Petitioners did so against three attorneys, and their respective law firms.

After the hearing, the trial court found Mr. M and Mr. H in contempt. The court (*Dinky*) found Mr. M in contempt for using confidential materials in preparing, strategizing, and negotiating the separate lawsuit and in attaching a confidential document to a pleading in that lawsuit. And the trial court also found that Mr. M had disclosed confidential materials to the media after the court had ordered that such documents not be disclosed. The trial court found Mr. H in contempt for allowing the filing of the confidential document in the separate lawsuit. Though Mr. M made the filing, Mr. H was his co-counsel. As such, the court (*Dinky*) held that Mr. H was responsible as well.

The trial court (*Dinky*) also sanctioned Mr. M and Mr. H under Tennessee Rule of Civil Procedure 37.02. The trial court first sanctioned both attorneys for the same actions for which it had found them in contempt. The court then found other actions of the two attorneys sanction-able. As to Mr. M, the trial court sanctioned him for disclosing confidential materials to law enforcement and three attorneys not involved in the case before the court issued any ruling on the protective. The court categorized those actions as an abuse of discovery *(oh yeah, but he didn't care when the hyenas abused discovery in my case. In fact, he'd testified for them against me and helped them to abuse discovery against me and then allowed them to keep lying even after their discovery turned up nothing).* The court also found that he was not candid with the court and attempted to defraud the court *(while Dinky was simultaneously allowing the hyenas to do it to me and refusing to hold them accountable).* As to Mr. H, the trial court sanctioned him for Mr. M disclosure to the media. The court found that Mr. H "had knowledge of and was complicit in concealing the improper disclosure" from the court. The court reasoned that Mr. H had also abused the discovery process, failed to be candid with the court, and attempted to defraud the court.

Based on its finding of contempt—and, alternatively, its finding of sanctionable conduct—the trial court awarded damages to Petitioners in the form of attorney's fees and expenses against Mr. M and Mr. H and their respective law firms. Considering affidavits filed by Petitioners' attorneys, the court awarded Petitioners $622,696.12. The trial court also granted counsel for Petitioners leave to supplement their affidavits with fees incurred for time spent preparing for the contempt hearing through the date of the contempt order.

## C.

About a month after the contempt order and before the hearing on the supplemental fee request, the judge of the trial court referenced Mr. M while presiding over a hearing in an unrelated case. In open court, the judge said:

> There was a lawyer, Mr. Bryce M, who I have released a one-hundred-twenty-two page memorandum *(please keep in mind that this was the asshole who'd mocked my attorney for filing a ninety page complaint against three defendants over my actual poisoning, the abuse of my children—physical and mental—as well as my own abuse, and that of my fans whom they'd attacked— A judge who openly laughed at the fact that my husband had attempted to murder me, poison and abuse us. Then, to the tune of over one-hundred- thousand dollars for a single week of work forced my "new" attorney to rewrite that complaint so that the hyenas could force me into bankruptcy and drop the case—then also forced Mr. M into bankruptcy during this to drop his case, as well. Yet, Judge Skeletor had the nerve to write over one-hundred pages because his itty-bitty baby feelings were hurt. Seriously?)* and order on, who, among many, many other things, submitted a false and fake package, along with another person, to the Board of Professional Responsibility and the Court of the Judi-ciary.

> Well, come to find out that it was fake. And it was wrong. Channel 4 News picked it up and made it a headline.... Totally false. Totally false.

> The Board of Professional Responsibility saw what it was and said, "We're not going to investigate it, Judge Dinky." And I said, "Oh, please do. I'm begging you to investi-gate because you know how people are. They'll read half the story and say, 'Ah, that was a put-up. They're helping Judge Dinky out.'"

I don't want that. I hired a lawyer and I said, "Let's do it right." Full investigation, dismissed, and it should've been. Now, Channel 4 News published it as if it were true. Now, what do I do when I'm sitting there watching that, and my family is watching it, and all of my friends are watching it?

And as a judge it's probably good that I don't say a word. It's very difficult. **But my day will come**. And it's just about here.... I feel like it's necessary for me to be crystal clear, transparent and clear. **I did not like what Mr. M did at all, and my day will come**.

After the trial court made these comments, Mr. M, on behalf of himself and his law firm, moved to recuse the judge. In his recusal motion, Mr. M argued, among other things, that the above comments showed the court's bias against him.

The trial court denied the recusal motion, finding the statements made in open court "irrelevant to the issues in the present case."

Two days after the denial of Mr. M's recusal motion, the trial court awarded Petitioners $126,073.09 in supplemental attorney's fees in a separate order. In total, then, the trial court held Mr. M, Mr. H, and their respective law firms jointly and severally liable for $748,769.21. The trial court designated the original order of contempt and damages and the supplemental order of damages together as a final judgment under Tennessee Rule of Civil Procedure 54.02.

## II.

Mr. M petitioned for an accelerated interlocutory appeal of the denial of his third recusal motion. See TENN. SUP. CT. R. 10B, § 2.01. And Mr. M and Mr. H appealed the final judgment of contempt and damages. We consolidated the interlocutory appeal with the appeal of the final judgment.

The parties' arguments focus both on whether the trial judge should have recused himself and on the merits of the contempt and damages orders. We find the recusal issue dispositive. As to that issue, the parties argue over various possible grounds for recusal. We focus on the trial court's comments about Mr. M in the unrelated proceeding.

### A.

Rule 10B of the Rules of the Supreme Court of Tennessee governs the procedure for "determin[ing] whether a judge should preside over a case." TENN. SUP. CT. R. 10B. When a trial court denies a motion to recuse, a party can either take an interlocutory appeal or raise the issue in an appeal after entry of final judgment. Id. § 2.01. In both scenarios, we review a trial court's ruling on a motion to recuse de novo. Id. *(So much for all of Melissa's bullshit that she couldn't get Dinky to recuse himself or the Appellant Court to agree with us, eh?)*

In Tennessee, litigants "have a fundamental right to a 'fair trial before an impartial tribunal.'" Holsclaw v. Ivy Hall Nursing Home, Inc., 530 S.W.3d 65, 69 (Tenn. 2017) (quoting State v. Austin, 87 S.W.3d 447, 470 (Tenn. 2002)); see Kinard v. Kinard, 986

The previous year Mr. M filed two recusal motions, which were denied. He sought accelerated interlocutory review of the denial of his first recusal motion. See TENN. SUP. CT. R. 10B, §

2.01. We affirmed the denial of that motion. Chase v. Stewart, No. M2017-01192-COA-T10B-CV, 2017 WL 3738466, at *4 (Tenn. Ct. App. Aug. 29, 2017). Mr. M did not seek interlocutory review of his second recusal motion.

S.W.2d 220, 227 (Tenn. Ct. App. 1998) (reasoning that litigants "are entitled to the 'cold neutrality of an impartial court'" (quoting Leighton v. Henderson, 414 S.W.2d 419, 421 (Tenn. 1967))); see also TENN. CONST. art. VI, § 11. It "goes without saying that a trial before a biased or prejudiced fact finder is a denial of due process." Wilson v. Wilson, 987 S.W.2d 555, 562 (Tenn. Ct. App. 1998).

**Tennessee has long recognized that "the appearance of bias is as injurious to the integrity of the judicial system as actual bias."** Davis v. Liberty Mut. Ins. Co., 38 S.W.3d 560, 565 (Tenn. 2001); see In re Cameron, 151 S.W. 64, 76 (Tenn. 1912) ("[I]t is of immense importance, not only that justice shall be administered… , but that [the public] shall have no sound reason for supposing that it is not administered."). **Of course, a judge should recuse when they have "any doubt as to [their] ability to preside impartially in [a] case."** Davis, 38 S.W.3d at 564. **But a judge must also "disqualify himself or herself in any proceeding in which the judge's impartiality might reasonably be questioned."** TENN. SUP. CT. R. 10, Rule 2.11(A). This test is "an objective one." State v. Cannon, 254 S.W.3d 287, 307 (Tenn. 2008). **It requires recusal "when a person of ordinary prudence in the judge's position, knowing all of the facts known to the judge, would find a reasonable basis for questioning the judge's impartiality."** Davis, 38 S.W.3d at 564-65 (quoting Alley v. State, 882 S.W.2d 810, 820 (Tenn. Crim. App. 1994)). *(Can someone please explain to me why the Tennessee Judiciary Board of Review failed to take action against Dinky all the times I reported him to them?)*

A party seeking disqualification or recusal must support a recusal motion with an affidavit or declaration and "other appropriate materials." *(You mean like the hours and hours of recorded screaming fits and transcripts that I provided to them where I and my counsel were insulted for no reason? Where we were called names in violation of their edicts and yet no one would act on it to remove the shit stain from my case? Oh, okay.)* TENN. SUP. CT. R. 10B, § 1.01. **When a party brings forward a trial court's comments as evidence to support a recusal motion, we must determine whether the comments "indicate that the judge has prejudged factual issues."** (*Like saying I had bribed the* USA Today *when no evidence had been provided? And granting a subpoena to harass people based on the judge's stupidity and bias?*) Alley, 882 S.W.2d at 822. "Any comments made by the trial court must be construed in the context of all the facts and circumstances to determine whether a reasonable person would construe those remarks as indicating partiality on the merits of the case." Id.

Here, Mr. M submitted the declaration of Mark Twain. In this declaration, Mr. Twain detailed the comments that the trial judge made about Mr. M in his case, to which Mr. Twain was a party *(Mr. Twain was the one who had called me during my case and asked if I wanted to bring a class action against ole Dinky and crew over this and many, many other gross violations).*

Petitioners challenge Mr. Twain's declaration as "inherently suspect, at best." We disagree. Courts instead presume that testimony provided under oath and penalty of perjury is true. See, e.g., Hogue v. Kroger Co., 356 S.W.2d 267, 271 (Tenn. 1962) ("This court certainly will not ascribe to the oath-taker the infamy of a perjurious mind. We think, with every presumptive support, that people normally are honest and tell the truth." (citation omitted)). In its order denying the recusal motion, the trial court treated the comments as if they had been made, so we do also.

Petitioners argue that Mr. M waived the right to seek recusal of the trial judge based on the judge's comments. A party waives the right "to question a judge's impartiality" if the party does not assert the grounds for recusal "in a timely manner." Kinard, 986 S.W.2d at 228 (citations omitted). A one-year delay in asserting grounds for recusal constitutes waiver. Chase, 2017 WL 3738466, at *3; In re Samuel P., No. W2016-01592-COA-T10B-CV, 2016 WL 4547543, at *6 (Tenn. Ct. App. Aug. 31, 2016).  Here, Mr. M filed the third recusal motion twenty-two days after the judge's comments. Under the circumstances, we find that Mr. M acted in a timely manner.

In his comments, the judge claimed that Mr. M "submitted a false and fake package... to the Board of Professional Responsibility and the Court of the Judiciary." The media ultimately "picked it up" and published a "[t]otally false" story about the judge. But, the judge continued, the media published the story "as if it were true." So, the judge wondered, "what do I do when I'm sitting there watching that, and my family is watching it, and all of my friends are watching it?" *(The same thing you forced me to do, you bastard, when your friends lied about me. Suck it up.)*

The gist of the comments is that the judge blamed Mr. M for the court's exposure to negative publicity, possibly drawing the scrutiny of the judge's family and friends. The judge was "crystal clear" and "transparent" about not liking that "at all." The court also did not like "many, many other things" Mr. M had done. And the judge envisaged that "my day will come."

Taken in context, "a reasonable person would construe th[e] remarks as indicating" that the judge may have sought retribution against Mr. M for a perceived wrongdoing unrelated to the contempt charges. 5 See Alley, 882 S.W.2d at 822.  This possible motivation provides "a reasonable basis for questioning the judge's impartiality." See Davis, 38 S.W.3d at 564; see also State v. Cobbins, No. E2012-02025- CCA-10B-DD, 2012 WL 5266427, at *22-23 (Tenn. Crim. App. Oct. 25, 2012) (recusal warranted based, in part, on trial court's comments that it was "[m]y time" and "my day had finally come").

Petitioners insist that the trial court was "impartial and entirely fair" to Mr. M and Mr. H.

The record reflects that the judge showed extraordinary patience and was thorough in his review of serious allegations against Mr. M and Mr. H. We do not conclude that the judge was actually partial. But that is not the standard for recusal. *(Yeah, but it should be.)* See Kinard, 986 S.W.2d at 228 **("[T]he public's confidence in judicial neutrality requires not only that the judge be impartial in fact, but also that the judge be perceived to be impartial.").** Under Tennessee's objective standard, the judge's impartiality might reasonably be questioned. So the judge should have recused himself. See Cook v. State, 606 S.W.3d 247, 255 (Tenn. 2020) (reasoning that Tennessee's objective standard "'may sometimes bar trial by judges who have no actual bias'" (quoting In re Murchison, 349 U.S. 133, 136 (1955))).

In the order denying the motion to recuse, the trial court provided more context. The judge explained that Mr. M had been providing information about the judge to Mr. Twain.  Mr. Twain then used this information to file a complaint with the Board of Judicial Conduct. That complaint was later dismissed *(As we know from Mr. Gentry, the Judiciary Board rejects 100% of all complaints filed against Tennessee judges—they bragged about this in a state legislative hearing because the citizens of Tennessee don't matter to them so why should Dinky care about having been reported*). In the judge's view, Mr. M and Mr. Twain "have obviously worked together for the sole purpose of... attempt[ing] to publicly embarrass or ridicule the Court." *(Yet Dinky works with attorneys—his former law associates—to humiliate, rob and embarrass others on a daily basis. Pity he can't take what he dishes out to the rest of us.)*

Petitioners argue that Mr. H did not properly preserve the recusal issue for appeal. In response to our order directing the parties to respond to Mr. M's Rule 10B petition for recusal appeal, see TENN. SUP. CT. R. 10B, § 2.05, Mr. H, on behalf of himself and his law firm, joined the petition. And as a party, he was entitled to raise the denial of the recusal motion in his brief, which he did. See Tenn. R. App. P. 3(h) (broadly allowing any party to raise any issue "upon the filing of a single notice of appeal"). Although Mr. H did not join Mr. M's recusal motion in  the trial court, the Rules of the Supreme Court of Tennessee speak of recusal as to proceedings, not as to parties. See TENN. SUP. CT. R. 10, Rule 2.11(A).

Petitioners also contend that, because the judge made the comments after the contempt order, the comments cannot be evidence of any predisposition against Mr. M. See Alley, 882 S.W.2d at 821. We again disagree. The unfavorable news story for which the judge claimed Mr. M was responsible ran in February 2017. And the trial court issued the contempt order in July 2018. So the impetus for the judge's thoughts about Mr. M may have existed for almost a year and a half before the court entered the contempt order. That the judge did not air those thoughts until after entry of the contempt order misses the point.

**B.**

Having determined that recusal was appropriate, we must consider the impact on the final judgment of contempt and damages. Retroactive recusal generally is not the appropriate remedy. See Watson v. Cal-Three, LLC, 254 P.3d 1189, 1193 (Colo. App.  2011) ("Recusal provides prospective relief; it does not necessarily invalidate orders previously entered."); 46 AM. JUR. 2D Judges § 210, Westlaw (database updated Nov.  2020). But, in Liljeberg v. Health Services Acquisition Corp., the United States Supreme Court set forth a test to determine whether retroactive recusal is appropriate under the federal recusal statute. 486 U.S. 847, 863-64 (1988). We find it appropriate to apply the Liljeberg test here. **Tennessee courts "may look to federal interpretation of similar federal laws for guidance in enforcing [Tennessee] statutes."** Van Tran v. State, 66  S.W.3d 790, 821 (Tenn. 2001) (Barker, J., concurring in part and dissenting in part); see Barnes v. Goodyear Tire & Rubber Co., 48 S.W.3d 698, 705 (Tenn. 2000) (interpreting Tennessee anti-discrimination laws), abrogated on other grounds by Gossett v. Tractor  Supply Co., 320 S.W.3d 777 (Tenn. 2010); Arnold v. Morgan Keegan & Co., 914 S.W.2d  445, 448 & n.2 (Tenn. 1996) (interpreting the Tennessee Uniform Arbitration Act);  Thomas v. Oldfield, 279 S.W.3d 259, 261-62 & n.3 (Tenn. 2009) (interpreting the  Tennessee Rules of Civil Procedure); State v. Clayton, 131 S.W.3d 475, 478 (Tenn. Crim.  App. 2003) (interpreting the Tennessee Rules of Criminal Procedure). Tennessee's recusal standard is identical to the federal standard, save for noun and pronoun usage.  Compare TENN. SUP. CT. R. 10, Rule 2.11(A), with 28 U.S.C. § 455(a) (2018). And Tennessee courts have often cited the United States Supreme Court with approval on recusal issues. See State v. Griffin, 610 S.W.3d 752, 760 (Tenn. 2020) (citing Williams v.  Pennsylvania, 136 S. Ct. 1899, 1907-09 (2016)); Cook, 606 S.W.3d at 255 (citing In re Murchison, 349 U.S. at 136); Bailey v. Blount Cty. Bd. of Educ., 303 S.W.3d 216, 239 (Tenn. 2010) (citing Chapman v. California, 386 U.S. 18, 23 n.8 (1967)); Kinard, 986 S.W.2d at 228 (citing Offutt v. United States, 348 U.S. 11, 14 (1954)); Alley, 882 S.W.2d at 821 (citing United States v. Grinnell Corp., 384 U.S. 563, 583 (1966)).

**The Liljeberg test "consider[s] the risk of injustice to the parties in the particular case, the risk that the denial of relief will produce injustice in other cases, and the risk of undermining the public's confidence in the judicial process."** Liljeberg, 486 U.S. at 864. **As to the parties in this case, the purpose of the right to impartiality "is to guard against the prejudgment of the rights of litigants and to avoid situations in which the litigants might have cause to conclude that the court had reached a prejudged conclusion."** *(In other words, when all the attorneys kept telling me how Dinky would rule and that I couldn't go before him because there was "no way" I could or would get a fair trial.)* State v. Benson, 973 S.W.2d 202, 205 (Tenn. 1998) (citing Chumbley v. People's Bank & Tr. Co., 57 S.W.2d 787, 788 (Tenn. 1933)).

7 Although one of the two hearing dates on the contempt petition occurred before the media story ran, there is still a "reasonable basis for questioning" whether partiality may have affected the trial court's contempt order. See Davis, 38 S.W.3d at 564.

As noted above, the basis for the judge's thoughts about Mr. M may have existed for nearly a year and a half before the July 2018 contempt order. It likely existed at least since May 23, 2017, when the trial court entered the order denying an earlier recusal motion filed by Mr. M. That order indicates that, by then, the judge suspected that Mr. M was behind the news story and unfounded complaints about the judge made to the Board of Professional Responsibility and the Court of the Judiciary. The contempt order itself references the Board of Professional Responsibility complaint in an adverse credibility finding against Mr. M. So once the court revealed its thoughts about Mr. M in open court, one might reasonably question whether the court "had reached a prejudged conclusion" as to the contempt order. See Benson, 973 S.W.2d at 205. Although the contempt order is the product of over two years of litigation, under these circumstances **"there is a greater risk of unfairness in upholding the judgment in favor of [Petitioners] than there is in allowing a new judge to take a fresh look at the issues."** See Liljeberg, 486 U.S. at 868; see also Olerud v. Morgan, No. M2010-01248-COA-R3-CV, 2011 WL 607113, at *2-3 (Tenn. Ct. App. Feb. 18, 2011) (vacating orders of the trial court entered before a recusal motion was filed when the basis for recusal "was discovered... after the court entered critical rulings in the case").

Second, to deny retroactive relief could cause injustice in other cases *(Don't even get me started).* Our supreme court has cautioned judges about inappropriate remarks *(But apparently, not enough as they all do it from my vast experience in the kangaroo circuses they run in Tennessee).* See Cook, 606 S.W.3d at 257 (**admonishing Tennessee judges "to refrain from [making] inappropriate comments"**); see also Leighton, 414 S.W.2d at 420 (**"[T]he judge must be careful not to give an expression to any thought, or to infer what his opinion would be in favor or against either of the parties in the trial."**). Allowing a remedy for inappropriate remarks even late in the proceedings would encourage judges to reflect on possible grounds for recusal through all phases of a case *(Such as when Dinky actually testified for my husband against me during one of our hearings?).* See Liljeberg, 486 U.S. at 868 (Retroactive enforcement "may prevent a substantive injustice in some future case by encouraging a judge... to more carefully examine possible grounds for disqualification and to promptly disclose them when discovered."). *(Then why don't you fucking bastards have a way for citizens to disclose this without having to use an attorney? Again, what do we do when our attorneys are so afraid of the judge that they refuse to file the recusals? In this case, Mr. M was an attorney that Dinky had disbarred, which quelled other attorneys from standing up to him. And when the Judiciary Board summarily dismisses all of our legitimate complaints, where are we to turn? This is disgraceful).*

Third, allowing the contempt order to stand risks undermining public confidence in the judiciary. Surely, "'justice must satisfy the appearance of justice.'" Liljeberg, 486 U.S. at 864 (quoting In re Murchison, 349 U.S. at 136); Cook, 606 S.W.3d at 255 (quoting same). **Here, when the judge mused that "my day will come," the judge also said that day is "just about here"—less than a month before awarding supplemental damages and finalizing the contempt order.** And the judge mentioned that he had "released a one-hundred-twenty-two page memorandum and order on" Mr. M, which was the order holding him in contempt. So the basis upon which it is reasonable to question the judge's impartiality is directly connected to the contempt order.

**Because the trial court's impartiality might reasonably be questioned, the court should have recused itself.** And under the circumstances of this case, retroactive recusal is warranted. In finding retroactive recusal warranted, we express no opinion on the merits of the contempt proceeding.

### III.

We reverse the denial of the third motion to recuse. And we vacate the contempt and damages order of July 20, 2018, and the order awarding supplemental attorney's fees and expenses of September 27, 2018. This case is remanded for reassignment and further proceedings consistent with this opinion.

That was great, wasn't it? Except for one thing... They had dragged poor Mr. M through the wringer, too. And for all those years. Ridiculed and ruined him.

Sure, he'd had the satisfaction of proving that he wasn't wrong, but now he had to relive and refile it all again.

More money spent and all those years wasted.

Because of one shit stain who should never have been allowed to sit on that bench.

One who had abused me and my children while doing this to him and his co-counsel and Mr. Twain, at the same exact time.

Mr. Twain had his own nightmares to impart. The abuse of his grandchildren in Dinky's court.

And those tales chilled me.

So many lives ruined by one madman Tennessee had unleashed on us.

But at least someone had finally reprimanded him, even though they had failed to defend me when my civil rights had been so blatantly abused. And my friend, Nan, had told me that the order was highly unusual. "Honey, they don't ever name the judge like that in an order. He pissed off a lot of folks for that. I'm telling you. His friends are numbered and they're dwindling."

How I hoped and prayed that was true.

Because the last thing I wanted was for anyone else to have to endure the nightmare that my children and I had survived. These abuses of power needed stop.

I wanted Karma to do her job. As Dinky had said, I wanted his day to come. And I wanted it to be everything that rotten bastard fully deserved.

All of them.

In the meantime, I was going to put it behind me. I had my fans. My children, real and fictional. There was a bright future ahead, and I had no intention of allowing the monsters of Williamson County to take any more of my soul from me.

Let them all burn in hell where they belonged. We would rise and we would fly, on broken, imperfect wings. Stronger and better than we'd ever been. Lessons learned and made wiser from our pain.

We would bury the monsters and never think of them again.

A S I'D PREDICTED, THE ink wasn't even dry on our Marital Dissolution Agreement (MDA) in September, before ole Les came yowling at my backdoor for scraps. There really was no way for us to get peace, even though he knew he had no legal leg to stand on. They were still relying on Dinky, who had told me "You better not be writing anything bad about me," to cover their asses.

But for those curious sorts, here was what happened after the divorce was finalized:

**Terri Woods** continues to write, while trying her best to put the whole nightmare behind her, and to rebuild the career that they sought to destroy. After being homeless for the second time in her life, she still has no bed to sleep on, but she has her children (real and fictional), and will never stop fighting for what is right, even though she no longer believes in happy endings. Williamson County victims continue to contact Terri in order to share their own nightmares. It's a frightening number that continues to grow.

**Les Manly** refuses to leave his ex-family alone. After he was told by Cockburn, House, Alaimo and Tiller that they would no longer represent him (they'd run him out of money), he found another Middle Tennessee shyster to represent him on frivolous motions that violate Governor Haslam's law, Stalking By Way Of Court.

**Bonnie Cockburn** is no longer a lawyer. She ran her practice only long enough to ruin the lives of the entire Manly family (and everyone else she touched). She is again in the housing industry, after refusing to help Les Manly pursue more bogus charges against Terri.

**Mika House** took his ill-gotten gains and has started his own law firm.

**Barbie Border** is now a partner at Dinky's former law firm.

**Sal Tiller** also started his own law firm. Months after the divorce ended, he made a very public motion to announce he would no longer represent Les Manly.

**John Alaimo** not only continues to be a commissioner, but he has also now been promoted to a high level at the Tennessee Board of Professional Responsibility where he's able to intimidate and threaten anyone who stands in their way. He also offered a biased and erroneous condemnation against Constance Yabetz.

**Constance Yabetz** is currently disbarred for defending a mother whose child was wrongfully taken by the state of Tennessee. She had been in the process of surrendering the mother to custody when she was arrested. The state dropped charges against the mother and returned her child (after admitting they had no right to remove the child from the mother's custody). After Constance decided to run against Williamson County judges, new charges were filed against the mother and Constance for custodial interference (even though the state had admitted that it had no reason or right to remove the child). They offered the mother a plea bargain if she testified against Constance. Constance is currently attempting to get her license back, while she continues to fight the injustice in Middle Tennessee.

**Bill Oldham** is in the process of being sued by Mr. M in the case where Dinky was reprimanded. He allegedly did the same bad acts against Mr. M that he did to Terri.

**Karen Hogg** continues to work with children and ruin their lives.

**Kevin Hatch** was an attorney who stepped in to help Terri after the divorce, and who had intended to file suit against Bubba Dinky and Williamson County. He called Terri on a Friday evening to tell her and Nan that he wanted to read through their complaint one more time, and that he'd file it on Monday morning. He died of unknown causes Sunday night, just hours before he intended to file suit. No other attorney would step forward after that.

**Nan Savoir** continues to fight the good legal fight. She is now Terri's pro bono house counsel.

**Dinky, Newhouse, Seaver et al** continue to make the lives of the citizens of Middle Tennessee miserable.

# ABOUT THE AUTHOR

Defying all odds is what #1 *New York Times* and international bestselling author Sherrilyn Kenyon does best. Rising from extreme poverty as a child that culminated in being a homeless mother with an infant, she has become one of the most popular and influential authors in the world (in both adult and young adult fiction), with dedicated legions of fans known as Paladins—thousands of whom proudly sport tattoos from her numerous genre-defying series.

Since her first book debuted in 1993 while she was still in college, she has placed more than 80 novels on the *New York Times* list in all formats and genres, including manga and graphic novels, and has more than 70 million books in print worldwide. Her current series include: Dark-Hunters®, Chronicles of Nick®, Deadman's Cross™, Nevermore™, Lords of Avalon® and The League®.

Over the years, her Lords of Avalon® novels have been adapted by Marvel, and her Dark-Hunters® and Chronicles of Nick® are *New York Times* bestselling manga and comics and are #1 bestselling adult coloring books.

Join her and her Paladins online at QueenofAllShadows.com and www.facebook.com/mysherrilyn.

ABOUT THE AUTHOR